TIME ASYLUM

DANNY BLUE

Publisher:
Australian Self Publishing Group, Pty. Ltd. / Inspiring Publishers
PO Box 159, Calwell, ACT 2905, Australia.
Phone: 61-(0) 2 6291-2904
http://australianselfpublishinggroup.com

A catalogue record for this book is available from the National Library of Australia

National Library of Australia Prepublication Data Service

Author: Danny Blue

Title: **Time Asylum**

Book type : Non-Fiction

ISBN: 978-1-923250-84-0 (print)
ISBN: 978-1-923250-85-7 (eBook)

A special thanks to those who endured an early draft
Bek
Hetti
Alex
Helena
and Mum

The story begins on
page 346.

Table of Contents

In the Dark

"I'm guessing you're a little lost, am I right?"
Sancia nodded.

"Yeah well, me too." Dahl sighed. "But I think it's this way."

Dahl led Sancia through a thick jungle, over ground that had not yet been travelled, and with each awkward step he tried hard not to show a longing for concrete paths.

He was trying to lead them back to where they had come from, but finding the way was hard. Dahl was sure that they had to head southwest to find their way back to the clearing, and little did he know the clearing was northeast. But Dahl was a lucky man without a clue which way southwest was, so they were indeed heading in the right direction.

The sun, whenever it's light broke through the trees, burned. Dahl's forearms were already flaking, but Sancia's browned skin only reddened.

It rained torturous, heavy showers of warm water intermittently. Soaking their faces faster than they could wipe them. It was brief relief at all from the heat, but as soon as it stopped and the sun crept back, so Dahl pined for it.

Soon, Dahl found what he was looking for; footprints pressed into mud. Something had ploughed through the jungle, flattening grass and weaving between trees, and only these footprints remained. They were deep prints too, and far apart. Someone had been running from something. They followed the tracks but quickly found that they stopped as suddenly as they had started.

"Where?" Sancia asked.

"Damn." Dahl nodded. "I thought we were getting close."

Sancia knelt down to inspect the footprint and search for the one that should have followed but found nothing.

"Jump?"

"Maybe." Dahl nodded a little while keeping his head up on the trees above. He suddenly flung himself against its trunk and climbed, digging his foot in between knots and between branches until the small man was high in the tree. Sancia waited at the bottom, alone and terrified.

She heard noises in the jungle, wind brushed the bushes around and for a second Sancia swore she saw something between the trees.

"Heads up!"

Down at Sancia's feet he dropped a bag, followed by a body.

"I guess he didn't get that far." Dahl said as he slid down the moss of the tree, his grip looser than he thought, the tree slipped from his fingers and Dahl fell on his back in a clump of ferns.

Dahl scrambled to his feet and went through the dead man's pack, laughing with joy as he found three cubes tucked inside with a few pairs of clean underwear.

"What did I tell you?" Dahl said as he tossed cube in the air.

"Dinosaur?" Sancia asked, looking at what was left of the body.

"Probably." Dahl grabbed his pack and double-checked the zipper before flinging it over his shoulder. "This means we're close. We're almost back where we started."

Dahl started off again and noticed she hadn't followed. He looked back to see she was still standing over his body, muttering to herself in her own private language.

"Oh, I'm sorry. I forgot you're only a kid..."

"I'm fine." She mumbled.

"Sure?"

She nodded.

"Because it might get worse than that."

She started off and Dahl had to hurry after to her to get in front and lead the way.

So she watched his back, and she studied his walk. He strode two feet longer than he needed to, often straining himself to make those strides so that Sancia with her average length legs wouldn't step on his heels.

Sancia wished Dahl was faster. She felt like they were being watched. A feeling she couldn't shake since she had left the pier.

"Dahl, what is a dinosaur?"

Since taking her under his wing, Dahl found he was wearing his vocabulary thin. He stressed over his annunciation and started looking at his hands like they were puppeteering without a puppet. He did his best, but Sancia still did not understand what Dahl meant when he mentioned dinosaurs, and she was thinking it was just a word he used when he didn't know what something was.

"Trust me, you'll know one when you see one." Dahl gave in. "There's also lots of different types, so they won't all look the same. That makes it hard again."

As they walked along the bed of vines, crushing leaves and swatting mouse-size bugs away from their faces, Dahl kept on looking back to his new friend to make sure she was still there and hadn't wandered off to follow someone else. Perhaps someone who knew where they were going.

Another fat bug swam through the humidity of the jungle, it's irritating buzz slowly getting louder and louder until Dahl felt it near his ear and brashly swatted it in the other direction. He then chopped at a large branch that hung in his way, which bent a little and flung back in his face. Sancia caught him and pushed him back to his feet.

Ducking under the branch, they found a clearing where the treetops were thin, and the sun shed brightly on the worn ground. As the two of them looked over the clearing it was like happening across a memory they hadn't yet had.

The clearing was fuller now than it had been before. Mushed into the earth amongst the soft greenery were purples and blues, reds and blacks. Beige shorts, jeans, summer hats and caps, hiking boots, and

torn backpacks. After a while the bugs and maggots came and sifted through the remains. The wind rustled a few from their spot before they returned to itch into the open flesh.

They could see them all over. Every bump and rise in the clearing was a half-rotted body, mangled and stomped flat.

Dahl pulled Sancia into his chest and holding her head as he tried to look away himself.

"Are you ok?"

"Yes." She replied.

"They're all... dead."

"I know."

"I just don't want you having any nightmares." Dahl assured. "You only have to look if you want to kiddo."

"I can look."

Dahl still held her head towards him. He did this until he was ready, and Sancia waited, smelling the leather of his jacket.

"Dinosaurs?" Sancia asked, moving through the bodies and lifting a leg to Dahl like it was a big stick.

"Yeah, dinosaurs."

Sancia knelt beside the bodies and bowed her head as Dahl heard her speaking rapidly in Spanish.

"In nomine Patris et fillii et Spiritus Sancti."

They tried to be careful when lifting a mangled and rotting arm as they were bound to snap a bone or two. Dahl threw up a little in his mouth and spat it into a puddle.

"Is this... ok?" Sancia asked as she felt her skin pale as all the blood run from under her skin.

"This is survival. There's nothing we could have done. All there's to do now is make use of what's left." Dahl said solemnly. "Nothing we could have done. When birds fall."

The two got to work, digging through pockets and backpacks for colorful cubes to add to their collection. Neither of them going anywhere near the four matching polo shirt bodies in the middle, but both sparing a look in their direction.

For them it wasn't long ago that they had seen them, the squabbling family. The father was having trouble with their cube, having already started turning tiles with half an idea of how it worked. His family had berated him until finally he tossed it off in the jungle and stranded them there until their tour group retraced their steps and found them, or someone came for them.

Something did.

"Dahl?" Sancia asked after a while.

"Yuh huh?"

"Where's your family?"

"My family?" Dahl asked himself. "My family is... back at home."

"Why?"

"Why?" Dahl asked back, as though he'd rather Sancia answer her own question. "It's a funny thing, really. They didn't really want to come with me."

"Why?"

"Well, the thing you've got to understand is that..." Dahl's words lost momentum for a moment, and then he grinned. "Not everyone is brave like you and me."

"Brave?"

"Yeah, brave. You're a brave one kiddo."

Dahl had to pull hard to wriggle it free, the tight grip of the dead was a difficult but eventual one-sided fight. Dahl soon broke the bones of the dead fingers and wiped the cube clean on his trousers.

"He really didn't want to let that go." Dahl joked as he swallowed a stinging mouthful of stomach acid and smiled at Sancia's perturbed face.

It baffled Sancia how Dahl felt disgusted by something so harmless but still so carefree about his own safety. Not once on this entire journey had he winced at a broken twig or rattling in the trees. It was as though Sancia must do the worrying for both of them.

Sancia lent over the bodies strewn about the mud, trying to keep her eyes off their faces where dark red patches showed evidence of the teeth and claws that had ripped them to shreds. She tried to hold her

breath, as to not sniff in smells of their freshly rotting bodies, while she rifled through their pockets and bags.

Sancia couldn't imagine anyone this brutal, cruel and malicious, it was beyond thought and without reason.

If these dinosaurs were after the cubes, why weren't they shrewd enough to remember to pick them from the dead? And were they not threatening enough to take from the living?

It took a long time to search every dead tourist for their cubes. Dahl was just as careful as Sancia and withdrew every time he moved a body and heard a crack or ooze.

"Piece of cake." He managed.

"What?" Sancia asked.

"Easy I mean. Cake, do you know what… have you had cake before? It's de-" Dahl felt a rib snap in his hands. "-licious."

Sancia couldn't tell if Dahl was trying to lighten the mood or just had no sense of his surroundings.

But he was right. It was easy and Sancia didn't mind the dead as much as Dahl, having helped coronate many of her congregation.

Sancia's eyes were on the darkening descent of the jungle. She looked past the first few lines of trees as the jungle came together and closed over itself.

What if the dinosaurs came back?

Deep in the darkness, a pair of red eyes flickered.

She wondered whether he had taken her to a place not so different to hell.

"They're not coming back." Dahl answered easily as he saw Sancia stare out into the abyss. "We're safe, don't worry."

"How do you know?"

"Because. When you're with me you're safe."

"Why?"

"When birds fall kiddo."

Sancia looked up to the clear sky. She didn't see any birds.

"No." Dahl sighed. "It's just an expression."

"What does it mean?"

"It means…" Dahl paused and winked at Sancia. "I can't just tell you what it means. You're just gonna have to trust me."

"I don't thinks so." Sancia said.

"What?"

"Cake. I don't think I've had t." She added.

"Well kiddo, you've been missing out. When we're done here, I'll take you to eat the best cake we can find."

"To the future, right? Where you're from, your home?" Sancia asked.

"Not exactly. Home isn't really home anymore."

"Why not?"

Dahl tossed aside the remains of the backpack he was rummaging through and came over to Sancia. If were taller or Sancia were shorter, he would have knelt. His tone dropped and he took her arm.

"There are worse things than what killed these people in the future Sancia, much worse."

"Worse than dinosaurs?"

"Yes. Worse."

"Who?"

"People that like telling other people what to do. People that like controlling everyone else. There will always be people that want to tell you what's right and what's wrong. People who will tell you you're not smart enough to be right."

Dahl leaned back, tilting his head back, trying to drain any tears back into his tear-ducts. He sniffed and sighed.

"So?" He kept on talking to move past it. "Where next, huh? The future? We can go a few years or so ahead or…"

"Can we go back?"

It was her soft tone, Dahl crumbled. The four words he had been hoping she'd never say.

"I'm so stupid! I'm so sorry. I'm so so sorry. Damn! Why did I take you with me? Why? You probably have family waiting for you. Friends! I'm so stupid, I'm so sorry."

Dahl fell back and sat on the shoulder of what was a larger man and held his face in his hands.

"Here I am, going on and on about cake and dinosaurs and all you wanna do is go home. I'm so sorry, kiddo. I do this, I get caught up in something and I don't think, I never think! I'm so stupid. STUPID!"

Sancia winced and worried as Dahl smacked his palms against his face. And she cried with him.

"I'll take you back to your home, I promise. I'll take you back right now."

"Please! No." Sancia cried.

Dahl stopped crying and looked up at her as she knelt beside him with a look of terror on her face.

"But you said…"

"Please don't take me home. I don't want to go back." She said. "I want to stay with you."

"But you said you wanted to go back?"

"Yes. Back. To the before." Sancia stood up and waved her hand out to the clearing of broken and empty pocketed bodies. "We can tell them. Warn them."

Dahl laughed, rubbing his eyes with the parts of his hands that hadn't touched a dead body. This time he knelt. He sunk lower than her to try to diminish any chance of talking down to her.

"See the thing is kiddo, we can't change this. Going back to warn them wouldn't work. That's just how it works. We can't change anything."

"Even if we try real hard?"

"Even then." Dahl pulled her in and hugged her tight. "I'm sorry kiddo I really am. How about instead I let you have a go, huh? How about that?"

He pulled back just as Sancia was drying her eyes with an enormous smile on her face. He took a cube that was digging into his thigh and sat it in her hand and explained.

Dahl had to stop and start a few times. Waving his hand for Sancia to forget everything he had just said, so he could try to explain it again. Sancia was polite and let Dahl finish explaining, even though she got the hang of it from the second haphazard explanation.

"Right. Are you ready?"

She nodded and took the cube from him and calculated the twists and turns for three days' time.*

Dahl stepped back and watched as she disappeared, and he smiled proudly as though she had just ridden off on her first bike.

Dahl whipped out a cube from his now half full backpack and turned it. A sudden gush of wind flustered the trees and Dahl in turn. His fingers shook and he dropped the cube. Though, he was quick to catch it and bounce it back up, juggling it from hand to hand, trying to regain his grip.

He finally caught it against his chest, and he sighed with relief and twisted it again, confident with where he was up to and where he was going.**

---

*Go to Page 10
**Go to Page 13

It was raining when she landed, hard. It was so loud that Sancia found it difficult to get her bearings. It was so thick she couldn't even tell that the day was well into the night.

She fumbled to a tree and held her back against it as she waited out the rain.

She squinted and waited to see Dahl follow her to this spot. Nothing but the rain fell.

It didn't take her long to worry. And as the rain grew thicker like long endless streams, she saw less and less of what was in front of her.

With the icy rain she was soon so cold and numb that she couldn't feel the tree at her back.

The last time she was this numb something awful happened. She felt his hands again, touching her all over. She was numb to touch but not to pain. She could see his face even when she closed her eyes, because he wasn't there, but he was always with her.

She screamed. She finally screamed.

She thought she screamed. It was so loud she couldn't even hear her voice carry through throat.

She screamed anyway.

All noise lost to the rain.

When her throat was raw, the rain slowed and what water was left in the trees ran down their trunks as rough as rivers. Dahl still hadn't shown.

The water that washed to the ground flowed between the trees and Sancia followed it, walking with the water. It ran to a river, which gushed and wrought against the embankment as it overflowed.

Sancia stood at the river and watched it. She crouched and let her hands dip in the water to feel the strength of it trying to take her away. She could see the white light of the moon reflected in the streams, its perfect circle stretched and streaked in the broken mirror of the river's surface.

Then a new light appeared, orange and yellow and just as rough and imperfect even without the poor reflection.

Sancia shot her head up to see a figure standing by firelight on the other side of the river.

"You." She sputtered.

"Finally." He spoke. His face half lit by flickering firelight; his expression was hard to read but he was definitely panting.

It was one of the men from the pier. His clothes were the same, only ravaged by sweat and exhaustion.

"Please don't kill me." Sancia begged.

"Kill you?"

Sancia backed away and the man just stood still.

"We'd never do that."

"We?"

Sancia felt herself back into something, not as firm as a tree, but she could only hope. The second man grabbed her tight by the shoulders, forcing her small arms to stay at her side as he jostled her back toward the river. The other man stepped across and brought his fire close to her face.

"You have no idea how long we've been looking for you." He yelled over the stream.

"Sources took us to Australia."

"But Australia's a big place."

"Then we tracked you to a castle in England."

"Do you know how many castles there are in bloody England?"

"Please let me go."

"Go!" One of them shouted. "We shouldn't have let you leave! You can ruin everything. We have to take you back."

"Back?"

"Back to where you came from. You have to go back to have the baby."

Sancia held a hand to her stomach. She had pushed it from her mind, and they just ripped it right back.

"I'll never go back." She said.

"Don't say stuff like that." One of them sighed as he slipped out a three-pronged dagger with long serrated edges. "We can't let you just do whatever you want."

"We will do everything we can to make sure enough of you makes it back. You don't need all of you to push out a baby."

The man who held her dug his fingers into her shoulder with one hand and pulled out a switchblade with the other. He held it to the skin of her elbow; an arm she wouldn't need.

Sancia no longer wondered what dinosaurs looked like; they came in all shapes and sizes. They could be big or small, old and misshapen or deceptively striking. They were more dangerous than Dahl could ever have described, and she was so glad she ran from them the first time. Now she knew she would have to run again.

With all her strength and trust in her footing, she ducked and drove her elbow backwards into his stomach. She then twisted in place and let the dinosaur slide along the torrential river edge and fall into the water. Without looking back, she ran. If she slipped, she followed through and if she fell, she crawled. The angry voices shouting over the rain were close behind.

Over a thick tree root she fell, sliding down a short hill and twisting her wrist as she tumbled. There at the bottom the ground felt rough and crunchy.

She looked to her hands, dug deep in the ground and sifted through white bone and bits of teeth. Half a skull had been flattened and lodged deep into the earth. This place was death.

She shook her hands free and cried an ear-piercing scream, jolted short as one of the men lunged down the hill and took hold of her foot.

Sancia fell onto her back and kicked at his face until his nose broke and he let go. She hustled to her feet again just as the second dove towards her, slashing at her chest with his dagger.

Three spurts of blood shot out, but the rain washed it away as brazenly as it drowned out her screams. Kicking to her feet, she clutched at her chest and crawled on all fours into the dark.

Under and between her fingers the ground felt alive and flowing, but it wasn't from the rain. She looked down to see the entire jungle floor covered in crawling bugs.

Worm like insects with a thousand hair-like legs crawling over one another and if she stood still long enough they would crawl up and over her.

Sancia scurried through the jungle anyway, clutching at her bleeding chest, praying that everything would go away.

Not knowing the way, she ran whichever way she could. Behind her chased the dinosaurs. They were quick and knew the land better. All Sancia could do was scramble over the crunching and wriggling ground as fast as she could.

They were surely gaining on her.

She covered her face with her arms, as tree branches slapped at her. She tore between the trees, hoping each step would land on some solid and less horrifying ground. She knew that it wouldn't.

She knew where she was now better than ever, that when she had fallen into the ocean from that pier, she had sunk so deep that when she came out the other side. She was sure she was in hell.

Two more steps and the ground gave way, and she fell forward, plummeting into the dark and cold depths.

The rain that had passed the night before had washed the jungle and now everything felt damp. The mouse-sized bugs were out in greater numbers and as soon as Dahl landed, he was fighting them off him.

Dahl eagerly reached down to pick up a swatting stick but flung the stick the moment he saw a family of millipedes squirming underneath. In the sunlight they burrowed back deep into the earth and were gone as quickly as they appeared. Dahl tossed the stick aside and made off into the jungle, looking for Sancia.

"She should only be a few seconds ahead of me." Dahl said aloud, as though it would help. "But it was her first try, maybe it was irresponsible to let her try on her own."

He walked for a few hours, sipping water from huge leaves, and helped himself to a packet of chips he had found while ransacking the bodies.

He had counted the cubes in his pack when he had gotten the chips. Nineteen cubes in all. They had used up six. It was almost embarrassing how long it took him to work out how many trips that left him with, but he rationalized it was because he was worrying for Sancia.

"Oh man. Maybe I should have stayed put. If she was just a little off, I'm nowhere near where she gonna be." Dahl looked back the way he came, not entirely positive he had walked a straight path. His method of hiking was to just follow the least bumpy track. Looking straight back he tried to spy his trail but caught a hint of falling leaves and a soft wind.

Standing still and no longer with the noise of crunching chips in his ear, Dahl could hear the jungle, and a constant rush in the distance. So constant, like the hum of traffic. Dahl headed for it, figuring Sancia might have done the same.

Dahl came to the river. Its pace had slowed since the heavy rain the night before, and Dahl beamed at his own survival skills. He saw the river flowed to his left and not so far in that direction the water bent suddenly at the bow of a thick tree and a body had washed up on the embankment.

Dahl ran for it and almost cried at the sight of her.

Dahl rolled Sancia over and pushed on her stomach. In that one push, Sancia awoke and hurled up a lung and breathed deeply as she spat water from her throat.

"Ha ha! I saved you again!"

Sancia tried to answer but had to fight off her sore throat. It was morning and Dahl had dug his knees into the earth beside the river and was rubbing her back as she heaved for fresh breaths.

"You must have been thirsty." He joked.

"Where… were… you?"

"I was right here. Waiting for you, you must have turned the cube wrong. But don't you worry. I'm here now and you're safe."

Sancia felt her whole body come back to life as she sprung up expecting to see something on the other side of the river, but a sudden sting had her clutching at her chest. Dahl's face turned concerned, and he laid his hand over the wound and held it for her.

"What happened here?"

"Dinosaurs..."

"You're not serious? Really?" Dahl found it hard to contain his excitement. "I'm sorry, that's awful kiddo. Is it painful? What am I talking about, of course it is? But you actually saw them?"

"It was like a bad dream."

"You know, my son used to get nightmares. I used to feel bad about it because I would read him the stories that gave them to him. But I did it because when he got scared, he would run into our room at night and snuggle up with us. My wife hated it, but I treasured it. I don't care if you get scared. Everybody does."

"Can we go now?" Sancia asked. Dahl could hear the strain in her voice. She didn't want to ask again.

"We sure can kiddo. I think we've got plenty of cubes for now."

Suddenly, a crack of a branch from behind them was too loud to miss.

Sancia froze up, aching her fresh wounds, but was too frightened to care. Dahl fumbled for a cube but only brought out empty chip packets now strewn about the jungle floor.

The ferns and bushes shuddered and finally out stepped a single, white cat.

They both sighed and fell back in relief. Dahl laughed as the cat sniffed the chip packets whilst not taking its eyes off of them.

"Some scary dinosaur you are." Dahl teased the cat, leaning over on all fours to let the cat lick his fingers.

"Dahl!"

Click.

Dahl didn't know which he heard first. As he was bent over on all fours and the cat scampered away, he felt the cold barrel of a gun

touching the top of his head. He didn't dare move, but just stared at the brown shoes without a hint of mud on them.

Sancia sat frozen, staring unwittingly deep into the man's nothing of a face. He was no dinosaur.

"You two couldn't have been easier to find." The Historian said coldly as he let Dahl sit back and look up at the man.

Sancia felt a cold run over here. The man had no face. Underneath his brown hat there were only wisps of shadow; a shadow not cast by trees or the shape of his hat.

"Sancia, use the cube!" Dahl said through gritted teeth as he grabbed the barrel of the pistol and held it to his own forehead.

Sancia patted herself down and found her cube tucked away and turned it at random, closing her eyes in waiting.

Nothing.

"It's broken." She said faintly.

"Fools." The Historian growled, tapping at something clunky on his belt. "To think people like you are what we've been so worried about. Good riddance."

There was a loud bang and Dahl clenched his teeth. No pain, no cut to black. He opened his eyes to find the Historian falling backwards into the bushes as someone stood behind him holding a smoking gun. Someone many times taller and broader than Dahl, with a great white beard and wrinkles carved into his face like it was clay.

"Now, we're even Dahl."

"You've got to be joking. O'seus!" Dahl roared and ran to meet his old friend.

"Dahl you old rascal!"

Sancia watched in bewilderment as Dahl hopped to hug the complete stranger as the last few breaths wheezed out of the Historian a few feet from them.

"How d'you find us?"

"I was looking, that's how."

"You couldn't have come a little sooner?"

"Hey, if you're gonna be like that, I'll just jump back a few minutes and see how you would've weaseled yourselves out of that sticky mess."

O'seus was a sizeable man, especially when he stood beside Dahl. Sancia was just happy to see that he had a face. Or what she could see of it. He smiled with chocolaty brown eyes and sported a gruff peppery beard that moved with the breeze. He wore a thick coat which had the sleeves rolled up to his elbows and constantly kept sliding them back up as they slid down. His left forearm was browned by age and beneath a flurry of black arm hair, he had a tattoo of a sailboat with some swirly text beneath it. His accent was strong, and it made what clever wording he chose to speak sound as humorous as it was clever.

"No ok. I'm sorry. It is so good to see you." Dahl clapped a hand on O'seus' shoulder, going on his tiptoes to do so. "What are you doing here, really?"

"There's a teeny, weeny tiny thing I want to do, but it's risky and dangerous. Figured who better than you to come along to give it a go."

"I'm flattered, really. But what are you trying to change now?"

"Wouldn't you like to know." O'seas smirked.

"You can do that?"

O'seus turned his attention to Sancia who had approached him still wet with terror sweat.

"Do what lass?"

"Go back and change something?"

"No." Dahl answered quickly and without thinking about it.

"Sure." O'seus rebutted.

"Whenever you want?" Sancia followed up.

"I mean what I say, little lass." O'seus nodded. "Come on Dahl, it'll be just like old times."

Dahl thought hard on it. He really did. His head sank into his heart like it was a beanbag chair and it was tough to wriggle it out.

"No. Knowing you, it's something needlessly dangerous. And we don't want any part of that." Dahl looked to Sancia with a smile.

O'seus seemed peeved. He nodded graciously while grinding his boot into the dirt. "Fine. That's fine. Well, while I'm here, did you want to get out of here? I can take you somewhere far more interesting."

Dahl narrowed his eyes.

"And safe." O'seus followed along. "It's certainly safe. Plus, along the way, if you change your mind…"

"I won't."

"… But if you don't, at least from there you can go anywhere you want."

"Can we? Please Dahl?" Sancia said.

"I am getting sick of seeing nothing but trees." Dahl sighed.

O'seus looked around quickly and looked up to check the sun. He then took out a pen and pad and scribbled some numbers.

"You might need to see a few more, we need to move a few miles first… that way. Then we can go."

O'seus led them alongside the river and Sancia hoped they didn't have to cross to the other side. The river led to a part of the jungle where the trees thinned and became further and further apart until a great valley exposed itself before them and Sancia and Dahl finally caught sight of the magnificence of this untouched beautiful time.

O'seus started off down the valley and Sancia quickly followed, sticking to his left, trying to read his tattoo without getting an elbow to the face.

With someone buzzing around him so closely, O'seus couldn't help but notice and he put his giant hand over her head and led her ahead of him.

"You walk too close, girly."

"Your tattoo." Sancia started. "It's a ship."

"Aye." He answered, rolling his sleeve up in habit.

"What does it say?"

"You can't read it?"

"I can, I don't understand."

O'seus looked down as though he had forgotten it himself. The tattoo was branded across the edge of his forearm. It read: *There's no adventure here.*

"It's just something that I got before this all happened." O'seus smiled to himself, feeling the outline of his tattooed arm. "And every day it gets less and less true."

"I like it."

"Tell me this young lass." O'seus asked, slowing down to let Dahl find the lead and unwittingly take it. "What makes you so excited to hear someone talk about changing the past? You lit up like a spark back there. Something you're not proud of? Something you want to see changed?"

Sancia thought about it and placed the words together as she spoke. "If something happened, something bad. That means I deserved it, didn't I."

"You poor little thing." O'seus almost stopped to take in all his pity. "You seem to be in the dark about so much. In how many possible timelines did something awful happen to you, and how many did it not? What makes you think you deserve to be in the timeline of suffering? What awful luck you must have? To imply you deserve to suffer simply due to these odds is absurd. Now Dahl believes what happened to you is concrete and unchangeable, and the hapless sack will love you for it, despite everything. But I'm telling you, it never has to happen in the first place. Suffering is a choice."

"Are you sure?" Sancia asked.

"That cross around your purty neck." O'seus noted. "You believe in all that God crap don't ya."

Sancia instinctively grasped it.

"In the war between good and evil, God and the devil, fate and free will, the devil is the one fighting for your freedom."

"I don't like the devil."

"Oh, but he likes you."

Dahl suddenly realized that he was a few meters ahead of the others and turned to wait for them. He stopped by an enormous boulder

sticking out in the middle of the open valley. He tried to rest his foot on it like it was a bear he had hunted and killed, but it ended up looking like the boulder hunted him for sport.

"What are you two talking about?" Dahl asked.

"Nothing." O'seus winked to Sancia. "This should be about right, let's get out of here. I'm sick of walking in shite."

"Where are you taking us, anyway?"

"To a Senate. I have to be the voice of reason." O'seus bellowed this so loudly that the jungle wafted in response. "But afterwards…"

O'seus shoved his hand into his pocket and pulled out a folded piece of paper and handed it to Dahl. Even as he unfolded it, it amazed him.

"You can't be serious."

"Serious. It's the real deal."

"How did you…?"

"Come on, you think they'd dare not invite O'seus Forshaker to the Time Asylum?"

"Fantastic! Let's go already." Dahl exclaimed, hoisting his pack higher over his shoulder. "I feel like we're already missing out!"

"Don't you worry pal. The Asylum will still be there when we're good and ready. That's the one thing you could never quite grasp Dahl - just how patient time can be."

O'seus held out his hands for both Dahl and Sancia to take them, and he whisked them away with the breeze. All that was left behind was a small silver cross on a chain, sinking in the mud and burying itself.*

---

*Go to Page 527

Chapter Two:
Numb

Sancia landed face down in the snow. The shock of the ice against her face had her up and trying to find her feet. She only stumbled, clunking knee deep in snow and frost pounded into her back trying to knock her down.

It was white. White everywhere. She couldn't see anything but the blizzard. If there was a sky above her head she had no chance of seeing it, she couldn't see more than ten feet ahead of her nose.

As she made forward, parts of the white became shaped and an embankment grew clearer in the distance. Her legs would've frozen if it were not for her aching muscles pumping warm blood into her flesh with every painstaking stride. Her body would've gone numb if it wasn't for Dahl's leather jacket, still wrapped around her like a blanket.

She reached the embankment and scrambled over it on all fours, then she made it to the top and allowed her worn out body to slide down the other side and out of the winds path.

Her tumble let chunks of ice slip in under her clothes and melt on her skin. She stood up and shook herself and patted herself down on the coldest places then stood huddled with her back up against the wall of snow, tucking her hands under her armpits and breathed again.

Without the fierce wind shooting past her ears, she could hear herself think and now for the first heard her thoughts and trembled at what they had to say.

You're lost.

She searched through Dahl's jacket, finding nothing but his loose gold pieces and her only cube.

The cube that had carried her there, now with one trip left.

She did not understand what had caused her cube to behave so strangely. Had she had done something? Turned it by accident?

The storm seemed to subside. Sancia took her chance and made her way east, or to where she thought was east.

She had to make her own bearings and she decided that behind her was west and ahead was the east. east of what, she couldn't tell.

When she had helped ships make port, she had heard some man speak of places so cold that the rain became hard and course. Places where the sun chose not to shine and where many of them lost toes or ears to the chill of it. She had seen them too. Their skin had blackened, and they said that the blackest piece of them had died and fallen off on its own.

She hadn't noticed it yet, but she had been asleep for some time now. Her whole body had collapsed under the weight of her eyelids. A strange sleep, she had not stopped hearing or feeling the world around her. She had long lost the feeling in her legs, and now that she tried to make them move, all they wanted to do was buckle and let her fall.

She couldn't let it. She knew if she fell she wouldn't get back up.

She pressed on, hoping that the cold had an end. Maybe a coastline where the water hadn't frozen, where it got warmer and she could rest.

Each time the wind picked up she stopped to rest, gaining only a few minutes sleep at a time. She wondered how long she had been in this wintery tundra. Days? Weeks? She could have guessed either and believed both.

She had been suckling at the snow, defrosting the ice in her mouth when it landed on her face. It had a strange taste and with each piece, she only grew thirstier. Poking her numb tongue around her face for a speck of ice became something to do, something to keep her mind occupied. She knew that if she entertained the idea, that of parts of her turning black and falling off, she wouldn't be able to stop.

She survived for what could have been a few hours or days longer, growing weary and feeling less and less sensation in each limb as she heaved her way through the snow.

Each time she sunk a foot into the snow it fell deeper and was harder to remove.

The ice she suckled had stopped melting in her mouth - her temperature had dropped, her body heat was declining. But she couldn't stop. She could feel the path she had decided was leading her some place warm. There was a rise and peak only a few hundred meters ahead of her.

She felt every agonizing step to the top, no longer striding through the snow, her thighs were now counting down until their last step at the top.

She made it to the crest of the rise, stopped and staggered back, almost falling back down the hill as her legs begged to falter and rest. She looked out into the valley below.

Nothing.

Just a desert of white with more white in the distance. Her path before her ran down the hill and through the valley and on to the horizon where more white nothingness would go on and on. She gave into her legs' desires and sank her knees into the snow as she sobbed and laughed at the same time.

She finally succumbed falling flat on her stomach, pressing it deep into the snow and waiting for it to turn black and that made her laugh even harder.

She couldn't remember a time before this, before being here in the snow. She couldn't recall not feeling numb over every inch of her body. She had no recollection of being able to wriggle her toes, feel her own touch, or wanting to be in her own body.

There was a dark patch amongst the white along the side of the snowy dune. She opted to climb to her feet, but she lost the quarrel with her calves and her efforts had her fumble and tip over the edge of the hill. She rolled down the hillside, with no regard for her body or what it carried. She managed to shield her own head with her arms.

She now lay motionless at the bottom, only meters away from the dark patch. She laid there a while longer. The cold could only bring so much punishment, perhaps she could enjoy a break while it worked at her. She laid so long she was so tempted to await death. No more effort required, no more running from the inevitable. Perhaps it had already died inside of her, she had no way of knowing. If not, then could she swallow her tongue.

Again it felt like days. She didn't know if she had spent it staring up at the sky or with her eyes closed and asleep. Both were as dark as the other.

No inner dialogue, just silence and the void washed out and drowned by the fury of the blizzards howl. She roused from memories of her own screams or maybe screams from somewhere out there.

She was tired, and she figured she was frozen to the ground. If someone was out there screaming, they were on their own.

She rolled on her side and rubbed her hand over her stomach. It was half covered in snow, and she listened for it. She hadn't yet felt a kick or a tug. She thought of it like a fish caught in a strange net, swimming around and when it kicked it was flailing and thrashing, trying to spring loose.

She couldn't beat this fish with a stone, but she could wait until the cold became too much. It was a more quiet and calming way to go, Sancia figured.

She figured she would wait.

Lying there, rubbing her stomach, she looked out into the darkness of the white. The shades changed depending on how long she looked. Sometimes it was a deep black with a storm of white streaking across it, other times the white took over and there was just deepness of black. Black holes, black waves, black figures.

The black figures grew larger and made for her.

She felt her upper-chest and collarbone for the first time in a long time. The ice had stung it and she held it with her frozen fingers.

The black figures came closer. Dinosaurs. They had come back for her.

They'd cut her open, take what they wanted and leave her behind like discarded bones.

Sancia saw a hand reach out, she felt it on her skin, but the touch was cold, like the touch of a shadow. Beings with no faces. Dinosaurs with sly grins. His face as he held her down.

She kicked and shuffled. Urging compacted and frozen-tight muscles to push and squirm until she was out of the open and deep inside the dark cave. As she slid inside, her back against the wall of ice she kicked the snow back with her feet, making a wall between her and the opening to the small cave.

The dark figures did not follow.

She lost them in the snow.

Hours later she awoke, defrosted. Her hands and feet now receptive, clenching weak fists and flexing the arches of her feet.

She found that in her sleep she had held her stomach, which she dismissed and stuck them under her armpits.

She got to her feet and moved away from the cave wall and started inspecting her enclosure. With the pale light the outside let in, she could see how the cave widened at the mouth and its depth narrowed to a hole so small she couldn't fit down to its end, if it had any end - the light didn't make it that far. The walls of the cave weren't cold, instead warm enough that some of the ice was melting. She was in a kind of impossibility; the cave was a womb of nature. The heat ran through and under this immense cold. Its sweltering depth had carved this steam shaft out of the side of the hill and had thawed Sancia's frozen body.

But as one problem solved itself, the others remained. Sancia knew she couldn't last there much longer, no matter what luck Dah.'s jacket brought her. Her only escape was the half-used cube that she felt dig into her chest from inside the leather jacket pocket.

She could go anywhere with it, but that was the problem - she could go anywhere. As bad as it was here, somewhere else could be worse. She poked her head outside into the storm for the quickest of seconds but found no sight of the stars.

She found herself trapped beyond belief, silenced by the universe, shunned to the depths of its deepest corner. She laughed because of what she brought with her.

She wondered whether it would come with her, or if it would stay behind. Her belly seemed still. It felt hollow. It hadn't blackened, but some part had become detached.

"If I go, so will it." Sancia said aloud in her native tongue, or in her head. She wasn't sure. The storm was so loud she couldn't hear her own voice. But then the storm stopped, and the universe revealed itself.

She stared up into the brilliant array of stars, so many more than she ever had seen. The moonlight illuminated the white desert and the moon cast her faded shadow out into the distance. She wished she knew more about the stars, the constellations, the galaxies. She had spent her entire life looking down, tying knots and talking to no one.

No shadows or figures chased after her, nothing could find her here, in the universe's dark corner.

If she was ever going to leave this place, it would be like testing a doorknob to see if it was open or locked. She had to try.

Heavy breaths shook free from her quivering jaw. She was alive all over, yet she felt nothing in her gut.

"Little thing." She told it. *"I have to leave you behind... you know, I was left behind too."*

The stars were silent.

"Please don't follow your mother." She cried. *"You must stay here."*

She sighed, dragging in the ice with her breath and fell onto her back. She held her stomach and wished she could dig into it and rip it out.

"Is this what I was meant for? Am I supposed to carry this? Is this my punishment for not being as good as..." Sancia fumbled her numb hands for the cube and rested it on her chest, focusing on only it and not her stomach. *"I know a man would save himself. I'm just hoping that I might try."*

She fumbled the cube in her hands and unwittingly, unknowingly twisted and turned the cube, holding it at its last turn. She spun it's last five spins and placed the cube back on her chest, taking her last look at the stars and then to her belly.

*"Goodbye. I'm so sorry."**

---

*Go to Page 135

Chapter Three:
Out the Other

A loud thud rocked the barn as the roof caved in under Atticus' uninvited weight. Chickens flew out terrified and a brightly colored object bounced off the straw roof and down onto the path where mud caught it and clung tight.

For days and weeks, it settled before hooves kicked it free. It bounced down the hillside and sank into an open well. Deep in the water it drowned, its color fading more than it had already, and it settled at the bottom amongst the stones and heavy sticks until the winter came and froze the well solid.

✧ ✧ ✧

The thick rope bristled, ached and creaked like an old wooden step as the two men pulled from their end. The rope ran through their hands, up to a pulley, and lashed around a wooden cross attached to the point of the church. But the nails held tight, and it took two more men until it yanked free.

It snapped off the peak then they lowered the bulky cross onto the back of a cart. The cart groaned under the extra weight, and it unsettled the horse strapped to it. They then untied the cross and retied the rope to another wooden symbol shaped like a shield and they pulled again.

As the shield rose higher and higher, more of the kingdom could see the crest of their lord being mounted. The crest now sat as high as the barricade walls that ran around the castle Two foot-soldiers

that manned the wall stopped what they were doing to note the cross' replacement.

"There it be, he's finally done it." A foot-soldier said to the other as he put down his hammer to wipe his brow.

"Yes, for now it seems like the lord has a mighty hold." The second foot-soldier said, still holding a wooden pike steady. "But lords come and go, more so the ones that come as he did."

"Don't you let yourself be heard talking such ways. Or you'll end up like these poor fellows."

The first foot-soldier readied his hammer and continued to slam it down onto the top of the pike, ramming it in between bricks along of the top of the wall. The second foot soldier shook the pike and found it to be sturdy enough. Then the first foot soldier picked out a head from a sack beside him as the second whipped out a blade and carved the top of the pike sharp. With a practiced swing, the first foot-soldier slammed the opening of the neck down onto the now pointy spike and drove it straight through and out the top of the skull.

"How many more are in the sack?"

"Three." The first soldier replied.

"Christ almighty." The second sighed. "Why are we doing this?"

"He said he wants everyone to see their faces. And it's true, if I was an eye of a York and I saw one of these, I'd turn back and go the other way."

"Do you think it'll stop… them?"

"Them?"

"You know what I mean. Those… others. There's been talk that they come from the fog, they eat the nose off your face and put curses on you if you look at them ill."

"Heresy, complete heresy."

"That's why the Lord doesn't want anyone leaving the castle. He's protecting us."

"He's on guard for the Brittan's and the Yorks, that's what. Maybe even the French. And it'll do you no good to speak of the devil's work so blatantly on the Lord's Day."

"Which lord be that? The cross is gone."

"What say your faith?"

"My faith is in the lord that protects me from all evil. And if sticking heads on pikes shows my faith, then you can hand me the hammer."

The heads on the pikes froze each wintery night in the cold and defrosted over the course of the following day, kept in a horrific and perpetual state. Until the summer months came when they shriveled and sunk the flesh to bone, and with it, lakes and rivers cracked and the wells unfroze.

Deep down in a well, the pale yet colorful object waited for some time before a bucket broke its form. It sank to the bottom as water and the cube climbed inside and weighed it down before it ascended back to the surface.

They poured the bucket into a trough and snouts of all forms knocked it back and forth between them before finally a hand reached into the mess and retrieved it.

This hand wiped the colored cube on his harsh clothes and rushed to his horse to take it to the castle. Meanwhile, the cube rode in his pocket, rubbing dry and leaking the last of the murky water from between its joints.

The object was retrieved every so often to be shown as a token for access, before quickly being tucked away once again. The last time it left the pocket it never was hidden again. For a carefully fingered man grasped it, favorably feeling and weighing the cube in his palm before it was placed on a mantle with several other colored cubes, no longer lost but regrettably found.

Through the slums of the streets, clean boots left prints in the mud. The mud seemed to be what excused the fields from being roads. Varying sizes of stone marked the trail that led from the poor outskirts of the kingdom grounds all the way to the castle hall's gates.

The soldiers felt their rusting armor as they stood guard and waited for the arrival of anyone of colored cloth. Steel on steel screeched

whenever it grazed the surface of an adjoining plate resulting in a foul nails-on-a-chalkboard sound.

These soldiers watched as two knights escorted their Lord out from the fortress of the castle and unto the lands between it and the great walls that surrounded them.

Within the kingdom's realm, the markets were eternally lively, only stopping to jeer at any passing peasant up for the chopping block. The smell of livestock dwindled in the haze of fresh feces and straw. The smell only grew faint the higher up in the castle you went, or in the inside of the Blacksmith's shop.

Inside the shop, two children were playing with blunt swords the craftsmen had left out. The Blacksmith's wife was reading in the corner and the Blacksmith himself sat in front of his kiln, poking the flames with his left and rotating a rod with his right.

The sudden knock at the barn door alerted the family to withdraw from their activities and near disappear in the back of the shop.

The Blacksmith calmly rested his rod against the wall of the kiln and groaned as he got up to answer the call.

Standing at his doorstep were the two knights and between them stood the very Lord of the kingdom.

"A fair morning Blacksmith." Greeted the Lord.

"By his own power, the great Lord welcomes himself and wishes to inspect your shop. Refuse Blacksmith, and your head it will be." One knight barked.

The Blacksmith barely moved a toe from his spot.

"Come now you stern brutes, the Blacksmith seems more than co-operative. Isn't that so Blacksmith?" The Lord pressed.

"Come in." Answered the Blacksmith.

As they all went inside the Blacksmith's family kept quiet in the corners of the shop.

"Now do I have it right, Blacksmith, that you have crafted ten swords a week for my men for the last nine weeks. Is that correct?"

"Tis true." He answered.

"Wow, that's quick work Blacksmith. You're quite the sword maker. Would I be right in saying that you're an ancestor of this craft?"

"You would be."

"Interesting. Because, upon my last census, I found that you have only been a part of my kingdom for three summers. Tell me, where do you hail from?"

The two knights tightened up, ready to draw their swords at the first mention of a York or Brit.

The Blacksmith didn't answer. The Lord frowned and then turned his attention to the kiln, still hot.

"Ah, the fires of a blacksmith. Keeps the smell out wonderfully, a great place for anyone who wasn't yet accustomed to the stench." The Lord strode over to the kiln, de-gloving as he walked, he held his bare hands over the heat emitting from the belly of the kiln.

"I bet it's also great for warmth in these winters, especially for someone not familiar with the freezing winds and snow." He held his hands even closer to the kiln and breathed in its glorious heat. Behind, the Lord silently approached one of the Blacksmith's children.

"I'd say the comfort of the high towers fair you the same pleasures." The Blacksmith said.

The Lord retracted and turned away from the fire. The Blacksmith eyeing the boy to stay unseen.

But the Lord, busy touching his warm hands against his cheek, spun to see the boy as he stood.

"Ah Blacksmith, is this one of yours?"

The Blacksmith grew ever silent.

"I hope he hasn't fallen ill to the latest outbreak of Yorkish Pox. Many have, but I'm glad to see that by some miracle your son seems fine."

The Lord then opened the kiln curiously.

"I wonder Blacksmith, what have you been working on today?"

He reached in and pulled out the rod. At the end of it was a melted opaque bit of glass. The Lord held it up to his face, distorting his eye before the Blacksmith whilst inspecting it.

"My my my. You are a talented one. Is this glasswork I see? Talented hands smith, and a talented mind."

The Blacksmith gulped and looked at his wife, still hidden in the corner.

The Lord approached the knights. As he stepped there was a creak in the floor that was so sudden it finally shook the Blacksmith. The Lord smirked and came before the knights. He swung the rod in front of the eye-slits of their helmets, smoke drifting off the rod as he did.

"Now it seems to me that this kind of glassware is a little ahead of its time. Clear work, round shape. My my Blacksmith you sure are a clever one. How did you ever come up with it? Hmmmm let me think."

"Please, I sold no one anything that I shouldn't have. Kept to ourselves as much as we could."

The Lord pondered, whilst spinning the rod between his fingers. Then tossing it aside, he crouched by the Blacksmith, mouth to his ear.

"Do you vow to keep the sanctity of the kingdom true and strong?"

"Yes."

"Do you swear to honor your Lord before you in all his glory?"

"Yes."

"And do you hold him as your God and savior?"

"… Yes."

The Lord sighed with relief and stood back up.

"Excellent. We shall leave you to it."

The Blacksmith couldn't believe it. His eyes crushed the last tears he had shed in disbelief.

The Lord walked with the knights out the door and watched as they continued through the courts of the citadel.

The Lord then closed the door behind him and approached the Blacksmith.

"Before I go Blacksmith, I have one last question." The Lord pulled from his sleeve a faded mixture of color wrapped around a cube. He held it up and showed it to them. "This wouldn't be yours, would it?"

The Blacksmith gulped.

"My men found it on the grounds, and they brought it straight to me, as they do with the ones they find on the bodies of those that come at night." The Lord stepped further inside the shop. "I take it you know what this is? If it isn't yours, then you will tell me who's it is."

The Blacksmith frantically struck up a sword and held it out in front of him. His wife came out of the corner of the shop, also wielding a blade. The boy pulled his knife from its sheath, whilst the oldest daughter picked up the rod the Lord had tossed aside. She cracked it against the kiln, breaking the hardened glass into shards that armed the rod. The Lord was at the dangerous end of several weapons.

"Well, aren't we a lively bunch once the fuzz has left the room?" The Lord chuckled and then whipped out his own sword.

"Just go, leave this place." The Blacksmith's wife spat. "This was a peaceful and fair time before you came along. We made a home here."

"Does she always speak out of turn?" The Lord asked the Blacksmith.

As quick as the Blacksmith could be, he wasn't quick enough as the Lord slid his sword through the belly of his wife. Pulling it out, he slashed his son and his daughter who dashed at him. One by one they all fell. The Blacksmith tried to catch them as they fell. Huddled with their bleeding bodies, the Blacksmith wept.

"You're a monster." The Blacksmith cursed. "Worse than a Historian."

"Why thank you."

"I hope they get you. I hope they kill you."

"And I hope you don't make a mess when you bleed." The Lord snarled as he prodded the Blacksmith with his sword.

At the sound of the screams, the knights stormed back inside the Blacksmith's shop to find the Blacksmith nursing a wounded shoulder, his family limp and their Lord wiping his sword on his robes.

"More spies, my Lord?"

"Should we take their heads?"

"No, they're just traitors to the crest." The Lord sighed. "Leave them to rot but take him to the dungeons."

He poured gold pieces into their grubby gauntlets and they grabbed the sunken Blacksmith, too diminished by mourning and wounded to argue or fight, and they dragged him out of the shop and back up to the castle.

As they passed, people stopped and stared at the Blacksmith being escorted by the two knights, sending a shock wave of suspicion and hearsay. They looked to the sky. Night hadn't even come and yet they still weren't safe.

The treachery of the Blacksmith and his family was the talk of the marketplace. Many were quick to blame the witch magic that their Lord had warned them about, cursing the Blacksmith for not favoring his end of the deal that granted him magical powers to complete so many swords in so few weeks.

Others talked of the Lord being wise enough to catch the Blacksmith and his family for disloyalty - that they were spies from the south.

But a quiet and pensive old man suggested that perhaps the Lord was being paranoid. A term they had not yet come to know, but they all trusted the wise old man to know what they knew not.

The wise old man had been the one to warn them of the rats, to have them cleanse their hands and to feed the sick some fruit to save them from sickness. For this, the wise old man did nothing but sit and take the food and clothing he was brought.

That day the rainstorm chased the market closed and farmers filled up their carts and hurried along the worn path leading to his corner of the citadel. Once they would sew and farm vast fields, but ever since the Lord banned anyone from leaving the protection of the high stonewalls, the farmers had to make do by farming chickens, cows and wheat from behind the walls of the citadel. The slopes of the farmhands outside had now gone unattended. With each rainfall the evenly raked fields turned to well-fenced pits of mud. The Lord called this a strategic decision, creating slippery terrain. Slippery enough to keep his people

inside slowly going mad eating only eggs, bread and milk. They ached to slaughter a chicken or two for the meat, but as the wise old man had said it would be an even slipperier slope having no food at all. They fed well him for this wisdom.

That night the wind was odd, fiercely burrowing against the northern walls and then cutting off and battering the south for a few seconds and then blew against the north once again.

A shift in the air had the wise old man worried. It had happened a few times before and nothing good ever came of it.

He was not the only one to notice, coming out of his shack to look up to the high towers of the castle where the Lord slept and seeing the glowing windows from firelight.

Word had spread that each night the Lord insisted more and more knights were fending off the stairway to his chambers and had several of his best were to guard him while he slept.

Every morning was the same. No one reported any break-ins and no foot soldiers on the walls saw anyone climb over, but every morning the knights would carry out body after body and dump them on a pile where their heads would be cut off and then handed off to the foot-soldiers to stick on pikes.

The fires were lit across the high stone wall, from the eastern side a cascade of sudden fire passed down to the western wall and an onslaught of yelling and barking of orders filled the castle towers.

The castle had been stormed many times before, it still bore the wounds of old wars in the walls and in the grounds. Whatever army was coming, Yorks, Brits or the French, it was not what Lord had been preparing for - he was ready for much worse.

As the armies inside the stone castle gathered and spread the rising hysteria to such a point, many of them were stabbing tapestries that moved as they passed them by. The wise old man made for the Blacksmith's now empty shop. As he beat at the door, he found a few scared farmers had already barricaded themselves inside and were quick to let him in.

But the wise old man was quicker to kick them out. Booting them into the dark and open cold of night as he locked the door behind him, screaming out reasons why he needed it more than them.

Night had fallen over wherever this was.

Madness brewed in dormancy, only giving rise to more tension. On ground level, the close quarters of the kingdom felt even closer as each panicked citizen rushed about, avoiding all shadows and strange faces. Knights were on high alert. They finished storming their own castle and now ran about the grounds knocking over carts and banners. They swung their swords about in such alarm that they accidently slew many of their own.

It was a wonder no one noticed ten new feet landing amongst all the commotion, all in odd clothing for the times. Eight of the feet landed steadily, only one slipped and fell flat on his face.

"Fuuuuck!" Vaughn groaned, holding his nose again, not sure if it was old blood or new mud.

Vaughn hadn't yet noticed the ensuing madness about them. It was still dark but sudden and sporadic fires gave light to each darting civilian of the kingdom.

"What's going on?" Dahl asked pointlessly, seeing the same mess of chaos as the others. "Where d'you bring us?"

The group couldn't see much. In the darkness there were screams and in the orange firelight there were shadows. Behind them there was the wall, brightly lit up by the fires at each interval and with it they could see hundreds of spikes all supporting heads at varying stages of decay.

"They've gone mad. They're running from something." Nash surmised.

"What are they running from?" Sancia asked.

"Doesn't matter, we find Crowe." Galina said, just as a middle-aged man ran past entirely in the nude spreading goat blood all over his torso.

"And how do you suppose we do that?" Vaughn shot back. "What if he's head to toe in feces doing handstands?"

At that moment, a shrieking woman darted past their little huddle and holding a small wooden carving of a shield crest in her hands. She ran with it towards the wall and with all her might she tried to throw it over but couldn't find the strength.

The crest fell in the mud in front of the group of travelers and as she went to retrieve it she spotted the five strangers; all obscenely calm in comparison.

"Are… are you all demons or… or the French?"

"No." Sancia spoke.

The woman seemed unsure. She backed away, ready to do the five of them in to any knight that'd listen.

Out of nowhere, Dahl threw his hands up in the air and screamed as loud as he could.

"WE'RE ALL GOING TO DIE!"

Dahl broke into a run and the group shrugged and followed his cue, the five of them running about in the mud, slipping where they felt and ducking swords where they could. They all acted as insane as possible.

Dahl jumped into a pile of mud and did a backstroke. Nash jumped up and down, speaking in fake tongues. Galina grabbed anyone she could, asking if they were a crow. Sancia ran in circles chasing loose chickens.

Shocked, Vaughn stood still and watched as his friends acted like lunatics. But shocked even more that it seemed to work. The woman soon left them alone and continued trying to toss the shield. All strange behavior and madness existed as one. They saw crazy and matched it. The group slogged their way up towards the castle, eyeing each madman for perfect teeth and unblemished skin, Vaughn nodding at all with his hands in his pockets.

Tiring themselves out and finally finding a quiet spot against the castle walls, they found labeled doors to the *Lord's Bakery*, the *Lord's Doctor* and the *Lord's Blacksmith*. They checked each shop, finding the insides had already been ransacked and torn apart now. Only

scared huddled farmers and families hid inside. Vaughn saw that the blacksmith shop had a small crowd gathered before the door. They were kicking and beating at it, trying to get in. But the door remained shut, being a sturdier door to suit a blacksmith.

"Go away!" The voice hidden inside called out the doorknockers.

Vaughn and the others watched the crowd beating at the door. They were all so desperate, but not as crazed as the others. They clung to their children or loved ones and just wanted a safe, quiet spot to hide until morning. But the door remained shut.

Suddenly a cannon fired out the window of a tall tower. The boom echoed down, and more fire sprung up from outside the castle walls, igniting the woods in the distance. Something was under all their skin. A loud and invisible war was going on and Vaughn felt for these farmers and families. They wanted no part but to hide.

As a group, they all started ramming the door and Dahl, Vaughn and Sancia found it hard to not get swept up by the crowd. They were pulled near the front and met the door with their faces. Vaughn's nose convulsed with fresh, throbbing pain.

"Would you all just stop it?" The voice from inside barked. "Find your own hiding spot before you ruin this one!"

"Just let us in, please." One mother begged. "Wise sir, please! Let us in!"

"He's mad! The Lord's mad!"

"It's not safe out here!"

Suddenly a sliding slot in the door slid open, no bigger than a brick. The peasants shoved their hands in and felt around but whipped them back out and clutched the fresh cuts that they had earned.

Two beady eyes met with the door slot. The man inside spied them all.

"Now I don't want to tell you all again. This is *my* spot. If you want me to keep giving you all my wise words of advice than you all better…"

The man stopped, his eyes caught sight of Vaughn, Dahl and Sancia.

"You?"

"Atticus?"

"You wouldn't happen to have any cubes on you by chance, would you?"

"Only if you come out."

The slot quickly slid shut and most of the farmers rioted. They flung themselves at the door and dug at the sliding slot with their dirty fingers.

"Atticus?" Nash called out. "We're here to rescue you!"

"Can you come back later?" Atticus called from the other side of the door.

Another boom from above as a cannon ball rocketed overhead and over the wall. It made impact with something, probably nothing but Vaughn felt the impact rumble under his feet. Or was it the stampede of the mob?

"Coward!"

"Break the door down!"

A furious roar came from the foul smelling, rag wearing mob as they rushed the door and tried to beat it down with all their strength. Vaughn wrestled a path out of the way. The Blacksmith's doors had dark thick boards and well forged brackets - it wasn't coming down anytime soon.

"Why are we trying to rescue this prick again?" Vaughn asked Dahl beside him as they slid out from the crowd.

"We have to try!" Nash called. "We have to make him come out!"

Despite the clanging of swords that echoed down from the towers, despite the rampant fires springing up wherever stray arrows struck, despite the screams they heard and winds they felt. Vaughn, Galina and Nash made for the Blacksmith door again and eased back the mob with steady hands and an arm with a hole in it.

"Atticus?" Nash tried. "We're here to rescue you. Just open the door."

"Are you crazy?" Atticus called back, not opening the slot this time. "I've been stranded here in this pigsty for who knows how long. It stinks, I can't shower, everything tastes like grease…"

"Atticus come. We take you to safe place." Galina added. "I hose you down myself."

There was a silence as he pondered the offer. Vaughn felt an anger rising as he was forced to stare at a wooden door in the cold, damp night while the rich man made up his mind.

"Nope, they'll tear me apart. I'm not coming out."

The sound of horseshoes and metal hitting stone came from just around the corner.

"I'll tear you apart!" Galina kicked the door. "You insolent motherfucker!"

Sancia clung to Dahl as they pushed past foul-smelling armpits and backsides. The crowd now violent, clawed and scattered out of there.

Everything got louder and rounding the corner of the citadel three knights on horseback tore into the crowd, splitting them as they scuttled in all directions like cockroaches. They cornered Dahl and Sancia. They nabbed Galina and Nash by their untimely collars. And a firm hilt hit Vaughn square between the eyes.

As morning came, very little light broke through the stone and mortar. Streams of it in solid beams shot through the walls, parting the group caged down there. They stood and lent on their feet side to side, feeling the mud beneath them and pondering if it were more than just mud.

Too tired to stand any longer they gave into sliding their backs down the walls until they were sitting in it.

Vaughn awoke, a hint of light landing on his eyelid and burning through until he roused and kicked frantically awake. He found he was locked in the same tight cage as the others, down in the dungeons.

As more sunlight came through, they could see the rest of the dungeon walls. Next to Dahl a foot hung loosely. It was only when a warm beam of sunlight touched it did the man it belonged to sigh with little relief and release a trickling down the wall, bouncing onto Dahl's shoulder.

Dahl sprung up and looked above him as the others did. The wall was at least twenty meters high and ordered in neat rows and columns were more feeble people. They were chained to the walls, and either

were completely withered or still withering away. Right next to the urinating man above Dahl was a man with a black bruise the size of a palm on his shoulder, his torso covered in dry, black blood.

"No one talk." Galina said. "They listen."

"Yeah, right." Vaughn stretched his forehead and felt the sore spot where a lump was forming. He looked up as he did, eyeing all the poor, limp figures on the walls. "I'm sure all these guys are here for diligent notetaking."

"We can't break." Nash stressed. "No one should know who we really are."

"What was that all about, huh? Why didn't Atticus open the door?" Dahl asked.

"They would have torn him apart if he had." Nash answered.

"I'm sure he deserved it." Vaughn added. "What reason does Atticus have for being on that list?"

"Vaughn don't be so…"

"So, what? Negative?" Vaughn almost laughed, and he pointed to the wall-clung man now squeezing out more mud to add to the cage floor. "Unless I'm that guy, I don't think I could be in a worse – Dahl seriously move!"

Dahl quickly skittered out of the way before the shit dripped down the walls to where he had been resting. They sat in silence for a bit as the morning sunlight moved up the walls. Dahl leaned into Sancia, and they spoke softly between themselves. Nash and Galina had fallen into a deep conversation, their eyes falling on Vaughn every so often as he clung to the cage bars and swung lazily off them. He watched the tortured man and woman hanging above them, some only waking to moan or cry.

The one just above Dahl was more awake than most of the others. He had been watching them carefully.

"What're you looking at?" Vaughn snapped at him.

The hanging man with the wounded shoulder suckled his mouth wet to talk. "They didn't get him again, did they?" He said softly.

"Get who?" Vaughn asked.

"I was hoping they would. But it's no use. Every night they come and every night they fail."

"Can you stop playing the pronoun game?" Vaughn barked. "Who are you…?"

"The Lord. He barricaded the kingdom. No one is allowed in or out. Every night they come to try to put things right. They don't like it when things change."

"Historians." Galina gasped.

"He found me out, me and my family. He doesn't like sharing. He wants to be the only one. When he finds out who you are and that you're here, you will be up here with me. Or worse, out there with them."

The hanging man nodded to look out the slight crack between the bricks. Dahl tried to hoist himself up but was too short. He stepped down and Vaughn tried himself, boosting up higher he got an eye to the crack-hole, and he had a clear view of the huge wall that ran around the castle. There, placed evenly like streetlights along a road, were wooden pikes and rotting atop the pointy ends were the heads. Just as haunting as they had been the night before.

The prisoners waited for the withering man above them to take his last breaths. There was nothing they could do and the more the man gasped and begging for water or food, the more it sunk into their own minds that they would soon be next. Not one guard had come and brought them anything to eat or drink. Sancia was dealing worse than the others. Her stomach ached. She kept tossing and turning against the hard bars of the cage at her back.

The smell had long aged out as a nuisance, though none of them were pleased that it would be the last thing they smelt. The only member of their party with higher hopes for his nostrils was Dahl who was still looking up at the bars and down to the far side of the dungeon at the doorway, expecting it to swing open at any second.

"You've got to use the back of your mouth, curve your tongue back and just flick it forward."

"Like this?" Sancia asked, opening her mouth wide so that Dahl could see how her tongue had folded.

"Yeah, just like that."

Sancia let fly a wad of spit as she tried to click her tongue like a horse. Dahl cracked up and Sancia chuckled despite her aching stomach. Even the corner of Galina's lip lifted, if only a little.

"You'll get the hang of it." Dahl said playfully.

"If we get out of here." Sancia dropped the mood.

"When we get out of here." Dahl smiled. "In the meantime, it's something to pass the time."

"It's probably the last of our time, I don't want to just let it pass." Vaughn snarled.

"That is life though." Galina said softly. "It passes around you. Pull you with it."

"Don't you start…" Vaughn sighed.

"It's all set. Sometimes we convince ourselves it's not and we are free. But we only feel free. Life is tricky. It let us feel like we choose and decide, so we don't complain. Free will just something to numb pain."

"You make it sound so bad." Dahl replied. "Don't you ever see the beauty in destiny?"

"I thought I had this destiny once. I try do what I thought I was meant to do. All destiny wants is to use you and spit you. I thought I was… I thought I could… no. Destiny? All too pretty a word for fate."

Galina rolled her shoulder blades back against the bars and rubbed at her calf.

"You could only try Gal." Nash assured her with half a grin.

"I think it's so comforting." Dahl shrugged. "I used to think a mistake was a mistake. I used to go through life worrying whether I was making the right choices and worrying about old choices before that. But there are no mistakes anymore. Everything you do is the right thing. Everything that happens to you is the right thing."

Sancia pushed off from Dahl and lent against the cold iron bars instead. Something had hit a nerve.

"Dahl you just…" Nash started.

"What?" Dahl said. "I don't get why everyone has a problem with this. I hate to beat a horse to death about this, but I don't understand how the lack of free will doesn't make you all feel even free-er?

"Dahl." Vaughn sighed.

"Yes?"

"Shut up."

At that very moment, a loud creak of the large wooden doors let in two men in metal suits. They ran with their swords out, red with blood that they couldn't and wouldn't explain. Now that day had come they seemed more composed. But the darkness of the dungeons brought back the fear of the night and they poked the walls and iron bars of the cages until they stood before their new prisoners.

"In the name of the lord, you will speak the truth." One started, his voice gaining confidence as he went on. "What side are you loyal to?"

"What side?" Galina asked. "Yours, course."

"False bearers and escapees get the wall!" The knight threatened. "We found you running from the royal guard."

"You were chasing us." Vaughn blurted out.

"We are not from the other side!" Nash pressed.

"If none of you will speak the truth." The other knight declared. "Then the truth will have to be taken from you."

"That doesn't sound good." Vaughn sighed.

Suddenly the cage was unlocked, and the two knights grabbed what they could. Thwarting any attempts to save him, they snatched Vaughn. They beat and hooded him before he could even crack a joke.

Vaughn didn't know where he was being taken, but as the smell grew worse, he suddenly found himself hanging upside down. His nose ached from this disagreeable angle, and he looked up, which was down. Below him was a bucket of blackness. As his eyes adjusted, he could see the blackness was moving. Small little black clumps, with tiny legs and rounded bodies. They scrambled over each other trying to climb out of the bucket.

The spiders were just as unhappy as Vaughn.

Vaughn looked down, which was up, to see a rope bound his legs and ran to a pulley. The knights held the more appealing end of the rope, ready to give him some slack.

"You will speak to the Lord, everybody does." The knight almost looked disappointed at the fact he might not get the chance to let the rope go.

Vaughn could hear the clunking of footsteps entering the chamber. He saw feet and followed them up to the face. The Lord was dressed in chain mail, it hung heavy under his thick woolen clothes that looked like he was wearing his bedding around with him. Atop his head was a crown, strapped down by a leather belt that ran under his chin.

"Well, well, well, who's laughing now?" The Lord smirked.

Maybe Vaughn would have laughed, if the man hadn't a history of fumbling a good joke. The only commendable thing about him was his timing, having left the Asylum before the Historians had arrived. No longer stammering drunk, no longer appealing for applause, the man Vaughn had nicknamed the Comedian had found a way to entertain himself.

"If this is a joke, I don't get it." Vaughn answered, turning his upside-down head to the knights. "Listen fellas, do me a favor and let go of the rope."

"I don't think so." The Lord declined, and with a hand he ushered the knights to tie the rope to a hook and leave the chamber. They did so with brief hesitation but quivering coordination in the presence of their lord: The Comedian.

"So, heard any good jokes lately?" Vaughn said as he tried to swing his head away from the spider bucket.

"Cute, that's real cute."

"No, I'm serious. You were a huge hit at the Asylum. Everyone applauded when you left. Well, because you left."

The Comedian grimaced and sighed hard to let it go.

"You know I'm surprised to see you. I gather your friends downstairs are also from that party?"

"Yup." Vaughn's eyes left the Comedian and came back to the bucket of spiders, now climbing atop one another in a small terrifying tower to get closer and closer to the top of Vaughn's head. The Comedian stepped over to Vaughn and slid the bucket away with his steel-clad boot until it was clear of his head. He then untied the rope from the hook on the wall and Vaughn fell to the floor, yet again on his nose.

"Are you impressed with it all so far?" The Comedian asked as Vaughn slipped free of his bonds.

"With what?" Vaughn got up slowly to his feet and rubbed around his nose as it stung and made his eyes water.

"I'll show you." The Comedian led Vaughn out from the torture chamber, and they followed a hall that led to a tower of stairs.

"Cool," Vaughn nodded to the stairs. "After this I can show you *my* sex dungeon. It's not as clean, but still..."

As they walked up the steps, they passed windows boarded up with planks of wood leaving only a slit to see through. As they got higher Vaughn noticed streaks of blood across the walls but no bodies. The Comedian stepped around them. Every knight stationed at each doorway or turn of the stairwell raised their helmets as their Lord passed, revealing their faces and nodding.

The Comedian noted every one of them until finally he came to the top chamber of the tower where no less than eight knights guarded the door. All eight raised their hands to lift their helmets, but one struggled. The left side of his helmet had suffered a blow and dented it in, making the sliding part jam. The hoard of knights panicked, as the Comedian readied himself, reaching for the blade at his own side. After much whimpering and unsteady breaths, the knight finally jerked the helmet up and the Comedian had a good, long look before finally nodding and parting the knights to lead Vaughn through with him.

Inside the Lord's chamber were warm fluffy sheets fitted to a foam mattress. There were bowls of fresh fruit, kegs of filtered water and bags of packaged food. Vaughn could see upon his mantle were several colorful cubes, and there were two wide windows on either side of the

room. These windows were fitted with inch thick glass and looked out over the kingdom.

Both Vaughn and the Comedian stood and looked down as the people in his land darted around unsure of themselves or others. The fires along the walls had burnt out and knights were being assigned new routes and rotations to keep watch as others crammed fresh heads onto pikes.

"This is what I wanted you to see."

"What am I looking at here?"

"My knights cover every corner of this castle and its grounds. I have them on constant high alert. It helps to slip a little Ritalin into the water supply."

Every word was a crumb Vaughn crushed between his teeth. He noticed from this high the unusual crest atop the church, and the Comedian followed his gaze.

"Ah yes, when I found this place it was in a constant state of war, the French, Brittany and Yorkshire all clamber over one another for this place. All in the name of religion. Once I took the throne, I renounced its falsities, centuries in advance, and now these people honor me for it."

"Is that who those heads belong to?"

"Those? Of course not, we haven't had an attack from the other nations in months. I've built an Asylum Vaughn. A real Asylum. Granted, I might have bent a few rules, changed a few aspects of history. So, who do you think those heads are?"

Vaughn knew. "Historians."

"We can all see their faces now." The Comedian snarled. "They attack almost every night but like I said, with my men's rigorous vigilance, they don't stand a chance. So, are you impressed now?"

"Immensely." Vaughn said through gritted teeth. "Do you have any idea what you've done?"

"I perfected what Atticus could not. I made a real Asylum."

"And you've destroyed the lives of everyone who ever lived here."

"Pfffft its one timeline. You know how small that is? Hell, go jump somewhere and find yourself one you like. Leave me with this one; I've cleaned it up nicely. Made it my own." As the Comedian spoke,

he circled Vaughn, considering head height and his rough size. "You people are too judgmental and honestly, selfish. There's plenty of timelines to go round."

Vaughn couldn't even tally the amount of havoc he had wrought on the universe, how many twisted strains it had put on the timeline. How beyond screwed everything was becoming. Vaughn feared the unfunny Comedian might have created a world wherein Pete wouldn't even be born. He looked at his own hands, imagining them fading with every unforgivable detail.

This was no laughing matter.

"Why are you showing me all this? What do you want me to say? What cheek did you want me to kiss?"

"I wanted you to finally get the joke. You all laughed me out of your Asylum so I will make you all the laughingstock of mine." The Comedian finished eying off every aspect of Vaughn's appearance. "The others, I mean, not you. I have another, better use for you."

Night fell again. Vaughn tasted a soggy cloth that had been jammed in his mouth and was causing a bout of silent and painful coughs. His own breath was choking him, as every attempt to breathe solely through his nose came with the ache of the broken cartilage.

The Comedian had him tied up under a high thread count, which was the only positive Vaughn could muster. He hadn't touched anything as soft as this in days. The crown strapped to his head poked through the pillow and under the blankets he was forced to wear the bizarre robes of the Comedian. They were like large, bundles of tapestries more than royal wear.

Vaughn couldn't hear a thing outside as the army of guards had been dispatched to the wall for the night. So were the knights that lined the spiraling staircase that led up the tower. Vaughn was alone and awaited the timely arrival to come that night. They had strung him up, bait as it were, for whatever no-faced assassin the Comedian rightly feared would come for him.

He couldn't tell but wind reached his window. It shook the glass plate ever so slightly as though it were a warning and then left him to wait.

Gracing the stairs with gentle footsteps, a shadowing figure climbed with exponential ease. A blade was drawn and dangling from a tight, right hand but found not one chest to drive it into.

The hooded figure kept climbing until they had reached the top of the tower.

Vaughn craned his neck, dragging his pillow up with it, so he could watch the door. The lively torch fire outside the chamber that lit the edges of the doorway was suddenly extinguished.

Under all those layers, his skin went frigid and cold. He thought of nothing but his own inane breathing.

The darkness fiddled with the doorknob. Vaughn half hoped they had locked it in some force of habit, but the door brushed open.

Standing there, now towering before the hallway torchlight, the ominous figure eyed the room.

The blade splintered light as the wielder played with his grip. Vaughn watched as they inspected the room, poking rolls of toilet paper, ripe bananas, running a finger along the top of the fireplace mantle where the Lord's collection of cubes had sat. Finally, they heard the breaths Vaughn was trying so hard to stifle.

The figure suddenly pounced onto the bed, straddling Vaughn between their legs and pinning down what was already pinned and helpless. The ominous figure tore the sheets back to reveal Vaughn's terrified face as they held the dagger beside Vaughn's ear ready to plunge.

"Vaughn?"

Vaughn needed more than that to open his eyes. He had them tightly shut and his own strobing heartbeat deafened him.

"Stop it Vaughn. Open wimpy eyes."

Vaughn wondered why being stabbed felt so much like nothing, perhaps it was the shock. Had his adrenalin chased away the pain? He opened his eyes a tad.

"Galina?"

Galina lowered the knife and leaned in to get a closer look.

"Vaughn what the hell? You go off by self and I find you sleeping with bad guy?"

"I am not! He took my clothes off, wait no. He dressed me… well it's not like that… look he's using me. I'm bait. We've got to get out of here before someone dangerous comes."

"You think Galina not dangerous?" Galina raised her brows as she swung her knife around.

"No, yes. Just untie me, would you?"

Galina sliced the bonds with her knife, slightly upset that's all it was good for, and helped Vaughn to his feet under all the bulk. Vaughn then dropped his head out of its hole and sunk into the washing pile he was wearing, slipping out the bottom in just his slacks. Galina looked around and found Vaughn's dirty white shirt, hoodie, and pants had been tossed loosely in a corner.

"How d'you get out?" Vaughn hissed.

"Atticus found us, set us free. I knew he was on list for good reason."

"He's using us, he's got to be. We have cubes and he doesn't."

"At least he don't sleep on job."

"You know what, fuck you. Leave me here then." Vaughn retorted.

"Come." She smiled. "While coast clear."

The two of them snuck back out of the Lord's chamber and back down the stairs. Vaughn marveled at how easy it was to go down and shivered in worry at how easy it would've been for someone less friendly to come up. At the base of the tower where the stairs ended, a strong flicker of firelight and even stronger threats and fury rose, echoing up the tower.

"I don't think we can go this way."

"It's up or down." Galina said, nodding back up to the Lord's chambers.

The heat of the fire warmed the stone walls, Vaughn felt it under his palms that rested on the wall. Galina backed up a step, scratching at her calf with her boot as she looked down to the chaos below and back up to where they had come from.

Through the slits in the towers boarded-up windows, Vaughn saw how high they were. The moonlight shimmered off the knights that parried fantasy along the wall and about the grounds. Swords struck and slit paranoid peasants and wildfires sprung up from the flickers of burning bodies.

The only part of the castle Vaughn could see was the second tower. It's windows were dark.

Vaughn spied through timber boards and saw something moving in the darker tower. A few silent stalkers scurrying about.

"Gal. Look."

Galina saw them too and with her knife, pried the barricading boards loose from the window and tossed them aside.

"Nash!"

One window level down, the Asian man popped out his head and waved to them both, an uneasy grin on his face. He knew.

"Ok Vaughn, you first."

"Me first what?"

"Jump."

"Fuck."

Vaughn looked down to the opposite tower. Nash's window was a good ten meters lower than theirs. The jump wasn't even that far. Four or five arms with ready hands stuck out, ready to grab him. And right down below - a solid stone landing.

His leg shook. His knee wanted to buckle as he placed his foot on the window ledge. Galina shoved him almost all the way out, her firm hands on his butt.

"Jump."

"I'll go when I'm ready."

"Ready?" Galina shoved hard and Vaughn flew. He felt stiff wind and nothing else. Weightless and helpless, he flailed his arms and legs and hoped to be caught.

His foot hit the window ledge and the rest of him toppled back.

But a firm hand caught his sleeve. Dahl held fast and fell faster as Vaughn's weight pulled him out of the tower and out the window.

There they both hung, suspended by a chain of struggling grip as Nash reeled them in and back inside the tower.

"Fuck fucking fuck." Vaughn shook off his nerves and the thoughts of falling.

"Ready?"

Galina's voice sailed down to them. Vaughn still stood closest to the window. He saw her knees bend and her hands reach out.

He'd have to catch her. Vaughn felt his hands sweat and sweat. He wiped them on his pants, slippery still. Limp? He wasn't sure.

Fuck, she jumped.

He reached out and hoped, almost closing his eyes.

Galina fell into his arms. He held her tight and didn't let his grip go. He had her. He caught her. Shaking and reeling with relief, Vaughn struggled to help her step into the tower and keep his firm hold. Galina bent awkwardly, and as she did, the moonlight caught a glint of color from the cube slipping from her pocket.

It squeezed it free, and the cube dropped silently.

Rushing past Vaughn, Atticus darted to the window and dove for it, both arms outstretched and his knees scraping the edge of the window ledge.

On reflex, Dahl, Sancia and Nash grabbed his legs and pulled Atticus back up. The old man slunk back inside the tower, a daze of relief on his face as he panted heavily.

"What was that Crowe?" Nash blasted him.

Atticus still panting, held up the cube he had caught and smirked.

"That is not our only cube." Galina growled.

"Well, excuse me for helping." Atticus grumbled.

Galina held out her hand and he begrudgingly handed it back.

The group snuck down the silent tower and out into the open.

Moonlight lit the wet grass. They followed the path not covered in footprints to stray to the far corners of the castle grounds.

As they moved, they left behind distant wails of tragic figures. Haphazard and clumsy assault on terrors unseen as swords clashed and more fires sprung up amid screams and wind.

"Are you ok?" Vaughn asked, nodding to Sancia once they had gotten far enough to talk.

"I am." She answered.

"Good." Vaughn turned to Atticus and his voice hardened. "Crowe."

"Um…"

Vaughn noticed Atticus' eye drop to look for a nametag that wasn't there.

"It's Vaughn, you fucking prick!"

"Vaughn, calm down." Galina hushed.

"No, screw this. He's just here because we have something he wants. He wants our cubes. He is using us."

"It doesn't matter." Nash yelled. "He's on the list. He's coming, no matter what."

"Fuck!" Vaughn stomped away from the group, holding his head and trying not to crush his own skull. He let go and could hear it starting up again; the screaming, the fires, the chaos.

He felt like it was truly broken. The way they ran and screamed reminded him of the people he had seen on New Year's Day in the city streets, breaking stuff, yelling and screaming. This is what time travel did to people. He looked back to Nash and Galina, the people that were supposedly set on fixing all of this, who were more concerned with making sure this asshole was safe.

He couldn't grasp the plan, he wasn't sure there was one. If Dahl, Atticus, Wyla and himself were all pieces of some big puzzle, he wasn't sure he wanted to see the finished picture.

Vaughn cared more about those not on the list. Sancia and Pete hadn't hurt anybody, and for that O'seus hadn't planned on saving them.

After all this, Vaughn thought, *when I get home, and the others have all returned to where they're supposed to be what will I do? Where will I go?*

Vaughn didn't know. He didn't know if this would ever be over. Whether this madness would ever stop and let him let go of all this irritation. He didn't feel like he had made any progression from being pushed through time to now being pulled.

Galina came up to Vaughn and put the cube in his hands, trying to help him learn. But all he was learning was that he wasn't really in control. He still had to twist it and turn as she said.

Though, it did make it a little easier knowing where she planned on going next.

Just as Vaughn began to solve the cube Dahl wrapped a hand over his shoulder.

"Just wait." Dahl said.

"For what?" Atticus hissed.

Dahl pointed up ahead over the wall. In between the hills covered in woodlands there peaked a golden shine. It was flooding through the trees and bathing the fields and eclipsing the walls.

"Just look." Dahl said, letting go of Vaughn's shoulder and taking Sancia's hand. "Isn't it beautiful?"

No one denied it. There they stood, a pack of misfits. Covered in wounds and dressed in muddy clothes from all eras. Vaughn was still wearing the Comedian's crown, which he felt when he scratched his head and promptly ripped off and tossed it aside.

They all stood and watched the sunrise together as the kingdom slowly went from chaos to recovery at the sight of sunlight. The heads on spikes atop the wall dried up, and the fires and smoke seemed less daunting.

Dahl beamed even brighter than the sun, and Vaughn watched him instead, Dahl somehow came out on top despite being locked up half the night and getting literally shit on. Nothing could slow this man down; nothing could shake his cheerfulness. Nothing could sink his buoyancy, not even actual shit.

"Great, it's up." Atticus groaned. "Can we go now?"

"I just thought that'd be neat." Dahl smiled.

"It was." Sancia grinned.

"Let's just go already." Nash hurried. "Wyla is next on list."

"Perhaps we should head back to the Asylum first." Atticus demanded. "Just a thought."

"No. List first." Nash repeated.

"Actually, list and Asylum can wait." Galina cut them off, having already decided for them all. "Lead the way Vaughn."

"That's right." Vaughn said, looking at Atticus. "Can't go back yet, we're still down one bartender."*

Inside the tower the wind had passed. The guards noted that they had all seen a figure pass in and out of the tower, how could they not spot those strange shadows.

One guard nodded to another to go find their lord's hiding spot, a small chamber in the guest tower where the Comedian had slunk under the bed and was hoping not to be found.

The guard entered the room and knocked four times against the chamber door with his steel boot, signaling for his Lord and commander to come crawling out. The Comedian thanked the guard and promoted him to knighthood with the indifference of a waitress offering a second helping of complimentary breadsticks.

The Comedian was led to the top of his tower where he found his clothes strewn about the floor. As the Comedian held the robes in his hands, he found his eyes darting about in search of invisible answers floating about. As such, the door behind him silently closed shut and in the darkness he found he was not alone.

He quickly drew his sword and held it out in front of him in what he hoped was the right direction.

"Who's there?" The Comedian found that even in the moonlight shining through his bulletproof windows, he could not see a face. Quickly he fumbled through his pockets for a cube, finding one quickly and turning it at random. He waited, sword still pointing out but not a waft of wind. Nothing.

"I'm not joking. I will use this." He waved his sword around like it was a remote.

A shot rang out. Bats flew from the rafters and the guards wondered who had fired the cannons.

---

*Go to Page 467

The Comedian stumbled back, dropping his sword and meeting it on the floor.

"The thing about bulletproof glass." A voice spoke from a faceless darkness. "Is that you have to keep it between you and the bullet."

The faceless being stepped forward. The moonlight beamed directly where they stood, and the shadows swallowed it up. As the Comedian lay dying, the Historian dug through his pockets to find several cubes, one worn more than the others. He pocketed them himself.

The Historian then stood in the center of the room as he flicked a match and a fire slowly started in the corner, licking up and tearing into the pile of two-ply toilet paper. As he twisted the pale, worn-down cube, the Comedian lifted his head and spoke.

"Did you want to hear a joke?"

The Comedian couldn't tell, but the Historian smiled.

"It better be good."

Chapter Four:

Knots

A powerful sea wind broke through into the bay and swept the ports clean. But the men kept walking, taking the wind brushed sand in their sunburnt cheeks with no concern.

These men were sea born men who found better footing on swaying decks than firm ground.

They steered their attentions to storing as much food as they could in their bellies before their next voyage and drinking as much wine and rum as they could get their hands on, whenever those hands weren't on a woman's soft body.

On the fourteenth pier, a young deckhand was lapping a support rope around the pier's post. Her knot was true, and she proved it with a firm tug.

Sancia wore her hair back in a knot just as tight, though the knot would always let slip a few strands of dark black hair by the end of the day.

She moved off her knees and down to the next post where she had tossed the second rope and, again, wound her knot around it. The boat she secured was only a vessel for the larger ship she could see docked out of the bay; its silhouette bold in front of the setting sun.

She stared as the sun eased its light, slowly setting and easing on her eyes. She watched until sundown and then sprang out of her crouch with a youthful spring the old would ache for and she raced from the port back into town.

The entire village chewed into the mountain that hung over the bay. To reach it you must pass the tavern that sat beside the Port Smith's lodgings and then it was a brief walk up a steep rise to find the rest of the village. And right at the top, lording over the village and the bay was the old monastery.

On her way home, Sancia first passed the tavern. In the night sky, the tavern was the brightest light in the village, it lit the first part of the path Sancia took home, the rest she had to do in darkness.

She never went inside, if one drop of liquor were to spill on her shoes then father would know about it. But she always stood in wait just a little so she could see him once again.

She watched many sailors spill outside grasping a mug and a woman. Those who hadn't been quick enough, simply shrugged and settled into their card games and pints.

Sancia had always kept her distance from these bolder men, with their forearms as thick as her thighs, and their skin stained from the sun.

She kept herself clean, or as clean as a young girl smelling of fish and salt could be.

Sancia struggled to slip by the other women who were trying to get a closer to the Duke's son, Rupert. Every woman in town fancied him, although he was closer in age to Sancia, just five years older at a ripe twenty. His hands knew only the touch of brass swords and silver spoons.

These more mature women wore tight clothes that pushed up their chests and had beautiful patterns up and down the material. Sancia wore only smocks or cheap cloth that had long sleeves she had to keep rolling up and pants handed down from Emilio, held up by one of the first knots she had learnt to tie.

As the night grew dimmer, she headed up the moonlit path to her home. The darkness had settled, and her eyes had adjusted, accustomed to walking without sight, and she made her way home judging one step at a time.

The monastery was worn. The great wooden door had a busted hinge and a weak chain. Sancia only had to push it open enough to squeeze through the gap so she could slip inside undetected.

She walked the stone halls to her room. It was at the end of a long hall of unused rooms and regrettably the only other occupied room was Brother Emilio's, and he had chosen the room beside hers.

"Late." A voice said in Spanish.

Sancia froze and saw that his door was ajar enough for her to see him sitting in his robes cross-legged on his bed.

Emilio was a few years older than Sancia, and he was taller and stronger than she would ever be.

He should have been the one Father Domenici sent to look for work in town, not her, but Emilio was older and would one day be the man of the monastery.

"They had me scrape the mollusks off again." She answered.

"Let's hope God forgives."

Sancia couldn't see well, but there was movement from the bed where he sat. It worried her he might pounce on her and cry for Father Domenici. But he stayed on the bed.

"Goodnight Brother."

"Goodnight."

Sancia snuck into her room and found her place beside her bed, where the stones were the smoothest and her knees could rest in the dimples of the floor.

"In nomine Patris et fillii et Spiritus Sancti." She began and then paused her tongue and it slowed to English. "Thank you for all your blessings, for allowing me a place in your home. For this I am forever in your debt. Amen."

"Get up. Up!" Sancia was thrown from her bed to the stone floor. She instinctively landed with her knees rubbing together and bent to pray. Father hit her less when God was around.

"That's right, pray. Pray for even more forgiveness. I doubt he has much left for you now."

Father Domenici restrained his leather strap and instead wrung it in his hands as Sancia prayed.

"In nomine Patris et."

"No no, if you want to pray in my church you pray in God's language." Father retrieved the bible from Sancia's side table and let it fall with a thud beside her on the floor. It opened to a random page and the English fell out of it.

"Pray. Pray that you might one day realize how lucky you are." Father growled. "When I found you at our door, I took you in without hesitation. Did I care about how we would feed you, clothe you, shelter you? No. The cost of it mattered not, but know of its worth, that this house of the lord crumbles under the weight of your responsibility. Tell me, where is your payment for the week?"

"I do not have it." Sancia whispered.

"What!"

"I am paid at the end of the week. That's today. Today I shall have your money."

"My money? You think it is my money? It is your debt, what you owe to God to rebuild his house now that you have sucked it dry. And I shall expect double."

"Double?"

"I know that you have been working late every night, much beyond you're agreed duties. Nothing goes unnoticed under the eyes of the lord. He watches and still he waits for you to show him praise. Everyday disappointed."

Sancia dared to look up as much as she could without raising her head. She could see standing just outside the doorway was Emilio. He was smirking. Her stomach tied itself up.

"You have been coming home late therefor you must have been working late. Do not think you can keep any money from God. It all goes to him; it is his to spend." Father calmed himself and walked to the door. "Now, you are late again!"

When Sancia was nine years old, Father Domenici sent her into town by herself for the first time.

The monastery housed only the three of them. Though, occasionally missionaries from other villages and overseas would visit. Every

Sunday the church would fill with a few elderly patrons as it always did, but their tithings barely kept the roof over their heads. So, he set Sancia to work.

Father Domenici expected her to work cutting up fish or scrubbing piers, so that is exactly what she told him.

But she had followed a sailor as he was boarding a ship and asked to go with him. He had turned her down. When he saw how disheartening this was, he offered her a job tying up their boats and helping them unload the cargo.

Eight years later and Sancia was fluent with a rope in hand and was as adept in every part of a ship as the other sailors were.

That afternoon Sancia finished unloading crates and barrels with the rest of the crew from a cargo vessel named the San Juan. It was a treasure frigate, about ninety feet long; only its treasures were dried meats and spices and sailed with half the men than usual. They all waited for the ship to clear the bay, passing the Duke's galleon that had settled outside the bay. Too large, at near one hundred and fifty feet long, no dock would take it. The Duke had recruited men from all other ships and turned deck crew into gunners. As they waited for the next ship to make port, Sancia and the others found a comfortable post to sit on.

The port was busy that day with villagers from the markets collecting their orders from the ships. Boats rocked between piers, waiting their turn to be unloaded.

The villagers never paid her much attention, they wanted their fish, their herbs and their meats and not much else. Sancia, like all the sailors, were simply another step between them and their supply.

While waiting, Sancia caught a glimpse of a pair of men standing away from the crowd. They stood by the empty crates beside the hoard of villagers and were talking wildly. Sancia thought they could be royalty, or at least very wealthy. Their suits were clean, black and were cut sharp in a style unfamiliar to her.

As if they felt her eyes on them, they turned and saw the young girl watching them and they waved.

"You're in trouble."

Sancia froze and turned to see Miguel.

"Trouble?"

"Yes." Miguel continued, walking over to the post beside Sancia and inspecting the rope. *"You tied a buntline knot, it will be too tight if the weather picks up like it is, it won't be easy to slip free if we need it to and if the boat drifts off it'll take the pier with it."*

Miguel untied her rope and Sancia knelt beside him and watched him tie a better one. Memorizing the movements.

"There. Much better." Miguel pulled on it to show it was strong but would untie easily with the tug at one loop.

"I'm sorry."

"Don't be sorry. You're still learning. There's only so much you can learn by staying on the port and praying to some invisible man all day. You'd learn faster at sea."

"I know." Sancia muttered. Miguel had always been nurturing toward her. He had been the one to offer her that first job.

"Oh, and here's your pay for this week. Why don't you come for a drink tonight and spend some of it? You must have saved up something by now. Come tonight and get to know the men in my crew. We want to get to know you too. They have nothing to call you other than 'girl'. And if they like you, who knows, you might just find yourself aboard a ship sooner than you think."

"I heard it was bad luck to have a woman on board."

"Men who believe in luck are fools. Besides, bad luck from a hard-working deckhand is better than luck from a lazy one."

Sancia struggled to show a smile, but her stomach tightened at the thought of it. She hadn't the will to tell him the truth. The pier was as close as she could go. She yearned to step off the docks and onto a ship, but she could not leave the church behind. She owed it to God to pay off her debt for saving her. She remembered what Father had said. She owed God his praise.

Most ships left the bay and returned every few days, but some ships, some ships left the port and docked nowhere ever again. She knew that

if she were to leave, she would end up on one of these ships, God would make sure of it. She had to show him something.

"Can I go now? I know it's early, but the next ship is the last and from what I've heard it's only carrying bundles of cloth." Sancia asked.

Miguel narrowed his eyes and Sancia felt the sores on her back against a stiff knock of wind.

"Unless you would like me to stay, or to scrub the pier?"

"No." Miguel laughed. *"You can go."*

Sancia dawdled down the slippery deck and once she made it to the shore, she took off in a run, her hand tight around the sack of coins. She couldn't help but grin as she ran. The road was hard and uphill; the ocean was downhill and behind her. It would have been so easy to take Miguel's offer. But she had avoided temptation. The sun split a cloud, and the heat was strong as it fell on her. God was finally proud.

When she came to the peak of the road outside the monastery, she found Father Domenici standing with the Duke and his son Rupert. She didn't know why she felt like he had to hide, and now that she had hidden, she felt compelled to stay that way.

"… If you could just extend your favor for another few months, perhaps…"

"No more." The Duke said. "No more perhaps. No more extensions. I've already called your debt as a loss, I will not make myself an enemy of a man of God, so you won't need to fear me taking what I'm owed. But I simply cannot afford to keep you afloat anymore."

"But a man of God such as yourself. God's voice in this town. Surely you know how much these people need this church?"

"Need? No. I may be a fellow believer such as you, but this whole catholic business thing has been on its way out for years. No one is praying in London, in Italy, or in Madrid, not anymore. The world may have lost its way, but don't you lose yours with it."

Sancia could see Rupert had no care for the adult's conversation. He was marveling at what was once a beautiful church, it must've been the only building on the bay bigger than his own house.

His eyes wandered so much that they caught Sancia's from behind his tree. He smirked and nodded.

Sancia didn't dare nod back. Her stomach was housing butterflies, which fluttered and cocooned the moment she saw Rupert look up to the monastery. Sancia followed his gaze and saw Emilio standing at the window, watching them as they left.

"You! Girl!" Father Domenici grabbed her by the ear. "Where's my money?"

Sancia scrambled for the bag and held it up to him like a shield. Without even counting it Father felt the bag and decided it's worth.

"It should be double! You think God would be proud of this? You think you can rob God!"

He took her hand and crushed her fingers as dragged her inside. Sancia kicked and struggled to keep her feet to ease the pain as Emilio followed behind with a smile on his face, closing the church doors behind them.

That night he slipped into her room and sat on the edge of her bed. Sancia curled her knees up to her chest and tried to keep herself small.

"Why couldn't you just do what he asks of you?"

He parted his legs so that his robe let show his calves down to his ankles. His legs were smooth and clean, not like hers; covered in scratches, cuts and bruises.

"Such is the impure, unclean and unwelcome under God's loving light."

Emilio lent forward and grazed a bruise forming on Sancia's thigh.

"Why don't you make yourself worth something? Don't you feel shame?"

The way the words left his lips, it was as though his vile words were words of praise. He lavished each word he spoke and pressed his thumb hard into Sancia's bruise. She winced, and he smiled. Her stomach tied itself up in a way much like how Miguel had shown her.

The next day, Sancia worked even harder. The waves licked the sides of the pier, inviting her in as she scrubbed the boards clean. Some splashes landed on her arms and the salt burnt her sores.

"They look worse than before."

Sancia raised her head and saw Miguel standing over her.

"My knots?"

His eyes looked to her bruises, running down her neck and up her legs.

"Why do you let him do that to you? If you left with us, no one would ever hurt you like that again."

Sancia feigned that the sun was in her eyes, which would be why she didn't look up to meet his.

"Do you know what a test from God is?"

"No, I don't."

"God tests those he wishes to reward. It would be easy to leave, get on a ship and go. But then I would have abandoned God. I owe him my life. Everything that I have, I have because of him. I'd rather take God's offer."

Miguel ran his hand through his hair, long as Sancia's but unkempt and unknotted.

"Look I don't know much about God, but I'm sure you can pray to him on a ship. You're a hard worker and a fast learner. We've got a boat heading out tomorrow morning, a few fresh faces will be on board, and you can be one of them. What do you say? Will you think about it at least?"

Sancia smiled. *"Are you sure?"*

"Yes. How cruel would I be to..."

"Ok."

"Ok?"

"Ok I'll go with you."

"You will? Good." Miguel nodded, satisfied. *"Meet us here on the pier in the morning, bring all you own, as we won't be making port here for a few months."*

Sancia nodded, sucking in her cheeks to keep any tears from coming out.

Once her knots were tied, the ships unloaded, and the piers scrubbed fresh. She rushed up the hill to pack her things. She tried not to think about it. If God was watching she hoped he had mercy. The truth was that God wasn't watching, but that's not to say Sancia wasn't being watched.

Sancia tried to walk home, but Miguel stood out front of the tavern and waved her over. Her first steps inside got her a few feet in and her nerves rooted her there. But there was a great cry of celebration from the sailors, led humbly by Miguel, who held his pint up gloriously and met with Sancia.

"My girl! I knew you would come, I'm so happy you are here. Everyone?" Miguel called to the other men. *"Sancia here will sail out with us in the morning."*

Many drinks and spills later, Sancia had forgotten all about the monastery and she forgot all about her troubles. A big-breasted woman pulled her in tight and sung her praise. They toasted many rounds in her name now that they knew it, and danced silly dances as they chanted sea chanteys. Even in her wild and playful state she noticed the same strangely dressed men sitting by the bar, a drink in hand and nodding at her. She thought nothing of it. Soon, she would travel so far and into many a strange place that she would have to get used to the uncommon, the unfamiliar, and the unknown.

Miguel saw Sancia was tying the barman's rag in and out of knots, so he suggested she leave before it got too dark, to get some sleep, and that she needn't worry. The sea was huge. Even God can't find her out there.

Sancia stumbled home, her stomach erupting and burning her throat with volcanic remnants of ale. She had it on her lips, in her clothes, and wore it all over her skin.

She was not as quiet as she usually liked to be, wedging the front doors wide enough to squeeze through, and by the time she reached the foyer Father Domenici was waiting for her.

He curled his nose up. He had gotten used to the smell of salt water and fish, but the burning smell of any alcohol sickened him, and he took to Sancia like he hadn't before.

Father Domenici led her by her hair into the chapel and locked the door behind them. He marched down the aisle and let her go at the altar. There Sancia dropped to her knees and prayed, her instincts had left her only her muscle control.

"Es spirtu sancti."

"Oh no. That won't be necessary." He rarely spoke in Spanish.

Father Domenici grabbed her hands and lashed a rope from the curtains around her wrists and lapped them around the stone leg of the alter. Sancia watched the knot tighten and bind, too slow to struggle. She knew this knot; she knew it would hurt.

"Please, it hurts."

"You've brought this on yourself. God can't save you anymore than he can save the devil."

Hours later Brother Emilio heard through his door Father Domenici walking Sancia back to her room. Once he knew she was alone, he opened his door and slipped inside of hers.

He expected to find Sancia coiled up in her bed, hugging her knees, but he found her digging through her things and shoving them into a sack.

Emilio smelt the ale too, and when their eyes met, she froze and gave the silence time to shout.

"What are you...?" He started but Sancia packed fast, with so little to her name, she finished in seconds.

"You're leaving, aren't you? They finally asked you to go, and you finally accepted. I can see it in your eyes."

Sancia saw that he was between her and the door. A shout would have her cornered, if she stepped within reach he could grab her, and he would trap her.

"You're taking me with you."

It shocked Sancia. Emilio darted out from her room and into his. She followed, dragging her sack behind her. He didn't have to pack. He dug out a similar sack from under his bed and held it up to her.

"Don't you dare think for one second you're getting out of here and leaving me behind. I've had enough with this place. These old ways are fading, the toiling and slaving away for the old man and his stories. The entire world is laughing at us. No one cares about God anymore. He's last centuries bad habit, this is the future Sancia, and I will not be left behind with it."

Emilio stormed out of his room and took her by the arm, twisting it so she kept up with him.

"What about God? You're abandoning him, all those things you said before..."

"It's all rubbish, Sancia. He's not going to punish us. If anything, he'll reward us for not praying to him and helping ourselves, now come on, you're slowing us down."

Sancia picked her feet up, still sore beneath her feet where the skin was still red and blistering. She ran with Emilio as he steered her out of the monastery and down to the docks.

The tavern was gearing down. The music had stopped, and the lights were going out one by one. Outside, she saw Rupert leaning heavily into a young woman. He grabbed at her breast, and she fought him off and gave him a slap. Emilio tore Sancia away and shoved her into the tavern and toward a large pack of men. He held Sancia out in front like one would a ticket.

"Ho there, crew mates."

Miguel turned his head, noticing his friend. *"Sancia, who is this?"*

"He is Emilio."

"And I would like to join you all on your ship tomorrow. If Sancia is going, so shall I."

Miguel and his men chuckled to themselves, even with tired eyes and woozy heads they could still size Emilio up. His pale face told them all they needed to know.

"Well, of course." Miguel offered much to the rabble of his fellow crew. *"But just like Sancia, you must pass the one test all our crew must undergo."*

Miguel laid a firm hand on Emilio's shoulder and Sancia stepped back as the other sailors grinned.

"To the pier!"

The group cheered and hoisted Emilio above their shoulders as though he were a crate of salted meats and made towards the docks.

Snow quickly melted and Vaughn immediately felt the rush of sand in the wind pass his cheeks. It was a warm night with a dark blue sky lit by a blunt white moon. He heard a sound all around him, like a wind that was calm. He looked around for it and saw where the sand ended. A great ocean, laid out like a blanket before him, stretching onto the horizon, and the moonlight streaked across it like someone had spilt white paint.

Vaughn had never seen the sea.

It was bigger than he had figured, movie and television could grasp nothing bigger than the screen; it really did just keep on going. But it didn't make him feel free or relaxed like many claimed it would. Vaughn felt closed in, trapped. The small bay on which he stood seemed to be locked in by this endless and restless water. The desert around Fracture was encompassing enough, but he at least he could walk across it.

Vaughn was still holding Sancia in his arms. She let her hand fall, and it grazed the sand, then she cried. The very touch of it brought her back to reality.

"I'm back, I'm back." She said in her own tongue, looking up and seeing the bay's village towering over them. *"I had to come back."*

Vaughn carried her up the silky sand that deceptively sunk under his footing deceivingly so. He brought her up to the pier and saw the long stretch of docks along the bay housing boats that rocked gently and quietly like they knew the village was sleeping.

Only the square shack right down the very end of the harbor had a light on and voices coming from it. It reminded him of the Observatory, carrying on long into the night and ignoring everyone who had to sleep through it.

Vaughn found a wooden cabin, tall and thin, just like the others at the end of each pier. The door had a chain loosely wrapped around it and Vaughn unraveled it until it was loose enough to pull open the doors and slip through the gap, guiding Sancia's head through first.

Inside, the tall ceiling had long boats hanging by chains and ropes above, some with broken boards and snapped ends.

The whole place smelt like salt and fish, and Vaughn tried to find a place to put her down. He found a bundle of rope, thicker than his hand, coiled up on the floor like a giant brown snake sleeping in the corner. It made a nice nest and Vaughn lowered her into it. Sancia gripped it and groaned again as she felt her stomach trying to burst.

He looked again to her wound. Her whole shoulder had gone black, the gauze swallowed up by clotting blood. He was sure she had lost so much blood that her little body couldn't afford to lose another drop.

"You should be dead." He said. "I'll get some help. Is there a hospital or something? You should be at a hospital. Wouldn't you rather be at a hospital?"

"I had to come back."

"But why?" Vaughn fought. "Why don't you want help? Why are you putting yourself through this?"

"Because, I want it to be over." She said.

Vaughn pushed off, tugging until she let his hand go. He lapped the boathouse, pacing around stacks of lengthy oars, bundles of rolled up sails, a collection of spear guns, and a few anchors that had gone crusty from sea urchins. Sancia moaned a little but found calm and relief between the sudden burst of pain. She looked around at everything Vaughn passed fondly.

"I was going to sail. I was going to cross the ocean, put the sea between this place and me."

"I know what that's like." Vaughn said softly. "To want to get away from somewhere."

"You do?"

"But I don't blame myself, or even Atticus really. But it still felt… forced."

"You couldn't stop it, just like I couldn't. It had to happen to me. It all had to happen."

"But it doesn't have to…"

"Vaughn, I hate it. But it does. I don't want to fight it anymore. I just want it to be over."

"Want what to be over?" Vaughn stomped back over, chains rattling above at the slightest shake. "Nothing has to be over. You don't have to die here just because someone told you so. I still don't know how you're not dead. But don't tell me it's your destiny or some shit."

"Vaughn, soon you'll see that there's no point fighting what you know will come."

She passed out again or fell asleep. Vaughn couldn't tell the difference.

He slipped out to get some air, or maybe just to spare her from the noise he was making, while pacing and thinking out loud.

It was nice there. The wind that carried over the sea and to the shore, it smelt like salt but at least it didn't smell like smoke and coal. He slipped off his shoes; tucking his socks inside and walked through the sand, letting the little granules get between his sweaty toes. The sand on the surface was cold, but as he dug and wriggled his toes deeper, it got warmer.

He walked along the bay, ducking under piers and weaving between support poles. The wet sand glistened but was freezing, so Vaughn kept to the dry stuff.

As he neared the end of the shore and out from under the last pier, he could hear the taunts and cheers of what could only come from drunken mob mentality that egged itself, on as drunken mobs do.

Vaughn strode up to the tavern and saw a group of nine or ten men lifting a small and thin young man, no older than twenty, onto their shoulders and out to the end of a pier.

After they were gone Vaughn's eyes were drawn to a man lingering outside the tavern. A thirty something man, inky hair, tanned skin, shapely beard, dressed in even sharper cut jacket and a ruffled shirt neckline. He was chatting to a familiar girl in a tanned shirt and pants tied up with a length of rope.

Had she slipped out and beaten him here?

She seemed fine now, no wound in her shoulder, smaller, more innocent. Sancia had never looked younger than she did here.

It was happening again. He was watching someone before they knew him. It made Vaughn wonder about how knowing someone depended entirely on when they are - not who they are. Right now, whoever Sancia was, she wasn't the girl he knew. Just like how Dahl wasn't the man he knew at the airport and Wyla wasn't the woman he knew at the Crowbar.

All the same, he was still curious. Vaughn checked himself out; his clothes weren't all that strange and out of place here. Dark pants, white shirt - you couldn't see how blue his shoes were in the dark.

He innocently walked towards the tavern from the piers as though he was a well-to-do fisherman in need of a drink. Getting closer, he saw Sancia lean back on the big empty wine barrels that sat along the outside of the tavern as the older man leaned in.

Vaughn didn't know what to do with himself as he got so close. He was standing within two steps to the door and man eyed him, just hovering around near the door. He spoke fast Spanish to Sancia as she hoisted herself up to sit on one of the wine barrels. Vaughn caught it - the man sliding his hands up her legs.

"Don't just stand there when you're so close." The man spat at Vaughn still awkwardly standing. *"Just keep your eyes to yourself."*

With his attention drawn away, Sancia slipped free from the man's grip and hustled into the darkness towards the trail leading up to the rest of the town.

The man quickly lost interest in Vaughn's and hurried after her.

Vaughn followed too. The steepness of the bay quickly became apparent, the incline had a well-worn path that led towards all the houses and buildings of the village. Right at the top, contrasting its shadowed shape against the sky, was a tall and dominating church, which unlike Fracture, no one had paid to light this hill up at night. There was only pitch-black darkness wherever the moon didn't touch, and the tall church spire split most of that light.

His eyes were adjusting as he tried to manage the steep hill and follow where the two of them had went. Shards of moonlight lit parts of the path as the hill leveled out to a wide road weaving between shops and houses. Vaughn followed one long shard that ran across the road and between two buildings.

There, just out of the light, Vaughn saw the rope that had strung up young Sancia's pants now wrapped around her hands. The loose threads holding her shirt together had come free, and the man's sharply cut jacket lay on the ground.

What moonlight would have touched them was cut off by the church spire, keeping them in darkness. This was not supposed to be seen.

Vaughn felt his throat tug as he heard her whimper, he felt his lip tremble as he heard the thuds against the wooden wall she was forced up against. He felt his legs jolt and his muscles harden, fighting to run over and stay put simultaneously. He saw her arms wrestle against the knot that bound them, and Vaughn felt his fingers twitch, but only twitch.

Vaughn desperately searched for a splash of yellow paint, a relief, a sign, a forced duty. Surely, he was meant to be here, at this moment; surely his path led him to intervene.

O'seus would surely have him intervene. He would tell him to intervene, even if he wasn't supposed to. He'd paint that name that followed Vaughn all his life and he'd do it with a good reason for once.

But there was no paint in sight.

Without it, strangely, he felt his body had frozen up. With every thrust, Vaughn ached to burst and rip him off her. But all that happened was the next thrust and cry.

Do it, help you fucking asshole! Vaughn tore at his own brain. He surged all energy to his calves that pulsed and jerked to run. But he was still standing still.

You're not going to save her. Thoughts ran through his mind, throbbing like a stubbed toe.

You're not supposed to help.

You're a bad person, Vaughn.

Feel those fingers? Gone limp again, haven't they.

This is supposed to happen.

You're not supposed to help.

She's supposed to suffer.

Or you're just a bad person.

Yeah, you're a bad person, Vaughn. Limpfingers. You are the worst. You're downright awful.

Finally Vaughn's legs moved - his feet left the ground. Only they took him back down the hill. It was all over. Those thoughts had subsided, and it left him numb, mouth agape. He reached the docks again, the moon now behind the church and the sky that met the horizon was getting lighter, a soft blue.

Vaughn's feet were heavy. He was heavy. He was a dense pile of numb garbage.

How was he capable of something like that?

As he stood on the wet deck, he looked to his hands. His palms seemed to look back at him. Each finger almost shrugged. They didn't take the blame. His hands judged him and he wondered whether they really acted of their own accord or his. Was he Limpfingers or just limp?

Behind him he heard someone coming, Sancia had also stumbled away numb and in such a state of shock she hurried down to the last few piers, each step finding more speed before Vaughn had to run to catch up.

He saw her run on the sand, trying to tie her shirt threads back together as she made for the water, and there she sank to her knees in hip deep water and shoved her head under.

When she came back up she was already crying, really crying. She wailed and screamed like she wanted everything to be over.

She spat out water and vomit, croaked, and then spat up some more. She heaved until she was scratching her throat with the inside of her stomach.

Sancia stayed there, kneeling in the water, drifting in and out of consciousness with the lashing of each wave against her balance and the saltwater stinging her blisters. The night hurried off and the light of the morning warmed her skin and burnt through her closed eyes like an uninvited guest.

And Vaughn watched, having hidden behind a post of a pier. So desperate to hold her and tell her it would be ok, but just as desperate to throw himself in and not come up because nothing ever was.

Watching her, he barely noticed the rising sun shedding more light over the shore. He hadn't taken a moment to see what the light was showing him, so they surprised him just as much as they surprised her.

"Sancia."

The young girl turned her head and Vaughn saw them too. Standing in the sand were two men in plain black suits, which must have thrown Sancia through a loop just as much as it threw Vaughn.

"Sancia?" The men tried again.

She nodded ever so slightly.

"Congratulations. It's a boy."

Sancia got to her feet and stepped out of the water. She ran her eyes up and down them. Their clothes were clean, and their hair kept neat. She noticed their teeth were peculiarly white and straight.

"We're fans. Big fans."

"We couldn't help ourselves."

What?

"I have seen you before." She managed to say.

"We're supposed to keep our distance, just watch and say unseen, but we couldn't help ourselves. We just had to say hello."

"Hello?"

"And now that it's done, we thought it couldn't hurt to give our congratulations."

"Congratulations?"

"You were just with a man named Rupert, we know, we saw."

They saw too? Vaughn thought. *Had they also done nothing?*

Sancia felt her mouth taste bad again. She took a step back, heels licked by the waves.

"Well, good news. You are pregnant and will give birth to a very important boy who is part of a very important bloodline that will one day be the reason we can even be here to congratulate you."

"I'm sorry, I don't understand." Sancia struggled.

"You will have a son. That son will have a son, and that son will have a son…"

Sancia stumbled away, making for the pier and holding onto a pole that held it up and now held up her.

"… And that son will have a son and eventually that son will be Luis· G. Stein."

"In fact, he is why we are here. He wanted us to make sure you were ok and that nothing bad happened to you."

"We're not supposed to talk to you but, like we said, what's done is done and if I were in your shoes, it would kill me if I didn't know that I was part of something so, just… so… important."

Vaughn wasn't sure just how good Sancia's English was or how much she had understood, but he figured she had understood enough. She held a hand to her stomach just as Vaughn had seen her hold it before. Not with love, not with care, but the same way she held her shoulder as it bled.

As Sancia staggered about the shore, weaving between supporting poles of the pier above. The two men followed spouting more praise and revelations.

Vaughn could only watch as Sancia tried to get away from her fans. She scrambled up to the top of the dock and onto the pier, while the men tried to keep sand from getting in their shoes. She darted down the docks, running towards the sunrise, the ocean, the open

sky and away from them. Vaughn watched her run and the two men run after her.

He watched her reach the end of the docks and down the last pier, the two men desperately chasing behind her. Vaughn saw her take barely a second thought as she launched herself off the end and sink deep in the ocean.

Vaughn saw the two clean suited men skid to a halt at the end of the pier. Neither jumping in, instead kneeling along the edge to look for her, hitting each other over the back of the head for letting her get away.

She has to live. Vaughn thought. *She can't die. She can't drown.*

But he wasn't seeing her head come up. Nothing but waves getting stronger and tides turning as the morning came.

Winds of the waves rushed past Vaughn and he counted the moments as they went by. For every moment that past he was sure he would do something by the next one.

You're not going to save her.

You're a bad person, Limpfingers.

Maybe you're supposed to help?

Is this supposed to happen?

From the pier above him, as if from out of the open sky, a small figure leapt into the air, his leather jacket spreading like wings as he dove into the water. He beat against the waves with courageous strength and little skill, but still the man dove deep and sprung back up, holding the girl in his arms.

The tide was too strong for either of them to fight it and it slammed them against opposing waves, rushing them back under repeatedly. But he held onto her tight and kicked against the waves that tried to pull them out to sea. Finding his feet, he dragged the girl to the shore where she coughed, sputtered, and rolled about in the sand. He rubbed her back as she coughed up salt water and swallowed up air.

The two suits in the distance spotted them and charged down the long pier, hurrying to catch them from one end of the docks to the other.

Vaughn watched, stunned and still, as the small man spoke, and Sancia smiled. Vaughn hadn't seen her do that for some time. Dahl

called her kiddo and smiled back. He brought out a colorful cube from his jacket pocket and wiped it dry.

The two suits were moments away, skidding down the smoothed deck of the pier as Sancia stood and looked out over the village, up to the church and then out to the ocean as she left it all behind, hopefully to never return.

By the time the two suits got to them, all they found was damp sand and the wind.

They whacked each other hard and fought as one took a cube out and shook it in the other one's face. They quickly left with no clue where to look first, leaving Vaughn alone on the shore.

The sun was all the way up. The day had started, and the village was coming alive.

But what was left of Vaughn?

He wondered back to the boathouse at the end of the docks. He would wake Sancia and then he would think of something. He would apologize for one, he would probably cry. He wouldn't forgive himself. *And why should she?*

He snuck under the chains of the boathouse and found the empty coil of rope where Sancia had slept.

On a crate beside it he saw the glint of color from their last two cubes, one more faded and worn than the other but still more colorful than anything here.

She had left them both, left him. No note, nothing.

All of it tumbled around in his head like his brain was tipping out a box of jigsaw pieces and he had to assemble it in the air as they fell.

Why hadn't he done anything? Two times he could have helped, twice he could have done something. But he didn't and now he was wondering if it really wasn't his fault.

Maybe. None of it was his fault.

Everything in Fracture, everything with Jake. Never being able to leave that stupid town. Everything he had blamed on Atticus now seemed much bigger than any of them.

What was it Sancia had said? There was no point fighting what he knew would come.

That's what he had been doing, that's why there wasn't any sign from O'seus marking his path here. Because this wasn't where he was supposed to be.

Everything that had happened to Sancia, as bad as it was, had to happen. He couldn't have done anything about it because he wasn't supposed to be here.

He was supposed to be somewhere else, at the end of that hallway. It was still there, perfect in his mind. The flashing red lights, the smoke, the sirens, the alarms. Waiting for him to come and be where he was supposed to be.

He really didn't have a choice at all.

Why fight it?

As Vaughn took a cube and spun it, he was so preoccupied with where he was going, he hadn't the moment to spot a spear gun was missing from the rack before he jumped through a tangent in time.*

✧ ✧ ✧

Father Domenici pulled hard on the curtain until the rings snapped and it fell. It folded into a pile on the stone floor like the all the others, mountains of cloth bundled beneath each window.

He had to remove it all, every symbol of the church. Bare the walls clean so that whoever bought the place could dress it up as they saw fit.

Father Domenici couldn't help but place blame on the empty room at the end of the southern hall. Though the lack of tithings had nothing to do with it - the Duke had finally called in his debts.

Father Domenici had offered the service of the church to put him under God's watch to keep him safe, wherever he was. But the Duke had renounced him and given Father Domenici only a few days to collect his things and depart from the stone temple.

Go to Page 443

Sancia kicked the door down - the lock busting off the wood and sending splinters everywhere. She stalked into the halls and found the chapel doors open, with movement coming from inside. Sancia ached to hold up the hefty spear gun, the spear itself weighing so much it pulled at her arm and her near dead shoulder.

She startled Father Domenici, who turned to see his young slave now hardened, grounded and twice her size. The cuts he had inflicted on her arms and legs had healed over into scars. Her hair much longer and wrapped tight, her clothes though ragged, were cut from a cloth yet to be woven and darkened by as much blood as her body could supply. Her legs wobbled and she rested the back of the gun on her engorged belly.

"Sancia?"

Sancia wanted to say something profound, but she couldn't keep the shakes from her fingers.

CRACK! The spear shot out to the surprise of both Sancia and the Father. It flung down the church aisle and struck him through his thigh and the tip broke through to the other side.

Eyes wide, he fell back, landing on the tip and screaming more than he had ever screamed before.

Sancia stepped up beside him, holding the empty spear gun and the line now attached to his leg. She had so much to say, yet so little words. She had enough strength left to pull, yanking his leg up, and he moaned on command.

Sancia suddenly howled in pain, doubling over as she dropped the gun but held onto the line. She dug her fingernails into her kneecap, and she bit her lip red.

But this time Sancia bent into her pain, she took long, wide breaths and held them in with a tight mouth. If she didn't breathe, it didn't hurt.

After a while she had to let it go. The room was getting fuzzy. Her vision rocked from side to side. The distant sound of the sea grew as though the waves broke against the stone walls of the monastery.

After a few deep breaths she recovered, the room stopped spinning, and she felt the floor beneath her feet and wrapped the line around her fingers and fist as you would a leash.

She dragged him. She dragged him through the halls and to where the curtains sat slumped on the floor beneath each window. Here the spear wriggled a wider gash in his leg and the tip slipped back through, hooking a chunk of his flesh and tearing it out.

Sancia barely heard his screams as he had always ignored hers. She instead bent and stroked the fabric, gradually reeling it in and twisting it tight. She bent over, bending into another convulsion in her stomach, almost throwing up on the Father. She wrapped it around his neck as she would a post at the dock. His neck was the ship. He would tug but she wouldn't let him go. If her knot were strong enough, it would hold; it would rein him in so he wouldn't drift off again.

And this was a good knot.

Of course he struggled, Sancia wasn't ready for much more of a fight and fell back against the wall, pulling him down with her.

He choked and flopped about like a fish, a fish she pulled in tight between her legs as she cried out to another contraction.

It was bigger than the others; deeper even.

It dug into her so excruciatingly, so she had to let out her pain and she pulled on the curtain tighter.

"God this hurts! Tell God that it hurts!" She cried as she pulled, forcing fresh blood to seep from the rotting hole in her back.

Father didn't reply with much more than a groan.

"I thought I knew pain; you made me know pain. Why did you hate me so much? I never understood why. That's what hurt the most. If I had a reason, something to hold on to when you beat me, it wouldn't have hurt so MUUUCH."

Again another throbbing pain, this time it throbbed. With each pulse, she pulled tighter and screamed with it.

"I hope this feels the same for you, I hope you're just as confused. I hope you die not knowing why."

Then the throbbing subsided, enough that Sancia could breathe out of her mouth again.

She loosened her knot, and the Father slipped and rolled off of her.

How long had he been gone? Had he heard any of it? How long had she been talking to no one?

She pushed him off her and pushed her back against the wall to stand, but the throbbing came back and this time it didn't stop.

"I know that you're coming, and I want you to know that you're wanted. I do want you and I will love you, no matter what you are. I don't want you to not know love like I did."

Her voice rang out a choir; the entire village could hear sweet, terrifying music from the monastery again. She screamed and pushed and screamed and pushed. She cried and pushed and she wept and pushed.

The closest villagers ran to the old church and found the tall wooden doors broken in, the wide and cold halls swept cold by winds which brought with them a piercing cry.

The women ran in first - they recognized that cry as every mother would.

And they found the newborn child held on tight by its young mother, finally out of blood.

Chapter Five

The Past of Least Resistance

Snow covered the Austrian hills in a blanket, thick and clean. Branches gave way under the weight of the last fall and spilt a fresh thud of doughy snow. A man stood tall amongst the mighty forest of age-old trees. O'seus Forshaker carried himself through the woods as though the snow he sunk his boots into were a red carpet, ushering him into the woods.

His illustrious beard wrapped around his carved jawline and his eyes tore through the hills to the tiny village he headed for.

As he dug each step a few feet deep in the snow and heaved a clean path, he clutched a stout axe and rehearsed his grip eager for a swing. He marched for a few hundred yards, only stopping to breathe in deeply whenever the wind blew pleasantly.

Coming up to the village, a collection of men stepped forward, concerned of his axe and intentions.

Ignoring the gun at his side, they insisted he leave the axe behind, as they did not allow visitors to cut from their woods. No doubt they caught onto his smile, resembling the whites of the snow enveloping their cabins. Not a man familiar with dreary winters too harsh for hygiene.

O'seus protested that this axe was not for any stump or thicket, barely noticing his free hand stroking its blade. He argued that it wasn't even his but in fact for someone else. With a deep howl from the mountains, the villagers laughed and waved him through, deciding amongst

themselves that anyone willing to walk into that empty mountain through that storm could have whichever tree he desired.

Once he had passed through the tiny village, O'seus stopped and withdrew a map folded roughly in his coat. Sherman's map showed detailed rises and edges of the mountain in the spring, but this was winter, and snow covered all definition of the land. Luckily, a little imagination was all it took to uncover the track and he found his guesses true as each stage of the map proved he was correct. Though this map showed a roundabout route that encircled the mountain, O'seus found a track that cut through to the center. He clambered up and down steep inclines and took sharp turns, as he continued the forest thickened and was unforgivingly repetitive. Each creak made O'seus wonder whether the trees could rip up their roots and huddle up close when visitors drew nearer to the sought after.

The cabin was smaller than the ones from the village, but ripe with life. The Austrian man in front was dusting snow off hefty chunks of firewood. He could bundle eight split logs in each arm and still find free fingers to grab his axe and move on.

O'seus laid his axe down and shuffled to unclasp his rifle from his side. He knelt in the ice, his knee finding firm earth beneath, and lifted the rifle to his eye. The view was poor, snow fell so thick, and his warmth fogged up the sight. He dropped the gun and looked to his axe. He only needed it to chop up the body.

He looked to where the snow fell and listened for the hum of a snow machine; how easy could it have been to cancel this weather, just as he had on the set of his last historical award winner.

This snow was relentless, it would not stop today and O'seus didn't have time to wait for tomorrow's forecast. As he did with his films, he knew when a storyline was over or just beginning.

Eyes back on his target, O'seus pressed on. Black trees and white everything else; the staging couldn't be more perfect for an ambush.

So he followed as the Austrian dumped his latest load by the cabin door and then ventured out for more.

Keeping his distance within eyesight but out of earshot, O'seus was careful not to leave any partnering trail of footprints where the Austrian might pass.

Darting behind trees and snow dunes, O'seus played his dangerous game, approaching stealthily behind the Austrian who plummeted his axe through any dead wood too big for his arms to carry.

The Austrian would sparingly stop mid swing and dart his gaze around before returning to the logs.

He was bundled up in a homemade pelt coat and multiple straps across his midsection to hold it down against the winds. So much so that one could only assume his frame was a gigantic one to be spitting those logs in less than a swing. Half the work seemed to be accomplished by his menacing look he gave each log before trimming limbs from its torso.

Once he had all his wood chunks balanced in arm, he took back towards the cabin.

O'seus followed and found that he was making for home a fair bit faster than before. Perhaps it was the weather, a storm might brew, O'seus had no way of knowing and stuck to following the Austrian.

Weaving through trees, up and down the embankment until O'seus had lost sight of him. He scoured what little distance he could see ahead of him but there was no discernable movement, no sign of a heaving creature lugging half a tree in firewood.

A rustle, a thud of soft snow, and an axe butt to the temple. O'seus was taken.

He roused awake inside the dank cabin. His first thought was to hold his hand to his wound, but his wrists had been tied to the beam up above his head. There he knelt on the floor of the cabin, back to the support beam in the middle of the room. He could feel the unsanded boards used for the floor running splinters into his shins, the heat from the fire melting the snow off his back and the bottom of his boots.

The freezing winds howling outside and the frail walls of the cabin being the only thing that stood between O'seus and the gusts that felt like a tidal wave being held back by curtains.

The Austrian groaned as he got up from in front of the fire.

Small, careful steps navigated him around O'seus. Inspecting his outfit and silence, the Austrian knelt beside O'seus, allowing his face only an inch between his. O'seus noticed his grey and blue eyes, his left pupil strayed loose, and it was off-putting. O'seus found he was avoiding looking at it in fear of being rude - rude to his captor.

The blood of his wound had long ago thickened and clotted, but O'seus had more concern for the rest of his blood, rather content with it staying where it was.

"Wer bist du?"

O'seus, missed it, his head still swirling, he would need it again.

"Wer bist du? Warum bist du hier?"

O'seus gathered his mind and forced it still.

"Beantworten sie meine fragen oder ihre zunge liegt auf dem boden." The big Austrian threatened.

"Don't touch my tongue." O'seus finally understood and answered in German. *"I was lost in the woods and saw your cabin."*

The Austrian hardened his expression.

"No one gets lost out here. No fools walk these woods in this storm."

The Austrian moved out of sight behind him. *"Tell me, where are you from? Why do you wear such odd clothes?"*

"I don't know what you mean."

O'seus scanned the room, sighting the door at the far side of the cabin as the only means of escape.

"Your German is awful, sounds like bug bite your tongue."

The Austrian came back into O'seus' line of vision, holding his pack. O'seus suddenly felt the absence of its weight from his shoulders, and his stomach dropped ten feet. Inside his pack were things, things the Austrian was not meant to see. Particularly the map of the mountain forest that led him to this house.

"Let's see if what you carry speaks more truth than you."

The Austrian unlatched his pack and poured the belongings out onto the floor in front of O'seus. He winced as he did, knowing for sure the map would now lead to his throat being slit.

But at a quick glance, the map wasn't there.

Maybe he still had it in his pocket, he was sure he had put it back in his pack.

The other items were curious, but not incriminating.

His cube and instruction manual fell about the uneven floor, as were some energy bars and a small sack of gold nuggets.

The Austrian inspected the manual first, thwarted by the unknown language.

He lowered from his crouch and sat flat on the floor, eyes now even with O'seus.

"If you are not going to tell me who you are than I must start by telling you who I am. My name is Johann, and I fought in the Prussian war. In this war I learnt many things, how to handle a weapon, how to watch your comrades die beside you on the battlefield. How to kill a man."

Johann startled O'seus by whipping out a hunting knife from his boot. He started playing with it, swinging it by the handle back and forth like a pendulum.

"But what I truly learnt, what war teaches all men, is what you are capable of. If you are capable of killing a man and then killing another, and another. How to watch a man breathe his last breath, how to remember the dead by memory and not their broken body in the mud. I even know exactly how long I can endure torture before I break."

O'seus just looked straight at Johann, not daring to blink in fear of missing the knife move.

"So you should tell me who you are and what I want to know, before we both find out exactly what you are a capable of."

O'seus only stared at the floor, at his cube, praying for it to take him away.

Johann sighed and grew up from the floor; O'seus would have sworn he was inches from the ceiling. He disappeared behind him

again, but not too far, feeling his breath curse the hairs on the back of his neck.

"What are you doing here?" He asked again.

Again O'seus pled innocent, knowing that anything but the truth could possibly see him free.

Johann then tossed out a scrap of paper in front of O'seus with the rest of his belongings. The paper was the map, his photocopy of Sherman's original.

Before O'seus could gulp, he screamed as Johann curled his knife under the tip of his fingernail.

"This map leads to this house. It was in your pack."

He drove it deeper.

"I thought I'd see if you were an honest man before I killed you. Maybe you were a messenger or a scout."

O'seus felt his fingernail tear away from his skin. Why didn't he think of that?

"But at least I know that my judgment hasn't worn thin." Johann lent right up close to O'seus' ear. *"You're going to tell me everything before you die."*

The knife finally cracked the fingernail completely off his finger, slicing open the flesh underneath as it did. O'seus felt cold sweat consume him. The cabin grew dark and then black, but he knew he was still conscious. The pain gone for now, but the vomit from his stomach was dissolving in his throat.

"More... will... come." He croaked, and then he blackout out again.

Outside, the near pure white floor of the forest blended with the white sky. You couldn't see a thing.

As a man named Thomas fell seven feet to his doughy landing, he could not see the two other men that landed only ten feet away, nor could they see the two other men that had settled only ten feet from them. Thomas was slim, but his wrist was strong. He carried a single knife with him and had never once needed anything more than it and the element of unthinkable surprise.

He and the small army tread through the thick snow, creating a perimeter around a certain cabin. As they got closer, Thomas thought he heard swift movement to his left, but all he could see was white. Then it happened again to his right - a plain white haze.

Thomas then felt his collar get snatched in a vicious grip. Something lurched his body forward to meet a knee with his nose.

The white floor now had a strong splash of red, like modern art, the canvas ruined as someone knocked Thomas back and dragged him right through the bloodied snow by the leg of his pants.

Fretfully resisting, Thomas wriggled and flipped like a dying fish on the end of the line, his calls for help resounded into nothing in the vast solitude. Occasionally the mysterious figure stopped to boot him in stomach and end the screaming, one solid kick to the teeth and his screams became moans, whistling out of his blackened jaw. The dragging continued until he felt the rough bite of the cabin deck.

Thomas scanned the room and silently screamed as he saw the body of another anachronist tied up to a support beam in the middle of the room, blood strewn about the floor where his hands were tied.

"What are you going to do with me?" He whimpered. His eyes flickered towards the door as he waited for the rest of his group to break it down.

The mysterious man turned to face him. Thomas saw his eyes were stale and grimaced through his woolen balaclava. He reached into his coat and pulled out a cube.

"You also carry strange object. You will tell me everything you know about me and how you found this cabin." He asked with a thick accent.

"I… don't... don't… speak German."

Johann smirked, then grabbed him by his hair and lifted him to his feet, walked him over to the door and back out into the forest. The storm had calmed and the trees in the distant were discernable. Johann tugged at his scalp and walked him around to the back of the cabin, while Thomas whimpered in pain. Thrown to his knees, he nursed his head and kept his eyes down, awaiting a blow that would permanently numb his pain. Any minute now, he thought, any second and someone will come.

Johann didn't strike him or slice a hole in the back of his head he was waiting for him, the trembling Thomas in the snow. Knees sinking through to the mud, he sensed Johann move in front of him. He lifted his head and immediately wished he hadn't.

A few feet in front of him were the broken, limp bodies of his fellow crusaders. The smell had frozen along with the lump of carcasses stacked behind the cabin. The dead, drooping man had his ice-covered eyes fixed on Thomas, a frozen drool of blood from his lip and a horrible gash from his stomach to his sternum.

"These men," Johann started. *"Also didn't know what I was talking about."*

Johann reached for the axe. Behind him, a man darted from one tree to another, gaining distance, waiting for the right moment.

"Now I don't understand why you are all so interested in me, and I can't help admiring your resolve. But it seems to me that a bunch of soft little boys went man-hunting."

Three silhouettes now appeared surrounding the cabin, Thomas darted his eyes to them and then straight back at Johann. He prayed he hadn't noticed.

Johann did, and his axe dug itself deep into the first attacker that had launched out from the forest. The others followed, trying to gain advantage of Johann's axe being busy lodged in the belly of their comrade. They swung at his head, but Johann ducked and their axes knocked back the first poor crusader, dislodging Johann's axe. Johann used the butt of his axe to break the nose of the attacker to his left and with a free hand he grabbed the axe of the attacker on his right, mid downswing.

The whimpering Thomas knelt there stunned, watching Johann effortlessly thwart the oncoming onslaught of crusaders with axes and knives. He made tissue paper out of them. He held back the swing of their weapons as if they were toys. A single blow from the weight of Johann's seasoned fists or elbows saw the men to the icy ground. When the last man was finished, Johann let the body collapse in the snow, now a furious red, before resting his boot on a shoulder blade and ripping his axe free.

Thomas scurried off into the deep white, crawling low and past thick tree roots that protruded from the snow. He made a lot of noise but couldn't hear a thing over his heartbeat. He didn't hear the man stand over him. He didn't hear him breathe and didn't hear him swing his axe over his head.

When O'seus next awoke, he thought he couldn't see. He thought he was dreaming. He only heard the sounds of chunky footsteps and muffled groans. He hadn't opened his eyes yet, and if he kept them closed, he could stay in a safe sleep.

But the shock of the cabin door slamming closed had O'seus break his dream into a nightmare. Johann looked worn, tired. O'seus felt the time he had been out has been long, the vomit he had drooled whilst unconscious had hardened over the corners of the map that still lay in front of him. His cube, however, was gone.

Johann still hadn't noticed that he was awake and O'seus thought to try for a subtle escape. But the moment he tried wriggle his hands free of his bonds he flinched in pain as his raw fingertips rekindled its pain.

The big Austrian noticed and dragged a stool over to O'seus, opting not to sit on the floor this time. Without speaking, O'seus knew the question.

"My name is O'seus Forshaker and I hail not from Austria or Germany. I am from the Scotland, originally. And I do know who you are. Johann Georg, you were a decorated general in the Austro-Prussian War. You won the Austrian Imperial Order of Leopold medal for your months in the trenches alone. You will soon find yourself a wife and have a son. Your son will have a child of his own. And that child will destroy the very country you suffered your allegiance for all those years ago."

Johann said nothing. In fact, O'seus wondered whether he had spoken in German. Then Johann leapt at him, seizing O'seus by his collar.

"Just who are you? Why do you know so much about me?"

Before he could choke out an answer, O'seus felt his head grow light. The sudden rush at him stressed just how much blood he had lost. His

hands and arms had long turned numb, his knees turned soft as his entire body boiled.

"I came here to... to..."

Johann guided his head to the floor as O'seus, still with his arms behind the beam, slumped to the floor. His body had lost too much blood, and the cold had taken him.

"To what? What?"

"To stop it..."

When O'seus next awoke he found his head rested on a soft blanket, his hands were bandaged and he was no longer bound to the beam but was lying in front of the gentle fire.

He felt Johann at his side, holding a bowl of soup and guiding a spoonful to O'seus.

"Eat. You won't faint anymore."

O'seus gratefully sipped the hot soup, never minding the plain taste or how much it burnt his tongue. He felt the blood rush back to his body, no longer feeling like a floating head.

"You feel better, yes?"

"Better enough to torture again?" O'seus replied.

"You speak as though I was the one hunting you."

He couldn't help it, O'seus felt his thoughts straying to a moment in one of his films, *Man Go Wild*. The hero of the story, Emmett, was in this exact same situation.

Well, not exactly. Emmett had been on holiday with his family in the countryside. They had rented a cabin for the weekend, but the problem was, someone else had been using his cabin.

The family sprung themselves upon an escaped convict who quickly slaughtered his family but kept him alive and tied up just as O'seus was tied up now.

He couldn't quiet remember why he had the character tie him up instead of just killing him too, something about making a phone call to the county sheriff to make sure no one came out there looking for him.

Whatever the reason was, Emmett was a family man, and O'seus had cast a much smaller actor to portray him than O'seus himself.

In the movie, Emmett had gotten himself free by gently loosening the ropes and rushed his kidnapper, giving himself just enough time to escape.

O'seus weighed himself up against Johann and pulled a little on his bound wrists.

The ropes might've been tighter than in the film. And Johann was quite a lot bigger than him.

Johann felt O'seus' eyes on him, running him up and down, trying to size him up.

O'seus quickly took his eyes off Johann and had a better look at the cabin. The wind blew through a crack in the walls and rustled the map across the floor.

"I keep having a dream about it." Johann started. *"In the dream I'm back in the trenches. All I can hear are canons and gunshots and all I can taste is mud. At first this dream feels like a memory, I recognize the men around me. But how can that be? Because in this dream, my comrades suddenly turn. Their guns don't point over the trench but at me. They come at me with knives. It feels real. But I can't explain it. It must be a dream. But ever since, I've found it hard to keep my trust in someone. So I built this house and live here alone. If you can't trust the men fighting alongside you, who can you trust?"*

O'seus shook his head, knowing full well why he couldn't trust those men.

"There have been others like yourself. Others who also carry strange possessions and the same map as you did."

O'seus said nothing. He felt foolish for the first time in a long time. He just finished his soup and savored the silence, but Johann decided to fill it.

"So you're going to tell me everything. No more fainting, no more lies. Explain to me why I have a pile of rotting men just outside my house. Why I am being hunted?"

Johann got up with the empty bowl of soup and started thinking aloud.

"At first, I thought you were military, here to tie up a loose end. But none of you fought like soldiers."

O'seus noticed the door didn't seem so far now that his hands were free, but by how much blood he must've lost. He judged getting back to town would cut it close, especially with a tail.

"Not to mention none of you seem to speak Austrian-German very well at all."

"I said that I was from Scotland."

"That's a long way for so many to come for just one man." Johann pressed.

"Oh, it's a lot more than that. I'll tell you what you want to know, but only if you take me into town first."

Johann frowned.

"I'm hurt, and I won't last much longer unless I get some medical attention."

Johann stood up and towered over him.

"What? I'm not going to run away or anything. Trust me."

"People should only trust those close to death. For they have no reason to lie."

Johann paced towards the cabin door and opened it. Like a bull at a rodeo the wild wind burst through the threshold and tore through the cabin.

"Why don't you just take off for town now," Johann yelled over the storm. *"That's if you want to freeze to death on the way."*

O'seus let the wind whip his face as he stared solemnly back at Johann.

"That's enough." He cried out.

Johann smirked, closing the door and barring it shut with a length of wood.

"Now that you realize just how much bargaining power you don't have, why don't you answer my questions? Tell me who you are."

"I'm a time traveler."

"Liar."

"It is always the truth that is the most unbelievable." O'seus said.

"What does that mean?"

"It's a line from one of my movies. I always liked how it sounded."

Johann didn't like this and O'seus heard his kidnapper's fist tighten. He heard it.

"Why are you here?"

"I'm just a guy trying to give a sad story a happy ending."

"What does any of this have to do with a son of mine?"

"That son of yours will have another son. That is who this is all about. In 1933 they will elect this son of yours to office in Germany, and in 1939 will cause the deaths of millions of people."

"I don't understand." Johann really didn't. This stranger was talking about a son and wife of his that he just didn't have.

"Or at least, you once did. But because of men like me, you never will. Your family line ended with you. We're just here to make sure that stays true. Unfortunately, someone else takes your grandson's place. He's who the world knows as the epitome of evil and yes, we will go after his grandfather too, and then next and the next. Until finally it stops, and no one takes their place."

Johann got up and started pacing from wall to wall.

"We need to do this, we will keep trying to fix the past until the future we find is the best it can be. The final draft, I call it."

"So you're from the future?" Johann asked. *"Then why kill me? Why not kill my grandson? Why not leave me alone?"*

"We tried. This was easier." O'seus try to shrug with his hands tied.

"Do you think yourself just?"

"Excuse me?"

"If what your saying is true, that means you are here to kill me for something I have not even done. Nor meant to do."

"That's right."

"So you think you are just."

"I do."

"Just. For killing a man with no ill intent?"

"Actions are actions, intent means nothing over consequence. You are always responsible."

"Then show me." Johann crouched down in front of O'seus, still in disbelief but made of questions. He grabbed his pack and thrust it into O'seus' chest. *"Prove to me what is so bad it must mean my death. Show me and I'll let you live."*

O'seus sighed and reached into his pack and withdrew the cube. Johann's face drew quizzical at the abnormally colorful object.

"I've only got one trip left in this thing."

"Show me how it works."

"It's pretty complicated."

"Show me!"

"No!" O'seus threw the cube across the cabin. As Johann went after it, he got up and made for the door. Quicker on his feet than O'seus, Johann double back and tackled him, crashing into his dining table.

"You bastard," Johann crawled up to O'seus' face and shook his torso. *"Don't you dare..."*

Johann noticed O'seus hadn't lifted his head. He put his hand behind his skull to lift it up, but it felt wet. Blood wet his palm. Johann dropped his body and gradually found his feet again.

He made for the cube, already lost for direction when feeling the gravity of the cube in his hand.

He turned it and turned and turned and turned. The cube spun on its axis in any and every direction, and Johann spun it many more times before stopping to admire the pattern, only to feel a pull through a tangent he had unwittingly opened.

As Johann strode up the mountain, he shook his head, trying to recall the way to the first marker. He took off from the path worn by hunters and diverted onto a separate trail he had worn in himself.

He thought of the map that O'seus had carried, knowing it was still there on his floor, next to his body.

Careful not to step and snap a twig or awaken any silent dens, Johann eventually made it all the way to the rock on which he had carved the next marker.

He had hidden his cabin well, too well. Any time the mountain steered you one way, a stranger path was the correct one to take. This is where Johann left his markers, a trail of markers that only he could distinguish what they meant.

He knew it was easier when the snow melted away, and the terrain was easier to identify. But he had to do something about the body, his body, which meant he had to deal with his trail of white ice.

As he drew closer, he saw that the wind had ripped the door to pieces. He entered his old house and looked at it as though he hadn't seen it in years. Everything was so eerily familiar. It was like having a photograph of a moment that you look at every day and then seeing a different photo from a different camera from a different angle.

The blood had gone cold and solid quickly, the dead man on his floor no longer resembled an enemy but one of the many bloodied friends he walked over as he had at through war grounds long ago.

He thought of his name again: O'seus Forshaker. It was so guttural. Just like the clunk he couldn't forget, the sound of his head cracking against the floor.

Johann's heartbeat was in his ears; it was too loud inside. He burst through the door to outside, beating his fists in dirt to calm his nerves. But the smell, he couldn't ignore it. The cold had frozen the body pile, keeping the odor in. But now he could still smell it, now it had melted.

It sent him back to the war. He was on the battlefield again. The thick snow had melted to find the grass below only to be set alight and burnt away, leaving only hard worn earth and an ashy sky. Bullets whistled past his head. He had the weight of his bayonet in his arms. The stench of the pile was now the beaten horses, with flies infesting their eyes. Once again, he found that he stood alive in a dead sea of blue and white generals and soldiers. Now only the color of the cloth on their backs separated them; unified in death.

He stumbled to the pile and sort through it for any signs of life. It was hard snapping apart their limbs and peeling clothing taking no skin with it. But his hands found cubes, dozens of cubes.

He tossed them aside and made for a hatchet, loosely in the lifeless grip of a crusader. He felt his heart break as the dull bones broke with his pull. Fighting off the tears and pain, he roared and thrust the hatchet into the wall of the cabin. Each time he launched the hatchet's steel fin at his house, he felt a life taken in the stoic future he had seen. He took every one, a hundred lives tore down the back wall of the cabin, and a stiff swing took down the support beam and the roof sunk in.

If any hunter or wanderer wanted to be the next to find Johann's cabin, all they had to do was follow the unceasing sound of steel to wood.

Johann stood still the whole time his cabin was burning. Not until it, and every bit of bodily remains turned to ash, did he move.

When he did, he turned only to see a figure in the distance. Someone had walked towards the light of the fire. If it was someone from town Johann was ready to give himself up, to fall to his knees in the dirt and beg for a quick death.

But this man had only just arrived.

"You did it already?" The stranger saw the fire in front of Johann. "He's dead?"

"Yes. I'm burning it all."

"I guess I'm too late, huh."

Johann nodded, wondering if he would need his hatchet again.

"What's your name?" The stranger asked, seeing Johann's face lit up by the flames.

"... O'seus."

"O'seus. The O'seus?" The stranger asked, both relieved and impressed. "I'm Nash."

"You were here to kill him, right Nash?" The new O'seus asked.

"I was." Nash replied with a sigh.

"So you want to save the world."

"I do."

"Good. Then you're exactly what I'm looking for."

Chapter Six:
Delays, Derailments and Departures

Vaughn waited outside the train station again, as Hammond was inside leaving another note for himself, and both were leaving puddles behind.

Vaughn's soaking wet socks rubbed uncomfortably in his shoes as they dried up. The sidewalk hissed as the blistering sun ate up the salt water, it dripped from his clothes, and he pushed his hat deeper onto his head as he kept his chin down while he waited.

Chin down, ears up. Vaughn heard an impolitely loud and joyous laugh. One he would find difficult to forget. He lifted his head just in time to see a particular young couple, hand in hand, their Yankee caps tipped forward, strolling past him along with the crowd.

He wouldn't see them again, but they'd see him.

When Hammond returned he tightened up his coat and headed down the street with aim. He held in his hand a torn sheet he had ripped from a phone book. The Fish Bowl was a bar in Greenwich Village. The sign out front had a red neon sign yet to be turned on. And you could see the cobwebs and dust gathered on it, especially where the letters curled.

Inside was loud, even for the middle of the day. The counter and seating were all arranged differently, the round tables only seated two, but everyone had crammed four stools around them. People were littered

99

so tightly along the main bar that others had to order drinks over their shoulders.

Hammond pushed through, sighing at the sight of so many. It wasn't as though the person they were looking for would be wearing nametags or waving to greet them.

"Which one do you think it is?" Hammond asked.

Vaughn looked around with Hammond. Any one of them could have been him, Smokey hadn't been too specific. In fact, he hadn't been specific at all.

"I suppose we wait to see who doesn't leave until tomorrow?"

The voice reached out from the depths of the corner of the bar, a voice Vaughn recognized it immediately. It ricocheted against all walls and tables just to make it to Vaughn's ear. A voice that made his short hair curl under his hat.

"… well I could tell it was a Rittenhouse Rye from the moment it touched my lips. Only the Rittenhouse has that insatiably bitter oak taste that… pardon me… burns your tongue and…"

Vaughn knew that man. He was usually terrible with faces, but he could never forget a showboat.

And what a boat. He took up three quarters of a booth, body odor wafted out from between his neck flaps and double chins all the way over to them. Jowls, once again, stunk up another bar.

"That's the guy."

"You sure?" Hammond asked.

"I'm willing to bet on it." Vaughn said determinedly.

Hammond made for Jowl's table, not for a second removing his hat. Vaughn followed the back of Hammond's head. Almost all the hair had gone from his neck, what skin was left and hadn't yet flaked off, and his flesh was so pale that the blue veins rippled through it like the fingers of thin tree branches.

Hammond stood over Jowl's booth and waited for him to notice.

Gulps and a shuffling of feet followed their arrival as two men scattered from the corner booth's leather seats and out of the bar, leaving Jowl's all alone with three half-drunk pints on his table.

"You gonna buy me a drink first?" Jowls hiccupped.

Hammond sat down and Vaughn slid in beside him as Jowls slipped all three drinks toward himself and got started on finishing them.

"You're not scared?" Hammond asked.

"I'm too drunk to be scared." Jowls howled with laughter that spat all over them.

"Your story." Hammond started. "Had you finished it?"

"The good parts, yeah. Frankly, the rest after that is rather unbecoming."

"What happened?"

"Well, I had won fair and square, despite what they had forced me to drink, and then I offered the bartenders my gracious mercy. I would let them stay, as I am not so evil-hearted. But then they all jumped at me, held a gun to my face, and they forced me out of there. Out into the open. They left me to die out there. Then I was jumped, and I woke up someplace I had never been before, I had to make my way back home."

"That sounds terrible." Hammond shook his head; his voice was light and friendly for a change. He waved his hand, and the bartender nodded, bringing over another round of drinks that Hammond pushed in front of Jowls.

"It was, believe me. A weaker man wouldn't have had made it. But I choose not to let it get me down. No matter how courteous you are, people can still think they can walk all over you."

"Sounds like a real tale, a man's tale. Something that would have had defeated most."

"But not me!" Jowls cheered with a glass in hand.

"But not you." Hammond followed.

"You know, it's a real nice change to meet ...pardon me... just some real nice guys such as yourselves." Jowls was slurring his words together, and Hammond simply pushed the next full glass toward him.

"You guys sure are nice."

"So which bar exactly was the one that treated you so unkindly?"

"The bar? It was more of a party. A very secret and selective party. But I guess there's no harm in telling you guys as it's over now. It was one of those, 'you had to have been there' kind of things."

"What kind of party? Who was the host?"

"Some rich old prune, Atticus something. It was in this huge building, with a telescope in it. It was on top of this big mountain in this shithole of a town."

"What was the name of the town?"

"Why are you so interested, huh?"

"I like to have context when I hear a story."

Jowls straightened up. He looked past Hammond and into Vaughn's shadowed face. If he could see through the veil, he would have seen the face of absolute repulsion.

"You know, I never saw you guys there. But I'm not very good with faces. Perhaps you were interested in going? Perhaps you have the proper means of travel?"

"Perhaps we do."

"Ah, so we've come to the real price of these drinks."

"I think we have. What is it worth to you?"

"You two don't seem like the partying type, do I have that right?"

They were silent.

"Maybe I'm overstepping my bounds a little by sharing. It's really supposed to be a secret. I'm guessing if you were to attend this event you would plan on making quite a splash? Maybe I shouldn't..."

"I believe the term is crashing." Vaughn piped up.

"Is that right?" Jowls mumbled.

"And from the sounds of it, these people didn't welcome you too kindly. Perhaps they deserve a little comeuppance? Wouldn't you say?" Vaughn pressed.

"Perhaps..."

"That story you were telling, it kind of tapered off a little at the end." Vaughn kept up. "Maybe your story doesn't have to end on such a low note. Maybe you can rewrite the ending. Maybe we can help you with that?"

"That's true." Jowls went silent for a while, possibly just so he could reorientate himself with all the dizziness the drinks were bringing. "In that case... Fracture, Central Australia. May 10th, 1991, started at six or six thirty. It's on top of the mountain of the same name."

Hammond scribbled it all down on a napkin, but Vaughn needn't bother.

They thanked their drunken friend and calmly left the Fish Bowl as Jowls slowly lowered his head to the tabletop to rest for a while. His skull laid sideways on a half empty glass, his ear inside the rim, he could only hear bubbles.

This was their last visit to the train station. Vaughn was learning the stations and train lines by heart from announcements made every few seconds. Hammond pushed through the antlike lines of commuters and found the locker bay. He flickered a code and swung open the door. From it he pulled a bag, Vaughn could see it had a shiny, silver lining, and was full of cubes with room for even more. Hammond thrust it into Vaughn's hands.

"What's this for?" Vaughn took the bag from Hammond. It was heavier than he thought. The strange lining made the whole bag heavy.

"Protects the cubes inside." Hammond asked. "How d'you know it was him?"

Vaughn lugged the heavy bag over his shoulder.

"He was loud." Vaughn said.

Hammond paused, but only for a second.

"That's a good point."

Hammond led them both to the public toilets. It was empty and hummed echoes of the trains on the other side of the walls. They stood there in yellow puddles and surrounded by black scribbling. All the graffiti was in black or blue pen ink, not one chaotic slur or etching was in yellow spray paint. Hammond choked up another gross ball of pus and spat it at a closed toilet. It landed on the seat

"Don't worry." Hammond breathed in deeply. Neither of them could smell much anymore. Lucky for them. "I'm fine."

"I wasn't worried." Vaughn said honestly.

"Good, because we're very close to the end."*

---

*Go to Page 317

Hammond was still wiping his hands clean of the moaning man. He hadn't bled on him or anything, but there was something repellant about him. Something about his neediness and absolute helplessness that just felt unclean and unsavory.

He was in his own head. As he walked towards the locker bay yet again, he fought with himself inside whether he was following or giving the orders. It depended on whether he was writing or reading the notes.

He tried not to feel too abandoned as the last locker he opened had only his old gloves and files. Files that were once so important to a much younger Hammond but mattered not in retrospect.

He would at least leave this note, hopefully prompting another.

Touching the pen to paper he lent on the locker door, feeling very much felt in charge, like he was taking control of his destiny and had found a way to make fate his own.

But opening the door and finding yet another note inside was like falling off his feet and being pulled by his necktie to where he was supposed to go.

And reading it was like slapping him awake.

Wyla is still alive at the Time Asylum.

What?

How was she still alive? He had taken care of this. Gotten rid of her like all the others. Just the thought of her made him think of a cockroach, ever crawling and ever living no matter how much you stomped. Wyla was crawling around in his head, and he couldn't get her out.

But how?

How had she survived? How had she not bled out?

How had she outwitted the place where all the lost things go?

He had more questions than just how, but his future self hadn't much to answer with. Scrawled at the bottom of the note like an afterthought was written.

A man called Smokey knows how to find her. You'll need Pratt.
1:30pm – March 21st, 2009

The co-ordinates that followed seemed exact. But his mind wasn't ready for exact. It wasn't ready for calculated thought.

You'll need Pratt. *Which Pratt would it be this time?* How many of his pets had multiplied by now? How long until people stopped being people and instead becoming the cogs that the universe needed them to be?

If he had any less fate than them, he would only be so lucky.

Yet he was the one controlling his own fate. At least he knew who was behind the wheel. As long as he kept on writing these notes and leaving them for himself, he could be sure of that.

The man grumbling into his locker unnerved the woman with the locker beside his. She rushed to an attendant and as she went to point him out, she found that the locker was closed, and the strange shadowy man had long gone.[*]

✧ ✧ ✧

His foot stuck out just a little too far. Hammond flailed at the top of the steps leading down to the lower platforms. His shoes had very little room and his smooth heel twisted on smoother polished marble.

"Watch it, buddy."

"Yeah move it pal."

Hammond staggered back and caught his breath as he eyed the long fall he almost had.

It was day again. The rush of incoming passengers changing trains from the No.12 to the No.5 were coming and Hammond had to step out of the way of each of them, knocking shoulders and elbows heavily guarding their cups of coffee.

This stream was too strong to bother parting around him, they washed over him and he felt less like a rock and more like a pebble.

––––––––––––

[*]*Go to Page 125*

Hammond was in brightness, and no one cared. No one saw him. The shade of his hat gave him the complete anonymity that he hadn't felt since before he had run for office. That, and how little they cared for someone was in their way.

He was used to his face being up on buses and billboards. Printed on pins and bumper stickers.

For the last ten years of his life he had been in the public eye and now, here he stood - amongst them and less than one of them.

He marched to the locker bay, diverting to the newspaper stand to buy a pad and pen, chuckling as he found one with the same yellow paper that all the notes he had read were written on.

Popping open No.016 Hammond found that the newspaper article was missing. Having not been left there yet. He should have figured as much. He jotted the note he had first found, telling him to jump ahead and he placed inside the locker the same cube he had taken from it, then slammed it shut.

Curious.

His eye caught the locker beside his, No.012, and he wondered if he could guess the code. So many numbers ran through his head, but he knew that whichever he chose it would have to be the right ones. He would make sure of it.

No.012 popped open too, the metal hinge creaking as he flung it open and found what was inside.

Wyla will be at Volta Tower June 24th, 2024

Other, hurried to finish shoving their things in their lockers and slammed the doors to get away from the manically laughing man, hunched over his locker with his head inside in the dark metal box.

This is what made him different from them. This is why he wasn't just another nostalgia-hungry tourist.

He was a hunter and they left him trails.

Everybody had a trail. Everyone had a path. Just like how everything has a beginning and an end.

Like a book he took too long to read, the characters would still be there on the page, waiting for him.

Waiting, somewhere. Still.

He had to get Pratt first.

How could he forget?*

Flat footed they landed, amidst the crowded intersection that all stared at a red light waiting for it to go green. Their tangent had squeezed them in between. From a distance, if someone were to look up at the crowd, they would just assume their faces fell under timely shadows, or that they were a blur between bobbing heads.

Most couldn't see further than two blocks anyway. The sun was too bright, their armpits were too sweaty. It was so hot that the garbage piling up alongside the road cooked. Trash bag stacks lent against bus stop signs and benches. They just kicked it aside. Some shop owners hosed it off and garbage water ran into the gutters and quickly dried up as it sizzled on the pavement just as the rubber tires of dozens of traffic-stalled cars sweltered.

They played an inadvertent symphony with their car horns, a detail that would keep you up at night but one you would barely notice during the day.

Unless you were here for the details.

Two men in thick brown coats with long dark faces traced the sidewalk. What they hunted had come this way. They had seen it.

They knew that they had taken a left off 5th and onto 47th.

They knew they were going to get their ankles wet as a green grocer sprayed rats from his door.

They knew that they were going to stop by a newspaper stand on Vanderbilt Avenue and buy one of each daily edition and skip to the stock pages.

---

*Go to Page 122

They knew the young couple were somewhere close, imposing on history.

The taller and larger of the two shadowy figures audibly gasped as they turned onto Vanderbilt.

"What!" Pratt went rigid. "You see them?"

"Not them, no." Hammond kept on, his eyes up and to the great pale bricked building that was now ahead of them. "Just how it used to look."

"They went onto 42nd next…remember their wearing Yankee caps and…"

"I know, I know." Hammond crossed the street instead. Pratt ran after him as they took the staggered maze that weaved between car boots and bonnets to the other side. "Did you know I used to do this every day?"

"Do what?" Pratt asked as they stepped back onto the sidewalk and got swamped by a crowd leaving the station.

"This is why they do it, isn't it?" Hammond was stroking the wall as Pratt bit his lip, staring at the gum and piss stains that dribbled down the wall. He at least could smell the stench of rubbish and urine and worried how infectious that brick wall was. But Hammond was grazing every bump, inhaling every waft of trash and embracing the heat. "They do it for the memory. You know I used to come this way every day, take this entrance and take the same train from the same platform every day. And it smelt…"

Hammond breathed in deep.

"… it smelt just like this."

"That's great. Look, we're falling behind. They will only be on that corner for another two minutes. Then we will lose them and will have to find another Ogle around here."

"I'm going to look around for a little."

"Hammond c'mon."

"Wait here."

Hammond left Pratt fidgeting on the spot and slipped inside Grand Central Station.

Streams of light rushed through the tall windows and laid stretches of spotlight across the marble floor.

Hammond recalled feeling young again. He remembered how he had hurried. How he had nothing on his mind but the polls, good or bad, they lingered in his thoughts all day. He didn't have music in his ears back then. He'd either read or sit quietly with his thoughts at the end of a long day or the start of the next one.

He remembered using this place as his own personal poll. He'd judge the people he saw, how they acted, how they dressed, what they were interested in. How so many didn't read more than the front-page of the paper and how that upset him but also how it made him feel better than them. He was informed, he was aware.

And that's still what he thought now. He was aware that he was walking through memories. That this had all passed long ago and was just a re-enactment, just for him.

Hammond walked to the middle of the busiest section of the station, where the marble was most trodden, and he stood still. He lifted his arms up and out and smirked as he felt them all rush around him like a rock in a stream. They didn't walk through him, this wasn't a fantasy, he was there, and he was in the way.

He considered himself a very big rock.

Just for fun he walked over to the wall of lockers and stood in front of locker No.016.

That had been his locker, and still should be. He wondered if his code would work, or if he could remember it.

He slipped his finger over the raised numbers and spun his old code.

Click, snap. It opened.

Curious, Hammond thought. He swung it open and expected to find a spare coat, a few binders maybe, but not this.

There, in the hollow locker, was a cube acting as a paperweight for a bit of notepaper.

This had to be for him.

He slid the paper out from under the cube and to the edge of the inside of the locker. He read the one line scribbled cleanly and neatly between the lines, followed by his own signature.

Take the no. 3 train to Brooklyn. Once you pass the Williamsburg Bridge, jump forward three days and four hours.

"Where to?" He was asked.

"Sorry?"

The teller hadn't even looked up. If he had, he would have been shocked by the general lack of this customer's face. Hammond hadn't even noticed he had left the lockers and wondered over to the ticket teller. It was as though his body was on autopilot.

"Tickets?" The teller pressed, emphasizing the 't' of tickets. "How many tickets? One way or return?"

Hammond walked away with a ticket in hand. *What was he to do next?* He remembered his old routine again, his feet already leading him to his platform.

The locker was most definitely for him, and he hadn't dared to leave the cube behind for someone else to find.

Hammond continued to follow his feet as they led him how they remembered; down the fourth gate, to the second platform and to his favorite bench, the one right near the end where the light would buzz as he read his paper.

He even got on the train.

This is when Hammond remembered he had left Pratt outside, thinking he would only be a few minutes. Once the doors had closed and the train began to move he could feel the distance growing between them. He knew he'd be waiting and now waiting a while. But did it matter?

He pulled out the cube to answer his own question.

No one else on the train noticed the power he held.

He felt the rush of excitement he hadn't felt in a long time.

This is how travel was supposed to feel. That's where it all went wrong. If only time travel could be as efficient, as smooth, and as inviting as this train. Hammond watched the doors slide open and people walked on just as others moved past them to get off.

It was perfectly similar, people choosing where to be and hopping on the train, waiting a bit and then getting off somewhere different.

Hammond got out of his seat and walked to the doors as he waited for the train to round the corners of the underground and make it to the next station.

He stood the entire journey, watching for the bridge up ahead, getting closer and closer.

He gripped the cube in his hand and readied his step for his next stop.[*]

Vaughn was quick to notice they were still in New York. Through his veil of haze, he could still smell, nothing but piss and garbage.

"I thought we were going to find… that man." Vaughn said. "Why are we still here?"

"We are here." Hammond answered as they walked back to the train station, only now coming from the south side on an entirely different day. "Because I still have to leave the note for myself first, just in case."

"Just in case?"

Hammond didn't bother explaining further, hiking up the slight incline of the street was a struggle, he stopped to cough a few times and Vaughn saw blood spots flicker on the pavement.

Hammond was slow but persistent; he would keep going even without arms and legs.

Vaughn gave him some distance as Hammond hunched over his favorite locker to write notes to his strange pen pal. Vaughn waited and

---

[*]Go to Page 128

lent against a pillar and watched the people pass. He held his head up, almost trying to get noticed but he never was, people really didn't care.

His eye caught a young couple in each other's arms, happy-go-lucky, the only ones looking around as they strolled through the train station. Vaughn pushed back against the pillar and followed them, finding them standing in line for a hot dog just outside on the main corner. Vaughn smelt only broth and saw clouds of steam coming of the vender's cart.

"See something?"

Hammond stood behind Vaughn, turning his head up and down the street until he too caught sight of the young couple fumbling for proper change to pay for their hotdogs. Both wearing matching Yankee caps.

"You see them too?" Vaughn asked. "Who gets a hotdog on a hot day like this?"

Hammond didn't answer. He merely pushed passed Vaughn and started tailing them. Vaughn had no choice but to follow along.

They had to keep their distance from the cheery couple ahead of them if they didn't want to be seen.

The couple took side streets off the main roads, and under scaffolding with high apartments overhead and crammed shop fronts along the edges with foreign smells and lots of things cooking. All the shops were selling odd foods or packaged items with foreign labels.

Between the alleys, Vaughn saw clotheslines hanging between open windows, old women on their fire escape balconies, resting their crusty feet and waving a fan.

Small children ran past them, and Vaughn felt his pockets rustle, still quicker than most, he held onto his pants and they got nothing.

They didn't dare grope Hammond. The children saw his face, or lack thereof. He'd be their nightmare fuel for years to come.

As the couple turned into a side street, so did their stalkers.

"That's right, lead the way." Hammond muttered.

It was easy to keep sight of them as much of the street crowd split to get out of their way. They were a disturbance. Vaughn was counting the seconds under his breath. The seconds rippled exponentially.

The couple entered an apartment complex. Hammond caught the door before it closed, and they followed them inside. As he did, he clicked a button on his belt and a strange whirring noise spiked in Vaughn's ear before fading quickly.

"After you." Hammond said.

Vaughn moved forward with his first foot on the first step as Hammond thrust something solid into his chest. Vaughn took it, the icy steel refreshing on such a hot day.

"In case they run." He growled.

The couple took the stairs and so did they.

It was a cheap building, yellow peeling wallpaper revealed crumbling, cream colored plaster.

The couple's apartment was the first on the right and they argued over who had the keys. She dropped them and Vaughn wasn't ready for the screams.

The two tourists staggered back, finding no tangents opened to let them through as Vaughn and Hammond closed in. She banged her cube against the wall to get it to work, but it was now just a toy.

The window above them shot bright sunlight directly under Hammond's hat and onto his face. The shade became an even stranger sight to see.

They didn't need the gun to take the light from their eyes, but it helped.

The man grabbed his girlfriend and pulled her up the stairs.

Vaughn pointed in between the banisters and held the trigger down.

SPLAT!

That calf was full of blood and shot half of it across the wallpaper.

The woman screamed.

Vaughn moved up around the staircase and again twitched his finger.

Hammond and Vaughn could hear fear from behind the other apartment doors.

Someone was using a phone; the police would be there soon.

Hammond didn't seem to be in a rush, stepping up the stairs over their slowly crawling bodies and fishing through their pockets for extra cubes as their legs bled out and down the stairs.

"Thought you got away huh?" Hammond grinned, standing over them both. "Such an untimely...ough ough ough."

Hammond's laugh turned on him and he coughed useless evidence all over the bodies. He held his hand against the wall and waited until he wasn't dizzy.

"Now can we go?" Vaughn asked, gun at his side.

Hammond took the girl by her bleeding leg and pulled her down towards him. She struggled only reaching for her partner. The looming Historian took one cube and twisted it relentlessly. So many turns and spins he could almost unscrew the cube from itself, then simply placed it on top of them both.

Sirens wailed in the distance, shouts and screams echoed behind closed doors begging to be left alone and that they weren't the ones who called the cops.

There was a lot of blood left behind, he must have hit some arteries.

"Now we can go." Hammond straightened up and cleared his throat. "We've got a boat to catch."[*]

---

[*]Go to Page 380

✧

Part Six:
RED

New York city was amid the hottest summer on record. Window fans and coolers hummed and expelled heat out into the street where the blistering wind picked it up and passed it along to the next open window. Trapped in metal hotboxes, drivers incessantly honked their horns only stopping to wipe sweat from their foreheads. Traffic moved so slowly the rubber tires melted ever so slowly into the road, and pedestrians walked following the shade - darting out in the sun only to catch a cab that would take them home slower than if they had walked.

The sun was too bright to keep your eyes up for long, so nobody noticed few new feet appear on the sidewalk, nobody cared to listen to the children that swore they saw two men in brown coats and brown hats suddenly appear on the sidewalk. The only thing that mattered was the cool breeze that preceded them, even if it was only slight.

Hammond returned to the familiar heat and tucked in his coat while the faceless man beside him broke into an immediate sweat.

Hammond had taken off, and Vaughn went to follow him when he felt a tug. Something had caught his sleeve. He looked back to see a man pulling his arm back just as Vaughn did.

The man's eyes went wide and his face pale when he saw nothing looking back at him; under that hat he saw a ghost. Vaughn could see the very fibers of their sleeves had somehow interwoven, as though that's how they had always been.

Everyone at the intersection was moving on except for Vaughn and this increasingly erratic man.

Vaughn pulled some more, tugging so hard that the shirt tightened over the rest of his body to make slack.

Hammond was quickly slipping away, and Vaughn was close to losing sight of him.

The man screamed which shocked Vaughn so suddenly that his next pull ripped his cuff completely off at the seam and he ran, leaving it behind.

The man kept screaming, but Vaughn found his facelessness got him through the crowd with ease. When looking for a culprit, people look for a face, scary eyes, a bloodthirsty smile. He never realized just how invisible you become when you hide only your face.

The streets hadn't thinned, people herded from one block to the next, all hot and sweaty, internally combusting, despising the hot bodies around them for being within smelling distance. He found Hammond had lent against a window and was staring mutably at the multiple televisions setup on the other side of the glass.

"The Big Apple bakes as records show hottest day in thirty years..."

Passers-by stopped to watch the same weather channel on several screens as the weatherman stood in front of an angry cartoon sun with his sleeves rolled up and his hair slicked back with sweat.

"And it doesn't look like it will let up anytime soon. Back to you, Carl."

"Thanks for that Wallace. More news following the violent disappearance of two New Yorkers in their early twenties. Police say this is just another sign of violent crime and danger that has become all too normal for this city."

"It's not just the heat that's making everyone go nuts, we've been dealing with break ins and drug dealers all over the city. And yeah, you're gonna get the occasional act of random violence. We keep telling everybody it's best to stay inside at night and keep to

the main streets, don't go wandering and further than Ninety-First Street..."

With their dark faces reflecting in the windows as more and more people gathered to watch Hammond took off and again Vaughn struggled to keep up. The sting of the dry heat drenched him in sweat and all he wanted was to dive into a body of water or take his hat off to fan his face. Hammond moved through and split the crowd, as no one wanted to touch each other any more than they needed to. Some stopped to have a quick scowl at Hammond as he passed them, muttering how crazy he was in his long, heavy brown suit.

Hammond only ever looked back at Vaughn like an owner to their dog on a leash. Vaughn followed faithfully. They paused at a traffic light and Vaughn, like all the others, moved to stand in the shade one building was bearing over half the crowd. They all shuffled to stay inside the shade kicking aside trash that bundled alongside the bins, overdue for collection, and was growing to be part of the scenery.

"You're being quiet."

"Am I?" Vaughn responded.

"Usually I can't shut you up."

The light went green, and they crossed the street with the crowd. Hammond was better at slipping through crowds and traffic while Vaughn got smacked in each shoulder as he passed people going in the opposite direction. The cars didn't stop either, trying to make a turn and arrogantly pushing through pedestrians with their bumper. After the third time Vaughn lent into it, shoving back harder and becoming an immovable object.

"They really are everywhere, aren't they?" Hammond said as he watched the driver cut through the crowd. He leaned in and made sure the driver saw him. The driver turned to abuse him but went pale while looking for his face.

"People that think they can do whatever they want just because it works out for them, it makes sense only for them." Vaughn added.

"They make it easy though. Easy to spot, just look for the selfish. Don't need a damn Ogle anymore. Makes me wonder why I got into politics. I never liked people."

Hammond was heading somewhere, and Vaughn followed along by his side now, sharply elbowing people that tried to push past like he wasn't there.

"What do you think it is about them? Do they lack that basic sense of self-preservation? Is it a natural yearning for self-destruction or are they all just plain selfish?"

Hammond stopped again, though it wasn't for the conversation. They had come to a short set of stairs leading up into a big, pale, brick building and Hammond was peering inside before going in. Vaughn had noticed how Hammond spoke properly now. He had more strength in his voice and his walk. He was more composed, and the saliva stayed in his mouth. Not at all like he had been at the Asylum.

Hammond was waiting for something, or someone.

And when Vaughn heard the moan, he assumed that must've been it.

It had to be a loud moan to be heard over all the traffic of the station. There was the horror in it that made people turn. A moan that went on and on with some crying in the middle, edging up to a scream but not quite reaching it.

The onlookers saw it in his face, the absolute dread, and of course, the horror.

The trains ran on schedule, but many missed their ride, as they couldn't help but watch, compelled to witness the suffering. A solemn circle surrounded the man with his ankles deep in the marble floor of New York's Grand Central Station on a Monday morning.

His face was white as the roses he carried. His eyes hollow, throat sore and moaning from the absolute agony that was digging into his shinbones. But that's all he could do.

Hurriedly, the police pushed through the crowd.

"Oh, my..." The first policeman said, as he swallowed his breakfast again.

The surrounding marble had been stained blood red and clean to the touch. The second cop dropped to his knees to grab at his leg and pull.

"The floor... it's dry."

The crowd was abnormally pale for so hot a day. They all watched as the cops tried to pull the man free, even the people in the back could hear the strain of bones cracking with each ambitious pull. Those near the front could see how perfectly his skin molded to the marbled floor, as if he was always there.

They had brought in men from outside, a road worker with a jackhammer and one with a drill. They grew sick when they saw it, but pressed on, digging and drilling into the floor as two police officers held the moaning man up. Twice he screamed himself unconscious and awake again.

After each bout of drilling and hammering, they would look and see that they had been boring through brick and bone. Chunks of cartilage chipped out and scattered across the floor. The tradesmen with the jackhammer doubled over and vomited a few feet away. The driller backed away, cold.

It was a persistent effort. No one questioned why. It was all that kept their blood pumping and their minds from inducing panic that they just had to get him out. They themselves felt trapped and no one could rest until the nightmare was over.

Hammond pushed easily through the crowd and up close to the moaning man, ushering away the police with strange authority. No one looked to his face, all eyes were on that of the man stuck in stone.

Hammond pressed his invisible nose right up close to the moaning man, who had gone silent in his presence. He knew what type of people wore brown hats and suits; were what type of people hid their faces. The moaning man figured himself the first to not run from the sight of them.

"Quite a mistake you've made." Hammond hushed. "Tourist."

Caught amid the crowd, Vaughn couldn't see much, but what he could see warranted the dry heaving and pale faces as he only needed

to catch a glimpse of the seamless meld of marble and skin. Just like his sleeve. Vaughn couldn't take his eyes off the only part of the man he could see; his ankles.

Hammond reached into the moaning man's pocket and found his cube. He then took off his large coat as the moaning man shook. The hand that still firmly gripped the tattered bunch of white roses shook the last petals from their stems. As he looked deep into the nothingness of the man standing before him twisting the cube, fully aware that his ankles were the least of his problems.

Hammond lifted his coat high and draped it over the moaning man. With a firm hand he forced him backwards, tipping him back and lowering him to the ground with his coat still covering his entire body.

Hammond was sly, but Vaughn caught it. Moving to the middle of the commotion, Vaughn told everyone to back off and back to their own business as Hammond slipped the cube beneath the coat.

"Such an untimely death." Hammond whispered.

Moments later he cradled the empty coat, supporting it with his hands underneath to give it some sense of weight and dimension.

Vaughn eased the crowd aside, tucking his hat forward and keeping his head down. They could see now the moaning man's body was free, apart from the blood and bone still solidified in the marble. Only the mangled white roses and rubble of broken marble remained strewn about the station floor.

The show was over.

Hammond walked until he was out of sight before he whipped his coat back over his shoulders and wiped his hands clean as he headed for the locker bays.

Still following, Vaughn watched as he opened one and hastily slammed it shut. He slammed it a few more times and Vaughn saw his back arch up as he sighed deeply and coughed a lot.

"I'll be back." Hammond choked.

"I'll wait." Vaughn blurted.

"Yes, you will."

Vaughn couldn't see, but Hammond eyed Vaughn strangely. Had he noticed that an understudy had been playing the part of Pratt?

Either way, Hammond slipped off down towards a lower platform and Vaughn stuck his hands in his pockets to keep them from any mischief as he was left behind to wander the heated streets of New York alone.

✧ ✧ ✧

What a morning.

The station's security bordered off the bloody stain with traffic cones and caution tape, sweeping up rose petals and small chunks of marble as the rest of the station moved on with their lives as normal.

Hammond was gone, having slipped away on another tangent, leaving Vaughn to wait outside the north entrance of the station, tracing his foot over the pavement cracks with his hands deep in his pockets.

Perhaps he was picturing his own ankles a foot deep in concrete, his fingers fiddling with his sleeve. Perhaps. From behind such a dark cowl, from beneath such a deep shade, was Vaughn even there anymore?

There was no way of knowing if under that hat, Vaughn was crying or if he was laughing or if he was grinding his teeth. Or maybe he was just staring blankly at the shoes of those that passed him by.

Strangely enough, on the west side of the station another was waiting, just like Vaughn.

He too was dressed in the same brown coat and hat, face concealed and waiting for the same man.

Only he had been waiting longer.

Hammond had left him waiting for some time now. So, this man had spent the last two days coming back and forth waiting a few hours every day for his Historian partner to return.

He was pacing.

Now enter another Hammond, back from wherever he had gone with a note he planned to give himself, crushed up in his hand. Mad as all hell he stormed through the crowd, knocking people aside as they were now all the same to him.

It was still the same summer heat as before, and nothing about the station looked any different from one day to the next.

This was a repetitive temple. Just how he remembered it.

The same people moved through the station twice a day for most of their lives; it was not so much a location to them as it was a

checkpoint in their days. Simply somewhere they had to pass through to continue.

Where Hammond stood he could see three exits and was unsure of which was where he had left his partner, waiting like a dog leashed to a pole.

He checked all three and like some absurd joke, he found Pratt was waiting outside of two.

These two shadowed faces hid beneath identical brown hats. So well hidden, unseen and unimposing that Hammond figured the universe hadn't even noticed.

What had all his time travelling done?

Two Pratts? Hammond thought and almost spoke aloud. How long had they been waiting? How long had they been existing?

He had been putting it off his mind, but the itching feeling had crept back into his head, in the sweet spot between his brain and his skull. It forced him to stand so still he would feel the floor rushing back and forth beneath him, like standing in the tide. The marble floor, now liquid and flowing. Everything was.

He looked at random strangers with the same disbelief as he did both the Pratt's. Nobody was meant to be here, everyone was in the place of someone else, reading lines and impersonating what had happened before.

It was all a fucked-up re-enactment, a high school production of a Broadway show.

If he thought too long, he would think about his wife again. Her picture was still in his wallet. He took it out and unfolded it; the crease running along her forearm which was brushing the hair off her face.

Why did he still keep it when he didn't even recognize the woman in it?

Because this was the lie now and he was waiting for it to change, or for some other stranger to step in and play the part of his dead wife.

It was getting harder to see himself as anything more than the tourists he hunted.

Before blaming himself too harshly, Hammond became aware again of the paper, crisp in his hand. He unfolded it, reading her name again and sighing deep.

It was not his fault, but hers.

If it was all the same to the universe than it was all the same to him.

Which Pratt he chose, didn't matter. Underneath that hat could be anybody's face.

Somehow Hammond had become exempt. He had jumped around so much he had slipped behind the curtain and found a mistake. He retained the ability to see through the veil pulled over their eyes by every change they caused and ripple they splashed.

He had even seen that the one responsible for it all had fallen victim to it too. Not that it made her any less guilty.

Hammond saw no difference between either of the two Pratt's, one was not more or less than the other. He simply took the one that was the closest.

"Were you waiting long?"

Pratt turned to see Hammond stepping down the steps and over towards him, both men in permanent shade and arousing strange looks from curious children and pigeons.

"Two days Hammond?" Pratt said in a huff as he slid off the edge of the steps and to his feet. "I tried to track them. I must've walked half the city but without knowing exactly where they were going to be I had no chance. It's a big city, Hammond, too many people. We've completely lost them."

"Hmmm."

"You haven't listened to a word I said have you?" Pratt snapped. "If you had, you'd have heard that we lost them. I know that pisses you off more than it does me, so what do you suggest we do about them?"

"Small fish. Let them swim."

"You want to let them go? That doesn't sound like you."

Hammond grinded his teeth. Pratt sure felt like Pratt. But how would he ever know?

"Pratt, we've been wasting time chasing ants. There's a better way."

"Pouring boiling water down the nest?"

"That, or we kill the queen."

"Ok, you're losing me. Ants, fish, just tell me you know where we're going next."

"I know where we're going next."

And they left, while Vaughn still stood idly outside the train station.

Vaughn, the Pratt not taken, had slumped by the edge of the train station. He was careful not to rest against any dried piss stains or where anyone could walk. Hanging his head between his knees, he breathed through the heat and stared at his borrowed shoes.

A few coins landed at his feet, one nicked his kneecap, and it stung a little.

He was blending into the scenery all too well.

"Up. Come on."

Hammond was standing over him, blocking the sun, and Vaughn pushed off the building to his feet and followed him.

Hammond led them both to a diner that smelt like burnt eggs and coffee. In this heat the smell sweltered into a gas that rose and clung to the ceiling and when you caught a whiff it roasted in your nostrils.

Hammond chose a far corner booth, and the waitress was too busy blowing her sweat-wet fringe from her face to catch their lack of facial features.

"Coffee. Hot." Hammond ordered.

"That's how we make it."

"Coffee? Really?" Vaughn tested; he couldn't help it. His tongue was sweating just thinking about it.

"Yes." Hammond pressed, as though he had been asked a thousand times before. "Coffee. When I say hot, I mean hot."

"If you want burnt water hun, I'll bring you burnt water. If you want coffee, I'll bring you coffee." The waitress was having trouble

with one clumped strand of thick hair that every time she flicked it up and out of her face it would clutch another strand and bungee jump back down.

"Coffee then."

"Coke with lots of ice." Vaughn asked.

She left, and Vaughn noticed Hammond rubbing his arms despite the heat.

"Are you cold?"

"I think there's something wrong with me." Hammond said.

Vaughn gulped.

"I think it's my mind. It's slipping. I can't remember things like I could before and what I can remember I don't know if I can trust. Does that make any sense to you?"

Vaughn moved his head.

"I know it's happening to everyone. It feels like ants in my brain. I know that every time they change something, my memory changes with it. I know that at any moment they could wipe you or me or anyone else from existence. At any moment I could be that waitress. That waitress could be that taxi driver outside. And no one would care, realize or ever know it happened. I know that's how it works but..."

"But what?"

"But I think I'm starting to feel it." Hammond said softly. "Do you think it feels like dying?"

"I don't know."

"I think dying would feel like something. Being erased is not dying. Death means you were once something. Carbon, molecules, atoms. Being erased... *Being* in the first place isn't easy. It's all about timing and coincidence. Time can never repeat the one perfect scenario that created you, only poor substitutes."

Hammond spoke like he was scrunching his upper lip into his nostrils. Vaughn could tell because when he breathed, the air struggled back out in an aggressive and guttural squeeze. It was like he was snoring internally. It was like he hated his words.

The waitress brought them their drinks and Hammond cupped his hands around his mug and sighed at its warmth, as Vaughn took a deep sip of his coke and too felt his body temperature sooth.

"Just look out there. Everyone just living out their lives." Hammond gestured. "In politics you're always afraid that the people will figure out they don't need you. Because then you'd be out of a job. They could ignore us, not vote for us and walk away. But despite all that, they keep following anyone that stands up and points. People need to be led; people need fate despite their free will. Which is good because free will is scarier than death. Strangely enough, when you think about it, the very fact everyone has free will means everybody doesn't."

"What do you mean?"

"You're surrounded by free thinking and free acting people, and everything they do affects you and your choices, so much that you lose all your freedom. It becomes its own form of a deterministic constraint, and it dwindles your own free will in comparison. Why even have it in the first place?"

"No idea."

"It's best you stick with me then."

"Why?"

"Because unlike everyone else, I control my fate."

"How's that?"

Hammond slammed a palm on the table and beneath it Vaughn could see a crumpled up note, now smoothed out over the table.

Wyla is still alive at the Time Asylum
A man called Smokey knows how to find her. You'll need Pratt.
1:30pm – March 3rd, 2009

Vaughn had no way of translating the co-ordinates underneath the date and time, but it wasn't what he focused on.

"The Time Asylum?"

"Ever heard of it?" Hammond asked.

Vaughn shook his head.

"Me neither. But if she's going to be there, then so are we."

"Where did you get this?" Vaughn asked, sliding the note back to him.

"I keep finding them in my old locker. That's what I meant by controlling fate. That's my handwriting. I will write that note and leave it for myself to find. And then I'll find the next one, and the next one, and the next one. And when we get to that Asylum…"

Hammond slammed yet another hand on the table, this time clutching a white cube in his frail hand.

"All the ants will be gone."

There was a lengthy silence as Hammond rested his back into the booth, pocketing the white bube in his jacket. You could hear the slow crinkling of the leather seat as he sunk deeper into it.

They sat there for some time, until the ice in the coke had melted, though that was not a strong indicator of a long time passing. The heat could thaw the hamburger meat in the diner's freezer, yet Vaughn was feeling colder and colder.

"Do you ever stop and think that maybe, I'm just saying maybe, we're just the bad guys?" Vaughn asked.

"Tourists risk all of us, all the time, every day. Time is a glass window that they break to pass through."

"And we fix the window? Put the glass back together?"

"You can't fix broken glass. No, we're going to do what this note tells us to do. We may not be able to close the window, but if it leads us just right, we can get back at those that broke through it."*

"Hey! Get off the tracks!"

Hammond fumbled his footing as he fell onto the large iron tracks just as the train was leaving.

---

*Go to Page 111

He was back at the station. The train gone, and the hum of human traffic with it.

Above him the platform was empty, all had boarded and left but a station attendant who had seen him fall but not jump onto the tracks. He was coming up fast for such a rotund gentleman, all the way from the far side of the platform. Hammond heaved himself out of the track's pit, finding the touch of the platform's smooth concrete soothing his tired fingers. He hurried up the gate's steps before the heavily panting station attendant could spot that he lacked a face.

Upstairs night had fallen. It left only a few nocturnal travelers with big heavy bags and men with mops. Hammond could hear the music that played all day. It was a pleasant jazzy tune; a croaky sax and another horn Hammond couldn't place. The tune filled the entire station. Even the sleepless travelers swayed to it and tapped their fingers on their luggage handles.

Hammond walking his crisp shoes across the stone floor. Finding that no one was watching, he took a quick step, then glided forward and did a little spin. He stopped in the middle of the station and in the grand spotlight of the room the faceless Historian danced and tapped his feet. The janitor sat his chin on the tip of his mop's handle and watched as Hammond moved to the uneven yet rhythmic tune, always in a constant shadow.

As the music slowed and fell quiet, moving onto the next song, Hammond tapped his last step and finished with his arms out, bowing, and the janitor clapped politely before turning back to the deep red and white stain on his usually pristine marble floor that he could not scrub clean. He shook his head at the few chunks and cracks that scarred it.

Hammond nodded his head. The buzzing lights of the station made sure his shade was most unnatural, and he bowed slightly then continued on his way.

Should he check again, he thought, *what would he find this time?*

From across the muted station where pins had echoes and footsteps were thunder, he saw the same locker No.016 staring back at him, almost swinging open its door to invite him over.

Could more secrets be hiding behind thin steel and three numbers? If it did, that would be his choice. If he so chose, the locker could be filled.

He knew how that should have made him feel, that sick taste the tourists gave him. But things were different now. The endgame was in motion and tides were turning.

He chose his locker, and entered his code, and the door sprang open. Again, inside was something for him.

This time it was a note clipped to a torn-out newspaper article. He slipped the thin newspaper free from under the note and saw it was a photograph of the winners of a high school science fair. Clothing styles spoke of the era, decades from where he stood. In the photograph was something cubed and colorful. It looked strange, arranged in pieces, showing off the inner workings along with diagrams and poster boards behind them.

It was all for the winning exhibit.

Along the bottom of the photo was a list of names of who was in the photo, and Hammond ran his eyes across them. There was one he recognized. It stood out immediately. Luis G. Stein's name was on the far right, as was the pubescent boy it belonged to. But he was not the one in the middle, holding the device. That name belonged to the ebony skinned, curly-haired girl with wide eyes and a proud smile on her face.

She was in the middle. She had won.

"Wyla Bavishni." Hammond breathed as he read her name.

As he crumpled the newspaper clipping in his fist, he slipped the note he had written to himself under his eyes and read it four times over.

Now you know who the real enemy is. He told himself.

Leave the article and go back and write the note that brought you here.

Hammond balled the paper in his hand until the oils in the skin of his palm softened it into nothing.

The sultry summer night outside suddenly found its way to his bones, but didn't penetrate, he was colder still.

Hammond stormed outside to find in the darkness of the New York night. Standing under a lamppost with his hands wafting the air onto his unseen face.

He could hear sirens in the distance; you always could back in these days.

"Best be safe tonight."

Hammond turned to see the janitor emptying his mop bucket out over the curb. The soapy brown water washed into the gutter and glistened under streetlights.

"This city ain't the safest place at night." The janitor noted. "There are some dangerous people running about out there."

"Oh, yeah?" Hammond grumbled curiously. "More dangerous than me?"

The janitor looked at him oddly. He caught sight of his face, or lack thereof, and hurried himself back inside the warm glow of the train station. While as the ghost he had just seen slipped off on a tangent as swiftly as the wind.*

---

*Go to Page 105

Chapter Seven:
In One Era

Dahl let out his breath and then inhaled a gulp of salt water as his body splattered into the ocean. He wriggled and writhed as the currents rolled him over and over. He lost his breath and sense of direction a few moments before passing out under the deep blue.

The coastline was plain, swept flat with winding lines running along it. The weak tide routinely washed over it, breaking down any shells or compacted stones back into sand and then mixed it in with the rest. Occasionally stuff would wash up from the tides, seaweed, driftwood, expired creatures. But this occasion made for a treat, Dahl's unconscious body washed up on shore, carving a disorderly chunk out of the coast. Face down in the wet sand he laid there, until the next wave cascaded over his body and swam underneath him, climbing up his nostrils and enticing him with its salty scent.

Dahl sputtered a throat full of seawater onto the sand and coughed until his chest was sore and then coughed some more. Ironically all he could want for was water to clear his throat.

He gasped a dry breath and found the strength to lift his head out of the sand and see where he was and he saw that he was not alone.

Another body was lying down the shore, face down and wasn't moving.

Dahl pushed himself to his feet and trod deep steps into the thick and loose sand over to the body. The beach was freezing. Where he was still wet the icy wind stuck and froze him some more and he didn't have his jacket to keep him warm. With only

his long sleeve shirt on, he hoped Sancia had needed his jacket more than he did.

The short walk stripped what little strength he had left, and he fell to his knees beside the body. Immediately Dahl hated himself for not knowing basic resuscitation, but wondered what harm he could do if the man was going to die anyway.

"Hello?" He tried. "Cough if you're still alive."

He pushed on the man's shoulder, hoping to roll him over. Suddenly the man shook awake and scurried in place in the sand, as though he was still swimming in the ocean.

"Geh von mir runter, du idiot, ich kann nicht atmen!"

The man rocked himself over and felt the calm of the somewhat more solid ground beneath him.

"Wer bist du, wo bin ich?"

Dahl recognized the man, only by his features that were now falling off his face. The German's wildly oversized glasses had lost their lenses, and the frame sat on the very tip of his nose. His eyes seemed less cartoonishly wide and owl like, now small and beady.

The German's moustache had come off and lay in the sand, and Dahl could now see his yellowed teeth and the frown ironed into his face.

The events of what was only moments ago came rushing back to Dahl with the touch of the soft tide cooling his feet as he sat in the sand. He hadn't a cube on him, but he remembered the German drunkenly grabbing at him before everything went haywire.

Dahl leaned over and frisked the German, who immediately slapped him aside and tried to regain his feet. He hadn't walked all evening without the help of his shaved headed friend Elliot, and she was nowhere to be seen. But the German took his time and gradually remembered how to put one foot in front of the other, so quickly in fact that soon he had already marched off in search of something else.

"Buddy wait up!" Dahl called. "You have a cube, right? Check your pockets! Hold up, wait for me!"

Dahl ran after the German as he stripped himself of his wet coat, useless glasses and drenched shirt and walked up the hill in just his slacks and grey singlet.

Dahl patted down the coat as he tailed him. Finding a clunky item hidden inside it, he dug and found a cube. The water drained from the slight cracks, but Dahl knew that was not why it wouldn't work. It was too light. He shook it as though it would help, but only flicked bits of salt water from it.

Useless.

Dahl turned and tossed it towards the ocean, making a third of the distance and watching it bounce and slow in the sand.

"Now what do we do?" Dahl sighed.

He turned to his German friend and found that he hadn't stopped to wait for him. He was already halfway up the hill. Dahl raced after him, shaking the sand from his own clothes as it clung to wherever he was wet. He repeatedly wiped his hands on his pants to get the sand off and as he climbed the hill, he bent to wipe his hands on the grass until they were clean enough to wipe his face. The grass was rough, and it scratched his hands more than it dried them.

From the rise of the hill, Dahl saw what the German had stopped to marvel at. Tall beige and brown buildings just off in the distance, with some smaller buildings scattered out around them. They were only a few hundred yards from the closest and Dahl sighed with relief that he didn't have to worry about starting a fire on his own merit.

They both walked towards the city, stepping from dirt onto pavement quickly and passing a few cars and locals. Dahl didn't recognize the number plates or models. The buildings had little glass and more concrete and whenever he heard music it sounded like nothing he had ever heard before.

Ahead a few men in long clothes that Dahl thought were ponchos were en route to pass them by. Dahl was more than happy for them to do so, given the stern scowls they had on their faces.

"Hal 'ant bikhayr?" One spoke in a dialect Dahl could barely place.

"What?"

"Limadha 'ant mubalil jda? Yib 'an tatajamad."

The men frowned at Dahl's wet clothes and bare feet. They pointed to the beach and back to them as one man slipped off his long robe and handed it to Dahl. The German sprung alive, knocking the hand aside and puffing out his chest as words as fierce as snot came out of his mouth.

"Fass mich nicht an, du dreckige leute."

"Hey, buddy. Take it easy." Dahl tried.

"Fass mich auch nicht an, du dummer mann."

The German pointed a fat finger at the man still holding his own robe and rubbed his finger along his face, then rubbing it as though paint would wipe off.

"Nein! Wissen sie, wer ich bin? Ich heiser Gunther Kurtzoph. Wo bist du manieren du schweine?"

Now these men were mad, shoving the robe in Dahl's arms but with less pleasantness. The German either sensed none of the hostility or all of it, as he shoved one man aside and made to keep on walking.

The men jumped him, ripping the German off his feet and to the ground before dragging him off the streets and into a cluster of houses. Dahl was left standing there all alone, still holding the robe with a thank you on his tongue.

Sancia's numb back hit hard ground. She felt the cold leave her lungs and she instantly defrosted. Her fingers went first. As they regained their sense as she felt rough grass stems and dirt. Then her neck itched, and she managed to reach instinctively and scratch. She had forgotten the sensation of touching her own skin and it made her feel less alone.

Her chest started again, holding off breathing until it knew she needed to breathe again.

Her eyes soaked up the blue sky, stinging her eyes and gradually becoming tolerable.

She tilted her head to the left and right, seeing nothing but desert on either side, few trees, and not much else.

She ran her hands down her body, rubbing it all awake, finding it was all still there. Her arms, her neck, her legs, her stomach.

Her stomach was still there too.

She moaned from the back of her throat, slowly letting more and more out until the feeling became more real. She wasn't waking up - it had followed her.

Her moan found endless breath, sank to her diaphragm and rose to a scream. She screamed hard, pounding her fists into the ground and pushing her back up from the ground, trying to rip herself apart or burst into pieces.

She lay there for a while, not wanting to roll over and face what she knew she had to face; she was lost.

This place was no better than where she had come from, she figured any luck she had had only kept her from landing far out in the ocean where she would have happily drowned.

She thought about falling off the pier again, sinking deep and feeling somewhat comforted, moments before the struggle started and fear had kicked in.

Looking around, she had little refuge. There was a big rock she could tuck herself up against, trees she could do nothing but stare at. The rest just seemed to keep going on for miles and miles to the hills on the horizon.

She struggled to start and keep a fire. Playing with the sticks kept her mind off her gut that groaned and hurt her when she bent over, threatening her to eat.

Her mouth was rough. She would have killed to have some of that wet, cold snow now. If only she had pocketed some when she left.

She went hungry and thirsty all night, barely getting any sleep because of it. The rock she tucked herself up against was cold, but the wind that swept over the desert was colder. Digging down into the sand, she felt it get warmer as she dug. She scraped a ditch and rolled into the warm sand buried underneath.

The next day she barely moved from her ditch. Her arms tucked beneath her had gone numb, she knew the second she moved them they

would ache from the contortion she had forced them into as she had slept in her little dugout.

Flies danced across her face, lifting hairs from her forehead and hovering over her ears, making her twitch and finally pulling free her arms to swat.

I'm lying here all day, she told herself. She figured if she did nothing, she wouldn't get hungry, if she didn't sweat she wouldn't need to drink, parts of her would die off, she would grow thin, she would go dizzy. Maybe it would die first, then at least she would finally be rid of it.

She smiled at the thought, then rolled up and out of her warm ditch and went searching for food.

She walked in circles, her feet hitting the ground hard with each step that shuddered up her entire body.

She went to sleep again hungry, curling up in her ditch and biting her cheeks from the inside.

With her ear resting on her arm she could hear her body, every heartbeat in her ear, every breath, every throat gurgle, every muscle twitch and every slight movement in her stomach.

Her body slunk into itself, her weariness helping every part loosen and perpetually float. She could feel her mind drift back, as though she was falling into backward somersaults over and over again.

And she let herself fall, she let herself be ugly and wilt. She let herself go for each disorientated moment. She floated in disorientation, drowned in dry water and boiled in a warm blanket.

Here, her mind tore that last membrane - its final leash.

Untethered to her, it floated too, turning back and filling the void.

It reminded her that she knew what drowning felt like. It showed her the dark jungle and the dinosaurs that lived within. In this place her scars were old holes that had been filled in and men with shovels dug them back up.

She paired the voices with the faces, all the people she had seen at the Asylum. The worse things that could have happened to them she saw with pristine clarity, and she knew it was her fault.

All because of what she carried with her.

It was there too. It would be a boy - it could only be a boy.

This boy floated in the void and barely saw its mother. It wandered the void and Sancia followed, arms out, ready to catch him if he fell. The boy was looking for something. Someone. Its father.

The boy found him there, waiting for him with the same outstretched hand as he had once offered her.

And the boy took it, and she threw herself between them.

They were strong and it took all she had to pry them both apart.

She could feel the pressure mounting on both sides.

Her arms folded into her shoulders.

Her wrists bent at odd angles.

She screamed and pushed.

They only crushed her tighter and tighter.

Then there, coming out of the darkness, there they were again dinosaurs on the hunt. Deep claws and black suits. They had found her, even here in her dark dreams, and they wouldn't let up.

She felt them clawing at her, scratching and scraping and scaring and…

… sniffing. Voices yelling and a pointed shotgun touched her nose.

Smells were thick here. They lingered from daylong simmering broths and clung to brick, tile and curtain. It was a small restaurant, but the owners kept the tables rotating. People knew to finish and then quickly leave so the next hungry customer could sit and eat.

There were no menus, everything was always the same and everyone knew what to order and everything came in steel trays, and everything always went back soaked in sauce to be washed again. Barely two minutes survived between one customer and the next.

"Asrae hunak nahn nafad al'atbaq." The chef barked at the dishwasher, as a fresh cart of dirty trays rolled up to his sink. *"'Ant bati' jiddaan Dahl."*

"You got it."

The dishwasher waved a soapy gloved hand and swept the fresh pile into his sink. Lifting any more than ten trays were almost too much for the scrawny man, he kept his hair back with a strip of fabric with patterns he had no clue how to translate. He stood in sandals and didn't mind if his loose button shirt got wet down the front.

Dahl slid the steaming trays from between his fingers and onto the rack with surprising nimbleness, wiping his cheek with the driest part of his hand towel before tossing it over the rack and exhaling through a smile.

"Break boss!"

"Kl ma aismaeah break break break." His boss teased before nodding.

Dahl waved him off and shook off his gloves, biting the fingers despite the soapy taste and checked on his pruned fingers.

He slipped into the back where the rest of the staff took their breaks. One of the waiters was on the phone, the cord running across the break room table where two of the waitresses were playing cards and kept flicking the phone cord off their game.

A small TV was balanced on a pile of magazines and phone books that sat on a chair in the corner. The small buzzing box had been through a lot. The knobs were missing, so it was stuck at this volume and on this channel. It was all in Arabic, so Dahl had no clue what was being said.

He preferred it. He knew what he was supposed to do, he got paid what he thought was fair, and he never had to answer their questions. Dahl had always felt there had been a language barrier between him and everyone else he met anyway.

He watched the TV like a child, spotting places, names and colors that he knew and felt smart all the same. The news was flickering in pale color on the screen, aerial shots and rushed camera footage

showing a very important place somewhere in the city. Crowds of angry people and police were swarming around an adolescent girl. Dahl ran out from the break room and burst into the restaurant, frightening the customers as he reached over a table to change the TV's channel in the corner, biting his lip as he searched for the channel he understood.

"… the young girl was found by the prince and his guard dogs as they were hunting in their private estate. Police and the royal guard are still concerned with the matter of how she got inside the perimeter and whether she will be granted any pardon for her crimes…"

Dahl got as close as he could to the TV screen, leaning over trays and getting sauce on the corners of his loose shirt. It was her. It had to be. It was the spitting image.

"*'Lilaa 'ayn tadhahab Dahl. No break. No break.*"

"Oh yes, break." Dahl smiled as he made for the door. "Big break."

Dahl did not know if he had been fired for running out so erratically, but he just kept showing up and washing trays until they paid him again. Soon months had passed.

His meager pay was enough to keep his room a few streets away from the restaurant above a small shop where Sancia kept to herself all day, cooped up inside the room.

Dahl put it all on luck, raving about the odds, the chances, the improbability of them finding each other, and Sancia found it hard to fight off it herself. It had to be his luck, not hers. She would never leave his side again to keep it.

The city was loud. The window didn't shut properly, and Sancia preferred it. Hearing voices and traffic outside keep her from losing herself and she felt less alone.

While Dahl was out at work, Sancia would go down to the same three shops below their room and walk the aisles deciding on what to make for their meals.

There was one aisle she steered clear from, the one with formula, diapers and bottles. Though she eyed it and felt a pull to it, like it was waiting for her to break.

She couldn't. If Dahl saw any of that stuff he would figure it out for sure. *What would Dahl think of her? What would everyone think?*

Sancia didn't know how much longer she could lie to Dahl, and she knew that the day would come when someone else would answer it for her.

At night she would toss and turn and when Dahl asked what was haunting her she had no strength to lie. She told him it was dinosaurs, and he nodded and rubbed her arm.

Every time she walked back and forth from the shops she wrapped her arms up tighter in Dahl's leather jacket, which she had refused to return, and Dahl had refused to take back.

She still couldn't shake the dream from her mind. Every man even slightly well dressed and clean-shaven froze her solid until they passed her by. Anyone of them could be one of them - one of those dinosaurs.

One morning Dahl was on the floor, trying out some stretches he had learnt, peering through windows and watching others before heading off to work.

Sancia rolled over in her bed and stretched out, ready for another day just like the rest. She didn't mind, these days were becoming too few. Days when it was still easy.

"You should stretch too, it's good for you."

"I'm fine."

"Are you really?" Dahl quizzed. "You're still young but you groan a lot when you bend over. I see you. Are you sure you're not sick? Is it the food? It took my gut a bit of getting used to."

"It's not the food."

"Well whatever it is, I hope it goes away soon. I worry about you, kiddo."

"I know, and I'm sorry."

"Don't be sorry. It's not like you wanted to get sick. And I'm worried it's something serious."

"I wish it was, then I wouldn't feel this way for much longer." Sancia mumbled.

"Don't say that. Don't ever say stuff like that. I'm dumb but I'm not stupid. I know you're bored here, cooped up inside all day."

"I'm not, I don't want to do anything."

"You sure?" He pressed. "Because I could get you a job if you like."

"I'm sure. I want to stay and do nothing."

"Ok, well when you change your mind… birds will fall, I guess. Boy, you're a stubborn thing." He kissed her forehead and went to work.

✧

Part Five:
WHITE

From heat to heat, the three of them touched their toes on pavement to the sudden sounds of screeching tires and brake pads. An intersection slammed to a halt as cars spun out and collided to avoid the sudden strangers.

Vaughn winced, and tucked up his knee and covered his face as Galina and Nash stood firm. They waited for the last car to stop before grabbing Vaughn by the hood of his jumper and dragging him off the street.

The locals scrambled from behind the wheel to get out and chase after them, many wanting their blood to pay for the dents and damages, but Galina and Nash were quick and slipped into the rush of pedestrians.

They kept moving and Vaughn saw it best to just follow along, not to look back to whoever was behind him brandishing a tire iron. He tried reading the signs, or recognizing the huge sheets-like flags, looking for a symbol to get a feel for where he was. Vaughn was awful in school, especially in geography. The moment he learned how many countries there were and how far he was from all of them, he never bothered learning a thing.

He figured they were somewhere in the Middle East, perhaps India or Egypt. Was Egypt in the Middle East? He expected desert and

turbans, but all he saw were cars and takeaway food. Had television and movies lied to him?

Galina and Nash finally slipped into a shop that felt like a milk bar, only Vaughn didn't recognize any of the candy bars or the strange drinks in the fridge. They picked an aisle at the end near a rack of breads and wraps and ducked down in a squat to take a breath.

"Good aim." Vaughn teased Galina.

"You try, huh?"

"Nope. So, where are we?"

"Abu Dhabi." Nash answered.

"Not my first guess." Vaughn said, grabbing a can off the shelf and studying it like it had all the answers.

"So where will he be?" Galina asked her friend.

"Around here. He's been spotted around here many times before."

"So, what?" Galina huffed. "We just wait and hope he come back?"

Vaughn was getting hesitant. They were getting looks from the other shoppers and the woman behind the counter in a long, white shoal. And for good reason. They were a group made up of a pale Ukrainian woman, a Chinese man and a sweaty white kid with the broken nose and an obvious Aussie accent.

"We buy something, look less suspicious." Galina said.

"With what money?" Nash asked.

"Fine. So, we leave."

The three of them nodded to the woman at the register on their way out, she nodded back to all but one of them and called loudly to the others in the back room.

"Musaeada! Shakhs ma yasriq shayyana!"

"La tadeuhum yughadirun!" A voice called back in the same foreign language.

"Kasr dhiraeayh hataa la yafeal dhik maratan 'ukhraa." She responded, pointing at Vaughn who froze as two men rushed out from the back room, both with big dark beards and eyes on him.

Galina and Nash turned back inside as they saw the men grab Vaughn and rough him around.

"Let him go!" Galina cried.

"Leave him alone!" Nash ordered.

But Vaughn just sucked in his lower lip and waited until... yup, they found it.

The strange can of food he had been playing with had somehow ended up in Vaughn's pocket, and the woman had noticed the sag in his front.

The men pulled it out and slammed it on the counter.

"Ma hdha? Hmmm?"

"Vaughn, what did you do?" Nash hushed.

"I didn't mean it..."

He stared at the can and at his own hands, at it again. One of the two men stood between them and the door, barely letting the other customers in and out. The second held Vaughn's arm and looked to the woman at the register for what to do with him.

"Hal yjb 'an 'uksiraha?"

"We don't... sorry..." Nash tried.

"You pay or jail." The woman sounded out.

"We don't have any..."

"He go jail. He won't like. Promise. Promise." She assured them, as though the idea sounded tempting.

"But we have nothing..."

"Aintazar daqiqat, la tatasil bialshurta." A voice said from one of the other aisles. "I'll pay."

They all stopped and watch as a young girl came out from the bread aisle holding out a crisp note and ending the madness.

The girl was young but mature, her long ponytail of thick black hair tucked down inside her brown leather jacket. Her dark eyes stayed on the woman at the register until she took the money and waved to the men to let Vaughn go.

They did, patting him down where they had grabbed him and thanking the young girl before returning to the back room.

Galina and Nash approached the young girl to thank her, sizing her up underneath that oversized leather jacket.

"Thanks little girl."

"She deserves more than a thank you." Nash sighed with a laugh.

"Damn right she does." Vaughn stepped forward and hugged Sancia tight. "She's gonna come with us."

They followed Sancia up the stairs in the back to the rooms above the shop. Pushing open a loose door, they stepped into a cramped room that was very lived in. Rugs and curtains over the walls, ceiling and floor made it seem like a blanket fort Vaughn had built during sleepovers. Two beds, a small rack of food and shoes at the door. There was a pot simmering some curry with so much spice it summoned a sneeze. Vaughn held his nose and swore at the pain of squeezing broken cartilage.

He could see that the leather jacket made her seem bigger than she looked before, just as Dahl always hoped it would do for him. He figured Nash must've done his math right - that Dahl must be here.

Perhaps they had lived here for a while and Sancia had grown into herself. She knew her way around that pot of curry well. Vaughn felt bad that it had only been days for him. How long had it been for her?

"I don't understand." Galina said. "I thought we look the for man, John Dahl."

"We are." Nash said. "He's here, right little girl?"

"John is working. But he'll be home soon."

Vaughn padded his face clean, careful around his nose. He noticed Sancia spoke much better English, no longer hesitating when trying to string a sentence together.

"How long have you two been here?"

"A while."

"Sancia do you know what happened to us? At the Asylum?" Vaughn asked her. "Do you know what that was? What made us leave? What pushed us out?"

"No."

Vaughn sank back, his right side closer to the big pot, the heat warming his arm.

"And the luck that you both ended up in the same place and the same time." Nash said.

"Dahl's the lucky one." Sancia said quietly.

"You say Dahl be here soon?" Galina asked.

"Yes."

"Good, he's man on list, we wait."

When Dahl came through the door, it was hard to read his reaction. The moment he spotted Vaughn he was pleased. But Galina and Nash unnerved him, taking a little getting used to speaking English to more than just Sancia. But Vaughn figured it wasn't his lack of practice that got him muddled when they told him about the list.

"So, you're all here because my name is on some list, huh?"

"That's right."

"And you want us to leave with you, abandon everything we have here. Is that right?" Dahl pressed.

"Yes." Nash rolled his eyes. "All you have here."

"I think we'll pass."

"Excuse me?" Nash said.

"No." Galina stamped.

"Why should we?" Dahl asked. "We're doing great here. Now, I'm fine with you all dropping by for a visit, but I don't think some list means much. Frankly, I'm waiting for you to drop a shoe."

"Drop shoe?" Galina quizzed.

"What's the catch?" Dahl said smugly. "Why should we?"

"Because you don't belong here Dahl." Nash lent in, he knelt, and Sancia saw the long gash up the side of his torso where his shirt sunk in, she swallowed a mouthful of something. "You don't speak a word of Arabic and you've got this poor girl, stuck up here making meals for you."

"I like cooking."

"See. She is happy here. We've talked about it, we both are." Dahl spoke firmly. "Now, as you are our guests, you can stay for dinner and then you can leave."

As they ate Dahl was sure to pour most of the leftovers into Sancia's bowl before she even asked. He kept her close to the air conditioner too, the few puffs of cool air keeping her from heat exhaustion.

She smiled and when they finished, she went to sit by the open window as the night settled in.

Galina took a pillow and joined her, wrapping an arm around Sancia and pulled her in tight. Sancia resisted at first but then lent right into her, ignoring the odd hole in Galina's forearm and closing her eyes for a second to dismiss the storm outside. Vaughn watched as Galina rubbed Sancia's back and stomach until she dozed off in Galina's lap. Dahl lowered his voice and didn't stray an eye from her.

"She still gets nightmares most nights." Dahl told Vaughn. "She thinks someone's out to get her. I know something's wrong, but either she won't tell me or I'm not smart enough to get it."

"We're happy to bring her too, even though she's not on the list. She can come too Dahl." Nash added.

"You know me." Dahl grinned. "Always up for adventure, but for those like her, I think she needs peace and quiet. Besides the three of you, no one's given us any trouble. She likes this place, keeping out of sight and not doing anything. I think she doesn't want to rock any more boats. This whole *time travel thing* might not be for her. Makes me think I shouldn't have taken her with me."

Nash and Vaughn didn't know what to say. To Dahl, they must've looked like two expert boat rockers offering Dahl and Sancia a ride on their rickety ship.

"It's late. I guess you can stay 'til morning, I know how hard it is to get any sleep on the move."

The night was hard to detect. With the window open and the traffic just outside, they seemed like the only ones who needed sleep.

Vaughn could see out the window as the lights took over the darkness and a large mosque stood out far in the distance, glowing as though it was covered in daylight, beautiful and ornate.

Dahl made them up a place on the floor using their collection of pillows and Galina lay near Sancia, neither of them asleep.

Vaughn watched them from his lumpy pillow bed, eyes just open enough to pretend to be asleep. They spoke in low voices, and he struggled to catch all that was being said, some words so low it sounded like nonsense. He must be tired.

"Does he know?" He heard Galina ask Sancia.

"No."

"You can't keep quiet long."

"I know." Sancia sighed.

More talk that Vaughn's brain was too tired to decipher. He tried to rest on his side without letting his sore nose touch the pillows or rug. His eyelids were heavy.

"I don't want it."

"That you deal with later. Nothing you can do here, trust me." Galina hushed.

"Do you think they can find me here?"

"We find you. But we weren't looking."

The next morning as Sancia approached Dahl, Vaughn watched as she uneasily crouched by his side, and they spoke. It stunned Vaughn at how quickly Dahl became convinced. He sprung up, kicked off his sandals and pulled his boots out from under the sink.

He was so happy to ditch this place as easily as he had found it, taking nothing of value except the white, discolored envelope he slipped from under a book on the mantle and into his pocket. The envelope he carried everywhere.

"Right, if we're going to go, let's go."

Galina huddled them all in together, holding Sancia but not too tight. Galina handed Vaughn the cube and he held in unsurely.

She told him to grasp it by a certain few tiles and then which way they should be turned. She counted them out and Vaughn tried to remember as easily as he mimicked, suddenly ripping open a tangent from one time to another.*

---

*Go to Page 36

Chapter Eight:
What Goes Around

They landed softly and Vaughn felt his arm fall free from O'seus' grasp. It was night here. He felt the humidity and the sweat under his hoodie.

That's all he needed. He was home.

Vaughn turned to face O'seus, expecting him not to be overly happy with Vaughn after what he had done.

But O'seus had already gone.

Vaughn spun on the spot looking for him and prayed that Pete had been quick enough with the cube to get out before O'seus returned.

He had no way of knowing, he had to hope. Vaughn hated that.

Seeing the crooked guttering along the sides of the milk bar, the broken windows of the sewing shop, the divots of missing pavement along the road and the overbearing white orb in the distance.

He was home, and it looked the same as he left it.

Vaughn hadn't realized he had been tense for so long. The moment he found himself in a familiar place so many of his muscles relaxed he felt like he'd keep going until he couldn't hold himself upright. He had no idea how stressful it had been jumping and appearing in places that were total mysteries.

Vaughn bent and took a piece of gravel and tossed it at the sewing shop. He was the one behind most of those broken windows, inside were just piles of old sewing machines still waiting for repairs and for some reason lots of old rugs leaning up against the shop front door.

Here he could break as many windows as he liked.

Vaughn walked his old streets, telling himself he would just do a quick scan to look for changes to his timeline, or something to that effect, before heading home. But Vaughn knew deep down he needed to see it all again, drink in the familiar but not admit he had missed it.

Still lording over all was the Observatory atop the mountain. It was quiet up there, possibly for good. Maybe Vaughn would visit it again, maybe not. He had flashes of the place in tatters in some far-off future and wondered if he will contribute to the damage to the sewing shop. He could do with some therapy, and he was running out of broken windows down here.

As he neared the pub Vaughn heard the music and the cheers of its patrons. It must have been a Friday or Saturday night, for that many to be at the pub it usually meant there was a game on.

Perhaps he would join them. Squeeze himself back into his life like he had never left.

Seeing the Crowbar again, Vaughn smiled and tucked his arms into the big middle pocket of his hoodie as he walked towards it.

He saw the car still parked in front, only it was missing the dead body that caved in its roof.

He checked and saw no yellow graffiti taunts in the alleyway behind the pub. He saw nothing stopping Vaughn from slipping back to normality.

The old man had released him, he was home, and he was…

Shit.

He was already here.

All those muscles he had relaxed now stiffened. There he was, literally, kicking open the back door of the Crowbar to chuck some trash in the bins.

Vaughn watched himself fling open the bin lid and toss the rubbish bag in before it slammed shut. He watched as past-Vaughn lit a half-smoked cigarette and puff a few times before flicking it against the wall and stomping back inside, back to work.

Vaughn waited. Eyes closed, standing still in the middle of the road.

He wouldn't have moved for a truck.

Any minute now. he told himself, wrapping his arms up tight to his stomach through his hoodie, ready for the ground to rumble as it rips apart. Any second, and there'd be as many of him as there were Petes.

Any second.

Nothing.

Why wasn't it happening? Why hadn't he caused another incident? Despite all their arguing, wasn't this the one thing that everyone agreed was an absolute certainty?

Had he broken that too? Had he broken absolutes?

Vaughn pressed his luck, flipping his hood over his head, and rounding the pub to the front doors. He slipped inside and sure enough, he found it full and lively. The rush of coal miners had come that day at the end of their rotation, flooding the place, and cheering loud nonsense at the small television hanging above the toilet door. They roared and scared the crap out of anyone coming out of the toilets that still had crap left to scare out.

Vaughn saw that his past-self was behind the bar, Jake too, laughing and serving drinks.

How far back had he come?

Vaughn wondered how O'seus could have gotten it so wrong? Had Vaughn distracted him at some critical twist of a tile? He couldn't be sure.

But he felt sure.

This was somehow his fault.

What night was this? How long was there between this night and the Asylum?

Hooded Vaughn took a seat along the counter and slid a half-drunk, abandoned glass in front of him to ward off any service. He was just there to listen.

Past-Vaughn was giving a few miners a great deal of attention, as Jake hung halfway over the counter to talk and make jokes. Past-Vaughn

didn't stray too far, acting like he wasn't listening and refilling their drinks before they even put down their pints.

"Surely you guys get good money from this place." One miner shouted over to Jake. "You two are here all the time!"

"Actually, I'm only ever working when you come in." Jake joked back, losing the sarcasm, as he had to yell.

"You should come down to the mines!" The second miner offered, looking right at Jake's ear as he yelled at it. "Much better money. Sick pay, holiday pay. Health covered. Fucking great."

"Yeah, maybe." Jake shouted back, crossing an eye to his friend behind the counter, unsure how much he was hearing.

"Yeah, I heard ya." Vaughn mumbled to himself from under his hood. He wondered if this was *the night*. If it was, he couldn't stand living through it again. He couldn't pull himself away.

But, if it really was going to be *the night*, as he thought it was, someone was missing.

That someone suddenly busted through the big pub doors and swaggered inside. He moved like he was dragging his knuckles along the ground, his forehead leading the way.

Fucking Carlos was here.

Yup, this is definitely the night, Vaughn nodding beneath his hood. *Fuck.*

Carlos was the worst. He'd been laid off from his job operating excavators after failing two drug tests, but he still would go down with them all. He hung out with the others while they worked. No one did shit about it. He was a mountain of a guy, all of it in his neck, so thick you weren't sure he could turn it. No one would stop him from walking around and jumping on diggers or trucks and mucking around until no one felt safe.

No one would stop him because no one *could* stop him.

"We winning?" The brute asked the crowd watching the game.

"It's only 3rd quarter." One said, knowing Carlos' team was down.

"Fuck!"

It was common knowledge that most small towns had more drugs floating around than in the big cities. With such big paychecks and so little to spend it on, Vaughn either saw it go in the register or up their nose.

"Carlos mate!" Baz came out from the back with an obvious edginess to him, he kept looking back between the glass bottles on the shelf, the register, and Carlos. "Come to watch the game with us?"

"That's not a game, it's a fucking stitch up!" Carlos sized up Baz, getting up in his face, walking through the crowd like they were tissue paper.

Carlos liked to size everyone up like he was about to box, head dodging from side to side, hunching his shoulders in and shadow boxing. Baz had his head already craned back to avoid a swing, eyes still darting to the precious breakables behind the counter. If Carlos sniffed, Baz flinched.

"Ahhhhhh!" Carlos grabbed the back of Baz's head and pulled him into his thick chest. "I'm just fucking with ya mate! You gotta relax mate!"

Baz tried to laugh along, patting Carlos on the shoulder like a good sport. Carlos came over to the counter and slapped his hands on the backs of both the two miners in front of Jake. They both bit their lips not to wince.

"Either of you two muthafuckers got anything good?"

"Sure. You paying this time?" The first miner wished he never said it even from afar. Vaughn could see his lips trying to suck the words back in as they came out.

But Carlos grinned and just tightened his grip on their shoulders. "Mate I've got it covered, all right? I got so much fucking cash from selling me bike it's not funny. But I left my wallet in the car. What do you think I'm some cheapskate?"

"Fucking of course not Carlos."

As they laid it all out on the counter and hid none of it from sight, hooded Vaughn eyed his own hands behind the bar. While all eyes

were busy trying not to watch Carlos drag his nose across the sticky countertop, Vaughn slipped a few fingers in the register.

Hooded Vaughn wished Jake had just said something there and then.

He knew he had been caught.

Not being able to watch anymore, Vaughn tucked his hood even more over his face and slipped out of the Crowbar. This was just as Carlos lost it at the umpire and started shaking at the television, ripping it out from the wall. Baz hopelessly tried to calm him down before he broke it over his knee.

Vaughn hurriedly skipped across the road, knowing his past-self was hot on his tail. He lent against the shop window across the road and watched.

Soon enough, out came Past-Vaughn, slyly stepping over to the parked cars across the road. He checked each model and peaked through the windows, looking for the right one.

An orange ute, flash and shiny on the outside, filthy on the inside.

Vaughn could see himself peering through this window and he felt himself biting back the urge to go knock himself out.

"Just keep moving." Vaughn whispered under his breath.

But it was like watching a movie you had seen before; you know the scene, when the character does the very thing that you know they shouldn't, but they don't know that.

And every time you watch it you hope that this time, this time they won't do it.

But every time they do.

Once he heard the glass break Vaughn knew he couldn't do a single thing.

"What the fuck Vaughn?"

As past Vaughn was walking back from the parked cars, pockets stuffed with bills, Jake stepped into the light - he had seen the entire thing.

"Uh… hey." Past-Vaughn had said. "Just on break."

"What the fuck did you do?" Jake snapped.

"What?"

"Don't *what* at me. I fucking saw you!"

Past-Vaughn just shrugged, trying to slip his hands out from his pockets without any money spilling out.

"What are you on about?" Past-Vaughn defended.

"Fuck, I thought it was just the register, then I see you doing this shit? He'll fucking kill you. Really, he'll kill you so much. You're so fucked I can't believe it."

Past-Vaughn was in a state of panic, Vaughn remembered it well, his mind had gone blank and nothing but the words DO NOT COMPUTE flashed where words and a capable argument should've been.

He went into a cycle of denial, shaking his head, and acting like he wasn't sweating bullets.

"I seriously don't know what you're on about Jake." Past-Vaughn shook. "Don't know what you mean."

"Fine." Jake turned to go back inside the pub.

"Wait!"

Past-Vaughn broke out of his trance and ran back to the orange ute, tossing the drugs and the bundles of cash back through the windows, bills flying loose. He started putting distance between himself and the car, running back after Jake.

"I put it back!" Vaughn yelled. "I don't have anything. There's nothing to worry about Jake. Jake!"

Jake stopped just before the door and stepped back on the street to meet Vaughn.

"And what about the cash from the register?"

"Oh, fuck." Vaughn broke his quick run back to Jake, half turning and groaning. He had thrown it in the car with the rest of Carlos' money. "I'll go back and get it. Then it's all good. No one misses out."

"What the fuck's wrong with you, man?"

"Nothing. It was just a joke. I wasn't really gonna take it."

Jake started back inside, and Vaughn danced between going back for the register money and catching Jake before he went inside.

"Jake wait man, dude. You're not gonna tell him are ya? Jake, c'mon. Don't be a dick."

"I'm the dick?"

"No, I said, *don't be a dick.*"

"If I was the dick Vaughn, I would be the one breaking car windows and taking other people's money."

"Yeah, fucking Carlos' money. Who gives a shit?"

"That's no excuse!"

"Wasn't making one!" Vaughn was even more panicked. Jake was getting close, he had to run in front and stand between him and the door. Another big cheer went off. Someone must've punched someone else. They cheer more for that than a goal.

"Jake. Jake, please. You're not gonna tell him, are you?"

"No Vaughn. I'm not." Jake said, looking at the floor, the windows, the balcony roof, anywhere but at Vaughn. "Because that's not what a friend does."

"Friend huh."

"Don't make this weird."

Jake went around him and Vaughn waited a little before he ran back to the car to get the register money back.

It was a struggle, most of it landed on the driver's seat on the other side and Vaughn had to reach right in.

He stepped back and cleared the glass shards that stuck up like teeth along the windowsill, then he hoisted himself in, resting on his stomach with his legs sticking up in the air as he counted out and separated Carlos' money from the Baz's.

Hooded Vaughn saw them coming long before Past-Vaughn did.

Busting out of the pub, Carlos was jumping on the back of one of the other miners who groaned and bucked him off like a bull before his back broke. They were pissed and high and couldn't figure out which of the five cars parked in the street was his.

He had to do something, even something little.

Past-Vaughn was almost done reaching through when he was startled by a slight crack. A bit of gravel had hit the windshield and startled him.

He stopped dead, body floating half in and half out of the car, trying to keep balance.

Stopping, he could hear more than his own heavy breathing and he finally caught the sound of Carlos getting closer.

Vaughn dumped the cash and fell back out of the car just as Carlos and his mate came along holding out his key.

He saw Vaughn, standing beside his ute, with a broken window and glass on the street.

Vaughn was lucky he was quick.

He tore off as Carlos chased after him, footsteps clapping against the road and echoing off into the dark streets.

Hooded Vaughn stepped out and came to the corner to peer down the road to watch the chase.

He remembered running. He remembered the air-drying the back of his throat as he ran and lost his breath.

But he remembered out running Carlos too. He was too big to catch him.

He had been lucky.

Or had he been? If he hadn't had thrown that little rock he would have gotten caught, no question.

Vaughn had always felt his hands had a mind of their own, but never had they felt to him as separate from him as they did right now.

His hands were pre-destined to throw that rock just as he was pre-destined to get away because of it.

Vaughn wondered about the streets, not knowing where he could go. He couldn't go home. He couldn't go anywhere yet. It would still be days before Atticus would come and invite him to work at the Asylum. What would he do until then?

Because of the temperamental power grid, most of the lights in Fracture didn't work at night at the same time. The Crowbar took up a lot of juice and caused many momentary blackouts.

Street lamps usually stayed off, only flickering on for a few seconds.

Most light came from above, not the moon but the path of streetlamps that spiraled up to the Observatory, all running off Atticus Crowe's private power grid.

So, when a building blocked the mountain and the moon wasn't out, you couldn't see a damn thing. Just dark, black shapes of things standing out from slightly less dark, black things. So much so you'd sometimes forget you didn't have your eyes closed and you'd try to open them even more.

Vaughn did what all the drunks in Fracture did as they walked home at night; he walked blind.

But even in all this darkness, if a stark, white shape scattered across the street, it was noticeable. Getting closer he saw the shape scatter again, darting from one side of the road to the other. As he got closer it didn't fret, it almost waited.

Vaughn got close enough to see that it was a cat, silent, white and slick. It watched him and Vaughn felt like he had seen a cat like this before, but from where, he wasn't sure.

Suddenly the streetlamp above him flickered on, two or three more lamps did too, and Vaughn saw someone panting on the next street corner. Carlos had burned through the energy he had snorted up earlier and was now running on his own. He had lost sight of the Vaughn he was chasing, but luckily, he had found a new one.

Vaughn bolted but Carlos had a second wind and tackled him quick, slamming Vaughn against a car and down to the ground.

Smack!

Vaughn felt his nose turn hot and numb. Breathing from it hurt and trying from his mouth only let in warm blood that he spat out and moaned.

Carlos wobbled to his feet, spitting on Vaughn and stumbling back up the street to his car, knuckles dragging along the way.

"Ah fuck." Vaughn tried to keep his nose from spilling too much blood, clutching his hoodie and pulling it up to stop the bleeding. His jumper was ruined anyway. As dark as the hoodie was, he could still tell his blood stains apart from Pete's.

His nose was definitely broken. He couldn't see, but he could feel it bowing strongly to the right after the powerful right hook.

The white cat came back, its paws silent on the road, almost floating instead of walking. With the streetlights on, Vaughn could

see the glow in its eyes, like it was watching. Recording him. Spying on him.

Oh fuck.

Vaughn scrambled to his feet, clutching his nose firm with his palm and darting a look in all directions, ready to spot and scream when he saw them.

As if perfectly timed, the streetlights went out again.

Fracture didn't feel like Fracture anymore, it felt like a haunting reflection. Everything was the same, but different. Like every street sign or parked car was out to get him.

He saw the figures move, some light from the Crowbar shaping their silhouettes. He couldn't see their faces; he didn't suspect they had any.

Faceless and relentless they came for him, and Vaughn ran, kicking the cat out of the way as he ran into the darkness. Not wanting to look back to see them gain on him, grab him, lift him off his kicking feet and off the streets.

Vaughn roused from a throbbing source of pain, like an alarm strapped to his face. Somehow they had knocked his nose when they took him, and it had been so painful Vaughn had passed out.

As things came back to him, as things after unconsciousness usually do, Vaughn became more and more aware of his situation.

He was in a chair; he had been for some time as his butt was sore. He felt like his legs and arms were tied to the chair, but they were not, just limp at his side.

He could hear a mumbled conversation. He could take in the words but not yet place them together, and he was still quite shaken.

All around him were chunky boxes of machinery, parts and pieces. Sewing machines in an incessant state of repair. The walls were holding up so many rolled up rugs that Vaughn wasn't even sure how they had found a way inside the shop. He spotted the windows up high on his right, some small beams of light getting through the holes he had broken long ago.

He saw them talking, leaning up against a line of rugs, keeping to the darkness. They kept their voices low and soft. The taller of the two ever twisting their neck to spy on their hostage. Vaughn raced to snap his eyes closed and feign unconsciousness a while longer.

He imagined their faces as dilapidated as the old man that had crashed the Asylum. As they spoke, Vaughn could picture loose hanging teeth, threads of gum holding on dearly as they breathed malicious intent to one another. Perhaps they were choosing his fate, deciding what history Vaughn had destroyed. Which punishment best served to a boy who had possibly wiped a species of bird off the map through sheer existence.

Vaughn wondered only shortly, even seconds lent to thoughts that incessantly deep had his chest cave and his lungs gasp.

"He's awake."

Vaughn's entire body tightened as the voices came out from the corner of the repair shop, still shrouded in darkness.

"You… you gonna kill me y-y-yet?" Vaughn tried to growl, but his nose caught his temper and tweaked it.

"Kill you? After coming all this way to find you? I don't think so."

One of them found the right switch in the fuse box along the wall and flipped it on. Shockingly, it didn't short out and Vaughn winced at the sudden brightness then winced again for twitching his nose.

The two figures had faces. They were real and hadn't at all deteriorated. They seemed like perfectly normal people that just so happened to have kidnapped him.

"Who are you guys?"

"Galina." The woman said, stepping over a pile of rugs to get closer to him. Galina was tired, purple shade under her eyes from a lack of sleep and it made it hard to judge her age. Probably in her thirties on a good day. Her Ukranian accent skewed her words, her hair was pulled back so tight a ponytail it looked like it hurt her forehead, and she kept rolling back her sleeves and rubbing her hands up and down her forearms. "And that's Nash."

Nash, standing near the fuse box, waved and followed Galina's pathway through the clutter of the store. Nash was Asian, had a short,

rushed haircut, and he was about Galina's age but wore a lot less worry on his face.

Vaughn quickly noticed that down the right side of his torso, his shirt dug into his flesh like it had been tucked in with a knife.

"I'm Vaughn." He found himself saying.

"We know stupid." Galina crouched in front of him. "Your name is on top of list."

"List?" Vaughn asked so suddenly he crinkled his nose again and tears rushed out.

"Here, I fix." Galina hobbled over, staying in her crouch, she placed both her thumbs on Vaughn's nose and pushed.

Vaughn swore so much he invented new curse words.

"Very welcome." She smiled, urging Vaughn's head forward so the loose blood could stream out onto the floor. She tapped on the back of his head like you would a bottle of sauce at the end of its run and then lifted Vaughn's head back up to rest his neck against the back of the chair.

Vaughn pushed through the pain and found it subsided quickly, down to a slight throb. He took a chance and twitched it. His nose responded and barely stung.

"Fuck!" Vaughn moaned.

"I said you're welcome."

"Yeah thanks." Vaughn replied, sniffing until he found no blood and he could sit up normally again. "So, you're not Historians?"

"If we were Historians, you'd be dead." Galina said. "They'll kill anyone outside of own time, even if only a few days."

"So, who are you then?"

"We're here to save you." Nash said. "You and everyone else on list."

"What is this list? Why am I on it?"

Galina dragged a chair and turned it around so she could lean her elbows on the backrest as she talked to Vaughn. Nash sat behind her on the edge of a desk, shoving off a sewing machine to make room.

"We come from future we don't want and everyone there is working to make sure it's different." She said. "Man in charge gives us list of names of people to save, your name on list."

"Who else is on the list?"

Nash took it from his pocket. It had been folded over a few times and handled so much that the folds were dark and stained. He opened it and handed it to Vaughn. He read the names, darting up and down the list.

Vaughn Ashton
Wyla Bavishni
John Dahl
Atticus Crowe

Next to each name was a series of notations and scribbles that Vaughn figured were directions that he couldn't understand. But that didn't bother him, he was too busy scanning the list over and over for a name that wasn't there and angry at a name that was.

Atticus, of course. How could you forget?

"Why these people? There were so many of us at the Asylum, why just these four?"

"Hey, don't ask us. O'seus must have his reasons."

"O'seus? Figures." Vaughn grimaced, wondering now how much of an accident it was dumping Vaughn days away from the right time. "I guess that's it, you found me. Can you let me go now?"

"This isn't a game of tag, you're coming with us."

"No, I'm fucking not."

"Excuse me?" Galina shifted in her chair, switching elbows to rest on and Vaughn saw it. He almost hurled in his mouth it disgusted him so much.

"What the fu-u-u-u-ck." He said like he was gargling jelly.

Galina pulled back her arm to see if there was a bug or something smeared on it. She noticed nothing, just her plain old forearm with a hole in it.

"What? This?" Galina stuck her finger through the hole. It was worse than Pete's finger nub, Vaughn couldn't stand stuff like that. He had another look and saw the hole go right through the hefty muscly part of her forearm. Lining the inside was a metal cylinder and her flesh had perfectly healed around it.

"Now I'm definitely not going with you." Vaughn shook his head.

"The hell you aren't, we've got a job to do." Nash pressed.

"And I'm sick of being pushed around!" Vaughn yelled. "I'm sick of it! The next time I go anywhere it's going to be because I chose to go and not because someone decided for me."

"Ok smart guy." Galina sneered. "What will make you change mind?"

Vaughn had an answer, but he held it back. Even he was shocked by it. He had figured he was done with all of this time travel crap. He was so close, just a few days until he could take back his old life. So then why didn't he feel that coming out of his mouth? Why was it something else instead?

"Pete." Vaughn said softly and hesitantly. "I'm not going with you unless we also save Pete."

"Pete who? What's his last name?" She asked, scratching at her calf with her foot.

"I don't know."

"Where is he? What time is he from?" Galina tried.

"I don't know."

"Come. You have to give us something?"

"He was at the Asylum, if that helps."

"Galina no." Nash stepped up. "Just the names on the list. That's it."

Galina turned and eyed Nash. She didn't even have to get up from her chair.

"If we can't get first one then what's the point?"

Nash threw up his hands and stormed off, kicking rugs that were denser than they looked. He hopped to a desk and rubbed his toe. Galina followed and they debated in the corner in a hush as Vaughn sat and wriggled his nose around.

He got off the chair and stretched, feeling a nice crack in his shoulders.

The two of them seemed desperate, as though that list meant everything to them. Vaughn felt tempted to tell them otherwise; to tell them their fearless leader would find only failure and that Smokey would overrun their precious Far with plans of his own.

He didn't really care what their plan was. He saw them as a way of finding out if Pete made it out ok, that he was safe and happy. That's all that seemed to matter.

Nash eventually agreed but wasn't too happy about it. He explained in great and exaggerated detail how painstaking it would be finding Pete - lost in time. Then told him that he had to catch a cat.

Galina saw his confusion and explained that there were family-friendly home versions of the Ogle. Ones that Vaughn had already seen and hated. Often resembling white cats, white birds or white goldfish. She attempted to explain their temporal hive-mind network and how they were designed to survive trips through time without malfunctioning, as so much technology was susceptible to do. But now the Historians use them for their facial recognition software, that's how they are able to track and identify people living out of their time. She regretted the fact that they were reduced to using the same trick.

Even seeing her own reflection as she stood by the old murky windows, she detested the very idea, instead leaning a hand on the window to cover her face. She frowned and took her hand away, only to see how black and dirty her hand had gotten just from leaning on the window. But to Vaughn that was just Fracture.

"Urgh." She groaned. "This town is disgusting."

"I know."

After that, Galina sat down with Vaughn and neither of them spoke for a while. The sun was rising, and the heat of Fracture crept in fast. The sewing machine repair shop swelled in the heat and the rugs blocking the windows did more to turn the place into an oven than keep the heat out.

Galina left after a while, slipping out and returning with some water and plain doughnuts from the milk bar. As they ate, Vaughn saw a crumb slip from Galina's mouth and fall right through the hole in her arm.

"Ok, seriously, what's with that?"

"This?" Galina stretched out her arm and mulled it over. "It's long story. I rush. You don't want to rush cube twist, trust me."

She finished up her doughnut and followed it up with a mouthful of water before going on.

"You know who invent time travel?"

Vaughn shook his head.

"His name Luis G. Stein. He came from nowhere. He say he discover time travel in basement. Then suddenly he is everywhere; most famous man alive.

People that knew him say he was strange, paranoid little man. With all his money he buy all the smart minds to design so much useless technology. For whole year before New Year's Day he never left penthouse and after, he never go back. Stein went hiding.

Still, crazy people look and find him, why? He is their constant, their rock that no universe could take, erase or change without paradox. So Stein use them. He make them go into past to watch and protect family. Make sure no one fuck with him and his bloodline."

"Man, that is paranoid."

"Which is why it's so easy to believe stories that Stein send crazy people to steal bomb from the past and bring back to blow us up. Only little crazy man do something like that.

Of course, not all believe it. We waste time arguing and fighting. Some don't want to admit he can do it. Say it's too hard, cannot be done.

And then we find videotape. In archives of Chinese military. We search for proof that someone steal bomb."

"What did you find on the tape?"

"We found ourselves. Video of us - we are already there. We argue for days. Some of us believe that we had to go back to stop it, others say going back cause very thing we try to stop."

"So did you go?"

"I wished we hadn't."

Galina was upset. She told her story like it was the first time she had let herself remember it. They sat for a while and Vaughn rubbed his wet finger along the inside of the plastic doughnut tray to collect the sugar. They still had to wait for Nash.

"So now I ask you question." Galina turned. "This Peter, why you want to save so bad? Who is he to you?"

This was the second time he had been asked that, but this time Vaughn found he had an answer.

"He's a friend. And that's what friends do."

Soon after, Nash returned with the head of a cat, and he used it to project images onto the blank wall of the shop. He found a face match and jotted down the location and info he needed on the same piece of paper that had the list.

Vaughn felt that, if nothing else, he had gotten Pete's name on that list. He made him someone to care about. Now he was someone that couldn't be easily disposed or ignored.

As they readied themselves for the jump, Galina tucked in her arms and legs. Nash did too and Vaughn copied them, not wanting a hole or a weird wound in his side like them.

"Here we come Pete."

"We'll get to Pete, but the axis line up better for the others first." Nash added and Vaughn eyed him.

"Don't worry." Galina said, stepping between the two of them. "You trust us. We find your Peter."*

---

*Go to Page 143

$\Leftrightarrow$

Chapter Nine:
A Job Offer

It's called a sigh. Vaughn had one with his cheek pressed hard into his arm as he lent on the counter, watching a fly delicately move around water rings. Vaughn took a deep breath.

In that breath Vaughn hoped the world would stop, that eight hours would skip forward.

Anything to get out of this place, out of work, out of town and, if possible, out of Vaughn.

Vaughn exhaled. Sighs pass. The fly flew away, and he poured another drink.

Vaughn looked up to see barfly no.4 slowly slipping from his seat at a tall table, precariously balanced so he'd finally fall at any moment. Vaughn would have slipped himself if it weren't for Baz whacking him on the back and startling him back up into place.

"C'mon, look professional. Pick up some slack."

"Make me."

At this time of day, after four hours on his feet, Vaughn's very low tank of enthusiasm usually ran dry. He didn't even have the mindless static of daytime TV to keep him prompt and awake, the loose cords still hung from the wall next to the loose brackets.

"Vaughn." Baz whined. "If Jake wasn't too sick to come in today or at all week, this wouldn't be an issue. But just because I've got no one else doesn't mean you can act like your indispensable."

"What, me? Indispensable?" Vaughn jeered. "Shouldn't have told me that."

"Just shut up and serve."

Vaughn lifted his head and saw an old man seated down the end of the bar. He had his head down, keeping to himself with his nose in a book.

The old man had been there all morning, taking the time to enjoy his book.

He timely closed his paperback, carefully saving the page he was on, stood and moved four stools up the bar towards Vaughn.

"Your name tag is upside down." The old man observed.

"That's so I can read it" Vaughn replied. Not a beat to be missed.

"Just in case you forget who you are?"

"Just in case."

"Does one often forget one's self?"

"One does not refer to oneself as one. But if two did, than I'm sure one would find oneself at a loss whether one was one or two. So, it helps to have a name."

"I'm not sure that made sense."

"Neither do I."

"I take it you're… Vaughn then?" The old man asked, peering at the upside-down badge.

"Sure is, and yourself?"

"Scotch, neat thank you."

Vaughn rolled his eyes and wiped the water rings from the counter, laid out a napkin and placed the glass on top. The mildly wet countertop glued the napkin to the polished wood, and the old man's disinterest in drinking his scotch glued the glass to the napkin.

"So what're you reading Scotch Neat?"

"The Great Gatsby, one of my favorites." He answered. "Have you-"

"Never read it."

"Well, you asked."

"I'm paid to be polite."

"If you could go back in time to any point in history, where would you go?" The old man asked.

"Dunno. I've never thought about it before." Vaughn answered, rolling his eyes, hoping the old man would see and end the conversation.

"Never thought about it! I couldn't imagine. Don't you have any sense?"

Vaughn woke up his brain. "Probably back in time a bit." He breathed, thinking of a night just passed. "Give myself some tips."

"A waste! Weren't you taught about history in school? Ancient Egypt, medieval times and the Great War. How could you not fantasize about leaving it all behind and becoming a knight or a gladiator?"

"What's wrong with right now?" Vaughn said, hating that he kind of agreed with the old man but was bent on being difficult. "Are you saying my life ain't any good?"

"Ease over effort then, huh? You are living in an age of superfluousness. The roaring twenties, now that was a golden age. A man could find invest in anything and find wealth around the corner, the outfits, the parties, the music. That's why I absolutely adore this book, I model my life after Gatsby."

"So?"

"So?" The old man spat.

"Yeah, so. It doesn't matter, man. It ain't real."

"How do you know?" The old man leaned in, raising an eyebrow.

"I don't, and I don't care."

"I bet you've never left this town, am I right?"

"I'm gonna go stand over at the other end of the counter now."

"Before you go, I was wondering if there was anyone here who would be interested in some extra work? I'm hosting a little gala."

"Bartending work?"

"I would hope."

"Well, it may not come as a surprise that I'm not exactly ready to follow you into an unmarked van just yet."

"I had no idea I came off so creepy."

"Not so much creepy as you are an ass."

"Charming. Well, as it so happens, this ass is used to getting what he wants. The job's contract only. One night's work."

"When?"

"Tonight."

"Tonight?" Vaughn scoffed.

The old man finally took a swig of his drink, the napkin tagged along. "Problem?"

"Yeah, you should have hired someone weeks ago."

"As it so happens, my first choice was flying in from Melbourne and his plane crashed. Horrible isn't it."

"For you?"

"Who else?" He answered, looking around him.

"So I'm your next choice?"

"From what I've heard, you're the only bartender who can make a cocktail within a hundred kilometers. My my, you organize an entire party, balloons and all, reserve the entire Observatory, fill the bar and the hardest part is getting hold of a bartender."

"What's the crowd gonna be like?"

"That's the thing, I'm not sure what kind of turnout we're going to have."

"See that sounds like to me I'm going to be working my ass off all night. And did you say the Observatory? That place can host a lot more than this dump. There was that party up there last month or so…"

"Am I sensing you don't want the job?"

"You're on the right track, what's the pay rate for argument's sake?"

"Oh, I don't know, I was thinking $1000 an hour?"

Vaughn drooled.

"Should I have started with that?"

"I think you should have."

"I'll keep that in mind for next time. So, you're on board?"

"A party, huh?" One barfly hiccupped. "Well, I'd be honored to come."

"Uh, no thank you." The old man waved them off. He eased himself away from the counter, any confidence he had exerted had slipped away.

"Now don't be rude." A second fly jumped in. "You don't want us to get upset, do you?"

"I'm actually just leaving so…."

"Hold up there, Vaughn," said another rotund barfly, shuddering floorboards as he approached the bar. "Do you even know who this is?"

Vaughn shot looks at both the burly barfly and the old man, before shaking his head.

"I'll give you a hint." Another barfly offered. "His name is on the building."

"Your Atticus Crowe?" Vaughn realized, a lifetime of aggression suddenly rising to his throat.

"Pleased to meet you." Atticus said. He wasn't too thrilled being identified but held out a hand anyway as though it was according to plan.

"Should've known, actually. A thousand an hour, I should've known." Vaughn said, not taking his hand.

"I assume you're worth every cent."

"Hey Crowe." The burley barfly leaned in beside Atticus, his arm the size of his torso. "I hope the potholes in the road didn't mess with your fancy car's suspension. That would be a shame."

"Not to worry, it's fine, thank you." Atticus waved it off with the politeness of a politician.

Two barflies nearest to the front windows leaned close to them, peering through the curtains.

"Hoooo weeee, that's a fancy car. Must've cost a few bucks to get that shipped from overseas." One of them said.

"I'd say the same amount it would cost to fix an entire town's electrical grid. Wouldn't you?" Added the other. "I hope those blackouts don't bother you too much, Crowe."

"Now, now enough with the jabs, fellers. All in good fun."

"Shut ya face, Crowe." The burley barfly slammed his glass down on the counter. "Don't you take one cent of this snake's money, Vaughn, it's not worth it."

"You'd be selling your soul for a five-cent hand job." Another chimed in.

"Vaughn, why don't you tell this slimy piece of shit where he can take his money and shove it."

"Love to." Vaughn turned to Atticus. In his head he was swimming through a pool of money. Atticus saw the hesitation. He also saw the Crowbar rousing to life. He swept up his paperback and his coat from the back of his stool.

"Why don't you get your rich ass out of here and maybe, maybe I'll come tonight or maybe I won't. Either way, it's my choice and I'm gonna leave you guessing."

The crowd cheered. Offering a rumbling chant of exit music.

Atticus pushed past the jeers and rough housing of the bar. They cheered as he tried to leave and stood tall with bellowing songs of victory. Vaughn threw up his arms in triumph alongside them while simultaneously mourning the loss of the offer. Baz collected a tray of shot glasses and hurriedly filled the entire rack as the chanting crowd snatched them up and they started a chorus of celebration. They threw money from their wallets to fill their guts with whatever Baz served up.

"Well, if you do decide to come." Atticus yelled over the crowd as they got louder and louder. "It starts at six."

"Noted." Vaughn yelled back, raising a finger in return.

"We'll be there with bells on Crowe!" The two barflies laughed, raising their mugs in the air.

"If you are going to come, please be punctual. Time is the essence."

"Of the essence you jerk."

"I know what I said."

Atticus then pushed through the crowd of sticky barflies. Each one throwing their weight into him like he was the ball in a pinball machine, but he made it to the door. By now they had raised Vaughn onto the shoulders of the burly barfly and was high fiving all the regulars as he downed shots that they poured.

"Hey Atticus!" Vaughn called out to him.

Atticus sighed and turned. "What?"

"Na nah na nah. Na nah na nah. Hey hey hey, goodbye!"

The entire bar sung along with him, growing louder and louder so that their victim could hear them even over the sound of his German engineered sports car humming to life and drifting away.

Vaughn toppled to the floor, barely staying on his feet as the burly barfly stumbled to a stool, having had six too many. Vaughn himself relieved his dizzy head with a celebratory line of shots before stumbling back behind the bar as though he was fit to work.

"Ok Vaughn." Baz said, holding his hand on Vaughn's chest to keep him away from the expensive bottles of liquor. "Why don't you go home early? You're done for the day."

Vaughn drunkenly eyed Baz's annoyingly genuine offer and batted his hand away. "I'm fine. Let me handle the tough stuff, you can pick up empties or something like a good boy." He slapped his face mockingly and continued towards the beer tap, filling up a glass with way too much head.

"Vaughn I'm serious. I can't let you work like this. You're sloppy as fuck."

"Don't you tell me what I am. You don't know what I can do." Vaughn outstretched his arms and closed his eyes as he tried to mix a cocktail with his eyes closed. 'See."

"Vaughn I can't have you like this too. First Jake gets sick, now you, I'm running out of bartenders!"

Vaughn cackled with laughter. "You believed that shit. Holy crap, you're gullible. I mean I had little respect for you before, but you can't go round believing every little thing you hear."

"What are you...?"

"He's not sick!" Vaughn laughed. "He's too chicken shit to see me that's all."

Vaughn got serious. He lowered his brow to show just how serious he was. "But don't you believe a word he says. It was all me, all me you get it? He had nothing to do with it. He's a liar and a good person and I'm not a liar and a bad person. Wait... I think I got that wrong..."

Vaughn leaned over to Baz, who stood as solid as a brick wall, barely breathing through his grinding teeth, and Vaughn whispered in his ear. "Little tip, maybe start trusting your gut the same way I trust mine-"

Vaughn hurled a little in his mouth, he held up a hand to pardon himself and stumbled out into the back alley through the fire exit and threw up a putrid slime that hit the wall and slid slowly to the ground.

Pleased with his aim, Vaughn staggered back inside and found the closest wall to nestle his head against as he rested his eyes. His legs started to buckle and as he continued to try walking, sliding himself against the wall until he was caught and hoisted back on his feet by the strong arm of a stranger. Vaughn groaned with thanks, turning his nose up to the thick smell of smoke woven into the man's grey sleeve.

"Come on, let's get you outta here."*

---

*Go to Page 346

Chapter Ten:
The Observatory

Vaughn had the feeling he was falling, then a sudden kick, and he felt the cold of the asphalt as his back slammed back against it. A shattering of glass and he sprung up and rubbed his ass before standing jaw-dropped in the middle of the road.

Vaughn spun and saw no vomit stain, no garbage bins. A soft wind whistling by his ear had eclipsed Baz's voice. His ears popped from the altitude.

The sun was setting orange over the town, the gases of the mines in the distance wavered the half circle of the sun, like it was dancing as it sank.

Vaughn was up high; he wandered to the edge of the road to the railing and found he was staring down at the town. He could spot the Crowbar, its lights flickered on as the night was warming up inside.

He checked his watch. No way it was night already?

On closer inspection, his watch had stopped. The minute and hour hands shook loose when he held his wrist up to his face and they swung limp, dangling from the center, swaying to a stop, both pointing at the number six.

On the ground were the remains of the gin bottle he had taken. How much had been spilt and how much had he drunk? His mouth tasted foul, and he had no idea how he had gotten here.

Fuck. Again?

Vaughn hated being known as 'the blackout guy', but he couldn't even be sure at what point he had blacked out.

He recalled the last thing he could remember. He was at work. He was talking to that dirty, dark-haired woman, and then he was in the alley.

But he was in his pajamas. The same pajamas he was wearing now, his apron covering his modesty somewhat.

What was it she had been saying? Her words were muffled in his mind by the still echoing sounds of Baz beating at the fire exit door.

Vaughn studied the road, it led towards the town, spiraling down until it led back to the Crowbar. He looked up and saw the road led only one way.

Vaughn knew exactly where he was, he was halfway up Mount Fracture, the mountain that towered over the small town. He couldn't see it from there, but he knew what was at the top. He figured he was almost halfway up the mountain and he had already unconsciously started up the road. He still had dreams that started like this.

Fuck, which is the dream?

Vaughn was only nine at the time, but he could still remember the swell of resentment and the rants that turned into debates, that turned into fights his parents had over this unnecessary development.

The constant blackouts and power surges were still as constant now as they were back then, the roads still had cracks and potholes from all of Crowe's construction crew, coal waste still poisoned the river.

Atticus Crowe had made a killing by buying and selling off every bit of land around them, and when he finally felt the need to give something back to his town of hard-working employees, he built them an Observatory.

When construction finished, the public weren't even surprised to learn he had written it off as public development in a tax loophole, and then booked it out repeatedly for his own parties and functions.

The Observatory was a thumping beat of the rich and powerful atop the hill that lorded over the town, but as Vaughn always thought; it was definitely an Observatory, it just wasn't the stars the town used it to observe.

Mount Fracture's Observatory was now over fourteen years old. Vaughn could barely remember looking up at the strange mountain and not seeing that glowing white orb of a building at the top.

The mountain had a thin gorge that separated the two sides of the mountain and was only five or so meters apart at the top but widened slightly as the fracture opened up at the bottom, allowing a quiet river to flow in between.

The town had a more traditional indigenous name, but because a big mountain had a crack in it, Fracture became the advertised name and no one said shit about it. Crowe branding the mountain's name on signs all over town didn't help much either.

From a distance you couldn't even see it, the two parts seemed as one. It was only when you looked closer that the lightning like split seemed apparent.

The shorter of the two sides of the mountain was protected by the national parks, with a hiking trail that led through the bush and met the opposing cliff at the summit.

As for the taller side, a wound all the way to the top where the Observatory sat. It was the only smoothly paved road in town.

Vaughn walked the path up Mount Fracture. The pure white glow of the lamps lit him up, and he hated it. The streets lamps that guided the winding road were more than enough.

Vaughn remembered the walk up before they revitalized it. He could overlay his memory of the worn dirt path over the top of what his eyes could now see. The pavement faded and the uneven dirt track he recalled took its place. Not once in those fourteen years had he returned to the summit, not since they took all the fun away. Yeah, that was why.

As he reached the summit, the egg white orb of the Observatory rose over the crest of the hill, like a moon rising. The arrogant glow of the Observatory dwarfed the glow of the lamps. The floodlights at its base lit it up so brightly that its radiance polluted the sky and from atop the hill you couldn't see the stars.

Vaughn approached the building with aching legs and sore feet from standing all day. He looked for a bench to collapse on, but there wasn't

any. Instead, he leaned hard on the railing and caught his breath. He hadn't made this climb for a while. He was out of practice.

"Ok seriously, this is strange even from a drunken perspective." Vaughn thought aloud.

Why was he at the Observatory? Had he dreamt a day's events as some nightmarish precursor to working this strange gig?

"Vaughn?"

Vaughn turned to see a young man swiftly walking towards him. He was wearing a white shirt and black pants, just like Vaughn should have been wearing. He also had a grin that made his eyes pop out and seem cartoonishly big. Even though he was far off his quick pace had him in front of Vaughn quicker than he was ready for.

"Please don't ask me if I know you." Vaughn asked, having flashes of the dirty woman again.

"I don't know you." The stranger said curiously.

"Ahhh ha, but then how d'you know my name?"

"I was told you'd be here. Plus, you're wearing a nametag." He pointed out. "I'm Pete."

Vaughn looked down and noticed he was still sporting his nametag, askew as always, clipped to his apron. This Pete seemed a little disappointed that Vaughn hadn't known he was coming. Pete was about Vaughn's age, black, and had an odd accent. Vaughn never thought himself one to place accents and whenever he met one, he couldn't place, he just assumed they were from New Zealand as a lot of miners he had met were. Vaughn hated moments like this, he felt racist whenever he struggled to determine race. Besides, what did it matter?

Pete too was exhausted from the climb.

"So Pete. Crowe's party, that's tonight?" Vaughn asked.

"Yeah. It's tonight."

"Hmmm." Vaughn shook his head. "I guess it is."

Vaughn tightened his fists, and they wrapped up firm. He had hoped they would be weak the way they are in the morning when you wake up. He had hoped he was dreaming.

"Are you ok?"

"Yeah, just a little off. I thought it was yesterday." Vaughn shook his head playfully and pulled a silly face.

"You'd be a bit late if it was yesterday. Doesn't start for another half hour."

"I guess we're both a little early. A first for me."

"Yeah, didn't exactly time it right either."

"Are you here to work or what?" Vaughn asked.

"Yup, yup I am. Here for this thing, whatever it is." That explained his outfit. Most bartenders dress alike as though they are expendable and replaceable and not actual people. Except for Vaughn, who felt naked in comparison, he wished he at least had some thongs on his feet.

"Didn't tell you what it was all about either, eh, it's a mystery all right." Vaughn said. "You're not gonna make fun of what I'm wearing are ya?"

"You do you, man." Pete joked. "Style's not really a white guy thing."

"Gee thanks."

Vaughn peered over to the narrow path that led around the Observatory. He wondered whether it was still there or if health and safety had gotten word of it by now.

"I was thinking about checking out the edge. Have you seen it?"

Pete excitedly followed along as Vaughn led him around the east side of the Observatory. This mammoth white building took up so much space on the top of the hill that the small gap that led around the back almost went unseen.

The gap widened as they rounded the Observatory and came to the back of the building where there was a small backyard size of land between the Observatory and the cliff's edge. There was a railing that ran around the edge of the cliff, but right at the highest point the railing had been broken and bent back so that rebellious teens could still get a running start. This was what was left of the once glorious Fracture Point.

"I haven't been here since I was a kid."

Vaughn walked right to the edge so he could sit with his feet dangling over the lip of the cliff. Without hesitation, Pete followed suit,

apparently never being one to fear heights or anything anyone else dared to do.

Straight down was the cavernous drop into the river below, and five meters across was the slightly lower half of Mount Fracture. From this height Vaughn knew all it would take would be a small leap and you would find your footing on the other side of the mountain. A small leap and then it's a long way back to the bottom and back up the winding road to where he was now.

"Amazing isn't it? It's like the two mountains are reaching for the other, but we know they'll never make it." Pete commented. "Looks like you could jump it easy too."

"Looks like it."

"Have you jumped it before?"

"Before this building was here, everyone used to come up all the time after school and jump across one by one."

"Anyone ever not make it?"

"Your accent's cool." Vaughn blurted.

"Thanks?"

"Maori?"

"No."

"Thought not."

They just sat there for a while as the dewy grass stained the bottoms of Pete's slacks and Vaughn's pajama shorts. There was a stressful hum in the air that Vaughn figured came from the generator that was hooked up the back of the Observatory, thus excluding it from the threat of power outages. Vaughn shook his head.

Finally Pete broke the silence.

"Do you usually work this sorta thing?"

"Oh yeah, I regularly work the last minute, mountainous gala event circuit. It's lucrative."

He smiled at his own joke to let Pete know he was kidding. He seemed overly gullible. "Nah you can usually find me at the Crowbar. You?"

"I'm between places right now."

Vaughn took one last look at the town before it descended into the dark of the night. The lights slowly came on for some buildings and others would struggle for the next few hours.

"I hate this town. I never got that patriotism for your hometown stuff, I guess if Fracture had something to offer, if I enjoyed anything about this place. They put this Observatory and railing here to try stop us jumping. There has been no water in the public pools for two summers. And d'you know the record store closed?"

Pete shook his head.

"Not enough business to keep music going. Music! People didn't care for it. Fucking joke. I'm guessing your from outta town then?"

"Sure am."

"Just here for the gig? Hey, why don't you take me with you once the party is over?"

"Ok."

Vaughn was stunned.

"Seriously?"

"Yeah. Why not?"

Pete was a curious guy, he was badly hiding how cool he thought Vaughn was and Vaughn was quick to stop himself from getting a big head. Pete's interest in Vaughn had relaxed his nerves and almost got too comfortable. Vaughn could feel himself wanting to open up to Pete immediately.

"I stole $9,000."

Is a sentence Vaughn both desperately wished to say and prayed never to pass through his lips. He sometimes worried that his brain would glitch and that would be the first bit of honest garbage that he'd spill. Luckily Vaughn got distracted as Pete rested his hands on the grass beside him.

"Ah what the fuck!"

"What?"

Pete whipped his hand back and held it out of sight but it was too late, Vaughn had seen on his right hand Pete was missing his index finger, the wound hadn't even healed properly yet and it was still a bit purple.

"Sorry, but I wasn't expecting…" Vaughn started. "How did you…? You know what, it's not my business."

Pete held his four-fingered hand to his chest and looked away, trying to look interested in something off in the distance whilst sniffing back a bit.

"Hey man, look, I'm sorry." Vaughn said as sincerely as he could. "It's just that… your hand is really, really, really gross. That's all."

Pete chuckled.

"I wish I could wash my eyeballs out. I'm going to be having nightmares for the next week. Just picturing you trying to pick up a ball or use a spoon, just you doing everyday things as though you're not some kind of non-human, monster of creation."

Pete scrunched his face up, trying not to smile. "You know, it's real, I have lost a finger. It's serious."

"For sure, I agree. It's serious… seriously messed up, that's what it is."

Pete burst into an ugly laugh, he could help it. He held his hand over his mouth, making Vaughn react in more terror and disgust. Pete held it out at him, and Vaughn screamed like a goat. He jumped up to his feet and stood there laughing for a bit, then looked back towards the entrance to the Observatory.

"Think we should head inside now?" He asked.

"Probably."

Stepping inside the doors, there was a vestibule that created an airtight lock between the Observatory and the outside. Vaughn wiped his bare feet on the steel-grated floor before walking on the soft red carpet that had been laid entering the main floor. But the carpet was not the first thing he noticed. Vaughn instantly swooned under the cool breath of air conditioning that silently fought the heat back. He wiped his sweaty forehead, and he felt the cool kiss of the Observatory air.

The decor of the Observatory cried faux regal. If anything wasn't made of brass or gold, it was wrapped in velvet red. The carpets

were patterned to distort, corner pillars that led to the open ceiling were draped in magnificent burgundy curtains revealing huge round, porthole-like windows.

They were the type of curtains that you would never use at home, the kind designed to be roped into a corner, a spectacular waste of fabric. Pete wandered right over to these reigned in drapes and grazed his hand and then his cheek up against them, loving the soft touch.

Just like tasting a peppercorn in your teeth, Vaughn scowled as he noted how clean the windows were. They were up so high the ash from the mines couldn't reach.

There was the telescope, its bulbous frame took up half the volume of the inside of the building. The Observatory seemed to be designed to host this giant eye and shaped itself perfectly around the scope, with the same perimeter of space surrounding it to the ceiling or roof. This created the feeling of constant space as the rich, red-carpeted floor circling all the way around it.

Both the windows and walls were decorated completely the same all way round, with the same selection and arrangement of four-seater booths, that Vaughn felt that if the front door and bar hadn't been there that he might have gotten lost.

The music was the next thing Vaughn noticed, the big-band music swelled from the speakers in the corners of the ceiling and Vaughn traced the music to the sound system built into a cupboard behind the bar. Superhigh tech; multi-disc rack. So many knobs.

The bar took up nearly the whole Observatory, following around the grand circle. It was shaped perfectly to match the telescope's body behind it and obviously an impressive deal of money had been seen to make it feel like it belonged there, arguing that astrophysicists have a lot more fun than they let on.

The bar felt strong and permanent. Vaughn shook the bench and saw no movement. The telescope that boasted its presence amongst this decor had a bold collar of shelves. Shelves that backlit the widest collection of booze Vaughn had ever seen, even at a liquor

store. Vaughn wondered how and why an Observatory would even be dressed up in this fashion. He doubted now if the telescope was even functional.

"Finally." A voice rang out. An old man rounded the bar circuit, hands behind his back. Atticus Crowe was already peeved.

Tight. Tight would be the best word to describe Atticus Crowe. But only cloth deep would your impression be if you only spoke of his attire.

His old bones still struck solid posture, his skin still clung to his muscle like they were sinking together on the Titanic, and his hair, whilst white as snow, was so firmly matted down you could skip a stone off it.

He was the symbol for why some assume wealth can buy youth; a mascot for baby blood tonic and skin lotions. Vaughn would wager his age anywhere between forty and eighty.

Atticus walked with his hands behind his back, only to make it easier to suck in his belly as he walked. A belly grown from caviar and truffles. A belly yearning for relief from his tight cummerbund.

"Maybe I'm a tad ignorant, but is this how all observatories look?" Vaughn asked.

"Don't be ridiculous." Atticus snapped. "Come over here, boy!"

Pete quit playing with the curtains and stepped up towards Atticus and Vaughn.

"So Vaughn." Atticus spied his nametag. "I'm surprised to see you, after how we left things this morning. I'm still not sure if I want you here."

Right. This morning, Vaughn thought.

"Well, here I am."

"And this is what you chose to wear?" Atticus said, seeing Vaughn's dirty feet and lack of pants. "Is this some form of protest?"

"You get what you get, I suppose." Vaughn shrugged. "My apron covers it."

Atticus looked him up and down and then saw that Pete was dressed slightly better, at least having pants on.

"For crying out loud," Atticus remarked, twisting his mouth as he inspected Vaughn and Pete. "Is this all I've got to work tonight, huh?"

"You don't know?"

"Son, I host many events. I can't keep track of whom I hire and what not. Obviously, I'm down to the bottom of the barrel, especially if I'm hiring locally. But I guess this is what you get when you try to help the everyday people."

"You can just call us people."

"For a thousand dollars an hour I can call you both Susan." Atticus sighed. "Come, I'll give you the abridged tour, and Vaughn straighten up your name tag like Pete's, this isn't a dive."

Atticus led them swiftly around the bar to the opening at the back where there were three doors against the east side wall. The one on the far left was lavishly labelled as the lavatory; the second was marked as staff only and Atticus quickly swung in open for them to see a small set of stairs leading down into the dimly lit room with shelves of glassware and a dishwasher.

At the third door Atticus stopped and stood in front of it. The label read storage.

"It's just full of junk, so don't worry about that."

Atticus moved away from the door, and Vaughn had a quick peak. It was dark but Vaughn could make out a fold-up Ping-Pong table, a piano, a few chairs and a television on a cart. The piano was actually pretty nice, Vaughn recognized the brand name glazed in gold lettering, the television was bigger than the ones he had seen in any store, and he didn't know anyone that owned their own Ping-Pong table.

"I said not to worry." Atticus growled and almost slammed the door shut back on his nose. "It's just a load of junk. No need to play about in there. Don't let anyone else in here either, ok?"

He then led Vaughn and Pete over to the bar flap and walked through the bar, showing off all the bits and bobs that may have well had been bits and bobs to Atticus.

"Here's your whatsits and whosits. Pipes and levers, that kind of thing. Ah ha here's the big toy."

Atticus bent down and flipped a lock free and suddenly Vaughn noticed the giant ladder that stood before him, now swaying freely.

"The top shelf would be a bit of a stretch without this."

Vaughn recognized it as one of those ladders that are in those great big gothic libraries he had seen only in movies. He took a few steps up and started reading a few of the bottles, some he recognized as being ridiculously valuable.

"Both of you be careful. If one of you dares to fall, you're done, you get me? You can walk home on a broken leg."

Atticus then left the bar with Vaughn halfway up the ladder. Twelve tall shelves of tantalizing mixers Vaughn had to play with. No menus were displayed, so Vaughn assumed there was free rein to make whatever the customers ordered.

Vaughn's hands chose a bottle of tequila, "Crowe, this is expensive stuff…"

"Mr. Crowe." Atticus corrected.

"Really?"

"Really, really."

"Mr. Crowe, exactly what kind of party is this?"

"That…" Atticus paused, darting his eyes as he chose his words carefully. "… Is none of your concern. You are here to serve drinks and clean up after my guests. I am paying you more money than you could make in a year, so please try to stay out of the way and be inconsequential."

The night had become a stormy one, a soothing summer's heat had become a sweeping howl of winds that ushered many citizens low in town to stay in for the night. Atticus seemed unaffected straightening his tie as the last minutes of the clock moved to 5:55 as if he was expecting his party to start at 6:00 on the dot.

Vaughn and Pete were accustoming themselves to the bar, Vaughn already filling his deep apron pockets with brass bottle openers and other fun stuff his hands discovered, while Pete struggled to clip his

nametag to his new apron, fiddling with it with his missing finger it almost made Vaughn hurl.

They then got to work discovering the racks of clean glasses, slicing up some lemons, orientating themselves to not get in each other's way.

Vaughn had his eyes on all the bottles that when he looked up to the overbearing shelves above, he worried that each still bottle was seconds from falling and crashing down. He scanned the labels, each one making him double take until his neck hurt. They were brands and years that Vaughn had no chance of ever seeing again, double, triple, quadruple distilled, all of them older than Vaughn.

Atticus was lapping the room, occasionally pulling a curtain back and peeking out one of the porthole windows. When the next song came on, it made Vaughn and Pete jump. Atticus had a remote for the sound system in his jacket pocket with which he had sneakily hit the skip button and the sudden boom of *'Fly Me to the Moon'* filled the Observatory.

"I'm thinking 50s themed, going by the music. What do you think?" Vaughn asked Pete. But secretly, Vaughn thought come six o'clock the doors would open and a parade of lizard people in clown makeup would dance in and start climbing the walls and licking the curtains.

He was trying to recall the conversation he had had with Atticus, when he was offered the job. He was drinking then, and he recalled the blur of passing out. Perhaps he had made it up the hill and fallen for a moment's rest before he awoke. Perfectly logical. All the rest was a dream. If not, he was dreaming now.

"Could be, could be." Pete replied.

"Do you suppose then that this is this one of those role-playing things, but for rich people?" Vaughn whispered after Atticus passed them by on his seventh lap of the grand room. "He's done those before. Don't know if you heard, but he had medieval dress up one. Knights, jousting and everything. There was horse shit all through the streets the next morning."

"Who knows?"

"Yeah good point. He didn't really advertise the thing, did he, all very hush-hush."

"What if no one comes?"

"He'd be very disappointed." Vaughn said. "But he's paying me for the full night no matter what. He can afford to take a loss."

Vaughn had taken the lead behind the bar with no debate from Pete. He assigned them both a section and order to which they would do things. Pete was to pour the basics from the tap while Vaughn would mix the specialty drinks and climb the ladder. Vaughn was especially pleased when Pete didn't argue about the ladder as he had been dying to ride it along its tracks, flinging himself almost from one side of the circular bar to the other.

For now, they took stock of their equipment, the bottle openers, the ice buckets, the drinks on tap and the fruit in the fridge. Pete had found some olives and nuts and now had gone to his knees, diving into the cupboards under the bench to find a bowl for them.

Vaughn passed him by, dodging this human obstacle, and noticed the bounce of something in his apron he had forgotten about. He reached in and pulled out a brightly colored toy; the toy that was no longer humming - the toy that was supposed to be part of his dream.

Vaughn felt the weight of his possession; it wasn't that heavy, but his awareness of it seemed to sag one side of his apron. It was the brand of awareness that throws you, like when you notice you are breathing and can't help but focus on it until it almost chokes you.

What possible explanation could there be for it other than the ridiculous, Vaughn hated accepting the ridiculous. He had always wondered why some people went insane - what was it they couldn't understand? What confused them? With this children's toy in his hand, he finally understood.

Pete finally found a few bowls to his liking. They didn't match, but he held them up to Vaughn anyway, shrugging. Vaughn gave his nod of approval and Pete happily poured nuts into some and olives into the others.

Vaughn had to say something; he had to ask Pete if he was real. What a horrible thing to ask a person, what a horrible thing to second-guess the existence of others. If Pete was real, then the morning he thought he had, hadn't been. Jake hadn't quit, his manager hadn't blackmailed him, the dirty woman hadn't spoken to him, and no blue-shoe-wearing stranger had fallen onto that car.

But they had felt so real, and from what Vaughn could tell, this party felt more unreal as time went on.

As tacky as it was to share dreams, he felt like he needed to tell his new friend. He couldn't just keep it from him; he couldn't do that to Pete. He thought of Jake again. That face he had when he caught him. He couldn't hold his tongue; words were going to come out.

"Maybe get some toothpicks for the olives."

Chapter Eleven:
The Irregulars

The first time Vaughn tried to leave Fracture was when he was thirteen, his teen angst had built up to a breaking point and he knew he had to do something about it, or he'd start punching walls. He had packed a bag of what a thirteen-year-old would regard as essentials such as magazines, his walk-man and no clean underwear or toiletries. There was only one long road out of town, and even in his naïve youth he didn't for a second consider walking.

The bus that came in and out every two weeks had just arrived and let off all the miners who stumbled like zombies into the Crowbar. Vaughn knew that the bus was heading for Broome, and it would be empty, and he planned to fill it.

Vaughn waited for the bus driver to leave it unattended, and when he did, young Vaughn snuck aboard. Even now looking back on it, he still considered it a simple, smart plan. All he had to do was duck under the seats and he would get a free ride out of there. His plan was to hit the coast and then make it down to Adelaide, and later to Melbourne. But no matter where the bus went, he would keep going; hitching rides, hitching boats, hitching planes, he figured a young kid like himself would have no problem hitching.

On the bus, with his nose peaking up to sit on the windowsill, Vaughn watched his town fly by. He remembered it really did feel like that. He was so used to the streets passing at a walking pace, anything faster than that was flying.

But not even fifteen minutes into the ride down the long and plain road out of town did the bus break down. Smoke fumed from the engine and the bus driver had to pull over so suddenly that it jolted Vaughn from his hiding space.

He had to walk back. The driver called for help and told Vaughn to stay with him so he could get him in trouble properly. But Vaughn had no intention of punishment. He walked back. The fifteen-minute ride was now a three-hour walk back into town. That was the day Vaughn learnt just how relentless the sun was, how little mercy the ground had for him as it bounced the heat back at him, like he was stuck in a toaster; grilled from both sides.

Though he had made it so far, the tip of Mount Fracture was still visible above the horizon.

That's the furthest he could get, and he wasn't even out of Fracture's sight.

Vaughn felt like the world was out there, but he had a rope tied to his ankle and it ran to a post at the center of town.

Many things seemed bad about Fracture but for those three hours, the worst thing was the heat.

His parents didn't notice he had left as he came home in time for dinner, they just asked him plainly how his day went.

Most parties begin half an hour or even a full hour after they are set to start. Most choose to be fashionably late. Vaughn expected the guests that night to uphold this ancient tradition and was shocked by the sudden surge of guests that found their way into the Observatory as soon as the clock struck six.

Atticus positioned himself by the door and shook every hand that took his. Vaughn noticed how bizarre some of them looked, hairstyles from many fashions, but mostly wearing the same non-descript outfit.

Some were dripping wet; others shook dust from their coats and a few apologized to Atticus about the snow melting off their shoes into the carpet.

"The Atticus Crowe!" They marveled. "We made it! Isn't this just fantastic."

"I can't believe I'm actually here."

"Well now, that you're here you can relax." Atticus said to his guests. "Get yourselves a drink and settle in. Enjoy."

Vaughn didn't recognize a single guest, not that he expected to. Obviously, they were similar rich folk from out of town or if they were from Fracture; they had never left their homes to mix with the everyday people.

Pete was the first to get to work. He collected a handful of glasses and laid them across the counter and filled them with yellow beer from the tap. The spout shot out beer faster than Pete was ready for, and the first few beers had far too much head.

Vaughn, on the other hand, shot into work mode and stuck himself to the more intricate orders.

"A severed wine, please."

"Goldneck? Do you have Goldneck Gin, or anything from Brazil?"

"I'm not sure." Vaughn stammered.

"Maltese lemonade."

"Ahhhh…"

"A Curly Sue."

"What's the price of milk here?"

"Do you make cocktails? A Slim Ricky is my favorite."

"Mmm yum I'll have one too."

They stumped Vaughn, for the first time in Fracture he wasn't sweating because of the heat. He climbed the ladder behind him and was relieved to find the brand of gin the woman had asked for. For the other drinks, he had to ask how they were made, luckily it appeared they were just strange names for drinks he had made a thousand times before.

"A bourbon, double." A sizeable man ordered. Yeah, one for each chin, Vaughn smirked.

"Two gin and tonics." Another requested, shaking the dust loose from his coat and beard.

"Could you slide one of those down this way? They're ignoring this end." Asked a stern lipped woman to the dusty man.

"I see you." Vaughn snapped.

Dusty turned and looked to see her forehead bore a freaky purple vein that throbbed as she frowned, and he quickly did as she asked.

A man with a bulbous bowler hat had grounded himself front and center of the beer tap and found every spare moment Pete had to shove his freshly finished glass under Pete's nose for a refill. After this third glass, Pete found an exit to move along the bar to serve some others.

"You know your name tag's a little askew." Bowler Hat told Vaughn, moving down to harass him.

"I'm aware."

"And you're missing your shoes."

"I'm having an off night."

Vaughn was close enough to the sound system that he figured he could quickly turn down the loud brass trumpet without Crowe noticing. But everybody else did.

"Ah look at that, so retro. I love it."

Retro? Vaughn thought.

Guests huddled around the sound system and admired it while Vaughn rolled his eyes slinked away to the east side of the bar. He rounded the curve and found a woman in military uniform, planted deep in her spot at the counter and slowly making her way through the more alcoholic drinks on the menu. When she got to the bottom of her glass, she would swing it back as though the droplets at the bottom were mouthfuls and then she would moan in disappointment until someone would feed her another drink.

She said nothing else but murmurs in response to others at the party who aimed for free seats beside her before snapping at them like a croc.

Vaughn's intrigue was cut short by a rotund man who had pushed his way to the front of the queue.

"What would you like?"

"Surprise me." Answered Jowls. Vaughn hid a smile to himself. He had unconsciously thought of naming him as the jowls that wobbled as

he spoke or turned his neck. Vaughn thought of Nixon as he collected the ingredients for his smoky margarita, a drink of his own concoction he whipped up whenever someone asked to be surprised.

"Here we are, one Surprise Me."

Jowls tasted the drink and smacked his lips enthusiastically.

"Acceptable at best."

"Ooo that looks good, I'll have the same?"

Suddenly orders for more creative drinks were being shouted across the bar at both boys. Pete was all too happy to shake his head at any of the strangely named drinks thrown his way and passed them off to Vaughn. He just wanted to keep it simple.

"And for you?" Vaughn asked the next in line.

"A glass of red." A ghostly pale woman asked for her head was wrapped up in a shawl and even her fingers had wrinkles. She took the drink with one hand and carried a white rose in the other.

"Thank you, precious." The old woman turned her head and spied a few free tables and booths around the perimeter of the Observatory. "Are those tables free?"

"Sure, sit where you like." Her politeness puzzled Vaughn. He watched as the woman then sat at a booth with a young couple already sharing the other side. Vaughn giggled as the couple collected their drinks and moved on. The old woman was as solemn as a cemetery.

"Hey Pete, check out Madame Rose over there."

"She's all yours." Pete sneered.

"In her dreams." Vaughn scoffed. "Do you think she's doing that thing with the rose? Do you think she's waiting for someone?"

"Poor thing. Maybe tonight we'll witness the start of a blossoming relationship."

From the call of another bizarre drink, Vaughn rolled the ladder around the wall of bottles and kicked in the brakes. He climbed up and overheard the first words from the woman in the military uniform that weren't mumbled slurs of a drink order.

"Hank, you son of a bitch." The woman offered an arm to the man who had just arrived, her various medals jingled against one another,

as they did one came loose and fell off, the woman saw it fall and bid it lost forever.

"Hank!"

But the man who she called Hank shook his head and stuck to his group of friends, turning his back to the woman and asking his friends if the crazy lady was still looking at him.

From up on top of the ladder Vaughn could see Atticus was walking laps around the Observatory, still shaking hands with everyone he met. Vaughn leaned back, putting all his weight in the strength of his hands as he could see a few people going into the storage room and wheeling out the Ping-Pong table and piano.

"Hey bartender!"

Vaughn snapped back to see a staggering man stationed at his counter, he swayed from side to side but had a steady finger pointing at Vaughn.

"Heeeey! Mr bartender man. Another one."

Vaughn climbed back down the ladder with the bottle in hand and started on a drink.

"Another? Have I served you yet?"

"Oh, of course not shhhhh. Hey? I'll get it right, just shhhh?"

"Get what…?"

"A talking dog walks into a bar. No. Just a dog, a dog walks in and is all like hey, why won't you let me in? The bartender's all like, 'cause there's a sign 'no dogs allowed' that's what the dog was talking about. And the dog's like I'm special, 'cause he can talk and stuff. No wait. And then the bartender asks, 'what makes you so special, huh?"

The man cackled with laughter while Vaughn stood waiting for the joke to continue.

"Oh, so that's the whole joke." Vaughn rolled his eyes. "Hilarious."

The man's laughs became whimpers and soon enough he was sobbing. Those around him backed away slowly, but Vaughn was caught in his vacuum.

"Hey come on, it wasn't that bad." Vaughn tried.

"Oh, fuck this!" He snapped, faltering back from the bar. He looked quite upset with himself and stormed angrily out of the Observatory.

"Someone should help him; he shouldn't try to leave in that state." One guest said.

"Who knows where he'll wake up?" Another replied.

"And with a hangover."

"All of you saw it, I landed within twenty feet of the front doors."

"You're a real math whiz." Someone joked. "I won't tell anyone that you walked all the way here yesterday and then jumped."

"Yeah. It's called strategy."

"I didn't risk it, I landed in town and walked up." Said the woman with the purple throbbing vein. "We're too high for my calculation."

"I landed in town too. But a few days ago, just had to wait around a few days. I gotta tell you, there is nothing to do in this town."

"What kind of a dump is Fracture anyway? Never heard of the place until a few days ago."

It harmed not one ounce of pride in Vaughn. "It's a hole that's for sure." He added.

"Well, if your gonna hide a hiding place, a hole's the place to bury it."

"You got that right." Vaughn grimaced.

"You got any chalk?"

"Huh?"

Vaughn turned to find a few giddy guests trying to peak over the counter.

"Why would I have chalk?"

"I found some!" A voice called out to them.

Vaughn stood back up and saw a girl had stuck her head out from the storage cupboard. She had found some chalk in Atticus' forbidden storage room.

"Oh, no you're not supposed to go in there…" Vaughn started, his level of care matching his volume.

"Thanks anyway." The giddy guests quipped as they double tapped the bar with their hands like a drum and scooted off to meet with the

girl. They regrouped with a bunch of other more youthful folk who all threw their hands in the air when they saw the chalk and started walking around and drawing on the carpet.

Vaughn smiled and waited for it to become Atticus' problem.

"Don't keep me waiting barkeep." A sloppy voice called.

Jowls ordered another drink, this time pointing to the uppermost shelf to a stained blue bottle of Shiraz. Jowls was an alcohol expert, at least, that's what he had been telling everyone. He said he travelled the world in search of the perfect brew.

"You can take it or leave it but the best beer every brewed was during the prohibition. Don't believe me? I drank it straight from the bathtub to my lips. I gotta tell ya, some people work best under pressure."

Vaughn looked him up and down and figured he was hiding his age well under all that excess fat, or he was a terrible liar.

His mouth bubbled as he spoke, like he was stirring his words before he spat them out. Two girls beside him looked away whenever he hit any word with one of his S's careful not to get hit by a stray shot of slobber.

"How about some of that Chartreuse up the top there young man?" Jowls wobbled.

Again, Vaughn was ordered to leap to the ladder. But in his revolt, he did it so sarcastically that he swung around, almost knocking into Pete.

Vaughn steadied himself and climbed up the ladder, slowly rolling across to reach the bottle.

From up that high, he had a bird's-eye view of the party. He looked out to the youthful guests, all-scrambling around the floor and marking chalk X's on the floor with their names next to it. Surely from this far up Vaughn would see a pattern, but it was all seemingly at random. Strangely, the other guests were careful not to walk over the X's, dodging them not to scuff the marks.

But strange chalk markings were none of Vaughn's concern; some new guests had caught his attention.

Entering the observatory was a short middle-aged man wearing a leather jacket too large for him and on his shoulders, rode a young girl

with a thick ponytail tied up in a thicker knot who was small but looked heavy enough to crumple the man she was riding.

They caught his attention, but what kept it was the woman that had walked in with them.

She wore red and black-checkered jumpsuit with a crazy mess of jet black, curly hair on top.

He couldn't make out what they were saying over the chatter of the party, but he watched them with wide eyes as they found Atticus and ushered him to the far side of the Observatory and into the forbidden storage room.

Vaughn wasn't one to recognize a face or a name at the best of times, but some people make more of an impression than most.

And Vaughn knew that face. That was the clean face of the dirty woman who gave him the colorful toy that sat in his apron pocket.

Chapter Twelve

The Video Tape

Vaughn hurried down the ladder and handed the bottle of Chartreuse over to the crowd who happily took up their own shot glasses and helped themselves.

He made for the storage room door, dodging through the guests and hopping chalk marks until he had his face pressed against the storage room door. With one hand, he gently eased the handle and opened the door a crack to see inside.

They had left the lights off, only the glowing blue standby light of TV lit the room and those inside it. It was wheeled into the center of the room on its cart and the short, middle-aged man handed a Beta videotape to the dark-haired woman who popped it in the player and the TV buzzed to life and hypnotized the young girl who stepped towards the glowing blue screen as it flickered to life.

On the screen, a logo spun in circles before finding the center of the screen, reading *Volta* with a squared pattern behind it.

Vaughn had barely a chance to try to recognize the logo before it started. A handsome man stepped into frame and began speaking as a soft jazzy tune played.

"Welcome to the world of the future, today. My name is James Biggs, but you know me best as one of the several voice options and faces of your very own Ogle. Well, I'm here today to guide you through the ins and outs of our latest product so you can have the safest and most enjoyable trips of your life. So, let's start by taking it out of the box..."

Suddenly Biggs' voice sped up and so did his movements. The dark-haired woman had found the fast-forward button.

"Whoa hey!" Atticus leapt up. "What are you doing?"

"That's not what we came here to show you, just wait." She kept fast-forwarding until the picture violently changed from a bright and colorful palate to an angry mix of black and grey. Having gone too far whipped her finger off the fast-forward button and rewound to moments before the sudden change and hit play again.

"Now I know what you're all wondering, James Biggs, you handsome devil, just how do I figure out how to calculate the day stream rotations? And boy, do we have an easy rhyme for you to remember..."

Again, Biggs was cut off, but this time by the stretch of the tape and a dreary room bounced up and down the screen until the picture settled and the audio became clear.

"Atticus Crowe."

Vaughn could see Atticus stand up straight, sucking in his gut again.

"This is a message is for Atticus Crowe. We are seeking a response in order to gain an approval to sanction..."

"Excuse me?"

Vaughn snapped back, his left eye adjusting to the bright light of the rest of the Observatory.

The man who had startled Vaughn was the cocky math whiz from earlier. He had a constant skip in his step though he was standing still, his suit was very nice but crinkled and rough like he had slept in it too many times and his eyes were stuck on Vaughn. Well, one of them anyway.

"What?"

"Is this the line for the bathroom, is it? The line for the bathroom?" Math Whiz sputtered.

"Do you think I'm standing here peeking into the bathroom?" Vaughn asked.

"I dunno, maybe. I dunno. But if you're next..."

"Bathroom's the last door. That way."

"Gotcha." Math Whiz did a cheeky finger gun too close to Vaughn's face and hurried off.

Vaughn wondered about the rudeness of some people and then went back to peeking through the door, shoving his face hard against it to get a good look.

The tape was over now, a blue screen again. But the dark-haired woman had taken up the video camera that sat beneath the TV on the cart and was filming Atticus now. Vaughn could see Atticus' face on the TV playing back, and he could see Atticus was trying his best to look good.

"Oh are, ok this is new for me... ahem." Atticus straightened his tie. "Hello. This is a response to your video. Atticus Crowe's response... my response. Atticus, Crowe. Me."

Atticus coughed as though his throat was the problem and continued as Vaughn stood there absolutely perplexed. What the hell was going on?

"As per your request, I give my full approval for the function I am hosting here to be used as a refuge from 6pm to 6am, as a non-violent, all welcoming..."

"Vaughn."

"WHAT!"

Vaughn turned again to find a startled Pete standing beside him with two steel shaker tins.

"Sorry, I just... I don't know how this... what were you doing?"

"Nothing!"

Vaughn sucked in his cheeks and held his breath. Pete looked so worried over the cups that Vaughn calmed and centered himself.

"Nothing, I'm not doing nothing." Vaughn lent his head on the door casually. "Getting swamped without me are ya?"

"Yeah, but it doesn't matter if you're busy. What are you doing anyway...?"

Suddenly Vaughn fell back as the door he lent against opened and Atticus and his new friends stepped out. Vaughn found himself only a few feet away from the dark-haired woman who had given him the chills and a Rubik's cube.

"Why are both of my bartenders not behind the bar?" Atticus growled. "And instead standing outside the very place I told them not to be?"

Vaughn heard none of it. His mind was scrambling itself as he stared at the dark-haired woman and tried to make sense of it all.

Clean and unscented, the dark-haired woman struck Vaughn as a very indefinable woman. Her black hair and skin had him made her undefinable accent even more curious. She was probably in her 30's, clean and fragrant, yet she was the exact woman he had briefly spoken to maybe hours ago?

"I think I'm dreaming." Vaughn breathed, looking at her.

The words hung in the air, Vaughn wondered whether he had said them at all, or if his mind had shouted it out.

"What was that?" The dark-haired woman asked, moving towards him with a raised brow.

"Vaughn. Not appropriate." Atticus snapped, looking back and forth between them.

"No, I meant... Don't I know you?" Vaughn continued, each word losing more momentum than the last. "You were at the pub earlier today... yesterday...?"

She took a moment. Eyes fluttering. She seemed like a mess of chaos contained in a jar and her mouth was the lid. Her outfit was organized madness; Vaughn didn't know how she got in or out of it. Her hair had a style all its own, each curl rebelling from the rest yet still perfectly structured to frame her face and center you on her gaze.

Her gaze, which fluttered from Vaughn to the edges of the room and back twenty times over, impatiently patient. She reminded Vaughn of someone reading a whole board of mathematic equations, what looked like nonsense and chaos to most made sense total sense to her and she kept coming back to the problem in front of her - the one not wearing any pants.

"I'm sorry, but I've never been here or met you before." She answered, her eyes welling up with intrigue. "But I'm Wyla nice to meet you."

"What are you doing?" Atticus pressed through gritted teeth, as Vaughn shook her hand.

Vaughn did not understand, but this was definitely the same woman he had seen at the Crowbar, the one who had slipped the Rubik's cube in his hand. But standing there now, there was something different about how she approached him. She was one of the last things he remembered before waking up halfway up the mountain. But gone was the enthusiasm and interest she had had for him the first time. Now only confusion and intrigue clung to her face, whilst urgency and embarrassment clung to Atticus's.

"Actually, you know what. I'm mixing you up with someone else." Vaughn waved it off. "I do that all the time. I see a lot of people and I must have mixed you up with someone else. My bad."

As Vaughn waved, reaching up to his face to hide it with a fake head scratch Wyla caught a look at his watch; she stared at it strangely and then threw a look to Vaughn.

Vaughn shot a look to his watch; it was still broken, the hands swinging freely around and around the face whenever he moved his arm.

"Don't apologize, happens to the best of us." She finally said, sizing Vaughn up and monitoring him as he subtly unclasped his watch and slipped it into his apron.

The short middle-aged man coughed.

"And this is John Dahl and Sancia." She added.

"Just Dahl…Sancia, say hello." Dahl urged.

"Hello." Sancia too had a thick accent that was hard to pick up as her voice broke and she lost it halfway through.

"Why don't you get them a drink and I'll be with you all soon." Wyla said.

A sudden rush of wind swept around their feet. Not a lot, not too hard. Just enough to make you notice it.

Vaughn looked around for an open door or window. There wasn't one.

All he saw as Pete and the others making their way to the bar, he did a jaunty run to catch up and get ahead of them.

Dahl walked with the form of a larger man, his arms swinging with wide girth from his waist. He powered through the crowd and slammed himself onto a stool opposite Vaughn at the bar as though his weight shook the room.

It didn't. The seat hardly creaked.

Vaughn was amused seeing how his thin arms were when sneaking out from his thick sleeves. His brown leather jacket boasted virility and threat, but Dahl protruded from it like a turtle from a shell.

Shadowing Dahl was Sancia. The timid girl couldn't stop fiddling with her ponytail as she stole a seat beside Dahl. Sancia was quieter than Dahl, as though she expected her presence to be a burden and merely waited to be asked if she wanted a drink, and even to that was she sheepish.

She asked for a glass of water and immediately finished it so she could slide the ice from the glass onto the counter. She played with the ice cubes hesitantly in her callused palms, whilst Vaughn groaned internally, thinking of the water stains to the countertop.

"By the way, your name tag is a little crooked." Dahl noted.

"I know." Vaughn groaned, quickly playing with it, twisting it straight before it flicked right back.

Vaughn stood close to Sancia, who returned to her half-melted ice cube, sliding it off the counter and back into her glass.

"Could I have some more water, please?" She carefully chose her words to form the sentence and held out her glass.

"Sure." Vaughn took the glass and tossed it in the sink, serving her a fresh one without any ice.

Pete had moved down the bar to take on the demand, rushing to help with the simple stuff that he could pour. Vaughn looked around for Wyla as he so desperately wanted her to be on the other side of the counter. But he couldn't see her. Strange, as her crazy hair would stand out anywhere. But all he could see Atticus, rushing over to the door to welcome the latest guest.

"Where'd she go?" He asked.

"She'll be back." Dahl answered.

"Not what I asked."

"Yes, but we're not supposed to say, so there, we're not supposed to say."

"Say what? What's with all the secrecy tonight?"

Vaughn noticed that few of the guests had sat at the bar, as though they wanted to keep their conversations to themselves. Only Dahl and Sancia had stayed seated at the bar, but even they seemed only to be doing it out of politeness.

There was a tension in the air. Everyone had noticed Wyla had left, and it led to a great deal of out of earshot discussion. Dahl seemed easy to Vaughn, saying he wasn't supposed to say anything already seemed like he had said too much.

"So, you two from around here?"

"Not exactly."

Dahl played with the bowl of toothpicks, taking one out at a time and building a little toothpick tower.

"And what's the relation here?" Vaughn pried and nodded to Sancia. "You her dad?"

"Ahhh, no."

"No?" Vaughn narrowed his eyes. She was a lot younger than Dahl.

"No, but I am doing my best." Dahl answered, he smiled warmly and looked over to Sancia proudly. "She didn't have anyone, so I thought I'll be her someone until she figures it out. I think we both needed some family."

"He saved me." Sancia said, she lent her head on his puffy jacket shoulder, instantly deflating it.

"Did he now?"

"I saw a young girl drowning, and I just jumped in. I had to, even though I'm a terrible swimmer." Dahl bragged.

"That's stupid." Vaughn replied. "You could've just made it worse and drowned too. No point in the both of you drowning."

"I knew I would be all right. Besides, it was no shirt off my back."

"Well, I guess we can't all be as heroic as you Dahl." Vaughn said pushing his palms into the counter. "Sancia, was it? You can have more

than just water. We've got non-alcoholic mixers and stuff. Just let me know ok."

"Ok." Sancia smiled.

"She's just so polite, isn't she?" Dahl beamed, wrapping his arm around her and pulling her in tight. "Aren't you, kiddo?"

Sancia winced, and Dahl instantly let go. She eased up and slid her shirt down slightly to check on her collarbone and Vaughn could see three deep cuts, healing but still plenty red.

"Sorry sorry sorry I keep forgetting?" Dahl winced with her. "Still bad, huh? You poor thing."

"You get that before or after almost drowning?"

"I am ok. Thank you." She said quietly, wanting the attention to leave her.

"Right... How did you get..."

"Animals."

"What?"

Vaughn turned to find Pete whipping a towel over his shoulder and sighed after the crowd he had died down.

"Animals. They just don't stop, do they?" Pete sighed.

"That's hospitality."

"I can see." Pete turned and slid two beers in front of Vaughn.

"I poured you one." Pete said. "Figured we were due by now."

"Well, aren't you a lovely so and so." Vaughn smiled and reached for the glass, Pete slid it over to him his right hand, four fingers touching the glass. Vaughn hesitated.

"What?"

"Nothing."

"Is it the finger thing?" Pete sighed.

"The nub is still a little off-putting."

"Fine." Pete took his hand off the glass. Vaughn took it and wiped the sides down dramatically and took a sip.

"Thanks bud."

Pete smiled, a little too much.

"What?"

"Nothing."
"No seriously, what?"
"I stuck the nub in that."
Vaughn spat out his mouthful and choked as Pete laughed.

Gradually the rush calmed. Everyone held a glass in their hand and had found a seat or a booth or had formed a loose circle amongst the other circles circling the telescope. The ever-growing group of weirdos still walking the Observatory floor with chalk and occasionally cheering still had Vaughn confused.

"I don't think we're allowed to touch them. They're playing some sort of game." Vaughn noted. "And it's taking up half the Observatory."

"That's not going to get annoying anytime soon." Pete moaned.

"Did you know we're working until six am?" Vaughn asked.

"Are you serious?" Pete groaned, but then shrugged. "Though, think of the money."

"That's what I keep telling myself, just gotta make it 'til dawn."

Both bartenders rolled their eyes, looking out to the circular room now full of staggered chalk marks and staggering guests. Some chalk crosses followed the same trajectory as others that ran around the grand room, but most people had no common clue how to play the same game, drawing their mark seemingly at random on the floor.

Two people were arguing over which way was west and which way was east and soon enough nearly every guest attending that night had gotten over their detest for the youth and had marked their own bet, now everyone graced the floor with respect and care, as they got tipsier and rowdier.

Some were picky, most were rude, one he had seen got on his nerve as Vaughn's pet peeve was people making water rings on the counter. Worse still, Vaughn grinded his teeth seeing a guy playing with the rings with a straw.

Vaughn handed Pete a tray stacked full of drinks and sent him back weaving through the circles like a bit of cloth caught between the cogs

and gears of a big machine. When Pete returned with a look like he had been through a car wash and Vaughn grabbed a tray to do the run himself.

As he moved through the crowd collecting foam-stained glasses, he couldn't help but inspect the guests for was wallets and valuables. He had to physically shake his head to stop himself from looking.

Just collect the glasses and get back to the counter, he thought. But it would be so easy.

Vaughn's hands once again decided for him, so many loose pockets, and Vaughn dug through them all in such a quick succession. First finding satchels of rocks and wallets full of international money. These people were proper rich, on Atticus' level; he could see how they could all get along so well. The next pocket Vaughn dove into stopped him in his tracks as he could have sworn, he felt a squared plastic object nestled securely in one woman's pocket.

"Is someone touching my-"

"-How are we doing tonight?" Vaughn grinned toothily and moved on before she complained.

Vaughn felt inconsequential. Like furniture that decided it was its turn to talk. He moved on and instantly the guests resumed their conversations.

"Don't get me started. How dare they say it wasn't political? They made themselves the bad guys, those commercials were so in your face..."

Vaughn hurried the tray of dirty glasses across the room to the storage room. He saw the two doors. The storage room with the television on his right and the storage room full of clean glassware on his left; he chose the door on the left.

He rested his elbow on the door handle and with the slight opening he nuzzled his foot between the doors and kicked it open and followed the stairs.

Down he went into the grimly lit room, his breath from the cold fogged his view for a moment; the freezers were working overtime. He sat the tray of dirty glasses on an empty shelf, sighing with relief

that he didn't have to clean them, and found a fresh batch of glassware ready to go. On his way out he was mindful of the stairs, as they had gathered a thin layer of ice from some spilt water.

Vaughn finally made it back to the bar, Pete looked avidly relieved as the line for fresh orders had him beat. Vaughn's hands showed off, and the crowd dwindled. Dahl still sat front and center of the bar as Sancia had laid her head on the counter to get some rest.

Dahl had his back to her, his arms flailing wildly as he retold stories to those that were listening. Stories that sounded like movies he had seen, books he had read, stories that Vaughn only caught snippets of as the flail of his coat entranced him.

"It was my idea to study the times the security swapped shifts, O'seus thought it was pretty smart too, because of that it was easy to find a small hole in the schedule to slip out undetected and later, back in."

As he flailed, a white corner caught Vaughn's eye. Something poked out of the top of one of Dahl's jacket side-pockets. It didn't stay there for long; Vaughn found his hands had already taken it.

Vaughn was never sure how people lost things. At all times he was aware of what was in his pockets. If he lost a thin slip of paper from his pocket, he would immediately sense the loss of weight to his carriage and recover it.

Yet here he was taking an item from the pocket of a stranger, and he was none the wiser. Oblivious to their very person, Vaughn felt he could have slit a wound in their side with his corkscrew and they wouldn't notice the blood loss, if it weren't for the pain.

It's people like Dahl, Vaughn thought, people who lose things, who would have slipped on that icy step - people who aren't careful enough.

Vaughn gently fondled the envelope, sliding his finger under the open seal, hoping for something, anything. But it was empty. Vaughn turned over and saw on the back, scribbled in pen was an address and some numbers.

It meant nothing to Vaughn; he just thought it apt that Dahl would carry around an envelope as empty as his head.

As Dahl flailed yet again, so wildly, Vaughn leaned over the edge of the counter to slip the envelope back into its pocket.

Watching Sancia to see if her eyes would open as he reached, Vaughn found it staggeringly harder to return rather than to take. But soon Vaughn slipped the tough corner of the envelope between the opening of the pocket and with it, he pushed and slid the whole thing in-deep just as Dahl turned to order another round.

Vaughn continued his rounds, finding himself at the edge of the room, near all the booths. Madame Rose was a heavy smoker; she had kept the booth all to herself, but the smoke wasn't the deterrent. She carried with her the gloom of aging and that seemed to depress the crowd. Even the rose seemed to wilt a little faster around her. But Vaughn dealt with gloom all day, every day from the barflies at the Crowbar. He brought her over a glass of water and offered to put the rose in the glass; she blushed at the mention of it.

"Don't feel it necessary to accompany an old woman in pity. Besides, I'm waiting for someone. He should be here any moment."

"I wasn't going to." Vaughn answered.

"I suppose you can sit for a moment or two if you really wish."

Vaughn glared at her as he reluctantly sat. She didn't care to look at him; her eyes were on the door.

Vaughn occasionally glared at most of his customers, finding that crucial second when they look back at him to change his expression back to something more accommodating. If he were too slow, they would see the face of absolute evil glaring at them as they wasted his time with their long-winded and aimless stories. But with Madame Rose, Vaughn could glare all day long and she wouldn't notice.

This took the fun out of it.

"What's with the flower?" He chose to ask.

"It's for Lester." She leant forward and winked at Vaughn. "He's got one for me."

"Figured."

She scrunched up her face and lent back in her chair, checking the door. "But he's late."

"You two going to hook up? Get wild in the bathroom?" Vaughn tested the waters.

"Lester and I agreed to meet here with a flower each."

"Yeah, I got that."

"Where's Lester? He should be here by now." She got worried, and Vaughn worried himself that he might never leave that booth.

"Hey, maybe that's Lester over there?" Vaughn tried.

As she turned Vaughn slunk out of his chair and slipped into the crowd. As he left, he could hear her asking the next person she could grab by the sleeve if they had also seen Lester and if they wanted to sit with her.

Lester wasn't the only person in demand. Vaughn overheard a few people asking about Wyla, just as anxious as Vaughn for her return. As well as someone called O'seus. Many people were under the impression that this O'seus person was due at any moment.

Vaughn kept an eye out as he carried his empty tray back to the bar and tossed it with the others. A quick scan of the place had him feel dizzy. The design of the place, he could go round in a circle and feel like there was a never-ending line of guests badgering him for drinks just as there was a never-ending collection of empty glasses sprouting along the counter.

As Vaughn swept them up, he came to the empty seat of the man who had been playing with the water rings, Vaughn ached to wipe them up but paused to see that the water rings had taken a strange shape.

He twisted his neck, reading the streaks of water droplets upside down.

Limpfingers, it read.

Really? Vaughn shot a look around the Observatory, furiously looking for any familiar face. It pained him to try to remember which of the fifty to sixty people in the Observatory had been the one playing with water rings at his bar.

Which one of them fucking dared?

"Vaughn, my mouth is dry!" Jowls badgered him.

"So is my humor, but you don't hear me bragging." Vaughn growled through his teeth as he refilled Jowls glass. Jowls was quick to take his

drink and carry it off with his friend as they debated the correct barrels in which to store and use whisky. Scooting off their stools, they left their empty glasses on the counter, with white dribble swimming at the bottom.

Vaughn only had ten hours left. Ten hours until he had a big ol' paycheck coming his way, he could pay off his debts, if he so felt. He could take out his parents, if he so wanted. And he could leave and never come back, which was all he could think about.

He couldn't wait. He looked at Pete - his ticket out. Perhaps they could go on a road trip together, drive along the coast. Everything's cheaper when you split it.

It was all so perfect. He had almost forgotten about Jake, who he suspected was sneaking about tagging insensitivities on the floor with chalk.

He looked at Pete, who pulled a face back as he poured six glasses at once that he had lined up across the counter.

No, don't be stupid. You barely know the guy, Vaughn thought, what makes you think he would drop everything and travel so far just to hang out with you?

Vaughn slid Jowls' empty glasses together and with a finger in each one he carried them to the rack and stacked them with the others.

He noticed a scrap of newspaper he had been using as a coaster had stuck to the bottom. Vaughn peeled the newspaper clipping off the bottom, careful not to rip the wet paper before he could read it. He almost wished he hadn't.

Attention Time Traveler's, Voyagers and Trekkers.
Hello there Black Hole Divers, Deep Space
Swimmers and Celestial Portal Riders.
And Welcome Quantum Leapers, Chrono
Jumpers and Space Skippers.
If you find yourself without a country
or a time to which you belong,
If you are lost and need to rest,
If safe haven is what you're craving,

Then you will find that there's
always time at The Time Asylum,
A place for those that have no other.
May 10th -11th 1991
6:00pm til 6:00am
Mount Fracture Observatory
Open Bar.

If it wasn't written in ink, it would have been mental. If it weren't so strange it would have been funny. If it didn't answer so many questions Vaughn swore it could have been a prop from a play.

The answers fell into such easy places; it explained how he got to the Observatory and how he did so from tomorrow. It explained the strange stories, the clashing of fashions and the bizarre drink requests.

Almost kismet. Vaughn's head sprung up at the sound of her voice. She was back.

Vaughn stormed from the bar and found Wyla mid conversation. Without a second hesitation he grabbed Wyla by her strange sleeve and dragged her to the storage room where he slammed the door behind him and waited for a response.

"Tell me I'm dreaming again, I dare you." Vaughn growled.

"You're not dreaming." She answered, not even bothered. "You've just figured it out."

"Figured what…"

"Funny, isn't it? How irrationally logical the mind can be when facing the strange." Wyla nodded to the wrist where his watch had been. "When did it happen?"

"Just before I came here." Vaughn answered. "That's how I got here. You told me I was dreaming."

"When?"

"Before."

"You think we've met before?"

"I know we've met before. You're how I got here. You gave me a toy and told me I was dreaming."

"You said that already."

"Why did you say it then?"

"I don't know. Perhaps to make it all more palatable. Do you still have it?"

"Have what?"

"The cube?"

Vaughn mechanically reached for it and presented it to Wyla, who scooped it up, felt it for its weight, then pulled it back, keeping it.

"Hey that's mine!"

"You just said I gave it to you. Sounds like it was mine first."

She studied it, the way one would study a dead bird. She didn't want to look at it for too long, let alone hold it.

"Ok."

"Ok what? What does that toy have anything to do with it?"

"This is no toy. This ubiquitous cube is the reason you are here."

"I don't get it."

"Yes, you do."

"So that's a… Time Machine?"

The words sounded so stupid when said aloud. He simply stared at the simple thing in her hand; it was as if it became more and more precious the longer he looked at it.

"Trust me kid, no matter what it looked like it would be shocking. Rubik's cubes have forty-three quintillion combinations you know."

"I don't know."

"Didn't think so."

Vaughn found the corner of his finger in his mouth as he chewed at the skin. It was a little raw there from earlier that day. Wyla narrowed her eyes noticing and Vaughn whipped his fingers away from his teeth.

"Why did it stop working?"

"The cube?"

"My watch." Vaughn clarified.

"Machinery. Technology. Anything even slightly complex breaks down when jumping through time. If you want to get into it, it's truly interesting."

That wasn't really the question Vaughn was dying to ask.

"So how does it…?"

"No."

"What?"

"No. Something else. Ask something else. But you can't ask that. We don't want you taking this and running around through time when you're supposed to be here working for Mr. Crowe, now do we?"

"So, I'm not allowed to use it now, but you can use it on me?" Vaughn pointed to his cube he had handed over so eagerly. "Give it back!"

Wyla carelessly threw the cube back, and Vaughn was almost too surprised to catch it. He held it as though it were glass that could shatter.

"I thought you said I couldn't…"

"Without knowing how it works, it's just a glorified toy. Have fun." Wyla moved for the door when Vaughn stepped in front of her one last time.

"Should I be worried?"

"About what?"

"I've travelled through time. What if I've changed something?"

"You probably did." Wyla shrugged.

Wyla opened the storage room door and just before she left, she turned.

"Oh and don't tell Pete."

$$\diamond$$

Chapter Thirteen:
Arguments from Ignorance

Vaughn already knew there was something different between himself and everyone at the Asylum. Of course, the first thing that anyone would have pointed out was how diverse the guests all were. He had never seen so many different brown and black skin tones, not only all at once, but as a majority. Was there some sort of incentive to change and mess with the past that his skin color just didn't have?

Jake once had made the point that whenever you are surrounded by a group of alike people, you should notice and understand why. Jake certainly wasn't the only aboriginal in Fracture but in the Crowbar on a Friday night, he stood out and was smart enough to point out why.

Vaughn had noticed, but now he finally understood. It had nothing to do with his skin or theirs.

The party appeared to have dulled down now that Vaughn re-emerged from the storage room, with Wyla a few seconds ahead of him, as though the entire room were trying for an act of normality. It wasn't going to work. This room, it frustrated him, and Vaughn was well and truly shaken like a can of soda, ready to pop if someone pried at him even a little.

Vaughn stumbled to the counter and found Pete in a moment of quiet. The guests were all watered, and he had found a moment to himself. He swayed in the slow beat of the big band music that swelled in the silences like water filling a hole at the beach.

"Where were you?"

"Took a little break." Vaughn managed, somehow stifling the surge of word vomit that he expected to come first. He figured he needed a drink.

"Oh, man, that would be great. I'm going to take a quick break outside. Get some air." Pete said.

"Ok."

"You all right?"

Vaughn was not all right. He was grappling with the concept of time and space while trying to get liquid into a glass.

No, Wyla said it was fine.

She also said that he might have changed the past - or the future - simply by existing in the wrong place. It was enough to make his stomach gurgle.

"Yep. Tip-top."

Tip-top?

"Ok then. Call me if you need a hand."

Vaughn found his patented slouch over the bar granted him no comfort. He took the cube from his pocket and stared at it.

A glorified toy, he thought as he began twisting and turning it.

He had seen a kid at school play with one, impressing his friends that he could solve it. Vaughn never even had a go until now.

It was simple. Vaughn found that each side had a middle tile that couldn't change. And it wasn't a process of solving one side at a time; it was solving it from the top, down. Each time he wanted to move a tile somewhere without ruining his progress, he would have to rewind his moves to reset the pieces he had already solved.

All of this problem solving never moved up higher than his wrists. All his brain had to do was remember what he had seen before, and soon enough he had a finished cube in his hands.

Was that it? He thought.

Ready to drop it the second it started shaking or expanding or whatever the hell it was supposed to do, Vaughn held it steady.

Nothing.

He started mixing it up again. Assuming moving the pieces clockwise might send him to the future.

But again, nothing.

"It's out of juice."

Vaughn looked up to the man just a few seats down the bar that had been in a deep conversation but had been watching him closely.

"What?"

The man left his conversation and came to find Vaughn at his counter slouch. He wore a classic suit and great thick suspenders, which he toyed with under his thumbs.

"You can tell by the weight, and it rattles a little like an empty spray can. Each cube only gets you there and back again. Looks like this one's already been to both."

Vaughn looked to his cube, then back to Suspenders. "So, it's useless then?"

Suspenders sighed deeply and shrugged. "Unless you like puzzles." He turned and walked back to his seat.

Vaughn caught sight of Atticus now poking his head in between conversations, resting hands on numerous shoulders and persistently asking if they were having a nice time right after they had taken a sip of their drinks. He spotted Vaughn and what he had in his hands.

"Hand it over."

"Did you know about this?" Vaughn asked Atticus as he stormed over in shock. Vaughn took out the newspaper clipping of the invitation and held it up to Atticus' face. "Did you know when you sent this out? Did you know people would actually come or was this all supposed to be a joke?"

"I hoped." Atticus responded, as a wry grin crept over his face. "I figured it was the only sure-fire way to find out. Especially since…"

Atticus slipped the corner of an envelope from his inner jacket pocket. Vaughn caught a hint of an address to some newspaper company.

"…I haven't sent out the invitation yet."

Vaughn felt his words tingle down his back. The old man was pleased with himself, tucking the unmailed invitation back out of sight.

"Now give me that."

He snapped his fingers to the cube still in Vaughn's hand.

Vaughn shrugged and handed it over. It was useless anyway.

"What are you going to do with it?"

"It doesn't matter what I do with it. I don't need my staff skipping out on me."

"But I've got so many questions."

"You think I'm paying you to ask questions?"

Vaughn sighed as Atticus sauntered off, pocketing the cube and patting the pocket.

Vaughn, alone behind the bar, couldn't think of where he would even skip off too. Either so many places and times flashed through his mind at once that he couldn't get a handle on just one, or he was still stuck on Wyla's casual comment.

Besides, he couldn't skip out now, Pete was on break and people had sat up along the counter again. Having seen Vaughn with a cube, perhaps they weren't worried about him eavesdropping things he wasn't supposed to hear.

How dumb did Atticus think his bartenders were anyway? Did he think they would serve all night and not notice the existence of time travel on full display all around them?

Again, another example of someone seeing them as furniture; drink dispensers with nametags.

Fuck, it's gone crooked again.

"'scuse me. That bottle there looks nice and dark."

Vaughn looked to see a chunky man with chins to match his double vision. He was pointing to both a bottle of bourbon and a bottle of vodka.

"Another double?"

"No ice."

"Easy." Vaughn nodded. "And for you?" He asked the woman who followed and sat beside Double Bourbon, the one with the large purple vein across her forehead. Vaughn was worried it might burst.

"Another glass of white." Purple Vein held her empty glass up and refused to let it go as Vaughn refilled it.

"Can I ask you both some questions?" Vaughn tried.

"About what?"

"What do you mean about what? About fucking time travel! I want to know what I've changed and the consequences of it. Does it just affect me, or does some guy in Japan now get hit by a tidal wave? Has anyone tried going back and killing..."

"Whoa whoa easy there. Don't worry about that stuff."

"Why not?"

"Because you can't change anything. Didn't anyone tell you that?"

"But Wyla...?"

"Look, some people got it in their heads that because in movies and books that time travel means changing the past and altering the future. But logically is just doesn't make any sense."

"But why not?"

"Too many paradoxes. Illogical conclusions that can't explain your very existence. Chicken and the egg stuff."

"But sure even something slight can..."

"Do you think anything you're doing right now in your life is changing the world? Affecting the future? Do you think the smallest thing you do each day matters at all?"

Vaughn felt very small, very quickly. "Well, no..."

"Then why do you think a small thing in the past can change so much of the future? We're all just tourists to history. Do you think we'd be allowed to do it if it wasn't perfectly safe? You think they'd have sold cubes to just anyone if they knew even just one could do such damage?"

"Hang on. You can just buy these?"

The great purple vein started throbbing through her forehead as she explained that these cubes were as easy to buy on the street, like a phone or something called an Ogle.

Vaughn didn't know what an Ogle was and thought it strange that phones would be something people were regularly buying in the future. Vaughn always thought that phones came free when you bought a house, stuck to the wall or side table.

He had trouble catching back up, his head had kept nodding (his bartender politeness had seen to that), but he had gotten lost. He was thinking about futuristic phones with cords that didn't get tangled and could call other planets, so much so that he had missed how both Double Bourbon and Purple Vein had started bickering over the restrictions of China and Korea. Both argued the same point; that the western world had correctly welcomed the freedom for businesses to stock and sell cubes and that they were damn proud of their countries. That quickly became the most knowledgeable conversation he had ever caught snippets of.

"Besides, wouldn't you rather it in the hands of everyone than under the control of specialty government agencies? History belongs to everyone."

"So nothing's stopping you from changing the past and...?" Vaughn asked.

"Weren't you listening? You can't."

"So time travelling is ok? Safe, I mean." Vaughn asked, still worrying about grass he had bent out-of-place by walking up the hill over an hour ago.

"Perfectly safe, if you know what you're doing. It's the people who don't want you doing it you gotta look out for."

"What people? Who doesn't...?"

"Hold on a second, what do you think you're telling him?"

A few other guests waiting at the bar had overheard and Vaughn watched as one by one they gathered around the debate, adding their own flair of opinion. Garnished with distaste for the opposing side.

So many of them believed, as Purple Vein and Double Bourbon believed; that time was linear and solid like the counter they beat on as though it was evidence.

But there were a loud few, including Wyla, who stepped on these claims and used bigger words. Waved their hands a lot more and slammed them down to the counter as though they hoped it would crack to prove their point.

As Vaughn stepped back and away from the debate, serving guests one by one anticlockwise around the bar, he began noticing that each conversation was in fact just another argument.

Given the fact that most of the guests were strangers, Vaughn figured that'd make them politer to each other.

But instead they argued like crazy, and it didn't take much to get it started. They dug and prodded with smug questioning to determine what side of the coin they were on and once they knew, they went at it. Mouths open and ears shut.

Those that thought that time was unchangeable and solid found another that believed time was a spectrum of infinite worlds and timelines, all minutely different, thus in most cases appearing the same as the one that preceded it. And they all thought they had the piece of evidence to prove their case, just as they had the exact argument to disprove the evidence of the other.

"Look, I've been a lot of places, done a lot of time travelling and I've witnessed no changes, everything was always the same after I left."

"That's just you, you're one guy. What about all those people that claim to see wars stopped or elections going the other way?"

"Liars! Attention seekers with a bad story."

They found each other and argued like they were drawn to each other, like positive and negative magnets, and Vaughn felt like the bit of finger skin that gets caught between them when they snap suddenly together. So, he kept on moving. Round and round the bar.

He just wanted a simple answer.

When Pete came back inside the Observatory, breathing in cool air conditioning that wafted against his face, Vaughn sighed with relief. He tossed him back his apron and they smiled at the clock as it counted another hour towards their paychecks.

"So is there much work back home?" Vaughn asked. He wondered if he could get himself a cube and take Pete with him, all while keeping his promise of not telling him.

"Uh, yeah. Once you get it they work you like a dog."

"So, like a job?"

"Look, I'm happy if you to want to come stay with me after…"

Vaughn's stomach dropped. He had read too much into it. He thought, again, of Jake.

"Oh hey, no. It was dumb of me. I was just talking shit, you know?" Vaughn slapped his rag over his shoulder three times, never getting it right. It didn't hurt enough.

Pete's eyed widening; he looked just as distraught as Vaughn.

"No no." Pete stammered. "I was just going to say. Home for me is just as much as a dead end as here. I was going to say we should go somewhere new, somewhere different."

Smiling more than he wanted to show, Vaughn sucked in his cheeks and nodded as cool as he could.

"Yeah." He said. "Sounds even better. I'm down for that."

Vaughn and Pete nodded at each other. They kept doing that; they had been doing it all night. Like they were nodding at an understanding between them, both yearning for a hug that neither would initiate. If the other had even lent in, the other would buckle in a heartbeat.

But Vaughn nodded at Pete and scooped up a tray of drinks and stepped out from behind the bar into the Observatory.

Careful not to step on any chalk marks, Vaughn offered and relinquished drinks with ease. They were free, and so the guests barely acknowledged that their drink-carrying robot had a face and a nametag. And they didn't drop their conversations, so Vaughn caught more time travel debates.

Vaughn learned that each side of the debate had a name for themselves.

Those that believed you can't change the past, present or future were calling themselves Monos. Short for Monochronists that believed in Monochronism.

The others referred to themselves as Polys. Short for Polychronists that believed in Polychronism. Believing that time was vulnerable to change, and as Vaughn understood, at any moment one of them

could jump backwards in time and stop the person who called them that.

But, as Vaughn overheard, many from both sides had called themselves tourists, despite the offence is caused for some. Apparently, it was a derogative term that they didn't approve of. But to Vaughn this was exactly what they were.

He figured if he were to jump from one country to another, living freely for a few days before moving on, he would happily consider himself a tourist. And there was no discernable difference to how these Monos or Polys were living their lives; they were tourists.

Vaughn noticed Double Bourbon had cradled himself in a booth and had lined up empty glasses out of his elbow space so he could rest most of his weight on the table.

"You should take it easy. The night isn't even old enough to vote yet." Vaughn said, sliding his tray on the table, stacking the empties on it and sitting down beside him. "Can I ask you something, big fella?"

"Name's Moe."

"Moe, I wanna know Moe, why are you all here? Surely there are better places to go than Fracture? Better things to see, better drinks. Most of you don't even get along."

"It's not about getting along. We get along fine in the grand scheme of things. And to tell you the truth, there isn't much to see, few places to go really. You think history is so big and long, but when they can track you by your face, it gets real small real quick. There's no place they can't find you."

Vaughn lent in. "Who's looking for you?"

Moe lent in just the same and whispered. "Them. Historians. They don't like us and they... yeah. They really don't like us. That's why most of us are here. No place left to go. At least here we know we have twelve safe hours where we can rest. Twelve hours to relax. Because they're going to come. They will be here when the time is up. And you'll see everybody scatter and run. But not me."

Moe lent back in his booth, the leather squeaking. His double chins and bourbon breath painting the rest of the pretty picture. He wrapped

his hand around something in his jacket pocket and mumbled again to himself as he took the last full glass of beer off Vaughn's tray.

"But not me."

Dahl and Sancia had moved from booth to bar over and over depending on the crowd. Dahl didn't mind them, puffing out his shallow chest and boasting like the rest of them, but Sancia sunk in numbers and as soon as Dahl noticed he would grab her hand and move again.

She would cling to his oversized jacket and go with him wherever he led.

This led them back to the bar as Vaughn returned from his rounds.

"Looks like you're burning both candles." Dahl said nodding to Vaughn, wiping his forehead despite the cool breeze that kept rolling by in this closed off Observatory.

"It's tough work."

Vaughn served Sancia another glass of water and Dahl reached for the bowl of toothpicks, slowly adding to his tower from before.

"So Dahl, where's your actual family?"

"What do you mean?"

"You said before you needed a new family. What happened to them?"

"I don't know."

"You don't know?"

"Marcie didn't like it." Dahl began. "I think we ruined Thanksgiving fighting about it. She said she didn't want to be with someone as stup… someone who didn't understand time travel like she did."

"So what did you do?"

"I left." Dahl said bluntly. "I left her with the boys and the leftover turkey."

Dahl picked up on Vaughn's judging look and he slipped his glass forward for Vaughn to fill.

"You're judging me aren't you."

"Should I?" Vaughn said. "I don't give a crap, personally, that you left her. It happens. But it's how you just said it. Like you don't think it was a bad thing."

"Oh, I felt bad." Dahl nodded. "Broke my heart to go, I felt awful. Until I didn't. When birds fall you know."

"No, I don't know."

"Once I left, and I found out the truth about the world, about fate and destiny. That we have no choice in it, and how that's a beautiful thing. Why should I feel bad about that? And things like time travel just makes sense to me now. If you want to make sense of it all too, just ignore what they're all arguing about. They haven't seen what I've seen. If you listen to me, you can turn over a new table and today will be the next day of the rest of your life."

Positively baffled Vaughn left Dahl nodding like they had an understanding, but all Vaughn understood was that Dahl maybe knew less about than anybody else.

Pete called out to Vaughn for more strange cocktails, and Vaughn heaved a sigh and got to it. Pete watched over his shoulder to learn, so Vaughn slowed down to demonstrate.

He figured Pete had come from Coober Pedy or somewhere around there. Out there, Pete might have only been trained to pull the lever and hold a glass under it. For the first time Vaughn considered himself slightly lucky to live in Fracture, to have worked for Baz.

"There, it's simple." Vaughn nodded to Pete. "I think you've got it from here."

Pete smiled and took over. It was just a margarita. Those that were just arriving seemed to ache for them to combat the heat from outside with several of them.

As Vaughn watched Pete roll glasses in salt, he wondered how much Pete had picked up from the guests, if he had figured out that some he was serving might not have been born yet.

Wyla had told him not to tell Pete, as she believed time could be changed, perhaps she saw it best that he and Pete knew as little as possible.

She seemed upset that Vaughn had figured it out, and Atticus was keeping an eye on him to make sure Vaughn didn't touch another cube. He could feel it, he caught it at times, and he hated being micromanaged. Was it so bad that he knew? What could be the danger?

Vaughn lent over the counter, watching the guests while Dahl still sat opposite him. He looked through him like he did his regular barflies down at the Crowbar. Occasionally regretting initiating conversation by thinking out loud and forgetting who was going to answer.

"Why don't Historians…"

"No no no no no." Dahl quickly pressed. "Shhhhhhh."

But he was too late. The eyes of two guests behind Dahl went wide. They whispered to each other, nodded and agreed to leave. Luckily Vaughn saw Atticus catch them with his arms wrapped over their shoulders and he persuaded them to stay.

"Are you trying to scare everyone?" Dahl asked. "A good thumb rule is to not say that word out loud unless you wanna scare the pants off everyone."

"Why?"

"Because we're here to get away from them."

"Are they not allowed in or something? How would we know…?"

"Oh, you'll know."

"So why do you call them Historians?" Vaughn whispered.

"We didn't."

Wyla lent in and sat beside Sancia, who lent more towards Dahl to avoid getting some of Wyla's rogue strands of curly hair in her face.

"They named themselves. When the cubes were released, they took onus of history like it was theirs and we had no right to it. They said history was a privilege, not a right. They act like they have this inherent need to save everyone; but they have it confused for their need to be in control."

"I don't get this." Vaughn stated. "I don't get how with all your futuristic knowledge you can invent time travel but not know how it works. How can you play a game when you don't know the rules?"

"First." Wyla started, seeing Dahl's tower of toothpicks still taking up counter space and deciding to start a project of her own. "Just because some people are born in the future doesn't mean they are any smarter than those who came before them. Every day people seem to wake up and decide they want to spend their days debating well-known facts and arguing with experts to make themselves feel better. There will always be those that don't trust what they don't understand.

But second, time travel is subjective. It's not something we know how to prove. You can't take a step back from it all and see it from everyone's point of view, only your own. Take color, for example."

"Color?"

"Perhaps the optics and retina of your eye makes you see and receive the information uniquely when it comes to color. Consider that maybe everyone sees the color blue differently to you, that some people see blue as green and others, yellow. We are taught the sky is blue, but that is just what you or I give the name to the color we see. It's perfectly logical that everyone has a different favorite color, but perhaps it is the same color, but we don't know if we all agree. How could we? We'd have to see it through each other's eyes."

"Huh."

"Objective perspective, that's all I'm saying. For anything more than that, all we can do is speculate." Wyla's toothpick tower was less than a tower and more of a strange square, and she was assembling it with her eyes on Vaughn. "It all comes down to belief, but that doesn't stop people from acting like it's a fact."

"So when you said you think time can change…?" Vaughn asked.

"I'm saying that because I understand the science of multiple dimensions and it is within my expert opinion." Wyla held out her toothpick construction, no tape, no glue. Just overlapping toothpicks. She collapsed it and expanded it like an accordion, from a 2D square into a prism. Dahl's jaw dropped and Wyla smiled. "My carefully drawn conclusions and a gut feeling."

Wyla pushed it away for the others to play with and nodded to Vaughn for a new drink.

"My parents brought me up wanting me to be a loving mother and a good wife. But I wanted to be a physicist. I guess that was the first time I learnt I could change my fate."

"So naturally you're a Polychrono...whatever?"

"Yes, I am a Polychronist, though I wish that these terms didn't have to exist, and we could just call ourselves 'normal.' The multiverse has been a scientific speculation for a long time. When the cubes were announced so many of us stepped forward and spoke about it, claiming and giving evidence of split timelines and that is the only rational explanation of how it works. But then you have people who, just because they didn't get the math, couldn't follow the big words, they didn't like how it made them feel. They felt talked down to, belittled and when that happens, they decided they wanted to do the same to us. They made it 'simple' and POOF! Monochronism was born.

"Sounds frustrating."

"It was. We had written articles, toured talks and lectures leading up to New Year's Day. You hire a mechanic to fix your car, right? You'd get a doctor to remove your appendix. So why was this suddenly up for debate and not left to the experts?

Convenience. No one cares how an appendectomy works, they just want it out.

Worst of all are the people that believe in Monochronism or whatever else. They are always the same people, the under-educated, anti-establishment sort. They have middle-class jobs, regularly get stooped by the government or have a history of being contradictory. They've got a chip on their shoulder, have been wronged by authority and lost their trust. The people that get real spiritual, buy lots of candles, read star signs, start their own podcasts or write their own blogs on topics they haven't ever studied. They ask big questions and find simple, little answers that fit on a fortune cookie or bumper sticker. But that's just not how the world works."

"So when you gave lectures and stuff, why didn't the people you convinced spread and tell their friends and..."

"Oh, nobody changed their minds. Not one."

"Huh? Why not?"

"Once someone makes up their mind, they only look for evidence to support them or refute others. It's hard to pop that bubble. But worse than that, people hate to look stupid. Admitting something they believe - something they've fallen for, is wrong? That's harder to do than swallow it."

"What about you then?"

"I... guess that's true for me too. The one hypocrisy I'll happily live with."

The guests were getting restless. Someone found the Sound system and switched it to the radio. Tuning in to what they referred to as classic hits. They all cheered and sang and dance along.

It was getting too loud for Vaughn, and he had been itching for a smoke. He told Pete he was taking another break and Pete either nodded or didn't hear him over the crowd busting out 'classic' lyrics.

Vaughn pushed through the crowd, waving off orders and pointing them to the bar as he headed for the door. He kept hearing more raging arguments dissolving into exhaustion as they grew more intoxicated, and the words they wanted to argue were harder and harder to articulate.

The vestibule opened up and a thick ceiling of smoke hung above him. Outside were a few silent tourists, enjoying the peace that fresh air offered. Vaughn noticed that they were careful not to step too far from the entrance, and he wondered whether the protection of the Asylum only covered the inside of the Observatory.

The smell of coal returned to Vaughn's nostrils just as fast as the heat ripped sweat from his pores. He immediately missed the air conditioning and sealed off windows of the Observatory.

One man had dared to venture out further, standing near the railing and watching the night sky through the clouds of green smoke he exhaled. Vaughn walked up to him and stood beside him, leaving enough courtesy space between them.

The man was dressed in an all-grey suit, and his face was almost totally concealed with the green smoke from his cigarette. He was feigning to feed the little white birds that had gathered around him, and they were falling for it.

"You smoke?" The smoking man asked.

"Usually." Vaughn answered, recalling the last pack he had thrown to the ground moments before he was whisked away from the alley behind the Crowbar.

"It's a nasty habit."

"One of my many. Can I bum one?"

He acted like he didn't even hear him. The smoking man was unsettling, and it was strange how slimly the man seemed despite how smooth and dry he was. His suit looked like it was once nice wool but had been washed so many times it now rubbed like carpet.

As he lifted his hand to his mouth Vaughn saw his arms were lanky and elongated, his elbows bent way lower down than he expected.

"So I hear you just found out our dirty secret."

"That's right." Vaughn said uncomfortably.

"And what do you think?"

"I'm…not sure yet. I still don't understand why there isn't a solid simple answer."

"People are complicated. And their beliefs, however irrational, are more so. I wish more of them realized their responsibility."

"What responsibility?"

"You should be responsible for your beliefs, they're not just for believing in."

"Responsible how?"

"You smoke." Smokey said.

"So do you." Vaughn retorted.

"And I am responsible for what happens to me." Smokey took a long puff from the cigarette he held between his long pointy fingers. "Think on it when you make up your mind."

"You got it Smokey."

Smokey laughed. "So that's how."

The cigarette that clung to his lip almost toppled into his mouth. Not that Vaughn could really tell, his face was impossibly shrouded by smoke only revealing one section of his face at a time, like puzzle pieces. If he had them all he could piece it all together but for some reason Vaughn struggled to arrange this puzzle in his mind.

Vaughn left Smokey by himself, if he wasn't going to bum him a smoke and only talk in riddles, then good luck to him.

The low hum of the party was suddenly louder when he went back inside, like he had popped his ears after altitude. Inside the Asylum the crowd was joyous, too preoccupied with their stories and drinks to even move out of Vaughn's way.

Fuck, what do I believe? Vaughn thought. Time traveling cubes, Historians, Monos, Polys? It was all so much and yet he had no clue what to make of it.

He wanted to ask Wyla some more questions. But she was hard to find. The Asylum had filled up generously - there was barely any room to move.

As he weaved through the crowd it was impossible to judge a path. They were all riotously dancing and dodging chalk marks, suddenly jutting out of place and slamming into Vaughn.

They were having a grand old time and Vaughn had to squeeze through it until he found an opening.

The Observatory had left a little area open in the far west side where the youthful group had first gathered to start their little game of chalk and cheering.

Vaughn saw one of them place a cube on the ground and leave it there. It was Dahl, he had joined in the fun and in his daftness, he had plainly left a cube on the floor.

He just left it there.

Maybe this was it. Vaughn thought. If he were to just get a hold of one, maybe he could use it. Figure out for himself what exactly was going on.

He wasn't sure where he would go, or even how to use it, but he figured he could copy the next person he sees.

Taking his shot, Vaughn wondered inconspicuously over to the cube and helped himself to it. Bending his knees but not his torso he scooped it up.

He felt immediately it was heavier than the other cube he had held, and it felt like it was pulling him down.

He raised it to his chest and looked at it.

It was starting to vibrate, it buzzed and hummed and before Vaughn could even tip his head in confusion it swallowed him up whole and he was gone.*

"Oh dam!" Dahl said as he turned to see him go. The youthful group went quiet, looking at each other, sobering up in shock.

"Did he just...?" One hushed.

"Well, he'll be back in real soon." Dahl shrugged. "Time heals all wounds when you're having fun."

---

*Go to Page 248

Chapter Fourteen:
Trust No One

Pete had taken a momentary break in the bathroom. He had taken a stall, and despite the dankness of a unisex toilet, he was enjoying the privacy. Though he tightened up when he heard someone in the neighboring stall. He wondered if they had been there the whole time. Pete calmed to a point. His pants at his ankles had him in a more vulnerable position than he was comfortable with.

"Don't mind me, just doing what I've got to do." Said the stranger, as though he knew of Pete's concern.

"Feel free." Pete stammered back.

"How lucky you are to find yourself at the Asylum. You must feel lucky. I bet lots of boys like you wish they could be here. But they're not as lucky as you, are they?"

Pete's knees felt weak. He wanted to get up and wipe, but he knew his legs would shake and collapse if he did.

"I just hope tonight goes well, that everything goes according to Mr. Crowe's plan. We owe our lives to him; he is our savior in every way. I hope everything turns out... as it should. Enjoy the rest of your night."

Pete heard the toilet flush and the man walk out of his stall. He could only see dark movements through the cracks of the man, washing his hands calmly and re-entering the party. Pete was alone again in the bathroom.

He chanced to stand up and left his stall to stand at the basin. He ran the water and watched it go down the drain.

He could only hear himself breathing. Out and out, but rarely back in. Vaughn prayed he hadn't gotten stuck in a wall or a tree or worse… another person. He prayed he landed somewhere with ground to stand on. He figured there was as much chance of volcanic lava or ocean beneath his feet as there was ground.

But Vaughn only fell a simple three feet to soft and crunchy grass. His entire body stiffened, and he landed with a thud against the side of the mammoth white dome at the top of the mountain.

Again he pushed through the doors to the Observatory. Again, he waved off any commotion and drink orders. Again, he endured threats from Atticus to throw him out if he took a break without permission.

Again it all didn't matter, as it shouldn't have had the first time.

He was there for Pete; he was there looking for his friend.

He shot a look to the clock - it was just after 10:15, plenty of time.

Vaughn looked for himself. Again, he was nowhere in sight. His only bit of luck so far.

Pete, however, was standing idly behind the counter, nodding and smiling to the guests. He hadn't yet taken a shard of glass to the throat. Far from it. They had only just become friends.

Vaughn did the math quickly in his head and figured he had known and thought about Pete for ten times longer than Pete had Vaughn.

"Hey buddy." Vaughn appeared exhausted and wishing to collapse, but that couldn't take the smile from his face. He was finally going to do it; he was going to save his friend.

"Hey!" Pete said. Only Pete could say it like that, Vaughn thought, classic Pete. Perhaps he was delirious.

"Can we… let's, let's get out of here, huh?"

"What are you talking about?" Pete raised a brow and narrowed one of his owl-like eyes.

"Let's go, I mean it." Vaughn stamped. "Fuck this place, fuck Atticus. Let's go get a drink ourselves. Let's get out of these dirty clothes, eat

something. Fuck, I'm hungry. Let's go back to my place and kick back and relax."

"You don't think we're a bit too busy." Pete at this point turned and faced the guests to refill glasses. "We've got time."

Vaughn found it hard not to bite through his lip. *Should I just tell him?* He thought. *Pete dude, you're gonna fucking die!* Vaughn held back, only biting halfway through; and the metallic taste of his blood was the first thing he eaten had in a long time.

"Pete." Vaughn said through his teeth and bleeding lips. "We're friends, right?"

"Yeah. I think so." Pete smiled a bit too big.

"So, as a friend, could you do me this favor and leave with me?"

It might have done the trick, but Vaughn grabbed Pete's arm and spoiled it. Pete pulled back, felt Vaughn's grip and wrapped his hand over Vaughn's arm, the hand with the finger nub that Vaughn detested. But Vaughn was unfazed. At least it was the right finger that was missing.

Pete yanked back, Vaughn didn't let go.

Now Pete's smile had faded. He looked at Vaughn with fear, a fear familiar to Vaughn. He had seen that look before. He had recognized it in Jake, and now it was in Pete.

Vaughn let go and Pete pulled it back and held it at his side, as though Vaughn would snatch for it again.

It was a moment Vaughn wished hadn't happened, but more than that, he wished it hadn't of happened in front of all those people.

They weren't forgiving of it, jokes and snide comments split the two of them up and Pete rounded the bar until he was out of Vaughn's sight.

Vaughn straight up ignored the guests and kept looking to Pete, wondering where he could go from here. Should he chase after him, grab him, and drag him out of there kicking and screaming?

He didn't know if he could take another look from Pete like that. It felt like he had kicked a puppy.

He slumped and lowered his chin to the counter. The heavy drinking crowd soon came to the realization that they couldn't just push their empty glasses into Vaughn's face to get served.

"I get it now, Dahl."

"Get what?" Dahl asked, puzzled.

"Fate. I hate it, but what can you do, you know?"

Dahl nodded and cheered to a sentiment he didn't quite grasp. Vaughn figured there was no convincing Pete. Perhaps Fate worked with infinity. He was doomed to watch Pete bleed out and disappear just as he was doomed to never truly leave Fracture.

Dahl moved down the counter even closer to Vaughn.

"I find it helps, when I'm overwhelmed by everything that's going on, it helps me to think about how I'm not in control. I'm in the car and I'm not driving. It makes everything easier. It's enough to make sure you don't get scared of nothing. Even Historians."

Dahl said with a whisper and a wink. But Vaughn's eyes went wide as the very word made the man sitting a few stools down uncomfortable. He shifted in his seat.

What was it they yelled again? Vaughn tried to remember. What did they yell when they learnt the Historian had escaped?

Strap him up by the suspenders. Yes, that was it.

The man in the suspenders had settled into his glass. He was the man that had only spoken a little to Vaughn before, keeping to himself mostly.

They had said if he were to see a Historian, he would know it.

Well, Vaughn knew it. He knew the timing of the Historian's looming escape and he knew the instant of Pete's seemingly unavoidable accident. Both events, barely moments apart. It couldn't be a coincidence, could it?

Vaughn gritted his teeth hard and hoisted himself back to his full stature, eyes never leaving the man in the suspenders still minding his own business.

"Dahl."

"Yeah?"

"Obviously with all the time travel going on and such, you can understand that when I say I know something about someone without it having happened, you can just take my word for it. Right?"

"Can't see why not?" Dahl said plainly, as though thought didn't pass through him as much as around it circled him.

"Good. Ok." Vaughn lent forward, elbows digging into the countertop, and he leaned to Dahl's ear, close enough to smell the leather of his jacket. He pointed with a stiff finger down the bar towards Suspenders. "That guy there. Historian."

Suspenders' neck whipped back as a firm hand shoved his back toward the counter and then for a second collected his flailing head and smacked it down on the wooden bar. The big man, Moe, had snapped himself sober and the entire place shuddered at the sound of him crackling the cartilage in Suspenders' nose.

"What are you doing?" Suspenders cried out, spitting out the blood that ran into his nose.

Wyla stayed put, finishing the last few drops of her drink as Moe tried to push Suspender's body through the wooden counter.

"Tell us everything first, you Historian asshole!" Moe growled.

The Asylum panicked, many rushed for the exit and others followed to lock it after them. People fumbled for cubes, either to use them or to hide them deep in their pockets.

"Take the hat off and you think you can be one of us huh?"

"I'm not what you think I am!" Suspenders yelled through his contorted blood-smacked lips.

"And what do we think you are?" Wyla asked.

There was a lengthy pause during which all the guests could hear was the slow cracking of his nose as he spoke.

"A Historian." Suspenders sighed.

"He admits it!"

"Tie him up!"

"Kick him out!"

"Kill him before he kills us!"

"Please!" Suspenders pled. "My name is Crandall. I'm just a guy. I'm not a Historian, I'm not anything!"

Everyone looked to Wyla, who seemed reluctant to come to the same speedy judgement as everyone else.

"Well, he doesn't look like one of them." She thought aloud. "And even if he was one there's no rule banning them completely, just the ones hunting us down during."

"Don't give him a chance!"

"You know the rules; we are not safe outside our time zone. He was going to wait out the asylum then…"

"Then what? Take us all on, fifty to one?" Wyla dared.

"We've got to do something! He knows too much already."

"What he knows." Wyla started. "He already knew. He could have told others before he got here."

"I say we end him." Moe offered, grinding his teeth. "There's the cliff outside he could be accidentally thrown over."

"Hey come on!" Crandall sputtered. "I'm not here to hurt anyone! I was just trying to get away! I had to go somewhere!"

"What were you running from?"

"The Incident." Crandall said simply. "No one could survive it. We all had to run. Not just you. I was in London when I heard the rumble. We thought it was an earthquake, I wish it was. But earthquakes don't look like that. When it happened and you Monos and Polys found out first, the rest of us weren't the first to be rescued. No, I had to watch as the roads and sidewalks quickly flooded. I had to rush myself to as high a ground as I could find before I was rescued.

Then after what he did, what Stein did, now it's not safe anywhere. This is all that's left, this party, the last safe moment in all of history. Damn right I wanted to use it!"

His words had commanded a silence, snapping the fiery tongues of those who still judged him by his beliefs, cold and still.

"Killing you would be jumping ahead of schedule." Wyla finally spoke. Crandall lost all use of his knees, sinking to the floor. Wyla

turned to her crowd. Especially the ones ready to burn him at the stake. "Look, I hate them as much as you do. But I have to admit, not all Alterchronists are Historians."

"All Historians are Alterchronists." Someone countered.

"We need to be sure."

"We lock him up then." Atticus offered. "That storage room has a lock on the outside. No way in or out. It seals up tight."

"All right." Wyla agreed. "Until we know what to do with him."

Moe and Dahl took Crandall by his shoulders, Moe doing most of the lifting.

"Fine. Ok, I'm going." Crandall said and stopped struggling. They didn't let up, Dahl and Moe held on tight, dragging him across the red carpet of the Observatory.

Just as they got him near the door Wyla's eyes widened. "Wait!"

She jogged over and caught up.

"One more thing" Wyla shoved Crandall up against the door, reached into his pockets. Crandall rolled his eyes and sighed. Wyla pulled three cubes from his jacket and one more from a sack tied around his ankle. Crandall seemed impressed she even found it.

"Ok, now you can lock him up."

The storage room had been cleared almost bare, leaving more of a cold tiled floor, small windows, a few spare chairs and the TV cart. Crandall walked himself inside, looking around before turning to face his captors as they slid the door closed.

"This is pointless Wyla." Moe barked. "We should stick him with sharp things until he tells us everything he knows so we can at least be prepared."

"Does no one else remember what they did to us?" Wyla asked the group. "What they did to us just for travelling at all?"

"Wyla, that's why we have to make him pay, *because* of what they did."

"No." She said firmly. "It's because of what they did that we don't. We'll let him sweat a little."

They all hung their heads, disappointed for many reasons.

"We're not *them*." Wyla finished.

Vaughn was as mad as the rest of them. Behind that door was the Historian he was sure would find a way to escape and murder Pete. He was sure of it.

The simple chilling thought of it had everyone on edge, some so close to it they took to sculling their drinks and heading out.

In classic Atticus form, he made sure to catch every guest, offering them words to calm them down. He was a master at it. Most stayed after their talk. But they were solemn; not drinking, not talking. They huddled in corners, pulled back the large red curtains and kept their eyes on the vestibule doors.

Talk of an Historian invasion had sparked some debates over belief as there were before, but a new topic had arisen, talk of *The Incident*.

Vaughn had gotten wind of it before, but never in detail. The more he learnt, the worse it made him feel. Gradually piecing together, the horrifying conclusion that it was the very thing he had run all those years from now and all that time ago.

Merely recalling the rumbling he had felt, made him shake with chills. It was like the feeling of sticking your hand in a deep and mysterious hole and pulling it out just before the monster bites it, but all over his body.

Just like everything else, everyone had an opinion. Seeing as no one could survive it long enough to know what it was, guesses were as good as fact.

"Can we all settle and agree on one thing at least?"

"Which is?"

"That *the Incident* happened because someone travelled through time and interacted with themselves."

It was a quick and silent consensus. No one denied it, least of all Wyla.

"Agreed."

Janet was trying to demonstrate her thoughts before the big vein in her forehead gave her too much grief. Vaughn recognized that she had so often critiqued the others all evening that now it was time for her thoughts to be judged.

Janet was not going to be made fun of. She reached down the counter for the bowl of cashews that everyone had been treating as decoration, chose a few, and laid them out on the counter. She held up one in front of them all.

"Say this nut, this one very special and unique nut, had a problem in his past that he wanted to fix. He also had an idea. He went back and told his past self that he would step in and save the day for him. Or better yet, he knocked himself out cold and took his place without permission. The same outcome would still happen." Janet stated.

She placed the special nut down with the others, all eyes still tracking it. "And this would still lead to him getting his hands on another cube and going back to try again in a different way, each time adding another and another version of himself to the mix, knocking out the last and trying again." Janet added more nuts, one after the other, to the first two. "All trying to solve an unsolvable problem. For us this would all appear to happen so fast you wouldn't even see the process, but just a wave of them all coming at once."

Most nodded, it was simple enough, and that's what they needed. But Wyla stepped between them all, concentrating her attention on the pile of nuts still in the bowl. It was her turn to hypothesize.

"Now I agree with you that he originally went back to his own past, but as we Polychronists know that the tangents of decisions can only splice a timeline once and not twice. He had already existed in his future. Going back and possibly messing so directly with his past, though as possible as it seems, it can alter the predetermined future. As it were, the future is predetermined, it has already been written. It is the past that isn't set in stone."

Wyla signaled with a click for those to her left and right of the bar to pass up the closest bowls of nuts.

"My theory is that his monumental decision to affect his own past, for whatever reason you want to dream up, caused a collapse in the integrity of the thin membrane that holds each parallel timeline apart. Thus, every version of himself from other timelines poured out at once."

Wyla then proudly poured out the contents of both nut bowls all over the small pile of nuts, drowning the original two nuts and making a damn mess all over Vaughn's bar.

"Was the demonstration necessary?" Vaughn groaned.

"Very." She winked.

Both sides were debating for the same facts, Vaughn found it strange. They agreed on nearly all the circumstances, yet when it came to the end of their argument, they twisted it to support their time travel beliefs.

Vaughn was totally lost. He was caught looking back and forth between everyone's various points as they all handled and spoke of the cashews as though they were people.

To Vaughn, they were all nuts.

"What do you have to say about those that swear they have already gone to visit their past or future self with no consequences at all?" One man argued. "Your entire argument is ruined."

"I can't speak to stories like that." Wyla laughed it off. "But if you want to take one of the tests of time travel, by all means."

Wyla and others put their differences aside to squash this moron.

"I say to you, not anyone else, go ahead and try it yourself." Wyla said. "But for me, personally, I would never dare even step a toe into the same time as I will be or have already been. I wouldn't dare."

"But what if it was like this?"

Another argument started the second there was silence to put it in. This guest slid all the nuts out of the way and hoisted a tray of clean glasses onto the counter. They waved all sorts of nonsense and piled up the glassware into a pyramid like tower, symbolizing the fragility of time with the theatrics of Jenga.

But it made Vaughn wonder.

All this talk of doubles and triples, rips through space-time and the very fabric of being. It was enough to make him sick, though he hadn't much left to bring up.

But it wasn't the thought of running from such a seismic event, but now the very idea of being ground zero.

He had seen this glass tower before, he had been there when it came falling down. He had swept up the shards.

In fact, the memory was playing back again in his mind like an old rerun. Every time they removed a glass to prove a point, Vaughn's leg gave way and he almost screamed.

He had to stop doing this. Jumping around through time. He hadn't meant to overstay his welcome and he certainly didn't mean to flatten all of existence with his mere presence.

He had to get out. He had to do it quick, and he couldn't just go back another two hours or forward four or six. He had to get away. To after all of this. He figured once the Asylum was over and the sun was up, he could just go home and lie down until his anxiety let him sleep.

Backing away, out from behind the bar and between the crowd of uneasy guests, Vaughn fumbled with his cube. This one still had one trip left, and he was going by the logic that moving tiles clockwise meant forward in time. A good as guess as any.

How many tiles, who's to say? But every time that reckless tourist removed a glass to prove a point, Vaughn sped up his guesswork.

It started to vibrate, and he held it tight. A soft wind swept the floor clean as he jumped through the tangent.*

---

*Go to Page 562

Part Two:
GREEN

Chapter Fifteen:
The Bet

Wet grass that grew along the edge of the cliff lifted in the breeze as a pair of bare feet fell a short distance, landing and crushing the grass back down.

He staggered and collapsed on his back, panting heavily. Vaughn had to consciously slow his breathing, after his panicked gasps started to dry his throat. He struggled to breathe in through his nose and held his breath before breaking and exhaling. The grass was prickling up his thighs where his pajama shorts didn't cover, and it itched. Once he calmed down, he sat up and immediately kicked himself away from the edge of the cliff like it was a rabid animal snapping at his toes.

"Well, fuck me."

Vaughn saw that the cliff's edge he had landed on was not the higher of the two, but the lower. He stood and judged the distance; above him on the other side, the cliff edge was sticking out like a tongue from the massive, glowing Observatory behind it. It towered over him, and he sighed. He had never been on this side before, he never thought he ever would be either. He picked up the cube that had brought him here and squeezed it, trying to crush it. It wasn't heavy anymore. The cube fell from Vaughn's hand, and he had to flap his arms to keep himself from following after it

Vaughn stepped carefully down the rough terrain with his bare feet. Despite the rough padding the years of barefoot walking had given him, he still felt every stone or stick hiding amongst the grass.

Vaughn knew he had time travelled before, but he had just done it with some awareness for the first time and he wondered if he should have felt... something.

Like maybe the wind would taste different. Maybe the sky should be full of flying cars. He listened for a roar of a dinosaur or gunshots of an old war.

Nothing.

He just smelt coal and dripped with heat.

As he moved through the trees, he could see the town below a little better. The same buildings, the same flickering lights.

How far through time had he gone?

He felt fine. He figured that time travelling was more of a threat to his mental condition than to him physically. All he could think about every time he took a step and broke a twig were the consequences.

He didn't know what he believed. He wished he could believe what the Monos had said. That would make it so easy.

Then he could burn this entire mountain down, and it wouldn't change a thing.

Of course, that meant that it destined him to be a bush burner. He didn't like that.

But he also didn't like the idea that he was in an alternate reality. A parallel world created by his very act of grabbing that cube.

That's why he sniffed the air, wondering if it smelt new or different.

It sure looked the same, felt the same.

As he walked to the bottom, he wondered what he believed without thinking about it. Though, it was hard shutting thoughts out.

What was it that Smokey had said? Be responsible for your beliefs?

Vaughn thought about when he was in school, and he first discovered that there was a religious kid in his class, believed in a man in the sky. This made him laugh, and then it made him annoyed that the kid didn't let up.

Almost nobody was religious these days. They even learnt about it in History class, how they discovered all those tablets and scrolls a

few hundred years ago that pointed out all the inconsistencies that tore apart every Holy text.

Vaughn argued with him. It was ridiculous. He remembered everyone joined in, but he was the one sent home for bullying.

Vaughn's mother had told him off for being inconsiderate and Vaughn couldn't understand.

"I just said he was wrong mum." He had moaned. "When I get math questions wrong, I don't get upset."

"That's not why he got upset." His mum had told him. "Belief is different."

Vaughn's mum told him that people's beliefs tell them who they are. If you take it away from them, they don't know who they are. It's part of them.

"You're not saying what they believe is wrong, you are saying who they are is wrong." She had said. "There's a big difference."

He walked on. The steady walk down took at least twenty-five minutes longer without shoes. The climb back up took even longer as the path was wound around the mountain. He was worried Atticus would fire him for being gone for so long.

But it wasn't his fault. What kind of moron leaves an active cube just lying around?

As he came to the bottom, some thirty minutes later Vaughn sighed and smacked his mouth for water. He wished he hadn't drunk so much already. It dehydrated him and any saliva he found rolling around in his gums tasted awful and he put a hand against a road sign and as he lent spat into the dirt.

He looked at both the road up the mountain and the road leading into town. He knew where it led; the Crowbar wasn't far, his house a little further.

It felt so welcoming, almost asking him to shrug the night off and go home.

Vaughn knew what was on the sign he had lent on, the great big sign for the Mount Fracture Observatory in big black letters.

He took his hand off it and as he wiped his soot-covered hand on his apron, he caught a glint of yellow in the corner of his eye.

Someone had spray painted over the sign. Yellow spray paint.

It wasn't someone's street name that they had practiced in an exercise book during class. It wasn't a giant cock and balls, nor was it some non-conformist protest like 'fuck the whales'. It simply said in big, wet, yellow letters:

Limpfingers.

There it was again. Vaughn hadn't thought about it for months, years even. Yet today, or more accurately the last twenty-four hours he had come across it four fucking times.

Here it was, on the Observatory sign, and for whatever reason, he felt compelled. Like it meant something, like someone was prodding him, hard, with a sharp stick, in the back.

Vaughn followed it back up the mountain road and back to the Asylum.

Someone was taunting him.

As he came to the top, for the second time that night, Vaughn found that all the smokers had retreated inside. Smokey, too.

Vaughn scuffed crushed cigarettes with his bare heel as he made it to the door, pushing it open and entering the Observatory.

Immediately he sensed something was off. Maybe someone had turned the music way up. All he could hear were the smooth tones of the big band vocalist as the entire Asylum clung to hush and low chatter.

Vaughn had wanted to storm over to the gaming gang of chalk hooligans to give them a piece of his mind, but they had all retreated to a booth and were in deep discussion. Most people were.

He looked for Dahl and found him now standing over at the bar with Wyla and Sancia. Pete was standing still behind the counter, head down but eyes on the crowd.

Vaughn looked around for an eye to catch. He caught Wyla's who looked up for a moment from a circle that had gathered around the bar. She smiled at Vaughn and slowly nodded.

This was not the same room he had left, Vaughn thought.

What kind of topsy-turvy world was this?

A sudden crash! Crash after crash after crash.

Right in the middle of the circle at the bar, a stack of glasses came tumbling down. Pete ran over to help. Everyone spread out wide from the shards, breaking open the circle to reveal Dahl, who caught sight of him.

He expected more of a reaction; he expected at least an apology or an answer, but Dahl just looked at him with the same concerned face he was giving everyone.

Vaughn approached Dahl, carefully treading around the glass and sensitive conversations.

"Dahl what the hell was that back there?"

"I know, I barely moved my arm and the entire thing came crashing down."

"No not that, before. With the cube you put on the ground. What the hell, man?"

Dahl's eyes widened. And Vaughn grew sick in his stomach.

Maybe in this timeline he hadn't left at all. Maybe Dahl would have no idea what he was talking about.

"Oh! You're back!" Dahl whispered. "That was only supposed to be thirty seconds. I must have gotten it wrong. Better late than sorry, I suppose."

"Dahl what happened? Why is everyone…?"

"One of them." Dahl said with a whisper and a nod.

"One of…oh."

Vaughn whipped his head around, seeing if he could spot them. Could anyone one of them be one of them?

Would he know one if he saw one?

"Vaughn!" Atticus snapped.

Oh fuck. I'm fired. Vaughn thought. How long had it been? An hour? Two?

"Clean up this glass, what are you? Thick?"

"Yes, sir." Vaughn said cheerily.

He hopped on over to the storage room to grab a dustpan and he found that a few guests had positioned themselves like guards in front of the storage room doors.

Vaughn asked if he could get through, and they said no. He asked again, motioning to the left door and the two looked at each other, then let him through.

Vaughn gave them a strange look, as he dramatically heaved open the door like it was such a chore and ducked inside, down the slippery steps and grabbed a dustpan and brush.

As he cleaned the glass up, Vaughn listened to the crowd who looked to Wyla for instruction.

She calmed them, and along with Atticus, suggested that they still stay inside the Asylum while it lasted.

Many disagreed and Atticus ran after them as they left, disappearing outside.

Once the glass was clean Vaughn found Pete and took him aside, leaning up against the tall shelves and toying with the ladder with his foot, rolling it back and forth as Pete crossed and uncrossed his arms.

"I don't know, I was on the other side of the bar." Pete mumbled. "You know, when they got real mad at that one guy and tossed him in the storage room."

"For no reason?" Vaughn asked. "What did he look like?"

"He looked like a guy. Vaughn, I don't know what you're doing. Why are you asking me all this?"

"Why?" Vaughn was taken aback. "Because I want to know what's got everyone so worried?"

"Everyone else worried? You're the one who was begging me to leave with you."

"Begging? I..." Vaughn didn't know how to finish that sentence. Maybe asking to leave with Pete after the Asylum was pushing his luck. How had he read it so wrong?

Pushy. You're too pushy, Vaughn, he thought, kicking himself without moving his foot. "You know what? Fine. Move, I've got glass here."

Vaughn nudged Pete out of his way with his dustpan full of glass and took it back behind the bar, on the far north side, away from the others where he poured the glass into the bin. About thirty glasses had broken. Vaughn wished he could break a few himself.

Jake's words were pressing into him again, and he wondered if he should second-guess his socializing skills. Vaughn did what he usually did in these self-doubting moments, when his brain ran through its greatest hits of crappy social experiences, disassociate.

He had to smile through it. People still wanted a drink and Vaughn wanted to join them. It was quieter around this side of the bar and there was less small talk.

"You ok?" Wyla had found him, wandering around to his side, she had scooped up a book she had found along the counter and was flipping through it. "I bet you wish you were dreaming now."

"My dreams rarely last this long." Vaughn said. "And they end before the good part."

"Dahl just told me you jumped again. You're not having the best luck, are you?"

"That's what I really wanna know. How come he put a cube down that was already set to go off? And why did I land outside and not where I started?"

"You did land where you started." Wyla said simply. "It's just that everything else kept moving."

"Huh?"

"It's a kind of inertia. Cubes work by detaching themselves and their companions from the gravitational pull to the Earth, only *without* gravity is time travel possible. But dealing with this is what we call location displacement." Wyla answered professionally. "The Earth doesn't stop spinning just because you left, so the team who had to program these little things had to calculate the day stream rotations. A way to calculate time gone over distance travelled. For example, if you travel ahead twelve hours, half a day, you will end up on the other side of the planet. Unless you make adjustments for…"

"Is that what they are doing with the chalk?"

Wyla smiled. "Wasting cubes? Yeah. They're playing a game, trying to guess what thirty or fifteen seconds looks like in space. They play for cubes and use cubes to play."

"They have that many?"

"Most do." She said, taking out a cube from her jumpsuit pocket. "I don't like carrying more than one or two."

She dumped it on the counter and twirled it under her finger. She looked at it like it was a bug she wanted to squish.

"You're smart, aren't you?" Vaughn asked.

"I'm not going to deny it. I used to work for the man who… invented these cubes."

"Really?"

"Yup." Wyla spat cut the 'p' of her yup, drew in her bottom lip and bit it. "I headlined the division at Volta that produced the patent on temporal mechanics. It sounds fancy, but all it took was learning how to make things not combust and break when travelling through time. It's why your watch stopped working."

"Sounds complicated."

"It was a living." Wyla took a weighty pause, and Vaughn knew not to fill it up. "I hated working for him. All it made me think was… why him? You know? Couldn't I have…?"

Wyla took a big swig of her drink and slumped between her shoulders, almost smacking her chin on the counter.

"Makes you wonder about yourself, you know? Your potential. Was your life wasted? What was it for in the end?"

"Hey now." Vaughn eased. "It's clear that you're easily the smartest person in the room. Probably in lots of rooms. Everyone looks to you and you answer all my questions."

"You buttering me up, kid?"

"I want to know for real who these Historians are. I can't get a straight answer other than *the bad guys*."

"When the cubes came out. At first no one really believed it was real. People made fun, made jokes. But the ones that weren't laughing, they were the ones who believed the most. Like I told you before, these aren't

learned professionals of history, they call themselves Historians because they want to preserve the version of history that they know. And what type of people do you think want to preserve history and not change it?"

"What kind?"

"The people that profited from that version of history. And to keep things as they were, they track us, hunt us and kill us if they find us outside our time zones. That's why the time Asylum is so important. That's why we're all here. Because of Atticus, they have to play by his rules. For twelve hours, they can't touch us."

"But it's only twelve hours."

"That's a lot of time to a time traveler. That's twelve hours for us to rest. Twelve hours for us to relax. For these twelve hours we can finally stop to catch our breath."

Vaughn kept moving along the bar. He could have squeezed more out of Wyla if he had the time, but ironically there wasn't enough time between him and Pete to serve everyone when they wanted service. The bar being a circle made it seem endless. He would do lap after lap, moving clockwise as Pete moved anticlockwise. Pete was looking to give Vaughn a nod as they passed each other by, but Vaughn just buried his head and tried to look busy at each intersection.

When he finished up another long island iced tea Vaughn almost collapsed in delight to find no one waiting next in line. He let his knees relax and lent his full body weight on the counter, resting his head on the sticky surface.

He could see that Sancia was also resting on the bar, her head nestled in her arms and her eyes facing Vaughn.

He smiled at her, and after a second she smiled right back.

Vaughn pulled a face, and she grinned.

Vaughn pulled up his head, face sticking to the counter and ripping at his skin as he winced and she laughed.

He poured Sancia another glass of water with ice. She sat up and took it, breaking the creases in her frown.

"They're all pretty shook up about these Historians, huh." Vaughn whispered.

"It's my fault." Sancia said hanging low at the bar, her head in her hands, ponytail falling over her shoulder.

Vaughn bit at the inside of his cheek and laid his hand on hers. She winced like a frightened puppy. Vaughn felt her seize tight until he took his hand off.

"Don't say that." Vaughn assured. "That's just silly."

"Everywhere I go I'm trouble. Everyone suffers because of me. I'm cursed, but Dahl is very lucky. We are like *escamas*?"

"Escamas? What's that?"

Sancia held up both her hands and tipped them up and down until they were equal.

"Oh, right. You balance each other out."

Sancia nodded as she lowered her arms and groaned, stopping to nurse her shoulder. Vaughn snuck another look at the painful-looking scars, almost feeling the wound on himself as he rubbed his own collarbone.

"What did that to you, anyway?"

"Dinosaur."

What do you say to a thing like that? He felt a chill run down his spine at the sheer thought of life really being that vast. He felt smaller like he suddenly felt a kinship to those flakes you feed your fish, like he was tumbling down through a suffocating void about to be swallowed whole.

"Well, your safe now." Vaughn choked. "They can't get you here."

"I don't know about that." Sancia shuddered. Not making Vaughn feel any easier.

"What do you mean?" He mouthed.

"They found me once."

Pete was still acting odd. Or at least, Vaughn wasn't giving him a chance not to be. Still moving from patron to patron, hoping for lighter conversation.

Moe had his bourbon doubles all lined up in front of him and Vaughn needed a new drinking partner, or just someone to sit next to so no one

else would bother him. He had enough on his mind without someone else unloading.

He picked a bottle of rum he liked the look of, one with a pirate sleeping under a coconut tree on the label and slid next to him with two glasses three quarters full.

Moe made for the second one.

"Actually, they're both for me." Vaughn said, sliding the second glass closer to his seat. "You can go back to sulking if you like, don't mind me, I just need some quiet time to get my head straight."

"I'm not sulking." Moe wiped his eyes and tried to look put together.

"Oh really, what are you doing then? Trying to see through your palms?"

"I'm thinking."

"Can you do it quietly?"

"You should be scared!" Moe snapped.

"I'm fucking too confused to be scared."

"That just means you don't know enough." Moe reached into his coat and grasped something.

"I know too much if you ask me." Vaughn sighed. "I've got a headache from thinking about it all, hence the rum."

They sat in precious silence for a while, one rum down, head feeling a little better. Vaughn sat perfectly still as the night carried on around him. No one had stopped the sound system so the music never got the hint.

"He died when I was little. Never got to know him." Moe sputtered.

"Oh, are we still talking?"

"My dad. His cancer became treatable when I grew up. It was almost too good a thing when cubes were invented."

"Did you do what I think...?" Vaughn asked.

"I wasn't gonna keep him. Just get him what he needed, and I would have a dad again." Moe's tears dried quickly on his cheeks as they shook. "But then they took him. They took him right out of my hands and... they..."

He broke down into tears, tears he tried to turn into anger but only stifled them for a moment before more tears came.

"… and… I hate them! I hate them so much!" He would have bitten the table in half if it came between his teeth. "That's why I…."

"What?"

"No, you'll tell."

"What am I, seven?"

Moe kept on fondling something in his jacket.

"When this thing is over. We're all fucked. They'll be here and they'll have us. No one wants to say it, most have convinced themselves not to believe it. But it's true, they are sticklers for rules and the second this thing is over, they are going to march through those doors and I'm going to be waiting. I want them to do it."

"And if they don't come?"

"They'll come."

Moe tucked his head down, not wanting Vaughn to see. Buried in his jacket pocket was a gun he cradled in his sweaty palm.

Nowhere to hide, Vaughn thought.

A bartender's work is never finished as long as his guests are still standing. Too soon was Vaughn called back to his station and berated with orders.

"You there, how about another?" Jowls returned with his unenthusiastic entourage.

"Sure, what will it be this time?" Vaughn sighed.

"A Jackermonkey Moonrise, no ice."

"A what?" Vaughn shook his head and just moved to the next guest. "How about you?"

Vaughn tried his best to ignore Jowls, but as he served each guest and moved down the bar, Jowls moved along with him and shook his namesake at every drink he made.

"Shame, can't even make a simple Jackermonkey Moonrise." Jowls muttered loudly.

"I still don't know what that is." Vaughn pressed, as though he was trying to debate a child.

"You don't know what that is," Jowls listed. "*She* ordered a New York Sazerac you made a New Orleans. *He* ordered a Corn and Oil but then he's drinking watered down rum. Come on man, can you do anything right? Just let me in and I'll show you how it's done."

"No. We're the bartenders here. You're the guest, and a rude one at that." Pete defended, stepping in next to Vaughn. "Besides, you wouldn't fit behind the counter."

"How dare you? I'm ridiculously overqualified. I believe there's no drink on this exuberant menu that I have not tasted nor would struggle to identify."

"Oh, really?" Vaughn raised a brow, turning his attention to the tall shelves of alcohol at his disposal. "I think you're full of shit."

"Damn right." Dahl burst in for support. "Why don't you put your money in your mouth if you're so clever."

"Fair enough." Jowls laughed a hearty laugh, his belly swilled like a pot of premixed packet soup. "I lay my last cube on it."

He retrieved a colored cube and slammed it on the table. The surrounding crowd swooned at his proposal, forgetting any talk of Historians.

"Cubes? How about something with higher stakes?" Pete offered before Vaughn could burst with a yes.

"Like what?"

"The loser has to leave the Asylum and never come back." Pete stated confidently, nodding to Vaughn. Vaughn bit his cheeks to hide his grin and nodded back as the crowd murmured over the wager.

Jowls thought on it barely for a second. "Done. The game gentlemen: you have the chance to offer me three drinks of your choosing. If I misidentify even one, I will leave."

Purple Vein made her way over to join in on the commotion. She withdrew a long necktie off a gentleman seated close to the excitement and wrapped it around Jowl's head as a blindfold.

"But when I win," Jowls said as she tied the knot. "You two will be out of here and I will serve these fine people's drinks in the like of

which they have never tasted, and once tasted will wish it was a skill to spill their guts of the swill that you...."

"-yeah yeah we get it." Vaughn flicked the man's nose once his eyes were sealed behind the blindfold, and left Jowl's swatting the air to get him back.

Vaughn and Pete looked at one another, then to the high rise of bottles of all shapes and sizes. Pete flung the ladder on its track to Vaughn who caught it as though it were a battle-axe. They were at war after all.

"Fuck him up."

Vaughn climbed the ladder. From this height he could see everyone not at a booth had gathered around Jowls the blind, awaiting Vaughn's service. Vaughn spied the bottles. His first thought was to pick something unusual. But this would be a mistake. Something strange would stand out and he'd pick it. He wasn't one for underestimation.

He chose three bottles, each one a different whisky. All whiskies are different in their own way, some sweeter most dry all seeping flavor from whatever oak barrel they were aged in. but how much difference could he taste when they were mixed together?

The crowd fought over one another to see the labels of the bottles, trading incessant comments on his choices. The exchange of whispers almost gave it away, someone had to physically cover Dahl's mouth before he spoiled it.

Vaughn added a shot of each and then a dash of bitters and a half a cheeky spoon of maple syrup mess with his senses. He slid the drink across the counter until it touched Jowls' fingers. He smirked, lifted the glass to his nose and sniffed. The silence was deafening.

He tipped the drink in his mouth, swilled it, shook his fatty neck about and swallowed.

"Is that some maple syrup on my lips?

Vaughn bit his tongue.

"Rittenhouse Rye, a whisky from Tennessee by Mr. Daniels, oh yes there's a smoky Bunnahabin no.12 in there too." He paused and smirked. "You snuck some Macedonian bitters to try and throw me off, huh? Do attempt to make a game of it, kid."

He had impressed half the crowd as they applauded to overlay the groans from the rest, and Vaughn spun the bottle of bitters with his finger to read the label.

The fat man even picked it was barrel aged?

If Vaughn had sleeves, he would have rolled them up. Instead, he just straightened his apron, still barely covering his thin boxer briefs as it hung dolefully around his neck and started round two.

Vaughn picked a fresh glass and slammed red and green dried chilies on the counter he found in the fridge. He crushed them thin under a thick knife and signaled Pete to grab the hot sauces, peppers and salts he spied under the bar. His audience giggled.

Vaughn took a bottle of tequila, the crowd became downright jittery when they saw the percentage, and poured out a shot, getting some on his finger and wincing as he sucked it dry and tasted remnants of the chilies.

Using a wide-rimmed glass, Vaughn rolled the edges in his own mix of Tajin seasoning and chili salt. He shook and poured his bright red margarita.

Vaughn's audience couldn't hold off their chuckling and Jowl's grin wavered, but again, raised the glass to his nose for examination.

A few red drops spilled down the side of the glass, glowing hazardously it should have burnt through the glass. Jowls' nose recoiled as a flake of chili slipped up a nostril and stung, but still he hesitantly sipped his drink.

"He's going to hurl for sure." Someone whispered.

"It's gonna come out his nose."

Vaughn pushed all thoughts of losing from his mind and enjoyed the expression that followed his sip. But there was none. The spicy syrup slid past his lips only to swim around his cheeks as though it was as tepid as milk.

"Please, I have a tongue as stout as my stomach. A dull remix of a margarita with a spicy Tapitio 110 Blanco. Then a mix of what I can only discern to be some mean-spirited Ancho, Chipotle and Habarnero peppers. Sriracha and Valantina hot sauce and on the rim a casual mix

of sea salt and Tajin. Come on boy, I know spices as well as you know canned dinners."

Again the crowd moaned and writhed. None of them wanted the game to end.

"How about a really hard one this time?" Pete teased Vaughn.

"Oh good idea, should've suggested that earlier." Vaughn jumped back up the ladder in a huff.

Vaughn took a deep breath and climbed up the ladder. Along the top he grabbed six different bottles of light green and crystal-clear liquor. He passed the bottles down to Pete, some thin and tall, one stout and square, one had a twist in the neck and Pete's four-digit hand almost let it slip. Almost.

With a shot of each and a few extra touches, Vaughn diluted his mix in two throwing jugs and added a crushed sugar cube. His audience lay dormant, reconsidering the drinks they had ordered earlier.

Vaughn ushered Dahl to lean back from counter as he flicked a light and the set both jugs on fire. From beneath his blindfold, Jowls heard the crowd roar and felt the warmth lick his face, but he reveled in anticipation.

He extinguished the drink in a tall glass and emptied a third of it into a final glass of crushed ice and added a lone sugar cube.

Vaughn pushed it towards Jowls and only then realized he had been holding his breath the whole time.

The glass sat inches from Jowls' fingertips; you could have heard a pin drop or the flaps of a fat man's neck wobble.

Pete nodded and patted his friend on the back, Vaughn still felt a finger missing but that's not what made him shiver.

It ran through his mind.

Pernod.

Absinthe Roquette.

Berthe De Joux.

If I can pick 'em surely the fat man and his fat face can too, he thought. Was there anything he wouldn't pick?

Jowls' hand reached for his third drink when an even swifter hand shot out and slapped the drink aside, spilling it over-the-countertop.

There was a gasp, a symphony of gasps and scoffs. Jowls lifted one side of his blindfold with his thumb and scoffed at the mess before him.

"What in the blazes are you doing?" Jowls roared. "Throwing in the towel so soon?"

"I changed my mind." Vaughn snapped back. "I'm gonna make you something else."

"But you can't…"

"You didn't touch it. Doesn't count."

"This isn't playground rules boy. This is a gentlemen's bet. Are you going to show any honor and…"

"Fuck no. You gonna give up or what?"

Jowls shook his turkey like neck and swallowed his pride as he slid the makeshift blindfold back over his eye and crossed his arms across his chest, resting them on his belly.

Vaughn breathed in and breathed out deep. He hadn't yet realized how many eyes were on him, all waiting to see what could replace the masterpiece he had knocked aside.

"What's the plan, man?" Pete whispered in his ear.

"This one is special. This drink comes in two parts." Vaughn said aloud. He took a rotund bottle of Bailey's from the shelf and poured out a shot then dusted some cinnamon on top. "But it requires a bit of participation on your end."

"Ok I'll bite." Jowls grumbled.

"No, you'll swallow." Vaughn jabbed. "But not until both parts are in your mouth, got it?"

"I'm not a simpleton. Serve the drink, boy."

"You got it."

Vaughn slid the Bailey's over to Jowls, and he scooped it up and tipped the creamy drink in his mouth. He puffed out his cheeks, face bulging even fatter, and waited as Vaughn poured two liquids into a second shot glass. The crowd leaned in, eager to see what ultra-rare drink he had found on Atticus' library of shelves.

Vaughn used one finger to nudge the simple glass over to his foe, and he held back a grin.

"In good health."

Jowls once again found the glass and took it to his nose. He held it there longer than he had all the others, but sure enough he popped it in his mouth and held it meditatively before swallowing.

He didn't swallow; he barely swished it from one cheek to the other. Suddenly the plump man ripped open his mouth, expelling everything he had. The crowd squealed and staggered as a herd back, giving a wide birth between them and the curdled drink now dripping down the side of the counter.

"Baileys, lemon juice and vinegar you ruddy malcontent."

"We call that the cement mixer."

"I don't care what you call it, it's ghastly and unsportsmanlike." Jowls nicked the rag off the counter, wiping the edges of his mouth and tossing it into the puddle hardening on the bar. "Especially the added cinnamon. Still…"

Jowls removed his blindfold and eyed the two bottles in front of him.

"I was right, wasn't I?"

Vaughn sighed.

"Then I believe the win is mine, gentlemen." Jowls started his own applause. The Asylum followed along, somewhat disappointed it had ended so abruptly, and some sniffing the mouth-warmed and curdled Baileys and felt nauseous.

Vaughn looked to Pete who didn't seem as disappointed as he thought. He was stifling a wide grin and nodded with respect. They both had known the game was up the moment he picked the color of the chilies. The boys moved down the bar, lifted the flap and walked out onto the floor. The crowd of guests were solemn but understood the finality of the bet.

"What's all this fat man?" Atticus spoke out, rushing to stop the boys on their way to the door. "You can just as likely dismiss my bartenders as you can eat them."

"Oh, but I can. That's the nature of a bet, you see. It would be crueler to let them stay, then they would not learn from their mistakes."

Atticus kept his arms up, and Vaughn just moved around them. Four hours, that's all. Was four thousand enough to start a new life? Why did he take such a stupid bet?

Vaughn and Pete made it to the vestibule; Vaughn could see a few guests outside sharing a smoke. As they saw them, they were quite confused why both their bartenders were sadly staring out at them. The heat seeping in, the stench of oil just waiting to welcome him home. But just as Vaughn's hand touched the door, Atticus made a declaration.

"I am the host of this event. The treaty is signed in my name, I will have the final say here."

"We can stay?" Pete squealed.

"Sure, I myself have never lost a bet in my life. Once in Phuket and I was having drinks with a Russian gentleman, and we placed a simple bet on two snakes. My snake was the weaker of the two and he knew that, so he allowed me to place another bet on two equally strong looking rats. Double or nothing."

It took the Asylum a moment to take in what Atticus had said, but the general gist was that another bet would be made and that went over fantastically with the crowd.

Jowls sighed and made his way over to Atticus, shaking his chins in his face.

"It has to be a fair fight. No more drink mixing either. A demonstration of their skills against mine."

The crowd broke into excited whispers, most too loud to be categorized as whispers. Vaughn caught on that they were mostly excited that the fat man would not be serving them their drinks.

Pete looked to Vaughn. "What've you got?"

"I can mix drinks rather fast." Vaughn shrugged, thinking slipping all their wallets from their pockets wasn't exactly an admirable trick. "What have you got?"

Pete went to shrug. But then asked, "Wasn't there a piano around here somewhere?"

"Piano? You can play piano?"

"I can..." Pete cut off and looked down at his right hand.

"Do you really need ten?"

"Piano is it?" Jowls overheard. "Splendid."

Jowls got his full weight behind Pete and pushed him with ease over to the other side of the Observatory, where the piano had been brought out.

Pete looked at the instrument like it was a shark's mouth and the tide was pulling him in. Jowls slammed him down on the seat and politely lifted the fallboard.

"Play something *funky*." Jowls growled in his ear.

Pete's heart fluttered; it had been a while. Vaughn and the others had followed him over and watched nervously. He tried to call the warmth back into his fingers, recalling the movement in his hands. He winced every time he moved the spot where a finger should've been.

Some in the crowd mentioned the missing finger, and a nervous tension rustled through the audience. It was now no longer a story of good vs. evil, but rather a story of redemption and fortitude. Would the music be a tenth as good as it ought to be, sure, but what did it matter if the pianist couldn't buck up the nerve to play? Pete's fingers just hovered over the keys, desperate to start but just as desperate to slam the fallboard down and crush themselves.

Pete felt the seat move, Vaughn had sat down beside him.

"What are you doing?" Pete asked. 'Can you play?"

"Not at all. But it's never too late to start." Vaughn winked.

Pete whispered thank you.

"Ah ah ah." Their foe interrupted. "What do you think you are doing?"

"We challenged you as a duo, we will contend as one." Vaughn stated proudly.

The entire Asylum looked at Vaughn in anticipation. A few chuckled and others grinded their teeth for the two brave boys.

Vaughn had sat down on Pete's right; figuring they were the higher sounding keys. Wyla came up between them both, dangling her black curls in their eyelashes.

"Boys, I hope we're in a timeline where you know what you're doing."

Pete was muttering various songs to himself to which Vaughn might scrape by. Few would be good enough to win or even easier enough to play.

"Just play these three notes over and over." Pete demonstrated. "In rhythm if you can. I'll try to match you if you fall behind."

"Thanks man. You ready?"

"Does it matter?" Pete giggled through the nerves.

"I guess we're about to find out." Vaughn said, nodding to his friend as they both took a breath and readied their nineteen fingers.

Chapter Sixteen:
Enabling Consequences

Jowls was walked to the door before he could collect his last drink he left at the bar, the habitual smokers followed and acted as guards as Jowls kicked the dirt free from beneath the cleanly cut grass, begging and sulking like a child for them to let him back in.

Inside, they welcomed Vaughn and Pete back behind the counter with a round of applause, some even holding the counter flap up and open, graciously beckoning the boys to serve them again.

"Drinks on the house tonight!" Vaughn and Pete cheered and shared another high five, to which Vaughn immediately cringed and pulled back his hand.

"Really? Still not cool with it?"

"You know, you'd think by now I would be, but nope."

The crowd laughed and organized themselves in front of either Vaughn or Pete, depending on the beverage they desired. Some commented on Vaughn's nimble fingers as he shook, mixed and stirred, complementing his skills and deciding he had been faking his hesitance in front of the piano. Meanwhile, Pete was dying to get a word into him, as he was fully aware Vaughn had done anything but fake it.

"Where d'you pull that from?" Pete finally burst when the lines died down.

"No idea." Vaughn lied, looking at his hands as he dried them with a hand towel. "Must be a natural."

"Whatever it was, you sure saved our butts."

"Dude I just followed you. You were amazing, I could barely keep up."

"Hate to interrupt but let me try this again."

Vaughn turned back to the party to find the try-hard comedian had returned. He seemed to have sobered up and was readying a second try.

"Try what again?"

"Shhh shhh just listen mmmk?" The Comedian muffled. "A dog walks into the bar, but there's a sign that says no dogs allowed...

"I know, I know the dog asks the bartender why and the bartender says, 'what makes you so special'?" Vaughn finished for the Comedian. "It wasn't funny the first time I heard you screw it up."

The Comedian scrunched up his face, a frown dropped, and he grumbled internally before storming off in a huff.

"Just let the poor guy finish it next time, would you." Pete said, fawning for the Comedian as he left.

"I'll try." Vaughn shrugged.

The Comedian tried to get himself out of sight, but Vaughn could still see his head weave through the crowd. He walked strangely, like he was following in an awkward maze. Vaughn peered over the counter and saw to his surprise they had restarted the chalk guessing game. Rubbing the old chalk onto the carpet, new X's with their names were scribbled and a soft breeze accompanied the next game.

The guest list had doubled while Vaughn was gone, and with the sudden rush of their bet, someone turned the music up and dancing started. Downright riotous behavior crowded the Ping-Pong table as someone jumped for a serve and the table snapped apart and collapsed in two. A roar of laughter followed and fueled the crowd.

It was here, in the chaos, that Vaughn saw a book alone and unguarded. It was the same book he had seen Wyla flipping through and being passed around by the guests in conversation. He slipped it from the edge of the counter and looked. It was called *The 47th Detective*. It was a heavily worn copy with pages bending at the top. The spine had white wrinkles like it had been read thousands of times. The front cover had a picture of an empty birdcage, making Vaughn wonder if the bird was what all those detectives were looking for.

Vaughn had only sneaked a look at the open pages when a hand slammed the book back down to the counter and Vaughn jumped.

"Don't bother kid." Bowler Hat growled.

"Reading is good for you, right? No harm."

"No harm. This book has caused more harm than you could imagine." Bowler Hat looked around to make sure they were alone. Most guests had stuck to the front, south side of the Asylum, leaving the northern-eastern side relatively isolated, what with the décor of the storage rooms and toilets enchanting the guests and all.

"Look, because I'm likely never to set foot in your time again, I will let you in on my secret. I first read this book when I was seventeen years old. It was my favorite book. I must've read it over a hundred times when I was in high school. For my 18th birthday my mother got me a first edition copy, it was my most treasured possession, and made me want to be a writer. I tried to write stories as good as this one, but no ideas could ever come to me. I took all the classes in high school, top grades in Literature studies and all that. But still whenever I sat down with a pen, I had nothing to say. I went to college and studied creative writing, and I graduated with honors. Surely now I would have some idea of what story I wanted to tell, I thought. I already knew the best story ever written inside and out. That should have given me some clue, don't you think?

But after I graduated, I still had nothing. I even took some of those pathetic night classes for stay at-home mothers that want something to do with their nights. It was so humiliating, but I topped that class too. I knew it all already, every facet of writing and editing. But as always, at home all I could do with a blank page was fold it into a neat ball.

I don't know, I guess some people are just better at being educated than learning."

Bowler Hat went to take a swig, but his glass was empty. Vaughn was quick to refill it.

"Then one day an announcement comes on the news, some scientist thinks they've invented time travel. Months later it happened, it happened, and I found myself holding one of these cubes in my hand.

People were talking about their harebrained schemes for fame and fortune. They wanted to go back and steal priceless artifacts before they went missing, mine gold from places centuries before civilizations would ever unearth it, and my first thought…"

Bowler Hat let down his head and sniffed. Carefully he wiped his eyes in the most gentlemanly way possible and continued.

"I thought hey!" He tried to cheer through his blubbering. "Let's go back before The 47th Detective was ever written and claim I wrote it first! Great idea, right! That's what I thought. And by I, I mean another I. Because this me thinks it's a damn awful idea."

"Another I…?"

"Me from the future, brought the book back and gave it to fifteen-year-old me. Two years before it was supposed to be written and published. He told me this exact story. Everything about my life I just told you, I haven't lived a second of it. I never got the chance. I took that from myself. I remember every word I told me, that's all I have left of it. I had no intention of being a writer, but when you tell yourself something, you listen.

"So you're A.J Sampson?" Vaughn asked, reading the cover upside down.

"Shhhhh not so loud!"

"Sorry." Vaughn looked and saw barely anyone had moved.

"After I had published it, I felt horrible. I got to do all the press tours and book signings and it just felt so poisonous. But I was the snake. A prodigy they called me, but a liar I was.

I knew what I had to do, I hunted him down."

"Who?"

"Torrance Whittaker, the original author of The 47th Detective, his name was on my original copy. He was working at a car service station, washing cars. I watched him wash cars for a week. Every day he came, washed cars and left. I could tell, even if he didn't show it, he had it caught in his throat, a song in his heart that he didn't know the words to but desperately wanted to sing."

"Did you talk to him?"

"Hell no."

"But he was your hero!" Vaughn getting mad for him.

"He was, to an alternate version of me he was. But what was he now?"

Vaughn went quiet.

"You wanna know the saddest part? It isn't that I ruined his life, or that I ruined my own life. It's not that no one will ever know he was the true mastermind behind one of the greatest books of all time. Not even the fact that he lived the rest of his life with an itch someone else scratched first."

"Then what is?"

"It's that I hate this fucking book so damn much. And I think I'm the only one."

"So why didn't you just go back and stop yourself from ever stealing it?" Vaughn dug at his story, the simplicity in it all.

"And cause another incident? Like *The Incident*?"

"We wouldn't want that." A voice groaned.

Bowler Hat's head shot up like a cat at midnight. Neither he nor the bartender had noticed Wyla sitting a few stools down, back turned but ears pricked and primed from under her dark and misleading curls. Wyla had been hunched with an almost empty glass in her hands. She was looking down into it, tilting the glass so the liquid would tip to one side and then back flat again. Wyla would wait until it would settle, and she could see her reflection, and then she would tilt the glass again.

"No, we… I ah… of course not." Bowler Hat hesitated.

He tried to get out as Wyla swung a wide swing on her stool to face him and slid over, her cheeks grazing over each stool until it found the one beside the author.

"Were you listening the entire time?" Bowler Hat asked with a quiver.

"Just the part about stealing someone else's idea." Wyla slapped her hand down on the copy of The 47th Detective and slid in over to herself. "This is my copy, by the way."

She flopped it open to the first blank page to push a finger to point to a strange signet scribbled in black pen. A 'W' that overlapped itself and twisted in an endless loop. It was a complex and rushed signet, yet Vaughn expected nothing less of Wyla, written in the front of her book like she scribbled it for fun on everything she owned.

"I think I better go." Bowler Hat said quickly, only for Wyla's hand to slap down hard on the book on the counter. Bowler Hat jumped, his hat rising slightly off his head.

"Well?" She growled. "Aren't you going to sign my copy?"

"Oh, um… sure." Bowler hat awkwardly brought out a pen and flipped past her pre-signed page and to the first few pages where only the publishing copyright and contents pages took up space and scribbled his name. It looked pathetic compared to Wyla's twisted signet.

"You know, I have had this book for a while, it was my copy we read it in school. I used to really like it too."

Wyla went to pour the last of her drink down her throat but opted instead to pour her heavily dosed drink all over the front cover.

"Vaughn could I borrow a light?"

As he handed it over he should've known better. She flicked the top and dropped it on the book and watched it promptly burn.

Bowler Hat toppled back off his seat before she could douse him in alcohol and slipped off into the crowd and out the door. Wyla sighed heavily, her breath fluttering the flames as the plastic colors of the cover melted into the pages, burning back to show off her signet once again before Vaughn swept it off the counter and into a box of ice to cool off.

"Are you going to light anything else on fire?"

"Why does fate make people feel so lost and doomed?"

"Probably the helplessness. Can I have my lighter back?"

"I don't see how in a fated universe I have any choice." Wyla sighed as she handed it over.

"So now you're saying you can't change the past?" Vaughn pushed.

"Now, that's hard to say."

"What is?"

"Now."

"It's only one syllable." Vaughn said. "I can't say phenomenon without fumbling over it."

"As an equation, now is just 'if's' over time."

"But if there were no if's, only the idea of an if. How does anyone not feel like crap all the time? I really do feel like my life was supposed to be something different. Like this one doesn't suit me. But what if I'm wrong. What if this is really it?"

Vaughn knew exactly what Wyla meant. He had always felt like his life wasn't his own. Like a pair of pants that don't quite fit, but you don't know why.

But maybe this was always supposed to be it.

Maybe he could never leave Fracture because he wasn't destined to.

He wondered what Wyla thought her life should be. He figured it was something to do with the cubes. She always seemed viscerally annoyed whenever she saw a cube, only using it like child brushing its teeth, out of necessity, not even wanting to carry one if she didn't have to.

They rattled her just how Fracture had rattled Vaughn.

Another cheer went up from those still playing that strange game, some math whiz had finally won, his had scribbled his X on the counter right by Vaughn and someone had placed their glass on it. The sudden shock of the cube popping back into existence knocked the glass askew and over the edge.

Vaughn's hands acted before he could even think, and he caught the glass swiftly from its fall. There was a small applause from the Asylum, a thing that Vaughn hated. He shot them all a smile he used for close call catches and enduring Happy Birthday songs.

"Nice save." Whiz joked, running over to his X to marvel at his own lucky brilliance.

"Yup." Vaughn replied. "Good thing too, we're running low on glasses again. I gotta go get some fresh one."

"Can you make a Dark & Stormy?" A smooth voiced curled.

Smokey caught Vaughn seconds before he collected the rack of dirty glasses. Smokey held his forearm tight so Vaughn could catch a face full of green smoke that smelt like old people.

"You can let go. I'll be two seconds…"

"I'm on it!" Sweeping in behind Vaughn, Pete had grabbed the rack of dirty glasses. "Won't be long."

Smokey let him go and shrugged, as did Vaughn now free to make up the drink and move on. Vaughn did a wide sweep with his cloth and surveyed the bar up and down while he waited for Pete to return, hoping it didn't get too busy again.

"Curious isn't it." Smokey quipped.

"What's curious?" Vaughn asked.

"What if it was supposed to fall?"

"Supposed to? It's just a glass."

"Ah yes," Vaughn could see Smokey's yellow grin from behind the veil of lime green smoke. "But that's where it all starts. May I?"

He took his own glass, finishing the rum, and placed it along the edge like the other had been.

"Say I wasn't a time traveler, and you had no idea about time travel nor had you been influenced by time travel. The glass falls, and it smashes on the floor." Smokey motions its fall with a flailing arm and Vaughn was worried he might hit the glass in doing so. "This would mean what?"

"That it broke?" Vaughn guessed, rolling his eyes.

"That it was supposed to…?" Smokey led him.

"Supposed to happen?" Vaughn finished for him.

"Exactly. No pressure, no responsibility. Milk spills and you don't have to cry about it."

"And you do?"

"I'm morally obliged to cry over spilt milk." Smokey surmised. "And now, so are you."

"Me? Why me? I didn't even mean to do it!" Vaughn sucked on his cheek. He hated how whiny that made him sound.

"Sure, you're tainted, damaged goods. Your life from this point on will be untrue to its original course."

Vaughn felt his migraine coming back from how hard these thoughts had him grinding his jaw. "Can we not talk about this right now?'

"That's the spilt milk we have to cry over. I knew a man who was going to become a neurosurgeon but never went through with it, claims time travel affected his original place in the world and whenever I bring it up he just blames that fickle bitch Time travel knocking him off course."

Despite the clear warnings that Vaughn was growing more and more irritated by the words flowing from his mouth, Smokey continued, prodding at his temple with each word.

"It's a weird business, being an anachronist. How we envy the innocence and ease in everyday decisions. If an ordinary person breaks a glass; they were supposed to break that glass. We break a glass, and we must worry over the repercussions. Was it always supposed to break? Will its absence be noticeable? What course of actions will deviate in its loss or will another glass break in its place? There are always three ways to look at it."

"At breaking the glass?"

"Yes."

"Surely just two. Breaking it and not breaking it."

"Breaking it. Not breaking it. And not knowing there's a choice and letting what happens, happen. Every day you affect the world around you. Unconsciously making choices that drastically change the outcome of the future. But when you consciously make a decision, even if it doesn't have anything to do with you. Now you're morally tied to the outcome. But only once you become aware of it."

Say you're suddenly the driver of a train heading towards a group of people, do you pull the lever and switch tracks, killing only one person. Or do you leave it on its current course, killing even more? Not being a time traveler means the train still exists, but you're not behind the wheel."

"I told you I didn't want to talk about time travel."

"Who said we were? This affects every single moment of your day. It's knowledge. The more you know..."

"The more it's your fault, I get it." Vaughn said.

Smokey leaned in towards Vaughn who drew his face back from him. His personal, green tobacco cloud overwhelmed him.

"But the real game begins when you start to make those decisions." His words were sloppy and delivered in a thick, sloshy whisper. "Decisions you have to live with forever. That's when you start to realize it's all your fault."

Vaughn couldn't listen to one more word. Smokey was all-encompassing. He either hadn't realized or didn't care that everyone around them had left. He hoped Pete would return with the glasses and give him an excuse to leave, but he hadn't.

He was hiding out with the glassware taking a break, Vaughn thought. Sneaky bastard.

Vaughn loaded up a platter of a popular selection of drinks and took off toward the storage room, as though he was just doing his rounds. Within a few feet from the bar, his platter was empty except for one glass of white wine that he downed himself and tossed the tray aside.

He reached the storage room doors, giving the right door a glare as the dust from inside the drab room floated out into the open. Vaughn then turned to the left door and opened it.

"Pete?"

He paused, a spasming, fluorescent light flickered, and the room was illuminated for a few seconds at a time. Vaughn stepped down onto the first step but stood frozen at the top.

He could hear a wheezing in the air.

A shuffling.

Soft moaning.

"PETE!"

There on the stairs sputtering and wriggling was Pete.

Shards of broken glass sticking out of his neck and chest, his hands painted red from clutching his own wounds.

Vaughn called for help. No one could hear. He ran back into the Asylum and called again. A silence washed over the party, only the music ignored him.

Many rushed to follow Vaughn back down to the stairs where he scooped up Pete and tried not to hold him where glass had cut in.

"Hey Pete, stay awake ok, I got help."

"Vaughn?" Pete eased his eyes open.

"Yeah, Pete, it's Vaughn." He wrangled his crying face into a smile for Pete as he held his hand, blood covering them both - he almost lost his grip of his four-fingered hand.

"Vaughn I..."

The people pushed a woman through the crowd to the front that someone had decided was a doctor. It was Purple Vein. Her vein pulsed as she frantically worked to keep the blood from flowing.

"He needs to be taken to a hospital," she said, putting pressure on a burst artery in Pete's arm. "I can't help him here."

"Someone call an ambulance!"

"Does anyone drive?"

"Oh, man, the blood!"

Through the cries of the crowd stepped the man, all in grey. Smokey's boot tread close to Pete's head that Vaughn held in his arms. Smokey casually lifted Pete from the floor and into his arms. He was rough but direct and pushed back through the crowd, back into the party, hoisting Pete over his shoulder as he pulled out a cube from his coat.

"What are you doing? Where are you taking him?" Vaughn cried, still on his knees, frozen solid. He could see, even though he had lost a lot of blood, he was still very much alive. If Vaughn could get him to a hospital...

"Someplace where he can get some help."

"Where's that?" Dahl asked.

Smokey turned his head back to his audience behind him. "The Far."

The crowd stopped following him and whispered to one another.

Smokey promptly disappeared, and the crowd stood in awe.

They watched the spot where Smokey had stood, and they all looked at each other solemnly nodding their heads as though a job

well done then returned to all their tables and seats. While Vaughn knelt in the blood that was quickly drying and sticking to his skin, the door swung closed and shut Vaughn away from the speculations and gossip.

"Did he say the Far?"

$$\diamond$$

Chapter Seventeen:
Burdened by Fate

Vaughn knelt in shock beside the drying pool of blood. The light still flickered, and Vaughn's hands shook as he held them suspended in the air. He didn't dare to turn them over, knowing they'd be darker on the other side. His apron was ruined. It had caught the full extent of the accident. He figured he'd better get off his knees before he started to stick to the floor.

"He'll be ok." Vaughn told himself as he swallowed what felt like a packet of gum at once. "They'll make sure of it, he'll be... he'll be fine."

Vaughn found the power to stand, and he dry-reached at the sound of the blood sticking to his apron. He stumbled back a step and his toes kicked something behind him. He looked down and saw on the ground lit by the flickers of the fluorescent light was a cube.

Someone had dropped a cube.

Someone had dropped it and didn't pick it up.

As he re-entered the party, tucking the blood-covered cube in his apron. The music was noticeably louder, as though Atticus thought he could drown out something like that. Vaughn couldn't avoid them - they hit him with an onslaught on condolences.

"We're thinking of him."

"And you too."

"Our hearts are with you both."

"You poor thing."

Vaughn's fists became harder and harder to keep clenched as he walked through the crowd to the door. He figured the next person to say something he was going to clobber.

Vaughn burst through the vestibule, the blood on his apron shocking the few brave smokers outside that hadn't heard the commotion. Vaughn scanned the darkness of the mountaintop, hoping to find Pete walking back in good health, just as they promised.

But only the wind greeted him, licking the few blood spots on his hands, wrists and shins, icing them cold. Vaughn wandered aimlessly, and for the third time that evening he stared down the deep dark crevasse that was the edge of the cliff.

He felt his left foot lifting, as though one more step was in front of him. Luckily, his hand had already grabbed the rail and pulled him back from the edge.

Vaughn sank to his knees. He felt the rip of his skin peel off the rail. Blood was always surprisingly sticky. He wiped it on the grass. The apron was covered even more. He reached around and untied the knot, emptying its pockets of stuff like his broken watch, a bottle opener, a corkscrew and the tauntingly colorful toy he had collected.

Now he had one more.

He let his damp and crumpled apron go. He thought it would float like paper, but it fell heavily with Pete's blood.

Vaughn hung onto the new cube he had just found, unsure if it was out of curiosity, desire or both. Either way, it felt heavier than the others. He tried wiping most of the blood he had gotten on it off on the grass.

Vaughn dragged his feet back to the Observatory and slipped along the edges of the crowd and into the bathroom. He dumped all his stuff under the sink counter and almost dropped to the floor as he washed his hands.

In the mirror, his eyes had welled up, he was still pale from the sight of so much blood. He wiped the sweat from his forehead onto his scalp, scratching his palm with his prickly shaved head. Standing there in just his white shirt and pajama shorts, he noticed they were

remarkably clean, as he had managed not to touch it while his hands were still sticky.

Another stepped into the bathroom, Purple Vein - the doctor. She saw Vaughn, paused, and then continued to the sink beside him to also wash her hands. After some time, she spoke.

"It's going to be ok, you know."

Vaughn looked at her in the mirror, and the doctor looked back through her reflection.

"What's your name?" Vaughn asked her.

"Janet." She smiled a little, her forehead vein fading somewhat.

"Ok Janet. That man, who was he, really?"

"I know him as well as you do, we all do." Janet turned over her hands and started scrubbing the other side.

"No one knows who he is? His real name? Where he came from?"

"I'm sorry, no."

Vaughn shook his head. "We just let him go. Just stood there as he took him."

"He did say he was taking him to *The Far*." She said, unbuttoning her sleeve and wiping away the blood that had gotten on her wrists.

"I'm getting really sick of not knowing what the fuck you all are talking about. What the fuck is the Far?"

"The Far is said to be the furthest point in time we have gone. I didn't believe it myself but here we are." Janet ripped some paper towel to dab at her neck and hands.

"How do you know?"

"Because people trying to go further, have never come back. They say that the greatest minds of all time have assembled there; the best scientists, best physicists, the best doctors and surgeons- "

Vaughn interrupted her by slamming his fist into the soap dispenser. The aluminum box shuddered, and soap leaked out in a steady stream. Vaughn kept his eyes on the doctor. With that, she hurried to the door, turning as she left.

"Your friend is going to be fine. He's in good hands."

Vaughn stayed at his sink, his hands gripping the porcelain so tight he thought it might crack. The sickly, pink soap dribbled onto the tiles and Vaughn had a flash of Pete's blood from his neck.

He was ready to storm out there and crack a skull or two with a glass jug.

Instead, he simply beat the soap dispenser again for good measure.

"Easy there, with the punching."

Vaughn saw in the mirror a cubicle door had popped open and he could see the math whiz was casually sitting on a closed toilet. Along with his wrinkled but sharp suit and slicked back hair his posture and attitude made it appear as though he was instead sitting behind an office desk waiting for Vaughn to join him for an interview.

"You need to relax more. You're so wound up, no wonder you're busting." Whiz leaned casually to one side where, along the top of the flat steel sheen of the toilet paper dispenser, Whiz had a line of white powder. With an eye still on Vaughn, to show he was an attentive and caring new friend, he snorted the line cleanly and without a nostril touching the cold steel.

"Hhhhaaaarbbbbbbbbeeerrr." Whiz shook his cheeks and let them wobble loosely.

"That's great. Really, that's fantastic. Tell me, do you do kid's parties? You're very talented."

"I tell ya, I don't know how everyone else out there does it. I need it just to focus."

"Stressful is it?"

"For me, yes. Also, it helps with my allergies." Whiz nodded, pouring out some more white power from a small plastic bag and pushing it around with his finger. "I can't do what these other tourists do man, that's what they are anyway, tourists. They holiday and dabble in foreign culture. They aren't living, they're visiting. That's not what I do, man. I live, man. I get into it. I land somewhere and I get my hands dirty, get involved. Meet people and live with them for a few weeks, take jobs I'm not qualified for and bail when I feel like moving on. I'm in it, I'm there, I fuck a few locals, eat some good

food and then I gotta get the fuck outta there or I'm going to have a fucking heart attack."

"And that calms you down?"

Whiz leant forward again and did another line as if to say *fuck yes*.

"Fuck yes. You have to keep it fresh. That's the key, and I'm sharing it with you for free. You got to change it up, man, or they'll get ya. And if you don't take some of this stuff, that many jumps will start to catch up to you."

Whiz was about to do his next line when he looked up to Vaughn accusingly.

"What am I, a drug addict? Get in here."

Vaughn stepped into the cubicle cautiously. It wasn't like he hadn't had some before, but he couldn't be sure it was the same stuff he was used to. He could feel the wet tiles beneath his already disgusting feet. Urine is sterile right?

"You into drugs?"

"Not really." Vaughn shrugged.

"Me neither. I just like the smell."

Vaughn did half a line, and that was enough to make him cough and blow the rest away. Whiz didn't mind, he already had the bag back out of his pocket and was sticking a wet finger in and sucking on it.

"What if you had a kid or something?" Vaughn thought to ask as he pinched his nose and squeezed out a few tears.

"Fuck, I'm sure I've got a small army of the little fuckers somewhere, running all over the place, man."

Vaughn thought of Pete's parents, somewhere they were waiting for him to come back. They had no way of knowing what had happened to him and Vaughn was only just realizing he had no way of contacting them.

"What are you crying? It's not that strong. Or maybe it was, is. Fuck, I don't know, I might have a tolerance."

"It's not that."

"Oh right, the other thing. Well cheer up anyway, he'll be fine."

"Why do people keep saying that?" Vaughn yelled. "You a Poly or something? You think there's a million different Pete's out there in other dimensions, doing ok, is that it?"

"Fuck no. I find that insulting man." He started rubbing the leftover powder from his finger on his teeth, exposing how white and straight they were. "There's always something bigger, that's how us humans have always seen it. It determines our logic and direction of thinking that led us to look out into the universe to a galaxy bigger than our earth, a universe bigger than our galaxy. A Big Bang bigger than anything else.

That's why it's hard to comprehend the madness of the thought of anything before the Big Bang. It boggles the mind, shakes it up like a fish in a fishbowl. It's the reason so many turned to religion, way back when, to settle the anxiety that comes with having thoughts of such a timeless time."

Whiz talked real fast now, Vaughn was dumbfounded by how he still hit every syllable, like his brain was firing on all cylinders. He was just talking to keep his brain going.

"Traveling before the big event; the big bang, the big kahuna. Staring at the tiny ball of such dense energy, of everything in existence. Could you even see it? Could it be touched? How hot would it be? Could you even feel hot without the atoms around to communicate the heat? Could you even approach it? What would be your surroundings? We picture a dark black world but would black even be in existence? Darkness is the absence of light, yet darkness is not yet proved to be there in the absence of everything.

For darkness is a thing. Wouldn't you say? Wouldn't you fall? Would there be gravity? There definitely wouldn't be oxygen. Gravity would imply a construct of a world of rules, implying that there is a world around our world. Not one we understand, but one only to help settle our stomachs over our own existence. Though, we would then go seeking an answer and origin to that world. Does everything have a beginning? Surely not, no. Eventually if you go back far enough, there would have to be a time in which something just was until suddenly

it became something else. This is also true to going away. How could life and everything just go away? There's nowhere to go. The only possible answer is a loop. Yes, a loop."

Whiz stopped to take a breath, and Vaughn realized he had been holding his. Whiz patted down his pockets for his little bag, twisted and tied it up with a rubber band. Before he could even twist it open, his eyes went wide, and he got going again.

"A continuous loop. It stops, then begins, continues and then ends right back where it started. Never coming from somewhere, never disappearing. Expanding as much as it would like and then contracting back again, like a rubber band. Every atom was spat from the Big Bang and shot off on the own direction and intercepted, interacted and intertwined with other atoms on their ultimate search for the edges they could reach."

Whizz undid the bag but only to get at the rubber band, which he stretched as wide as he could. Vaughn winced at the thought of it snapping.

"A big snap, these atoms slowing down and running out of steam before like an elastic band snapping back and retreating. You see, you see it, don't you?"

He let the rubber band go from both ends and it snapped back loose and dropped into his lap. He picked it up again and held it in front of both of their faces. Vaughn figured it was the coke had him so interested and intrigued.

"I'll do it again. Watch, watch!"

He again held up the rubber band and pulled it tight, and as he pulled it to its limits his pull slowed, it was harder to pull it tight, so it stretched slower the more it expanded; until finally it stopped at its limits before snapping back to its original size.

"See? See? That's how it works. It goes back in reverse and back into a ball. Now, if the same bang happens again, what's to say that their trajectory wouldn't be the same? That they aren't continuously repeating the same journey back and forth, over and over again?"

Vaughn just had to interject. "You're telling me that universe is like a videotape that we can play from the start. Rewind and start over again and it's exactly the same every time?"

"Yes."

"And that's supposed to make me feel better?"

"It's got nothing to do with how you feel. I don't care which way or another."

"I don't believe it then."

"Why not?"

"Of all the people I've met tonight, they all shared how they thought the universe worked…"

"And?"

"Of all of them you seem so damn sure, they at least have the modesty to admit they don't have the answer to everything."

"Is confidence a problem?"

"If the universe is as complex and mysterious as you make it out to be, how could you or anyone believe that you were smart enough to have figured it out, and what more, be the only one to have figured it out? How incredibly arrogant, how unbelievably unlikely."

He expected Whiz to be at least offended; he expected he would get off his toilet and yell or punch or push. But Whiz was miles ahead.

"That's exactly it though, probability, unlikeliness. What if there were an infinite number of monkeys at an infinite number of typewriters, they'd eventually write something that made sense right?"

"Right…." Vaughn answered, not even asking this time.

"So, by that same logic, in an almost infinite amount of human life occurring between the chaos of life's beginning and the order of its end, one person must be miraculous enough to think up the secret to life, the universe and everything. It's probability."

"So if you are right, if you are that incredible miracle, are you saying that I shouldn't get upset over something that has happened time and time again? Something I couldn't change."

"What? No, that's not what I've been saying at all. Have you even been listening to me?" Whiz stood up, wrapping his fingers around the bowl to do so and flushing the toilet out of habit and exited the cubicle leaving Vaughn left standing in it alone. "You wanna be sad, be sad. Just because something is predestined doesn't mean it shouldn't affect you, that you shouldn't take any less responsibility or care. If you know how you're going to die, don't walk blindly across a busy road. Love your fate, but don't depend on it."

"You know what? Fuck you and your fate."

Whiz didn't seem startled; he applauded Vaughn's outrage.

"Fuck all of you." Vaughn shouted. "You're all so overconfident, overambitious, you keep overelaborating, overestimating, overemphasizing, now it's all over-complicated, overpowering, to be honest, overwhelming."

"That's a lot of overs." Whiz noted.

"Yeah, well, I'm over it."

Vaughn stood up, and they both washed their hands in front of the mirror, checking their hair and shirts were as askew and disheveled as they wanted them to be. Whiz went through his pockets, flicking the rubber band around the plastic bag and pocketing his coke.

Maybe it was the coke talking, but Vaughn had had enough of being told what to think, what to feel, how to act, how to dress. He was done with being pressured to let life just play out in front of him or to believe there was so much of it that he had no say.

"Hey, you wanna get fucked up tonight?" Vaughn asked him.

"I'm an alcoholic."

"Oh."

"That's a yes. Let's go, this place smells like shit."

Vaughn and Whiz burst out of the bathroom with their chins up. They eyed off and sized up everyone else in the Asylum. It was theirs. They owned it. Vaughn strode along to the bar, pushing aside people waiting for a drink, and he jumped up on the counter.

"Happy hour starts now!"

Whiz came up behind and climbed the ladder, skipping two steps at a time, he tossed Vaughn bottles and Vaughn poured it over the crowd who held up their glasses or opened their mouths while he held another bottle to his mouth, trying to drain it past the label.

Someone broke the knob off the Sound system turning it up and the knob bounced onto the floor and vanished as music ramped up as Right Said Fred's *I'm Too Sexy* had everyone on their feet doing their best strip tease on the person next to them.

Vaughn could see three people making out in a booth, scaring off the few trying to distance themselves from the sudden energy that they didn't share.

As Vaughn and Whiz drank to an even ratio to everyone they served and were lost to the blur of either cheers or shouts for them to share a little more.

Vaughn bumped against everything. The space behind the counter had definitely gotten smaller, he was sure of it.

He found a space of near dry counter and almost lost a finger as Dahl jumped up on the bar and started singing over the music with his own rendition of Frank Sinatra's *My Way*. Unapologetically, he got most of the words and lines out of order, but he sang even louder through those parts to make up for it.

"HEY!" Vaughn shouted in Whiz's ear, resting his cheek against his face and scratching at his stubble. "I got an idea."

"What!" Whiz yelled back, eyes moving about the room like he was watching a Ferris wheel go round and round.

"Let's go. Let's get out of here. Let's… let's go to the fucking Far man."

"Far out!" Whiz shouted. "You wanna go to the future, huh?"

"Yeah. The Far."

"You wanna go far, huh?"

"Yeah, far."

"Fuck it man, let's do it! Let's blow this popsicle stand!"*

Go to Page 477

Vaughn shook as he found himself suddenly clustered between them, incredibly lucky no one had been standing where he now stood. The crowd rocked to one side and back again, and Vaughn was rocked with it.

They were yelling and chanting, but far from the anger and fury of before.

The music had been turned up and the sound system was crowd surfing above their heads and being passed around. They circled in song, linking arms over shoulder and sung until their throats were raw, violent and ever competing stories were told with as much theatrics as they could muster. This audience grew stale and rioted for a mutiny between stories until a new storyteller stepped forward with one that could entertain. One overzealous bard of time travelling tales wrapped himself in one of the long flowing red curtains, ripping it down from its rail and re-enacted the traits of the royalty he had mingled with.

The chalk game had persevered since it had begun, yet they were finding it harder and harder to find their cube in the forest of feet that staggered in no comprehendible pattern.

Vaughn saw no sign of a three-person brawl. He saw no knife wielding or dashes of blood from anyone's knee.

This was earlier for sure. But how early he couldn't say.

He wondered if he was here. Would he overlap? A lab-rat for the third test of time travel.

Vaughn tried to break free from the crowd but found that he couldn't.

His apron was caught. He tugged, but it hadn't latched onto any zipper, button or buckle. He saw that the tails of the coat worn by the woman beside him lifted and the fabric had welded like metal. The seams were seamless. There simply were no seams.

Vaughn pulled until the corner of his apron ripped and came free, then he snuck around to the safe side of the bar. His eyes scanned every

face, every movement, every person now serving themselves and their friends behind his bar. He looked for himself - surely he would be around somewhere.

Vaughn put a foot on the ladder and scooted a sharp kick to the floor and flung himself around the bar. He made a full circle and didn't see himself once, nor Pete.

He figured if he had, perhaps he'd remember it.

"There you are! Quit mucking about!" Atticus roared. "Damn, where do you keep getting off too?"

"Serving drinks?" Vaughn tried, taking a bottle from the shelf and jumping off the ladder.

"Well, stay behind the counter will you. Now that it's just you..."

"It's just me?" Vaughn's stomach dropped.

"Yes. Obviously, the black boy was making a mess and I do expect you to clean all that up when you get a chance. There's bleach under the counter."

He was too late, Vaughn had missed his chance. If only he had more time...

Atticus watched as Vaughn took the bottle and made whatever drink he could with it and pushed it into the hands of an unsuspecting guest. The guest pushed it back and Vaughn had to insist as he waited for Atticus to get off his back.

Vaughn looked at the clock above the vestibule doors. It was 1:05am. It had been that time before.

"Ha HA!" A man said, approaching the counter with an armful of cubes. "How d'you like that!"

"Like what?" Vaughn hurried, unsure whether he should feign an understanding to keep up appearances. Honestly, Vaughn felt like doing anything else besides making small talk with guests. His feet wore pain like a shoe, his legs wanted to buckle, and if he lay down, he might cry from exhaustion. For these guests, the night had been only a few hours. But for Vaughn, who had been awake since tomorrow, time was literally going backwards.

The man held an annoyingly toothy grin. He had won the latest chalk & cube game and had come to celebrate with his winnings spilling over the counter.

"What a great night! Can you believe it?"

"Are you kidding me?"

"I nailed that, damn straight in the middle of the X. I'm a fucking genius."

Vaughn frowned. This asshole seemed familiar. Had he nicknamed this guy already but forgotten it?

"Earned me all these cubes too. I'll put 'em to good use. Someone like me can navigate the earth and land just about anywhere I like."

"Oh yeah, you're pretty special."

Arrogant Prick? Nah, that's not it. He thought.

"Cheer up, man. Think like a winner. Tonight's going great. Only a few upsets but that's all part of the trade, is it not?" The man slapped Vaughn on the arm as Vaughn was contemplating ending the night then and there.

The cube Wyla had handed him was light, empty, and hadn't gotten him anywhere closer to finding his friend. He would have to finish up the night without his Pete, their plan to leave together a fantasy. Fuck, would he have to be the one to tell Pete's parents?

How would he even word it? How would he even go about finding them?

He took Wyla's cube from his apron pocket and held it in his hand, comparing it to the cubes piled on the counter.

"Hey, how about you let me tell you a little joke? This one always kills." The man persisted.

Vaughn tilted his head, like a dog would. He did recognize him. Only more sober this time.

"A dog walked into a bar…"

"What makes you so special!" Vaughn finished it without thinking.

"Hey don't ruin it!" The Comedian spat.

"I'm sorry." Vaughn couldn't help his grin. "But I've heard that one before."

"Oh, yeah?" The Comedian said, checking the clock on the wall. "No matter."

The Comedian shoved all his cubes into his pockets and for good measure, swiped the bottle that Vaughn had left on the counter.

"I'll see you later." The Comedian smirked as he left Vaughn again and headed out the door.

"Yes, you will." Vaughn sneered as he watched the Comedian leave. He smiled to himself and fondled his new and heavier cube he had switched out from the Comedian's stash.

How does this fucking thing work? Vaughn thought as he turned his back to the Asylum with the cube in his hands and grappled with the thoughts that asked him how he had managed to time travel so many times already without setting the cube himself?

He had seen it done. He had to hold himself back from letting his fingers repeat the twists and turns of Whiz, Elliot, and Wyla.

There were no numbers or letters of the cube, no arrows or symbols of any kind, and no obvious trick to it. Perhaps if he were to just copy what Wyla had done? She had sent him back two hours, perhaps if he repeated her maneuvers, he could do the same.

Two hours would do it.

"That's it! Nobody leaves!"

The Asylum came to an abrupt stop. The only thing ignoring the sudden order was the sound system, as a few guests fumbled to recover the broken dial and turn it down.

They all saw that Wyla had taken to standing on the table of the booth closest to the storage rooms.

Both doors were open.

Vaughn could picture all the blood still slowly drying in the darkness through the door on the left, but the door on the right had everyone tense and attentive.

"Has he gotten out?"

"Who did this?"

"What's going on?"

Wyla waved off the shouting until they were ready to listen.

"Who let him out?"

"Oh man, oh man!"

"We should have strapped him up by those suspenders of his and never let him go!"

"We're all doomed!"

The panic in the air Vaughn felt was familiar. He had felt it before. When he first left the Asylum, ending up outside and walking all the way back up, he had returned to a tense hush much like this.

What had happened all those hours - for him, days ago - had happened again. They had been terrified by something and now that something or someone had gotten loose.

A Historian had been locked in there.

As Wyla entertained suspicion and calmed those that called for strip searches and violent action, Vaughn slinked away from the bar. If he were going to jump back again, he didn't want to meld with anyone the way his apron had to that woman's coat.

Vaughn found a quiet corner, far away from the crowd. Only one person was watching. Madame Rose smiled blindly, her rose still wilting slowly as her glass of red wine swirled in her hand.

"Have you seen Lester my dear?"

"Believe me." Vaughn said as he twisted the cube just as Wyla had. "If I did I'd let you know."*

✧ ✧ ✧

"We have to stay calm ok." Wyla pressed as the crowd raged on. "Remember, he wasn't an actual Historian, just another Alterchronist."

"What's the difference?" They shouted.

"We could see his face, for one." Wyla rebutted. "And he was here for the same reason as the rest of you. He just wanted to have a bit of peace. And we can keep that peace if we all calm down."

---

*Go to Page 236

"You all best listen to her." Atticus added, standing on a table, almost falling backwards as he did. "This is still the Time Asylum. You are still safe. I don't want to see any of you leaving. I would hate for anything to happen to any of you."

"But they will know we're here now! What's stopping them from…"

"The rules." Wyla called. "Remember, they are more sticklers for rules than we are. Sure, they may be waiting for us when this is all over. But we only get one Time Asylum, and we are not going to abandon it so early."

The crowd seemed to calm. Wyla was firm, and she seemed to believe every word she was saying. This meant a lot to those that listened. Atticus caught the others, tucking them under his arm and calming them himself, like the good host he was.

"So what if they come at dawn? The only thing we need to do is make sure, when they kick down that door at one minute after six, is that none of us are here to meet them."

The crowd cheered. They saw it as a win. They all could picture the utter disappointment their enemies would have across their faces when they found the Observatory empty the next morning. Despite not having faces to see.

Newly invigorated, the crowd went back to their stories, discussions, and their drinks. Again, Atticus went bloody red, as he found neither of his bartenders in sight. He faced an onslaught of drink orders anyway, something well below him.

Atticus threw in the towel, literally tossing the rag at the pleading guests and made his way out from behind enemy lines.

Hank, a well-built torso with legs, pushed through and held a glass under the tap and helped himself. The others followed suit as Hank hoisted himself up onto the bar and looked out into the crowd, taking a few more sips and making loud satisfactory noises while he scanned the room that revolved around him.

"Nadia?"

The worn-down woman who had been relatively quiet all night lifted her chin from the top of the bar. She had been trying to watch the rest of the party through her sepia-tinted drink and simultaneously keep her head up as her neck had gone limp. She was fantastically drunk.

"Huh?"

"Nadia it's me, Hank!"

Nadia turned her cheeks up and in what seemed like slow motion, lifted her mug in the air and praised the moment.

"It's Hank! The man back from the dead!" Nadia roared, making those that had chosen the seats beside her jump. "Hank my dead friend, come, sit, drink!"

Hank hesitantly joined her, and Nadia ordered another round from a stranger to join their collection of near full glasses.

"You're from after it, aren't you? What happened to you guys?"

"No no no shhhh." She drained her mug and drew in her next drink with open arms. "It's all very covert."

"Well, tell me what happened then."

Nadia leaned over to speak in his ear. "It's a secret." Nadia burst into laughter, Hank catching every loud note. "How are you doing, Hank? I thought you were dead."

"I'm not."

"Congratulations!"

Hank sighed and whirled his mug until a small whirlpool invaded his drink. "I assume you know as little as I do about what went down on those subs."

"Almost less you could say." She answered. "But your sub went down, Hank. You went down with it, right?"

"Well no. I can't speak for the others, but I got out just in time. Swam to the top."

"You swam to the top?"

"That's right."

Nadia nodded with her face showing she was sizing up his story in her head.

"That's… impressive. So why you didn't come find us?"

"I thought you guys were toast. So, I wandered for a while, caught some sights. I waited around until the next election and hitched a ride back with a few tourists who were there to try to swing the votes. Luckily, those guys told me about what happened. They were on the outskirts and got out before the fallout hit. Stein setting off the bomb and calling it self-defense? Makes me wanna squeeze his neck 'til his eyes pop. I guess we never had a chance, huh."

Nadia slammed her glass down on the bar, spilling most of her beer overboard.

"Here here!" Nadia declared, sticking her arm out straight with a violent upright fist and disturbing the last few audience members they had left who hurried to get away from them.

"And August? He didn't make it out?"

"I could ask you the same."

"Huh?"

"Antin and Gal."

"Right." Nadia took another deep drink. "They went back, I stayed. Not much else to tell."

"You stayed?"

"Someone had to."

"Lucky girl."

"Lucky me."

Hank gestured to the room around them. All of their audience had moved on, they were left to talk freely, and they sighed. Solemnly, they surveyed the Asylum as though it was a cemetery.

"We should warn them." Hank said.

"If they know they know, there's no stopping those meant to be there when it happens. You're fucked. I'm fucked. We're all fucked. Unless you matter, then I guess you're not."

"It's frustrating isn't it? Makes me feel like the bad guy."

"We're all disgusting people in the dark." Nadia said as she passed out with her head hitting the counter with a thunk.

The sudden thud had stirred another. He had too been in a deep personal conversation with his drink and that bond had been broken.

He slammed his glass against the bar, eyes glaring at Nadia' sunken head.

"Wake fucking bitch up."

"Whoa steady on there, man." Hank offered. "Let's keep it mutual."

"Mutual? *Ya pokazhu vam vzaimnoye!*" The Ukrainian muttered under his breath.

"What did you say?" Hank pushed.

"I say you blew me up!" The Ukrainian broke out from his seat and stumbled over to Hank in a fury, no other stools were in his path, but the Ukrainian found a way to walk into all of them. Like a baby fawn finding its legs.

Hank's retaliation wasn't much better. The liquor ran through his veins and sloppily pumped the blood into his muscles. As though a line of communication had been cut from his brain to his body, he made a move forward to meet with his adversary but fell back over on top of Nadia who was sound asleep.

Now Hank struggled to lurch himself forward and off her but failing.

"*Ty vzorval menya!*" The Ukrainian kept shouting as he fought valiantly against a stubborn stool in his way. "You blew me fucking up!"

"We didn't do it! We tried to stop it!" Hank yelled back, rocking back and forth on top of Nadia, like an old man trying to get out of an armchair.

"She go because you go. I try stop it but you all go. You go and ignore Milosch." The Ukrainian slumped to the floor and started to cry. "You go and now she's gone."

The crowd of guests that had evaded the drunks in disgust chose not to move back in sympathy but kept their distance by moving around to the opposite side of the room.

Hank managed to get down on all fours where he found it best to crawl over to his Ukrainian friend.

"Milosch?" Hank asked, batting away a pathetic swing at his head from the crying man.

"You should not have gone. It happen anyway, you stop nothing!"

"You kept saying that nothing would happen."

"If you stayed nothing happen? But you go, fucking shit happen!" Milosch said.

"Must've been a loophole." Hank offered.

"Loophole? You say loophole! Fucking loophole?"

Hank tried to stand, slamming his back against the bar, halfway there.

"Where are your girls?"

"Shut mouth right now." Milosch crushed a tear.

"Are they safe?"

"No one's safe." Nadia roused and grumbled. "Not unless, not if…"

"What she said." Hank kind of agreed, his jacket sliding up to his chin as he slid back down to the floor. "There was one last safe place, but it's blown to bits."

"If it was really that safe then it wouldn't have blown up now would it." Nadia slurred.

"If you want angry Milosch…" Milosch started.

Nadia continued, as though Milosch had only threatened to give her a foot rub. "A truly safe place would be impenetrable, well-guarded and protected. You couldn't just make a law or wire the place up. A true defense is a good offense."

Milosch pushed himself off from the floor and stumbled over to Nadia. Hank waved his arms to try to defend her, but Milosch knocked them aside and landed a solid punch in Hank's eye. He quickly flopped still.

"And what more, it can't be safe for a few hours or a decade." Nadia didn't let up as Milosch held her by the collar and pummeled her face in. "You'd want to make it safe for a very, very, very, very, very…"

Milosch beat at the interval of every very.

"… Very, very, very long time."

Milosch held back his fist to let the flesh of Nadia's cheek reform back into a target.

"And the biggest mistake," she continued. "Would be everybody where it is! How safe can you be if everyone knows where you are? Look at how many pathetic motherfuckers found *this* place! Like you, little man."

Nadia who, with her cross-eyed direction, pointed at Dahl who took it to heart.

"Who invited you? Who invited any of you?"

Milosch took another swing, but this time Nadia was ready. She suddenly sobered up, dodging the punch and throwing Milosch off balance. As quick as a trained soldier, she slammed Milsoch's head into the counter and then held Milosch's broken nose up to her own bleeding face, spitting out blood as she spoke.

"You are not here to control the world. You are only here to observe it, to feel the futility of it, to be a slave to it. You like to think you can control time? You think you can do whatever you want, change whatever you want? At what point will you all see it, that he's..."

Nadia caught herself and bit her lip. "... That the universe is using you? It's dragging you by your shoelaces. All you're ever doing is affirming consequences. You're all enablers. True causes of your own suffering. And I hope you do, I hope you suffer."

Nadia could see she had built up a crowd and she didn't waste a second of it, now addressing the rest of the Observatory.

"It's like magic isn't it? You all like magic, right? People love magic. It makes you think you have some control over your world. That's what it's all about. That's what it's always been about. Control. But when it turns out magic is real, guess what? You're not the magician, you're not the bloody wizard. You're the bunny in the fucking hat!"

With that, Nadia dropped Milosch who went limp, and she collapsed in exhaustion alongside Hank.

Outside the wind incessantly blew the ash from the tips of lit cigarettes and into the smoker's faces. But they needed their nicotine as much as everyone inside needed their next drink.

And they were used to it by now, so familiar with people popping into their view of the now sleeping town below, that when a lanky figure in an all grey suit appeared clutching the shirt of a young black man, they thought nothing of it.

They thought nothing of the fact they couldn't see his face behind all that smoke, nothing of the peculiarity that one bartender was outside rather than in.

And they thought nothing of the absolutely terrified and confused look on Pete's face.

Part Three:
YELLOW

Chapter Eighteen

Traitors

Familiarity comes before recognition. Vaughn was always familiar with the taste of grape flavored lollypop well before he could name the flavor.

As Elliot, the unconscious old man, and Vaughn landed they felt the spikey grass under their feet. They suffered the sudden heat washing over them like a hot towel and smelt the smog in the air invade their nostrils. This was indeed familiar.

Vaughn looked around, seeing a dark purple sky, the cool blue light from the ever-glowing Observatory disturbing a black night. He saw the flickering of the few lights down below in town and they all could feel the hum of the party still going strong as it vibrated through the ground, to their feet and up to their stomachs.

He was back.

Vaughn was on the lookout for changes as they entered the party. The carpet was still red. The air was still cool. The music was still playing sounds of brass and percussion and there was still an endless line of guests waiting bar service.

"Vincent!"

Flummoxed, Vaughn dropped his half of Elliot's unconscious friend and turned to find Atticus storming over. And yes, he was looking at Vaughn.

"Huh?"

"If you take one more break, I swear you'll be out on the streets before you can say…"

“Vaughn.”

“What?”

“My name is Vaughn.” Vaughn said, with less conviction than he had ever had before. “Isn’t it?”

“Right, right. Whatever.” Atticus waved off. “Whatever your name is can you get back behind the bar before I have to chain you to it?”

Elliot was baffled.

“Wait, hold up. You’re from here?” She said. “And you didn’t say anything?”

“I didn’t *not* say it.” Vaughn tried, shrugging his shoulders for forgiveness. “Can I get you something?”

“Ah, a vodka soda. Thanks?”

“You got it.”

Vaughn did a quick jog to the bar only to dig in his heel and swerve to the right and to the bathroom. He pushed his shoulder through the door and was careful not to slip on any wet tiles as he hurried to find his stash of stuff tucked under the bathroom sink. His corkscrew, his bottle opener, his busted watch, the cube still stained with dashes of Pete’s blood, but most pressingly he fumbled for his nametag. He checked it six times to see that his name was spelt right.

Sighing greatly, Vaughn left the bathroom and snuck himself back behind the bar. He found a new apron, dumped his loot in the pockets and anxiously pinned his nametag on as if it was all that was keeping him pinned to this reality.

He didn’t exactly feel like doing his job - not that he ever truly did. As they pushed for their orders, nudging ahead by a nose or an outstretched arm, Vaughn monitored the room.

There was a fragile tension. The eastern side of the Asylum was completely abandoned, over by the storage and bathroom doors a curtain had been ripped down and now draped on the floor by a broken rod.

All booths and drinking circles had moved to the western side of the Observatory. Though, Vaughn could see one booth on the abandoned side that seated three unconscious and drooling guests, left in isolation.

Vaughn could spot and recognize one, the woman in the military uniform. She had her head resting on her right arm and her left dangling to the floor. The other two he couldn't place.

Vaughn took to serving once again, this time his eyes firmly on the patrons. Confirming a checklist in his head of those he knew and who was new. Dahl, Wyla, Sancia, Moe, Janet, Bowler Hat, Madame Rose, check, check, check.

He whipped up Elliot's vodka soda and brought it over to her as she inserted herself and her limp friend into a booth. She took the drink and nodded back as though any of this was normal.

Vaughn felt his heart slowing to a less anxious pace, starting to feel his chest was sore from enduring the panic for so long. He felt his infinite selves in multiple dimensions falling back into one body, his transparent self-solidifying as he calmed. As long as nothing strange came out of nowhere, like the sky being green or insects the size of houses, he figured he would be ok.

"Hey, how d'you make a Cosmopolitan?"

Slow motion.

Vaughn's mind moved as fast as his neck, turning his head to look over to his left where he saw him, standing with him behind the bar. He was holding two clear bottles of straights and had a queer look on his face, and his mouth ajar waiting for Vaughn to answer.

"P..P..Pete?"

He was back.

He was there.

Standing there with that unreadable look on his face, just as he had when they first met.

He was fine.

He was fine?

"PETE!" Vaughn slammed a hug into his friend, who held the bottles out and away as he was held. "Buddy! Holy shit. Fuck you're back, you're here!"

"Yeah, Vaughn, I'm here." He grinned, unsure of what to do with himself, still holding the bottles and his initial question. "Are you good?"

"Good, hell yeah I'm good." Vaughn sighed, beaming an enormous smile. "I thought you were, well, you know."

Pete nodded, rubbing his nose with the top of a bottle. "So you gonna help me out?"

"Huh?"

"I have no clue what a Cosmopolitan is." Pete said, tucking his chin in awkwardly. "You gonna help me out or what?"

"No problem. Here we'll switch."

Vaughn shut off the tap he had left running, the glass of beer beneath it had been overflowing. Pete wiped it up and found fresh glasses as Vaughn stirred up a Cosmo, his eye still on Pete.

He couldn't help it. He had lost him so quickly and he felt stupid now that he left looking for him. It felt like he had given up a week just when he could have waited.

Dahl's words came back to him at that moment; *everything works out if you let it.*

He should have been patient instead of rushing off and putting himself through what he had seen.

Now the night could go on, just passing 2:00am. They could work an honest four more hours and be done with this place. Not that he knew how much longer they could. With all the guests piling in as the night went on, they were running low on liquor.

Vaughn peered up each column of shelves, each one missing more bottles than the last. He had to deny certain drinks and started offering alternatives.

Pete kept finding the taps, dribbling little but froth and making that awful sucking noise like the saliva hose at the dentist.

"Has the entire world turned upside down, or is it just you?"

"Huh?" Vaughn stammered.

A guest at the bar was pointing and nodding to Vaughn's nametag with a cheeky grin on his face.

In his panic to assure himself of his own name, Vaughn had pinned the nametag upside so he could read it best. The not-so-clever guest waited the entire time Vaughn made his drink, holding his breath as

Vaughn found a way to mix Midori with Scotch that didn't taste like balls and then blasted him with the inept burn.

"How astute of you." Vaughn replied.

The man laughed at his own magnificence and swept the fresh drink from the counter, spilling some on Pete's shirt.

"Oh, great!" Pete sighed, starting to clean himself up and held out his hand to Vaughn. "That's just great. Could you pass me that rag?"

The rag was glued to Vaughn's hand as he was frozen solid with epiphany.

"Vaughn?"

Pete looked exactly the same as he did before, he sounded the same and he even acted the same. And when Pete reached his hand out towards Vaughn, he still cringed, but not for the same familiar reason.

Pete was still missing a finger, but the ghastly nub that triggered Vaughn's goose bumps, that nub was not where it ought to be.

Pete's right hand had all four fingers, but he was missing his thumb.

"Vaughn the rag?"

This wasn't his Pete.

How could it be?

Vaughn had stumbled through the twilight zone and into where he knew not.

His nametag was the only thing with the right side up. To him, the Observatory was spinning, warping, and if he took a step forward the floor would rush beneath his feet and sweep him up.

Pete was still waiting for the rag and Vaughn gave it up, careful not to touch the stranger. They all were strangers. Or was he the intruder? Stumbling into his neighbor's house having mistaken it for his own. So similar, yet so unfamiliar.

This wasn't where Vaughn belonged. He had to get out. He had to go.

Vaughn staggered back, moving around the bar and breathing heavily down his own shirt.

"Hey, I see it too."

Vaughn turned to see Wyla had lent over the bar. She ushered him over and spoke low.

"I know, I see it too." She repeated.

"You do?"

"Yes." Wyla whispered. "But we mustn't draw attention to it."

"To it? To what?"

Wyla crooked her neck again and led Vaughn away from the bar and over the quiet side of the Asylum. They crept past the booth of unconscious drunks and took the one next to it. Wyla waited to answer Vaughn's question.

"His neck." She whispered.

"What about it?"

Wyla was giving Vaughn the weird looks now.

"There's no scar, no blood on him. It's like he was never hurt."

Vaughn latched firm onto Wyla's hands before she could pull back and he breathed aggressively into her face. He wasn't letting her go. She anchored him. The room stopped spinning and his balance returned.

"He was! He was hurt, wasn't he! You remember too!"

"Of course." Wyla studied Vaughn like you would a mental patient. "From what little I've heard about The Far, even they couldn't heal a wound like that without a scar."

"But the thumb, the thumb!" Vaughn almost yelled into her eyeballs.

"Hmmm." She said, leaning back to think or at least get away from Vaughn's breath. "That could be it."

"What? What?"

"This proves it." She said with utter confidence, pleased that the very situation that made Vaughn such a wreck had her filling with comeuppance. "He's from another timeline."

As though their revelation were smelling salts, a sudden uproar came from the isolated booth beside them. The unconscious ones were rousing. The three drunks had woken to find they had been shoved out of the way, and they weren't too pleased to find they had been resting their heads on each other's shoulders.

"Off. Get off Milsoch!"

"How long's left?"

"Who knows?"

"Get offa me, Hank!"

The one named Hank, a beefy man with tattoos up and down his arms, went to stand but was slammed back as if by an invisible barrier as he held his head and winced. A black bruise was forming under his brow and either that or his blood alcohol level had him pegged. Vaughn could see the tattoos were made up of scribblings of math and physics equations, medicinal recipes, and important dates. He leaned over more to listen.

"It's all so fucked up isn't it, we're eating ourselves. It just goes round and round and round. We're eating ourselves." The woman in the military uniform groaned loudly.

"Come off it, Nadia. We don't want to hear it anymore." Hank growled.

"Stein is the only one that won't be eaten." Nadia sighed. "Praise to him."

"Now I know you're talking crazy."

But Nadia went on. She was talking to herself, somberly reveling in her own revelations.

"It's a bitch. It really is. It's hopeless to deny it, hopeless to stop it. That one end, it's coming, and it's going to happen how it happens."

"I know. I know and I'm sorry." Hank begged. "Have I said that yet, I don't think I have? I am sorry."

"And it doesn't care how it gets there. Fate doesn't care about us. We're little, unimportant." Nadia said as she tried to stand. "All we can do is try to find something stable to hold on to."

Nadia gripped the edges of the table. It shook and her elbows buckled in, and she plonked back in her seat.

"If both you don't stop big talk..." Milosche huffed.

"I'm sorry to you too, Milosch." Hank cried. "We didn't know."

"For sorry man, you do a lot of thing for to be sorry." Milosch snarled.

Hank shot right up, not at what Milosch had said, but at the thick, cold blade he had dug into Hank's knee. Even in his sluggish condition, he was still quick to draw.

"You kill her, yes? You make her go. You stop nothing! You cause…
everything! I'm right, yes?" Milosch growled. "Fucking traitor."

"Milosch, don't." Nadia begged, too weak to stop him and unaware
of the knife carving into bone under the table.

"Milosch Milosch Milosch." He mocked. He spat at her and drew his
attention back on Hank, now baring thin eyes at him. "Hank kill her.
He traitor no? I don't let traitors get away."

Vaughn and Wyla ducked down in their seats as the other guests
screamed at the sudden slash of blood from Hank's leg splashed and
stained the red carpet and tainting a few chalk X's.

Hank had to fight off Milosch, who launched himself on Hank as
they plowed into guests, knocking drinks and breaking up friendly
banter.

Atticus, unsure of what to do with himself, held his hands up and
kept anyone from bumping into him as he shouted for calm.

"Hey!" Atticus called out. "There's no fighting at the Time Asylum.
I could have you all thrown out."

"Fight. Fight. Fight. Fight!" The guests chanted, forming a drunken
circle and trading unprofessional commentary on fighting styles.

As everyone got swept up in the commotion Wyla took Vaughn's
hands and pulled him in towards her.

"Go." She said.

"What, where?"

"Back. You want your friend back?"

"Yes." Vaughn nodded as he shot a look to the faux Pete, trying to
get a good look over the crowd to the fight.

"Well then, you have to go back and get him." Wyla took her cube
from her pocket and started to twist it all before Vaughn could even
fathom what was happening.

Over in the fight, Nadia had jumped on top of Milosch and was
banging on his back and biting his ear to get him to stop. But this
only enraged him, the fight tossing itself in towards its audience and
the whole crowd shuffled back. Two guests bent over their table and
knocked Wyla slightly as she counted her twists and turns.

She shook her head and handed the cube to Vaughn.

This was not like she had before back at the Crowbar. This was different, this was honest. This time she looked him in the eye, and he trusted her.

She nodded, and he took a deep breath. He was about to do this whole-time travel thing all over again.*

------

*Go to Page 291

Chapter Nineteen:
Last Call

All of it went away, all the light, all the noise. All of it sucked into a vacuum and left only what was ringing in Vaughn's ears.

The next thing he heard was his own gasp for air as he popped back into space, slammed his shoulder into white concrete and bounced off to the ground, tasting dry grass.

"Urrghhhh." Vaughn rolled over and eased his shoulder. The cold was gone. He felt like he was being defrosted in a microwave. All his bits and pieces felt pain again, leaked sweat again, was tickled by the grass again.

Vaughn was still holding it in his hands - he couldn't let it go. He held the cube like it tethered him to a boat out at sea. If he let go, he would slip away and drown.

What was that *The Incident*? That explosion. He felt like the fire of it had nipped at his heels, like he had been only seconds from it. His hands looked back at him as he held them up to his face. If he hadn't been so quick... if he hadn't gotten himself out... he wouldn't be... where?

Was it the incident? It didn't feel the same. He had time to run from that. There was no running from that blast, that sudden bang.

Time was more dangerous than he could imagine, and the Time Asylum was surprisingly making more and more sense to him.

And somehow that's exactly where he had wound up.

On his back, he looked up and saw the bright lights beside him hit the leaves of the gumtrees against the black sky. The white building

beside him curved enough to rebound the light off and it still had that energetic rumble coming from the other side.

The party was still going strong.

"That'd be about right." Vaughn sighed.

At least he still had his bag of cubes. The jacket ruck sack had split, one sleeve had come loose, and Vaughn got to his knees and swept them all back in and tie it up again. Standing to his feet, his legs jittered, still rocketing blood up and down his calves. It was enough to make his muscles shake, ready to run or to buckle. He couldn't keep them still.

As he rounded the Observatory, he saw guests were still arriving. There were still the habitual smokers but now two guests were manning the doors. They shared cigars with new guests, the newest shaking snow off their boots that quickly melted into the dirt.

Vaughn stepped over, minding his feet that were begging for a pair of shoes. He didn't even need to ask to bum a smoke, one of them handed him a cigar and Vaughn fell against the wall of the Observatory and took a long drag. He told himself not to shake anymore as the ash from the tip shook and caught on his apron. Calm down and breathe.

Vaughn saw the smokers were watching how when new guests arrived there was a large man sitting on the curb desperately nagging each of them.

Jowls wasn't winning anyone's favor, showing too much desperation not to be left alone in this dreadful town once the party was over. As each guest came and went, Jowls would dance over and ask to borrow a cube or get a ride along with them, always facing denial.

This took his mind off things. Seeing Jowls' desperation had Vaughn's leg jitters slowing and with each long inhalation of caramel smoke he felt almost normal again. Vaughn flicked the tip of his cigar and handed it back to the smokers.

"What time is it?" Vaughn asked one of them.

"Don't know." One smoker said, holding up his broken watch. "Been broken for a while now."

"You're time travelers that don't know the time?" It stunned Vaughn. "How do you even deal?"

"You get used to not knowing."

Vaughn hung his head back, arching his neck and leading with his Adam's apple. He had no idea how much longer he had until this was all over. He wanted a shower; he wanted to crawl up in his bed while his bed was still his bed, and his house was still his house.

He figured it had to be sometime after they won the bet. He wondered if his Pete was still here. And he figured he should have a quick peak to make sure his past self wasn't.

Before he could get the door open two bodies slammed the doors back in his face knocking Vaughn to the side. The men were fumbling over one another, digging elbows and gnashing teeth as they rolled out onto the grass.

Milosch on his back, he slammed the soles of his feet into Hank's stomach and Hank fell back. He crawled in a hurry to get away as Milosch found his footing and kept after him. Hank kept running but Milosch had blood on the brain. Without the light of the Observatory, the darkness of the path down the hill was all-encompassing. Hank quickly slipped into it, as he dug for a cube in his pockets.

Milosch had to knock back the needy fingers of Jowls as he followed Hank, but finding nothing as he went further and further into the darkness, looking up instead of around. Hank's trail had gone cold and swept clean by the wind, so Milosch took a cube of his own and tried to follow him.

Vaughn watched, stunned. He had only missed mere minutes of the fight and as he went back inside, he found the crowd had gotten a second wind of energy, riled up from the rumble and desperate for the last bottles on shelves behind the bar.

Vaughn cocked his head back to see the clock above the doors, 3:56 in the morning; he had a little over two hours left.

Wyla caught Vaughn's eye, noting his even more ragged appearance, and nodded. He nodded back, not knowing what they were acknowledging. He hadn't succeeded. He hadn't found Pete. He hadn't changed or accomplished anything.

If anything, Vaughn was feeling like time was even more stubborn than he was.

It kept bringing him back, forcing him to live out every hour of the Time Asylum, no matter the order, no matter what he tried or what happened to him.

The Asylum needed someone to serve it drinks, and it didn't care what became of its bartenders, or even if they came out of it the same as they went in.

Vaughn counted the fingers on Pete's hand as he approached the counter. He was still missing the thumb. Vaughn cringed at the sight of it and sighed, stuffing his rucksack of cubes under the counter for safe keeping. He peaked down into his pocket and saw next to his corkscrew, bottle opener, broken watch and the folded-up newspaper tear out was the cube he had collected earlier. The one he had found beside Pete's bleeding body; it still had some blood on it.

He wanted to throw it, but he couldn't even bring himself to touch it.

Instead, Vaughn gladly handed out straight bottles of alcohol to any that asked and gave out straws instead of glasses.

"Any luck?" Wyla asked as she came and sat opposite Vaughn, swinging her stool and resting her back against the ridge of the counter.

"Only bad."

Sancia looked up from her resting place along the counter. At some point Dahl had taken off his jacket and hung it over her like a blanket. From underneath a padded shoulder she smiled at Vaughn like she understood all too well.

Dahl was still dancing about, joining in with the more uproarious of the guests. They were beyond drunk, if they weren't all in a tight circle, dancing around each other they would've collapsed.

They linked Dahl in the chain, his feet scraped across the red carpet now stained by so much spilt drink, he couldn't touch the ground.

Over in the corner Madame Rose's flower was bending over, sadder than her. She kept a keen eye on the door - Lester still had time but it was running out.

Moe was watching his lap, still cradling the gun in his hands below the table and muttering to himself.

Vaughn couldn't help but picture what would become of the Observatory. Flashes of the yellow-painted words all over the counter and floor came to mind. As neat as the curtains were now, he pictured the anger it would take to rip the thick brass rods from the walls.

His eyes strayed to the storage room, still missing the accused Historian, and only Vaughn knowing where he had gone. Crandall was probably halfway down the shaft by now, not knowing to what end he would come.

"Some night, huh?"

Pete had come to Vaughn with the same voice and face as his real Pete. He didn't want to be fooled, but he was too tired to care.

"Yeah, it's been a long night." Vaughn replied.

"I kind of don't want it to end."

"And I kind of wish it never started." Vaughn spat back, making Pete a little uneasy, his giant owl eyes unable to hide the slightest twitch. "And in a couple of hours we'll both be equally disappointed."

This night had no moon and the light from the glowing orb of the Observatory cast its light only so far. The lamps that led down the winding path of Mount Fracture allowed a certain shade of darkness, and the smokers stared into it as they mulled over their thoughts.

Then, out of the darkness, two figures tread towards the glow of the Observatory. The smokers awaited the next guests of the party with little concern. But as the figures got closer and still remained figures, their concerns grew. These figures were faceless no matter how much light the glowing building cast onto them. Their faces remained veiled in the shadow of their wide brimmed hats, while their bodies were clear in the light.

No matter how strange they seemed, Jowls took his opportunity to ask for a cube.

"Excuse me, gents, but could I trouble you for a moment?"

"Catch."

Jowls caught a cube that had flown through the night air and into his hands, and before he could react it warped him out of existence. Cigars fell from lips to grass, as the smokers couldn't believe what they saw. They thought they had more time.

The two smokers both bolted around the sides of the Observatory and were confronted with the gorge that split the mountain.

As the first one jumped and made it to the other side, the second went to follow but was tackled by one of the faceless men with absolute conviction.

As they plummeted to the river below, the faceless man kicked off from the smoker and now fell a few feet above him. But with a quick twist of another cube, he was gone, and the smoker rocketed alone down to the shallow river below.

On the lower side of the mountain, the second smoker hid. He had made it down the gully of trees and bushes in complete darkness, panting loudly as he did, until he had found a sizable tree to duck behind and catch his breath. He cursed every loud heave of air he inhaled and exhaled, opting to cover his mouth until he calmed down. A twig snapped, and he had to peek as he saw one of the faceless men silently striding down the forest path. *Please let him pass and not find me*, the second smoker prayed. He watched the faceless man intently, knowing what he was and how little hope he had if he found him.

The second smoker then remembered the cube in his bag, it still had one trip left. He slowly slipped the bag off his shoulder, watching the faceless Historian wander further on down the hill. As the second smoker unzipped his bag as silently as he could, another hand reached into the pack and retrieved the cube from inside. The smoker was frozen, as he stood face to no face with the second Historian who

twisted the cube with no consideration and pushed it deep into the smoker's jacket pocket.

"Such an untimely death." Spoke the faceless Historian as he watched the man blip into nothing right in front of him.

The other Historian returned from his search down the hill and together they took a cube and jumped ahead, ready to crash a party.

The doors swung open and for a moment nobody noticed those that had just walked in. Dressed in dark brown suits, crinkled well-worn hats and absent faces, they tread purposefully into the Asylum. The second Historian dealt with the door, locking it behind them. The two of them stood and went unnoticed until one old lady stood and pointed.

"That's not Lester."

It took just a scream after that; quickly they had everyone's attention. Vaughn looked up like the rest and saw the crowd part ways to uncover the two faceless men being given a very wide birth of space. Vaughn felt those leg jitters coming back. They were like the ones he saw before, dressed in brown suits with brown hats and the same void right where a face should be.

"Hello." The taller of the two Historians said, spitting his words from his lips, he was out of breath.

"Bastards!"

Several shots rang out as Moe struggled to his feet, firing his gun in the air as he used the same hand to pull himself out from the booth. As he lined up a proper shot, he flew back. Eyes went to the shorter Historian, holding the smoking gun. So quick, like he knew it was coming.

Moe dropped dead on the floor, blood matching the carpet.

Nobody moved after that. They shook but didn't move. A few went straight for their cubes, shaking them as they spun the sides, but to no avail. There was a whirring noise in the air. Something was disrupting the mechanics inside all of their cubes.

Vaughn looked down to the sack he had under the counter and felt the one in his apron, now just inert playthings.

Out of the crowd, Dahl stepped up. He put his toes in line with the tall and ominous Historian and looked up without a second thought.

"If you're gonna shoot anyone, then shoot me." Dahl said.

"Dahl no!" Sancia shouted.

"Don't worry, I've got an ace-hole up my sleeve." Dahl winked back to his friends before turning back to the faceless man. "I can kick your ass with both legs behind my back."

The Historian plainly raised his own gun, aiming between Dahl's eyes. But Dahl didn't even wince. But the rest of the Asylum did.

"Waste of a bullet." The Historian sneered. He nudged the small man out of his way and stepped further into the midst of the Asylum. The taller Historian limped and still heaved to catch his breath, but what threat it cost him, his gun more than made up for. Dahl fell back and took a quiet seat along the bar besides Elliot and her unconscious friend.

The Historian surveyed the crowd and with each flick of his head the crowd jolted in a tremor. The shade he wore for a face wisped and sunk deeper the longer you looked. He had his audience.

The Historian staggered and moved through the crowd towards those at the bar, as the second shadowed man moved to the door clutching a big bag at his side.

Vaughn happened to be clutching a bottle of scotch by the neck; in such bright glowing light their dark shadowed faces were even more unnerving.

As the Historian limped closer, he could see just how well the veil of haze obscured the features of his face Vaughn could only tell he was a man by his deep voice.

The Historian finally noticed Wyla, still sitting at the bar with Vaughn.

"My, my, my, who might we have here?" The figure said, stopping at Wyla's feet, his clouded expression within sniffing distance of Wyla's stern face. "Wyla Bavishni is it?"

"Have we met?

"I thought you were…" He started, looking Wyla up and down. "Never mind."

The Historian stood in pause for a moment, his deep gasps for a breath subsiding, and he took off his hat. The haze around his face followed as he held his hat at his side. Now in full light all could see the gaunt man with a face that could have once been ripe and rosy but now cold and pale. His boney face was weak, and his temple sagged. His cheekbones had sunken in, and his chin had loosened so when he spoke it creaked and rattled against the rest of his jaw. He was a disturbing sight, but Wyla didn't hesitate at his complexion, just the idea of him.

There were whispers and murmurs from the others, recognizing the man through the deterioration.

"Is that…?"

"Howard Hammond."

'The senator?"

"Thank you for the introduction." Hammond grinned a crooked grin.

"You can't be here." Wyla's eyes kept darting to the clock. "Doing what you did. You broke the rules."

"Does it look like I care about the rules?"

"That's right!" Atticus stepped forward from the crowd out of necessity. "You're not allowed to be here. I didn't invite people like you."

Hammond quickly snatched at Atticus's tie and roped him in tight, close enough that his nose rubbed against Hammond's sunken cheek.

"You!" Hammond snarled. "Just for thinking up this… party… I should… I should gut you."

"Please." Atticus pled softly. "Aren't you here for them?"

The Asylum was silent, tentative to even breath but all now wishing a quick death to Atticus.

"Hey scab face!" Nadia snarled from her booth. "Is that what's underneath all those shadowy faces? Why were we running from you all this time?"

She thrust herself to her feet, ignoring her pounding headache and the bruises from her fight. She marched at Hammond with all the confidence the others had lost.

"What are you gonna do, huh? We're done, done with all of you, done with running, done with hiding. We're not scared of you anymore. So why don't you just…"

The second Historian rushed her. He grabbed Nadia by her official collar, lifting her up, and slammed her down to the ground. He beat her relentlessly, seeing her cheek bleed onto his fist and then beating that blood back into her. The entire party was stone silent, as the hits went from the sound of breaking hollow bone to a brick smashing jelly.

Once it was finally over and the Historian got off his knees and off Nadia, he took a cube from a strange bag that he had strapped over his shoulder and laid it on her chest. But he didn't twist it. Nadia suffered to breathe, choking on blood or bone, and everyone just watched.

The party was silent, most wishing they had made a break for it when they had the chance. Vaughn shot a look at Pete, as stunned as the rest of them. Eyes like glass.

"Now I know the rules, but as my friend Pratt here has shown, we do like to bend them."

Hammond began creating a circle and lapping it, showing off his graveyard tan to as many tourists as he could.

Hammond stopped and faced the crowd. He kept his back to Vaughn and Pete. The bartenders were again furniture.

"Now, this is how this is going to go. We will go around the room, and you will give us all your excess cubes. I am a fair man. I will let you keep one cube each. But one cube only."

The second Historian opened his bag and circled the place, holding it open, and no one budged.

"Do what they say!" Atticus cried out, begging his guests. "Then they will leave us all in peace. Please."

The guests all started patting themselves down and handing cube over fist. The bag the second Historian carried was quickly filling up, and he was made a lap of the Observatory quickly.

Vaughn looked down to his feet again, to the cubes he had tucked away. *Surely they wouldn't check everywhere.*

When the second Historian came to the bartenders, he shook his bag at them without saying a word. Vaughn felt the hairs on his lower back trickle. Nothing was looking at him and nothing was waiting.

The Historian lent forward and bent over the counter. He searched and quickly found the coat, bundled up with Vaughn's stash of cubes.

Fuck.

The second Historian then moved to Pete, who held up his hands, all eight fingers and one thumb but offered nothing. He had nothing. The Historian withdrew a cube from his bag and handed it to Pete and moved on.

As the second Historian moved from tourist to tourist, Hammond stood and breathed in the chill in the air. All eyes were on him, and he acted like he hadn't felt that feeling in a long time.

"Tonight is about what's fair." Hammond growled. "I was once a very rich and successful man, in every way. I knew the rules of the game that we call life, and I played the game well. Through my determination and wits, I made myself into the man I was destined to be. My family was precious to me, unique and irreplaceable. But they were taken from me, taken by something I could not have predicted and was hopeless to stop. Something I couldn't even grasp with my own two hands."

Hammond stopped and slipped a napkin from the counter to wipe his mouth as his bottom lip sagged to the left and he couldn't stop drooling.

"You tourists and your carelessness forced me out of my home, out of my success and out of my life. I was reduced to nothing, nothing but a shell of what I could have been. You all know the shell, you're

like hermit crabs, disposing of one life and trading it in for the next. Well, I'm here tonight to show you what it feels like to be a victim to someone else's chaos!"

One tourist couldn't hold it any longer, jumping to their feet and running for the door. He was stopped by another gunshot Hammond fired into his leg. It echoed thunderously in the open orb of the building as the frightened tourists howled in pain and clutched his leg. No one helped him.

"I'm sorry." Hammond laughed. "But no one is going anywhere until I say so."

"You're a hypocrite." Janet yelled.

"What? Oh, you mean the whole thing about rules and safe spaces? It is hypocritical, isn't it? If I still gave a damn about it. After all this time, all these timelines change after change overlapping each other constantly, repeatedly. It kind of dulls the hypocrisy until all you've got left is pure and unrelenting vengeance."

The way Hammond hit the 'v' in vengeance made a tooth come loose and it dropped to the floor. The small clink of the bone hitting a glass on the floor was enough to make most of them want to vomit. But it only made Hammond laugh and snarl, as he suckled on the fresh spot where his tooth had been, and the room recoiled.

"I don't think I can ever put time back the way it was. It's kind of like me now, falling apart at the seams. And all we both want is relief."

Hammond limped towards Wyla, his bones cracking as he did. It looked like a single blow would knock him on his back. Vaughn thought that if it weren't for the gun in this hand, he wouldn't seem like much of a threat. But it was more than that. Just the idea of him being there, the knowledge that their Asylum had been violated hours earlier than it should. Vaughn wondered if perhaps he had changed something with all his jumps through time.

"All I'm trying to say is that this is about what's fair. That's something you lot all understand isn't it? You love your sense of injustice. I guess the part of me that drove me to make something of

myself, doesn't exist inside of all of you. Replaced by an unearned sense of the world being too unfair to you. That's why you never learnt that you can't just change the rules of the game when you're losing. Why do you get to change things to suit yourselves? Why do you get to have a haven, a sanctuary to call your own, when you took mine from me so mercilessly? That's not very *fair*."

The second Historian finally finished. His bag was bursting with cubes, and he nodded to Hammond that he was really. Every single tourist still breathing had one cube each, as useless as the toy it resembled, in their hands. They all clutched or pocketed them, unsure why they were allowed to keep them. Vaughn saw Dahl fumble and clumsily drop his. It bounced softly on the carpet and was lost in the crowd of feet around him. He didn't dare leave his stool, merely kept his eyes up and nodded to Elliot's unconscious friend beside him, slouched over the bar as though was cool and he had everything under control.

Hammond took something from his pocket and held it in both his hands behind is back.

Vaughn could see from that what he was holding was just another cube, but this one was entirely white and slightly larger than the regular cubes. He turned it slowly in his hands, delicately passing each side over, not moving a single tile. Not yet.

"I hope you all enjoyed yourselves tonight, with what little time you had, and I offer you this as a parting gift. May this be the last time you escape the grasp of a Historian. Though you're probably not going to live to tell about it, but if we do meet again, let me know what this feeling tastes like."

Hammond twisted the white cube once and it hummed, playing an eerie ringing in everybody's ears.

Wyla leaned forward, curious as to what Hammond had just done. He spoke through what yellow teeth he had left.

"Tastes like justice to me."

Vaughn suddenly felt his apron pocket hum. He reached into it and pulled out his blood-stained cube. It was vibrating so intensely that it

seemed to barely move. Everyone else had found their cubes acting the same. Some tried to rip them from their pockets or toss them aside, but none were able. It was like everything the cubes touched sealed and gripped to it. All their cubes were now welded in their pockets or glued to their hands.

"Hammond what have you... you didn't...?" Wyla started as she held her cube, or her cube held her.

"Ah, ah, ah. Save it for next time." Hammond taunted.

Vaughn watched his cube perplexed as it jumped, spun and danced in his hands all without leaving his skin. His palm burned, and he saw the edges of his skin seal to the cube. All he could do was watch every move it made. Vaughn wanted to ask what was happening.

But there was no time. Every guest at the Asylum had the same mouthful of questions.

And every cube answered them all. All at once.

Every single guest at the Asylum was pushed through a tangent in time and Vaughn couldn't help but feel that somehow, it was all his fault.[*]

✧ ✧ ✧

A tremendous gust of wind followed and swept the near empty void of the Observatory. Hammond made his way over to the bar while Atticus just stood there, his mind adjusting to the mass eviction.

Hammond chose a seat at the bar and swept the barrage of near empty glasses off the counter to and to the floor, soaking in the sound of glass breaking.

The second Historian joined him, keeping to the outside of the bar, and poured them both a drink of the scotch the bartenders had left behind.

"That... that..." Atticus stuttered.

Both Historians spun around on their stools to watch him struggle with himself.

---

[*]*Go to Page 627*

"That wasn't supposed to happen like that."

"Excuse me?" Hammond growled.

"You're not supposed to push them all away!" Atticus roared. "Do you know how many cubes you wasted on them? Huh? There were, oh I don't know, thirty, forty of them left. That's forty cubes. You owe me forty cubes."

Underneath his thin veil of haze, the second Historian raised a brow, downing his drink and slapping the glass on the counter. Underneath that veil, his eye twitched.

"What are you…" Vaughn started.

Hammond pressed the back of his hand into Vaughn's chest and kept him seated. He then turned that hand to a fist and pointed at Atticus as he approached him, his size looming and Atticus's diminishing.

Still, Atticus stood firm. He looked at Hammond the way he had looked at Vaughn and Pete several hours ago. As overpaid labor.

"Look, you got your end of the deal, but I don't know why you made such a show of it. Tossing them over the edge has worked fine the last six times. But you screwed me. I do all the hard work. I set these Asylums up, I organize everything, I get them all here. Me. Me! I do that!"

Hammond stopped a few feet from Atticus, man-to-man, arrogance-to-arrogance. Both were looking down on the other despite their near equal height.

"Now I've got to start over, setup yet another Asylum, go through it all again because you brought that… what was that thing? The White Cube that…"

Hammond hocked and coughed. All that came out were devilish sounds from deep down behind his shade.

"We're not familiar with any deal." Hammond snarled.

"Then… why are you here? Why did you break the rules? Just to take them all out? Is that it?"

Neither Hammond nor Vaughn said anything.

"You can't touch me, you know." Atticus said snidely. "I'm in my proper time zone."

Hammond's shoulders lurched, and he snorted another chunk of mucus.

"You know." Atticus started, walking with his arms locked behind his back as he had all night. "When I first found a cube and discovered what it was and how it worked, I used it selfishly. I'll admit to that. I got filthy rich on stocks and investments that I knew would pay off. I crushed opposition, dropped companies before they went down, picked them as they went up. I set myself up with a means of getting as many cubes as I could without leaving my time zone. I was smart. Sure, I stepped over people, sometimes *on* people, to get ahead. But I have never done what you just did. I have never done anything so sour and cruel without anything to gain. That, sir, is pure evil. And I toast to you."

Atticus held up a glass of warm, orange champagne and saluted Hammond and invisible Vaughn. He got no reaction. Sighing, he took his glass and stepped towards them both, forcing a toast and clinging mismatching glassware without them moving a muscle.

Atticus grimaced from the dissatisfying toast. He approached Vaughn, still clutching the bag of cubes.

"Well, you can take off that stupid hat and give me what cubes you did collect so I can store them safe and secure."

He swung a hand for Vaughn's bag, but Hammond caught his arm, and he wrenched behind his back. Atticus dropped the glass and fell to his knees and then his stomach as Hammond used the last of his strength to bend it out of place. Atticus screamed and bit the carpet as Hammond placed a foot on the back of his head and held out his hand for a cube from Vaughn.

Vaughn dug quickly through the bag and handed one over. Only as it passed hands did he see how faded and worn it was. He watched the cube rest on Atticus' back and pull Atticus through a tangent, his groans passing with the wind.

"Finally, some peace and quiet." Hammond said softly as he returned to his seat at the bar. They both sat in silence and sipped at their drinks, one shaking uncontrollably, the other calm and still.

"I guess that's it." Hammond said. "It feels weird, like it's over, but it's... not. I thought it would feel different."

There was a droning from the speakers. The scratching sound of the end of the disc filled the air. Napkins drifted in the remnants of the departing breeze.

"You're being awfully quiet." Hammond said softly.

"Am I?"

"It's fine. Quiet is nice. I want a quiet world."

Air ran through the place with a strange freedom and under a low hum. Chalk was drawn across the floor like strange crop circles and the place was left behind with a wafting smell of slowly warming beer.

The two faceless men sat and finished their drinks and bid the place farewell, as one of them slapped his hands on the counter and the other took out one cube from the bag they carried. Vaughn twisted it in a way he had seen it twist before whilst resting a hand on Hammond's shoulder. The party was finally over.[*]

---

[*]*Go to Page 618*

What if there were no Tomorrow?

Amidst the swollen bubble of the Observatory a wind blew and welcomed back its bartender, crashing down on the edge of the counter and toppling over the side. Vaughn swore loudly and added in some other words for good measure as he found his feet. As painful as he knew it would be, he still put both hands on the counter, took some deep breaths, and cracked his back, stretching out every limb. He followed each stretch with an exasperated moan, laughing with relief for every bone that retired from aching.

An annoying hum clung to the air and rang in his ears forcing him to smack himself on the side of the head hoping it would stop. It didn't.

The party was well and truly over; a golden tinge of the sunrise came through the big round windows. The Asylum was out of time. It was no more and the laws that protected it once were now null and void. But Vaughn walked with no hesitation, despite Hammond's final face flickering in his mind.

Vaughn cleaned up out of habit. His hands were collecting dirty glasses and stacking them in a tray with a few that were clean. After doing half the bar, he had to physically stop himself and ditch the tray.

He had done enough overtime.

Vaughn found it strange to walk the red carpet of the Observatory with as much room to move as he would like. He danced between the

carefully drawn chalk marks on the floor, weaving like a show-dog between cones. When he came to a half-finished glass sitting on the floor he playfully kicked it aside and watched the drink soak into the carpet.

He saw the spill meet with the hardened, crusty, dark spots on the soft red carpet. He recalled standing over her, beating her. His fingers still ached.

Thinking of Nadia gasping for air through a mouthful of blood, then thinking about what she had done. It had him hoping that the tangent the White Cube had pulled her through was just as punishing as his fists had been.

Vaughn graced the piano with a soft hand across the top. A fine layer of dust slid off with his touch. He sat on the bench and lifted the guard and played. Each note he hit sounded poor and off key.

"Come on Vaughn." He found himself saying aloud. But they didn't move. In fact, they felt cold. He used a finger to wipe his eyes, then his cheeks. "C'mon hands."

The friend he missed and had only known for so short a time was fading fast from his mind. What did he look like? What did he sound like? How much of their friendship had he romanticized and overthought? The Pete he had left behind, was he still out there, thinking about and missing him?

A short breeze lifted the hairs on the back of his neck. Vaughn shot to his feet and scanned the room for any and all movement.

Where were the Historians now? He didn't like the idea of spending the rest of his life looking over his shoulder. Vaughn thought he had more time than this, but then for them, this could be a long time coming. Time was funny like that.

A pair of feet landed on the carpet somewhere in the Observatory. Vaughn moved around the giant telescope, not dampening his own steps or holding his breath.

"Figures." Vaughn laughed.

"Vaughn, right?"

"You got it right this time."

Atticus raised a lip and smiled into his nose. Vaughn saw he was covered in plaster dust and sweat. His hands were in his pockets where the material stuck out at jagged angles with so many cubes crammed into each. The old man was still catching his breath, his eyes still looking over his shoulder for a stray bullet, his mind still back on the 42nd floor of the Volta Tower.

"So this is where you went to." Vaughn said.

"We agreed to meet up here after it all was over." Atticus strode around the room, pulling on his jacket corners like it made it any straighter. His hair was still strewn about his scalp, no more than the flourishing grey bouquet it was before. He clenched his arms behind his back and kept walking, but Vaughn cut him off to where he knew he was going.

"And is it?" Vaughn asked, slipping up beside him, getting ahead and leaning up against the storage room door as casually as he could. "Is it all over now?"

Atticus narrowed his eyes. He didn't know what Vaughn knew and groaned as his bartender pressed his dirty shoe up against the rich red door, leaving a mark.

"I thought you left us behind." Atticus said, stepping back a little, hoping Vaughn would follow.

"Not quite." Vaughn didn't move.

"Well, I'm glad someone else made it out of there." Atticus realized he wasn't getting past Vaughn anytime soon and instead moved towards the counter to get a drink. Vaughn still didn't move. "Once all the shooting and explosions started, I knew we were done. If they were smart, they would have left as well."

"But they didn't?" Vaughn asked.

"No one could have made it out of that."

They both felt it, a second wind. It terrified Atticus and delighted Vaughn.

She fell, lying down, a few feet to the floor. Wyla groaned as her shoulder bled discretely into the red carpet, hands still gripping the cube that Vaughn had placed on her chest.

Vaughn left his post and ran to her. She was gasping, mostly from shock. Her mind ready to accept the ground to be volcanic, the air to be poison or for everything to be on fire.

Yet here she was, feeling nothing but the soft padding of the thick carpet and breathing in freshly air-conditioned air. She opened her eyes.

"Hey."

"Vaughn?"

"Easy, go easy." Vaughn said as she tried to sit up.

"I don't understand." Wyla hushed. Her eyes no longer darted around. They were fixed on Vaughn. How had he beaten her there?

"I thought it was you… but then… wasn't it…" She started.

"That was me." Vaughn sucked in his lip, but then nodded to her shoulder. "That wasn't, though."

He could see the bullet had gone straight through with just as much blood pouring out the other side.

As her breathing slowed, so did the bleeding. Vaughn grabbed a rag he had used all night that sat on the bar and balled it up and pressed it into her shoulder. She winced and held his hand as he held it over her wound.

"I thought you had left us. I thought you were with them. With him."

"Never." Vaughn winked.

"I thought, I really thought…" Wyla finally spoke.

"I had to." Was all Vaughn could say.

"Ah it's good to see you Wyla." Atticus stepped in over Vaughn's shoulder. "What are the chances the three of us got out of there? Slim, I bet."

"You didn't stay long enough to find out." She accused.

Then came a third wind, a little stronger than the others. All three of them scanned the room and saw two people stepping out of a tangent, one more so hobbling than the other.

It was Galina, her boots covered in rust-colored dirt and breathing fast.

Behind her stumbled another. His wooden legs made a strange clopping on the floor.

"Vaughn?"

"You remembered!" Vaughn lit up.

"I did, didn't I?" L laughed. "Good for me."

L stood and swayed uneasily, finding it strange to move in real time. He waved slowly and watched as his own arm moved as slowly as he ordered it. It would take some getting used to.

"And you remembered." Vaughn looked to Galina, flashes of her on the boat all that time ago rising to mind. He looked at her arm. "You remembered to find him for me."

"Bah, no problem. We had backs in corner, all gone shit. I look for you, but I don't find. I find no one. No Dahl, no you, no Sancia. I think we have no chance, so I leave. But I remember promise I make you. And, you know, saving people, it what we do, no?"

"I'm sorry about Nash." Wyla interjected and frowned as she helped herself up and onto a stool. "I'm sorry about everything."

"It's ok. Not your fault." Galina nodded.

"But it was mine." Vaughn started.

Vaughn finally explained everything. All that had happened to him the night before and all the time in between. He left nothing out, only pausing when he got to the parts that he knew would hurt. And they did.

Galina didn't expect to relive the memories she had at sea, rubbing her calf and thumbing the hole in her arm. Atticus looked away through most of it, and Vaughn tried to avoid Wyla's eye when he told them about his time with Hammond.

Once he was finished they were all so quiet. The only one not suspended by his story was L, who was still staggering around the Observatory. He chose not to listen to the sad stories they were exchanging. Mainly as he still got confused as to who certain people were and what was going on. But he was pleased to know that he could remember how many laps he had walked around the room. Passing all the booths and chalk lines, he stopped only when something caught his eye.

A white rose wilting in a glass of water. He didn't know why. He couldn't remember if he ought to know at all. But he did know that it had been a long time since he had cried like that.

They saw more sunlight creeping across the carpet from the big circular windows. A glance at the clock and Vaughn saw the time hadn't changed. But he was done with this place, and so far it seemed that no one else was coming. No one was left to come. He helped Wyla up off her stool, her wild hair trying to get itself stuck in her bloody shoulder. As she knocked it back, Vaughn couldn't help feeling like she was becoming more and more familiar as time went on.

All of them went outside, breathing in the surprisingly cool morning. Vaughn knew that when a day that started this nice meant it was going to be a hot one, and it was comforting to know that he had some idea what was going to happen next.

The sunrise was something Vaughn only now realized he had never seen before, having resented the sun for the heat it brought and because he never been up early enough to see it.

Did sunrises always last this long?

He still couldn't shake that ringing in his ear that was sounding more and more like a hum, but then the smell of smoke and coal drifted back to Vaughn and somehow it soothed him. He recognized it; it smelt like home.

"Quite a nice place this." L said innocently looking at the great big building that stood behind them. "A good place for a party, don't you think?"

"Everything all right, Vaughn?" Wyla asked.

"Sure. Yeah, everything's fine. The good people are gone and I'm still here."

"What do you mean?"

"What do I mean?" Vaughn started. "I feel bad about what I did. Which is strange, I used to think I was only full of hate and self-pity. I even forced myself to like that part of who I was, but I didn't know."

"Didn't know what?"

"That I was capable of caring." Vaughn looked down. The word felt sickly in his mouth, and he felt something in his throat he had to force down. "But I'm not like you. I believe what he believed, what that asshole..."

Just then Wyla pulled him in and held him tight and whispered something in his ear.

"I don't care."

Vaughn felt something lift in his chest, the literal weight everyone always talks about. It was heavier than he thought, and he had no idea how long it had been there.

After standing outside for some time, never once seeing a change to the uprising sun, Atticus frowned and sighed loudly. Crushing shriveled up cigarettes scattered about the ground; Atticus wondered whom he'd have to pay to pick them all up.

Vaughn caught Atticus' eye as it sneered at the ground.

"Hey old man." Vaughn started off, walking away from the group and around the side of the Observatory. "I've been wondering, have ever you seen the gap?"

"Excuse me?" Atticus frowned.

"Yeah, c'mon. You own this place, you have to see it."

Vaughn led Atticus and the others around the side just as he had Pete, squeezing around the corner and coming to the edge where he and Pete had once sat and dangled their legs, all that time ago.

"What?" Atticus groaned, resentful like a child being shown their own messy bedroom. "What am I looking at here?"

"This is the gap." Vaughn explained. "Jumping across is what people in this town used to do for fun around here, before you built this place."

"My, I never knew this town was so... cultured."

Vaughn wasn't looking over the edge like the others, he was looking straight at Atticus. He had left out the part of the story after the White Cube had sent everyone away and before ditching Hammond in the slowing time.

And Atticus hadn't said a word about it. He kept his mouth shut, silently hoping Vaughn had either forgotten or forgiven.

"I have to say Crowe, you throw one hell of a party."

He nodded and tried not to look Vaughn in the eye.

"I suppose all that's left now is for you to post the invitation to the newspaper, huh." Vaughn followed.

Atticus nodded again, slipping a white envelope from his jacket pocket, muddied on the corners.

"You had that with you all this time?" Galina gasped.

"Oh, he sure did. A great way to keep yourself safe wasn't it, Atticus. A little unfinished business as your insurance from the universe."

Atticus' quiet refrain suddenly turned. Sensing the power in his hands he loosened his shoulders and turned to face Vaughn.

"That's right." He snarled. "And you know what? It worked like a charm."

"I'll bet."

"I'm just going to post this and then we'll have all this behind us, won't we."

"That's right." Vaughn sneered.

"I guess there's just one last thing to do after that." Atticus said with narrow eyes.

"What's that?"

"We can't have you skipping around through time anymore. Not with all the trouble you've caused." Atticus crushed his tongue under his back teeth as he nodded to the lined bag full of cubes that Vaughn still carried with him. "So, hand them over. All of them."

Vaughn obeyed, sliding the bag over to Atticus with his foot. Galina and Wyla watched as they both stood by the edge of the mountain doing an exchange as tight and tense as a drug deal.

"That one too." Atticus held out his hand, eyeing the cube poking angles in Vaughn's pocket.

Vaughn pulled it out, the last cube he had left. It was half its weight, with one trip left and Vaughn knew what it was going to be.

"What, this cube?" Vaughn toyed.

"Yes Vaughn. All of them. That means that one too."

Vaughn held it out, moving his hand slightly to one side and then the other, noticing Atticus' eye didn't leave it, following it like a dog does a treat. Atticus was almost salivating. The bag at his feet full but this one tasted the best.

"You want it?"

Atticus licked his lips.

"Then catch."

Vaughn tossed the cube aside, over the edge of the cliff with Atticus chasing after it.

He didn't judge his steps.

Two, three too many.

Atticus toppled over, arms out, reaching for it but forever out of reach as he chased it to the bottom of the mountain. Galina, Wyla and L all rushed to the edge, looking for an Atticus sized splash at the bottom, but the drop was so deep there was nothing to see.

"What did you do?"

Wyla got up close and in Vaughn's face, but he didn't buckle.

"What did you…"

"He was the one who invited them." Vaughn cut her off.

"Yeah, we know."

"No, the Historians." Vaughn finished. "He invited the Historians."

"He… what?"

"It was Atticus, Wyla. He set the whole thing up. And it wasn't the first time. Believe me."

Wyla backed off a little, still in shock. But Galina stepped up.

"I believe you."

"Thanks."

"I believe you too." L smiled.

'Thanks L."

"But the letter..." Wyla suddenly realized.

"What, this letter?" Vaughn held the envelope up and smiled. His quick hands had made themselves useful. "Don't worry about it. I'll see it gets where it's going."

Vaughn walked away from the edge, leading the group back around to the front of the Observatory. He was hoping someone else had returned as well. That maybe Pete would be looking around for him. But it was a strange and windless morning.

The sun was still rising, taking its time, knowing no rush.

"Well." Galina said, stretching and putting an arm over Vaughn's shoulder. "We should go, yes? You come with?"

"I am so... so very tired." Vaughn sighed with a smile. "I've got to try to get some sleep before work. And then after that, I'm just going to sleep for a week."

"Don't tell me you're staying here?" Wyla quizzed.

"I am."

"But why?"

Why indeed, Vaughn thought. He took his eyes off his friends and looked past them down to the town below. Their ordinary days were only just beginning. TV shows would air, politicians would turn the course of history, great actors would grace the stage and screen, bands that he had not yet heard of would emerge from their garages. So much was happening, like the ground was buzzing, here and now, Vaughn felt it crazy to leave and miss out.

"Because to someone, somewhere, this is a golden age. And I'm a part of it, a real part of it. Not a tourist, but a tiny piece of the big picture. I belong here."

Wyla shook her head while Galina smiled and looked to Vaughn with a look of great respect.

"If you want, we can go back, change things so you don't end up here, in this town. It'll be like none of it ever happened."

"But it did happen." Vaughn assured. "Don't take it away from me now."

"Ok crazy boy." Galina ruffled Vaughn's thin hair and pulled him in for a hug and he tried not to let her armhole get too close to his face. "You be good. I'll know if not."

L came in for a hug too, stumbling unevenly and falling into Vaughn's chest.

"You take it easy, L."

"I will." L smiled. "Hey, wasn't there five of us before?"

Wyla and Galina spoke and hugged each other too. Both women happy to part and go their separate ways, but on good terms. Galina winked at them both, took L by the shoulder, twisted a cube and the two of them left.

All that was left was Wyla and Vaughn. She saw Vaughn was eager to stay, but eagerly tense, like he was waiting for someone.

"You know, you two were quiet a duo." She said.

"Huh? Who?"

"You know who. I would have guessed you had been friends for years."

Vaughn lowered his head.

"Don't worry. I think you'll see him again."

"I hope so."

Wyla hugged Vaughn and he held back his sense of smell as she still stunk like the tin cave she had crawled out of.

"Before you go Wyla, I need you to do me a favor."

"Sure, anything."

"I need you to go find me down there." Vaughn nodded to the town below, still waking up below the mountain. "I need you to find me at the pub. I'll be in a bad mood and hard to talk to, but you must talk to me. You must hand me a cube; tell me I'm dreaming and send me back to yesterday."

"I have to say all that?" Wyla asked, eyes darting all around as they used to do. "Why?"

"Why?" Vaughn smiled. "Because that's how it's all supposed to play out, that's how I ended up at this party in the first place. There's no point fighting off what I know will come. All I can do is step back,

look at it from a different point of view and understand it. And that's what I'm gonna try to do."

"All right, so I go down there, find you and give you a cube." Wyla held out the one she had arrived with; the faded one Vaughn had placed on her chest.

"Not that cube. That one's yours." Vaughn smiled.

"What are you…"

Wyla looked down, the cube she had been holding, the one he had placed on her chest, was still in her hand.

"I noticed that cube had more jumps in it than the others. It's also the cube that nut-job Stein was holding onto for dear life. Something tells me it wasn't his to begin with. Something tells me this cube is special."

She noticed its colors were faded more than usual, like it had been through a lot. She turned it over, careful not to slip a tile out of place and she came to the white side, the middle white tile than never moved from its place had a strange marking. She wiped at it with her thumb; it didn't wipe off. Her hand shook, as she couldn't believe what she saw, a twisted 'W' engraved on the white tile.

"Is it… what I think it is…?"

"I think so." Vaughn grinned.

"I think… I think this really might be a dream."

Vaughn walked the long walk down the winding road back into town. He was back in his own time. In fact, he had to keep reminding himself that he had work in a few hours, not that he needed to be on time today.

As Vaughn walked down the hill, he flapped the letter in his hands, barely proof that anything out of the ordinary had happened.

Proof only of another one of Atticus' crazy parties, but it needed a new envelope - the address was indecipherable.

As he made it into town, he ducked into the open post office for a new envelope, stamp, and a pen. When the lady behind the counter asked for payment, he checked his pockets and found he was still broke.

But Vaughn still left with that envelope, stamp, and pen. His hands still had a trick or two.

Outside was a mailbox and Vaughn lent on the side and copied the faded address onto the new envelope, slapped the stamp in the corner, and then tore open the old envelope to see what was inside.

He slid out an invoice to pay for a half-page advert in a Melbourne city paper. So far away that it would be a wild chance that anyone in Fracture would ever see it, and too far on the other side of the country for anyone to attend.

Along with it was the advert Atticus wished to print. Vaughn couldn't help but grin from ear to ear as he read the first opening line.

Attention Time Traveler's, Voyagers and Trekkers.
Hello there Black Hole Divers, Deep Space
Swimmers and Celestial Portal Riders.
And Welcome Quantum Leapers, Chrono
Jumpers and Space Skippers.
If you find yourself without a country
or a time to which you belong,
If you are lost and need to rest,
If safe haven is what you're craving,
Then you will find that there's
always time at The Time Asylum,
A place for those that have no other.
May 10th -11th 1991
6:00pm til 6:00am
Mount Fracture Observatory
Open Bar.

Vaughn decided not to go to work that day at all, even after his past self would have left. And even though his body pleaded with him for some rest, he instead headed back up to Mount Fracture.

He passed the sign leading people up the mountain to the Observatory. A man in an orange Fluro-vest had a brush and bucket of soapy water

and was scrubbing at the yellow spray paint. He wore a frown on his face and muttered animosity towards the youth of today.

Vaughn smiled as the 'L' of *Limpfingers* was washed away and he started on up the path to the top.

As he walked the streetlights were turning off one by one as the sun truly rose and the morning passed into day.

At the top of the hill the humming in his ears picked up again and the sun seemed to be closer to the horizon than it was moments ago. He found himself once again and standing before the Observatory, but he kept on, moving around the side of the building to find the mountain's edge calling waiting for him.

He had no longing to jump, just to sit, leaving room at his side for another if they were to join him.

As he looked out over the town glowing in this constant dawn with the Observatory at his back and air under his swinging feet, he decided this is where he'd stay.

For however long it took, he would not abandon this town, this place or this time.

He would stay and wait for his infinite friend.

Part One:
BLUE

Chapter Twenty-One:
The Morning After

Did he jump or was he pushed?

The unfortunately and illegally parked car was a now crater. The body had fallen through its thin, metal roof like a cartoon character falling through snow. Glass and blood everywhere. The onlookers pushed to the front, trying to catch a glimpse of the mangled man.

Did anyone recognize him?

Was there anything left to recognize?

Vaughn stood on the opposite side of the road, chewing his fingers. Small white birds cawed from the ledges above. He could see them scuttling along the rusted guttering by their shadows on the ground before him. They were the only sound of nature in the entire town and it was a caw that taunted you to collapse in the heat and die so they could peck fresh eyeballs.

Vaughn felt the soles of his feet burning against the pavement and he recoiled from the sun, positioning himself under a thin stretch of shade from a power line pole as he watched the cops assess the scene.

They pushed away spectators but most fell back on their own once they had gotten a good enough look. Especially one woman. She sobbed and wailed so hard a cop had to hold her as she fell to her knees.

Vaughn felt a lump in his throat that watered his eyes; perhaps she knew the dead man, maybe it was her son. Maybe she had just seen the lifeless body of the boy she had raised and loved; cold and broken. Vaughn swallowed hard and cleared his throat, pushing the lump down

uncomfortably. He couldn't help but feel that this, like everything else that went bad, was somehow all his fault.

"What a shit show." He muttered to himself and scratched his shaved head as he watched the cops looking at the car and then up into the clear sky, scratching their heads as well.

Just lifting his arm made him wince. He had moved and rubbed the mighty rash under his armpits where his shirt had gone soggy and was irritating the skin.

Fracture was always hot, bad hot. Sweaty and disgusting hot.

Vaughn saw it as just a small hot dot on the map.

Granted, Fracture had a few streets of houses, strips shops, that kind of thing.

And it definitely wasn't small size wise.

Add up all the acres of the cow farms and the buffer zone of land surrounding the mines and Fracture was huge. You'd have to walk for hours just to get out of it's sight.

There was only one road running in and out. And it was a long one.

And it wasn't even one of those small towns where everybody knows everybody. Many kept to themselves. Vaughn still didn't know half the names of the regulars at the pub.

No, Vaughn figured it was a small town because it barely mattered.

Map space figured little when the entire history of the town could fit on a postcard.

Or maybe it felt small because a few decades ago someone just straight up bought it.

Vaughn watched one cop try to pull the body off the car and almost rip an arm off. He savored the slight pause this random event had offered him, it gave him time to let his rash breathe and his head quit aching, but whatever it was, whatever divine intervention, it wasn't enough to get him out of going to work.

The blood and broken glass had discouraged no regulars from finding their way past the crowd to the door. It was not as though the alcohol had destroyed their empathy for suicide, rather an overhanging stench of depression had built them up a thirst.

Instead of happiness, the people of Fracture sought complacency; a more realistic and achievable goal. These people were used to routine, sameness.

Different would kill 'em.

A bus did come from Broome every two weeks, and Fracture was the last town you'd pass before heading to the mines. You'd see it on their faces, those passing just passing through, they had just arrived in Bumfucknowhere.

The dread of what was waiting for him at work, made Vaughn empathize with the bloodied, torn skin and jagged boned body currently sun baking on top of the trashed car.

Maybe he had said some things to his manager he would regret but fail to remember.

Things that, if he ever recalled the words leaving his mouth, would feel more like lumps of vomit surfacing instead of sounds.

Maybe Jake would be in. Maybe fuck.

"I don't wanna go, I don't wanna go, I don't wanna go." Vaughn said to himself as he bounced up and down on the spot. "I quit. You can't quit, you need money, money to buy things, pretty things, like rent. Then you'll be broke anyway, and the whole friggin cycle continues. Urggh this suuuucks."

To top it all off, Vaughn had woken up on the floor of his bedroom that morning with no idea how he'd gotten home, heavily hung-over and late for work; enough of both that he considered quitting.

Quitting work, not drinking. He wasn't crazy.

"Fucking fine! I'll go to work!" He argued with himself.

He crossed the road, careful not to get any glass in his bare feet, weaving in with the crowd to try to get a peak before the cops could barricade off the area. He hoped it was his manager, Baz, but suspected it was one of his regular barflies.

When he got close, the blood, the rips and protruding bones. He thought maybe he'd see Jake's face plastered to the roof of the car.

The dead man was neither. Not that there was much left to go by; his face was cookie dough. The cops were talking about specialist forensics

and whether they could move the body at all until they arrived. They had no clue what was protocol, and the only defining features of the dead man were his bloodstained suit and his blue shoes.

Vaughn wiped his brow. His sweat was dark, he had stood still for too long, the soot and ash in the air had landed on his forehead just as it landed on everything. The windows had to be constantly washed, otherwise they'd go dark. The bricks and pavements were always black and if you touched anything, you got black on your hands.

From the outside of the pub, Vaughn couldn't even get a quick peak. The windows were covered in unwashed filth, what sunlight got through, broke into eschewed shards across the yearly vacuumed carpet inside the pub.

The pub was a double story, with a fake and inaccessible balcony running along the sides. All that was upstairs were boxes of crap that each owner generously left to the next. Red brick and mustard-colored moldings ran around every door and window. It had one of those massive Carlton Draught signs rigged to the top just to signify how good the wine list was.

It had big chunky wooden doors that either pushed or pulled depending on your mood, and boldly adorned along the north side of the building, facing out to the main street, was the name Atticus William Crowe.

He was a man everyone had heard of, but barely any had met. That postcard of the town's history would tell you he made it big in the seventies on stocks and bonds; paper wealth in uncallused hands.

He bought the land, sold it to the mining corporations, and branded his name all over the sides of every street corner building. He only ever visited in rumor or hearsay, hosting parties and leaving behind the mess. Vaughn figured he probably had some penthouse in Sydney or on the Gold Coast and didn't even live in town.

Because of his branding, the pub was aptly nicknamed The Crowbar, despite the business name Baz had on the lease.

"C'mon get inside before you burn over your other sunburns." Vaughn told himself and pulled on the push open doors.

As per usual, each barfly had found their booth or barstool and was already mulling their mornings over a fresh drink.

"Gents." Vaughn saluted as he karate palmed open the heavy door.

"Looking good, Vaughn!" A barfly saluted.

Vaughn gritted his teeth as he made for the staff room door.

In and out, he thought, just ditch your bag and grab an apron.

Painfully, he pushed open the door and tried not to look and see Jake standing in close quarters with Baz.

The sound of a broken sentence hung in the air as they watched and waited for Vaughn to leave so they could continue.

Fuck.

Vaughn thought it best to get lost in his work and found that his hands had nabbed a rag and done a wide sweep across the counter.

Vaughn looked at his hands, curling up his lip to his nose and gave his right hand the stink eye. It was these hands that had gotten him into this mess.

Vaughn had found that at a young age, while his mind would spout evil thoughts and suggestions, his hands had already committed the crimes. Pick pocketing strangers, nicking cash from the register, sliding friend's possessions at parties up his sleeves, and easiest of all was his exclusive five-finger discount at the milk bar. Stuff was just stuff, regardless of who owned it, and it was only stolen if someone found it missing.

Yes, Vaughn found that his larcenous limbs were always lining his pockets with whatever was in reach. Now, again, they had done something he couldn't wriggle out of so easily. But he still couldn't help but let them unconsciously wipe down the counter.

When the door occasionally swung open, it shed its blinding light over the vampiric barflies that spent their days huddled in the darkest corners of the pub. Their lingering stench maintained their permanent reservation at their own seats, the kind of reservation you didn't want to break under threat of a slurred what-say-you.

"Vuughn."

Vaughn knew all their orders, what drink each barfly was calling for with each half-assed wave and garbling of his name. As disrespectful as this felt, Vaughn preferred the flies to stay where they were than to approach the counter and give him a lesson in beer breath: a second language.

And thanks to his hands, he needn't bother lending any thought to mixing them, so on an average shift he could just hang out with Jake and talk shit.

He had barely poured a drink, and he was already sweating.

Vaughn lifted his arms and aired out his armpits. His forehead was perpetually covered in sweat, which was mostly what he used his rag to wipe up.

He couldn't understand how they all could tolerate it. It was as though they didn't even recognize the heat of hell. The town stunk of smoke and swam in heat. Sweat and grease, salt and fat.

Vaughn was honestly shocked that today was the first suicide he had seen.

Everyone that dwelled in Fracture lived life like it was a chore.

Vaughn hated them for it, working ten-hour days, two weeks on two weeks off for a heavy pay slip.

And all they did was blow it. Half of them lived in The Crowbar for their two weeks off.

These flies started to buzz; the ones sitting along the bar had huddled close and were avidly discussing Fracture's newest celebrity currently being scraped off the parked sedan. It was a pleasant change of pace, Vaughn thought, allowing the drivel to flow out of their mouths rather than into it.

"They don't know shit." One barfly said to the other.

"Oh, I bet they know, have you seen Law and Order? They get a hair and…"

"Mate he's got no wallet, no tats, no birthmarks. No suicide note. The fella's barely got a face yet alone dental records."

"How d'you even…"

"The sergeant's a mate of mine."

"So like I said, they'll get a hair or something and they'll find out who he is and why he did it, like they always do. No mystery."

"Don't you think it's strange that we don't know the guy? I like to think I know everyone around here."

"His face was schmooshed, I wouldn't recognize you if you looked like that."

"Still, someone would notice if someone went missing. 'Specially someone who wore blue shoes."

"Have you seen Frankie around much…?"

"Pulled a third week."

"Could be a visitor from the shindig last night up top."

"True true could be one of them. Another one of Crowe's blowouts. Actually, fuck, I hope so."

"Kept me up all night, all that commotion. He must've known when he built the damn thing it would echo down to us."

"I fucking know that he did that on purpose."

"Wouldn't surprise me hearing that one of them got so wasted that he wandered down here, climbed to the top and jumped."

The two barflies raised their glasses and wacked them together hard enough Vaughn's ears rang.

"Excuse me, but are you two talking about the incident outside?" A stranger to the flies interjected as she approached the counter.

A disheveled woman, dark black hair all over the place with bits of gunk clogging strands together. In Fracture, anyone over the age of forty looked oven-baked, they had sunburnt and coal-stained skin which just looked leathery and gross. But this woman had a more exotic, darker skin tone, natural and kind of nice to look at. She was something different. New.

But fuck, did she stink.

Enough to make the debating flies wince and she sat right between them on the seat they had left empty to assure their own sexuality wouldn't be questioned. She eased down on the stool and rubbed her shoulder as she asked for a glass of water.

Vaughn slid her one, which she raised and toasted with a wink.

"What's it to you, darling?" The first barfly defended, shuffling one stool over. "Was that your car out there? No."

"Was it yours?" The dirty woman asked.

"Right oath it was."

"Oh, give it a rest." The second barfly interjected. "It's been parked there for almost five months; it's got one of those wheel locks on it because of parking tickets. Why don't you go out and let the cops know whose car got smashed?"

"Nuts to that, they can have it. Got a big dent in it anyway."

"I'd bet your insurance doesn't cover suicide?"

"I'd be surprised if it covered anything, fucking third party."

"I'm sorry, suicide?" The dirty woman pressed.

"You didn't notice the new paint job on your way in?" The car owning barfly jabbed.

"Yes, but I just thought I'd help point out the obvious part of the scenario that neither of you two seem to have noticed."

"You're not going to try to tell us that he was murdered or nothing?"

"What would you say is the approximate height of this building he supposedly jumped from?" She asked.

"Two stories." They said raising an eye to each other.

"Now do you believe a two-story fall could cause that much of an impact on your vehicle?"

Their silence said no.

"I overheard the police saying that they've seen falls like this before, but from forty story buildings." The dirty woman continued. "They can't fathom he fell from any less than eighty feet, possibly a hundred."

"Now how do you think that's true?" The second barfly argued. "I didn't see any unopened parachute on his back or nothing."

"Now that's not fair. Give the sheila a chance." The other barfly mocked. "Maybe it was hot-air balloon. Maybe he wasn't loving the view and hopped it."

But the dirty woman nodded, unfussed. "That's true, anything's possible."

"Ok that's enough, love. Why don't you take your wise-assing somewhere else? These seats are for loyal customers." The car owner turned in his seat and leaned over to Vaughn. "Ain't that right, Vaughn?"

"Oh, I really don't give a shit."

"Yer see." The barfly said, undeterred by Vaughn's comment. "What he said."

"Changing it up today Vaughny?" The second barfly said with a wink. "Looking good."

Vaughn shook his head. He barely ever knew what they were going on about, and he wished they didn't persist in talking to him. He moved himself further down the counter and pretended that he couldn't hear any new orders as the next drink he was to pour was one for himself.

As he sipped it, a mouthful at a time, as he stared at where the TV had been, usually playing crappy daytime programs that he'd watch on mute. But instead, there was just a broken TV wall mount and loose cords that Baz still hadn't gotten fixed.

He took another sip, and the sound of the staff room door stiffened his hands, and he knocked glass against his teeth.

Jake walked behind Vaughn.

Vaughn checked his fingers, he hadn't realized he'd been chewing them raw again, the skin that sunk under his fingernails peeled to shows new red flesh that stung to touch.

Jake fumbled behind him. But being behind the bar kept them in too close a proximity.

How best to approach this?

"Hey man."

Jake walked past coldly.

"Did you get a look at the thing outside?" Vaughn kept on.

"The thing?"

"Yeah, the thing."

"Did I see the dead body on the smashed car right outside?"

"… Yeah."

"What about it?" Jake said, keeping his back to Vaughn.

"… Bit odd, huh?"

"Odd? You think it's..."

"- Look, I'm sorry."

"Sorry? Did you push him?"

"What? No, about the other night. I fucked up."

Jake couldn't help but crack and turn to meet Vaughn; face to angry face.

"Just the other night?" Jake whispered harshly. "That's just when you got caught. You're only sorry because you got caught. What about everyone else? Don't you care about what your actions do to other people? Don't you have any empathy?"

"Tons. Buckets of it."

"So you care, but did it, anyway?" Jake finally turned around. "That's worse."

"Then fine, I don't care. Which one's better? What do you want from me?"

"I want you to care about someone else for a change. I want you to stop being such an asshole."

"Don't tell me what to do." Vaughn retorted. "My ends justify my means, so what else does it matter? Besides, I only got caught because..."

"Oh, don't fucking start. Don't turn this around on me. They were my mates. And even if they weren't what kind of fucking prick does that? They work a hard days' work down there and you do shit all and think you can just take it."

"Jake we were saving up to get the fuck out of dodge."

"No. No, I was saving up. You were stealing."

"Who cares? What were they going to spend it on that would be worth letting them keep it?"

"That's not how money works Vaughn you earn it not deserve it."

"Well then, you deserve to stay here. Down there with them."

"Funny you say that. I've just given my notice to Baz. I'm on the next bus."

"Perfect, fucking perfect. You can throw your life away digging in the dark like a mole."

"Is that… is that really what you wanna say. To your…"

"My what?" Vaughn said through gritted teeth.

"…To your best friend?" Jake finished.

"If you don't like it, then too bad."

"I don't like it."

"Then too bad."

Jake stood back, almost lost for words. So many things almost came out, and he held nearly all of it back.

"So that's it? I've known you forever. I stood by you after… I was the only one who'd even talk to you after… And now this is it, huh? You're fine with this?"

"Pretty much."

Vaughn knew it sounded harsh; he immediately wanted to snatch the words out of the air and cram them back down his throat.

"Shit, fucking fine with me. I was getting pretty fucking sick of listening to you go on and on about getting out of Fracture and never doing shit. All talk and no fucking game."

"Look, did you quit or not? Why are you still here?" Vaughn snapped and threw a towel at him.

"Consider me gone, *Limpfingers*."

Jake slipped into the back room as a shot glass narrowly missed where his head had been. A furious Vaughn dodged the rebounding glass as it refused to shatter and instead bounced off the door. He realized how quiet it had gotten. Was it a quiet fight? Had he really been yelling?

"Friend of yours?" The dirty woman asked, swirling her empty drink in her hand.

"Butt out." Vaughn said and sloppily filled the shot glass, offered it to the dirty woman and downed it himself.

"What's the matter?"

"None of your business. That's what."

"Well, maybe don't have your lover's quarrel in front of everyone. Now we're all curious."

"Well, like I said." Vaughn looked out to the rest of the pub and exclaimed. "It's none of your business!"

Vaughn's words resonated as the pub fell quiet and everyone watched Jake collect his things and struggled to keep his composure as he hurried back and forth, forgetting things and having to go back past Vaughn again and again. Each time Vaughn tried not to look and see the tears welling up in his eyes.

Vaughn felt that lump again. He downed a shot of gin to get rid of it.

"Hey Vaughn. Didn't old man Crowe offer you a job waitressing last night?" A regular jabbed.

Shit he did, didn't he. Vaughn recalled.

"Oh, ha ha. You all were here; you all saw it." Vaughn replied.

"He offered you a job, huh?" The dirty woman asked, shuffling into the counter, elbows sweeping up water rings. "Did you take it?"

"Sure fucking didn't." Defended a Barfly. "And you know that our boy Vaughny here told him exactly where to go, didn't you kiddo."

"You did?" The dirty woman was almost impressed.

He did. Vaughn could recall most of it, as hazy as it was. The old man had come to buy his favor, offering him a bartending job at one of his parties, up at the Observatory. Vaughn was sure he had turned down the offer... surely?

He was at least sure he had spoken eloquently and made equally eloquent points.

Actually, he wasn't sure of either...

"Damn right. We've got to send him a message. He can't just buy anything or anyone. Some of us have class." The barfly scratched the lint free from his exposed belly, popping out from under his wife-beater. "And he offered you a lot to do it, right Vaughn?"

"Yeah." Vaughn sighed heavily. "A lot."

Vaughn nabbed a bottle off the lower shelf, loosened the lid to pour three glasses across the counter and then tipped the bottle to wet his mouth. He had a long suck before he turned to put it back and then bumped into Baz.

"Fuck, don't sneak up on a guy like that."

Baz was a big man. His man breasts and stomach sunk off him to the floor like melted cheese.

"What's this?" He said, snatching the bottle out of his hand. "You're not fucking get shitfaced on my shit again like yesterday?"

"I wanna say… no?" Vaughn tried.

"And what's was all this about working for Crowe?" Baz asked. "You didn't go last night, did you?"

"I have some dignity."

"Is that right?" Baz pressed.

"Fuck you, are you done talking about me behind my back?"

"We'll talk after your shift's up." Baz said turning back, avoiding eye contact and confrontation.

"You let Jake quit."

"Yeah, he's moving up in the world now." Baz sighed.

"He's literally going down in it Baz."

"You should be out of a job after the shit, he told me. But as you know, the next bus comes tomorrow afternoon, and I don't have time to train someone else. So, you're just gonna have to apologize."

"Sorry." Vaughn spat out quickly.

"What? Is that a genuine apology?"

"Probably not genuine."

"Well, if you're not sorry now, you're sure gonna be. You're gonna pay me back. Out of your pay."

"You're kidding me."

"Hey, I could just go to the fucking cops out there and get 'em to take you away." Baz tightened the leash he just realized he was holding. "Taking money out of my till, fuck. Don't make me regret it."

Baz sighed heavily. His entire body sunk in, probably pressing on his heart as he held up a fist to push into it.

"I don't know what your problem is mate. Life's not as bad as you make it out to be. But now you've well and truly dug yourself the hole and jumped in."

"Fracture is the hole."

"Well, I'm sorry you feel that way, but from now on, or until I hire someone new, you're gonna be here every day open 'til close. Got it?"

Vaughn looked down to his hands, wanting them to fight each other to the death.

"Vaughn?" Baz pushed.

"Yeah, I get it."

"Good. Now get back to it and tomorrow I expect you to be in full uniform."

"What's that supposed to...?"

Vaughn finally looked down. It was like something out of a bad dream. How hadn't he realized he was still in his pajamas? A plain white shirt with drool stains and blue and white polka dot cotton boxer shorts.

Hell, he wasn't even wearing shoes.

He could feel the stickiness of the rubber mats behind the counter. Each time he pulled his foot up, he had nowhere better to put it. He was lucky his apron was so long, or he would have felt even more self-conscious.

"How d'you not notice?" Baz asked.

"I don't know. All right? I'm having a rough morning."

"Tomorrow, pants, white button shirt."

"Yeah, I know." Vaughn said, trying to add some sense of confidence as his voice broke through it. He dug through the drawer behind the bar, found his nametag and his wristwatch; haphazardly, he clipped his tag to his apron and slipped on his watch as though it adequately dressed him.

The regulars were all accounted for, but the crowd outside had also found their way in, squeezing themselves along the bar and into unwelcomed booths and tables. Vaughn served them all, feeling

a little rushed without Jake covering tables, and he and Baz were at some silent war for who should be behind the counter and who should pick up Jake's slack. They made do by ignoring them completely and beckoning those accustomed to table service to come to the counter if they wanted to get any of his attention.

Vaughn's hands were swift, any drink on or off the menu Vaughn prepared with little to no thinking as he hands remembered the tricks, the maneuvers and minutiae of each cocktail he had learnt by watching Baz.

Vaughn knew Baz owed him more than he let on. Before he started the barflies would only order off the tap and occasionally someone turning eighteen would order something fancy and Baz would have to make it.

From there Vaughn learnt quick and now the barflies had a more eclectic taste. Ordering Martinis and Bloody Marys between pots and jugs. And they all had their own favorites.

Baz figured either they had gotten over beer or they had seen how much vodka Vaughn poured into an Appletini.

Baz wiped his sweaty face with his rag as he held four pots in two hands and handed them over the counter. They were a very thirsty crowd this morning, and as hot as it was, it wasn't hotter than usual.

Though Vaughn had learnt all his moves from watching Baz. He wasn't as quick to speed through a cocktail, and Vaughn found it hard to hold respect for someone he had outmatched. Baz was only in his fifties, but years of Fracture had tunneled into him and Vaughn watched as he struggled to pull apart two shaker tins he had clamped together.

Hit it with your palm, you old twit, Vaughn thought but pictured himself in Baz's shoes in thirty years and bit his tongue instead.

"So, you turned down the invitation to go to the party last night?"

"Sorry what?"

Vaughn slid down the counter to where she sat hunched over her drink, strands of curly black hair almost creeping into her glass of

water. Vaughn was used to smells, but she really stunk, like she had been living in a cave for years. Her clothes had lost any sense of shape, just clinging to her body out of habit, and her breath was...

"Crowe's party?" The dirty woman insisted.

"Yeah, I know." Vaughn coughed, backing up. "But why're you asking me about..."

"Why didn't you go?"

"I didn't..." Vaughn wanted to say he chose not to but honestly couldn't remember that much after Crowe's visit yesterday, besides the taste of stale alcohol on his tongue. "I just didn't mmmk?"

"You don't know who I am, do you?"

Vaughn stood a back a bit. For the smell and to judge just what she was getting at. He wasn't great with faces or names.

"Look if you were here yesterday or before that I'm sorry, but when I drink I forget some stuff. Most of that stuff ends up being people."

"You know, you told me to come see you here." She lent in.

"Really, I don't remember a thing. Don't take it personally." Vaughn pointed to one of the regular barflies sitting close by. "He's still barfly no.4 to me..."

Barfly no.4 dropped his cheeks and stuck his head in his drink.

"...And he's here every fucking day." Vaughn finished. "So, can I get you anything that's not water?"

"At nine in the morning?"

"Hey, it's nine-thirty somewhere."

"Vaughn...?" The dirty black-haired woman pressed. She spoke in a way that made Vaughn feel like he was having an eye exam. "Do you want to know who I am?"

"Sure, I guess."

The dirty woman's black hair had him like a hypnotizing spiral, winding into her eyes, as she leant forward and spoke, her words slitted between his thoughts like corduroy pants on a corduroy couch.

"Do you know those dreams you have nights before something important the next day? In those dreams you're late, tragically and ridiculously late. No matter what you try everything gets in the way,

the sun sets at two in the afternoon, you can't stop your feet from walking in the wrong direction. And most of all, your caught in public in your underwear?"

"Yeah. So?"

"You're having one of those dreams, Vaughn. And I'm your subconscious."

"For real?"

"Dreams can be more real than we like them to be sometimes. And nightmares even harder to wake up from."

The woman was doing something with her hands below the counter, but Vaughn couldn't tell what.

"But you've got to wake up." She whispered intensely. "It's time."

Vaughn felt himself falling forwards, the room tilted, the chatter in the background found gravity and fell back, slamming against the blacked-out windows.

He felt his head growing heavy, too heavy for his neck, and that feeling sank to his stomach.

He reached out to the dirty woman who was pushing something forward from her hands to his. Vaughn's trembling hand felt for it and clasped the strange object. He looked up to her eyes; they were insistent and still.

He looked down and in his hands; he held a children's toy.

A colorful six-sided cube with six different colored tiles, all mismatched on every side.

A fucking Rubik's cube.

"You're absolutely right." Vaughn sighed, rapped his knuckles against the counter and walked away before he bit through his own tooth. "There's been enough bullshit for one morning. It's time for my break."

The dirty woman lent back in her seat and sipped from her glass and watched him leave as she softly counted backwards.

'Baz!" Vaughn yelled, stuffing the cube in his apron pocket and calling over to Baz busy serving jugs to tables. "I'm taking my break!"

"No, you're fucking not." Baz yelled back. "Vaughn. Vaughn!"

"What's that? Take a bottle for my troubles? Why thank you Baz."

Moving along the back of the bar, Vaughn nabbed a bottle of gin, a brand-new carton of smokes from the rack as he patted his apron down for his lighter and pushed through the fire exit door.

"Fucking little shit." Baz stomped over to the fire exit door and found it wouldn't open.

Outside Vaughn leant up hard against the fire exit door, foot firmly against the garbage bins, thus jamming the door closed to keep Baz and anyone else on the other side.

With his hands free, Vaughn tried lighting his cigarette when a strong thump from Baz knocked his shoulder. He sighed his flame out.

Vaughn glared at the vomit stain on the brick wall of the alley that no one had bothered to hose down before the sun could burn it into the brick. But no stain could possibly drop the estate value of the alley any lower.

Next to the stain were scribbles of spray paint and people proclaiming in near illegible writing that they were, at one point or another, there.

The whole alley was full of them. Everyone wanted to brand themselves in this town and Vaughn couldn't understand. Who would want people to know they were there, living in Fracture? A place where the only source of art had a great big disgusting vomit stain, streaking down and covering it all.

"Vaughn? Do you think this is funny?" Baz called. He tried the door, but Vaughn pushed his foot hard against the bin and the door stayed shut.

"Yup!" Vaughn yelled back.

His eye caught sight of a new name sprayed on brick, the yellow paint still dripping from the longer letters.

Limpfingers

Fucking Jake.

He ripped his eyes from it and chose instead to stare at the vomit stain.

Today would be the first day of the rest of his life. His life was now that stain. For fifteen minutes every six hours. He would have only that stain to look forward to.

Baz started to put all his weight behind his kicks. "Get your ass back in here right now!"

The sun was creeping into the alley and burning Vaughn's bare legs. The heat had warmed the gin he had taken. It was even worse to drink, but he did so anyway. What did it matter? This was his life now. His last grand plan to get the hell out of Fracture was spoilt, and the one he planned it with would never speak to him again.

"Vaughn! Open this fucking door right now!"

They were planning on heading for the coast, any coast. But when Vaughn really thought about it, wherever they went, Vaughn would find some way to ruin it. Vaughn ruins everything everywhere he goes; he was the stale chip in the bag, the unpopped kernel in the bottom of the popcorn, that one cigarette in the pack that just falls apart when you pull it out.

"Damn it, fuck!" Vaughn yelled, throwing the packet at the wall. The beat of Baz's pounding shook him, jolted him back to reality every two seconds. He wanted to cry, he wished silent yelling was possible, but he didn't have either of them in him.

What he did have was a toy in his pocket.

The toy vibrated, it hummed, and before Vaughn wondered what was going on, it was already over and he was gone.[*]

Baz burst through the fire door, which swung open with ease. He fell into the alleyway and found only a burst packet of cigarettes rustling in the wind.

---

[*]*Go to Page 176*

✧

Chapter Twenty-Two:
Mechanics of a Good Story

Sampson sat in his car. It was parked across the street from a mechanic in the car park of a dentist. Tickets flapped in the breeze, trying to loosen their grip from the windscreen wipers, but the rubber held on tight.

A ticket inspector and a dentist secretary repeatedly told him to move his car, but he just waved them off.

He sipped from his straw a glob of his juice, a rich chunk of pulp ran up the straw and into his mouth. Whittaker was onto the tires now, on his knees scrubbing the rims with a wire brush. This was his fourth car today and it was only 10:30.

A sudden knock on the window, Sampson dismissed it, assuming the ticket inspector had returned. But the knock was firm. Sampson checked and saw the knuckles were oil stained. He rolled down his window.

"Can I help you?" Sampson defended.

"I don't think you can. I think you're the one who needs help, sitting here watching us work all day long. Man, I saw you here last week doing the same damn thing, you think we don't notice. You with OH&S or something?"

"No." Sampson said plainly.

"Then we can either fix your car or you can fuck off."

"Gotcha. Can do." Sampson replied.

The man left his window and crossed the street, tapping Whittaker on the back and handing him a doughnut. Whittaker placed the dessert

on his bucket and wiped his hands clean. He got to his feet, taking the doughnut and walking over to an empty milk crate next to the roller door and sat down.

Now or never, Sampson.

He got out of his car and crossed the road. He felt his feet taking him a little off course, as though to straighten up when he made it to the path and ignore the man completely. But he corrected his aim and walked up to the man who had a mouthful of dough.

"Hello."

"Hi." Whittaker muffled.

Sampson had nothing. He hadn't thought this far ahead.

"Is that it?" Whittaker asked. "Do you want your car serviced? You'll have to make an appointment with Lucy at the desk."

"No, I'm here for you… I mean. I want to talk to you."

"What have I done?"

"Nothing." Sampson sighed. "And that's the problem."

Sampson found another milk crate, turned it over, and sat with Whittaker.

"I'm not sure if you noticed but there is a new book that got released not too long ago. It's pretty popular. Topping all the best seller's lists and everything. Have you heard of it. *The 47th Detective?*"

The car detailer nodded.

"Have you read it?"

He nodded again.

"Of course you have, who hasn't? Well, I can tell you why you liked it so much. The author might have stolen that book. From someone else. From you actually."

Whittaker said nothing.

"The author stole it before you even knew you had the idea, before you had even written it. Now this is the crazy part. That was me."

"You?"

"That's right. I liked it so much that I went back in time and gave the book to myself."

Whittaker was silent.

"What I'm trying to say is that I'm very, very sorry."

"You stole the idea from me?"

"The idea, the characters. The entire thing. I stole your book. I stole your success. I stole your life. Your future."

"Why are you telling me this?"

"Because I feel awful about it. Shouldn't I? I mean, surely it must have been eating away at you. Seeing your creation with someone else's name on it."

Again Whittaker was silent.

"Do you want money? Is that what you want, I have loads of it."

"What use is money when you have time travel, right?" Whittaker noted.

"Right."

"You know I saw you across the road, parked in that car last week."

"Oh yeah"

"Why didn't you say anything then?"

"I've had some time to think."

Whittaker lent back in his square chair. He folded his fingers between each other and rested them on his belly. He was relentlessly laid back.

"So, are you mad?"

"Mad?" He thought aloud. "No, I'm disappointed."

"I'm sorry."

"With myself. I could never do what you're doing."

"This is no time to be polite. Believe me, if you ever did anything as bad as what I did… first it was the excitement blocking it all out. I was signing the contracts. Then it was the fame, on the book tours, people lining up to get my autograph. It all drowned it out pretty well. But after a while it all goes away and all that's left is the guilt."

"I guess all's fair now, huh?"

"No, are you kidding me? That doesn't even begin to do it for me. Hit me, rob me. Overcharge me for an engine service. Anything you want."

"Anything?"

"Yes. Yes, anything."

Whittaker stood up and arched his back.

"There is one thing."

"Yes?'

"You are famous." He started. "Would you sign my copy of the book?"

Sampson couldn't believe it. As the detailer wandered into the garage in search of his copy, he wondered whether he would return with the paperback or a crowbar and have him sign it with his blood.

But Whittaker returned, cradling a copy of *The 47th Detective.*

He handed it over and Sampson took the book. The cover taunted him but then he ran his eyes down to the name below the title.

There on the cover, on the spine and on every page. It wasn't Sampson's name, nor was it Whittaker's. But the name H.J Hornback.

"It's a clever idea you had," Whittaker said. "But I had it first."

Chapter Twenty-Three:
The One-Minute War

The docks were wet. Rain had been falling for hours, stranger still it was the middle of summer.

Storage containers had channeled a section of the docklands so that one particular loading bay was kept out of sight and hard to find by any that didn't know where to look.

The Malaysian workers waved through truck after truck, as they loaded shipments into the backs. Between a few trucks there was a dark, black car with darker tinted windows waiting to be waved through by the workers. They drove past the forklifts and stacks of wet cargo to navigate the maze of storage containers, carefully making each turn not to scrape the sides. When they found the opening the black car slotted itself perfectly into a spot besides another.

Luis G. Stein got out of the car, clutching a black zipped up folio, leaving his driver to wait. He was met by a security guard standing ominously in the rain.

He followed the guard inside one forty-foot container and into complete darkness. Their footsteps echoed and neither could see where they were placing their next step. They came out the other side to find a hidden warehouse, the steel roof shielding them from the hammering rain dozens of meters above. Florescent lights hanging and swinging from chains, narrowly avoiding contact with the massive ceiling fans rotating car length panels and keeping the heat off the men below.

The security guard led Stein to the three men standing with drinks in hand and patting sweat from their brows. The rain did nothing to combat the humidity. Stein absent-mindedly waved cool air over himself with his black folio.

"Drink?" One of the three men offered. They were all wearing tie clips with the INDX logo.

"No, thanks." Stein held up a hand. "Let's just do this shall we?"

"You know, we could have done this at our offices." One of three mentioned. "Or even somewhere less… dramatic."

"No. Believe me. We couldn't." Stein shook his head. He was giddy and anxious. His eyes flickered to every corner of the warehouse. *Was it really going to happen? Was she really not coming to stop him?*

"We just don't get what you're so worried about." One of the other three jeered. "Or why you were as adamant about getting this deal done in such a rush."

"I have matters to attend to. My younger self is participating in a science fair soon and I'll need to be there."

"Nostalgia?"

"Sure, nostalgia."

"But it's fine with us. Your younger self is going to get a heck of surprise when he sees his bank account tomorrow morning." The third swooped in with a grin. He held up an INDX branded laptop and rested it on his forearm as he showed the screen to Stein. An eleven-digit figure next to a button that read 'transfer'.

"Can we see it first?" They asked.

Stein went to hand over the zipped-up folio in his hands but held it back at the last second.

"Just for my peace of mind… what do you plan on doing with it?" Stein asked.

But the three men just stood there, as though they were waiting for Stein to answer his own question.

"I can't help but wonder, you're CEO is buying it for such a high price, not that I think I'm over charging but really, what exactly does he plan on doing with it?

"Why don't you let us worry about that, ok?" They dismissed.

He finished handing it over and they unzipped it and flipped through the glossy blueprints and schematics inside.

"There's a copy on a hard drive in there as well." Stein assured them.

The three men nodded and slipped a finger over the keyboard and hit enter, sending the eleven figures to another account. Stein's account.

"So, how about that drink to celebrate?" They offered again as he folded the laptop closed and Stein checked his account on his phone. The howling storm outside wailed against the warehouse. They waited until it settled down. Outside, their drivers were a storm away. They celebrated with a few more drinks.

When they all stepped outside the heavy rain had cleared and they found it had flooded the entire dock. An oozing black liquid dripped from a crashed helicopter and mixed with the rain. Both their drivers were dead, having run for cover behind their bullet hole ridden cars. Blasts of all sorts had torn chunks of steel from storage containers like bite marks. The Malaysian workers had made a run for it as the crane had snapped loose and had swung mightily close to the loading bay.

All about lay hundreds and hundreds of bodies lying dead among small engine fires and damaged drones.

The war was over almost as soon as it started.

The three men from INDX were stunned.

"And you wondered why I was worried." Stein shook his head.

$$\diamond$$

Chapter Twenty-Four:
Condemned to be Free

Akin to a drop of water landing in a swimming pool, the five of them pin-dropped in the ocean and felt the current beneath their treading feet. It was slow and calm. They were lucky.

Galina kept her head under, she sunk, looking down deep, just seven hundred feet below her where she knew she would soon be.

Galina felt a hand grab the back of her shirt and pull her face from the water.

"Don't die on me yet, yeah?" Nadia said.

They swam to meet and hold on to each other, and the rest of their team. Galina clung to Nadia, knocking back her wet, black hair. She dug her fingers into Antin, a twenty something twig of a kid that shook in the icy water and was trying to keep his mind from sharks.

Antin held Hank's shoulder firmly, despite how much Hank tried to knock it loose, and Hank swam next to his friend August, neither touching the other but keeping within reach.

They coordinated turns to tread water for the others as they waited for their ride. On the horizon a small black dot grew larger and took the form of something more assuring; the encumbering freighter headed right in their direction.

"Who does the talking?" Antin asked.

"I will." Hank and Galina said together. Galina eyed him, knowing he wasn't one to seek help but more likely to order it.

"She will." Hank grumbled.

"We get on board, we lie low, keep to ourselves. Wait for exact moment. We get one shot to do."

"What if they're on board?" Antin asked.

"They?"

"The one's we're here to stop."

"Everyone's a suspect." Nadia answered. "But don't do anything stupid without the rest of us. We do all the stupid together."

The crew of the freighter were quick to help them aboard, seeing the five of them dressed in allied military uniforms. They were met with little questioning and were drying off on deck with the captain within minutes.

Galina's story was as she rehearsed. Their plane went down and they were awaiting rescue by air but were denied for the danger it would put the other pilots in. They were subsequently left to drown with medals post-mortem.

The captain shook his head and offered them space to stow away until they reached land, promising to keep it a secret to save both their skins.

Antin walked across the deck to a dry and secluded spot. There he pulled out a small zip up satchel wrapped in plastic. He was relieved to find everything was bone dry, and he got to work. Galina found him and sat by his side as he handled several pieces of a whole.

"Good thing scrapper like you was on that tape, no?" She said.

Antin smiled as he carefully twisted copper wires around a coupling and screwed a plate down.

"It's something to take my mind off... well...you know." Antin said, not taking his eyes off the wires. "What did the captain say?"

"He say we safe here, he not to bother us. Hope, when you fix radar, we know if boat on course or not on course."

"Why wouldn't it be?" Antin asked. "We know it will. I'm only rebuilding this radar just so we can find out when not exactly."

"Antin, if believe without doubt, then why you here?"

"Because of the tape." He answered, screwdriver between his teeth.

"Yes, because of tape. So are rest of us."

The ship they were on was carrying military aid and weaponry. Hundreds of shipping containers were stacked up around the volatile cargo so that this freighter looked harmless from a distance.

But there was still a danger of pirates coming for whatever they could find. The U.S. Army relied on them finding the outer layer of decoy containers stocked full with the latest Ogle's in pristine packaging, and that they would leave it at that.

Galina stood between two large stacks of shipping containers. She knew what they would inevitably use these irritating household appliances for. She had to hold herself back from cranking open the container and smashing a few to relieve some tension.

Instead, she just lent against the disgusting steel that had been painted in bird shit and mindless graffiti and waited. Galina knew that she should have been tracking the ship's speed and co-ordinates, just in case their being there had sped up or slowed down their trajectory. Only when Antin finished his work would she know for sure. They had just nine hours to burn.

Nadia had done a few laps. Antin was busy and Hank and August had found a spot to take a nap below deck, so Nadia listened in on crew conversations while she traced the path from one end of the ship to the other. She kept an eye on Galina, who had climbed up and sat atop a high stack of shipping containers with her legs dangling.

Galina watched her too, waving and whispering comments between friends that neither heard. From there Galina could see everything and was eye level with several vents that ran up to her height and blew a stream of smoke and steam. Strangely, Galina noticed a color of smoke that had no business puffing from below deck. A vile green smoke slipped between puffs that dissipated amongst the greys and whites.

Climbing down, Galina slipped below deck and found a trail of pipes that ran overhead and followed the wider of the pipes. Galina had to make a few guesses at a few corners of the corridors whenever the pipe slipped into the walls. Down here it was considerably warmer, and she felt her hair moisten like a wet towel.

She crept down lower and lower until the humidity was so strong that she felt condensation on the railings. No one was down here, strictly an engineering level. She walked the grated corridors until she caught sight of the pipe again. It ran clear above her head and directly into the wall of the last door at the end of the corridor.

She followed it and stood at the door. The sign read.

HIGH VOLTAGE AREA. SAFETY PROTOCOLS REQUIRED.

She pushed on the door, and it clicked firmly, locked from the outside and heavy to swing open. Immediately she ate a waft of green smoke. It tasted foul, like breathing into a couch cushion. As it cleared, she saw the room was small. A few generators pumped loudly and were sweating steam, and there, in the middle of the room, handcuffed to a steel chair that was chained to the grated floor was a man all in grey. His face still shrouded in green smoke, only his long, pointed cigarette broke through the unceasing cloud. That and his elongated words.

"Hello there."

Galina stepped back and went to lock the man back behind the door without saying a word, but he slipped a few more out.

"Galina, isn't it?"

She held the door from swinging.

"I know you?"

"I hope not."

"Why you down here?"

"I'm a stowaway. Just like you." The man was smiling, though she couldn't see it. "Well, not exactly like you, I was at least honest about it. And look what they did, they locked me down here, safe and out of sight."

"And you know me how?"

"Big fan." The smoke covered man held up two thumbs, one caught by its handcuff. He curled his words deliciously. "And I know why you're here."

Galina stayed quiet.

"You are here to deactivate the last active neutron bombs on the planet, all drifting this way on two separate U.S submarines. How am I doing so far?"

She bit her lip.

"You are doing this because you believe someone is planning on stealing one to bring back to your future to use against you. All because you saw fifteen seconds of yourself on a security tape. Isn't that all of it?"

"Pretty much." She said through gritted teeth.

"Thought so."

"So, why you here?"

"Because I have a message for you."

"What message?"

"There's a slight issue with your plan. It appears you have a mole in your group." He sang. "Someone's got an ulterior motive."

Galina gripped the door, wanting to slam it shut, but didn't know what side she wanted to be on.

"Maybe." Galina started. "Or maybe bad guy gets caught and makes up new plan to break up good guys with stupid lie."

"That would be a good plan, wouldn't it?"

"I suppose you want me to thank you and set free, yes?"

"Oh, please don't." The man slithered. "I've got guests coming soon."

Galina slammed the door, testing the lock and kicking it shut. She leant back and beat her skull against the hard door. She didn't want to believe him, but just as she had warned Antin that they might already be off course, them being there might be enough to make a change.

This is what Milosch had predicted, why he took the girls and why he had been so mad. Had he really been right all along? Was she bringing about the very thing she was trying to stop?

She walked out from below deck with uncertain aim towards the helm of the freighter. Circling the helipad, she ran it all through her mind as though her brain was about to take off. She kept coming back to the same thought over and over again. Even though she knew the concrete fact that nine 500 kilo ton, 20-foot-long Neutron bombs were

stagnating somewhere under the deep blue rough that rocked her from her place as she stood, something still plagued her mind.

The mole.

It had to be Hank.

If it was anybody at all.

If she believed it.

Standing over the big *H* meant for helicopters, she rubbed at her calf with her other shoe. She found a strange balance with the sea that either meant it had settled or she was not.

She felt alone. The wind hit her from all sides, and she felt open and vulnerable. All around her the crew were moving, lugging gear and seeing to their tasks with no clue what was going to happen in a few hours.

Then she saw him again. She had seen him before, back before she left. Or at least, she thought she did. Perhaps it was just her mind playing tricks.

Even from such a distance she could tell he was watching her; the Asian man who she suspected had been watching her every step of the way. She was his to look at, not the other way around. She felt like she was breaking some rule looking back and tore her eyes off him and to the opposite edge of the helipad.

No, it was just another member of the crew. She told herself.

Look back again and he's gone, see?

Galina climbed back up to her spot atop the storage containers. Nadia was waiting for her with a bottle of water. She drank half in a few seconds.

"Thanks."

"You look shook."

"I hate boats."

Galina rubbed her leg again with her foot and Nadia took a quick look at her leg. Galina was prone to bruises and scars, and Nadia had taken quite an interest in this one. In all their time together, Galina had never really given her a story to how it happened or even a good

look. So Nadia was surprised when Galina stopped, finally sighed, and rolled up her pant leg.

Her calf had several shapely indents, like knife wounds that dragged down her calf and rippled the skin.

"Bad no?"

"Does it hurt?"

"Only when someone ask."

Galina took her eyes off it and looked out over the ocean, but Nadia couldn't take her eyes off her leg.

"I used to hunt black bears with my father, my aunt and two uncles. We set trap, catch bear alive to sell to fat Japanese businessman as trophy. Pays good. We catch two, maybe three bear every year and we survive. And catching bear hard work, you must get close. My aunt get big scratch across chest from black bear, after, no more hunting.

So, cubes, suddenly all over news. We don't think much of it. Most of Ukranians don't care; time travel is silly American fantasy. But my father very smart, he get cube on Internet. Takes apart and make new bear trap, safe bear trap. No more scratch or bite. Bear step in trap and poof! Sends to Japan in cage and that is that. Simple no?

So, next day we go, set trap and wait for bear.

And we see huge, big bitch bear. Lot of money for her.

But, one thing about black bear, they are fast. You see bear, it see you, bear catch you no problem. Bears run fast, bears swim fast, bears climb tree fast.

Out in woods, I see bear. Bear see me. My father's trap in between. Uncle say stay, bear will go to me and step in trap. I don't see my father anywhere, but he never use me for bear bait.

Nadia lent in, imagining a big bear biting down hard on her own leg. Galina continued.

"I shit myself; I feel cold, I feel sick. Bear just look at me and I think I am about to die."

"What happened?"

"Bear do nothing." Galina rumbled the steel container with her heels and making whooshing sounds through her mouth. "Noise like this. But louder all around. Bear hear noise, I hear noise. Noise get louder more and more and everything shake. Bear think nothing of me and run back off into woods."

Galina beat her fists against the shipping container they were sitting on as though they were paws.

"That sound get louder and louder and louder. I hear trees snap and birds scream. Then I see what bear see, I see dark wave, higher than trees. You know what I'm talking about, yes?"

Nadia nodded.

"So many bodies. Wave eat woods, make crunching sound. I hear my uncle scream… and then I don't. I have no time to run. But what I did have was bear trap. So, I make choice."

Galina let her pounding fists rest. Nadia had grown very silent.

"I land in Japanese factory, in cage. I speak no Japanese. But now I have time to get out before wave come for me again. Now, I look at scar, I feel pain yes, but pain means I am alive. My husband, Milosch, he say it mean I trust stomach more than people."

Nadia bent down and got a much better look at it, while Galina flexed and showed it off.

"Milosch is an idiot." Nadia smirked.

"Before we come here, Milsoch tell me I will cause what we try to stop."

"Why would he say that to you?" Nadia said simply.

"What if he right?"

"He's not."

"Eh, I worry, what if I do wrong thing? What if I make it worse?"

"Gal shut up." Nadia pulled her friend in tight. "You're trying, and that's more than he can say."

At that moment Antin clambered up the side of the shipping contain as the boat sank and rose over waves, he had only one free hard to hold on and Galina helped him up.

"Finished." He panted.

"And?"

"Two subs. One on track to pass under us in a few hours. The second, just forty minutes after."

Nadia grinned and turned to Galina.

"See." Nadia said. "Everything's on track."

But Galina didn't answer. She was looking off and out to the side of the freighter, feeling the ship slow as the crew for the second time today had to toss the rope ladder over the side and help those lost in the waters.

"This look bad." Galina breathed.

Two figures were approaching in a small boat not meant to be this far out from land. They were too far away to be identified.

"This look real bad."

"Or this could be them." Nadia suggested. "The one's we're here to stop."

"Or worse." Antin gulped.

"Tell others." Galina snapped into action, rolling her pant leg down and nodding at Antin. "We keep heads down, hope they don't see us. If it is them, it's what we came here to do. So watch close."

"And if it's not them, if they're something worse?"

"That's why guns have bullets, yes?"

The lumbering freighter pushed through the ocean like a scoop through ice cream. Every moment getting hotter and hotter, only the mist from the broken waters cooled anyone that stood by the edge. That is only if you dared to stand out in the open - afraid of the sun or being seen.

Vaughn was sick from the bounce of the small motorboat they rode in, though Hammond was worse off. He had thrown up twice over the side, vomit spilling from a dark void. Each wave that the freighter sent their way soaked them down to their socks, then the sun baked them dry only, to get soaked again.

As they climbed aboard - Hammond first - they didn't take off their hats and let their masks down. Hammond was set on that, and Vaughn said nothing to dispute it.

The ship was the size of a modest shopping mall. Massive stacks of shipping containers, each of a different faded color, sat at both ends of the ship, covering areas big enough for soccer fields. Surely you'd think it'd be enough to sink it, if you didn't know how boats floated.

On deck, they kept their heads low and hoped the sun in the captain's eyes would suffice. They didn't kid themselves to think that none of the crew had any questions as to why two men in brown suits were on a small boat in the middle of the Pacific Ocean.

Hammond spoke for them and whatever he said granted them both passage onto the ship. It was only moments later that Hammond threw his gut into the railing and vomited over the side. He was not settling well with the slight bumps and fumes from the petrol engine, and now it was worse still as each wave lifted the freighter and turned Hammond's stomach.

"He better be here." Hammond gurgled as drool dripped from the dark void of his face. "This 'Smokey' fellow better be here."

As night set, most of the crew acted like it was day, routine carried over no matter the time, and Vaughn was less conspicuous at night when everyone was covered in shadow.

It was obviously some sort of military boat, with all the uniforms, guns and rankings. Still, he moved about the deck, looking for their target with the freedom Hammond's authority had granted him. He looked for smoke of a specific color and menace. The quicker he found Smokey, the sooner they could avoid anymore-unnecessary attention from men with guns.

Vaughn searched along the edge of the back half of the boat where there was a narrow section of deck between the shipping containers and the railing. All he found was some squeaky kid, about his age, resting on his elbows along the railing with his eyes on something in his hands. He too wore a military uniform, too long at the sleeves and no gun at his hip.

Vaughn heard a beeping and as he got close, he heard another voice.

"Still watching that thing like a hawk?" A woman stepped out from a gap between the containers. Vaughn ducked in against the wall, the moonless sky and his shaded face keeping him from sight.

Even though it was dark, and the waves were loud, Vaughn could still pick voices. She sounded very familiar to him. She looked even more so. Vaughn could see the squeaky kid was holding something that looked like a high-tech calculator. It lit up half of the woman's face, and half was enough. It was the drunken woman from the Asylum, only sober and speaking with clarity.

"Hey Nadia. I've got nothing else to do." The kid shrugged. "Waiting is the worst part."

"I know what you mean." Nadia said. "That feeling in your gut. It's the worst."

Both of them lent out over the railing to look deep into the dark fluid that was the sea below; hearing water, but not seeing it.

"No matter where we go, these stars stay the same." Nadia said looking up. "No matter what happens to us here, on Earth, those stars will stay exactly the same. They'll go supernova and explode. They'll slowly drift away from us as the universe expands. Nothing we do will have any effect on them. They'll stay the same."

"That's kind of nice to know."

"I think so. It's comforting to know there's something stable out there to hold on to."

The kid checked his watch and tugged at Nadia's sleeve.

"She said ten, right?"

Nadia nodded.

"Well, it's ten. She'll be waiting for us."

The two of them moved back and slipped between the shipping containers and out of sight. Vaughn didn't hesitate and followed right after them.

It was loud between all the containers. Any noise reverberated against the thick steel and thundered past Vaughn. Any gentle rocking of the ship knocked him from side to side as he followed their voices through the jagged, right-angled maze of containers. Finding a dead end, he heard the echoes coming from above where more of the maze went on, and he climbed up with weak fingers and even weaker upper body strength.

Wherever the containers were stacked even a little off center it created enough space for a person to sneak between. Some gaps were thin, and Vaughn had to suck in his breath to squeeze through. Now he was truly in amongst it. He had containers all around and barely any light. Groans and aches of the giant steel boxes getting roughed up by each uneven wave. It unsettled him, but he pressed on, losing track of their voices and now just feeling in the darkness for the next spot to put his foot.

A thin slit of light shone between two containers. It wedged out and fanned over the tiny, dense hallway Vaughn was in and he stepped up and peaked through it, only as wide as his nose. Somehow Nadia and that kid had made it to this cave made up of the shipping containers. A group of them huddled together and had their torches in hand.

"I think we should split up."

"We're not splitting up."

"Why? You tell me why. Antin says there's barely an hour between subs. How are we going to make both?"

"You heard of time travel no?"

Vaughn's mouth fell open. Those voices were familiar, he recognized almost all of them. There was a man with his arms covered in tattoos, scratching his head with the hand that held his torch, scattering light all over the place. This man was at the Asylum too, Vaughn had met him. Henry something, no Harry...no...

"Drop it, Hank. We go together."

Vaughn knew that voice too.

"Gal, you know it's easier. We'll be in and out."

"I'm not here for easy." Galina snapped. "I want all done right. If mess up, if you don't..."

Vaughn had to stifle back a gasp to keep himself hidden.

"Don't what?" Hank snarled back. "You think I'm the mole don't you."

"How did you...?"

"Antin told me you thought one of us is a mole. Of course, you think it's me."

Antin, the squeaky kid with the high-tech calculator, hung his head, not wanting to get any more involved. But Galina didn't shoot him any rough looks, she kept her eyes on Hank.

"Why you think I think it's you?"

"Because I wasn't on the tape. That's why." Hank said firmly. "You all saw that tape with yourselves on it and thought yourselves heroes. Well, me and August wanted to help all the same. We didn't need some security footage on some tape to tell us our destiny. Maybe we were supposed to split up. You take one sub, and we take the other. That's why we're not on the tape. Don't you see?"

"Galina come on, it makes sense." August spoke up.

"No. Mole or no mole. We stick like glue. We do what we come to do. Only mole would try to break us apart."

"And I think you want to get us all on that first sub, all of us on camera just to see if you can. You're going to test the limits of fate, all the while putting everything else at risk. Don't you get what will happen if we fail? Everyone we left behind all the people that are relying on us, including your own children, Galina, your two little girls..."

"Don't." Galina barely opening her mouth.

Hank took a deep breath.

"Whoever agrees with me raise their hand." Hank said. "We've got two subs and two groups. We don't have to hold each other's hands anymore. Let's just finish this."

Slowly August and Antin raised their hands. Nadia looked at her friend, still staring daggers as Hank, and she raised her hand too.

"Gal, we've got to figure this out. There's no changing their minds."

Vaughn could see that Galina had suddenly felt the weight of the ship and all the surrounding containers. It pulled her back into the reality she was in, everything was fragile, everything had a time limit. She had to make a choice.

He saw her scratch at her calf with her foot and bite her lip.

"Fine." She said. "Two teams. August and Nadia, Engine room. Hank with me, we take out bridge. Antin your eye on that radar, yes?"

"When you're down there." Nadia instructed. "Find a walkie or radio and use our frequency so we can find each other when all is done. Do you remember the frequency?"

"Don't worry." Hank nodded, winking at Nadia. "I got it down."

"Maybe you should tattoo it on your arm, in case you forget."

"I'll remember."

"Or just write it down."

"I've got it, Nad."

"Are you incapable of taking any suggestions at all?" Nadia asked, shaking her head.

"If we meet again." Hank started. "You can suggest us a drink."

Nadia sighed with huge relief when the two of them left, hoisting themselves with excessive brute strength up and out of the cave of containers.

"It's all about trust now." Nadia said. "We have to trust him."

"You trust him?" Galina asked.

"It's easier if I say yes."

"Uh, it's time." Antin said, checking his radar.

"Yes. As they say, show time."

Seconds later the torches were all off, the voices long gone, and Vaughn was in the dark again. He could hear them all take an effortless way out and they left him in the silence that hummed inside and out of the containers, like putting a shell to both ears.

"I'm so fucking lost." Vaughn whimpered, squeezing his way out from between the shipping containers as the freighter swayed and the huge metal boxes, capable of crushing bone like twigs, groaned and shifted with him in the gaps.

He wriggled out, gasping for air like he had been holding his breath. He could feel the ship rock like someone had slammed on the breaks. Someone had.

Rushing to the main deck Vaughn saw the crew on the move. With guns at the ready, they darted from deck to deck, all yelling codes and

positions into their radios and Vaughn could hear they were heading to the bridge. Wherever that was.

He looked for Hammond, checking every single railing and shadowy spot.

"You. Inside now."

A crewmember grabbed Vaughn's arm and pulled him below deck. He hadn't looked Vaughn in the eye, he was taken with so much chaos he had dropped what he was doing and was following orders from the few navy soldiers on board. He dragged Vaughn inside the rec room. There were half-eaten package sandwiches and chips strewn across the tables, sliding slightly with every bump from the current.

Sitting there, silent and nauseous, was Hammond. The TV was on, but he stared at a flopped open egg sandwich that slid side-to-side on the table as he ripped his fingernails through the foam in his seat.

"...*Tensions are mounting as the soldiers recovered from Abuja in Nigeria are for waiting safe transit home just as security leaks are coming through from unnamed sources that identify the attack was from the armed forces of the Republic of China. What this means for the current stronghold in the Senate is yet to be determined, as the US government has stated it will not retaliate or recognize any information from unsubstantiated sources. The attack on the US base just two days ago resulted in thirteen dead and seven injured...*"

Images of smoke-filled cities in Nigeria flashes on the screen as soldiers and locals ran to evacuate crumbling buildings. After Vaughn, several other members of the crew were brought in and told to wait while the soldiers searched the ship for some missing stowaways they accused of permanently stalling the freighter. Vaughn sat with Hammond, both slunk into the background easier than he ever thought possible.

"We're like sitting ducks out here." One crewmember whispered to another.

"Any chance they could turn us around and…"

"Engines right out. We're not going anywhere anytime soon."

"Choppers?"

"Not a chance."

Vaughn sat beside Hammond and both faceless men scanned every single person who came into that room. But not one of them smoked so excessively that they couldn't see his face.

"In the Senate today, there were more efforts to have China agree to move away from fossil fuels along with the one hundred and forty-five other countries including the United States that have signed the act. Sandra Stone has more. Sandra?"

"Thanks Wallace. Recent polls have shown that most American's still don't understand The Emission Independence Act. The latest data showing only fourteen percent feel they have an understanding of the Act, fifty-six percent have heard of it but are not sure and thirty percent state they have never heard of it. The Act is being voted on in the senate and the pressure from the UN to move the world towards renewable energy is reaching its peak. The US is aware of the cost, a bipartisan agreement as neither side wants to be left behind to pay the mandated carbon emissions subsidy like other countries..."

"... Countries like Nigeria wherein again, thirteen soldiers were killed and seven injured..."

"I remember this." Hammond said softly.

Vaughn looked up to him, Hammond was now watching the news and shaking his head.

"If I remember just right, five years from now it'll get out that we bombed our own base and let it leak that China might have been involved. They weren't but who was to say? We were stuck in debates in the Senate anyway. It loosened everything up. We were free to send a few of our subs right up to the Chinese border, holding up their shipping routes, until they agreed to be an energy Independent Nation as well."

Hammond breathed in and out uneasily, like he was holding his teeth from chattering.

"Things were simpler back then. Back now. Makes you want to..."

Suddenly Hammond rushed from his spot, Vaughn knocked aside and followed as they went through grated floored corridors until they

found a door that led out to the outside and Hammond flung himself up against the railing and hurled.

Hammond pushed his stomach into the railing and forced the vomit to surface. It dribbled from his throat, and he mostly spat into the ocean. His bottom front teeth leaned forward, wrenching themselves from his gums when he spat, and he sucked them into place and pushed them back down with his tongue.

He felt the sunrise on his back, burning its attention to his brown coat, he worried with the cloudless sky it would burn through his disguise.

Vaughn leaned over the edge with him, not saying a word and his expression as hidden as Hammond's. Both of them looked down to the ocean, where neither of them could be sure of the white goldfish they had seen skimming just beneath the surface and under the ship.

Hammond spat some more up again and groaned enough to make Vaughn ease his way down the edge and out of smelling range.

"He should take his hat off every once in a while." A voice said casually. "You too."

Vaughn turned and saw nothing, absolute darkness and deep, deep shade stared back from under the rim of a hat just like Vaughn's.

"Why's that?" Vaughn asked carefully.

"You know, the radiation?"

"Oh."

"You here for the same thing we are?"

"And what would that be?" Vaughn asked.

"Huh, funny."

Three more Historians stepped out onto the secluded deck with Vaughn and Hammond. The air was silent, the ship had stopped moving. Everything was waiting. The wind had even settled along with Hammond's stomach. There were muffled concerns coming from below deck and inside the bridge, as the sun had barely even risen, and the day had only just begun.

✧ ✧ ✧

They all heard the scream; it was as piercing as the gentle wind they all were waiting for. Rushing back inside, letting the crew and trained soldiers go first, the Historians followed noiselessly behind. They played shadows to these men, who all were running towards the screams and not, rationally, away.

Vaughn followed the Historians that led him upstairs to the higher level and out to a balcony that looked out over the main deck. He bumped into the back of the woman in front of him, her rough and unwashed split ends slipping out from under her hat's shade. They didn't dare step out into the light, not yet. Instead, Vaughn watched from the window at what had just washed up on deck.

Galina was screaming, her arm out at an obscure angle as she stood right by the edge of the dock looking over the water. Nadia stood beside her with a crewmember's head tucked under her armpit and a gun jammed against his ear. Antin stood behind her, going pale just by looking at Galina's arm.

Vaughn saw it too. Even from there he saw the steel rod of the railing running through her forearm and out the other side.

"Help, I need help!" Nadia yelled at the men surrounding them. None had a clear shot. "Did you hear me? Someone cut her free!"

The crew and soldiers looked to each other, one man waiting to move and was given the slight tilt of a nod to do so. He ran and returned with a hefty grinder that he held under his chest and uneasily edged toward Galina.

She just kept screaming at the strain any slight movement put on it. The railing pushed through her muscles and ached, her bones running up and down her entire arm. But second the grinder revved to life and touched the steel she found more voice to scream. The entire railing was vibrating and shuddering. Sparks flew and nicked her skin. The man with the grinder tried to cut as close as he could but left a few inches on both sides. When the second cut broke through, she dropped to the wet deck and held out her arm like it didn't belong to her. A hollow steel rod

running cleanly through, no blood, no scars, just a seamless join and a hole in her forearm she could see through.

"Alert the base!" The captain roared, finding enough saliva to wet his dry mouth at the sight of her. "We are under attack. Call it! Alert the base, we are compromised..."

A shot fired from Antin's gun, it hit the sky and killed the captain's orders. Both Galina and Nadia were impressed. Antin had them all toss their guns overboard as he threatened to blow the crewmember's brains all over the deck. He led them to a shipping container, took the keys from the captain and locked the entire crew inside, though he struggled to close the door without Galina and Nadia's help. Slamming the door shut, jamming the crank down and locking it, Galina whimpered. She had knocked the end of her arm pipe against the door sending shock waves up the muscle.

"Fuck it sting like bitch!"

As far as they knew, they were alone on the freighter just waiting for Hank and August to return. Nadia and Antin watched out both sides of the ship, out to the rocky waves in case the two men landed in the water. Galina moved to the bridge, checking on their position and hoping they hadn't found a way around the broken engines.

On the console, alongside countless confusing dials, buttons and screens, an intercom on mute flashed violently. With a hesitant finger, Galina pressed the button beside it and a voice filled the near empty room.

"... Mayday received. Retaliation actionable. Please respond with cancellation codes AMX-0417 in two minutes and nineteen seconds to cancel retaliation on naval carrier. Repeat, please respond with cancellation codes in two minutes and sixteen seconds..."

Galina backed away from console as Nadia and Antin came in, he was holding his radar out in front of him.

"Uh, Galina." Antin said uneasily. "You might wanna see this."

She knew before she looked. The radar he held showed both submarines beneath them. The one they had successfully invaded and deactivated the missiles inside was silent and unmoving. But the

second sub, Hank's sub, was turning around and coming back towards the freighter.

"What did you think it's doing that for?" Nadia asked.

"*... I repeat. Please respond with cancellation codes in one minute and fifty-eight seconds to avoid retaliation...*"

"Probably that." Galina breathed.

For a few seconds all three of them froze, taking in each second now, knowing it's worth.

"By chance do either of you know the cancellation codes?" Antin asked.

"They must have alerted the sub before we could stop them." Nadia figured.

"What do we do?" Antin breathed.

"Hank and August are still on that sub." Nadia urged. "Probably screwed now that they're on full alert. There's no way they're going to be able to do what they have to do in time. And even if they get out, there's not going to be a boat waiting for them when they're do."

Galina was biting her lip, eyes darting across the room, from Antin to Nadia and out to sea where she figured the incoming sub was turning back fast.

"We must think. Is this plan, did Hank..."

"Gal!" Nadia yelled. "This is no time to play 'who's the mole'. It's sink or swim time. What do we do?"

"We still have our cube." Antin said, eyes going wide, and he dug it out from his pocket and held it out. "We can get the hell out of here right now!"

"No." Galina said firmly. "If we leave and Hank is mole, he win. If we stay and blow up, he win. But if... if we..."

"... If we retaliate." Nadia finished for her.

Both women held each other's gaze for a strong moment, a flinching contest. Neither lost

"Then we retaliate." Galina said.

"*... Please respond in one minute and thirty-two seconds...*"

Upstairs, a firm hand held against Vaughn's chest as he made for the stairs. He looked back, one mesh of haze looking at the next. They shook their heads. These Historians were waiting for something.

"Not yet."

Nadia ran to the shipping container full of crew, keys jingling in her hand. She threw the latch up and heaved the door open, pointing her gun in first.

"Ok, everybody stay cool."

What little light shed inside on the huddle mass showed a petrified crew and lackluster soldiers aching, wanting to fight back.

"I want whoever's in charge of the torpedoes to raise a hand." She barked.

Two navy technicians slowly raised their hands.

"Great ok, take me to where the action is."

Nadia made them run in front of her and back to the command station inside the bridge. The two technician's legs shook as they took in the alarms, the repeating message of an imminent attack and the sight of Galina's arm.

"I want you to lock-on to that sub." Nadia showed the radar to them, Hank's submarine hundreds of feet below them coming in quick, gaining a closer and more accurate shot.

"Why?" One technician asked.

"I want to send them a birthday card! What do you think?" Nadia grabbed him by the scruff, and he scanned through their input signals from the submarine's warning alert and paired the co-ordinates.

"*... Please respond in twenty-six seconds...*"

"How is progress?" Galina shouted to Nadia over the alert.

"Give us a minute!"

As she waited, Galina flexed her arm. The pain was gone as long as she didn't bump it. Instead, she was feeling a tightness in her calf. She scratched at it with the tip of her boot.

"*... Please respond in seventeen seconds...*"

"Progress?" Galina urged.

"Done! It's done." One of the nervous technicians sputtered as he clicked the final button and armed three torpedoes. He, and the other technician who had done nothing but watch, staggered back, away from the console, giving Galina control over the last step.

The button lay under her fingertip, she grazed it. It felt much bigger than it looked.

"Uh, fire when re… re... ready." The technician stuttered.

"Yes. Fire when ready." A voice snarled.

Vaughn and the others appeared from the deck above, guns out and ominous faces glooming overall. Hammond stood by the front with another eager Historian.

Galina could feel their breath but couldn't see them breathe. She could taste their sweat-lathered clothes in the back of her mouth. She could feel the hate and the danger she was in, like they were the teeth of a very large mouth that was about to close in on her.

But this mouth stayed open. They were waiting for something.

"What you wait for?"

Vaughn looked up to Hammond. His patience was strangely still.

"... Please respond in nine seconds..."

"What do you all do?" Galina stammered. "Toy with us? You win, you got us!"

One Historian leaned over to the other and whispered, pointing at the hole in her arm so she tucked it away quickly.

"We're waiting to see what you do. We will intervene if necessary."

"Necessary?" Galina felt her breath trying to count and relish its final intakes. Her calf hurt so much it was hard for her to stand up straight.

She looked to Nadia, who was biting her nails intensely. Antin was shaking. The radar rattled in his hands.

"... Please respond in four seconds..."

Galina had to force from her mind everyone else was on board; soldiers, crew, and members of her own team.

Vaughn saw the flashes of thought across her face, eyes darting to all but the button. She thought of everything but still came back with nothing, left with just the button and a choice. One choice would get her killed, but she had no way of knowing which.

"So we find out." Galina winked at Nadia one last cheeky time and slapping the button and sending three torpedoes straight for Hank's submarine.

The torpedoes shot straight and on target. The first skimmed the tail and blew out the massive rotors. The submarine would have been stranded beneath billions of liters of water if it weren't for the second two missiles that struck and exploded the sub within seconds.

The blast sent shock waves through the water, washing the lumbering freighter back and rocking Vaughn and everyone else off their footing.

He looked around. The alarm had stopped, Galina and the others were on their backs, distraught and dazed.

"Antin quick!" Galina yelled. She grabbed hold of Nadia and Antin and closed her eyes as he shuffled their last cube, twisting it just right with his eyes shut tight.

✧ ✧ ✧

Eyes still shut, they felt nothing. Nothing but the rocking of the ship from waves knocking against the bottom of the boat.

Galina opened an eye to see one faceless shadow cradling a small part of their belt, tapping it with a sharp finger. There was no running while that whirring noise was on.

"Nice try." The Historian jeered. "Now we can kill you."

A second and much bigger shock wave finally reached and tossed the freighter like a spilt drink.

Galina and Nadia took their chance, dragging Antin behind them as his knees skidding along the floor and out to the deck.

They dove behind a few strapped down drums, carelessly firing at the swarm of Historians still clambering after them.

"We need to be on other end of boat! Far from them for it to work again" Galina yelled only inches from her friends. "We need to be fast!"

"And how are we gonna do that?" Antin cried out, closing his eyes every time he fired off a shot.

"With a little gusto kiddo." Nadia wrapped her arms around the drum and fired wildly. "We'll get some cover and make a break for it!"

Storm clouds grew, the clear skies they had moments ago were swamped and muddied. Rain pelted down and winds from both sides of the boat rocked it steadily. Through the storm Vaughn and the others blended well, like coats hanging from a clothesline as their shadows were washed away in the wind. Many Historians lost their hats, flying off their heads and into the brewing storm.

Suddenly their faces appeared, and they were open, seen and present. Galina spied them from their hiding spot, gripping onto the ropes as the freighter tipped down and back up. She could see a few faces now, she wished she hadn't - they were madder underneath.

Vaughn and Hammond held onto their hats and bent their knees to stay upright, moving with the others towards their targets. Scalps slipping up out of hiding and ducking back down when a bullet pinged off a drum.

Vaughn could see one on his right. He had an arm wrapped around one of the ropes, his gun loose in that hand, and in the other he was still gripping his radar.

"Antin, put radar away! No time for radar!" Galina snapped as she saw him holding the radar in front of his face. "Antin! Antin?"

Antin was fully enveloped by his radar. He snapped at his name and shared the screen with the others.

"What is that?" She yelled to him, inches away. "That dot. What is that dot?"

He kept staring at it, calculating distance as the number plummeted to few digits.

"Antin!"

"That," he said, barely getting his words to make sound as they came out of his mouth. "That's a nuke."

"How is that possible?" Nadia shouted. "No bombs ever blew up here. It's a fault, a glitch surely."

Antin looked to Galina. His look told her it was for real.

"Where's it come from?" She asked.

He widened the perimeter.

"It's already up. There's no way of..."

But Galina needed no more conformation than that.

"Son of bitch!" Galina's legs felt weak. "He did this! He was NEVER going to turn off bomb! He was never going to steal it! He'll kill us now! Start war so future will be gone!"

"What do we do? How do we stop it?" Antin stuttered.

"No stopping bomb." Galina said vacantly. "No fucking way."

"We've got to get out of here." Antin breathed.

"How long does it say we have?" Nadia rushed.

"Five minutes until impact." He breathed.

Thunder broke out above as more wind gathered, skimming across the ocean and tackling the side of the ship.

"We go home." Galina said. Her mind hadn't settled. "You have cube yes? So we go."

"What about now?" Antin said, apologetically repeating her own words.

"There's nothing we can do now. It's already done." Nadia looked to Galina. "It's out of our hands."

Shots fired and snapped chunks of the deck. The group ducked their heads even lower, as a wash of rain, waves and bullets showered down over head.

Galina stuck her head up. Everyone she saw was as faceless and dark as the last, getting harder to spot them in storm. She picked off any faces that lost their hats and appeared long enough to be shot. But still dozens and dozens of Historians walked ominously toward them, unaware or unafraid of the situation they were in.

"Fuck!"

She leaned over to Antin and checked his radar.

"Four minutes!" Antin yelled. "No, two minutes forty-five!"

"Fuck!"

"Don't they know?" Antin struggled to get out between hurried breaths. "Don't they know what's going to happen? They're going to die keeping us here."

Nadia was staring at the deck she knelt on, counting her breaths until they were low.

"Gal!"

"What?"

Nadia ripped the gun from her friend's hands and pushed her aside.

"You two run as fast and as far as you can, get to the other side of the boat. I'll keep them back long enough to get you out of here."

"Nadia no!"

"You have a family Gal. And Antin, you're too smart a kid."

"But Nadia..."

"I have nobody. Let me do this."

Nadia handed her the last cube and looked her in the eyes one last time.

"This isn't your fault, you got that?" Nadia said, the rush of a heavy storm beginning to brew under the thunder of gunfire.

"But...!" Galina yelled back.

"You remember that!"

Galina cried as she nodded.

"We've got less than three minutes!"

"Goodbye my friends." Nadia said.

The Historians didn't see it coming. In a flash of thunder and muzzle flares, two of their targets darted out from behind the steel drums and ran towards the shipping containers, while the other held down two triggers and sprayed shots with reckless abandon. She was left to fight them all off on her own.

2:55

2:54

2:53

Vaughn chased on with Hammond, swallowing any vomit he had been saving up, and growled through gritted teeth and radiated shade. Empty guns were dropped, and full ones were fished from coat pockets and thrown to each other. Vaughn had two thrown to him at once and both hands caught them with ease, slipping fingers through to the triggers before even getting a hold on the grip.

2:49

2:48

They chased after Galina and Antin as they tossed aside their guns and the radar, holding only their last cube as they slipped along the side of the ship, past the shipping containers, sliding their hips against the railing keeping them from dropping over into the ocean.

The tailing Historians slipping uneasily behind, a shipping container slipped free a few feet and broke through the railing, taking two Historians with it and cutting off their path.

Vaughn went the other way, running with two other Historians he couldn't tell apart. They followed his shortcut through the maze of the containers, lightning flashes illuminating their route and they broke through to atop the containers, jumping down and across container to container like they were skipping skyscrapers.

2:27

2:26

2:25

Galina and Anton were way ahead, almost to the end of the ship, Vaughn was trailing too. Climbing up his shortcut had slowed a few Historians down and were now way out of range to keep them here. Only two Historians had kept on their tails, and Vaughn eyed them easily.

Vaughn's hand shook. He had it, but he didn't take the shot.

2:11

Galina and Antin had too little distance as they reached the end of the boat. The two last Historians slowed and walked menacingly towards them, cornering them like animals.

Galina could feel the cube in her hand rattle uselessly. Tamed and numbed by the very presence of the faceless figures approaching.

Nowhere left to run, no time left to stall...

2:09

2:08

2:07

... and no time for the Historians to grab hold of a rail, as a sudden gush of saltwater rushed the deck and washed it the of Historians clean overboard.

2:05

2:04

Galina let out a laugh and clung to Antin's hand as she held the railing. As they steadied themselves and twisted their cube under wet and frantic fingers, Vaughn could see one last figure approach them.

2:02

2:01

Galina held on tight to Antin as the cube he clutched hummed and buzzed. Until a hand rested on her shoulder. She turned and saw him, the stranger. The Asian man who she thought she had seen watching her from a distance, many times before. Nash simply took her hand and the pair of them left swiftly, leaving Antin to disappear all by himself.

1:35

1:34

1:33

The radar still counted down as it rested innocently on the deck, waterlogged and still working. The Historians stood over it as they saw the number tick down closer and closer to zero.

"I'm coming out!" They heard her say.

Vaughn was only just coming back from the other side of the boat, as they all saw Nadia with her hands up, throwing over her guns and waving for a ceasefire.

They agreed.

More thunder rumbled around them, the clouds darkest above the freighter. It seemed to rain just for them. Nadia stepped right up to the most eager of the Historians. She wanted to put a bullet between Nadia's eyes more than anything. But she bit her tongue, as Nadia stepped right up and looked deep into her void where her eyes ought to be.

"You know what's going to happen, right?"

0:58

0:57

After a moment, her ghostly face nodded.

"Then drop your guns."

The Historians looked to one another, and one by one they vanished with the winds of the howling storm.

One Historian stepped right up to Nadia, a hand on top of his hat, keeping it from flying away, the other dug through his pocket and shoved a cube into her hands.

"Just do what you came here to do." He grimaced, leaving too. Now only Hammond and Vaughn remained behind.

0:31

0:30

0:29

Nadia shrugged, unconcerned if they stayed or not. She strolled calmly to the steps leading up to the higher decks. Vaughn watched helplessly as she kept going up, higher and higher until she stood up by a vent shaft; the highest point on the boat.

She looked to the sky, searching it for any sign of incoming death as the radar by Vaughn's feet counted down.

0:22

0:21

She found her place and bent her knees to ride through ever bounce and bump the freighter took as it rode mightier and rougher waves. In

her hands she held the cube she had been given. She tossed it up and caught it a few times, checking out how worn and faded the colored tiles were.

0:13

0:12

The wind became more furious, and Nadia found it hard to keep on her feet. She widened her stance and smirked at the tumultuous sky. She held her watch up and counted the final seconds to herself as they passed, then she started twisting her cube as a booming sonic screech sounded. Growing more intense as the huge warhead nosedived straight for Nadia.

0:09

0:08

"I hope you're watching this, Stein!" She screamed. "Because this is all for you."

Staring it straight in the eye, with the gusts of the temporal winds almost lifting her from the ground, she finished the final twist, swung her arm back and hurled the colored cube straight up in the air.

0:07

0:06

0:05

0:04

The clouds opened as the neutron bomb pushed through and rocketed down to the ground. It was only a few hundred feet from the earth when it met with the cube just as the tiny atoms and energy burst from within the little toy. A tangent snapped open in the sky just wide enough for the bomb to be swallowed up and zapped out of time.

Vaughn ducked and held his breath, clenching his eyes closed as he waited for it to be over.

But all he felt was the wind dying down and the storm suddenly subsiding.

He patted himself down, counting limbs and feeling for cuts or bruises. There were none.

He was still there, all in one piece.

Hammond hobbled on his feet, uneasy and queasy. He hocked and snarled and spat out a glob of blood and mucus on the deck.

"What the fuck was that?" Vaughn asked as he saw Nadia take out a cube of her own and vanish from her post, a much softer wind sweeping up after her. "Was that on your note too?"

"Let's just do what we came here to do."

They kicked down every door and navigated every corridor until they found him. Below deck, deep in the engineering section, it was empty and silent. In fact, the whole ship was empty and silent. All the crew was still locked up in a shipping container too scared to want to know what had happened on the other side of their steel cage.

The lanky man was handcuffed to a chair in the middle of the room, the chair was on its side and he stood beside it, cool as a smoked cucumber.

They had found who they were looking for. The machinery in the room had broken down and nothing was working, yet the room was full of smoke. Green smoke from his long cigarette. The green smoke did anything but match his outfit. He was a stick of grey even in the low light of the brig.

There was no mistaking him.

"So, you're Smokey?" Hammond asked, waving his hand to clear the air. Everything but Smokey came into view. The thick cloud didn't disperse, instead it hovered around his face and Hammond gave up waiting for it to clear.

Smokey chuckled as he relit a cigar he had saved halfway to oblivion, switching it out for his cigarette like he was celebrating.

"And you're Hammond." Smokey jeered. "See how this works."

Smokey nodded with a smile before turning his grey eyes to Vaughn. "Pratt, I assume?"

Smokey's hidden eyes lingered, lingered on Vaughn as he sunk deep into the abyss of them. A swirl of cloud, of nothing. Smokey's disguise was better than his; each puff of smoke from his mouth wafted around his face, only his grey eyes pierced the cloud.

"I suppose you want something from me?" Smokey rolled those eyes.

"I'm told you know how to find the Time Asylum." Hammond answered.

"Told by whom?"

"Does it matter?"

"It matters because whoever they are, they are spreading lies." Smokey grinned. "I do not know how to find the Time Asylum."

"Then…"

"But." Smokey winked at Vaughn. "I can tell you who does. The man you're looking for is at a bar called *The Fish Bowl* in New York. 1976, May 30th, at about 10:00am 'til noon the next day. He'll tell you what you want to know if you buy him a drink."

Hammond committed his clues to memory, whilst muttering *what are the odds* and scribbling it down on the yellow of his pad.

"And now I want something from you."

"Something from us?" Hammond growled. "What do I have that you want?"

"Not from you." Smokey said. "From him."

Both Smokey and Hammond looked to Vaughn.

"What?"

"I'd like to try on your hat."

"No." Vaughn blurted.

"Why?" Hammond asked.

"I like it, I want to try it on."

Vaughn looked to Hammond then back to Smokey as he took a deep, long and drawn-out breath before sliding the rim of the hat off his head and over to Smokey.

There he stood, face out in the open. Vaughn didn't dare look at Hammond, instead he looked straight into the mist of green smoke, waiting for either of them to speak his name or shove a bullet through his ear.

Smokey took the hat with his rigid fingers and curled his grip of the hat and pulled it into the smoke and placed it on his head. The smoke only darkened.

Vaughn shot a look at Hammond. His dark cowl looked at him, taking him in, knowing all his secrets and all he had to hide.

"Are you just about finished playing around?" Hammond asked.

"Hmmm" Smokey said joylessly to Vaughn. "It doesn't fit me as well as it fits you."

Surely he spotted him, knew him, or would know him. Waiting for a reaction was becoming worse than getting one. But he handed it back to Vaughn who snatched it up and crammed it back on his head and felt the relief from the shade quickly falling back over him, like pulling up your bed sheets on a stormy night.

"Can we go now?" Vaughn asked Hammond.

"The sooner the better." Hammond answered. "As for you Smokey, don't you let me find..."

But Smokey had taken his leave, unrestrained by his cuffs, leaving behind only a puff of green smoke in his wake.

Hammond sighed loudly, whipped out a cube, and Vaughn was quick enough to leave with him only by the touch of their shoes.[*]

---

[*]Go to Page 99

$$\Large\diamond$$

Chapter Twenty-Five:
Bite your Foot or Bide your Time

A stiff wind snuck through the bodega's automatic doors. Anyone that passed by would trigger it, which drove the lowly paid attendant crazy.

He swept his newspaper flat over the counter, gushing out the wind that had curled up under its pages, and he lent over it to pad his elbows as he scrolled through his phone, huffing a slight laugh under his breath.

"What's funny?" His co-worker, who had been restocking the fridges, appeared and tossed him a coke.

"Nothing, just reading something."

"Reading? You know there's probably an app for that."

"I like it."

"No one likes reading."

"I do."

"C'mon, gimme." He snatched the phone easily. "Oh man, this is just news. I thought you were scrolling through some tasty memes.

"It's important to stay informed. It's an election year you know."

"Ok *mom*. What was so funny then?"

"A quote from a senator, I can't believe some of the stuff they get away with saying."

"And that's funny?"

"Not funny haha, like shake your head funny."

"Yeah well, freedom of speech."

"That's not what that means, these guys are plain evil sometimes."

"If he was really that bad, then future generations would send back cyborgs to blow their heads off. And I don't see no terminators, do you?"

The breeze blew through the door again and a woman stumbled into the shop. Her jumpsuit was too fancy for her to act this crazy. She held a multi-colored toy in her hand and whatever wind was out there had blown her curly black hair in all crazy directions. Her eyes were steady yet wild. She kept the workers at bay as she scanned radically everything in sight. She was looking for something, but she just saw chip packets and energy drinks.

"Where's the milk?" She asked.

He pointed and she rushed over, only looking at the price. She seemed to do some math in her head then whispered to herself. "2020, maybe…2021"

"You looking for soy or something? We only have full cream or almond…"

The crazed woman stepped away from the milk and back to the counter. She saw the phone in the attendant's hand, his finger unconsciously sliding up and down the screen. She quickly snatched it. She slid her fingers all over it until she found what she was looking for.

"Whoa, hey gimme back my phone!"

"August 12th." She confirmed in a whisper to herself.

She dropped it and fell back into a rack of sunglasses.

"Oh man, the screens cracked!"

"New York accent." She whispered some more.

"Hey can you calm down bitch. You broke his phone. You gotta pay for that."

Wyla dove into her pockets and turned them inside out with a shrug to their bewilderment and contempt. Wyla then walked out of the bodega, watching each foot she put in front of the other.

"Mustn't touch, mustn't talk. Already talked too much."

Wyla ran. She tried hard to avoid bumping into the people on the street. She even tried not to slam her foot too hard into the pavement. She tried so hard that she slammed into a tailored brown suit.

Wyla landed back and sat on the concrete. She panted hard and replayed the moment over and over, ingraining the feeling of the material in her face.

The man in the brown suit offered a hand and the sun peaked out from behind his face.

"Are you ok?"

Wyla grew to her feet and almost immediately fell back off them. But Hammond still held her hand, looking into her face, trying to understand her fear. Though Hammond didn't quite look the same. He was large and plump, his cheeks were purple, like they were aching from overuse.

Behind him was a camera crew, lugging tripods and sound gear over their shoulders. Hammond was surrounded by people wearing big badges and hats with the American flag.

"You were running like you were being chased." Senator Hammond laughed.

"I… ah…"

"Running off to vote for me, I assume." Hammond boomed to the crowd and squeezing out laughs and cheers as Wyla's entire body developed pins and needles. She just nodded enough to skip a response. "No need to rush, the polls don't open 'til November."

Wyla looked him up and down. His skin was perfectly pampered, his teeth held tight, his eyes had no yellow.

"Well, I'd love to stay and chat with a supporter, but we've got to keep on moving." Hammond was talking to her, but not with her. He spoke loudly so everyone else could hear. "You make sure to vote ok."

"Sure… sure."

She walked spritely, careful not to break into her run again until she was out of Hammond's sight.

Wyla walked west and out of town. She found it easy to find her way. Everything was familiar and that's what frightened her. Careful not to bump or put off any fellow pedestrians, she strode out of the city, along the edges of the highway until she came to an off-ramp that barely led anywhere.

She stumbled down the edge of the highway and down to an industrial lot. Trucks and vans ran down the street. Each building bore a logo stamped over the top of an older one. Wyla continued until she found what she knew would be there. Had she not driven these roads before she couldn't have known she would find it, but both luckily and unluckily she found the 24-hour Storage Queen.

The woman, who Wyla assumed was the Queen of this storage kingdom, snorted loudly as she led her down the dank maze of storage units. She snarled at her as though Wyla was only there to usurp her throne.

Each unit boasted a hefty lock, and the only indicator of difference were their numbers. She finally stopped, and with her foot kicked up the roller door to a bare storage unit.

"This one's a hundred a month. Spacious and clean, as you can see." She spat courteously away from the empty unit as she snorted.

Wyla kept her eyes to the ceilings, Ogles were positioned to pan the halls, and she frowned.

"Anything with a little more privacy?"

The queen followed her eyes and snorted confirmation.

"Those are our deluxe units. Not for everyone."

Wyla pulled out a handful of her gold pieces and slipped three chunks into her sweaty palm, careful not to get her finger caught in the Queen's grimy fist as she curled it up.

"That should cover it."

The Storage Queen smirked and welcomed Ms. Smith to her deluxe corner unit, complete with a hallway of faulty florescent lights, broken Ogle and a turned head.

Wyla returned from the closest supermarket with a cart full of canned food, a fan, a self-inflating mattress and a cheap selection of books. She rolled the door down and shut herself off from the world.

Chapter Twenty-Six:
Determining Freedom

"Well, we found Pete!" Atticus screamed, heaving in as much air as he could. The others all did too, bending and deep breathing until their pulses stopped racing. Dahl could still feel the pressure that had squeezed in his chest. Sancia shook and kept lifting her feet from the ground to reassure herself they were no longer sinking in between bodies.

Galina and Nash were the calmest, or at least, were standing up the straightest. They practiced panting rapid breaths until they were calm.

Vaughn swayed and tried to keep himself from seeing it again. For the split seconds his eyes closed to blink he saw it.

Him.

Them.

No one paid Atticus any attention as he ranted. Kicking at whatever his foot could find. They were in some shopping mall car park and getting strange locks from people loading bags and children in their cars. The disheveled and anxious group dodged passing cars and shopping trolleys as they tried to remain calm and keep together. But Atticus couldn't help but kick at cars and thrash at strangers as they circled around them.

"That was way too close! Way too damn close!" Atticus growled as he stepped back into a car reversing out of its spot. He slammed his fist against it and made it wait until he was ready. "We should have left when I said so. We waited too damn long!"

The car beeped, and Atticus threw his hands up and stomped up and down the car park.

"We had to wait Atticus." Nash pled. "Vaughn was on the list too."

"List. List. List. This damn list. Aren't I on that list as well? Shouldn't I be kept from danger? I almost drowned amongst that that that…"

"So many." Sancia whispered. "So, so many."

"We got out, didn't we?" Galina offered.

"From now on." Atticus waved a finger in Galina's face. "From now on you have a new list. And there's only one name on it, and that's Crowe. Got it?"

Galina stared past the finger and waited for him to remove it.

"Put finger away or I take finger."

They all went inside the shopping mall, Nash traded in some gold pieces at a jeweler, and they all found some new and less travelled clothes.

Again, Vaughn felt refreshed putting on a new set of pants and a button shirt, though he only had to wipe his blue sneakers along the edges of an escalator to get them clean. He stuffed his bloodied hoodie and pants through the narrow hole of a bin and stuffed the cube he had stolen from Ida and his corkscrew in his new pockets.

Vaughn met up with all the others in the food court and he found it strange to see them all in such regular clothing. Especially Sancia, who had gone shopping with Galina and found matching pants and tops. Sancia had copied the way Galina pridefully kept her arms bare despite the obstructive hole in her forearm. Now Sancia didn't even try to hide her scars across her collarbone.

Nash and Dahl had dressed like two middle-aged dads; simple and in earthy, mismatching color tones. Nash still wore his old shirt underneath the new one, unable to separate it from his skin.

Atticus had struggled to find a suit that fitted him perfectly and had been kicked out of a few stores when he abused them for not tailoring on the spot. He now yanked at his sleeves that were a little too short with all the frustration that came from sharing a place on the list with Vaughn and Dahl.

Following Nash's instruction, the group took a bus out of the suburbs and towards the city. Atticus refused to touch anything, acting as though it was the worst torment anyone had ever gone through, somehow forgetting where they had just come from.

Vaughn sat between Nash and Galina and tried not to dry heave when he glimpsed her armhole. Though it was a heart-warming, nostalgic sting of stomach acid in his throat as it reminded him of Pete's missing finger. Looking away, he saw Nash itch at his side, and he pictured the slit along his torso.

Nash saw Vaughn's eye and tried to explain, under his breath, that accidents like that can happen when jumping through time. He got too close to a tree branch, and it imbedded in his side, pushing in his shirt and his skin sealed over. As he tried to explain that it didn't hurt as much as he thought while Vaughn went pale and shook his head, pleading for him to stop.

Galina smacked Vaughn across the chest and cupped his mouth.

"You make too much noise."

"You never know who's listening. Before you know it, they'll be all around us." Nash added, looking to the rest of the group.

They all knew what people he was talking about. They all feared the faceless Historians.

"Why do they look like that?" Vaughn whispered to Galina through the gaps in her fingers.

"Look like what?" Galina asked back, taking her hand away slowly. "Brown suits? Always brown. I know."

"No, the… the faces?"

"They don't like being watched." Galina's eyes darted above her head like a fly was circling. "They always watch, but don't want to be seen."

"By who?"

"People. Everyday people. And any Ogles pets."

"I hate those things." Nash shivered. "You see one of those. It means an Historian is not far behind. If you see it at all."

"That how they sneak on you." Galina continued. "Get close, do a Dead-End-Turn and poof! You not there anymore. Gone."

"Gone?" The bus bumped and Vaughn's voice cracked. "What is a Dead-End-Turn?"

Galina leaned over, dropping her voice even lower. "They don't kill you when they get you. They send you away, very far away. Further than Far, further than anything. Maybe send you to before Earth exist. Maybe send you to after all is gone. It called Dead-End-Turns because there's nowhere to go when you get there and no way back."

Vaughn's thoughts went straight to carrots as he picked at the skin around the edges of his fingernails. Carrots and sand. The man named L was still there, waiting and forgetting.

"I think I've been there."

"You have?"

"It was, awful." Vaughn muttered low. "I have to go back though, after all this, I have to make sure I go back there and save a friend, this guy who could very well have forgotten all about me just as easily as his own name. But I can't forget what I promised him."

"The things you do for friends." Galina shook her head as Vaughn quietly explained where he had gone, what the cube had done to get him there and how sorry a case L had been.

"Don't worry." Galina slapped his knee and winked. "We don't need list to save someone."

Vaughn nodded and then spent the next hour watching the suburbs drift back behind them and the city rise on the horizon, just ahead of the freeway.

The freeway fanned out into more and more lanes that all ran straight into the city skyline. Their bus swerved lanes and pulled over to the edge where a lone bus stop sign rocked in the wind. The bus driver raised an eyebrow as he let the group off along the turnpike. *Bunch of lunatics*, the bus driver thought.

Thousands of cars screeched passed as the six of them stood on the side of the freeway and headed down the embankment to the shipping yards and warehouses to the one big cream painted building branded with the name *The Storage Queen*.

The six of them walked down the hallway of doors, hidden in the shadows, led by the queen herself. Ankle fat curling over the edges of her heels with each step and her shoes clopped loudly on the hard-concrete floor.

She walked with a cigar bouncing from her lip and turned through the maze of undetectably similar doors until she found the one they requested. She stopped, blew a puff of smoke from her nose and held out her hand for them to fill.

Nash placed a thick wad of cash in her greasy palm, which closed shut and warmed the notes.

"This is the one." She snarled, turning and splitting the group, leaving them with the key.

One of them took to the lock and with an easy heave they threw the door up to the roof. The dim light from the hall awoke the unit, and a shuffling amongst the mess inside tried to hide from it.

To the squatter inside, these figures were shadows. The light shone through them and over her.

Wyla lay sprawled on the floor, bathed in the horrors of artificial light, as she could not yet see their faces.

She had been practicing her kicks, and the group kept their hands up as she shuffled away. She had made a fine carpet with pages and pages of paper from notebooks, novels, newspapers and food wrappers. She had spilt enough ink over everything, and they could smell writing fumes. Everything from train routes to flight patterns she could hear passing overhead from inside the unit.

She had calculated the rough cargo weight from each freight delivery on one scrap piece, and on another, done the math of the very unit she had stored herself in. Working out the exact cubic millimeter she had paid for, how many cubic millimeters she took up and how many of her she could fit into the storage unit before running out of cubic air. Across the unit walls a timeline of her life had been plotted. X's counting down days until she left her original present.

"I knew one of you would find me one of these days. Still not going to show your faces? Cowards."

As one from the mysterious group reached out at Wyla, she kicked again. The hand recoiled.

"Just do it already! That's what you're here for, isn't it? Eliminate me! Terminate me!" Wyla cuddled into a pile of tin cans with her eyes closed and a deep breath, she whispered. "Just get it over with."

Vaughn stepped out from the group. His hand stretched its fingertips to lightly touch Wyla's shoulder and nestled there. Wyla loosened her withdrawal and opened her eyes as they adjusted to the light.

"Weren't you the… the bartender? Is that you?"

"No, this is all just a dream." He couldn't help it.

"He's joking."

Dahl stepped from the group and knelt just before the mess that lined up perfectly against the edge of the door.

"We're here to rescue you."

"Rescue… rescue me?" Wyla whispered, darting her eyes from Vaughn to Dahl to Sancia and Atticus standing gleefully amongst her mess. "How did you even find me?"

"You were on their list." Atticus nodded over to Galina and Nash standing in the hallway of doors. Nash waved awkwardly. "Come on out of there so we can go."

Wyla shook her head furiously. She was happy to approach the edge of the storage unit, but she would not cross the clear line of filth she had created.

"Wyla, we're the good guys." Dahl said, kneeling in front of the unit like he was talking to a bear in a cage.

Again, she just shook her head and hobbled back into the dark corners of the unit.

Vaughn sighed and stepped on in, crushing paper and tin can lids as he went further inside. It went deeper than he thought, enough to store an entire house worth of furniture but Wyla had chosen instead to decorate it with piles of garbage. It looked like at first, she had a system, separating the rubbish into groups and keeping it divided. Then as it

got darker in the back corner where Wyla slunk, the piles mixed and conjoined, and she had formed a morbid couch from old towels.

"I'm just gonna sit if that's all right." Vaughn said, not waiting for Wyla's response.

It was a challenge to choose between breathing in through his mouth and possibly tasting or swallowing the foul air, but worse still was letting himself smel it. He alternated.

"So, you've been in here for a while, huh?"

Wyla nodded. He recalled how she once made a tesseract out of toothpicks while debating conventions of time travel. That had been her. This was that same person.

"Ever since it happened." Wyla said. "At the Asylum. I've been here. As much as I can."

"How d'you get food?"

"I pay that woman to bring it."

"Smart." Was it though? "Wyla why are you in here?"

"Because I'm also out there."

"Excuse me?"

"This is my time. The real me is walking around out there and this was all I could think of. I am trying, I really am."

"I'm not following?" Vaughn said, and Wyla rolled her eyes. Still the smartest person in the room.

"The incident. I'm trying not to cause another... incident." Wyla calmed as soon as she had gotten it out. "If I stay in here, out of the way, and leave as little imprint as I can, I can wait it out."

Vaughn slumped back and wished he hadn't. Something squished under his thigh.

"Wyla, I've seen the incident. I've been there."

"You have?" She tilted her head like a puppy.

"And yes, it was as bad as you'd expect." Vaughn studied her face. "But..."

"But?"

"But, I don't think it works that way. Are you prepared to think maybe, just once, you were a little wrong?"

"What did happen?"

"I can't… it's tough to explain. All I know is that I think it'll be ok if you come out. I think you'll be all right."

Vaughn took her arm and as Wyla got up and move towards the door she wriggled and dropped, eyes not leaving the line of filth separating her and the outside world.

"Wyla." Vaughn squatted with her, not giving up yet. "Come on, you've got to get out of here. Once we have you safe, then we'll all be safe, and we can go home. It'll be over, done. Wyla, I really need this to all be over. I know that out there seems scary. But I still remember what you said to me when you came to me that morning."

Wyla took her eyes off the hallway and finally on Vaughn.

"You told me nightmares are hard to wake up from. And I really want to wake up from this one. I want to go home. Let's get back to our lives, the way they were before."

"Yes." Wyla said pensively as Vaughn sighed with relief. "The way they were supposed to be."

"Yeah!" Vaughn smiled. "Yeah just how they were supposed to be. I promise you nothing bad is going to happen if you leave this place."

Vaughn tried one more time to lift her up. This time it felt like she weighed nothing at all. Wyla wasn't resisting. She stood up with Vaughn and quietly she and the others all left the storage unit. Sliding the door down behind them, they left the empire of the storage queen behind.

The sunlight was harsh. Her usually brown skin had gone paler without it. Wyla hadn't been out for quite a few years and her eyes had dark, purple rings underneath and took some time to adjust.

Wyla stepped up to stand amongst them, as though she wasn't the odd one out. Her toes sticking out from her shoes, her wild and dirty black hair turned brown. And she had a smell that, if the lights went out, they could have found her in the dark.

Wyla stood and waited for something to happen and Vaughn, for a second, worried he had been wrong.

But nothing. Nothing but the sound of cars rocketing by on the freeway just off in the distance.

"Well, that's it." Nash said, pulling out and checking his list.

"So? We good?" Vaughn asked the group, all seven of them standing in a circle. The list was complete and every one of them safe from acts of terrorism to time and space.

"No." Wyla said, her voice firm and demanding, as it had once been before, so long ago. "We are far from good."

"Anyone else hungry?"

Wyla stormed off toward the glowing sign of the burger chain at the next freeway exit. They had no choice but to follow her as she led the way, not wanting to waste one more word until she ate.

Nash paid with the rest of their cash and they all sat outside on the rickety, bird-shit covered table setting and munching silently on processed meat and cheese.

Wyla inhaled three burgers and coughed and choked between each bite. Nash took out the meat and just ate the cheesy bun, and Sancia held a burger in each hand and ate simultaneously.

Vaughn was the only one who didn't eat. His stomach rumbled and tried to eat itself in protest, but it set his mind at ease. The more he watched bits of matter crumble and disappear down throats of those that didn't belong, the worse he felt.

Once they had finished up and tossed their wrappers lazily towards the bin Vaughn exhaled his long silence and jumped to his feet.

"Finally." He breathed.

"So, now what?" Dahl asked.

"We go home, obviously." Vaughn said.

"No!" Both Sancia and Wyla blurted.

"I'm sorry, no?" Vaughn snapped. "What do you mean no?"

"We've got things to do." Wyla answered.

"I don't. I don't have things to do."

"Why do you think our names were on that list, Vaughn?" Wyla turned and asked Galina and Nash, sitting arms and legs crossed on top of the tables. "Do you know what we're supposed to do?"

"We were told only to find you." Galina answered. "That's it."

"Gal!" Nash snapped.

"What?" Galina replied. "That is all we know. I'm not going to lie. We did the job."

"Our job was not let them get into even deeper trouble."

"What you suggest we do?" Galina pushed.

"I'll tell you what were supposed to do." Wyla smiled. "We change it so it doesn't happen."

"Change what?"

"That White Cube." Wyla said firmly. "It was a White Cube right? Did any of you see it too? I only caught a glimpse before…That's what it was, that White Cube, that's what pushed us all out of the Asylum. And I'm so sorry."

"Sorry for what?"

"When I was in high school I made a mistake. My senior science fair project shorted out the fuse box in the gym. Total blackout, my fault. I didn't know what I had done wrong. But it taught me to predict any miscalculations before case testing. It made me a better engineer. But I never was any good at seeing beyond the tiny details. That White Cube was my design. If you could have gotten a closer look, you'd have seen my personal signet engraved on the side just like with all my devices. It's designed to randomize every cube within a certain radius and send whoever's around anywhere in time. Stein had all sorts of strange stuff designed for him once his paranoia took hold of him. And I ate it up. I focused on function, not application. Not for that cube, not for any of the other tech Stein had stashed away. It's all my fault. And now I get it, that's why you found me last, here, now, right?"

Wyla was looking at Galina and Nash like they all knew what only she meant.

"Wyla, we're not hiding anything from you…we don't have any ulterior motives…"

"But whoever sent you did, does. We're here to fix it. All of it. Stein's floor, at Volta Tower, that's where it all is. Every bit of tech I helped design. After Stein sold the patent to INDX and they began their mass production, he became paranoid."

"INDX?" Vaughn asked.

"*The* tech empire. Solar roads, Ogles, lithium mines, mass plastic printing and dollar-a-day sweat-shops. Even I worked for them, before they… let me go."

"You? *You* were let go?" Dahl questioned.

"I helped design the Ogles to last, not really a sustainable business strategy. That's why when they bought the patent for the cubes, they limited them to hold only two jumps. So you'd have to buy more. Stein hired me minutes after I was fired.

The things we designed for him at Volta, these things that could hide your face, disarm cubes, activate cubes, you name it."

"The hats Historians wear." Sancia added.

"Exactly. These are all things they got their hands on *first*. But it doesn't have to be that way. This is our chance."

The group quickly huddled closer around Wyla as she started laying out plans faster than they could comprehend. She pointed to the big city skyline to the east and the Volta building that stood amongst it. She laid out a quick and easy plan with a high degree of stealth and varying degrees of danger. Vaughn could only listen maddeningly as they were assigned tasks and missions, planning to all meet up at the last minutes of the Asylum when it was over.

"I don't know." Galina pondered the plan, but not for too long. "That would take big substitute."

"A what?" Dahl asked.

"It's what we call something you do to override the thing you want to change." Nash explained. "You want to go back and win the lottery; you'll make your parents get divorced. You want to save the Titanic from sinking, you sink a different boat. Something to counter-act the thing you want to change so that the universe has a harder time course correcting."

"But that would only make sense if you could change time." Dahl noted.

"Oh, here we go." Nash waved him off.

They argued like so many before them and just how Vaughn remembered it. There he was again, back at the Asylum. Listening in on all their debates from behind the bar, each one grinding into him a little more than the last.

They brought it back to their plan, not really addressing any of Dahl's concerns with the rules of time travel. Wyla darted about like she wanted a big chunk of chalk to map it all out on the pavement where they stood. Instead, she tried to visualize the entire building, floor by floor, until they theoretically reached Luis G. Stein's office on the penultimate floor and destroy it.

Vaughn found his heart was beating unusually fast, despite how still he was standing. He felt the flutter in his chest and his knee bounce rapidly. Looking up and over their heads, he took in the blue sky and a deep breath of cool air.

Overhead he watched as a plane soared over, passing under and over clouds. He wondered where it was going.

Suddenly the world felt bigger. He felt stupid all of a sudden, that he had forgotten there was more than just one way to get around on this crazy planet.

He cast his mind out, thinking of where they had come from, where Pete would be right now. He was on the other side of the world, yet to do what he was cursed to do.

"If we do it, there's no changing mind." Galina added up. "We've all got to be on board. We all have to agree to same plan."

Vaughn was brought back down to Earth again.

"You said Stein is the one who created the cubes, yes?" Sancia asked, finally stepping into the conversation. "The creator of time travel?"

"Yes." Nash answered.

"Supposedly." Wyla muttered.

"Good." Sancia said firmly. "Then I'm in."

"Me too." Dahl added. "Still not sure what I can do to help or if any of this is going to pan out, but hey when birds fall."

"I guess I'm in too." Atticus added. "As long as it's going to be as smooth as you say it is."

Galina, Nash, and Wyla were on board the moment the conversation started.

"Vaughn?"

Vaughn couldn't keep up. He had to repeat what was being said in his head before believing it. They were doing it again - they were messing with what shouldn't be messed with. Just when he thought they were out. Here was Wyla, ready to pull them back in.

"I don't like it." Vaughn shook his head. "Nope. Can I just nope out of this because I'm gonna."

"Vaughn." Wyla approached Vaughn and held his eye. "What if I told you that this could save him?"

"I don't want another Pete or a..."

"No, the real Pete, and everyone else. We could save every single person that was at the Asylum. Change all of this. Get our real lives back, like you said."

"This isn't what I meant."

"Vaughn." Galina urged. "Your name was on list. If this what you were meant to do, you can't say no. You're one of us now."

"No! Stop doing that!" Vaughn growled. "Stop contradicting each other and agreeing. We can either change the past or not. You can't have both! You keep saying that you want to save Pete, but I don't think you do. Do you know where Pete is right now? On the other side of the world. We can go save him right now if we want. We don't need to do any of this!"

"Vaughn, take it easy. We're just..."

"And no." Vaughn kept on. "I am not one of you. I'm not like you. I didn't choose this You all got to choose and then dragged me into this. No, fuck you guys. Why can't you just let me go home?"

"Why would you want to go home?" Wyla sighed with a frown.

"Why? I'll tell you fucking why. Because at home, before any of you showed up, I wasn't constantly second guessing my very existence. I feel like I'm taking crazy pills! I don't want to change everything. I might hate my past, but I really don't want to do this. We don't know! That's the thing. None of you know what you're messing with!"

"Trust us Vaughn, we know what we're doing." Nash said.

"How though? Everyone else thinks that too! Ah! It's giving me a fucking headache thinking about all of this! Why? Why does it have to be so fucking complicated? I can't do anything. I can't think, I can't speak, not without thinking about all the crazy shit that might or might not happen if I do.

I can't do it, but I can't ignore it either. I thought I'd try, I tried ignoring it, I tried pushing it to the back of my mind and just ignoring it. But it's there, that nagging feeling, that shitty feeling that pulls at you for putting it off.

It ruins my day. It's like a bad thought your brain gives you at night right before you want to sleep. But it's all the time. And I just…I can't do it anymore!"

"Vaughn…" Wyla tried.

"No, don't you fucking start. Five minutes ago, you were basically living in a cave and eating your own shit to survive. Fuck, you think you're so destined for a better life that you don't care what happens to the one you're in. Maybe it's time to face the music. Maybe you're not special, maybe you're not as smart as you think you are."

"You talk big, small boy." Galina said in a low tone.

"And you, weren't you crying over how you fucked up like this before? Trying to change something but causing it instead? How are you not seeing that this could be exactly the same?"

Galina scratched harshly at her calf. "This not like last time. O'seus knows."

Vaughn scoffed.

"Vaughn, there's nothing to be afraid of." Dahl tried to comfort him.

"Nothing to be afraid of!" Vaughn sputtered. "Did we not almost drown in Petes this morning? Quit the whole fucking tough-guy-act

Dahl, either you're too dumb to know how much danger you're always in or you're even dumber to think that the universe will keep you safe."

"Come on Vaughn, this is going too far." Wyla fought.

"No, you know what is going too far? Ripping someone from their life like they don't have a choice and dumping them somewhere they didn't want to go. That's what you did.

I didn't want to go to the Asylum. I hate that place! I turned Atticus down. I hate that Observatory. I hate that town and I hate that fucking mountain! The only thing I didn't hate died in my arms and that's probably your fault too!"

Vaughn stopped only to wipe his eyes. They were just watching him now, like he was on stage with a microphone with no one cutting him off. Vaughn felt it too, their eyes dropping, hearts breaking, connections fading. But he couldn't stop, no, he was on a roll.

"And you." Vaughn turned to Nash. "Besides the fact I vomit a little every time I see the gash in your side or her arm hole, I feel sorry for you."

He turned on Galina as well.

"Both of you. You didn't even know why you were saving us. You just did what some old fool told you to do."

Vaughn turned, quickly taking his eyes off them before his welled up. He caught sight of Sancia; still and quiet.

"Sancia..." Vaughn started, but Dahl stepped in front of her and shook his head. Vaughn bit his lip and moved on. Only one of them was left.

"But last and certainly least, Atticus Motherfucking Crowe. You know Crowe, I used to think it was you who ruined my life waaaaay before the others did. You had to make sure that the town I grew up in was a dead end, that I would be stuck there for my entire life.

But good news, I don't just blame you now. I blame every single one of you. It's half your fault and half your fault and half your fault..."

"That's not how math works." Wyla couldn't help it.

"I don't fucking care. I really don't. Fuck math. I feel like a ball of clay you all just keep pummeling with every cube you twist. Do you know how it feels to feel so out of control?

I'm glad the Historians came. I'm glad they ruined the Asylum. If it makes you feel any closer to how shitty I feel, then fucking good on em!"

Vaughn looked around him, his friends stepping further back until he was standing all by himself, swaying against the rush from the distant freeway.

He'd done it again. He thought of Jake for the first time in a while. He had done it again. He was still the same person he'd always been. No amount of time travelling could change that. He could see it in their eyes; he was smeared, like a bug on a windshield. That's how they saw him now.

"I'm fucking out of here." Vaughn crushed his foot into the ground as he turned and headed to the freeway bus stop. "See you in another life."

The bus had worn seats. The patterns were all the same checkered greys and blacks, and all faded in spots that had the most sweat. Paint had chipped off the handrails and the rubber hand flap that hung above felt greasy. Everything else seemed so new and improved. Vaughn barely recognized any car brands or models as he looked out the window, resting his forehead against the glass as the bus vibrated gently, jittering his teeth.

The only thing new about the bus was the crisp, white dome fixed to the bus's ceiling. The Ogle's glass eye scanned the passengers and emitted soft sounds of radio chatter.

No one sat next to him. He watched at each stop for when too many people would to hop on and he would have to share his seats. He didn't feel like talking or even being near anyone else right now.

He wanted to feel bad for himself some more, to look out the window with a solemn stare and to be completely and pathetically alone.

He dug his hands into his pockets to keep them warm and secure, finding nothing but a corkscrew and a cube he was saving. He didn't dare take out. He no ID and worst of all, like always, no money.

"I'm not fucking crawling back to them." Vaughn mumbled to himself, catching a transparent reflection of himself in the bus window.

He had no clear idea of what year it was or where he was in the world, but he knew he was in America. He could tell from the side of the road the bus drove on, the accents, and most of all the consistency in body fat.

More people hopped on at the next stop, dragging chunky suitcases behind them and dumping them in the aisles, making it harder for others to get off or on. Yup, this was the good ol' US of A.

Vaughn's old habit of fixating on conversations that didn't belong to him reared its ugly head, as two girls sat in front of him and put a white plug in an ear each and played with a screen in their hands.

Vaughn watched and listened as one girl scrolled through song after song and ripped her friend to shreds over her music choice as her friend laughed.

He wondered if the girls knew their headphones had lost the cord. He didn't see any slot for a CD to fit, nor was the screen big enough to fit one. Vaughn imagined even smaller CD's the size of a coin and wondered just how many coin-CD's that screen could fit at once as they were going through *a lot* of songs.

Finally, the bus pulled up to its last stop and everyone got off, including Vaughn. Immediately he heard the rush of jet engines and open space of the massive airport.

Herds of travelers ushered around him with shopping trolleys of luggage and entering the airport.

He wandered through the checkpoints, slipping past customs and following the signs to the international terminals. Vaughn's hands had never seen such easy pickings before. Swiping passports and credit cards was easy and everything was done through a computer screen, he had no one to look in the eye and lie to. It took him three swipes and scans to get a printed ticket and he found himself window shopping at the duty-free shops in no time at all.

It was only an airport mall, but it was still the biggest mall Vaughn had ever seen. The shops were as glamorous and decked out as the Observatory had been to him. He saw movie posters on computerized billboards and projected against the glass as he walked by. Movies he had never heard of with actors he didn't know. Strangely this felt the most familiar to him. An action movie was an action movie, no matter who was holding the gun.

He looked at his ticket and bit at the skin of his fingers, thinking about it. Whose seat had he taken? What would become of it? How long would it take for the butterfly's wind to subside?

This was exactly what Vaughn had feared leaving Fracture would have felt like. He felt small and unwanted, like a cockroach in a kitchen. He didn't know if he really meant to leave with Jake all that time ago or if it was all talk. He could never picture it in his head as easily as he could talk about it. He kept on saying that once they had the money, the hard part was over, and they could just leave. But in truth he made the hard part hard.

Just like with Pete, Vaughn didn't want to do it alone. And now that's where he was, alone. Far from Fracture, far from that all seeing, ever watchful mountain in Fracture.

He couldn't smell dirt or smoke or gas. He didn't sweat from his thighs or pits anymore. Fuck, did he miss it?

No, he missed Pete.

He had gotten the feeling that Pete felt as close with Vaughn as Vaughn did to him. He hoped he wasn't wrong, and Pete wasn't just being polite.

He hoped he made Pete feel as good as Pete made him feel. He thought of how Jake had last looked at him, then he put that face on Pete, and he almost cried.

Had he told enough jokes? Was he nice enough. Encouraging enough? Friendly enough?

He knew Pete was a better man than he was, but he really hoped Pete didn't know that.

He wondered where Pete had gone once he had thrown him that cube, if Pete was looking for Vaughn just as he had looked for Pete.

It made him feel awful thinking that he wasn't, but somehow worse if he was.

No one would come to help him as his name wasn't on their list, that fucking list. Vaughn was glad he had so much vapid color and sound being projected everywhere he looked. Especially if it made some awful, taunting, yellow spray paint hard to spot and easy to walk by. He even flipped it off.

He liked to think without it he might even be going in the wrong direction. With that in mind, he picked up the pace and headed for his terminal. His flight was leaving soon.

Vaughn walked the long stretches of halls as great white jets and passenger planes taxied by the windows. They made enormous noise but were muted by such thick glass and cut off from view by more projected ads. Ads that took up every available window like he was walking past a wall of televisions.

He caught advertisements for specialized tours to Ancient Greece, Woodstock, and Jurassic safaris but simply waved them away, as did most everyone. Then, up ahead were actual salesmen with shirts, posters and brochures. These salesmen were quickly dismissed but not for their annoyance. Vaughn heard the other travelers openly mocking these salesmen.

Time Travel's all fake! He heard them shout.

How simple life was when Vaughn felt the same.

As he reached the end of the long hallway he had to approach and pass the salesmen at booths and marquees, harder to wave away as easily as the projections.

They jumped on him, lightly grabbing his arm and forcibly stuffing brochures in his hands.

"How you doing today, sir?"

"Do you like to have fun?"

"Where you headed today?"

Vaughn nudged passed, but they caught sight of the terminal number on his ticket he held.

"Africa, huh? You would love our safari packages."

"No, thanks."

"This time next year you could be sixty million years in the past, getting a real deal, no holds barred look at Dinosaurs in the wild. Now how does that sound?"

"Not for me."

Vaughn kept on, but he couldn't shake the salesman.

"Our team are trained experts in paleontology and its highly recommended seeking a tour group than to go by yourself. Tickets are only…"

"Fuck off." Vaughn finally looked the man in the eye, and he fell back, leaving Vaughn to keep walking unattended.

Ahead he heard a screaming child, making dinosaur noises and reaching his tiny arms towards the animated and pixilated dinosaur.

The salesman left Vaughn and happily strode up to the child's parents waving his brochures.

Vaughn watched the young boy grab his father's pant pocket and yank as he pointed at the poster with a roar. The screaming child had a slightly older brother who leapt on top of their father to slow him down, while their mother walked swiftly on without them. They both yelled and clawed at their father, making dinosaur calls and biting their dad's shoulder like the animals they emulated.

They easily brought him down. Their father was small, he had thin arms, weak legs and an even weaker disposition. He didn't have the courage to swat a housefly and if it wasn't for his face Vaughn wouldn't have recognized him.

"Dahl?"

What had happened? Had the group split since he left? Had they disbanded and gone their separate ways, quickly adopted children and beaten Vaughn to the airport?

"Dahl what are you doing?" Vaughn stepped in front of him as Dahl limped forward, turning him down as he did the salesman.

"No, thanks." Dahl said, trying to step around Vaughn like it was his fault for being clumsy.

"John!" The woman ten steps ahead stopped and stamped her foot. "Would you just hurry, I've had enough today. I just want to pick up my mother and go home."

But Vaughn was persistent. Dahl hadn't paid him much thought, more occupied with the two boys digging through his pockets and taking his wallet and keys.

"Dahl seriously, it's me. It's Vaughn. Don't do this to me man, tell me what's going on."

"John!"

"Coming honey." Dahl gave Vaughn a quick look and passed around him. "Sorry, I've got my hands full here."

Vaughn stepped aside, and Dahl was pulled past as his two boys finally leapt off their father and ran towards their mother who had found an old woman standing by two bags and waving at her grandchildren.

"Sorry, what are you offering?" Dahl asked.

"I… what?"

"John!" Dahl's apparent wife stamped her foot to get his attention. "Please don't do this to me. Not today."

She slammed her foot as she passed the two boys to her mother and stormed over to her husband.

"Do not even try to buy tour tickets or even ask about them." She snapped, her makeup around her eyes had smeared and her cheeks were puffy. "I'm sorry but whatever trip you're trying to palm off on us, we're not interested. And you should think more about what you're doing."

"What I'm doing?" Vaughn stuttered.

She looked like she was about to cry again as she got right up in Vaughn's face.

"You and all the other people who think travelling through time is another fun family activity should think again. And stop badgering people. Get a real job."

"Honey, he's just trying…"

"John, I'm done arguing about this today ok. I'm done. I want to go home." She marched back over to her mother, gave her a brief hug and started off. She didn't care whether Dahl followed her or not.

"I'm sorry about her." Dahl said. "Do you have a pamphlet or something? I am interested."

"I ah…"

"Nevermind."

Dahl shook his head and followed his wife.

"What the fuck was that?" Vaughn stammered.

Vaughn had never been on a plane before. He wondered if the ones from back in his time had the same computer screens in the headrests as this one. He swiped and scrolled, finding weather stations, news programs and even a map of the world with their plane on it. He followed with his finger a long green line that crossed the ocean and spotted all the cities that they would pass over.

His ears popped and ached. He tasted the recycled air, and every now and then he tuned back into the constant hum of the engines. Almost everyone on board the flight was plugged in with little white headphones like the girls on the bus. They watched movies ten inches from their noses and ate from plastic trays and drank from paper cups.

This was the most luxury Vaughn had ever experienced.

He figured he would land and then find his way back somehow to where he had been before. He would find Pete before anything happened. He would tell him the truth, because he couldn't imagine lying to him again. He couldn't keep it up. From there they would be free. They could choose their own lives and negate all that had been written ahead of them.

As for now, Vaughn was having trouble choosing what to watch for the next nineteen hours. He shuffled through stations and as he slipped in his headphones, his channel swiping finger froze.

"... The attack was heard from several blocks back, we are already seeing footage caught on cell phones and Ogles in the area of the

explosion but there is yet to be any information on what exactly caused the explosion and who is inside..."

Vaughn leaned in. He would have been pressing his nose to the screen if it weren't for his drop tray holding him back. The reporter was in New York. She was standing outside a smoke-filled building and the camera crew were panning between her and up to the blown open windows of the top floor. And there, on the top of the building in big gold letters welded to the side, was the name *Volta.*

"Oh, man..." Vaughn choked as he read and re-read the name over and over. "What have they done?"

"... The police are trying to keep everyone back at a safe distance. There is glass all over the ground and chunks of rubble are still falling from probably thirty, forty stories up. You can hear the sirens and alarms over my voice, it's just chaos down here."

And that's when Vaughn saw them. Dozens of faceless people, standing about the streets and in the shadows lurking behind the veil of smoke now drifting through the street. They came out of nowhere, all in brown suits and brown hats. It was as though the explosion had sifted them from the crowd. No one stopped to look twice at these people. Without any faces they almost slipped by unnoticed. Except for Vaughn. The cameramen hadn't shifted their focus at all. The police even let them slide by with dozens entering the building at a time.

Vaughn knew that he was the only one who saw them. Anyone watching the news would assume their faces were simply overshadowed.

So many of them too, Vaughn knew his friends would be outnumbered.

Vaughn searched his pockets and pulled out his last cube, the one he had stolen from old Ida's stash. Galina had shown him all her tricks, as they took that long bus ride from New Jersey into the city she had walked him through every aspect of the cube to pass the time.

With it weighing heavily in his hands, he solved it under the tray so fast he had to peak to be sure he did it the way she taught him.

He remembered her patience. How her accent curved and stunted her words, and the fact she had saved his life once already. He owed her and he hated that.

The best parts of all the others came to mind; Sancia's innocence, Dahl's optimism, Wyla's wild ideas, Nash's determination. Even Atticus seemed helpless and worthy of saving to him now.

Did he owe them all? They had gotten themselves into this mess. Why should he be the one to bail them out? Besides, Vaughn on a plane, more than a mile up, what good could he do?

"...Of course warning of this attack on Volta's headquarters and other landmarks have been predicted in the wake of INDX's announcement their latest and most controversial device only a few months ago. If you can recall, those predictions came under the pretense that the anonymous individuals had come from the future and were thrown out under stipulation that the entire thing had been a hoax. Could this be our first concrete proof that time travel is something to be taken seriously?"

Again the cube in his hands lay heavy, solved but not yet activated.

Vaughn looked up at just the right moment as the camera crew had unsteadily changed position, setting the camera down on an angle for several seconds and focused at a bus stop on the side of the road.

There it was, yet again. Spray-painted in yellow for all to see, but only for Vaughn to understand.

Limpfingers.

If only he hadn't looked up at that exact moment, he would've missed it.

If he had kept his eyes on his empty tray.

If he had blinked.

Vaughn sighed and lifted and clipped his tray to the back of the seat in front of him. He slipped out of his seat and down the aisle to the bathroom. Inside, he felt cramped and uneasy. The walls might as well have been removed along with the rest of the plane. Holding the cube, he felt like he was about to skydive. He only had to move through space in order to make it there in time. He hoped he had been taught well. He hoped the co-ordinates he had taken from the plane's virtual

map thing were accurate. They had to be, or he was going to very dead, very quickly.*

The stewardess knocked for ten minutes before she used the spare key in her pocket. The rest of the passengers had been waiting for some time. Whoever was in the bathroom had either passed out or was doing something illegal.

Not only did she find an empty bathroom, but not one passenger could leave the plane once it landed. As it was the first plane in the airline's history to land with less passengers than it had taken off with.

____

*Go to Page 448

Chapter Twenty-Seven:
Deterring Fate

Vaughn felt a ping as a shot flew past him and almost clipped his ear. It stung his eardrums as much as it did his flesh. He shot his head up and saw smoke sifting out of the fresh hole in the wall he had been staring at.

More flashes of gunfire lit up the end of the hall where the stairs opened. It tore out chunks of plaster and floorboards. Vaughn danced and skipped to keep his toes, ducking and throwing himself behind a large indoor fern.

"ATTENTION ALL PERSONAL. THE BUILDING IS CURRENTLY UNDER LEVEL 5 THREAT. PLEASE STAY INSIDE AND LOCK ALL DOORS. PLEASE WAIT FOR SECURITY TO INFORM YOU WHEN YOU ARE CLEAR TO EXIT THE BUILDING.

ATTENTION TOUT PERSONNEL. LE BÂTIMENT EST ACTUELLEMENT SOUS UNE MENACE DE NIVEAU 5..."

Vaughn shuddered as sudden red lights flashed, a siren wailed, and warning signs emitted from a small white dome in the ceiling's corner, the Ogle somehow surviving the first explosion.

"You're not getting any further you motherfucking bastards!"

Vaughn whipped his neck to see Wyla firing wildly into the stairwell as Galina knelt beside her. She was fiddling with what looked like a phone book wrapped in brown paper with a few wires running out, hooked up to parts of a dismantled Ogle – he figured this was the second explosive device: the substitute.

Galina and Wyla had successfully taken control of the hall but faced an onslaught of no-faced enemies on one end and the building's security on the other.

"We know he's here!" Wyla screamed. "He's always here! I want Stein brought here now or we'll blow this whole place to bits!"

Several more Historians struggled to get through the doorway without taking a hit, but nothing was getting through. Whenever Wyla ducked to reload, Galina covered her with a war cry and a torrent of bullets.

Vaughn thought of the others. What parallel Wyla had they found in that storage unit? What had she gotten them all into? Where were Dahl and Sancia? Had Nash died yet or was there still time? Did Galina even know or was she trying to seek revenge as she set the last wire into the package. A package that started to tick.

Vaughn backed down the hallway, away from the ominous, flashing red and the blaring security warning coming from every dome in every corner.

He barely heard the door crash open behind him as a man stumbled out from an office with someone riding on his back and crashing them both into the walls.

Vaughn caught only a glimpse of her long-knotted hair. The man threw the young girl off his shoulders and sent her sliding down the hall. Sancia was quick to get back up, spitting strands of hair from her mouth as she screamed.

"I hate you!" She screamed, tearing back at him, clawing at his face.

"Who the fuck are you?" The man fought her off, his left arm covering his eyes.

The man was using his other hand to keep a strong hold of a cube, willing to take a few solid hits to keep his grip. He took a few more punches before bringing up his leg and booting her stomach, knocking her to the floor.

"Don't think that just because you're a little girl that I'm not going to defend myself. I've been preparing for this day ever since I sold the patent."

Luis G. Stein, Vaughn thought. He watched the wretched man hold up the cube over the young teenage girl he had just knocked down and was reminded of Atticus. Who was strangely absent here.

"You want what I've got?" Stein barked. "That's it, isn't it. You want what I've got, well TOO BAD!"

Vaughn ducked away as the two fought clumsily and sloppily. Biting, clawing and kicking. Vaughn squirmed to keep out of their way and back up the hall only to dodge a showering of bullets that tore the wall behind him to shreds.

"You want to know why!" Sancia screamed, holding onto her stomach and digging her nails into the floor. "Because it's all your fault! It started with you and it's going to end with you. This all goes away. Every part of it. Nothing that has happened to us will ever happen! None of it will be real!"

At that moment, a small man rushed out from behind Vaughn, leaping over him and spear tackling Stein against the wall and knocking his head against the tough plaster. With the upper hand, Sancia kicked his leg out from under him and rode Stein's body to the ground. She whipped off her belt and wrapped it around his neck and pulled as Stein roared, squealed like a rat and lost his grip on his cube that dropped and scattered across the hallway. Vaughn had just enough time to get a look. It seemed strangely like the cube in his pocket, faded colors and a heavier thud.

Then... black.

"ATTENTION ALL PERSONAL. THE BUILDING IS NOW IN LOCKDOWN. PLEASE WAIT FOR SECURITY TO INFORM YOU WHEN YOU ARE CLEAR TO EXIT THE BUILDING.... ATTENTION TOUT PERSONNEL. LE BATIMENT EST MAINTENANT EN LOCKDOWN...."

All lights were off, only the red flashes remained. The halls lit up sporadically, going from pitch black, to red flashes, to full light, and then black again.

Muzzle flashes lit up the rest of the hallway. Galina and Wyla backed up, sinking into the same corner as Vaughn, who was shielding his head with his arms.

Through a flickering of light Vaughn saw a room down the hallway right where Sancia and Dahl had Stein pinned. He caught an eye.

Atticus was here, though not in the same violent manner as the others. Vaughn wondered what part of Wyla's plan he played. He crawled and followed the old man.

The room Atticus sought out was the stark white he had seen earlier – or later, only now it was filled with large plastic crates that sat on the tiled floors. Crates that the old man was desperately trying to open. One cracked, the lip of the top popped up and Atticus dug at the contents immediately, pulling up handfuls of cubes and tucking them into his jacket pockets. Still flinching at every gunshot, Atticus hurried, cubes spilling out onto the floor. He was becoming too frantic, his eyes far bigger than his stomach, or pockets.

Don't you dare, Vaughn thought, as he snuck up on the old man; well-hidden between red flashes and darkness.

Though, as if he read his mind, Atticus caught Vaughn's eye in between a flash. In that fleeting second, he winked. And in the next, he was gone.

Stein dove for his dropped cube and both Dahl and Sancia dove after him. They grabbed his legs and cut his leap short. Stein howled, kicked Dahl in the jaw, he rolled to his knees and pummeled Sancia with a hefty and fed-up fist.

And with that, Sancia was a young girl again, dropping like a rag doll and losing all fight she had in her.

Stein pushed himself to his feet and staggered a second, flinching at every round of gunfire, unbeknownst to him who'd catch sight of him next.

"Finally." Wyla snapped, whipping her arm around and aiming it at Stein. "What took you so long?"

Stein was even more confused, seeing a crazy haired, raggedy woman through these flickering lights. He barely had time to duck behind a decorative plant that she shredded like lettuce. Both Vaughn and Stein could see the faded cube still sitting idly in the hallway, never flinching.

"I just want to talk." Wyla roared between bullets. Galina still at her side trying desperately to hold off the onslaught of Historians, she tugged at Wyla's arm, but was battered away.

"Really?" Stein called out. "I'm kind of busy right now, next time could you make an appointMENT!"

Sancia was up again and jumped on his back just as Stein bent to pick up his cube. The two wriggled and struggled and fell back through a door and into an open office.

Wyla tried to follow them just as Galina's gun choked and sputtered empty. The Historians saw their chance and moved in. Dozens of them charged through Galina grabbed Wyla and pushed her down the hallway, slamming against the walls without slowing down, getting her to safety.

Vaughn ducked for cover himself, sliding into the cold tiled floor of the room Atticus had been in.

His hand quickly slapped a green, pop-out button beside the door and the doors knew to slide closed in a hurry.

He lay there for a second, either frozen or paralyzed. This room was chilly.

Vaughn got to his feet and watched as dark faces under brown hats moved past the closed door, ignoring this room completely.

What was this room?

Besides the crates in the corner Atticus had cracked open, this room was organized and sleek. Vaughn could see many mounted items along the walls. Bags and suits lined with what looked like aluminum. More guns with chunky handles that looked twenty years newer than the gun itself. There were even hats of all styles and colors hanging on hooks, brown hats. But there, in the middle of the room, was a giant glass case big enough to fit an entire aquarium. And inside it was an

all too familiar shape. A strange frame held it in place with spider-like claws, so it floated in the center of the display case. This was the White Cube.

The White Cube that his friends were fighting for, here, suspended in this glorious fashion. Unlike all the other bits of tech in the room, this was the only one of its making.

This was it - the thing that ruined everything.

Vaughn peered at it closely. He could see a scratch on the corner of the cube, a bottom left tile on one side had a strange engraving that he had had seen before. A twisted and never-ending *W*, just as he had seen it in Wyla's copy of the book at the Asylum.

It was her signet as it was her design. In fact, it was on everything, the sleeves of the shiny suits, the handles of the guns, even the inside rim of every hat on every hook. Vaughn bit his lip thinking about how the woman outside ruining everything had possibly ruined everything. He bit it even harder when he realized he was hiding in the very room she sought to destroy.

Before he could bite all the way through his cheeks, he heard the door click and slide. He ducked behind a crate, low on his knees and held his breath. He saw the two dark-faced figures step into the cold, white room through the reflection of the glass case.

The taller of the Historians stepped up towards the White Cube and easily broke through the front panel with the butt of his gun. Vaughn winced as the bits of shattered glass scattered across the floor. He saw the Historian reach in and take it. He didn't need to see through the shadow cast from his hat to know which Historian this was - he knew Hammond would be the one to use it. He could tell it was Hammond too, the moment he stepped into the room. It was his deep breathing, his struggle for breath which grew cold and stale the second it passed through his dark mask and dead, yellow teeth.

The other Historian that tailed Hammond held up Stein's prized cube. He must've picked it up before Stein could rid himself of a feral Sancia. Its color, though faded, seemed vibrant compared to the dark void where Hammond's face ought to be.

"Take that bag Pratt."

The second Historian swiftly took the aluminum-lined bag, tossed in the faded cube, as well as any and the leftover cubes from the crate Atticus had left open.

"Did we get him?" Hammond asked.

"Stein got away." Pratt answered.

"And the little girl?"

"Taken care of." Pratt seemed to sneer.

Even from behind the door, Vaughn felt the jolt and shake of another explosion. Even the two Historians took pause to feel it's power. The ground didn't stop shuddering and Vaughn couldn't either. If that was Wyla's bomb, and this room full of gadgets he was hiding in was still here…

"Good." Vaughn assumed Hammond was grinning, his words whistled past his teeth. "One more to go."

"You sure she's still here? Maybe she left like her friend?"

"Oh, she's here, trust me. Ms. Bavishni is still in the building."

How long he waited after they left, he didn't know. For the few seconds the door had stayed open, all Vaughn heard were sirens and alarms. He heard screaming and turbulent winds. Smoke seeped through the top of the door and water from the sprinklers slipped in underneath. Vaughn didn't stray, staying safely behind a wall of crates.

Swallowing his nerve like it would dissolve in his stomach, Vaughn pushed to his feet and carefully opened the door. He stepped out into a smoke-filled hallway, still flashing with red light.

It looked like a small tornado had blown through, doing much more than just knocking picture frames off their hooks. In fact, it was looking more and more at how he had found it hours later, or moments ago.

The few fluorescent lights, not left hanging by their wires, flickered and spat sparks. The walls were cracked, and plaster shredded where every blow or bullet had missed its target. And at the end of this long hall and continuing in some other part of the building, Vaughn heard the fight was still going; they were backing Wyla into a corner.

Good. Vaughn found his first thought. *She started all this. She can see how it ends.*

As the smoke above him cleared - caught in the wind and blown clear - Vaughn could see more and more of the hallway, and he wished he hadn't.

There, just above the doorway at the end of the hall, he saw it again. A rushed and smeared piece of yellow graffiti. Another one of O'seus' handy work. Taunting him. Torturing him.

Limpfingers.

He had brought him all the way here and was pushing him further still.

He swayed on the spot, refusing to let his legs move. If he took one lousy step towards it he'd be validating O'seus. He'd be recognizing he has no power over the lunacy of an old man living off stolen meals and stolen names. He'd be finally admitting he didn't have a choice.

"No." Vaughn said, sure and steadfast. 'Absolutely fucking not."

He could hear a cough. It had been there for a few minutes but only now did he recognize it.

He went back down the hall a few feet to an open door hanging loosely from its frame. He recognized it to be the conference room that would later be sealed off by police caution tape.

The floor to ceiling window had suffered an immense blow. Bits of everything covered what wasn't sliding out the forty-second floor to the streets below. Wyla's explosion had taken a massive bite out of the building.

Vaughn looked back, the graffiti still calling for him. Urging him to press on and follow it through and ignore whoever was lost in the wreckage. He looked down at his fingers. He squeezed them tight, but they barely twitched.

He felt his body sway back into the hallway and towards the yellow dripping paint. He had to tear his mind from wondering what he would find on the other side.

That's when he heard a moan. It was painful, someone was hurt. They were whining with everything they had left. Vaughn saw movement, someone rolled out and coughed a puff of dry plaster.

Vaughn felt his fingers tighten and form a fist as he stepped inside, dropped to his knees and started sifting through the rubble as a harsh wind whipped against his face and flicked dust in his eyes.

He moved tiles, glass, brick and broken pieces of office tables and chairs. Then a hand reached out, grasping and scratching until Vaughn took it - his fingers dug in tight.

Sancia was pinned under a large desk, and Vaughn rushed to lift it. She howled, and he heard a squelching of bone and blood as the snapped table leg withdrew from her shoulder.

Under the table another body lay on top of Sancia, it was small and limp.

Ignoring the bleeding hole that went through her shoulder and out the other side, she pulled Dahl's body into her and held it tight.

Vaughn tried to hold back a lump in his throat that brought up tears and curled his lip. Dahl still had that charming, naïve look on his face, as though he still had one last stroke of good luck left.

Sancia bawled, wiping her eyes as smoke got in and stung them dry. Through the torn opening in the building, they could hear a hum growing outside. Vaughn saw four white Ogles rising on tiny propellers and hovering outside thé wreckage. Their shiny glass eyes scanning through the smoke that billowed out and covered the two of them.

Vaughn tried to help Sancia up, but she didn't want to let Dahl go. He tried to hoist her under her arms, but he only tore at her wound even more. She screamed and coughed up more blood again. *Damn,* Vaughn thought, *she couldn't just keep coughing that stuff up like it was free, not for much longer.*

"Sancia!" Vaughn yelled, his words nearly lost in the wind's howl and traffic below. "Sancia! We've got to get out of here now!"

She just held Dahl tighter. Vaughn wasn't sure she was even listening to him. Too much pain, too much smoke and wind, too much everything.

"Sancia!"

"Not without him!" She yelled back, finally recognizing Vaughn was there, alive and trying to help. She fumbled her hands through Dahl's leather jacket, checking pocket after pocket as Vaughn tried to heave her to her feet. She knocked him off and kept digging until she found it. Brown with drying blood. The crumpled envelope was still in his pocket.

After all this time? Vaughn thought, having almost forgotten about it. Sancia dug under the seal and read the numbers written inside as she still rummaged through his jacket until she found their last two cubes.

Vaughn barely had a second to take hold of Sancia as she twisted the cube and took both the living and the dead with her.[*]

Alarms again. He was eighty feet up and it was blaring in his ears. Vaughn stood outside the doorway of the conference room as he saw the last few seconds of Sancia, Dahl's dead body and himself before they disappeared.

He turned his eyes forward; knowing the only way was through. Through that door at the end of the hall, the one with all the gunfire, the one with the yellow graffiti hanging over it.

The one straight ahead.

Vaughn walked through it, stepping into fate the way one would step into an elevator, ready for it to take him away.

BAM!

Shots fired, Vaughn ducked and his confidence in his fate quickly disappeared as bullets ricocheted and snapped bites out of the walls, floors, and ceiling of the open plan office space.

Galina was shooting at a faceless Historian while taking cover behind a self-serve coffee station. Bullets pinged off the steel machine as the Historian emptied his rounds in all directions.

Galina roared and held her arm tight as blood seeped out between her fingers.

---

[*]Go to Page 552

Vaughn couldn't prove it, but he knew the Historian was smiling.

Fuck it.

Vaughn ran full bore at the Historian, driving his shoulder into his chest and throwing them both through a glass wall into a separate office. It shattered easily.

The Historian struggled beneath Vaughn's weight and got an arm free to sock Vaughn in the cheek. Vaughn fell back but held his knees tight and swung back up on top to land a punch of his own.

Vaughn didn't care how weak his punches were, he had never been in a fight in his life, but that didn't stop him from pummeling senselessly into the black void where a face ought to be.

The Historian roared, blocking most of his hits with his elbows and viciously pushing Vaughn off of him and then kneeling on his chest and waiting to hear a crack.

Vaughn gasped for air as his ribs pressed into his lungs under the bony knees of the faceless man, now reloading his gun with stray bullets from his jacket.

With his one free hand Vaughn searched his pockets, desperate to find another weapon as the faceless man had him by the neck.

Vaughn felt something, and he took it, slipped it between his fingers and shoved it into the void that stared down at him. The faceless man shot up straight, dropped his gun and bullets like loose change. He fell off him and to the floor.

Vaughn took this moment to catch his breath; still thinking how it could've been his last one. The faceless man lay beside him. He only heard groans and sputtering coming from deep shadow and Vaughn quickly recoiled, backing away from the man with a corkscrew poking out of where his face should be.

"You can keep that." Vaughn offered the gasping Historian.

His hands shook. He looked to them wondering if they knew no boundaries. Not so limp anymore.

"Ok, ok. Breathe, just breathe." Vaughn told himself. "You got this. He's just hurt, badly hurt."

As he reached down to the body, he heard a BANG and Vaughn flinched hard.

Another gunshot not too far away. Vaughn took stock of his reality. He wasn't out of it yet. There were only so many gunshots between now and the end of this fight.

He could tell; there was a feeling in the air.

They lost the fight; the efforts of his friends were thwarted. Whatever they had been trying to do, they had failed. They dropped, one by one. Wrong about time travel and paying for it with their lives.

Vaughn crouched and slipped the hat off the Historians' head. Slowly the face he had destroyed became visible. The man was still breathing around the corkscrew that Vaughn had driven through his mouth, almost down his throat.

The man was in his thirties, late thirties. His face needed a shave, but if Vaughn was being honest, he could have looked handsome without that corkscrew between his teeth.

He looked… normal. Vaughn couldn't get past it. He wasn't crooked and evil, he was just a guy like him.

He wondered what was the real difference between the two of them, what decided which of them lived and which of them died? Was it just fate? Was this man destined to die like this? Was that fair? Was what happened to Sancia fair?

The man was more than choking, his throat was gargling its own blood and trying to find a place to put his tongue with a spiral shaft of steel in the way.

Vaughn never truly thought of himself as a killer, but here he was, killing. On purpose this time.

He figured maybe if it was his fate, then it would feel less wrong.

If that was, in fact, true.

If everything these Historians believed was true, that the actions of others really did push everyone off course, then it would feel strange.

It wouldn't fit like a pair of pants two sizes too small.

Vaughn had to decide. And he had to decide quickly because those gunshots had stopped.

He had to choose whether he would follow his fate or believe it had been taken from him long ago.

Digging his hands in his pocket he found he had just one cube left, the faded one was still tucked away in his pocket. He picked up the Historian's gun, half loaded and heavy.

Looking at the Historian, he noticed they both were wearing white button shirts and dark slacks. The only difference in how they were dressed was his brown jacket and Vaughn's blue shoes. They were about the same shoe size too.

At last, something that fit.

Vaughn felt his mind go blank. He let his hands take over, watching what he did from the back of his mind.

He casually lifted the man's jacket, careful not to disturb the nearly dead man's body too much. His mouth was slowly filling up like a ditch in the rain. Tipping him even slightly sideways spilt blood onto the floor but Vaughn successfully slipped the jacket off his back, shaking his dead arms from the sleeves, and kept it clean.

Then he sat beside him, calmly sliding off his blue shoes and swapping them with the dying man's black boots.

Lastly, Vaughn picked up the hat on the floor and held it in his hands. He could see Wyla's signet sewn into the rim. Dahl said he'd know a Historian when he saw one, he saw one now.

Looking in a glass window, he stared passed himself and eased the hat on his head. He heard a soft hum in his ears as he watched his face disappear in the reflection, and only a small part of him wondered if he would ever see it again.

"Who's there?"

A tall brooding Historian strode into the room to see Vaughn standing beside the body on the floor. He knew this voice. Its crispy inflection, its low tone, its foul origin. It was Hammond.

Vaughn still held the gun and he turned to face the tall and empty-handed Historian. The gun heavy in Vaughn's hand.

It was all that was between them both, and it was loaded.

It was all up to his finger.

"No one." Vaughn said, pocketing the gun in his new jacket pocket and looking down at the near dead body.

"Then why is he still here, Pratt?" Hammond reached into his bag and pulled out a fresh cube and handed it to Vaughn, not wanting to get his hands any dirtier than they already were. "Get rid of it."

Vaughn took the cube, not knowing the wicked twist Hammond was expecting, instead spun it at random and laid it on his chest then stepped back as the real Pratt's body disappeared.

"Good." Hammond said. "Such an untimely death."

Vaughn nodded.

He then led Vaughn back to the open office floor where Wyla's body was lying face down in a splatter of blood. He couldn't see Galina anywhere. Chances were Hammond had already done away with her.

"Well, well, well." Hammond sneered. "Look who's bleeding."

Hammond reached into his pocket again, seemingly with an endless supply of cubes to hand to him, but Vaughn, now Pratt, brushed him away as he pulled out a cube of his own.

Though this one wasn't fresh, it was heavy and old. This cube was worn, the color had drained from it, and only the stronger colors remained.

As he knelt beside Wyla, she rolled over. Hammond had shot her in the top of her shoulder; her dark hair dyed an even darker red. She looked at Vaughn, she looked to his hands. She saw the cube he held, one meant for her.

She looked Vaughn right in the eye, through the shade, as though it wasn't even there. Vaughn ignored her as he meticulously wound the cube, thinking of everything she deserved.

Right before he laid it on her chest he leaned in and whispered.

"Sweet dreams."

Wyla's eyes went real wide. For the first real time she had no idea what was going to happen next and that scared her more than anything and Vaughn knew it.

With the cube on her chest, holding her down like it weighed three hundred pounds, Wyla swiftly disappeared. Pulled through a tangent with that look of shock and disappointment hardened on her face.

"Such an untimely death." Hammond said again.

Vaughn stood. The alarms were subsiding, the smoke was fading, and it was time for them to go before any of those hovering Ogles caught sight of them.

Hammond drew out another cube and started to turn it.

"What now?" Vaughn asked, pulling his brown hat down tight on his head.

"Now?" Hammond growled. "Now we get the rest of them."*

Vaughn skidded uncontrollably, rolling along the carpeted floor and slamming into a wall. He felt a tinge of dry dust in his nose. The carpet he landed on was drab, grey and rough. The dust he sniffed was all he could see. It hung in the air along with a whistle that swept through into the dark room he had found himself in and under the cracks of the closed door.

Vaughn walked to the dark blinds drawn down over the wall of windows. He tried to pull them up, but they were tight and had no string to pull. Instead, Vaughn just tore them aside and was stunned by the heights and sounds he saw. It was night, the city outside was lit up and a great number of cars and emergency vehicles were huddled beneath the building.

Vaughn backed away the window of the dark office and explored the rest of the building. As he walked the halls he saw that someone had strung caution tape across nearly every opening. The floor had been swept free of rubble, glass and broken plaster. In the corners were lumpy black garbage bags, full of the unidentified dead.

---

*Go to Page 115

The wailing sirens from down on the streets sailed up to him. One closed door was taped shut around the handle, *conference room 902*. Vaughn peered through the small window of the door and saw that this simple conference room had endured an explosion that had taken a ghastly bite out of the side of the building.

He couldn't make heads or tails of what was left of the hallway and offices. He

What he saw was the bloodied bodies on the floor. Most without their hats. Their faces expressionless and limp. It made Vaughn's stomach curl, but one face more than the others.

Nash was among them, body strewn apart and zipped up in a body bag.

Don't think about it, he told himself. *This is why you're here.*

He passed a set of doors that led into a strangely bright, white room. The room's ceiling light flickered just enough to show off how bare and empty it was. Nothing but bare hooks and shelves along the walls, glass on the floor and a big empty crate inside. It looked like a store after Boxing Day sales.

Vaughn stopped as he had to concentrate on the twists and rotations of his cube. He only had one last shot at it, and he didn't want to go far. He had to remember how to adjust for displacement. As he counted out loud and in his head. He stared at the wall. He studied a bullet hole that pierced the wall at eye level, at how the plaster crumbled but burnt cleanly at its edges as the hot bullet drilled had through it. Deep breaths and a final turn. Vaughn jumped through his tangent staring point blank at the hole in the wall.*

---

*Go to Page 434

Chapter Twenty-Eight:
Retirement

The room was full of unseen faces, as bright lights were focused on the front table, lined with the closest friends and family to the man of this hour. Howard's face beamed bright and swallowed a mass of words he wished to say but kept to himself, merely tucking in his lips and grinning through it.

It was like he could hear the buzzing outside the room. In all their pockets and from every projection on every wall; the news would be the same.

He had dropped out of the race for presidency. Still such a long way off, he had been forced out by his peers in an even darker and smaller room than this one.

Some of them were out there tonight, lost amongst tables, lit by weak electronic candles in jars.

"We're here to my father. A man who, by all metrics, took what little he could and made the most of it. Starting off in the mail room, making his way up with no degree, nothing but – how'd you always put it dad? A little pull of the ol' bootstraps? Anyway, you all know his story and his successes. So, let's celebrate the impressive seventy-two years you've had on this earth and… and hopefully seventy-two more."

That got a laugh. The room raised their glasses to his son's speech and there was a hum about the room as everyone disputed whether a man such as Howard Hammond was worthy of such kind words.

"Ah, look at me, I'm breaking up here. Gotta get off this stage before I start crying about little league. So, if you will all join me in raising

a glass to a father, a grandfather, a terrible golfer... and one hell of a senator. My Dad."

Howard sat uncomfortably with his back tensing too much to relax in his chair. He just had to say *senator* and not *presidential candidate*, didn't he.

He nodded softly to every cheering face as his daughter rose to speak next. She gracefully touched his shoulder, and he took her hand and kissed it.

"As you all know our mother passed almost a year ago now and we would just like to thank everyone for all their support, love, well-wishing and understanding. It was a hard time for me, for all of us, but I couldn't imagine how hard it was for you dad. How you kept on going, staying on the campaign trail. You were our rock. I love you for it. Happy Birthday, Daddy."

His daughter passed the microphone to Howard, and he let it rest on his stomach before he stood. The room was bigger than it felt. He had seen it lit up and full of supporters before. But tonight, the lights low, and the seating all tucked in close, it seemed rather small.

"So by now you've all heard the news." Usually Howard wasn't this abrupt, several better openers had run through his mind and worn themselves out before he could speak. "I know you've seen the news and yes, I've dropped out of the race."

Howard stood and played with the microphone cord to give himself some slack as he walked around in front of his table of guest, and stood looking over the small mass of constituents.

"This was my... fourth run for the white house."

The silence he followed it with was sour. It turned every face.

"I was so sure it would happen... But it seems like I might not fit with the times anymore. Maybe I'm a tad behind, maybe I'm an old man who should find a nice house near the ocean and keep quiet for a while. The world is changing all around us and I just can't keep up anymore.

The future is for the young. It's not for those of us who wish to see it stay the same. We have to keep moving forward, despite what's ahead.

If a ship is headed for a waterfall, there's not much we can do to stop it. So, I'm retiring. I'll give up my seat in November and that'll be that. Cheers everyone and thank you for coming."

Afterwards there was cake. Howard stood with a plate reading the icing as others reached around him and took a slice one by one. The cake had an edible photograph printed on the top. It was one of Howard's celebratory photos, taken when he won his senate seat. He had a big smile on his face, and everyone took a piece of him.

He moved his slow feet down to the bar where he could rest his near empty plate. He didn't feel hungry. The seats along the bar were sat on by men holding plates smeared with icing.

"They pulled us up on a few items that need adjusting, but the gist of it got through."

"Good, I need a win. Brings a smile to my face knowing that when those smug assholes get back from their little trip, we'll have them by the balls. At least it's something."

"I'd feel a whole lot better if we could have put an end to this sooner."

"All that court time and nothing. So, when the New Year comes, that's it. Those things will be on the shelf."

"At least we slowed them down."

"We slowed nothing."

There was a wide distance kept between the guests of the impromptu retirement party and Howard. Few wanted to have their words trip up after that speech.

They all had something else on their mind. A senator retiring just didn't seem important enough. Truthfully, Howard expected no such gasp. Truer still, he didn't retire to induce one.

"Does seem out of the blue though."

"Don't most senators age into the role than out of it?"

"Maybe it's because of his wife."

"I think he's a little… you know. He is getting on in years, up there. He's asked me three times this week what my name was."

"Son!" Howard roped in his eldest son Gene and had him sit beside him. Gene was returning to his conversation with three new

drinks, but now those drinks were for his father. "Thanks for the speech."

"Well, your secretary wrote most it."

"They seemed to like your jokes."

"Well I wrote those."

Howard pulled in his son who hadn't fully committed to his seat. His father pulled him in by the shoulder until he was almost falling off the back of it.

"I got your present."

Howard dove into his jacket pocket and brought out a half-wrapped gift. Gene nodded, knowing his own gift. A three-fold picture frame with each picture painstakingly picked out and framed. One of Howard winning an election, one of their whole family and the third was his mother, Howard's deceased wife, on their wedding day.

"I love it son."

"And I didn't need your secretary to help with it either."

"Do you think I'm old?"

"You're retiring."

Howard paused and rubbed the back of his head thoroughly.

"You're not that old dad."

"Oh." Howard lent back against his chair, letting out a deep fatherly sigh. "I feel like I'm going mad that's all. Like there's an itch in my head I can't scratch."

"Should I book another appointment with Dr. Sandlon?"

"That's not what's itching." He went back to the photos he clutched in his hands. He had it folded over showing his wife.

Gene sucked the tears back into his cheeks as he watched his father stare at every inch of it, he wasn't sure if he was admiring or analyzing it.

"Why can't life be like this picture? Forever frozen in time, perfect. I wish I could freeze time." Howard took in one of those stifled breaths that were on the verge of breaking into cries, like the crest of a wave never quite breaking. "Preserve it's perfect moments."

The party ended early. Those that made poor excuses to leave were perfect cover for everyone else to slip out too. After they all had left Howard still sat alone.

It was so silent now. He had never truly noticed the noise of people before.

And he noticed the same silence in his dear wife's face in the picture. He had missed her. It had been so long, but he never stopped missing her. Staring at the picture of his wife, preserved behind glass; eternally young. Her details blending and fading, her face was becoming less familiar in his old mind and the picture did little to revive it.

He closed his eyes and tried to picture her on his own, images ran through his mind's eye, he couldn't keep focus on her. He looked to the picture again.

There she was. Who was she?

Howard Hammond dropped the picture to the floor and stepped on it, driving the broken glass shards through the old photo as he took his long brown coat off his chair and left.

Chapter Twenty-Nine

Three Black Kings

Atop a tall casino tower was a lowly lit room filled with smells and fabrics of such pleasure they could not be smelt or touched for free. And amongst them played a melody that too needed to be bought to be heard.

The room was full of extremes. If there was a chair, it was then the most comfortable chair in the world. If there was an ice cube in a drink it was the frostiest ice cube money could freeze.

So being that if there was music, it was the most mesmerizing music you ever heard.

The piano player was groomed by his own melody; it brushed his hair, washed his clothes and unstunk his skin.

For one precious hour, they cheered the pianist with still hands and quiet mouths until the last note resounded and hung in the air before suddenly being swept away by conversations restarting, waiters shifting glassware and the recorded music drifting back in through speakers in hidden corners.

Pete sat back from the keys and watched them disappear as the maître de closed the fallboard, almost snatching a few of Pete's fingers.

"Mustn't linger." The maître de snarled.

"A little longer, you don't even have to pay me." Pete offered.

"We don't offer an hour a day to be economical, an hour is all we can endure of your unkempt appearance. If you haven't noticed, we uphold a dress code here. Why don't you take some of your generous pay and fix yourself up next time?"

"If you let me play for more than an hour, maybe I could."

"Here." The maître de shoved his pay into Pete's chest and with the same hand pushing him up from the piano to his feet. "Don't spend it all at once."

"Oh piano boy!"

Pete leaned to look past the maître de to see the usual table calling him over. Pete sneered at the maître de and walked across the blood red carpet. Yet it was so dark it looked black. The piano was lit so he could see the keys, but the rest of the glamorous room was deeply dark. The black curtains held the daylight off, and only dim lamps sat at each enormous table - no one wants to know what time it is at a casino.

Pete's eyes had to adjust, but he knew who was sitting at the table that had ushered him over.

"Another marvelous display of talent." Ugustus Mumbato congratulated Pete, waving an arm wrapped in white silk that ran down from his shoulder to his wrist. The material stopped there and his unbuttoned shirt exposed his dark-skinned chest where he wore a solid gold chain that dipped down and rested on his belly, chest hair getting caught in the chain loops.

"Thank you, sir."

"We love to come listen to you play, I tell my friends in the west about you, they are jealous, I had one of them from Exxon on the phone while you played and even he thought you were something special. Until he saw how you dressed!"

Mumbato laughed, and the gold chain bounced on his belly. The others at the wide table also laughed, having heard the joke or not.

Pete looked down at his cleanest white button-down shirt, missing only two buttons. Buttons that didn't matter, they were in the middle. He figured as long as he had the top and the bottom buttons then what did it matter?

Mumbato wasn't even using half his buttons.

The table was easily four meters wide, the light from the lamp in the middle barely reached the outer edges, and as for small talk, Pete wasn't sure how they even heard each other. Where he sat, he could

only make out three or four of them, the rest sat in darkness, some puffing cigar smoke into the air to show they were still conscious and in need of another drink.

"So, were you well paid today?"

"Yes, sir." Pete mumbled. Sometimes they would give him tips, not knowing what's too much or too little, often he got too much. As long as he didn't rock the boat.

"Let's see, don't be afraid to flaunt your wealth boy. At least not here."

Mumbato reached into Pete's breast pocket and pulled out the small wad of cash. Pete felt like he had ripped a rib from his chest.

"OOoooooo someone's a rich little boy, isn't he?" The table chuckled as Mumbato passed around Pete's money and they all mimed fanning themselves with it, taking a bite out of it or even slipping it into their pocket. Pete laughed along, but inside he was choking down anger, as he knew no one would raise a fuss if he never got it back.

Mumbato had the cash float back to him and he held it out for Pete to take. He snatched it quickly, but Mumbato hadn't let go.

"Now boy." He grumbled, fat lips smacking fat lips. "Don't run home too quick, after all there's a beautiful casino down there for you to play in. You might even double this little fortune. Make sure you play ok?"

If you couldn't handle the market stalls, then you had three choices around here. Work at the plastic printing plants, the oilrigs, or work for one of the three casinos. None of them paid very well, and you barely got to keep any of it.

Ugustus Mumbato ran his casino The Oasis and a key Exxon stakeholder. Jaheem K'wate owned the Lucky Pharoah as well as the owner of the plastics plant, and Faraji Rufaro never left his casino The Red Jewel, not even to check in on his oilrigs.

If you worked for any of these kings of Niger, then part of your noble duties was to feed your paycheck back into the casinos to keep them running.

Sure, there wasn't much left of your paycheck to begin with after the U.I.N (United Independent Nations) subsidy was deducted. And

sure, now and then you might win at the slots or at the green tables. But they would make sure you were back the next day just to lose it anyway.

Sometimes, they wouldn't even let people leave until they had no cents left.

Pete was a magnificent exception. Before his parents were killed during the occupation, they taught him how to play piano, and they did it with love. They didn't teach it as a trade but instead as a way to try to escape from this place, if only through melody.

Pete hated that he had to use his gifts to get by, but he couldn't deny he loved it while it lasted.

"Make sure you play." Mumbato pressed.

"I will."

When the war began, America and China each occupied major areas of Africa. They fought through to the middle, quickly building plastic printing plants and oilrigs to promote themselves as liberators. Built only to give the locals job security and even pass on the ownership and management of these facilities to the people.

Thousands of paying jobs created a sudden wave of people from the surrounding areas, looking for work. Ushered in like moths to a flame. But they soon found themselves cut off from the rest of the world, those roads home closed and guarded.

The borders were systematically closed off. No planes ever landed again, and they left people with only what food they could grow and what little resources they had left.

There were riots, but these quickly calmed down once they realized the ones with power were waiting for a riot as an excuse to thin the herd.

After that, most either learned to speak Mandarin or English.

When word of what the plastic plants were printing got around, it amassed an abundance of naïve hope, some even trying to sneak a few early colorful models out. This is how they discovered the power and ruthlessness of the company. They made examples of those that tried to steal a cube for themselves, and it sent ripples of fear into the Nigeriens.

And once the ads and marketing for cube sales went worldwide just a few days ago, the price increase for Nigeriens was staggering. Come New Years Day, even the upper class in America couldn't afford a cube in Niger.

While others saw defeat in the wealth they would need to earn to acquire a cube, Pete saw a goal. He had nothing to sell but his music, but that only bought enough to survive. They made sure of it.

He figured, watching the wealthy float in and out of time, that he only had to get one.

They stayed rich and in power, using knowledge and fortune from the school of the fourth dimension. He could do the same.

He just had to get one.

The maître de led Pete to the elevator, selflessly selecting the button for the basement floor. Pete had to walk through the underground car park and out the exit ramp as cars revved encouragingly for him to sink into the wall so they could pass.

As he made his way out of the concrete car park, the road turned to gravel and he made his way to the Lucky Pharaoh, easy to do without giving it much thought as all the streets either ran to one casino or another. The slope was so steep, with an incline running right down towards the giant open mouth of the Lucky Pharaoh. Sometimes the gravel and dirt were so loose that you could slip and helplessly slide towards it.

As he walked, he passed a street of market stalls owned by survivors and hagglers. Most of the villages outside of the city were destroyed by the pollution and that sent the farmers and their families to gather in the city center, forming a permanent marketplace for the economy to rebuild itself upon.

With the naturally skilled and the naturally consumerist populations meeting each other in the streets, it became the new normal for Niger. Now their streets were filled with people. Many homeless and ignorant people sat to the sides spouting bombastic thoughts that could get them killed, claiming the West had merely given the ownership of the rigs and plants to the first three outstretched and open hands they saw. Or

that if they had a cube, they'd go back and make sure they were one of them.

Pete saw one homeless man pull back on his blanket. His blanket fell from his face and he could see the dugout where his nose should've been.

It shook him back into reality as the homeless people shuffled out of the main streets and out of sight, Pete could hear the chaos building closer and closer through the crowds; The Ruffs were coming through.

This gang grew larger every day as people grew tired of beatings or paying for protection. Under that rein, eventually everybody joins.

Recently most of the city had signed up to pay the Ruffs their weekly fee after they successfully hijacked a Volta truck full of cubes. They sold these to the people at a top price, too high for Pete, and they paid. Anyone who could, would.

Pete wobbled on his feet as he tried to speed himself up, nearly blacking out as the blood rushed to his head and he remembered he had eaten nothing since the night before. He hastened to the marketplace, wafts of steaming soups and broths seeped up his nostrils, dangling beads and marques bumped against his head, and what he hoped was only food waste crunched under his bare feet.

After paying off debts at the Lucky Pharaoh, Pete made for the The Red Jewel. Inside was different in décor. Most casinos had a theme that let you imagine you were someplace else, but not here. It was as though it didn't mind letting you remember where you came from, as the entire bottom floor was just as rancid as this outside. It was only when you made enough money to go up a level did the conditions improve; what an incentive.

As Pete lined up to pay, he watched as one woman put one coin in a slot, pulled the lever and the lights went off. A sudden gush of coins poured into the tray, overflowing as she struggled to catch it all.

Pete made it home just as Amir did. He stunk as always; a cutting fume wafted off his jumpsuit as he greeted Pete with a routine hug.

"I heard something interesting today."

"Yeah?" Pete asked. They both had their hands buried deep in the inside of his piano. The keys lay on the floor, and they passed the same set of pliers back and forth as they tightened the strings and fixed the alignment of the piano.

"Someone down the conveyer slipped one out."

"I thought they.. ."

"He got one out, I don't know how."

"Do you mean a faulty one or…"

"No. Real deal. Hand it back?"

Pete passed back the pliers. This piano was like an old car. They had sourced parts for it from all over, adjusting and refitting as they went. Sometimes it didn't sound half bad. Pete desperately wanted to play for more than one hour at a time, and Amir liked having something to do with his hands besides refilling polyurethane tanks.

"How d'you find out?"

"Word got around. Hopefully not too far. I was going to ask you…"

"You want my manual?" Pete asked, not wanting to part with his one and only book.

"If you could lend it. I think if I bring it to him and help him work it out, he might let us use it. One jump each."

"Amir."

"What?"

"That's stupid. What use does anyone have with one jump? He's not going to let us touch it."

"Then we'll buy it from him."

"With what money?"

"We can start saving. Or you could try doubling what you get…"

"AMIR!"

"What? Imagine that. Coming home and having what you made still on you."

"It's not worth it."

"With your credit you could get a good run going at any of the casinos before they ask for what you owe. That's if you end up owing, you could win…"

"Nobody wins Amir."

Amir finally finished cranking tight the last string on his end. He plucked it with his finger and relished the high-pitched twang.

"Let's give it a go."

They refit the top and closed it all up. Then Pete dragged a stool over to the piano and tried the first notes of the same song he tried every single time.

To him, the first notes of Nat King Cole's *Unforgettable* were so iconic that he could recognize them anywhere. If he heard any two of the notes strung together in elevator tunes, casino pop music from overseas or even in the melody of speech he would think of *Unforgettable*. Sadly, it was usually only the first two notes he would get through before some other part of the piano would bust.

But not today. Today he got through half the song, Amir humming the words to himself as Pete played. The pitch was all off and Pete could only play so much before it bugged him. He stopped and took out his favorite record and listened to the song as it was meant to be heard.

Nat King Cole's voice filled their little apartment and Pete watched Amir. It was about this time that his story would start. Amir would tell some version of the same story over and over every night. Each time focusing on a different side of that same story depending on his mood and what he was thinking about. He never forgot to tell it. Now even the very fact the sun was setting was enough of a reminder.

It was the story of the time Pete's parents died.

During the occupation, they divided most of northern Africa up into smaller and smaller pieces between the Chinese and the Americans. No one knew what these foreign armies wanted, but had been willing to give up whatever it was if it saved their lives.

Usually Amir would talk about the digging, that's what he would think about most of the day, and so that's the story he'd want to tell.

During what the Chinese called *The Revolt*, they marched hundreds of Nigerians to a nearby farm where they were told to dig.

Once the hole was several feet deep, the soldiers determined which diggers were the weakest and they were shot.

The stronger half had to keep digging, to bury the weak.

Again, after a few more feet, only the strongest were left standing.

Amir would always pause as he mentioned how his whole body shook, that he had the push himself to keep digging no matter what, not wanting to be seen as weak, while struggling to find a place to put his feet as he dug, as bodies and faces of his friends would slide deeper in the hole with him.

After hours of this, Amir was lost in the hole, buried with their dead friends. The smart ones hid with the bodies and closed their eyes. As they shot those left standing once the pit was big enough.

The Chinese soldiers jumped into the hole and walked over the bodies, spraying rapid fire at the pile until it satisfied them.

To this day Amir would always end this story showing Pete the tiny flesh wound he got from the soldiers' gunfire and told Pete to remember to believe in luck above all else.

But today; no story, no new take or old retelling. Amir's mind was on the cube. That rumor had made it real in his mind.

"All it would take is one cube." Amir said no hints to whether he meant to change the course of his stories or to be free of the outcome.

Pete lent forward and took Amir's brittle and callused hands in his. "Look at me, we're gonna get through this, we're going to get that cube and get out of here. And we're not going to be stupid about it, we're not going to take any risks or put ourselves in any danger to do so. Because it matters more to me having you around ok? Wherever that means we are."

Pete nodded to the guests as he passed them, his hair ragged, his white shirt going yellow and his shoes leaving dirt in the carpet - they felt poorer by affiliation.

But once Pete reached the piano nobody saw the man, and for an hour Pete hid his identity behind his music. Each note softened the rough skin on his hands. Each bar of classical score washed his clothes and rinsed his hair. Each song that he seamlessly moved between,

allowing only a moment for applause, ascended him to the top floor of this building by neither stair nor elevator shaft.

"Beautiful playing. I wish I had your fingers." A middle-aged woman dressed in jewels flirted as he joined their table again. She probably wasn't speaking figuratively. Pete nodded kindly but bit off a small layer of his inner cheek. He was a toy to them, their way of seizing peace between those that scattered in the streets and those few that dropped spare change from the rooftops.

He wondered how well they valued this toy and whether he could use it to his advantage.

"Excuse me, sir?"

"He speaks!" Mumbato roared, turning away from his conversation to laugh at Pete. "He's not just sitting with us, waiting for us to add layers to his tiny fortune."

"I ah…"

Mumbato turned back to his conversation and showed Pete a great deal of his back, which Pete would usually find more appealing.

"I was wondering if I could ask a favor?"

This time when Mumbato turned it was slow, almost like he needed the time to decide what face to pull.

"And what… favor would that be?"

"I have a friend, he's got some debts with Rufaro and K'wate. I was thinking, seeing that we're friends, and it's a small debt, that maybe you could ask them to call it even? I could play more often if you want, for the same pay. I could play for them if you want, I could…"

"You know what kid." Mumbato said. "That took a lot of guts to ask that. No, seriously, I mean it. Real guts. Now I can't guarantee what my two brothers in business will say, but I promise you I will tell them what you asked me."

"Really?"

"Really. And you know what?" Mumbato squeezed out from behind the round table, scooting awkwardly as his belly rubbed against the sleek edge of the marble tabletop. "Come with me now and we'll settle it."

Mumbato pushed Pete forward, almost too rough. His hand and fingers dug between his shoulder blades, and he could steer Pete with a sharp poke.

They both entered the elevator and rode it down to the main floor where they got out.

Pete couldn't believe it, he was going with Mumbato to see the other two kings of Niger. He was going to have all his debts settled and would be able to save his own money from now on.

But Mumbato either didn't know where the exit in his own casino was or was going a different way.

Pete tried to push his feet into the floor to slow them down, but Mumbato pressed on, turning heads as the very owner of the casino made his way through it. He pushed Pete right up to the roulette table and took a seat.

"Before we indulge in boring business conversation, let's have a little fun, huh? Why do I get the feeling you don't have any fun?"

He reached into Pete's breast pocket and took his small wad of cash. He slammed the money on the number 17 and nodded to the roulette worker to ignore that it wasn't in the form of chips.

"This is all so exciting, wouldn't you agree?"

Pete was distraught as he watched the wheel start to spin and the small little ball bounce around on the inside. His skin prickled. Nothing but sweat ran through his veins. His stomach jumped to its death.

For a second Pete thought of the brilliance if he had won. Maybe in some perfect world...

"Black 35."

His stomach died on impact.

"Too bad." Mumbato frowned. "But hey, the fun's in playing not just winning, am I right?"

All Pete wanted to do was slink away from the table, possibly curling up underneath it and just watching people's feet for a few hours.

"You know what, Sammy?" Mumbato asked the dealer. "Put five thousand on red for him, he's good for it."

Pete's spine went so solid he had no chance of slinking. Before he could even breathe a fat ball of snot out his nose, the dealer had slapped five black chips on red and spun the wheel.

"Red 21." Sammy slid ten black chips toward Pete

A little breath entered his body.

"Don't even bother Sammy, let's go again." Mumbato slid the chips right back and put them all on red again.

Pete watched the wheel. Those ten chips would cover half the debt Amir had left.

"Red 14."

"Let's go, sir. I don't want to get greedy." Pete said as the deal slid twenty black chips over to him.

"Nonsense. You're on a roll." Mumbato slid all the chips back on the board, again on red. Pete bit through his teeth. What we're the odds...

"Black 10."

And there it went, someone was scraping his stomach from the curb, it peeled off like a stubborn orange peel; little bits at a time.

"Well, you can't win them all." Mumbato sighed. He lifted himself from the table and walked Pete away from the roulette wheel and through the casino floor. He wasn't pushing Pete anymore. Pete was walking purely from muscle memory. One foot went after the other whether he liked it or not. They got to the lobby exit and Mumbato turned and looked down to Pete.

"Now don't you worry; I will keep my promise and tell my colleagues about what you asked of me. Just because we're rich doesn't mean we can't enjoy a good joke. But I don't want to see you in my casino again. In fact, you won't be able to play a single note on my piano until you've paid your debts. Twenty thousand, that's what a lesson in manners costs my boy."

Mumbato shoved Pete into the arms of a guard, and they escorted Pete outside, kicking and thrashing all the way to the doors.

Dry dirt and gravel. Solid ground felt foreign to Vaughn and the others. The cold wet wind was replaced by hot air that tasted and smelt like burnt plastic.

Atticus held his nose, despite already travelling with people covered in shit.

So many hustled passed them, around and through, that no one had noticed six more squeeze into the shoulder-to-shoulder traffic. They thought themselves lucky to land somewhere that anyone wasn't. Nash held his side and rubbed it as Galina rolled down her sleeves and covered the hole in her forearm.

They were in some kind of marketplace. But the markets didn't seem to end as these streets were full of only vendors and stalls. People carried all sorts of baskets and bags of food and supplies. They knocked past them, each one huffing annoyance at the six idiots creating a roadblock in the middle of the street.

"He's here?" Vaughn tried to turn to Nash. He thrust the empty cube for him to pocket. "That's what you said. Pete is here somewhere. Right?"

"He should be." Nash yelled back over the crowd. "Look for a casino."

Nash was looking around as the others did. They tucked into a tighter circle.

"All right." Vaughn turned to them as a hefty basket of melons knocked against Dahl's back and thrust him forward. "Pete's not on the list, which means he's none of your concern. You all get out of the way, and I'll go find him and bring him back here."

"Vaughn no. We come."

"No."

"You sure?" Nash asked.

"Sure I'm sure. Just stay around here, if you can. I'll find you."

Vaughn slipped off, diving through the crowd, eyes peeled for detail. It was tougher just to catch where he had been and where he was going, let alone a face in the crowd.

Everyone he saw had dark, black skin like Pete, making it even harder. Whenever he stopped and stuck his head up like a meerkat to

get his bearings, he saw more of the same shops and shoppers in every direction.

"White sheets." Vaughn repeated to himself. He had eyed a huge white sheet dangling from a window above where the others were waiting and prayed it was the only one. 'White sheets, white sheets, white sheets."

When Vaughn looked up, he saw just three massive buildings towering over all. Two in the distance, both shrouded by a glaze of gas in the air that made everything ripple and wobble.

The third and closest building was only a street turn away and was laced with pulsating neon lights that shone even in the stark light of day.

Every other building was only one or two stories and hugged so close together it made the streets feel like the cracks in between.

Pushing through crowds, Vaughn pressed on until he stood at the entrance to the massive building. Vaughn saw the crowds divert and steer clear from the sleek and freshly swept steps that led up to the valet driveway and the many glass doors of the buildings.

It sure looked like a casino.

Vaughn hopped up the steps and under the awning of the valet entry. Thousands of light bulbs above him lit the entry more than the sun did the streets. Vaughn easily crossed the freshly swept pavement that hadn't seen a car pull in for a while, yet two valet drivers and three doormen stood by the doors. They eyed Vaughn as he approached the glass doors to look inside. Peering through as a few people came in and out, Vaughn saw a rich red carpet and flashing lights. Upon a second look, he spotted the slot machines and card tables. Vaughn's teeth jittered, his knee shook, he felt his heartbeat in his ear. He was going to see him again. He was sure of it.

Through the doors he felt a cool touch of air conditioning beckoning him in. It was so thick he could open his mouth and almost drink it in. He laid a hand on the glass door and as he went to walk in someone else was thrown out.

Two hefty security guards hurled out a young man. He kicked and scrambled free and stumbled forward into the vacant valet strip.

Vaughn backed out and watched the man sigh and start off on his way.

It was him.

From the back of the head he could spot him. He knew it was him.

It was Pete.

Pete was quick. Making an almost impossible path to follow through the hectic streets. Vaughn knocked shoulder-to-shoulder with every second person. Each time almost losing his sights on his distant friend as he slipped through the human traffic.

Vaughn ran it through his head, losing track with every bump and thump. This was definitely Pete. But which Pete, he wasn't sure.

He hadn't gotten a close enough look at his hands to see what finger was missing. Would it be the Pete he knew and lost? The fake Pete that returned to the Asylum? Or would it be the Pete he had left alone in the Far with his bloodstained cube?

Smack! Another firm elbow in his shoulder, and Vaughn let it happen. He only cared about his face at this point. He wondered just how bent out of shape his nose had gotten.

Pete diverged through the crowd and Vaughn wriggled between families to catch up, taking the next street on the right where the crowd cleared up and the street widened somewhat.

Was it a Pete from Smokey's zoo? A Pete trained and brainwashed and better left alone? Perhaps one from an alternate timeline, just as scared and alone as Vaughn?

Or perhaps he knew nothing. Perhaps this was where he was from. It would explain the accent Vaughn could never quite place.

'There's just too many Petes." Vaughn grumbled.

As he tailed Pete, he noticed that foul smell of burning plastic getting stronger. He wished his nose had been broken enough that it couldn't smell, but unfortunately all it could do was smell and then crinkle up like folded paper when he winced.

Pete unknowingly led him to the edge of the wide-open street in the shade of market stalls. Pete was looking out for those that walked in the middle of the wide road. It could easily fit ten lanes of cars between one side and the other. Yet most stayed to the sides; only the tough and

naïve walked down the middle. All the buildings had too many doors, each one only a few meters apart. People swarmed in and out of them, apartments as big as closets and no windows.

Pete sudden shot out into the middle of this street, heading for the stairwell doors and Vaughn followed.

But as soon as Pete stepped out into the open, Vaughn saw several figures drop what they were doing and grab him. They snatched Pete's arms and cranked them behind his back. They pushed him forward, passed the buildings and went towards the source of the smell.

Vaughn broke into a run. He wasn't about to lose Pete, not just yet. Though he wasn't sure if he was about to rescue him either.

Vaughn saw the smell. Visible stench, like waves of gas that Vaughn used to see melt off the hot roads or waft out of his toaster when he eyed it too closely. The kind of waves hung in the air and stunk like burning rubber.

It got in his eyes and Vaughn tried to wave it away as he walked straight through the black clouds to where the rats didn't dare wander.

Here nothing grew, and everything died. In this wide-open clearing, one big tombstone of a building sat just off in the distance. Smoke and gas rose from the windows and vents, and Vaughn thought he might not smell anything again.

Stamped on all sides of the big factory was the Volta logo, as well as on every sign that flapped and hung by straps to every section of fencing that ran all the way around it.

That's what it smelt like, melted plastic.

Nets clung to the sides of the building, strung up beneath each window. Circling the building, the dirt roads ended, and everything became paved. Cars, buses and vans lined the car parks as big, hefty trucks navigated the loading zone and waited in line as workers forked pallet after pallet on board while the truck's engines ran. No time to turn them off. Each truck branded with the same logo and awaited the same cargo.

When exactly am I? Vaughn asked himself.

Ahead, Vaughn saw the men dragging Pete through a split in the wired fence and into the parking lot of cars and vans. They found an eighteen-wheeler parked over eight parking spaces, empty crates and broken pallets dumped out of the back. The gang dragged Pete up to truck and knocked their knuckles against the steel of the back doors.

When the back doors swung open grey smoke seeped out. The men had turned the truck into a hot box. Smoke came out and the gases in the air ate it up. They reached out and hoisted Pete into the truck and sat him down at a fold-up table they had prepared for such a guest.

Vaughn snuck up alongside it, crouching behind a large crate that had tipped and nothing, but busted polystyrene spilled out. Vaughn could read some of the packing slip taped to the crate:

Deliver to Republic of Niger, West Africa.

Pete had come a long way from home, Vaughn figured, and now he knew what made him leave.

"What? No, I don't owe money. I've been helping my friend pay his debt, I owe nothing!"

"That's not what manager said. He said owner of The Oasis calls him and says you wanted all your friend's debt on you. We do as you ask, no problem."

"I..."

"Since you are here, maybe you like to meet K'wate?"

Vaughn felt the truck shift its weight as a man in the far end of the truck made his way to the other, sitting down opposite Pete at the rickety foldup table.

"Piano boy!" K'wate greeted. "You're a bad gambler. You owe many people a lot of money."

"And I can pay them all back, I just need time."

"Oh no, you're out of time now, too bad for you. He's coming." The gang laughed, sliding their fingers against their blades and resting their hands against their guns.

"Do you know what I'm famous for?"

Pete didn't answer. But that didn't mean he didn't know.

"I'm famous for making people pay through the nose if I have to."
K'wate chuckled, the sounds of a sleek knife grazing the table chilled
even Vaughn. "Or with it."

Vaughn had to see more. He had to get a sight of Pete's fingers or else
he risked taking Pete away from his rightful time. Though, Vaughn felt
that anywhere but here would have been Pete's first choice.

"I heard you play once."

"Huh?"

"Don't huh me! Piano Boy, I said I heard you play!"

Vaughn bit his lip. He had forgotten about that.

"So?" Pete asked.

"I play too."

Pete gulped.

"Now, as one professional to another, would you like to hear me
play?"

Pete nodded.

"I don't play any traditional instruments." K'wate started. "Real
music comes from instruments I bet you didn't know could be
played."

Vaughn could feel movement in the truck again. K'wate was
walking around in the truck and suddenly he lunged with his knife
point at one of his men's stomachs. Even Vaughn heard the man
whimper.

"Hmmm you hear that? Now that was music."

"I will pay you back. I'm good for it." Pete stammered.

"No, no no no. Boy, that's not why you're here. You're here because
I'm going to give you a chance to win all your money back."

"Really?" Pete asked. Vaughn cringed, waiting for the catch.

"We're no bad guys. You can win every dollar you and your friend
owe. All of it. You just have to play one game."

Pete was still skeptical. "What if I lose?"

"Then I get a new shiny instrument." K'wate smiled. "I will take
something from you. A toe perhaps… or a finger."

Vaughn gulped.

"Which one?" Pete asked, like it mattered.

"I still haven't made up my mind, yet. And I will take another one every day until you either run out or your debts are repaid. That's twenty days."

"Do I have to play the game?" Pete gulped.

"I don't think you want to ask that again."

"Ok. What's the game?"

Fuck. Vaughn thought. He shook his head at how stupid Pete was about to be. He snuck around the truck and moved towards the back opening until he could see the steel, checker pattern floor and the darkness that sunk in the back of the truck.

Pete was still seated at the table and K'wate had sat opposite him and was now shuffling through a deck of cards. As Pete ran through all the card games he knew in his mind, K'wate retrieved three kings from the deck. The two black kings and the king of diamonds.

He placed them all on the table and then flipped them all face down. Slowly he moved them around, rotating the order they were in.

Pete already knew the game and was watching the red king circle the others.

"Very easy, very easy. Just pick red king and you win." K'wate insisted. The cards started to move a lot faster. His hands were swift and exact. Pete tried not to blink, but his eyes went dry, and he had to. That's when he lost track of it. The three cards were now interchangeable. He had to guess.

But Vaughn saw it. It sank his stomach to the floor to see what Pete hadn't. K'wate had been quick. Only someone with devious hands would've seen what he did.

Three black kings now stood between Pete and his freedom.

"Ok you choose now." K'wate ordered.

"What a dilemma." Pete breathed.

"It's not a dilemma. It's just a game. Choose."

Pete took a breath and stared at the cards. His eyes swaying towards the far-left card, but he wasn't sure. The rest of the gang had grown ever silent, eager to see which one he would choose.

Outside Vaughn felt it getting strangely windy. That burning smell replaced by dirt flying up his nose and he tried not to cough or snort.

Pete had collected a pool of sweat on the back of his neck as he tried his best to gain x-ray vision out of sheer will. His mind must have been jumping between his most glorious dreams and what he imagined K'wate's knife felt like.

Oh fuck, Vaughn thought.

He had no chance of winning, that was for sure. But what would stop Pete coming back to try again, picking a different card and losing all the same? Vaughn wondered.

It was a never-ending cycle. Never-ending.

Fuck.

Vaughn didn't wait to see which one he chose. He didn't have the time. He had to get out of there as fast as he could.

And then Pete appeared.

He appeared right before him, standing in front of Vaughn in the middle of the truck car park. He didn't mind Vaughn, just going for the truck instead. Then it happened again. K'wate didn't have time to panic. He dropped his knife and screamed a new kind of music.

The other gang members didn't have time to scream or to run. They were trapped inside the truck as it quickly filled with Pete after Pete until they spilled out like a can of beans.

Vaughn ran as fast or than he ever had before. Making it back to the housing slums just as it started happening there as well. Vaughn heard the screams before he saw the horror. Petes were overflowing out of windows and balconies. And the people ran, not knowing where to go. If they got backed into a place with space left the Petes would drown them like sand filling an hourglass. And then Pete appeared.

Vaughn just legged it. He felt his feet hit the ground and shudder up his entire body, his path ahead closing slowly as the crowd screamed and scattered as though they were caught in rapidly drying cement. They ran and screamed, but nobody got far. And then Pete appeared. It hindered every move they made until each move was silenced and

trapped. And then Pete appeared. The only move to make was to run as fast and as far as you could and that's just what Vaugh did.

"White sheet, white sheet, white sheet." Vaughn breathed with each shuddering leap.

The world around him filled with more and more of him. Each one with the same innocent and tragic look on his face that Vaughn had seen before. The same face he had watched die so long ago. The same face he had almost abandoned before tossing him a cube. The same face he had burned into his mind and hoped he could make smile once again.

The Petes moved with conviction, barely noticing one another as they made for the parked truck at ground zero. And then Pete appeared.

Vaughn heard screams quickly silenced as chests caved in and air supply drained. And then Pete appeared, he appeared from the ground, he appeared in the sky. Out of skyscraper windows they fell like fools. Their bodies never hit the ground, for the ground was now a river of Petes, purposefully flowing in waves towards the parked truck. And then Pete appeared. It would only be a matter of time until this reached the rest of the world.

Against the tide Vaughn fought and swam, kicking his friend in the face as he scrambled towards the white sheet that still clung to the buildings and Vaughn could see his friends had clung to it, trying to climb up into the building and away from the ocean of Petes.

Vaughn fought his way toward them. He never thought he'd feel this relieved to see them waiting for him. He was shocked that they waited at all.

"VAUGHN!" Dahl called out, his calm and happy face now white with dread and lost in confusion.

Vaughn fought hard against the rip. And then Pete appeared. He clambered over body after body. And then Pete appeared. Until he reached the top. And then Pete appeared. And then Pete appeared.

But there wasn't a top to be reached. And then Pete appeared. The top was evasive. And then Pete appeared. It grew as fast as he could climb. And then Pete appeared. He was being swallowed whole. And

then Pete appeared. Like tree tops closing over the jungle floor. And then Pete appeared. He could barely see Galina's hand reaching for him. And then Pete appeared. But he found it. And then Pete appeared. She held on tight.

And then Pete appeared. Vaughn closed his eyes and held his breath. And then Pete appeared. And then Pete appeared. He waited. And then Pete appeared. And then Pete appeared. And then Pete appeared. For the cube to click. And then Pete appeared. And then Pete appeared. And then Pete appeared. For them all... And then Pete appeared. And then Pete appeared. And then Pete appeared... to... And then Pete appeared. And then Pete appeared. And then Pete appeared... leave.[*]

____

[*]Go to Page 409

Chapter Thirty

New Years

A seven-foot drop is a short fall if you were jumping. But imagine a floor on which you were casually standing, maybe even with a wall you were leaning on your, feet crossed at the ankles, and suddenly the floor and wall are ripped out from you like you were the champagne glass in a tablecloth magic trick.

You might not land on your feet. Especially if you were drunk.

Vaughn smacked his head against a car as stumbled back, the heels of his feet still shuddering from the sudden impact.

The daylight was bright, and he looked to the road he was standing on until his eyes adjusted.

In the distance were shouts and sirens.

Around him were glass and steel structures, known as skyscrapers. Vaughn had only seen them in movies. They didn't seem so tall until he looked up and found it too bright to even see the top.

Whiz grabbed his arm and got him off the road to a perfectly neat patch of grass along the footpath; four drunken legs were better than two.

Without everyone else around, he felt a lot worse off than he had thought he was. Counting standard drinks in his head as he lapped his mouth with his tongue for help.

Vaughn saw that along the path the grass patches were neat and organized, planted in between every two patches was a neat tree with no branches or leaves until the top. The trees didn't bend or outgrow

each other and reflecting in the windows of the buildings made it seem like there were twice as many, all standing to attention.

If it weren't for the distance shouts and sirens, Vaughn would have thought he had stumbled into a film set for an urban paradise.

"Where the fuck…"

Whiz kept on, straightening his crumpled suit and slicking back his hair as he quickly strode down the path ahead of Vaughn. Almost distancing himself from Vaughn.

"Oh man, oh man." Whiz kept mumbling.

Vaughn jogged to catch up. Whiz crossed the street. Vaughn did a head-check and went after him when a sudden CRASH knocked him back.

A 1955 Ford Thunderbird bounced where Vaughn almost stood. It's tires and suspension groaning. He could see his reflection in the sleek red paint job and remembered he was still in his pajamas.

Inside the creamy white interior, the driver kicked on the pedals and wrangled the keys in the ignition. Vaughn peaked through the windows to see the speedometer and all the other dials had failed, their indicators had dropped, swinging to the bottom just as his watch had. The engine didn't even whimper.

"Oh, come on!" The driver yelled.

Vaughn backed away from the car, almost tripping over his own feet as his head wanted to hit the pavement and go to sleep. But he had to run to catch up with Whiz, who had already crossed the street and rounded the corner.

Vaughn caught up and saw what he had been hearing.

On a long street of perfect glass and greenery were hundreds of people collecting around one building. No dozens, no, six.

Six people all holding cubes of their own suddenly vanished and the street was wiped clean by a sudden gush of wind.

With his reflexes numbed, Vaughn looked downright monk-like as a clock came plummeting down from above and went to pieces in front of him. Little bits broke off and stung his legs, prompting him to move off the road as more and more clocks came raining down, thrown out of high-story windows and busting to bits.

"Hey, man." Vaughn asked, just now realizing he didn't even know Whiz's name. "What's going on?"

"Tensions are high as retired New York senator Howard Hammond again made headlines as he relayed his thoughts on cubes to those that remain, now that they're available for purchase just yesterday, here's what he had to say."

"... I expect this to be a fad, nothing more. People will tire of travel and get homesick and soon we'll all look back on this day and laugh..."

"The ex-senator then went on to talk more on the key pillar of his new campaign, the refugee crisis in South Africa. Something he felt was more pressing to address."

"... That is why I am refusing to accept new refugees from any carbon emitting nations upon my re-election in four years' time, and I will fight to keep it that way in the house of legislation..."

"Minutes later, he also stated..."

"... Let's just get something straight here, time travel isn't real ok? I said it. It's a hoax, people are going to open those boxes and play with their toys to find nothing is going to happen."

Vaughn tried to wave it off, but it was everywhere he looked. Something was projecting news footage on every surface he turned his eyes too. His wave only changed stations; the news cycle was rampant and aggressive, and Vaughn couldn't keep track about what was proper news and what was just footage of angry people in suits behind desks.

"Let's now cross live to our Johannesburg correspondent with their response. Val."

It was nauseating. Being tipsy wasn't helping either, every minute he felt worse. Vaughn smacked his nose into the glass window and about to trip on a gutter and fall when a hand reached out and snagged his shirt.

"...Val? ... It seems like we're having some technical difficulties."

"Off." Whiz barked, and the images disappeared. Vaughn blinked rapidly and looked around. Up above him, a small white dome with a black glass eye was mounted just above the doors. It was now projecting the same newscast against the window below but on mute. In the corner of the news was the date January 2nd, *2025.*

"Is this the far?" Vaughn slurred.

"The Far? Buddy, I have no idea…" He was cut off by a sudden splurge of vomit that he wiped off his chin with his sleeve as a shaky hand dug for his powered medicine in his jacket.

Roars and shouts came rocketing up the city street as two sedans raced by, taking full advantage of the empty roads.

They got off the streets, heading for a closed off shopping district where it wasn't any better. Vaughn shrieked a few times before he noticed the people were dumping bags of white cats, and birds. Tipping white fish from their fishbowls onto the concrete and smashing them to hell with bats and hammers.

Vaughn saw wires and chunks or metal crack and chip off the animals and scatter as they were smashed and once they were done they took their weapons to the white domes mounted all around them and shattered them too.

The future was just as confusing as Vaughn had thought, as he kept turning corners into buildings and streets to find remains of rioting, people suddenly vanishing, and shouts always just off in the distance. It was sobering.

He just wanted to find Pete. He had to be here somewhere. He thought maybe he should look for the hospital.

The future was strangely smooth on his bare feet. Without the occasional bits of broken glass there wasn't anything rough to stand on. He wondered how bad they would feel come tomorrow when he had feeling back in all his nerves.

When would tomorrow even be?

Vaughn figured it had to be the first time he had been outside during the day and wasn't sweating profusely in the heat.

Whiz still walked ahead, unfazed by so much of it. As he walked, he struggled to get the rubber band off from around his bag of coke without spilling.

"Hey man? When's tomorrow?" Vaughn muttered to himself. "What time is it?"

"Sandra Stone here with the Four O'clock News. Reports are coming in about mass power outages and explosions in Niger, although it is

still as first predicted. These were not the results of uncontrolled riot attacks but outsider terrorism threatening the peaceful country and its people."

"That's right Sandra. As you can see in these images, the people are calm and friendly, going about their days as usual. It will take more than a few deranged separatists to break the spirits of these fine people."

"That's Matthew Handler, our international correspondent, Matthew could you tell us anything about the effect these outages will have for plastic exports from the region? Should we expect an emission drop and how will it affect the subsidies of hardworking Americans?"

Vaughn waved at them again. It was like it was being beamed right into his eyes. He squinted and strained to keep his eyes on the street, on Whiz, and on where they were going. A dome with propellers like four small helicopters had targeted Vaughn and was hovering over him.

"As far as I can tell no exact word has gotten out as to what is causing these ongoing surges in explosions and radio silence. As far as I can tell from my base here in the UK, no one has called in any riots from its citizens. We can only speculate on the evidence for terrorism. Like I said before Sandra, these are relentless and proud people."

"Thanks for that Matthew. Let's take a look at the public's reaction to the most recent tragic attacks in Niger a few weeks ago that left forty-five dead and several Americans injured."

"It's just awful, after all they've been through, they just want to live their lives and go to work like everyone else."

Vaughn definitely couldn't see. If it wasn't bad enough, the pixilated image blasted in his face anywhere he turned, but pop-up ads and images scrolling and flying across the news was more than disorientating.

"-They should find these left-nut terrorists and put them to work and make them see what a hard day is like."

"As a mother of four I rely on my subsidy to provide for my family and keep my children in school. Who do these terrorists think they are trying to take away money from innocent children?"

"The subsidy drops we had last year almost sent half the country broke, if it wasn't for the Volta spike..."

Vaughn felt ahead for the walls, maybe Whiz's shoulder, but found a handrail. He could feel that it slid downwards, and he felt in front of him with his bare feet, landing a toe on a step and he took it, hoping the projections would leave him alone.

He waved them off, but they persisted.

"In other news, it has been almost six months since the attack at the Volta research and development facility. Since then, many people have come forward as apparent time travelers who tried to take the company down before the release of the highly anticipated cubes, although their claims have since been debunked. Experts say that it was more likely tech fans trying to get their hands on a cube of their own, months before they were released just yesterday, ever since word that Volta was housing cases of stock shipped in from Johannesburg.

Certain governments have been investigated and cleared of any involvement amidst the ongoing trials in the high court. As it is day 689, let's check in on this case it continues to unfold. Bryan?"

"Bryan O'Halloran here outside the federal court. Again, the latest petitions by the senate against the public release of the cubes were blocked..."

"No!" Vaughn yelled. "Stop it, leave me alone. I don't wanna watch this!"

As though he had said the magic words, the projections rapidly flicked through channel after channel.

"... The merger will not result in homeowner rights being stripped from them as speculated. Rather, an influx of regulations that are designed to protect all current homeowners and lighten the tax on their subsidies. For the American people, we are excited to provide them with the safety net that their homes and assets will be protected under these new regulations in theses strange and unpredictable times."

The flashes were violent. It settled on a channel barely long enough for Vaughn to squeeze tears from his red eyes.

"...Look, our worries shouldn't be about any of this nonsense, who cares if it's real or not. What our primary focus should be on is the economy..."

"That's true. Many businesses won't be able to survive even a few days without regular stream of customers. Government bailouts for airlines and the big banks will be a must."

"When I say economy, I mean the stock market. Our bread and butter. We haven't seen a recession in decades, our economy simply isn't designed..."

Vaughn groaned and missed a step, his sore heels whacked against the next concrete edge, and he fell to his back and slipped down the last ten steps. Not knowing how far he had to fall, he closed his eyes and tried to pull himself into a ball and hope for the best. Little did he know how awkward he looked. He imagined himself tucking into a perfect ball and gliding down the stairs when, in actuality, he looked like he was impersonating a slinky and moaning with his eyes closed.

As he slammed against the ground at the bottom, he rolled onto his back and held his breath, eyes still closed, and exhaled, waiting for any broken bones to announce themselves.

He was fine. He thought.

"I'm ok everyone!" Vaughn smiled. "Don't worry, I'm ok-"

He rolled over quickly and heaved. Nothing. He spat a little and let the drool cling to his bottom lip. Nothing, not yet. However, the effort and pull on his throat woke him up and things started becoming more apparent.

Slowly he opened his eye, and without skipping a beat another projection literally caught his eye.

"You don't have to be a genius with children's toys to figure this one out. Start with what we call the White Cross. Just make a cross with the white tiles, there you go..."

This one he recognized. It was that handsome man he had seen, what seems like so long ago, on Wyla's videotape. He was on some trivial daytime program with a blonde talk show host and was playfully walking her through the kinetics of a Rubik's cube like it was a golf swing.

"Now that you've got your cube complete, yes dear there we go, you can start twisting each side relative to its numeration..."

Vaughn felt the back of his head for blood. It was aching, but no blood, which he figured was a good sign. His ankle throbbed, he tried to lift it and he had to bite his tongue through the pain. Probably just rolled it, he thought, but still.

Fuck.

The pain had broken through, his high fading. His sense of awareness told him he was fucked as the flickering light of the projections snuck under his eyelids.

Whatever was playing Vaughn had to let play, as more and more domes hovered over his body, emitting a whining noise like big chunky bees.

He could only see by squinting past the corners of the projections to catch glimpses of concrete and sky when a white cat on his right came down the same stairs he had taken and stood over Vaughn, meowing once and a sudden beam projected from its eyes and filled what gaps Vaughn had found with another program of a man walking through a library with a husky voice and a grand mustache.

"Liberty. Freedom. The Constitution. These are the tools we have used to build this great country of ours. It's in our schools, in our hearts and it feels damn fine to know I can walk into my hometown's public library and read about what my grandfather and your forefathers fought for."

It was a commercial, Vaughn figured. It was too cheesy to be anything else. Oh, look; Vaughn chuckled in his delirious state. Now he's in a field, chewing on a length of hay as the American national anthem rises in the background.

"Yes sir. There's some great history beneath your feet. It's what makes you feel safe, it's simple, and it's made us who we are today. Don't fix what ain't broke. Let the past last."

"Fuck OFF!"

Vaughn flung his arm at the cat, and the projections stopped. The cat whirred as it ran away, back up the steps and the flying domes hovered off. He was free to see again.

Again, he had to take in the daylight and where he was.

Just a few feet away, the stairs he had fallen led through this narrow side street and out to a main road. Without all the projections in his face, the sounds of shouting and sirens rang again, and he could see the wind whipping past, scattering empty cube packets.

"Are you ok?"

A woman stood with her head blocking the sunlight atop the stairs.

"Fine." Vaughn groaned politely as he could. He rocked himself to sit up and his ankle twitched. "All good, just rolled it, I think."

The woman trotted down the stairs. She seemed middle-aged, with a short haircut that curved at her ears. Vaughn saw she had a white surgical mask covering her mouth, and he wondered if she was a nurse. She knelt beside him and inspected his knee. He didn't fight it, he just let her mother him.

"Lift it up, darling. And if you can, you should ice it." Her southern accent came through the mask, and it made everything she said sound sincere and sweet.

"Yeah." Vaughn nodded and stretched a smile. "I will."

"In all this fussing, I'm surprised you're not just about beat."

"Nope. Got lucky."

She helped him up and Vaughn found his ankle wasn't too bad. He could walk at least, just with a bit of a limp on his left side.

She didn't let up, taking his shoulder and helping him as Vaughn staggered out into the street. He looked up to the left where the chaos seemed to come from, then back to the right for any sign of his ride.

"C'mon dear, you got the strength." She said.

"I was with someone." Vaughn breathed.

But she kept on, nodding only slightly.

"Don't you worry, we'll find them too."

"We?" Vaughn asked, as she led him to the left, a little faster than he would prefer. "Hey, if you want you can just let me down here, I'll find my way..."

"Of all the things a boy can get himself mixed up in...." She spouted, her big cheeks puffing up from under the mask and crushing the crow's feet beside her eyes. "I've just about had it with all of you."

Vaughn sensed they were getting closer to the shouts and screams, something he had no intentions of being a part of. But he could see the crowd now, and it was huge. Clustering around a bus, the crowd was shouting at something or someone. But Vaughn couldn't see it. But he didn't like it.

He planted his good right foot to the ground but found the sweet woman walking with him had some strength, pushing his hand in his back and nudging him forward.

Vaughn tried again to stop, using both feet, despite his ankle. The woman landed her heel in the back of his knee. He toppled over easily, and she held tight to his arm.

"Over here!" She called out. "Another one!"

"Lady! What the hell?" Vaughn shouted.

"I am so disappointed in you. All of you. Being so reckless. You deserve everything you got coming to you."

The crowd broke, and a few men came running over to Vaughn. They too wore surgical masks. They pulled him up to his feet and dragged him by each shoulder. Vaughn kicked and struggled. His white shirt ruffled up to his chin and exposed his stomach, and he worried his boxers might slip off.

The masked men frisked him for anything he could hide in his tissue thin boxers. Vaughn didn't need to ask what they were looking for. He wondered if he would pass a breath test or if he needed to worry about one.

The crowd shouted and spat hate at him. They all were wearing masks too. Some held cans of disinfectant and stabbed their finger down on the trigger. He felt somewhat protected by the men dragging him to the bus, shoving him on board and plonking him in a seat by a window.

The bus was near full. Vaughn was among others who looked just as nervous and confused as he was. Another man was crying his eyes out and Vaughn felt a little less caring about being stuck in his pajamas.

The bus suddenly jerked and took off, breaking through the crowd that still wasn't done with them. Some were waving signs of protest,

which they smacked against the windows and yelled muffled slurs from behind their masks.

Vaughn was glad to be rid of them as the bus took them down the street where he saw more people popping back into existence holding colorful cubes, only to be ambushed and jumped on by those waiting with bats and heavy kicks. Now and then the bus would stop for these tourists to be forced on, running low on seats these new passengers had to stand and shake with fear, not knowing what timeline they had returned to and if it was all their fault.

The bus took them to what seemed like the city's business district, with taller and less creatively shaped buildings. Other buses had arrived too, and the people on board were being funneled into the foyer of one of the larger office buildings.

They forced Vaughn to follow.

The world kept spinning and his forehead felt heavy. He had no strength in his neck and he kept nodding off balance, only perking back up as they moved forward and down the line.

As they entered the foyer more masked guards forced them to follow to one of the six elevators, filling each one with as many tourists as possible but leaving a wide gap for a masked guard.

Once they reached their floor, the masked guards forced them out and to follow the halls that led them to an open plan office floor.

The desks went column by column, twenty rows wide and sixteen deep, each with a masked attendant attending to a gun-lead tourist one at a time. Vaughn noticed how much of a distance the masked people were keeping. The entire building stunk of citrus disinfectant and bleach.

Vaughn realized he was now just waiting in line like all the others. He worried if he should be there, if it were best to let someone know that it was all some silly mistake, and he would be sent back to his own time with an apology and a handshake.

Ahead of him was one man that was so much shorter than the rest. He was wearing a leather jacket that was too big for him and was playing with an envelope in his hands, folding it in half and unfolding

it repeatedly before shoving it in his pocket as they called him to his session and shoved into a chair.

"Name?"

Dahl! Vaughn shouted in his head. *How was he here now! Had he left, or come before?* Vaughn dared only to drop his lower jaw and moan a little as he listened and quivered.

"No." Dahl contested.

The masked guard behind him used his gloved hand to grip Dahl's collar, lift him from the chair and push his face aggressively towards the white dome that was mounted to the desk.

"John Dahl." The masked woman behind the desk read as the dome projected his identification to her. "Thank you. Won't be a moment." The woman allowed the humming dome to run a full diagnostic.

"Ok, let's start with when you travelled to."

Dahl leaned back in his chair.

"Why don't you make me?"

"We will make you."

A gun cocked behind his ear.

"I see." Dahl said, touching his fingers together and resting them on his belly. "I believe I have a right to an attorney."

"Well, you're not under arrest, so… no you don't. You're not getting one."

"I see." Dahl said again. Vaughn figured it was all Dahl could think of to say.

"Did you travel alone?" The woman behind the desk said, eyes never leaving the images flashing onto the desk.

"I don't have to tell you anything."

"That's ok, we'll find out, eventually." She said, nodding to the dome. Dahl glared at it.

"Do you recall doing anything that you might think altered anything in any way while you were gone?"

"How could I?" Dahl said, rather confident with his answer. "I don't think we have to worry too much about the future. Everything's going to turn out just the way it's supposed to. When birds fall and all that. Now when are you going to let me go home?"

"Home?" The woman peered up from her desk. As they spoke, pictures of Dahl's house and his bills flashed.

"Yes, home."

"Your home?"

"Yes, my home."

"I'm sorry Mr. Dahl, but it says here that your home has been reissued into your ex-wife's name in your absence. But if she has also gone missing then, under the new real estate laws, the government will repossess it along with all its contents."

"What?" Dahl choked. "You can't do that! How can you just...! Wait, my Ex-wife? How can you do this, I didn't sign anything or..."

"Well Mr. Dahl, we tried to inform you through all legal manners but you were unreachable, almost as if you had disappeared off the face of the Earth, couldn't find you anywhere."

"Well, I'll just get another house."

"You can't afford it."

"Why not?"

"Like we were saying, all funds would either be transferred into your ex-wife's name or to the government. Second, seeing as so many properties were abandoned at the same time, the price dropped well below the price of a candy bar, and we all took the opportunity to expand our portfolios. And now with so many new buyers popping up all over the place, it's become more of a seller's market. Are you following?"

Dahl gulped

"And third, no one will sell a home to someone who has been declared legally dead and his social security number has been revoked."

"But I'm not..." Dahl sat back in his chair, rubbing his head as though the room was spinning. "Why do you keep saying ex-wife?"

"Legally, any governmental documents are liable to disclamation once either party are deemed missing or dead. This includes rental agreements, adoption papers, passports and marriage licenses, etc."

"You can't... you don't think. I... I?"

"I'm sorry, Mr. Dahl."

"Can I see her?"

"Your ex-wife? I'm sorry Mr. Dahl, I can't help you there. But for you and everyone else here, we are providing you with public housing and a decent wage for work. Now if you could just follow the officer out to the bus station, you'll be taken to your new accommodations."

Vaughn watched as they lifted Dahl from his chair, dragged out kicking and screaming back towards the elevators. Vaughn was then shoved forward towards the same seat as it was quickly sprayed with disinfectant, before he sat in it. He felt his pajama shorts dampen.

The woman inhaled and sighed dramatically under her masked, fluttering her fringe. To her this was just one long day.

Vaughn found his chair was too far away from the desk to touch it or read the messages projected onto the desk from above. He sat there anxiously, waiting for the best moment to tell them he didn't belong, unaware he was swaying back and forth with his eyes half closed and stomach gurgling.

"Name."

"Uh...."

The dome had already begun scanning him and his results projected in front of her, she didn't even look up at him yet.

"Vaughn? Vaughn Ashton?"

"Uh, I have to tell you guys something, I don't..."

Suddenly the woman looked up, her eyes wide. Then she spoke sharply.

"You don't look fifty-four."

"I ah, what?"

"We've got another one!" She called. The masked men came up and grabbed his shoulders. Vaughn was shocked back to life. He had to say something. He hadn't asked for this. He was dragged almost all the way here. If he could just explain himself, they would surely understand.

"Wait, wait, WAIT!" Vaughn shouted, stopping half the staff on the level for a few momentary seconds. "I can explain everything."

The woman lent forward over the desk, and the masked men let go of his shoulder.

"Please." She said. "Explain."

"Ok so…" This time he heaved, hard. Dousing the desk with vodka reeking of vomit and chunks of carrot. He got it all out, three, four deep heaves, and he was done. Bits dripping to the floor and from his chin, splashes as thick as snot stained the attendant's blouse, hair and face.

"Take. Him." She uttered near silently as yellow gunk dribbled down her cheek.

The masked guard grabbed Vaughn like he was a bag of trash, wringing his neck like the knot tying the top of the garbage bag. They hauled him up and out of the office and to the fire exit. The spot where he had sat was now getting heavily doused in bleach and the woman at the desk was crying.

They dragged Vaughn down the stairs out the back of the building. More buses. More masked men. A smaller yet just as furious crowd stood around them, chanting violent aggression and waving their signs. He could hardly take in what any of them meant. His head was still spinning.

History is a PRIVILEGE.
The Future is for LATER.
I Love OUR past.

They shoved Vaughn up against the bus like four others and hosed down with bludgeoning, icy water. He screamed just like the others. It was like being punched, but with a handful of knives someone had taped it together. Once it was over his body felt aggressively numb and he followed the others onto the bus. The crowd came up to the windows and beat at them, yelling so endlessly Vaughn had time to count their teeth before the bus started up and Vaughn was again being taken somewhere he knew not.

Wherever Whiz had taken him, this wasn't the Far. Pete was somewhere, but it wasn't here.

Vaughn was having a hard-enough time remembering how to breathe out without vomiting that it was all he could think about. He thought he would pass out. How long was the bus ride going to be? He couldn't keep this level of concentration up for much longer.

Breathe in Vaughn.

His muscles still trembled from the shock, his legs wobbled like jelly from the flights of stairs, his stomach empty, his pajamas soaking wet, his mind suffering through the realization that he was long from where he was supposed to be.

Quickly he had forgotten all about Pete. Whatever danger Pete was in, it wasn't Pete he had to worry about now. He had to worry about himself.

Now is Not the Time

They drove them far to another side of the city; the shakes and bumps of the bus fell into the background as Vaughn lent his head against the window. The vibration shuddering against his temple was somehow comforting his headache.

The scenery outside flew past and it reminded him of his failed bus ride out of Fracture.

He saw billboards with pictures that moved. Heavily pixilated and advertising videos that no longer mattered, products that no one would buy. Mostly perfume.

It all seemed so petty now, that, and everyone on this bus, and all the other buses in all the other cities all over the world; they wanted what Vaughn once wanted.

All the buses communed outside of a grand building, what looked like a town hall. Big wide steps led up to the wide mouth of an entrance with thick concrete columns holding it open.

Each busload could see out their windows, the others getting pushed and shoved in line to march up the stairs and inside. Alongside them more men and women wearing surgical masks were lugging crates stacked on crates with trolleys up the same stairs and inside.

As Vaughn's bus emptied, he overheard one prisoner questioning his guards, calling her all sorts of fascist. He received a sharp jab from the butt of a rifle in his gut as the guard screamed through her mask, never to call her anything but what she was.

"We are not fascists!" She shouted with her gun in their faces. "We are volunteers."

"Time travel deniers! That's what you are." The prisoner called from down at her feet, still holding his stomach. "Fucking crazy ass Anti-Doxers."

"You're the crazy ones!" She yelled, taking the man's hair tight in her gloved hand, pulling him up and yelling in his ear. "Now move it!"

Vaughn followed quietly, itching his legs with his bare feet whenever he felt a volunteer looking at him funny. He tried walking with some nonchalance, as though he were on a holiday tour and was there to take in the sights. He wondered when they'd serve lunch.

Vaughn's tour group were led to follow all the others up the stairs and into the town hall building. Inside, the first thing they all saw was the huge opening in the marble floor of the foyer where stairs led down to the bottom floor and masked volunteers were pouring crate after crate of cubes into cavernous tomb now beneath their feet.

"What are you doing with all of those?" One tourist cried.

"If we can't destroy them, we'll bury them." A masked volunteer said proudly.

Vaughn felt like they were burning money. A few even tried setting the pile alight, but all it did was melt some of the plastic then fizzle out. A few more were fiddling with the cubes. One had a wire jammed firmly between two of the squares and was wriggling it senselessly. Another had one in each hand. He was twisting them simultaneously with the sides of the cubes touching when suddenly both cubes went live.

The shock wave sent ripples through the skin and hair of the group as a violent hum shot out and mellowed quickly.

Vaughn stared at the man, the cubes still touching, his body frozen. One volunteer stepped forward to get a closer look. Sure enough, the man was vibrating ever so slightly, and it buzzed a low hum.

"What did he..." Vaughn breathed.

Tourists and Anti-Doxes all stopped to witness what had happened as the man continued to vibrate. Life hadn't left his body, but life had left his eyes.

"You see!" One masked volunteer growled at them. "You see how dangerous those things are."

Solemnly they were nudged onwards, past the vibrating man, trying not to make eye contact. Neither side made much of a fuss after that.

That night they locked them all in rooms of twenty. Each given a section of floor to themselves, and Vaughn had struggled and wriggled to get a section with some wall he could put his back to. These weren't prison cells, these were offices and meeting rooms with all the furniture taken out.

There were whiteboards and bland art on the walls, power sockets imbedded in the carpet for plugging in computers, and glass walls that weren't thick enough. Vaughn could hear crying coming from the other rooms, but the lights were off. There was no moonlight tonight.

Most of them just tried to get some sleep and Vaughn was the only one dressed for the occasion. He got cold and rubbed his legs with his hands to stay warm.

"What do you think they're going to do with us?" The man beside Vaughn asked.

"I don't know, they separated us from the others."

"You mean the people that belong here?"

"You're not from this time either?" Vaughn asked.

"No." The man sighed. "I was at home with my newborn, I was just holding him in my arms that day. When someone knocked at my door and told me he was my son, from the future."

The man said it like the words from the future still held weight and intrigue.

"He brought me here, telling me I would get sick and die before his first birthday if I didn't go with him. I went. And now I'm here. Somehow it all got so much worse. I just want to go home."

Vaughn looked into the man's eyes. He couldn't see much in this light but make out the defining edges of his face, but the man was near

tears. Confusion had taken over and after so much the mind just wants to cry it all away.

He did, beating at the glass wall he called, and he screamed to be let go. Crying out, he wouldn't say anything. He would just go back like nothing happened.

Two masked guards showed up to make sure the glass didn't break and let the man keep beating at the window.

No one stopped him. Even if it woke them up, they let him pound all his might into that glass.

"I'm not supposed to be here!" He kept screaming. "I'm not supposed to be HERE!"

Vaughn tried to get some sleep. It had been a long night, a long day and night.

A long morning, then night, then day and night.

Fuck, he thought, how long have I been awake?

Some hours later, Vaughn woke to a low rumble of voices. The man beside him had stopped shouting, crumpled like a crushed soda can, finally asleep on the floor.

A thin sheen of light spread across the sky outside. Morning was breaking.

Vaughn felt his eyes sting and the pain run behind his eye into the crest of his forehead. His temple stung. It was his worse sort of headache. He palmed his right eye and massaged the back of his neck to soften the sudden throbs that came with each beat of his blood. The vein that ran over his ear felt thick and with each pump it engorged and squeezed until he squished tears out his eye.

He hated being hung over. It gave him a strong sensitivity to light so he would usually sleep in until midday, almost sometimes later if he could.

He never threw up, but his head would always ache. The only thing that would make it worse was hearing others suggest solutions.

Couldn't he just live with the pain like a normal person?

With his eyes closed and holding his head steady to keep back the pain, he heard the rumble again.

Those voices became clearer the more he listened; two masked guards were talking just outside their room.

"The others don't want to either."

"Either we do it, or we let them go. I can't do it. And we can't just let them go back to wherever they came from."

"What did he say we should do?"

"I don't trust the senator anymore. I think he and a lot of the others are taking it too far."

Vaughn could hear it in his voice. The man's jaw was chattering as he spoke.

"If it wasn't for the senator and those who took charge, we would all be gone." The other man said. "Who knows what has changed since yesterday? If we hadn't stopped them, maybe none of us would be here at all. Maybe more of us should be here and now they're not. You don't want to be erased as well, do you?"

"No, I…"

"Then we'll keep doing what Senator Hammond tells us to do."

"Right. Once we have them all, we'll bury them with the cubes."

Vaughn was having trouble rousing himself awake. No one was giving up their floor space and his legs ached from not stretching out. There was no way he could hold his head or let it rest and be comfortable. He ached for a pillow and a soft bed.

His muscles felt like they were filling up with boiling water.

How long were they going to keep them there?

Was this their solution to their problem?

Vaughn had seen it that way; that he was a problem they had to solve. His very existence was causing others harm and ruin, even if he didn't understand it at all.

He had figured that these people, believed that no one should mess with time because almost any action can change it. He wondered how different they were to the Polychronists or Monochronists he had met in the Asylum.

Could there be yet another theory about how time travel worked? Vaughn wondered. If there was, these people believed harder than anyone else he had met.

True believers, a scary thought.

The day grew lighter outside as Vaughn and the others waited for their kidnappers to decide what to do with them. Vaughn was watching his breathing, wondering how awful it would be to get buried in that cube pit, with those jagged edges jabbing him in the face.

Was this really going to be it? Was this supposed to be his fate?

Or worse, a more isolating thought; perhaps he is just another Vaughn to be killed for running off to this future and the other Vaughns in the other timelines would go on. His death wouldn't be noticed, just like one grain of sand taken from a beach isn't noticed.

It had him trembling in fear, his entire body had lost control, it felt like the entire room was shaking…

Wait. The room was shaking. The others held tight to the floor and walls.

Screams and shouting from outside as the gun-toting, mask-wearing, volunteers ran terrified passed their glass wall, abandoning their posts and weapons.

The shaking grew more intense, tiles fell from the ceiling, light fixtures burst. The wide glass wall at Vaughn's back shattered in streaks from the corners and crashed as Vaughn fell back with it.

He covered his face as the others trampled over him, cutting their hands and legs on the glass to scurry over him like rats.

Vaughn just covered his face and endured the screams, the feet, knees and hands, the shaking and the glass bits cracking under his back.

He endured until they were gone, the last of them ran from the office halls and out towards the main foyer.

Vaughn wasn't careful getting up, his sore muscle-constricted legs weren't out to save themselves. He stumbled slower than he cared for down the hall to catch up, running from that he knew not.

All he knew was it was something worth running from.

As he came to the main foyer he could see the pit again, full of colorful cubes, a cement truck parked up to the top of the stairs, moments from spilling cement down its slide and into the pit of cubes.

Standing ever still and unaffected was the vibrating man, with the two cubes in his hands.

Doomed to endure whatever was coming.

Vaughn slipped past him and the cement truck and down the stairs.

Outside was chaos. Everyone was running east towards the sunrise, running like they were being chased.

Vaughn could hear it, whatever it was, it was loud, and it darkened all the streets it passed.

Not wanting to push his luck, Vaughn took off down the same road as everyone else. His legs flexed and agile again, his bare feet giving him a speedy advantage as he tore past the others.

Anti-doxers and tourists were now only separated by the speed of which they ran. Vaughn could see ahead of him other tourists that had escaped as he did. He didn't see them for long, promptly disappearing as he passed them.

Fuck.

He had no time to run back to the big pit of cubes.

Whatever was behind him was gaining. He didn't dare to look.

It could only be a mighty tidal wave, rising and overshadowing him. He knew if he looked back it would be the last thing he would see.

And right at that moment he saw it, again.

Sprayed over the entrance to an underground car park up ahead.

The yellow paint. The long dripping letters. Beckoning him.

Limpfingers.

Vaughn drove his heels in and steered himself to the left, sliding across ash-felt as he broke his speed and ran down the steep incline to the darkness of the car park.

The darkness swallowed up after him, the daylight shining over him down to the underground disappeared and just the fluorescent lights were left.

Vaughn saw, huddled by the stairwell, a group of people, all standing in a tight circle, around one cube.

"HEYYYY! WAAAAAAAIT!"

He was lucky they did.*

"What's all that commotion?" Howard Hammond snapped, rolling from his bed, praying for his retirement to start sooner.

He wiped some drool from his mouth and finally lurched himself off the bed, his jolly belly both holding him back and giving him momentum.

The rumbling he had been feeling wasn't from his upset stomach, instead it was coming from two floors below.

New York wasn't a usual host for earthquakes and he wondered whether his worst fears were being realized.

Quickly dressing in a nice brown suit, he rushed for the chocolate box in his dresser, where he kept his unused pistol.

No, he thought.

Hammond instead made for the suitcase under his bed, crouching for it as the building trembled and had him wobble and hurt his knees. He dragged it out and tipped its contents onto his bed. He hoped it would never come to this.

He took the clunky belt, and he ran it through the loops of his pants. Beside it sat another gun, only this one had a bit more girth in the handle and was branded strangely on the side. He slid it in his pocket. He disregarded the surgical mask and canister of disinfectant; weak signs of panic, he figured.

But he did like the hat, it matched his suit, and he tucked it under his arm.

Lastly, he looked at the cube it innocently rested on his bed, nested in the folds of the sheets. He felt sick just to thinking of holding it.

"Bah, leave it." Hammond growled.

____

*Go to Page 522

He took off, slipping on his shoes as he made it to his door. He checked the hall and wondered if his neighbors were home or if they had already left the building.

Simply, he took the elevator down. The hum of the machinery blocked it all out, and he even had time to adjust his tie around his neck and laugh at himself at such an overreaction to an earthquake. He really hoped it was an overreaction..

But as the elevator doors opened, Hammond had never been more shocked in his life.

Overflowing through the lobby were dozens, hundreds, thousands of bodies.

Wallowing, scurrying, collapsing and repeating over and over again, forming a liquid like wave spilling into the lobby and up to the elevator doors.

Hammond was quick to press the closing button. He hammered at it until it shut.

Shaking on the spot, the ex-senator rode the elevator back up to his floor, loosening his tie from his throat. With quivering hands, he placed his brown hat on his head and pulled it down tight.

When the doors opened again at the top, he saw from both ends of the hall more of the same person were fumbling and spilling until the halls were nothing but doubles.

He tore back inside his apartment, firing his weapon wildly, four, five shots, all bang on. Killing the doubles left, right and center, only leaving trillions to go.

Hammond locked himself in his bedroom, trying to slam the doors behind as he did. All he could do was throw his back against it as the weight cracked the hinges. Moments stood between him and his death.

He looked to his last shot, not the gun, but the cube still lying on the bed.

"I guess I have no choice." He said aloud. He leapt for it, twisting it and was pulled through a tangent.

And then Pete appeared.

Chapter Thirty-Two:
Double Time

And then Pete appeared. And then Pete appeared.

And then Pete appeared. And then Pete appeared. And then Pete appeared. And then Pete appeared. And then Pete appeared. And then Pete appeared. And then Pete appeared. And then Pete appeared. And then Pete appeared. And then Pete appeared. And then Pete appeared. And then Pete appeared. And then Pete appeared. And then Pete appeared. And then Pete appeared. And then Pete appeared. And then Pete appeared. And then

Pete appeared. And then Pete appeared.

And then Pete appeared. And then

Pete appeared. And then Pete appeared.

appeared. And then Pete appeared. And

then Pete appeared. And then Pete appeared.

appeared. And then Pete appeared. And

then Pete appeared. And then Pete

appeared. And then Pete appeared. And

then Pete appeared. And then Pete

appeared. And then Pete appeared. And

then Pete appeared. And then Pete appeared.

appeared. And then Pete appeared. And

then Pete appeared. And then Pete

appeared. And then Pete appeared. And

then Pete appeared. And then Pete

appeared. And then Pete appeared. And

then Pete appeared. And then Pete

appeared. And then Pete appeared. And

then Pete appeared. And then Pete And then Pete appeared.

Chapter Thirty-Three:
The 2nd 21st Century

He had always thought they were exaggerating. No one in Fracture took a word of it as truth. Even without a strong education, it made sense that the planet was on a continuous cycle of heating and cooling, think of the ice age; that's just how the world worked. The people weren't at fault.

But breaking from his tight wince and finally staring out over the absolute unrecognizable view, Vaughn wondered if maybe those scientists knew something they didn't.

The concrete car park he had ducked into was gone.

But at least it wasn't shaking anymore.

There was no grass or concrete and the air tasted like the ash in Fracture but thicker and warmer.

At least the screaming was over.

The ground was dry and brown, rust-colored dirt that despised a soft touch and burnt Vaughn's bare feet. Fresh plant life struggled to break through the ground that had rushed over itself like a wave, and when it did, the heat shriveled it up. Some old trees poked out from the new layer of ground that had blanketed the earth but curled up like an old man's spine.

Buildings still stood, petrified from what they must have seen. It looked as though a wave of earth had swept up and risen to devour all one-story buildings. Anything taller sprung up like weeds between pavers.

Just like the group Vaughn had hitched a ride with, many had come here, some long before.

An entire civilization of anachronists plummeting the short drop onto untouched ground, like marbles cascading to the floor sporadically appearing weeks and months apart.

And the world they found was not how they had left it.

He thought of them, those Time travel Deniers that had thrown him on that bus, locked him up and asked him all those questions. They must've been mad. He smirked.

Not much to deny now.

Vaughn skipped on one hot foot to the other as those he came with gathered themselves.

"You're welcome." One of them said, tipping an imaginary cap.

The group talked and took off quickly, already with places to go, or people to hide from.

Once Vaughn was on his feet, he could see at what was left.

The grey sky met with the brown dirt. And it went on and on past the buildings the horizon in plain sight from all directions. He recognized skyscrapers that looked like they had endured a beating, all glass in the windows gone, the wind whistled through and he could see tiny figures of people moving about inside.

qVaughn felt that the wind hadn't let up, constantly tossing the rusty dirt in his eyes, the vast sheets lifted like sails and sandstorms barraged against it.

Vaughn walked towards them, seeking shelter, he skipped his feet, hopping as his skin sizzled. He tried to keep to any shadow he could. He eyed the deep, black shade ahead, where the sun had been refused entry and walked a little faster to relieve his feet.

He felt like he was walking through a dangerous forest. The buildings were foreboding trees, whistling to each other, the sheets resulting like leaves. Any movement big enough and living things scattered. Something sent a wash of wind Vaughn's way. It passed him and shook an old tarp, loosely sending dozens of cats dashing for other dark cover. The hair on their backs was wiry and sharp. Their eyes red and yellow. They hissed through fangs and had biceps bigger than Vaughn's.

BANG BANG!

Cats mid scatter sprung up and ducked out of sight, as streets ahead two clunky cars sped through, rocketing gunfire as they raged past.

Their target quickly retaliated with more shots and sounds of metal being struck, quickly muffled by the shouts that followed.

Vaughn followed the lack of shouting, hoping to steer clear; he wondered past sheet metal fence line that bowed to every gust, on a large section someone had spray painted the words.

Nobody's Home.

Vaughn checked. It wasn't the same yellow painted graffiti that had taunted him here.

Though, had he not followed it he wouldn't have made it much further, he also wouldn't have gone back up to the Observatory. Thinking about it grew an ulcer in his mouth for him to chew at. Following any sign of words *Limpfingers* was like being led to safety but by a string pegged to your earlobe and it pulls. He so badly wished to unclip, but was he supposed to? He would be a goner for sure without it.

"If I see another one, then I'll know." Vaughn said to himself aloud, if he said his thoughts aloud like that it would get it out of his head.

Only now his head started asking itself where exactly he was. Could it possibly be *The Far* he was searching for?

Was this where Pete would be?

More gunshots and cackling insults followed by the sound of something crashing.

"Probably not a place to bring someone who was dying." He thought out loud again.

Vaughn kept wondering, hiding whenever he saw someone, which wasn't often.

It was true; nobody was home.

He soon passed the car that had crashed, the engine still smoked, the hood was bust, and Vaughn could see someone had rebuilt the entire thing with parts from microwaves and plumbing pipe.

BOOM again.

Vaughn ducked away, slipping through a window of a building close by, his foot resting on the windowsill that poked through the dirt floor.

A car bomb went off and people scuttled from buildings like cockroaches. Some running away, others making for the car to strip it for parts before scuttling away themselves.

Vaughn shifted his foot and actual cockroaches scuttled out from beneath the creaking windowsill wood. Bugs of all sorts snuck out from under splinters, not used to being disturbed for so many years.

He didn't have to wait long until it was quiet again. He snuck out and kept to the edges of the road, avoiding any cars or unlit rooms behind windows. He passed dump heaps where people had accumulated their garbage, yet no one would drive past in garbage trucks to retrieve it. There were mounds of smoldering muck, empty fast-food packaging, broken things and old tires. Flies buzzed around it all, following the scent from one pile to another with every waft of wind.

Above, the enormous tent like sheets that clung to the buildings lifted with this wind and he felt like he was going to get sucked up with it, it lifted his white shirt and made him conscious of how thin his pajama boxer shorts were.

He was avoiding the voices and signs of others, but this sounded different. As he neared the end of the street he was on he could see a gathering of people all walking towards and into a stone building. It was one of the larger buildings in girth with a domed glass roof, sans the glass. Now it had one big sheet draped over the top and strapped down, barely moving in the wind and keeping the dust out.

Vaughn came up to it; he could see piles of dirt amassed around it and beneath every window, as though someone had shoveled it out. As he stepped inside he saw the clean original tiled floors and piles of dirt swept into the edges and corners.

A muffled sound was coming through two big wooden doors to his right. He followed it and peaked through.

The speaking echoed profoundly in a dull monotone voice, the kind that would make the most exciting story sound like the phone book.

Vaughn found he had stepped into a large auditorium under the massive dome of the building. It slowly sunk with a gradual decline towards the center of the massive room. It was like walking into the depths of a bowl from the rim.

Towering over Vaughn were stands; great tall seating pews that reminded him of bookcases. They stood about a meter apart and a few people wandered between them before quickly finding a ladder and scooting up to sit with the others.

Swept to the bases of each tall stand was more rusted dirt.

Vaughn walked towards the center, wiping the grit from his feet and enjoying the cool touch of the tiled floor. No one looked down at him and he figured that was the idea. A seating structure that made it possible to walk from the door to any seat in the auditorium without drawing any attention.

Vaughn liked this. He felt like he could continue to go about unnoticed and hopefully inconsequential as things played themselves out.

It sounded like a hearing was taking place. As he neared the inside of the auditorium, he noticed the dirt that had collected at the base of the largest podium and then he noticed it was surrounded by ring of prominent stands with plateaus at the top instead of seating. Atop two of these plateaus a few important-looking people stood, glaring at one another. The rest of the center plateaus were empty. Most of the auditorium was.

A coughing fit caught Vaughn's attention. Atop the center most podium sat an old man in a black robe. He was resting his head in his palm that rested on his arm, which rested on his elbow, which rested on the bench. He twiddled a gavel in his hand and was either bored or tired by the whole thing, as those above were busy introducing themselves to whoever was listening.

Unbeknownst to Vaughn, Judge Norwell had been plucked from the past, just days before a heart attack, in order for the matters of the court to be fair and unbiased. The matters of the court were also unbeknownst to Vaughn, as were most things.

But what those that had plucked Norwell didn't know was that Norwell had a history of highly realistic dreams and hallucinations. At this moment, he saw no difference between the strange court that had summoned him and the dream he had had the night before of a kingdom of mice that resided between his walls.

"Honorable Judge Norwell. I, Gene Winters, will be happy to speak on behalf of any time travel deniers, Alterchronists, Anti-Doxes, or any others against the act of time travel, with the exception, of course, for our survival."

Vaughn shot a look up to Gene in the opposition podium. A bland individual, he wore his scowl better than his suit.

"Very well Mr. Winters." Norwell responded. "And for those in favor of time travel?"

"Wyla Bavishni and O'seus Forshaker your honor, representing the Polychronistic views and values." A familiar voice called out. "We are assisted by Mr. Dean Shute representing the Moncchronism movement."

Vaughn shuffled to a better position and looked up to see a familiar face. He couldn't get away from her, could he? There she was again, popping up when he least expected it.

She was wearing the same jumpsuit as she wore at the Asylum and was standing tall against the edge of her towering podium.

"How ye do?" He heard a man roar from up above alongside her.

Vaughn couldn't get a look at this O'seus fellow from below. Having heard his name around the Asylum, he wondered if he looked the same as he pictured him. He didn't sound like he imagined; O'seus had a thick Scottish tongue and seemed to enjoy the court's process.

"Your honor, before we start, might I suggest the use of a paper that was published before..." Gene paused and shrugged. "For your consideration, I can submit the Eleven Tests of Time Travel published by Dr. Kenneth Brown PhD to use as a frame of reference..."

The judge waved his hand to silence Gene. He instead sat still in his chair for some time before pulling from the deep pockets of his

black robes an ornate wooden box, which he placed at the edge of his desk.

"This is my wedding ring box, due to my heart condition and my age my fingers swell, and I can no longer wear my ring. It stays in this box with me at all times. Except for this morning, when I left it on my dresser between 8:00 and 9:00, unattended and free to any who wished to tamper with it. Just before I began this session, I checked the box and found only my ring."

Vaughn caught the odd silence in the room. Many were concerned whether this old timer was still fit to judge such an important case and whether his mind was all there.

"I want you all to write down this sentence on a piece of paper 'honeysuckle trees deliver sweetness to the bees' and then sign your name. This will be my frame of reference."

After a few hesitant seconds Gene, O'seus, Shute and Wyla all wrote their names, and the sentence given.

"Now, all three of you are tasked, by law, to return to this day after it is over and place your piece of paper inside the box provided in the time allotted. This will determine how I sway my decisions; a judge needs context. Questions, comments?"

Immediately Gene spoke up, obviously never too proud to display it.

"I will do this, as I know for a fact that actions can change the past and when you open that box for us all you will find my name inside."

"Excellent." The judge approved.

"But," added Gene. "This will mean that the universe shall correct itself and that when you said that the box was empty just before you began speaking you were in fact, lying. Or we will all remember you telling us all that my bit of paper was in that box."

The judge took this minor insult to his own testimony under consideration and nodded.

"Again, you would know where we all stand if you just take a quick glance at the document mentioned on your desk." Gene tried again.

The judge noticed the paper he referred to, lifted his gavel and nudged the published paper off his desk and podium. The thick thing fell and landed in a clump of sand and dust at the foot of Norwell's podium. Vaughn could see it was as thick as a manual.

The next voice rang out, not even getting up from his seat to address the judge.

"I cannot abide by this." Shute spoke. "As you have said, you checked the box and found it empty. This means it cannot be changed and my name, nor any name, will be found in that box."

"Understood. Mr. Shute, But I will task you to try anyway."

"If that's what you want." Shute responded.

The room was heating up, already the factions were at each other's theoretical throats. Wyla stood and approached the edge of her podium to be closer to the Judge.

"Either myself or Mr. Forshaker will go back and successfully place our names into that box." She said. "But in doing so we say goodbye to you all, as to change the past means for me to move into another universe, one wherein my name was always in the box. Sadly, none of you will be present to see me prove my point. In fact, if you do find my name, or any other in that box, I will be proven wrong."

"Well said." O'seus roared from his seat.

Wyla didn't wait for a response, like someone who owned everyone and everything in a room; she turned and walked back to her seat.

Now that each of the three factions had spoken, the room fell to a hush. The judge waited a few seconds before pulling the box back toward him, like a magician waiting for the magic spell he had pretended to cast to take effect.

He unclasped the box and slowly opened the lid to peer inside. What the audience of the court didn't know was that the judge, still secretly convinced he was hallucinating, had the smallest of epileptic fits at this precise moment and saw only a small beetle rummaging around in the box and nothing else. Assuming this was normal for the fantastical dream world he had dreamed up. He simply closed the box and continued the case with an increasingly vague perspective on reality.

"Hmmm. Interesting." He held out on them, and the court creaked with the groan of too many chairs bearing too much weight on their edges. "We may now move on to the matters at hand."

The court erupted into calls and shouts for answers. Several agitated spectators fell and crashed into the walkways below - their screams now silenced by the soundproofing design of the depths. The judge calmly placed the box back in his robes and talked over the chorus of complaints.

"Order, order in the court. This may be the first tribunal held for over a thousand years, but we should all aim to keep this great civilization running smoothly. Mr. Winters?"

Gene Winters stepped forward as the representative for the static party and Wyla Bavishni had been appointed to argue the case for the nomadic people.

"We will first hear the proposals from the static community representative. Mr. Winters, you have the room."

Gene stepped forward to the edge of his plateau and spoke simply, enjoying the sound of his own voice echoing back to him. "Thank you, your honor, I wish to first address the tragedy that brought us all here... the Incident."

The entire room fell to silence thinking of those they knew that hadn't made it out in time. Vaughn gulped.

"First, I would like to state that, though today I am speaking and debating for all unjustly removed individuals, I do not speak or represent the mob group known as Historians. Despite what I have been accused of, I have absolutely no affiliation with those people. In saying that, I would like to point out that these troubled people were reacting to a time of great stress and under that sort of pressure we can't all label our actions as reasonable. But as much as I do not warrant their acts of terrorism, as what they are doing is barbaric and hypocritical, I do wish that their cause to fight would end here, in this courtroom. I believe there are good people on both sides and both sides can come to an agreement today."

"Understood, understood. Please proceed."

"Gladly. First, we request that it be declared that due to dire circumstances, the true present of the 21st century should be relocated to today, we can say today is *January 1st, 2025 - post incident.* As there are no native people to this period to deem us unwelcome here, so we should self-recognize this time to be our present as our true present was tragically taken away from us by reckless usage of time travel."

Norwell contemplated this notion and surveyed the reactions of his audience. There seemed to be no hesitation or debate over this motion, but he asked anyway.

"Does the opposition have any disputes?"

"Just a clarification." Wyla stepped in. "We are allowed to live in this time period without revolt or persecution."

"We're not living here against anyone's wishes, only our own. So, yes"

"Fine with me."

"Decreed. Next motion." Norwell declared, making a note to himself.

"Second, we ask that it be deemed illegal to alter human history."

"Objection your honor!" Wyla slammed.

"A cliché your honor!" O'seus followed up with a laugh.

Wyla had risen from her seat.

"I object to the motion of the static party leader Winters, as they base it on prejudice and unshared beliefs. We believe that events cannot be altered so why should they hold us in contempt for something we believe to be impossible?"

There was a small cheer from the crowd and Winters drew breath.

"The practices you speak of are more harmful than you know. Just because you fail to notice the changes you and your fellow tourists are enacting. Doesn't mean they aren't happening." Winters sneered.

"That is based on faith alone." Wyla said. "Faith is not a path to truth. No proof has been or can be presented to prove that we have had any effect on the past."

"All right that's enough." Judge Norwell eased. "I shall confirm Winters request."

There was a great moan from the crowd.

"Hear me out, hear me out. I shall confirm his request on the pretense that to be held guilty of altering past events, they must prove they have altered it. Next request, Winters."

Gene looked sore. He eyed Wyla as he readied his third motion.

"Our last request is for Ronny Boltzmann to be found innocent for the murder of Arnold Stoch."

The court went into an uproar. The two major sides entered a fuming debate voiced predominantly with cuss words and heinous name-calling. Many wished to jump from one tower of seats to the other, but the leap was clearly designed to be slightly too far.

Instead they ran down their ladders and were fought off by kicks from those sitting above.

The Judge sent out his bailiffs to slip into the depths of the walkways and the loudest of the crowd suddenly were pulled into the quiet halls, excused for the rest of the trial.

"Order, I will have order." Judge Norwell continued to stand as he settled his court. "There shall be no hostilities held before my gavel. Now would someone please explain the situation?"

Gene left his seat and began recalling the occurrence.

"Stoch and Boltzmann were two friends that time travelled like most to all the popular destinations. They finally stopped in 1900's Poland to find gold stolen and buried by the Nazi's. During this time a feud erupted between the two, and Boltzmann killed Stoch."

"Your honor he is telling the truth, and for once I agree with everything he has said." Wyla charmingly agreed. "Based on the lack of argument over whether or not Boltzmann murdered Stoch, I urge the court to promptly find Boltzmann guilty and move onto more pressing matters."

"Ah your honor," Gene interrupted. "I have further evidence to support my request."

"Proceed."

Gene reached into his pocket and pulled out an apple and rested it upon his lectern.

"What is this?" Norwell asked, unimpressed.

"This is a miracle, your honor." Gene started, building to his point. "This apple rode in the pocket of a friend of mine as he was unjustly shifted from the comfort of his own time to today, bringing with him this apple."

Norwell's expression hadn't changed. Wyla wondered what he was getting at.

"Now your honor. If he hadn't taken this apple from its time would it be fair to say that it could not possibly be here today, having completely deteriorated and decomposed, am I right?"

"I suppose."

"And if I were to take this apple to a time before its mother tree had even been planted. Would that make its being there unnatural and wrong?"

"Mr. Winters, please get to your point."

"Sir, if I were to now stomp on this apple in its impossible past or today in its ridiculous future, how could you find me guilty of squashing anything that, by all reason, should not even exist?"

Norwell eased forward in his chair.

"By the same reasoning, how could one be guilty of killing a man that by all logic and reason should not yet be alive?"

As Norwell went to speak, O'seus piped up and yelling back from the comfort of his chair.

"What would stop me then from putting a bullet between your eyes right now then, huh? A thousand years out of existence?"

"Exactly. But as the honorable Judge Norwell has already confirmed, this age is now recognized as our correct present, so we are legally allowed to be here."

"Mr. Winters don't mistake my agreeing with you as a courtesy. You have my attention, but so far all I see is an apple, not a human being."

"Your honor, may I call a witness."

"You may. A witness to what?"

"To the murder of Arnold Stoch."

Again the court went up in a roar of whispers, but Gene clicked his fingers and outran one of his assistants, down from their seat, down to

the walkways and outside. The court waited patiently as the assistant returned, listening for faint footsteps until the assistant popped back up along with the head and body of another man who stood terrified on the right plateau.

"Mr. Winters, perhaps you have lost your mind, but this is not a murder trial."

"I am aware. Just making my point your honor."

"State your name for the court." The judge asked, waving his hand as he rolled back into his chair.

"What? Um… Arnold Stoch."

The court was in silent chaos, fighting to stay furious without falling as they wished very much to grapple over the others to get a look at a very famous dead man.

"Hmmm, a first for me, I must say." Judge Norwell tittered. "In all my years…"

"Your honor, I have only one question to ask the witness." Gene didn't miss a beat, carrying on as though he had the preceding's in the palm of his hand. "Mr. Stoch. Are you alive?"

"Yes." Stoch answered, thoroughly confused.

"There you have it your honor, how can you sentence a man of a crime he didn't commit. Mr Boltzmann couldn't have killed a man who is right here and now, alive."

"He what?" Stoch started but was cut off by the volume of the crowd and the bangs of the gavel.

"Silence! Everybody calm down. Gene, you make an excellent point. I shall take it under advisement. Please ensure Mr. Stoch is returned from the time whence he came. I will now hear from the nomadic representative." Norwell announced. "Ms. Bavishni. You have the floor."

"Thank you, your honor." Wyla strode comfortably to the left side of her platform and eyed Gene. She then motioned to the apple still resting along his platform's edge.

Gene took it and tossed it to her. Wyla nodded politely and took a sizable bite. The conservatives gasped and Gene looked horrified.

"Mmmm delicious non-existence." Wyla teased sarcastically. "As much as I disagree with my opponent's demands, I respect your judgments and have but two requests. First, we wish to have the right to be granted immunity to travel in time, with permission by the court. Maybe a visa or license to –"

"Hey HEY!" Gene cried out, erupting from his seat. "Your honor, what's the point in prohibiting people from changing the past when you're just going to allow them a ticket to go do it anyway? It's insane!"

"Thank you, Mr. Winters. For that unwelcomed insight." The judge rested his head against his hand and leant over his desk. "Ms. Bavishni?"

"Yes. Mr. Winters." Wyla teased. "But can't you argue that any visit to the past is an alteration of the past? Why don't we just ban time travelling all together? What's the point in constructing rules to a game you don't want anyone to play?"

Gene tried to stand nose to nose with Wyla despite their distance and spoke so low that only she could hear, despite the acoustics. But Vaughn stood beneath and between them, looking right up their noses.

"If I could motion to have each and every one of these fucking cubes destroyed, I would. But in a world where these… things exist, I'll pull the leash as tight as I can."

"Do you think I'm afraid of you?" Wyla said in a hush. "You know you're not wearing your brown hat right now, don't you?"

"Oh, I know what you're afraid of." Gene hissed, over articulating with his tongue. "What I don't understand is if you really want what I know you want, why are you on that side of this court?"

"Your honor." Wyla ignored Gene and raised her voice again so all could hear. "My friends and I want to use this miraculous invention to see the pyramids getting built, to see Alexander the Great conquer, to see and maybe even help the cavemen create fire. If we can't have that, then we have nothing."

"Your honor?" Gene turned the attention back on himself. "I know I'm out of turn, but I would like to request that we deem it illegal to

visit any time or event considered historically important. Just listen to what she's asking for, there are just too many variables in play; too many things that could change and it would undo everything we are trying to do here today. So, make it so."

"And what we would consider historically important?" Wyla asked.

"Any events put forth before the court." Gene answered. "Like the invention of time travel, for example. The true, original moment. These events can be lodged at any time. We have even compiled a list for reference."

Gene held up a binder that looked like it had twice the number of pages stuffed between its casing than it could hold. He dropped it down onto the edge of his podium with a loud thud.

There was an interminable pause. If Wyla thought she had been backed into such a tough corner as it seemed, she certainly wasn't showing it.

"What if we get permission?" She tossed this suggestion out as casually as someone dropping a grenade.

"Permission?"

"If the aim is to avoid messing with period-constrained individuals free will, asking their permission would allow it to be up to them."

"I couldn't imagine a circumstance wherein a period-constrained individual would be simultaneously unobstructed by time travelers whilst also maintaining their personal agency. It's a paradox of logic."

"You haven't heard of the Time Asylum?"

There was a hush about the court, as if Wyla had professed Santa Claus to be real.

"Hey wait a minute…" Gene was flabbergasted.

"As Mr. Winters suggested, it is a historically important event and should not be tampered with. Unless with paradoxically legal permission."

"That's such a…"

"As you said, Gene. No one should mess with important moments and most of all, if anyone knows anything about the Time Asylum is

that it was presented as a place safe and home with strict permission for those who come to it peacefully. Therefore, by your first rule, the Time Asylum is also home to anyone who is welcome there. Which, according to public record, is anyone not there in anger or violence."

"You can't do that!"

"I almost didn't. Thanks for helping."

Gene looked as though his boiling blood was frying his skin from the inside while Judge Norwell dwelled on this idea. "Hmmm. If I were to allow this, then I would need this permission from the person in charge of this event, to officially recognize it as a historically significant event."

"I thought you'd never ask." Wyla answered, walking as she spoke.

"Where do you think you're going?" Norwell asked.

Wyla turned and gave the judge a weird look. "To get permission, of course."

"And have you meddle with time by plucking him out of it against his will?" Gene spat. "No, I don't think so."

"I would go invite him myself, but I am not up to any more travelling today." The judge sighed.

"Actually." O'seus stood suddenly. "I have a solution."

O'seus climbed up to the judge and went about filming the video Vaughn had already seen, playing on a television in the storage room of the Asylum.

Once it was done, the Beta tape was taken from the video camera and handed to a short man waiting at the bottom of the stall ladder. Beside him stood a young girl who had just as confused look on her face as Vaughn did.

The short man pocketed the tape in his big jacket pocket and pursued Wyla, clutching the young girl's hand so as not to leave her behind. When they left, a small waft of wind followed in their wake. Leaving a dumbfounded look on Vaughn's face.

Gene grumbled and waited patiently with all the others and Judge Norwell tinkered with his robes.

Vaughn staggered back until his spine felt the firm surface of one of the stands. So much to take in, so little of it made sense. They argued like it was all so normal. They talked like metaphysical events were as disputable as parking tickets. They acted like it was normal for a person to leave and return, all with the space of a minute.

When Wyla returned she walked right towards and past Vaughn. He made sure he ducked in between two stands just in time, hoping not to be seen. Hoping for once to be inconsequential.

He didn't venture out again, he didn't need to watch, he could hear it well enough. This auditorium projected so clearly that Vaughn recognized Atticus' awkward introduction from the tape instantly.

"Hello. This is a response to your video. Atticus Crowe's response... my response. Atticus Crowe. Me. As per your request, I give my full approval for the function I am hosting here..."

As the words that Atticus had spoken echoed about the auditorium, Vaughn spotted excited tourists gathering at the bases of the tall stands, swapping cubes for information. Bits of torn out newspaper that Vaughn recognized as akin to the piece he had found and read, exposing the truth about Atticus' little party. He saw one of them was showing his piece of the invitation off to others while some of them kept theirs close to the chest, having just traded a cube for the privilege of secret information.

"... to be used as a refuge from 6pm to 6am, as a non-violent, all welcoming refuge for time travelers..."

Vaughn kept his back to the stands as they spread, darting from one stand to the next, gathering into groups to visit the Asylum together. Some of them Vaughn recognized, some of them he didn't. Figuring perhaps, based on how well they navigated the cubes, he might not have met them yet. Or they were there now, in his absence.

"... providing they follow the rules and not bring any weapons or harm each other in the set time allocated. Ah, signing off."

One tourist noticed the curious Vaughn approaching their tight circle and handed the torn piece of newspaper to him with a wide grin. The invitation looked just as Vaughn remembered it... almost.

Attention Time Traveler's, Voyagers and Trekkers.
Hello there Black Hole Divers, Deep Space
Swimmers and Celestial Portal Riders.
And Welcome Quantum Leapers, Chrono
Jumpers and Space Skippers.
If you find yourself without a country
or a time to which you belong,
If you are lost and need to rest,
If safe haven is what you're craving,
Then you will find that there's
always time at The Time Asylum,
A place for those that have no other.
February 23rd - 24rd 1991
6:00pm til 6:00am
Mount Fracture Observatory
Open Bar.

Vaughn felt his stomach gurgle, as though it was trying to tell his brain something before his kidneys let it out. He felt cold and couldn't listen to one more word being said. Some rules were being listed, hands were shaken, and pens fought over to sign some papers, but Vaughn took in none of it. The words still rang in his mind, bouncing from one side of his emptying head to the other.

February 23rd. It said *February 23rd.*

It shattered him. He felt his fingers in his hands, layering them over one another repeatedly, wondering what it meant. Wondering what he had done, how he had done it, and how he could take it back. The Asylum he knew and had come from was in May.

What had he done?

He hurried out of the Courthouse, still gripping the invitation and with a head start as the audience had to file down the ladders one by one. He took pause at the courthouse steps and almost yelped as he felt dust

tickle his bare neck. Looking up, he saw someone already carving the new rules into the blank stone above the arch of the front doors and he staggered out into the street to read them.

Today is the new today, January 1st, 2025
The old laws are the laws of today
You are not safe from these laws outside of your time zone
Do not talk to your past or future self
Do not make yourself part of history that you were not a part of.

Vaughn wondered if Pete was even somewhere lost for him to find anymore.

Had he abandoned him in a previous timeline? *Could he even get back?*

As he wondered about the streets that garnered bigger and more sudden wafts of wind from everyone leaving the courthouse. He looked out, scanning the buildings and wreckage that survived from the past for the marking again. Some yellow spray paint.

Maybe one to take him home, maybe one that would lead him to a nice warm comforting bed he could crawl up in and shut his brain down for a while.

Vaughn was not a smart guy, he had never claimed to be, and all this was making parts of his head hurt. His temple felt like someone had wrapped a band around it and squeezed it tight. His neck ached from holding his head up and his body wanted to drop everything above the shoulders.

He chuckled to himself at how unfazed he was by what was happening. The second they announced the rules, and the court was adjourned, both sides had gone at it. Things were set on fire and launched at each other, more cars rocketed down the streets, whipping up sandstorms of their own.

Gunfire and screams were as normal as birds chirping. Only there weren't any birds left, besides the white ones that fluttered from mantle to mantle to twitter and watch with a keen and shiny eye.

He should have been more scared. If somehow he was discovered, if someone were to find hesitance at the twenty-three-year-old boy, with no shoes, no pants just pajamas, aimlessly wondering the worn-torn future giving himself a headache from his thoughts, if someone were to take notice, maybe he'd be in trouble.

But for now he chuckled, it relaxed him. His mind retreated to one simple thought; at least he had gotten out of Fracture.

Kicking sand and rusted dirt, Vaughn kept on until he came to a strange building. Someone had taken an interest in it, it stood out from the rest, having been the only one not covered in filth. The windows were washed, the doorway swept, and the sign said 'open'.

It looked like a wholesome 'mom and pop store', despite the unwholesome flags waving in the window. Vaughn stared at the sign that swung above the door. Though it was written in plain English, he had to read it three or four times to be sure.

He had to give it to them; few businesses could survive in such a desolate economic climate, but Sherman & Son's Flight of the Fuhrer: An Interactive Adventure had found a way.

Vaughn pushed through the door and set off the bell chime, finding himself in a Nazi Museum. The walls were covered in flags and uniforms, medals and photographs. There were glass display cases of tools and Nazi inscribed paraphernalia, labelled and organized. Behind the counter was a stringently hand-drawn, detailed to the last detail, a map of Germany and its surrounding countries.

In front of the map was Sherman Sr, standing proudly while giving a group of fresh recruits his riveting pep talk, these recruits listened and poured gold out of their pockets and onto the counter.

"That's what we like to see, if only more brave men, and sorry, ladies too… if there were more brave men and ladies like yourselves, we'd be in a better world." Sherman Sr.'s eyes lit up as the gold flowed in. "Now follow my son here through to the back and he'll get you sorted."

Sherman Jr. had been busy sweeping the dirt that kept sifting in under the door. He groaned as he let the broom fall against a glass

display case and he led the newest recruits to the back, only for the next lot to step forward and dump their gold on the counter.

Vaughn saw that the girl Sherman Sr. had almost overlooked had a shaved head like Vaughn but a mean look in her eye. Beside her were a few young men, bouncing with nerves and testosterone.

"O'seus, back again I see." Sherman Sr. called, looking past Vaughn.

"Too true."

O'seus' brogue voice followed in behind Vaughn, kicking aside the neat piles of sand Sherman Jr. had been sweeping up. Now, no longer hovering above him, Vaughn could get a good look. O'seus was an older man, sharp in frame. His big jaw neatly covered in a white beard and looked down at Vaughn with his big chocolaty eyes. His brow was furrowed, but in a way that gave him character and charm. He had his sleeves permanently rolled up and so tight it cut off his circulation somewhat, causing bulging veins to run down his forearms.

Vaughn noted on one arm he had a tattoo of a ship cresting some waves, he didn't have time to catch the words scrawled alongside it.

"Third time's the charm." Sherman Sr. joked. "Oy! Don't touch the medals!"

Vaughn snapped his hand back, not realizing it had slipped an SS medallion in his pocket for some unknown reason.

"Just looking at it." Vaughn stuttered.

"Sure sure." Sherman Sr. raised an eyebrow. "If you're interested, you're welcome to apply."

"Doing what?"

"Doing what?" Sherman Sr. mocked. "Doing your due diligence by trying to knock off the most hated man in all human history. Gunther Kurtzoph."

Vaughn knew who he was; he didn't need the reminder of all the Nazi gear to recall what he had been taught in school. The only interesting part about World War history in his opinion was the almost cliché villain that led the Nazi party. He had been turned into a punching bag of the stereotypical bad guy. A constant comparison for anyone wanting to villainize a politician. And now he was a theme park attraction.

"So you guys go back and try to change the war?" Vaughn asked. "Or are you just doing it for the glory?"

"What's wrong with both?" O'seus asked, signing the paperwork and readying himself to follow Sherman Jr. into the back room.

"What about the other wars, other dictators and other major world events worth changing?" Vaughn asked. "Do you try to change them too?"

"No one cares about the wee little indie films, it's the big ol' blockbusters that they all want to pay their hard-earned cash to see." O'seus grinned.

"And why would anyone come here and pay someone else when they could just go back and try it themselves? It's not like we've never read a history book, we know when to go back to."

Sherman Sr. laughed like he had heard that question a thousand times.

"My friend, we are no tour group to take pictures with dinosaurs or a historic expedition to witness the signing of the declaration of independence. We do not sell the trip there. Hell, take a cube and go off on your own. Good luck. I won't charge."

Sherman Sr. then leaned his left elbow on the counter, as if was secretly sharing top-secret business secrets.

"But do you know where the Fuhrer was on July 3rd, 1941? What his day-to-day schedule looked like? Who his personal guards were? What he ate for dinner? How often he had a bowel movement?

"No."

"And do you think you will be able to blend in enough so that the thirteen million Nationalist eyes don't spot that you don't belong?"

Vaughn shrunk his eyes to the floor, playing out all the scenarios in his head, knowing for sure he would get caught and executed in a heartbeat.

"I'm not trying to scare you, quite the opposite. Do you know how many people that took their first-time traveling steps into Berlin were captured, tortured and killed or sent to detention camps?"

"A lot." The shaved headed woman chimed in.

"Right, so our charge is for safety. We rent out uniforms and equipment. We can set you up in the best locations, detailed backstories and separate you from other crusaders so no one can get in your way. Now how does that sound? You up for it?"

Vaughn didn't have to wonder for long. He was anxious enough about being in a place he shouldn't. He couldn't even grasp the amount of anxiety he would feel trying it himself.

"You know, I'd love too, but I don't have any money."

"We wouldn't take your money, boy. No one would." Sherman Sr. berated. "You got gold, don't you? Everyone pays in gold."

"I don't have any gold." Vaughn laughed off.

"Well, I can lend ya your share if you really want to…" O'seus started.

"I'm not going ok!" Vaughn shouted.

"Fine." O'seus scoffed. "You'd only slow me down anyways."

Vaughn watched as both the shaved headed woman, a few other men and O'seus followed Sherman Jr. into the back room and into the past. As they changed into their costumes Vaughn started following the map along the walls. Strings darting from pinpoint to pinpoint creating an intricate timeline of Gunther Kurtzoph's life, going back even before he was born.

"Generally, you to pick a place and time and then we co-ordinate the mission from here." Sherman Sr. said, seeing his interest in the timeline and standing over his shoulder. "Unless it's been attempted before."

Vaughn saw that clipped onto each event in time were lists of names of all the people who had or were gone to that time.

"Do many make it back?" Vaughn asked, seeing the dozens of lists.

"We don't accept responsibility or liability for what happens to someone on a mission."

"So, no."

Vaughn panning through the life of a man many had intended to murder, noticing most of his attacks were early in his life and some along his family tree.

"Obviously no one's done it yet." Vaughn said, noting the red Xs on every tag.

He noticed that there was a long strip of string covered in orange tape. Stretching from 1938 to 1939 and Vaughn noted all the notable events and moments that had gone untouched by customers of Sherman and Son's with no lists of crusaders attached to any event like the others.

"What's with this section?" Vaughn asked Sherman Sr. "Why hasn't anyone gone to any of these times?"

"That's the martyr period." Sherman Sr. explained. "Popular convention and experts have noted that if you assassinated him during that period, they would turn him into a martyr. They would carry out his plans with less ill intent and perhaps even the protection of honor and patriotism."

"Oh." Vaughn stood back from the orange string line, as if even touching it would affect its course. He couldn't imagine a history wherein Kurtzoph was seen as a victim of a hate crime. A martyr that was adored and celebrated.

"You know, this is all a bit much for me. I don't even know if I think it's possible, or even the right thing to do. There are too many implications, too much to think about, and right now I don't know how much more I can think about. All I'm looking for is a place called the Far. If you might tell me if I'm close or where I have to go?"

"The Far?" Sherman Sr. had a belly full of laughs and relished every chuckle. "You're a long ways off yet my boy. Why would someone like you be looking for a place like that?"

"I'm looking for a friend."

"It'd be easier if he were looking for you." Sherman Sr. offered.

"I don't think he... he's not... he doesn't know to look for me." Vaughn stumbled. "Just look, can you give me any hint? How far the Far is? How long from now?"

"If that was knowledge you could just ask for, then it wouldn't be The Far, then would it." Sherman Sr. winked and set back to the counter to

his rocking chair behind the desk. Vaughn figured he had had enough of this shop.

Vaughn marched out and let the door stay open a little longer than it was polite, letting more dust from outside swoosh in for Sherman Jr. to sweep.

Vaughn exhaled heavily, feeling his chest lower to settle on his stomach, and he made off in a wayward direction.

A sudden gust twirled the dirt in front of him and a woman dropped several feet to the ground right in front of him. She collapsed backwards and her travelling companion followed, crushing her.

Vaughn rushed to help, heaving the unconscious body off her torso and helping her up. She wore a dark coat, thick black wool with 'S''s on the collar. Underneath she had too many layers for this heat, green and white shirts and undershirts. She kept scratching at her gorgeous blonde hair.

"I got it." She shouted, waving off any help, pushing up to her feet and dusting herself off. "I got it all right. Would'ya let him go?"

"Gee sorry." Vaughn said and tossed aside the arm he still held of the unconscious man. "Only trying to help."

"Yeah well…" The woman sighed. She bent to pull the unconscious man up. He was barely breathing, his tongue swung from his mouth like a dog's tail. Vaughn had to laugh, he looked so ridiculous, wearing oversized clothes with hastily mismatched buttons, and sporting big square glasses that made his eyes magnify until they were the same size as his thick and imposing moustache.

"Your friend ok?"

"Fine. He's fine." She groaned as she hoisted the unconscious man's body up as best she could and dragged him backwards towards the wall of the empty shop across the street, kicking up dust trails as she did. "You mind not touching him while I change?"

The woman shocked him silly, as she slipped her gorgeous blonde hair right off her head and rubbed the shaved head underneath, scratching it with such relief. Like strange déjà vu Vaughn suddenly recognized the woman from moments before,

having watched the back of that shaved head as she signed up for Sherman's services.

"Same haircut." Vaughn tried his best to be friendly to a woman, motioning to his own shaved head. She wore it better than he did; she had a better head for it.

"Crazy right." The shaved head woman entertained, though she was more preoccupied with her friend. "I'm serious. Don't go near him. And tell anyone that passes by to keep their distance."

"Sure." Vaughn said as he heard furious gunfire and hooning cars in the distance. He watched her strip layer by layer of thick winter clothes as she slipped back inside Sherman and Son's.

Vaughn knelt beside the unconscious man, picking the dirt from his pajamas, and waited. Wind whistled out the man's nose and his body slipped onto Vaughn's shoulder. The unconscious man's glasses slid askew, and his moustache seemed like it was slipping up his cheek. He nudged him aside. The old man fell away, bending comically in the other direction.

When she came back out, she was dressed in her original jacket, shirt and jeans. But it was the face she wore that concerned Vaughn the most. She looked like she would punch hard. He scrambled away and to his feet as she rushed over and straightened up her unconscious friend's glasses.

"You better have left him alone."

"I didn't touch him." Vaughn said as he saw her fix up the man's glasses.

"Do you think you could help me out? I'm kinda stuck here."

"You think I have cubes to spare?"

"Not a cube, I'll go with you."

"You're turning down a cube?"

"No point having one if you don't know how to use it. I just need a ride."

"I'm not a taxi."

"But I am stuck here."

"Too bad, so sad."

She kicked the dirt back as she wrangled the unconscious man by his shoulder sleeves and out onto the street. She looked far out to the distance and sighed before digging her hands under his armpits and heaved him up to his feet and walked backwards. It tired Vaughn just watching. The man looked heavy, easier to move with a quick cube than dragging him.

Looking back and seeing how little distance she had covered, she groaned and dropped him on her leg and let him slide to the ground.

Then she walked the ten meters back to Vaughn, who pretended he wasn't watching.

"All right, you can come if you help carry him."

"What, you need my help now?"

"I'd drag him with one arm through the dirt myself but I need him in good condition. I'm taking him to someone who's paying a lot of cubes just to meet him. Can't have him all messed up. Supposed to meet them at a place called the Time Asylum, that's where I'm headed so if you want a ride outta here I'm afraid that's the only…"

"That's perfect!"

Was it? Vaughn asked himself. It wasn't before. But this place gave him too much anxiety. Besides, he wasn't any closer to finding Pete here than he was there.

"Good." She didn't see a boy in his pajamas as much of a threat and nodded for Vaughn to take the man's legs. "What's your name?"

"Vaughn. I'm Vaughn."

"Elliot." She sighed. "C'mon then, we have to walk first."

Vaughn took the legs and lifted them up to his hips and walked awkwardly with Elliot carrying his shoulders. After a few meters they dropped him and tried holding him sideways, but he kept drooping and dragging along the ground. Vaughn couldn't help but giggle as he saw the unconscious man was hanging so low that he was dragging his loose tongue along the ground.

They tried one more time, Vaughn bent and hoisted him over his shoulder and took the brunt of the weight as Elliot walked behind and kept him from slipping off Vaughn's shoulder. They walked like that

for a while. She steered from behind, leading Vaughn west, towards the setting sun as the buildings became more and more dilapidated and buried the further, they got from the center of the city. No one lived out here.

She ached. "Here, this is good. We've got a nice and straight time stream now."

They dumped the heavy body to the ground and Vaughn rolled his shoulder as Elliot took out her cube, counted numbers softly to herself and started twisting. Vaughn knelt and gripped the unconscious man's arm hard, keeping a firm hand on his ride as Elliot opened a tangent and he hitched a ride.*

As Sherman Jr. groaned and swept the endless barrage of dust and dirt from their shop, a sudden crack and shatter caught him in a fright. Someone had suddenly popped into existence above a glass display case of old war photos and journals. The case's wooden legs snapped, and glass scattered everywhere, covering the freshly swept floor as Sherman Jr. sighed and took a break.

"You know, that shouldn't be there." O'seus tried, still lying on the floor looking up to Sherman Sr. still standing behind his counter.

"I was thinking of moving it over in the corner." Sherman Sr joked.

"I'll pay you back for this." O'seus said, surveying the damage.

"Oh, I know you will. It's in your contract." Sherman Sr. nodded to the form he kept under his elbows as he leaned over the counter.

"As of now I don't really 'ave much on me, but if you let me…"

"Was always a fan of your films." Sherman Sr. said.

"That right?" O'seus turned and showed off his pristine grin, the one he saved for compliments.

"Oh yes. Loved how you captured that sense of adventure, the human spirit. Gave me goose bumps."

"Any favorites?"

Go to Page 304

"Time of Death was always a treat."

"One of my favorites too." O'seus winked.

"You know, for a two-timer like yourself, you seem like you could be up for a little extra adventure. And maybe a way of paying me back."

"Mr. Sherman, you've been 'olding out on me."

Sherman Sr. held a cheeky grin and nodded for O'seus to follow him. He had his son take up the front counter and he led O'seus down the hall and down the stairs passing rooms of strings.

O'seus eyed the string lines, wondering which he was going to be shown.

But Sherman Sr. kept moving past them, finding a door at the back of the room and unlocking it with a key that dangled from his neck.

O'seus was pumped full of intrigue. For the first time in years, he felt energy surge to his hands, and he could not keep them still.

The door led to another room. It sat in total darkness and once the door was closed Sherman Sr. hit the light and the room lit up, revealing another string line set up from wall to wall. It was smaller than the other, and Sherman Sr. had used red string instead of orange.

"What is this?"

"This." Sherman Sr. started. 'Is a dead timeline."

O'seus could see where the string ended, dangling in the air; it had been cut. Sherman Sr. had tied a fishing line to it and it hung almost magically on its own.

O'seus got down on his knees and followed the strangely similar line of events to what he knew was the past, but the differences were slight and surreal.

"Where did you...?"

"I don't know. I know little about it at all, I found this." Sherman Sr walked to the start of the string line, plucking a section in his fingers and holding it tight. "What I do know is that somehow it was split from the one we know, and where it split is right here."

Sherman Sr held the red string in his fingers, as though if he let go the entire universe would fall apart. The very moment he held had,

just like the other string line, crucial notes attached for the crusader to complete their missions.

"O'seus, I need you to go to this point in time and make sure this timeline stays dead."

"You believe as I. When I leave, I'd only be entering another timeline. You'd never see me again. You'd never know for sure."

Sherman Sr. sat on a stool in the corner; he loosened a pin from his coat and held it in front of his nose.

"My ancestors were victimized and radically massacred in this war. I have spent my life trying to honor them and recently, trying to be a hero and save them. I do know there are other universes, with an infinite amount of suffering. But if I can save even a fraction of them, I'd sleep easier, you know."

"Sherman old pal, you 'ad me at hero."*

---

*Go to Page 83

Chapter Thirty-Four:
The Epitaph

They landed as softly as they could, not wanting to drop or harm the body. But Sancia's grip faltered, and Vaughn had to quickly catch Dahl before he hit the ground. The soft, white, puffy ground.

"Sancia, seriously, your shoulder..." Vaughn watched the paper white snow catch and stain dark red.

"I'll be ok."

"No, you won't... please let me just...." Vaughn laid his palm on her shoulder. He could see the scars on her collarbone from the supposed dinosaurs, now seeming more and more plausible. He applied pressure to stop blood from oozing out, almost making vomit ooze out of him. The slight tinge of cold had already helped her clot and even though she tried to hide her cringing, Vaughn caught sight of the puffs of frost shooting out of her nostrils.

She squirmed, but after only a few seconds she pushed him off and swatted his hand away. She pressed on her knee as it dug into the snow and got to her feet as Vaughn dipped his hands in the icy cold and washed the blood off. She didn't care she was bleeding, the scars that had once made her wince and flinch now had a giant wound running through them.

This she could ignore.

She was adamant she could carry Dahl on her own, but she didn't have the strength.

"Can... can you carry him?" She asked.

Vaughn sighed gladly and gently lifted him over his shoulder, careful not to catch his face. He had to think of him as just a heavy thing or he couldn't do it.

He was much heavier than he looked and Vaughn sunk deeper in the snow, finding the earth just a few inches beneath. Vaughn had figured Dahl was just skin and bones, but now he was realizing he was so much more. This made it even harder.

Together they walked, Sancia buckling over every so often, holding her stomach and not her shoulder. He worried that she had internal damage and every moment he spent carrying Dahl, she was getting worse.

Vaughn barely even thought about where he was anymore. He was sick of it, even waving it off as a waste of time. He had given up - he was here, wasn't he? What good was wondering going to do him?

He didn't have much of a chance to recognize anything; it was all covered in snow. He had never seen or felt it before. It was crunchier than he thought, picturing all his life that it'd be soft like powder, but it was closer to the icy crust that he had to scrape off the back of the fridge at work.

At least the snow had stopped falling. The sky was blue and clear. The birds flew overhead and passed the yellow, almost white sun, and he thought again of the man he carried over his shoulder.

"What did he mean all the time?" Vaughn finally spoke, Sancia kept walking, her eyes on her feet counting. "When Dahl said *birds would fall.*"

"When birds fall." She corrected.

"Right. What was he… do you know what he was talking about? Did you get it?"

"Dahl knew a lot more than you think."

"So you knew what he meant?"

"No." She said, looking up at the birds flying overhead. "But I like to think it means when all is lost. That when birds were to fall, all would be lost and that would be it. But until then there's

no excuse, there's always time. When birds fall, only then we can give up."

They rose over the top of an incline to a valley housing a neat little suburb. The abandonment, the silence; it felt like another place that time had forgotten. They followed roads cleanly carved out from beneath the snow. As they ventured further, they passed large street sweepers and snowplows, parked correctly between white lines.

Every house had nicely shoveled driveways, freshly swept white lawns and perfectly white roofs. He could see through the windows that all the furniture was upright and free from dust. There were no passing cars or a thousand conversations blurring into background noise. It was peacefully quiet.

After they passed the third street of houses, he convinced Sancia to wait on the curb so he could run into the next house to look for help.

He wandered up the driveway across the road, still instinctively checking for cars, and reached the front door finding it unlocked and easy to open.

"Hello?"

Vaughn brushed the door aside and stepped inside. The walls kept the wind out, so the place was sterile and quiet. With no one answering, he made for the kitchen and tested the taps. Water ran and his thirst, which had been keeping dormant, suddenly ached and he wedged his head in the sink to rinse his mouth of this metallic taste.

"Susan, you have left the water running. I will turn it off, please state otherwise."

The tap shut off and Vaughn shot up straight, banging his head on the cabinets. He looked around for a voice, a face, or even a mad homeowner with a baseball bat.

But he saw no one.

Vaughn instead spotted the house's Ogle; it was hidden in the middle of the kitchen ceiling, obscured by a piece of duct-tape over the lens. He waved his hand in front of it and got nothing.

A piece of tape, he chuckled.

Vaughn checked the fridge and found so much of the food had gone hard or stale. Weirdly, there was a bright, white and blue birthday cake that had sunk in the middle like an upside-down traffic cone.

"Why is it everywhere I go nothing is normal?" Vaughn asked himself.

"Vocal recognition malfunctioning. Please do not lower your voice, Susan."

Vaughn felt for the Ogle, of all things, still working away while Susan and whoever else left with complete abandon. What kind of lives had these people all just up and left?

"Whose birthday is it?" Vaughn asked.

"Calendar. Joshua's 9th birthday, remember to buy dairy free cream for the party."

"What year is it?"

"The year is 2086 PI."

"PI?"

"Post Incident."

Fuck. So long after the court case, this is what the world looked like. Everyone that left had never returned like they thought they would. The future was empty, abandoned, unwanted, discarded, overrated, under-appreciated and completely forgotten. Had the offer of anytime at all really been enough to make so many take it? Was this really that undesirable? Were that many people so unhappy with their lives that most of the population got up and left it the moment they could?

Vaughn had never felt so normal in his life.

He checked under the sink and then in the bathroom. Finally, he asked the Ogle where their first aid kit was. It asked for him to stop using such a deep voice and that it was in her bedside drawer.

Outside, Vaughn brought the kit to Sancia and tried to apply what first aid he could. The antiseptic was solid, the bandages had dried up, all he could do was fold a patch of gauze and tape it to her shoulder and chest. She waited impatiently; trying to get up and keep going every second he wasn't sticking tape.

They followed the crisp, icy streets to the middle of town and came to a roundabout. There the streets stretched off in harmless directions, with huge mounds of separated snow on either side of the street. Looking down the street to their right, they finally knew where they were going.

At the end of this street was a large iron gate that clung to two brick pillars that had once been all that had allowed entrance to the grounds behind.

But the hedge walls that extended from the pillars had dried up, fallen and now laden with snow. The gate looked like a giant tombstone itself; a gravesite for the cemetery.

"Is this why we're here?" Vaughn asked Sancia. 'Did you know this was going to be here?"

She shook her head. "I just wanted to know what his big secret was. He never told me why he carried that envelope with him. I needed to know."

"And now you do."

They stepped inside the untouched of snow of the cemetery and looked for an open spot for their friend. Each gravestone had been dusted free of snow and stuck out like candles on a cake. The cemetery had a slight rise to the center of the grounds where a tree bloomed and coming over the crest of the hill they saw a man approaching gently with a broom in his hands and a kindly grin.

"Don't get many visitors these days." Said the groundskeeper. "Too many want to find their final resting place somewhere else in time."

"What happened?" Vaughn asked. "Is anyone else here?"

"No, only me. Someone's gotta keep things in order."

"But why?" Vaughn asked. "Why don't you leave like everyone else?"

"I like it here, it's peaceful. I can clean something up and it stays clean."

The groundskeeper had been busy. He told them all about the empty town he took care of, visiting house after house, sweeping the snow from the streets and keeping it all neat and tidy. He buried the dead he

found and occasionally dug graves when someone asked. He said that he mostly spent his days brushing old tombstones and remembering names others wouldn't.

"Would you like for him to rest here?" The groundskeeper asked, nodding to Dahl's body over Vaughn's shoulder.

"Um…" Vaughn looked for her. Sancia had stopped in an open patch not too far from the willow tree in the middle of the grounds. The leaves each held a handful of snow and dropped them in the wind. From atop the small hill, Sancia could survey the scattered tombs in all directions. The groundskeeper smiled, as though he allowed everyone to wander until they found the best place to bury their dead.

"Yes." She said. "Right here."

"What would you like on his stone?" The groundskeeper asked.

"John Dahl." Sancia said.

"And the dates?"

Vaughn looked to Sancia, and she searched her mind for a thought that didn't hurt.

"1978 to, when are we?" She asked.

"2086." Vaughn answered.

"And how about a message? The groundskeeper added. "Something nice like 'rest in peace' or 'in loving memory'."

Both Vaughn and Sancia broke a smile and laughed a little. She knew just what to say and told him.

"What does that mean?" The groundskeeper asked.

"It's just something he used to say."

"That's very sweet." The groundskeeper smiled.

The groundskeeper took the words to the workshop next to his cottage. Inside, the old machine still worked as long as he oiled it first and replaced the coils every so often. He slid a slab of black marble into place and powered the machine by peddling a bike he had hoisted off the ground. Many wires ran from the chains to the engine. Once it was done he shined the surfaced with a polish and returned to the site with a bag of cement, a bucket of water in a wheelbarrow, with two shovels and a broom.

Together Vaughn and the groundskeeper dug in silence, scraping back the snow to find the dirt and muddied it with each shovel's worth spilling out around them. Vaughn found he hadn't thought about anything for a while, the work was hard, and he found the effort of heaving dirt out of the hole had emptied his head.

When they had finished, they lowered the body down to the bottom of the grave. They had gone as deep as they could manage before the roots from the willow tree became too thick. It surprised Vaughn at how stiff the body had become since he had it folded over his shoulder. Maybe it was just the cold.

Filling the hole was easy since the dirt was fresh and loose, and the snow covered it smoothly. That's what the groundskeeper's broom was for. He carefully swept the spot clean. If it weren't for the tombstone, no one would know anyone was buried here at all.

'You get going soon, you hear?" The groundskeeper said. "I don't want any of those fellas in the brown hats following you here and messing this place up."

Vaughn nodded as the groundskeeper swept his brow, nodded to them both and saw his exit to left them to be alone. His job was done.

"Goodbye John." Sancia hushed. "I wish I thanked you for what you did. I wish…"

Suddenly she dropped, knees in the snow and she moaned - digging her fingers into her stomach. Vaughn ran to help, going straight to her shoulder, but she was still gripping her stomach.

He tried to do anything, something. But she just kept moaning, grabbing his hand and squeezing as she held her breath and went red. More blood spilled out from under the already crimson patch of gauze on her shoulder. She tensed her entire body until the pain left.

Vaughn helped her up. She groaned and held onto him. He noticed a pinkish stain in the snow between her legs.

"I put it off for too long." She said, between breaths. "You have to take me back Vaughn."

"Back?" He panicked. "Where?"

"H… H… Home."

She passed out, head rocking back with her neck limp as a noodle, and Vaughn again struggled to lift a body. She was heavier than Dahl and he dragged her by her waist to rest up against a big, thick and tall tombstone down the side of the cemetery hill.

He zipped Dahl's leather jacket up around her to keep her warm but dug through the pockets for the two cubes tucked inside. He held them, unsure where home was for Sancia - or worse, when.

He looked up at the name on the tombstone she rested her head against, then at all the others - watching and expecting more from him; the living.

A slight chill of wind froze Vaughn's nose and as he rubbed it warm he saw the willow tree drop its bundles of snow to welcome a new arrival that just landed and rolled down the hill.

Vaughn watched as the figure dusted himself off, shaking loose snow from his leather jacket, and was poised to apologize to anyone he had upset.

It couldn't be.

The small man darted his head around, unsure and confused. He scratched at a worn patch of hair and hunched slightly to make himself even shorter.

Vaughn left Sancia behind and ducked behind tombstones to pursue the man up the cemetery hill, while as the man followed Vaughn's old footprints in the snow to the grave under the tree.

Vaughn thought he was going to be ill. He had just buried this man and now here he was about to stand over his own grave.

Dahl didn't walk like Vaughn was used to seeing, the Dahl he knew would have stomped elephant prints into the snow, but this Dahl barely left an impression. He reminded Vaughn of the same Dahl he had bumped into at the airport terminal. He swung his arms low like they were still being tugged at by his two children and held his head down as though his tired wife was still berating him.

He was definitely not the same man Vaughn and Sancia had buried.

Dahl stopped, and Vaughn hoped he was well hidden. Poking his head out he saw Dahl had stopped by the grave with patches of Sancia's blood. It stood out. He then raised his head as Vaughn's throat caught a bulge and sent it down, and down and down in his gut.

He hoped maybe he would miss it and move on.

"Watchchu reading there." The groundskeeper had returned by the call of a fresh wind.

"Nothing... I..." Dahl stammered.

Vaughn knew exactly what he was reading.

John Dahl
Beloved father, friend, and hero
1978 – 2086
When birds fall.

"108." Dahl mouthed and followed with a grin.

"I'm sorry, what?"

But Dahl didn't answer. The groundskeeper took it as grief and stood by his side in a moment's silence for the deceased.

"What do you suppose it means?" The groundskeeper asked Dahl. "I've been thinking about it. Nice though, right? Like it means something."

"I don't know." Dahl read the line over and over again. "Means something important, I bet."

"I bet."

"Can I ask, where and when am I?"

Vaughn didn't believe what he was seeing. As Dahl walked out of the cemetery, he took out a crisp, flat, white envelope he kept in his jacket pocket. He slid out a piece of paper, a note he had not yet delivered, and scrunched it up and tossed it aside. Then he scribbled the time and place on the envelope.

Vaughn didn't need to know what he wrote, as he had read it before.

He watched Dahl and still couldn't believe it.

Now this was the man he had buried. A man who walked with his head held high, with each step a leap and solid bound. He was the man

he had known. A man with limitless confidence. A man who was his own good luck charm. A man who knew his own fate and loved it. A man who would trust that fate for the world, who would throw himself on a friend as though he was bulletproof. A man who did it, not because he wanted the glory, but because he carried the burden of his own fate like a shield.

Vaughn dashed back down the snow to find Sancia, who had roused and was holding a cube, counting twists and turns between deep gasps and strains. Each time she tensed up she almost lost count and she flailed for Vaughn's hand to hold to keep herself steady.

She persisted, kept counting, twisting and sliding from blue tiles to orange and yellow to white. Vaughn didn't for a second doubt or worry she might make a mistake and doom them both, just as he knew he could never tell Sancia what he had seen.*

The groundskeeper huffed and brushed the entire cemetery flat and clean again, finding their last indents by a tombstone where they had crouched, and he sighed as he brushed over the blood with clean and forgetful snow.

---

*Go to Page 69

Chapter Thirty-Five:

Things to Come

When Vaughn was eight he didn't remember much about his life, but what he could remember was being atop Mount Fracture to jump the gap with his friends. Even at that age it was an easy jump. You didn't think twice about it or look down not unless you wanted to instill yourself with fear as Vaughn had. He remembered he took a rock and dropped it, watching it tumble over itself and rocket to the bottom. He put his mind inside that rock and imagined what the fall must we felt like.

He couldn't remember that kid's name, but he did remember him falling. He was only a few feet in front of Vaughn. And he didn't watch; he didn't want to see him fall like that rock.

He was only a few feet away. Within reach.

Vaughn now knew what that rock felt like.

Because Vaughn was falling.

Vaughn didn't know this, but an important step to operating a cube was adjusting your altitude.

But there was little he could do about that now. He couldn't even stop himself from flipping and turning as he was too disorientated and exhausted from trying to breathe air that was too quick to catch.

He had lost his grip of the cube that had gotten him into this mess.

Vaughn wanted to think nice, pleasant, final thoughts.

But all he could think about was that they would find his body dressed in dirty pajamas.

The sudden stop was not so sudden, but it took his breath away. Water ran into his mouth as he sank deeper and deeper into the murky water.

It was quiet, cold. His body froze up on him and he felt naked.

He kicked, he kicked to keep from freezing, and he kicked to find the surface.

Breaking through, Vaughn gasped with a deep guttural heave that croaked and scared off the birds.

This deep brown pit had stopped Vaughn's fall. All around him were high walls of dirt and rock and this body of water seemed to be trapped inside of it. Vaughn hadn't felt or seen the bottom, having plummeted deep like a needle into it. It was too deep to be a lake or a dam.

He swam to the edge. Not knowing any strokes, Vaughn was pitifully dogpaddling, making pathetic whimpers from the cold and to get air as he tired himself out getting to the muddy embankment.

Vaughn rolled out until he felt the ground underneath his entire body.

He was sick of it. All of it.

He hated the feeling of constantly having the rug pulled out from beneath him with every new twist that came with time travel, and now that feeling had been externalized.

Rolling to his feet and wringing the water from his shirt, Vaughn started walking up the embankment. He noticed the path he took was an actual path, as wide as a road, and it circled from the water's edge then spiraled around the high walls of dirt and rock.

It was not until halfway up did Vaughn realize where he was. He had fallen into a quarry - one that had luckily filled with rainwater.

He got that shiver again, thinking about how deep the bottom of it went, knowing that mine shafts drilled deeper than this quarry and his little legs had been kicking about in it.

Before Vaughn could see out of the quarry, he had a gut feeling. He hated those. His gut was only ever right when it was something bad. He sighed heavily as he walked up the path high enough to see over the edge of the quarry's rim where he saw the ever present and ever

watchful peak of Mount Fracture in the distance and the white ball of the Observatory on top.

Vaughn couldn't help but double over, breathing deep to settle himself. His jaw was hurting; his teeth clenched so tight. He felt every whistle of breath he was taking through his nostrils, and he gripped his thighs so hard he figured he might try ripping off chunks of flesh.

Vaughn found a shovel, resting against a crane and he shook it loose from the rusty soil. He and held it up to inspect its strength before frightfully swinging the thing at the crane's bumper, beating a deafening CLANG into the silence.

Vaughn swung the shovel at anything and everything, machinery windows, tall piles of dirt. He beat the ground with it and winced every single time the vibrations shuddered up the handle into his forearms.

He roared and crushed tears as he swung, his frustration echoing out from the mines and out into whatever time he found himself in now. All the while the mountain with its little white bump of an Observatory watched on, silent and unapologetic.

Once he calmed down, or rather once the shovel broke and he tossed both halves in separate directions, Vaughn started walking. He passed rusted excavators, crushers and diggers long since abandoned and made it out of the mining plot, aiming for town. As he walked, the mountain was ever present in his peripheral. He tried to keep it from his mind.

Fracture was flat, but the trick of the light and gases that rose from the hot soil bent the horizon, and it usually looked like the world caved in on Fracture. But this heat, the trademark of his hometown, was gone. The sky was a grey wash and not its usual stark, pale blue. The sun was up there somewhere, beaming a glow through the clouds that made it hard to look up without squinting.

Fracture was somehow flatter than usual, and he had no idea what was ahead of him.

Vaughn found houses and streets. He stepped off the dirt and onto the end of a court where he saw the street had been torn up by the weeds underneath, roots overgrowing and breaking through.

Each house was overgrown with brown weeds and had paint peeling. The roofs had caved in on some. He saw through windows that some houses had been reinforced with posts and wooden beams, and others had smoke puffing through makeshift chimneys.

Every so often a short waft of wind would chill his calves and Vaughn would see someone new walking the streets. A couple arm in arm, shaking sand from their boots. An older woman, promptly pulling in her coat and tucking her neck into her collar due to the sudden cold. On the other side of the street Vaughn saw a young man land and fall to his knees. He was soaked and still held his hand out for someone that wasn't there.

Vaughn continued to the end of the court to the street and tried to aim for something familiar. Knowing his house wasn't too far, he took the road to his street, and he figured he could get himself a change of clothes and maybe some shoes. His feet were shredded and now had either developed a layer of thick padding or gone numb to the constant impact that he forced on them.

Seeing his home – and a home to whoever he could convince to stay and split the rent - Vaughn felt his heart flutter slightly. Like seeing an old friend weathered by the years since you last caught up, this house too was ravaged by time. The gutters were full of dirt and weeds, the windows so brown and dusty he could see inside, and the weatherboards had cracked in some places, had fallen off or only clung on by one last nail.

Other than that it was the same, only now someone else was living in it.

People were living in every house he passed. But he knew none of them. Vaughn didn't know these people coming out the front door of his home wearing big coats, thick enough to endure the cold. A cold that Vaughn plainly stood in, with just his slowly drying apron, thin pajamas and bare feet.

Vaughn walked away a little faster, rubbing his arms to keep warm and straying into the middle of the street when he noticed no cars were using it. Anyone he saw was either walking or riding a bike. Cars he passed had sunk into the road. Rubber tires melted like ice cream into the pavement.

He noticed the roads were longer. As he made it into the center of town, Vaughn could see the main roads trailing off into several distances with more and more streets and buildings sprouting off of them.

Fracture had gotten bigger while he had been away.

How long it had been? Vaughn couldn't tell.

Long enough to expand but also to break down. It felt like hadn't been used for a while.

It was instinct. A habit of walking the same route every day. Vaughn stood outside the same two-story pub he had almost forgotten about.

He noticed the car with the body imbedded in it from long ago was gone, swept clean, glass and blood too. Now the Crowbar was draped in wind torn sheets with construction logos printed on it.

"The old man finally decided to renovate the place." Vaughn chuckled to himself, thinking of Baz, wondering how old the old man was now.

Vaughn followed the first people he saw. Just up the road from the pub were a few familiar strip shops that had been reopened and people funneled in and out. Vaughn rubbed his hands together as he stepped inside. In the corner he saw a pallet of water bottles. Running along the side walls were pallets and crates of cans, and in the center of the shop were boxes stacked on boxes of packaged meat, toiletries, alcohol and medicine.

They all moved through the stacks of pallets, boxes and crates. As they squeezed past other rugged up shoppers, they all calmly decided which thick steaks or sausages they would eat that night. Vaughn figured they had snatched it from some unsuspecting delivery trucks in the past. Invoices were still taped to the sides of the boxes addressed to companies all over the world.

Everyone helped themselves - not taking too much, only what they needed - filling bags and boxes to carry home. They didn't pay any money either, no one did. Vaughn only saw the shoppers reach the counter and leave gold or a stranger token of payment.

One that made Vaughn taste his stomach acids.

Cubes.

He would need one of those if he was going to get anywhere before freezing to death. Everyone had big thick coats with fleece lining. They looked at him strangely in his apron and pajamas but offered him nothing.

There were coats on a rack, gloves, and boots too. Vaughn wondered if he could do the same as all the others.

Shivers of warmth ran down his back as Vaughn slipped the coat on. He picked an extra-large size to make up for his bare legs. Stepping out of the shop he counted down until someone chased him out and ripped it off his back. He squeezed the cuffs of his sleeves and kept on walking away before he heard…

"Hey!"

Vaughn shuffled onwards. If he didn't look back, they might give up. And for fuck's sake, it was only one coat.

"He's got a gun!"

Vaughn's motor functions seized up. His eyes went wide. He felt the end of a barrel pointed in his direction, so he shot up his hands and turned slowly.

"I'm sorry… I was just… so cold and I…"

Standing about fifty meters away Vaughn saw a man wrapped in enough coats and scarves that it altered his shape. This bundle of comfort was pointing his rifle right in Vaughn's direction.

"You're not from here, are you?" The man with the rifle said.

Vaughn shook his head.

"Figures."

"Dude, it's just a fucking coat." Vaughn pleaded.

He heard the rifle cock, a few onlookers gasped, and a shot was fired.

Vaughn ducked and held his head, hoping his hands were bulletproof. He wondered if his body was too numb from the cold to feel it right away. Where had he been hit?

He heard a clunk and a thud behind him. He pried his eye open to look.

Only a few feet behind him a bird crashed to the ground. Sparks and crackling emitted from its neck and parts of it started to glitch.

The man with the gun approached and stood over the glitching white bird with a scowl on his face. Vaughn saw it lose its form and reshape into a broken white dome before sizzling and powering down.

The man with the gun spat on it.

"Didn't think I was aiming at you did you?"

"What…no."

He held out a hand and pulled Vaughn to his feet. As he did, the man pulled Vaughn in close, and his eyes darted back and forth over every part of Vaughn's face. The man grinned then begged Vaughn to follow him.

He obliged as the man led him back towards the pub, sweeping away the construction signage and led Vaughn inside the thick wooden doors, closing them behind.

Vaughn had never imagined the place could be trashed any more than it ever was. But he was wrong. It looked like someone had swept the trash from the streets into the pub. Piled high all around the peeling carpeted floors and leaning up against all the windows was junk on top of junk. It piled up high too. There was a hole in the ceiling that Vaughn couldn't figure whether it had fallen through on its own or the junk pile needed to go higher and broke through itself.

Vaughn could only wade through so far until he was at the opening alongside the counter. Here the bench top was laid out with tools and wires. A few lamps clamped onto the beer taps and the man who he had followed was digging around for something.

Vaughn was less concerned with this man and more concerned with how stable the junk pile above their heads were. As the man pulled an old game console loose from the pile, like Jenga, it swayed a little. Vaughn was sure he saw a bathtub on the top.

"What are you doing?"

"I'm a scrapper." The man said as he stripped off any excessive jacket or scarf. "I scrap."

"Right."

The man was gauntly. His cheeks had grey stubble and sunk into his jaw. His long fingers were stained with oil between each bend and crack. He was so thin that Vaughn figured underneath all those coats was a body no thicker than a broom.

"I fix things that people take from time to time and make them work again." The Scrapper held up a laptop he had duct taped a cluster of new parts to and pressed the space bar, and the laptop lit up with an orchestral hum.

"Ok, so?" Vaughn asked. "What did you want with me?"

The scrapper turned to the back of the bar and took a picture frame off the wall and passed it to Vaughn. He wiped the dust from it and choked.

"That's you, isn't it?"

The picture was from a year ago, or however many years ago it was now. Jake and Vaughn huddled in close as Baz and his wife along with a few other close friends. All squished in along the bar for a picture on grand final day.

Vaughn had to swallow a lump in his throat before he teared up anymore.

"I look at the photo all the time while I'm working. The second I saw your face. I knew it was you." The scrapper said. "It's kind of like meeting a celebrity, a bit... I don't know. Antin and I used to look at the picture and make up names for you all. Didn't have the heart to take it down, you know."

"Who's Antin?"

"Another scrapper. He left with the others to go off and do something important. He and I used to dream up adventures together. Getting away from all of this, finding somewhere like the Time Asylum or The Far. Together, you know. Then one day he tells me some videotape decided it was his destiny to go off without me. Leaving me behind, you know. Kinda felt crap, you know."

"Yeah, I know what you mean." Vaughn was still holding the picture frame.

"Sorry if I scared you before. But in times like these, one of those… things… can mean the death of us all."

"It can?"

"Trust me, you see one of those things, be it a bird, a cat or even a freakin' goldfish, A Historian's not far behind."

Vaughn gulped.

"That's why everyone's so tense. Historians are just fuel to the fire. Many of us believe the rumors that his followers might try something drastic against us."

"Who's followers?"

"Who's followers?" He repeated in shock.

Vaughn shrugged.

"The man who invented time travel, Luis G. Stein. He's had a bit too much of the good ol' healthy paranoia. Thinks everyone's out to get him, you see, he's a little nutty."

Above them, the lofty pile of scrap creaked, and the Scrapper's eyes almost split like a lizard's, trying to spot another bird to blow apart with his rifle.

"He's downright cuckoo." The Scrapper continued, both eyes back to Vaughn. "His followers are even worse. They aren't like Monos or Polychronists. But an offset of Alterchronism. Which is just an offset of lunacy if you ask me. They think, sure, time travelling can alter everything, unless that everything is Stein and his bloodline. They figure that the universe would tie itself up in a big ol' knot trying to solve that lil' paradox."

"So they don't like you guys."

"Exactly. Paranoia is valid when you're threatened by everything. As long as we're out and about, we're a threat to the sacred timeline."

"And you all are just waiting around to see if they actually do something? Why don't you leave?"

"And go where? This is our new time zone now. There was a treaty and everything. The only other place safer than here…"

The scrapper stopped suddenly. He held up a finger and scrambled through his things. His long fingers prying and tossing things aside and until he found it. The Scrapper swept the counter clear and placed a gaming console in front of Vaughn. He only knew it by the logo. It had to be a few editions newer than anything Vaughn had played on at Jake's place.

The Scrapper pressed a round button and the disc slot popped open, revealing a scrap of paper folded up and hidden inside.

"I fixed some guy's video camera, and he gave me this as payment. I was going to go with Antin but nuts to him now, I say. Still don't wanna go alone though."

He passed the paper to Vaughn and shuffled his feet amongst the crap and scrap on the floor. Vaughn took it and unfolded it. He only had to read the first line.

> *Attention Time Traveler's,*
> *Voyagers and Trekkers...*

"What d'ya think?"

The newspaper tear-out shook in Vaughn's hands.

"This is for the Time Asylum." He muttered.

"You've heard rumors, yeah?" The scrapper took out a cube from one of his tool drawers and sat it atop a collection of spanners. "Didn't think you'd ever get the chance, did you?"

"Never thought I'd be that lucky, no." Vaughn bit into his cheek.

Vaughn dug through his apron pocket for his tear out invitation. He dug around and then felt it, damp and soggy, at the bottom of the pocket. He tried to carefully pull it out, but the top half tore easily, and Vaughn quickly held soggy scraps of grey blobs.

"So you'll go with me?"

Vaughn couldn't trust his luck. He felt for sure he had been stranded here, but now he could go back, try again or see if everything was back to normal. If Pete had returned, maybe he wouldn't have to leave again at all.

"Of course I'll go with you. What the fuck are we waiting for?"

The Scrapper smiled and slid the paper on the counter between them and was readying his cube. Above them, the towering pile of scrap groaned again. It wobbled slightly, side to side. The wind was picking up from outside and shifting the scrap with its unrest. The Scrapper looked up as Vaughn did, spying a break in the ceiling to the darkening clouds outside.

"Looks like a storm's coming." He said with little concern.

The cube in his hands was like a firm door the Scrapper could close on the rest of the world. Vaughn could see the strength he had in just one finger as he twisted the colored tiles around the cube. Vaughn held a hand on his shoulder as he twisted and turned while he looked down to the newspaper tear-out. He read Atticus' invitation with the old man's voice in his ear. The sentiment seemed less inviting the more he read, and even less as he reached the last few lines.

> *A place for those that have no other.*
> *November 15th -16th 1990*
> *6:00pm til 6:00am*
> *Mount Fracture Observatory*
> *November 15th?*
> *1990?*

As cube clicked its last turns and sucked the scrapper away Vaughn was left to watch. His hand had quickly sprung off his shoulder, letting him go on that tangent alone. Alone and confused.

A short draft breezed through the pub and the massive junk pile rocked only slightly as Vaughn had to catch his breath as it almost escaped him.

November. *Fucking November*?

He felt sick. Real sick. Whatever craziness he was stuck in, now his scrapper friend was lost in it too. Lost to some alternate life. Maybe there Vaughn would be waiting, some other version of Vaughn with some other version of Pete.

Or perhaps neither of them at all.

Vaughn couldn't let his mind wander, the more it did the more it concocted the most bizarre and yet plausible alternate versions of time. Each as plausible as the next, nothing was off the table and each contributing to the massive unlikelihood of Vaughn ever finding the timeline he belonged to.

He pushed his way out of the junk and trash at his feet, shuffling too hard and too quick. He didn't have the spry and thin legs of the scrapper and he kicked the wrong length of galvanized pipe.

As he pushed out the thick doors of the Crowbar and squeezed out from the construction safety fencing, he could hear the junk pile collapsing and burying everything inside with a short waft of dust puffing out from the building like a tomb caving in.

A few people on the streets looked on and tilted their heads to the side, confused and concerned only for a moment before getting back to their thoughts. Vaughn stood on the other side of the road, staring at the Crowbar from the footpath.

He rubbed his toes together, enjoying the cool pavement. His feet were black and dirty, microfibers of dirt and dust from so many eras now nestled between his toes. Looking down at his feet, thinking they needed a wash, he caught sight of something painted on the footpath.

"You've got to be kidding me."

There, at the tip of his toes, a yellow streak of paint.

Limpfingers.

There were more, three more, all leading up from where he stood. They led towards the Observatory.

His body was too tired to be cold, his legs pumped warm blood, and he figured if he stopped for a breath he might freeze.

He made it to the top, finding the Observatory just as it was. Only now the white paint had faded somewhat, the edges of the base had green and yellow veins from the fauna creeping up the sides.

The top had browned and faded the most, and the grass that had once been nicely manicured around the entire thing had died off into patches of brown weeds spouting out of mud.

Vaughn noticed a strange hum in his ears, but every time he tried to focus on it the cold wind whistled past and he lost it.

Vaughn expected the doors to be locked, and they were supposed to be. A thick chain and a broken lock coiled like a snake at the foot of the door. He easily pushed them open and stepped through the vestibule and into the Observatory once again.

"Holy fuck."

The place would have made Atticus cry. The carpet was torn up, and small fires had been lit and stamped out in several corners. All the curtains had been pulled down with such force they ripped the rods out too. The speakers had fallen from their brackets but were swinging freely by their wiring. All shelves behind the bar were empty, every single bottle taken, and broken glass scattered about like confetti.

None of this bothered Vaughn; it was spilt milk next to a dead body.

It was not what had taken his attention. Vaughn was shuddering at what did.

There were hundreds of them, all in the same yellow spray paint.

Limpfingers. Limpfingers. Limpfingers.

The words painted so violently over every inch of the Observatory. One was painted so big on the floor that it bent and crept up the side of the counter to complete a corner of a letter.

Vaughn wasn't so sure of what he had been following all this time, it now seemed like etchings of a madman on his padded room walls.

Deliberate along the floor, tracking a path through the broken glass, Vaughn traced a long unbroken line which ran to the door, which was wide open and exposing the darkness.

What did whoever painted these want him to see? Vaughn wondered.

Now that the wind was locked outside he could hear that humming again, clear and constant. The line along the floor had his bare feet dodging the glass and oddly enjoying the deep and soft red carpet once again. It led him to the storage room where the Historian had been kept, now wide open, hollow and dark.

Stepping inside, gently nudging the door aside before closing it behind him, Vaughn could see the yellow line continued. It ran to the very corner of the room and stopped on one of the floor's tiles. The trail had gone cold, but the humming continued.

Vaughn wondered just how the Historian had gotten out of this room.

There were no windows, no other doors and he had seen for himself Wyla search and take every cube from him before they locked him away.

Vaughn looked at the last tile curiously with a streak of yellow spray paint on its edge. The corner was raised slightly, and the grout had worn away.

On his knees, Vaughn dug his fingers around it and pulled the tile up with ease and he tossed it aside.

Almost instantly the humming grew louder, echoing up from the deep dark chasm below and up to Vaughn who was looking down into this seemingly bottomless shaft.

His elbows trembled, trying to keep his arms straight. *Was this here the whole time? Where did it go? Why was it here?*

His mind had taken off on this tangent of thoughts, while his hands had grasped the first steel rung of the ladder that ran down the shaft and he couldn't help but lower his foot down the shaft to feel for a rung of its own. The cold steel unnerved him even more, but he kept going.

The shaft was just big enough for a person to climb down, about one meter wide and who knows how deep.

Vaughn took the next rung, and then the next and the next. He had been climbing for a while. He figured he was deep inside the mountain now; the narrow shaft was getting colder. But he continued, finding the next rung with the touch of his foot. Each time fearing the absence of touch in the darkness, as though the ladder would suddenly end, and he would be stuck in this dark shaft with the nightmares below.

And suddenly he was right.

But he was too slow to react.

He put all his weight on his free foot.

And down he fell.

A rung caught on his warm coat, tearing it from his shoulders. It cocked him forward, and he knocked his chin against the ladder and fell flat on his back. He groaned at the pain, but only for a moment.

He hadn't fallen far. The ladder had come to a stop at the bottom of the shaft, and he was now lying where it led. Above him he could see the small square of light of the storage room.

A shiver of the cold ran across his neck and he shot up to his feet then squinted to see what he had gotten himself into.

He could hear a tight echo of his own panic, and that soothed him slightly. The room couldn't have been too big. Maybe as big as the storage room above him, like a bunker.

What kept him on edge was what he couldn't see, what he kept kicking whenever he moved around.

He felt for the walls in search of a light and he found it, a small toggle and with relief he flipped it.

He wished he hadn't. Now he could see another face. The white of a man's eyes.

"Fuck me." Vaughn stumbled back.

The man wasn't exactly standing still. But he wasn't going anywhere. He gained the courage to approach the source of the humming. Vaughn saw it was the man he had seen up above him and some time ago. The

man with suspenders, the one he had outed as one of those Historians they were all so worried about.

Now looking at him, standing there, vibrating ever so slightly at an incredible rate, Vaughn wondered what all the fuss was about.

Crandall, he remembered. That was his name.

Crandall was vibrating just as Vaughn had seen before, with an armful of cubes he hugged close to his chest. His face was compelling, almost too sympathetic to be the bad guy. Crandall had a sorry look in his eye that begged and asked; *really, like this*?

Vaughn had no idea how far back in time the asylum had been, but he knew for sure this man should have decayed long ago. But besides the vibrating, he was in perfect condition.

As Vaughn moved from Crandall to the rest of the space, he saw what Crandall's last view had been. The bunker was lined with stacks and stacks of cubes. Piled up to Vaughn's shoulders and against every wall, each cube too vibrated just as the ones in Crandall's arms. It was a vault.

What was a bank vault of cubes doing beneath the Asylum? And what had made them all go off at once?

Go on, touch one. Vaughn thought just as he found his twitchy hands reaching out and grazing the side of a cube nearest to him.

A cluster of shivers ran over his entire body so fast he had to dance the last of them off.

He whipped back his fingers and waited for the bad things to happen.

Nothing did.

"Ok then."

Vaughn tried again, delicately wrapping his hand over a cube and as each second passed with nothing bad happening, he firmly gripped it and pulled hard until SNAP. It broke off from the others and stopped vibrating.

He held it successfully in his hand, tossing it up and down playfully, assessing its weight.

It had a little heft, but not a lot. He figured whatever made it vibrate had taken one of its trips.

Vaughn took to the others, snapping free dozens of cubes, occasionally snapping too hard and breaking chunks of tiles off.

He gathered his collection and lumped them in his torn jacket by folding the arms in together and tying them up to make a little rucksack of his findings.

Vaughn nodded farewell to the crazed and pathetic historian and started back up the ladder to the square of light at the top.

As Vaughn neared the top and was seconds from hurling his rucksack of cubes and out into the room above when he heard something.

Low voices.

He peered out the top of the hatch. It was coming from the main room of the Observatory. Luckily for him he had almost fully closed the storage room door behind him.

He quickly shuffled up the last rungs of the ladder, slipped the tile back over the shaft and crept over to the door.

Maybe it was just a few tourists from the town below. Maybe they had come up to have a look around, maybe paint more oddly specific graffiti to confuse Vaughn some more.

Easing on the door, Vaughn inched it open so he could see through a wider slit out into the red and gold room of the Observatory.

Nothing. But he only had a narrow line of sight, they could have been standing off to his left or right and unless he opened the door some more...

A dark shape moved past the door and back out of sight again. He saw none of them, not a hair, not a nose, nothing.

"How long do we have?" The dark figure said.

"Only a few minutes, give or take..."

"How many exactly...?"

"Four."

The second figure also moved in front of the storage room door. Vaughn eased the crack shut a little more, tensing his jaw to keep it quiet.

He couldn't see a thing anyway. Whoever they were they were standing too close to the door to make out who they were. Vaughn had to wait.

"Should we tell them?"

"I feel like it wouldn't be the right thing to do."

"What's that saying? To be the cause of your own suffering?"

"I don't know it exactly."

"Beside the point. All I'm saying is that they got themselves into this mess."

"They can get themselves out."

"If they have time."

"Which they won't."

"No, they won't see it coming."

"This will be the last of them."

Vaughn's body shook as rapidly as Crandall did down below. These dark figures were no tourists. Vaughn couldn't keep his eyes away from the door. They moved towards the center of the Observatory floor, becoming more whole and Vaughn was waiting for that moment - that moment when their faces would show, and he could calm his unsteady stomach.

He saw their brown coats, brown suits and brown hats. But he never saw their faces. They turned and spoke to one another, but he never saw their mouths. He couldn't see their eyes. He saw nothing at all.

Despite the daylight streaming in, none of it hit their faces - nothing but shade. More shade than the hats on their heads could give.

Did they have a face at all? Vaughn thought. Or was it just a void you could reach into and grab nothing, but a nothing that could still bite.

He had been told that when he saw them, he would know it. But he didn't think it'd be true.

These were Historians, for real this time.

And there was nothing between them and Vaughn but a slightly open door.

He waited in the dark stale room, all his muscle tension keeping the door gap only an inch wide. It would only take the slightest movement

and they would find him, cowering in a storage room in his wet and dirty pajamas with a torn jacket full of cubes.

What were they waiting for?

They kept talking and looking out the windows. They seemed unconcerned with the state of the observatory. They shrugged it off as vandalism, vandalism that if Vaughn hadn't followed he would have been found for sure.

A soft waft of wind slipped through the door gap and tickled Vaughn's leg. His hairs stood up and he slipped forward and clasped the door shut.

Fuck.

Fuck. Fuck. Fuck.

He fell back and froze, looking at the door. Surely seconds from now it would fly open, and the two faceless beings would swallow him whole.

Surely.

Nothing. It took everything he had to open it again, hearing and seeing nothing before he opened it some more. He stepped out and traced a circle around the Observatory, peering over the counter in case they were hiding.

But they were gone.

Slipped away in the wind, as quick and as quiet as they came.

Though, he did notice something out of place. A glass sat on the counter on a corner of a napkin. Purposefully. Yet the napkin seemed purposeless. Just scribblings of what read like dance moves. *Right twist 7, left twist 8. Full turn 11.* And so on.

Vaughn stepped over more glass, strewn about curtains and trying to steady his breathing until he could go back to not thinking about it.

He wanted out, he was done with this place. If he never saw this place again, he would be more than lucky. In fact, he wished he had been the one to trash it. If he still had his shovel…

Vaughn gripped the strap of his rucksack and made his way back out of the vestibule and back out to the wet and soggy marsh that surrounded the Observatory. The storm that the Scrapper had predicted

was picking up wind. Vaughn felt it lash against him like it was trying to knock him off his feet.

Down below, Vaughn heard the tiny lives of the tourists that had taken over his town. The wind was rushing between buildings and scaring them off the streets.

Ominous clouds hung over Fracture, and just Fracture. Vaughn could see the sky clear and bright far in the distance. Rain fell and scattered, not knowing which way to fall.

Then suddenly the wind settled, rain fell again, and out of nowhere Vaughn thought he saw something blip into existence.

It was falling fast, like a small black bullet.

Down.

The sudden boom was too quick for anyone.

The massive cloud and fire ballooned and burst. It was louder than sound could get. But nothing was left to hear it.

No one stood a chance of escape. No one had time to act.

No one, except for those whose hands act faster than they can think.*

---

*Go to Page 313

Chapter Thirty-Six:
The Far

Vaughn's head crashed against the dirt. Vomit spat from his mouth while his throat dug for more. He wheezed and held his stomach as he felt his ribs unlock from each other. His legs seized up in spasms of cramps from the muscles, not wanting to loosen their grips from his bones. Every finger and toe ached, his eyes bled tears. His ears rang sirens.

Nearby, the man who had pulled him through time was on his feet but doubled over, catching a breath. He spat out a bloodied mess, rotated his jaw, lent back and cracked his spine. Vaughn passed out the moment the man hoisted Vaughn over his shoulder and started carrying him away.

When Vaughn awoke again he was close to a fire, a tantalizing plate of meats and vegetables were inches from his face - the smell had pried his eyes open.

Vaughn lifted his head, but a whopping headache pushed it back down. He only had as far as his eyes could stretch to get a sense of where he was. Somewhere dark, but warm. The fire must've been close as he could feel one side of his body was a lot warmer than the rest. His eyes hurt and there was a ringing in his ears like an explosion had gone off.

"Hungry?" The man said.

"What?"

The man stepped into view, his left hand holding a plate similar to the one in front of Vaughn's face and the right hand grasping the leg of lamb he was gnawing on.

"I will not put it in your mouth for you."

Vaughn tried again, but his body warned it had more pain to throw at him if he pressed it any further. He collapsed again and looked longingly at the plate of food.

"Where am I?"

"Somewhere quiet."

"Why do I hurt so much?"

"You should be grateful that you hurt, you could be feeling nothing at all."

The man crouched down beside Vaughn and tilted his head to the side so their features lined up.

"I saved you."

Vaughn could see thick yellow and brown mold between his teeth. Trying to see into his mouth was a task. It was so dark that he couldn't imagine it as anything but a dank hole. As he spoke his words came out in a raspy rumbling; a sound that you could sleep to. It was as though the words were stirred and spun in the broth of his deteriorating gums before they were let out.

"Saved me? From what?"

"The end." He said simply. "It didn't want to let you go. That rough, all over sickness that you're feeling, like having a terrible flu, that was a just a taste."

Vaughn watched the man spring out of his crouch and into a stand, moving just fine but holding his head.

"Why isn't it so bad for you?"

"Just stretch."

Vaughn closed his eyes and concentrated on making a fist. Just like those mornings when you wake up with a dead arm and you force your unreactive hand to ball up as tight as it can. His fingers twitched and then curled one by one, falling into line with an immense pain writhing up and down his forearm. They could move on command and without issue besides pain. Nothing was broken. He only had pain. Pain he could push aside and overcome. He rocked himself up to his knees and then fell to his side and twisted his whining legs into a

seated position, the things in his apron pockets digging into his thighs. The reward of food he could now reach kept his mind off his throbbing aches.

"Good. Eat, then sleep, and then we'll talk."

When Vaughn finally lifted his eyelids again he saw sunlight when there should have been, and its absence lulled him back to sleep. The man had to wake him later in the afternoon, when the sky was at its brightest black. He did so with a rough shaking of his shoulder.

Vaughn howled when he was shaken and rolled onto his back, where he took some deep breaths and stretched out his legs and pointed his toes down. It was the best relief he had ever had from a morning stretch, so much so he continued to stretch every part of his body, suffering the quick first hurt and then the easing pleasure of extending himself.

His ears still rang. He rolled his jaw and swallowed, but he couldn't shake off the faint ringing. He now saw where he was, just in the middle of nothing. The only distinction about this spot was the campfire. There was just concrete beneath them and nothing around but a haze that went on forever in all directions. But, if Vaughn squinted and waited, looking just in one direction, it was like the haze would dissipate just for him. He could see a little further where a line of tree stumps led off into the distance.

"Is it still night?"

"If you define day and night on the occurrence of the sun than yes, it is still night. But the time is 4:30 in the afternoon."

"What happened to the…"

"Not now. No more questions."

"What if I have a really good question? Like a really good one?"

"You ask too many questions already." The man rubbed his temple with this thumb and index finger, while Vaughn's headache had already passed. "Here."

The man handed Vaughn a neat pile of folded clothes with a pair of shoes on top. Vaughn nearly cried when he saw a pair of thick comfy socks.

"Figured you'd need these."

"Thank you." Vaughn breathed. "Seriously. Thank you…. ah… er?"

"O'seus."

"Wait. I know that name. I know you. Don't I? I met you." Vaughn recognized the name, but not the man. "From the future, right? Or the past from here, I don't know… You were at the court, up on the podium. I saw you at that Nazi shop. You were going to hunt Kurtzoph, right? That was you?"

Vaughn slid off his dirty clothes and put on a fresh pair of underwear, oblivious to being nude in front of the grizzly man.

O'seus sighed loudly, rested his head in his hands.

"Just get dressed."

Vaughn slid on the pair of jeans and laughed. He had never been so comfortable. He felt snuggled up in his fresh t-shirt, hooded jumper, thick socks and new blue shoes. He bundled up his dirty clothes and tossed them away into the haze, keeping only his corkscrew, the torn-out newspaper invitation and his two cubes. The pale one he had stolen from Ida and the other that had banished him from the Asylum. Bloodstains almost worn off. He figured he kept it because he hated it too much to let it go.

O'seus didn't look how Vaughn remembered. His face was withered but not with charm or quirk, but with stress and fatigue. His eyes were lighter, a greyish blue rather than the deep brown Vaughn could remember. What more, on his forearm Vaughn saw no sign of his tattoos. No ship cresting waves.

Vaughn sat back with concern as he watched this O'seus try to shake his headache. After a while he resorted to an axe he had at his side, and he sauntered off in search of the next tree in the line of tree stumps. He found one and hacked at it. This O'seus was a beast of a man, and his mere gaze at the tree was almost enough to topple it.

Vaughn couldn't stray from that thought: *this O'seus.*

They would burn the wood. The fire ate it up and burnt blue. Only a few chunks of the tree were enough to last all night. And while Vaughn poked it with the axe, O'seus would disappear and return with more

food, always on plates. He wondered which restaurant he had taken them from and how much each would cost.

He had trouble knowing if the days were passing or if this was just one very long afternoon. O'seus thrust the axe into Vaughn's hands one day, when his headache grew too bad, and he had Vaughn hack at the trees for him. Vaughn was shocked to find it was like chopping stone. The tree had become petrified, and Vaughn's hands vibrated to his neck. He dropped the axe and then dropped to the ground himself, shuddering.

O'seus watched as Vaughn tried to chop into the tree in any way he could. O'seus sat with a headache and moaned softly, tears squeezing from his eye socket as O'seus pressed his own palm into it. Now and then the headaches cleared long enough for him to take the axe from Vaughn and slam it halfway through the tree as though it were made of wood. He then returned to his spot by the campfire and let Vaughn stare at the axe for a while.

Vaughn hadn't asked any more questions, despite the list compiling in his head. He took this moment as a timeout, a moment where he could push all thought and worry from his mind and focus on the tree. A long moment.

He knew he couldn't stay here forever, despite the seemingly endless supply of meals O'seus was serving from some hidden kitchen. Vaughn also had the sense that O'seus wasn't going to keep him there as his weaker tree-cutting pet, O'seus seemed to be waiting for something, but he couldn't tell what it was or how he was counting the time.

"Up."

Vaughn awoke to find O'seus leaning over him with a hand to help him up. Vaughn took it and was flung to his feet, dusting off the crumbs of his last meal from his soft hoodie.

"What's happening?"

"Let's take a walk."

O'seus led Vaughn deep into the haze, passing all the tree stumps and trees. Until Vaughn saw a tree which had a string tied around it, and then the next and the next. These strings shot across Vaughn and

O'seus' path like lasers in a spy movie. They came from all directions and extended deep into the haze ahead.

They were all tied around chest height and O'seus was very careful not to touch, instead moving along them and following certain strings.

Vaughn tried to follow, catching up by ducking under a couple and getting lost. He was only three strings away from O'seus, he could reach out and touch him, but the strings were so convoluted and would cross each other at so many intervals he had to keep ducking.

Vaughn found so many dead ends where strings crossed and knotted together and sprouted off like weeds. Vaughn noticed things clinging to the strings, pictures, newspaper articles and handwritten notes. It reminded him of the wall in the Nazi shop that tracked the life of the infamous Fuhrer. But these notes were about so many people, ordinary people, anyone and everyone had notes and a line of string.

"What is all this?"

"Not so long ago." O'seus started. "I found this place and decided to use it to try to fix things. But I needed help. So, I recruited. I led people here, the best of them. Others I took."

"Took?"

"Some that were close to death. I gave them a new life." O'seus said easily. "Together we tracked everything, laid it all out to see just where things went wrong, to see if we could alter things to make the history of humankind meaningful and full of beauty. We were tired of seeing war after war, crisis upon crisis. We used Ogles as a database and put every single event we considered meaningful out in the open, making links and connections. That's what we did here. For a long time, that's what we did."

"So." Vaughn started slowly. He had asked this before and been told he was wrong, but this time he was sure. "This is *The Far*?"

O'seus took a long look around him, as though he saw a world around them crumble before his eyes.

"Yes." O'seus finally said. "That is what some called it."

Vaughn had gotten himself lost in a cluster of strings, and O'seus was twenty feet away. He had stopped at a bundle of knots, all running together.

"When we found a moment like this." O'seus lifted the bundle of knots with his finger. "We would investigate."

"But why?" Vaughn asked. "If you believe things change then why try to change them in one reality if there's so many other realities?"

"That's not how time works." O'seus sighed. "It's more like a videotape. When you rewind it back you, then record over what came next, erasing what used to be."

"That's not what I've heard." Vaughn said, thinking back to the Asylum. Not one guest amid all the debating ever brought up this theory. No *guest* at least.

"No, I wouldn't think so."

O'seus kept on, he was a master at zigzagging through the web he had weaved. He knew every twist and sudden turn, while Vaughn chased after him. Every time he got closer there'd be another string he'd have to dodge or duck under. Photos and notes scraped across his scalp. Every time he did, O'seus got even further away.

Brushing past clippings of old newspaper Vaughn thought of the one he carried with him. The one from the scrapper. He felt the folds of it crinkle between his fingers and he brought it out.

It still read November 15th. It was still wrong.

"Stop."

"We're almost there."

"No." Vaughn stood firm. "I can't keep going like this with you."

O'seus turned, and Vaughn waited for him to say something. But he just looked back at Vaughn, his light grey-blue eyes almost passing through him.

"You're not the right O'seus, this isn't right at all. I shouldn't keep… you shouldn't be… I can't just…"

"You right. I'm not the O'seus you once met."

"You know?" Vaughn was stunned.

"Know?" O'seus raised a brow. "I met the real O'seus once, he came to me when I lived in my cabin in the Austrian hills. It was far from anything, but he found me, and he tried to kill me."

"Why?" Vaughn asked softly.

"Because I was just like one of these strings, and where I led wasn't good. My death would change everything. I wouldn't bare a son, a son that wouldn't become the man he was trying to stop. He talked about responsibility. He said it didn't matter that I didn't know what my actions, however innocent, would create. By being integral it meant I was responsible, intent didn't factor at all."

"So what did you do?" Vaughn asked. He had stopped cold and so had O'seus. If he was talking about what he thought he was talking about…

"I killed him." The fake O'seus' words echoed from deep in his throat and came out foul. "I killed him because I had no reason to believe him. It was madness. But then, as I went through his things, I found one of these."

O'seus held up a cube.

"I used it, not knowing what I was doing, twisting and turning it in all sorts of directions. And I found myself here. Lost in this strange future, far from anything. After a while of wandering I found an Ogle, somehow it still worked, and I asked it my questions. I wanted to know everything."

O'seus held his palm over his right eye again, grimacing to Vaughn from five strings away.

"And that's exactly what it showed me."

It looked like it hurt, like this fake O'seus was holding all of human history from hemorrhaging and spilling out his eye socket. It reminded Vaughn of his own hangover headaches. It was hard not to sympathize.

"And you took his name, why? Because you liked how it sounded?"

"Because I couldn't use my own. Also, you might say I was inspired by his wisdom and the eye of a director. I was directing after all. Directing people here, rewriting and redirecting things."

"Is that what you were doing? Directing huh?" Vaughn asked softly and coldly. "Were you directing me, huh?"

O'seus looked and Vaughn and waited. He would make him say it.

"Limpfingers? Was that you who painted that?"

"I had to get your attention." O'seus rumbled.

"Fuck you, there's my attention."

"But I wasn't trying to direct you." O'seus turned and kept on moving through the strings.

"You sure about that?" Vaughn snapped, sick of all the strings in his way so he broke one. It fell and twenty other strings collapsed with it, Vaughn stepped over them to get to O'seus. "Because it sure as fuck seems like it."

"I wasn't marking a path for you to follow. I was marking the path that you will take. Your pre-determined path."

"My what?"

"Everyone here." O'seus motioned to all the other string lines. "These are all the set paths that all these people would and will take. After years of trying, despite all our efforts to change things, we realized that we couldn't. We kept coming to dead ends. Something always came up; something always stopped us. Nothing changes Vaughn, or when it does, it only gets worse."

"What are you saying?" Vaughn felt his throat rising and stomach trying to pull it back down. "What about all that stuff about videotapes and erasing the future? Was all this just for nothing? Why show me a path if I was doomed to take it?"

"Because I wasn't sure."

"Sure of what?"

"There's no way to know." O'seus held both hands to his head, digging his fingers into his skull until the throbbing subsided.

"Know what?" Vaughn could see his yelling was too loud for O'seus. "KNOW WHAT?"

"There's no way to know if something happens because I did nothing at all, or because I did."

Vaughn was fuming. He felt every bone shake and every muscle tense to hold them still. All this time he was following in his own footsteps. Everything he had done or will ever do was already decided

for him. His life was a car, and he was tied to the tow bar, being dragged along behind it.

Every bad moment of his life came to mind, every little shitty thing, unlucky encounters, and regrettable words and lost friendships. All had been decided for him. People like Atticus had been handed a life on a silver platter while someone like Vaughn had been given the scraps. None of it was about how good you were, how smart you were, what decisions you made or chances you took. Life had already decided your fate and here was this faker, casually spelling it out for him. He felt like throwing up, but his jaw had clenched too tight to let anything out.

"I know it's tough to hear, but it's the truth." Fake O'seus said, now zigzagging through the web of strings to get to Vaughn, not wanting to duck or break any.

"I don't want to hear anymore." Vaughn broke. "I'm tired, sick actually. Sick of people like you and everyone else thinking they know the truth. You're all the same, egotistical and selfish. Why would any of you think you were the one to finally figure it out? All I want to hear from you next is a simple answer to my question, and then I want you to take me home. I'm done. So, where's Pete? I know he's supposed to be here, don't tell me he's not."

O'seus kept weaving through, his eyes on Vaughn as Vaughn held his distance, ducking under more strings to keep O'seus at a distance.

"Why do you want to know?"

"What? What do you mean why?"

"You barely knew Pete." O'seus put simply. "What does it matter to you what happened to him? Why do you feel this need to save him?"

Vaughn was taken aback, and he tripped into more strings, falling. They couldn't take his weight, snapping at the knots and more snapped and went flaccid. O'seus was shocked, his precious strings falling to the ground.

Vaughn didn't have an answer when he thought about it, he just did. He didn't think he needed to justify himself. Especially when he had this feeling. He could spot it in how frantic O'seus was getting in every step Vaughn took to away from him. What was O'seus hiding from him?

"Why did you save me, anyway? Was it because you think you were always supposed to? Maybe I was supposed to die. Did you ever think about that, huh? Why save me when you could have saved Pete? Huh? Why didn't you save Pete?"

"Because. Everything I've been trying to do, everything I've spent years setting into motion, it's all because of you, Vaughn."

But Vaughn was done. He was way out of the fake O'seus' reach and almost out of sight. And he would keep going until he could no longer hear his voice.

"There's still something you have to do!"

O'seus wasn't quick enough to follow, as Vaughn tore down string after string and ran off into the haze. Behind him O'seus called out, caught up in his own strings. His voice resounded behind him. It echoed a great distance further than Vaughn expected, due to the extreme lack of silence of the world around him. But Vaughn didn't hear a word he said. He pushed him to the back of his mind as he weaved further and further into the middle of the web, following a thick strand with no intent on returning.

He felt in his pocket for the cubes still in there. They taunted him, as he was unsure how to use them. Even if he did, he had no idea what year he was in and what hell he might end up in if he were to try his luck.

Not that Vaughn much believed in luck in the first place.

He just wished he could get back home but he didn't trust O'seus to let him.

Vaughn found and followed a main line of string. It was straighter than the others, having so many threads run to and from it to keep it up. It seemed to be a constant amongst all the chaos of the other strings, dividing the web and making its own path.

Vaughn wanted to be more like this string. He hated it when someone told him what to do, even if that someone is time itself.

He thought of the others; Wyla, Dahl, Sancia, even Jowls. How much of what they did and had gone through was in their control. Could he

even blame Atticus for being such a prick? Did the old man have any choice?

Vaughn read the clippings and peered at the photographs pinned to the main string he admired. He didn't know much about history, especially Spanish history. This string seemed to follow a family line, names and titles being passed down with some great importance that Vaughn couldn't decipher without some of the knowledge he had ignored in school.

Though, what he did find curious was how this main hefty string that was covered in detail about Spanish shipping vessels, dukes, and a Jewish wedding was designed to collide with another thick string line that had come from the distance on Vaughn's right. They struck each other and the string that Vaughn had been following had won, stretching out into the distance and fading in the haze.

Curious what was pinned to the intersection, Vaughn traced it, moving toward the big knot that tied them together. Pages from an American High school 2009 yearbook. Photos from the prom and science fair that year.

Before Vaughn could get a closer look, he saw all the other strings, photos, notes and clippings rise and flutter in a sudden wind.

There, in a wide-open spot that the strings left open, appeared a man all in grey. He landed with a thud too heavy for a man his size. Vaughn could tell he was carrying someone in his arms, but it was too dark to make it out. Especially through all the green smoke.

Whoever it was, he dropped them to the ground, stepped over them and walked away.

Vaughn ran to meet them. As he got close, he noticed the body had dark black skin and was in a bloodstained white shirt. He was sputtering attempts for a breath out of his mouth but only blood dribbled out.

Smokey looked unsurprised to see him there.

"Vaughn? Nice to see you again so soon."

"Smokey, what is..."

Then he saw his face, the blood spilling from his neck; Pete was still dying.

Vaughn sank to his knees at Pete's side. He heaved Pete into his arms and held him to his chest. He had to hold a hand over Pete's

neck. Glass cut into his palm as he tried to stop the bleeding a second time.

"PETE!"

"Vaughn?" Pete stammered, dark red blood slipped from the corner of his lips and across his cheek.

"Hey Pete." Vaughn smiled through a gush of tears. "Hey buddy."

"Vaughn... I slipped..."

"I know, I know." Vaughn wiped his eyes with his sleeve. "It's all ok. You're gonna be ok."

But Smokey had done nothing besides drop his body on the ground and light a new cigarette.

"You're getting help right?" Vaughn begged to the lanky man as he wiped the bloodstain from his grey jacket. "That's why you brought him here? To save him?"

Smokey looked at the body, dragging a long breath from his cigarette, and shrugged.

"If I get to it."

Smokey walked on and into the darkness, out of sight as easily as he had exchanged pleasantries.

He left Vaughn there alone, clutching his dying friend. He wished he knew what to do. He felt like he was helping drive that glass into his neck just by doing nothing.

Pete's breathing was getting harder to listen to. He choked more than he breathed. He just kept looking at Vaughn as though he was apologizing for getting hurt. Vaughn could do nothing but scream for help, for someone to come rushing out from the haze with bandages and a gurney. Anyone.

"Vaughn... I'm... Sorry."

"No, no, Pete don't. Just stay awake ok." Vaughn said between screams.

"I wish... I wish..."

"Pete?"

"I wish..."

Vaughn was screaming for help when he died.

Chapter Thirty-Seven:

Infinite Monkeys

Vaughn raced after Smokey, who had disappeared into the ruins of the old city. Vaughn ducked under webs lines and snapped a few strings in his pursuit. His chase brought him to the remains of an old stadium that grew out of the haze.

The roof had collapsed, and the fallen chunks had imbedded themselves all around the outside of the entries like crooked tombstones. Vaughn followed a well-worn path; it led through a crack in the wall which Vaughn followed through to the other side.

The stadium had cracked in half. Vaughn stood awestruck on the curved side that still stood as he looked out to the other half that had crumbled into an open valley of haze that stretched into nothingness. He had to grab a railing to steady himself. Vaugh felt the steel groan as he noticed the same rust that had torn through all the ancient seating was all that was keeping the railing together.

Below, in the open field, was a grid of hundreds of camping tents with a hustling population moving amongst them. The string lines broke through gaps and cracks made in the walls and shot through walkways between tents. The strings intersected and interrupted the paths of the thousands of people who were rushing about as though there was still work to be done.

Vaughn stumbled back and felt a presence behind him as he did. He spun around to see Smokey stepping out of the stands to meet him.

"You motherfucker."

Smokey seemed to smile, not that Vaughn could tell through the smoke.

"Ever hear that expression: *an infinite number of monkeys at an infinite number of typewriters...*"

"Don't change the...?"

But they caught his eye and Vaughn took a harder look at the masses of tiny people busying themselves with tasks. They all looked familiar.

Probably because they all looked like Pete.

He saw Pete threading time webs, Pete taking notes, Pete sorting through photographs. There were Petes carrying bottles of water, Petes sweeping the dirt, even Petes standing over other Petes making sure they were working properly.

Vaughn felt a cold sweat break out on his forehead and run internally down his face and under the rest of his skin. His mouth hung open for so long it dried out.

"What do you think are you doing?" He asked through chapped lips and a sandpaper tongue.

"The old man wasn't cut out for it. You saw what was left of him and his strings. Someone had to step up and get things done."

"Step up to what?'

"Saving the world."

There it was.

Vaughn swallowed the vomit in his throat and tasted the acid that burned his tonsils. "Not like this."

"Well, actually." Smokey ushered a little white bird to fly over and land on his shoulder. "I think you were the one to say it."

The Ogle bird opened its mouth, and a voice played from inside.

"What about everyone else? Don't you care about what your actions do to other people? Don't you have any empathy?" The familiar voice sounded.

Vaughn knew that voice. It brought up heaviness behind his eyes in an instant and he fought to hold it back as the recording continued.

"Tons. Buckets of it." Vaughn's voice answered.

"So you care and did it anyway? That's worse."

Jake's words were as painful now as they had been then.

"Then fine, I don't care. Which one's better? What do you want from me?"

"How did you…?" Vaughn quivered.

"Shhhh." Smokey petting the bird under its chin with a bony finger. "This is the good part."

"I want you to care about someone else for a change. I want you to stop being such an asshole."

"Don't tell me what to do."

Vaughn's mouthed along, recalling it as though it was yesterday.

"My ends justify my means, so what else does it matter? Besides, I only got caught because…"

"Oh, don't fucking start. Don't turn this around on me. They were my mates. And even if they weren't what kind of fucking prick does that…"

Vaughn's voice continued, though he did not need it to remember what he had said.

"Stop it." Vaughn plead in a whisper.

"You don't want to hear the rest?" Smokey curved a grin, rolling the long cigarette between his lips from one side to the other. "Another time perhaps."

Vaughn didn't respond. And for a long time, the both of them stood and looked out at the empire Smokey had birthed. One of them with pride and satisfaction and the other with gloom, guilt and an unmatchable level of self-hatred.

"He's dead you know." Vaughn found himself saying after some time had passed.

"Of course he is." Smokey scratched the Ogle bird some more until some white feathers fell off and crumbled into tiny specks of metallic dust. Still, the bird's glass eyes followed Vaughn. "That recording is hundreds of years old. Everyone from that time is dead but you."

"I meant Pete." Vaughn held out his blood-stained hands.

"Oh." Smokey took his cigarette out and dropped it to his feet, lifting a foot and grinding it into the dirt. "I guess I never will get to it."

Smokey didn't seem to mind Vaughn walking out into his enclosure; his zoo of Petes. Vaughn passed through them, popping their heads up

like meerkats, only ever sparing a few seconds before rushing back to whatever work they had been handed. Smokey was trailing behind and Vaughn could sense the rapid hush that followed him.

"You know I have tried to change this."

Vaughn tried not to listen.

"I tried to spare you. But you couldn't stay away. You know it would have been a very different Asylum if you were never there. But you just couldn't stay away."

A chain of lumps collected in Vaughn's throat, each one he swallowed brought up another, strung together like sausages.

The tents were all the same dark green and were laid out in perfect lines like houses in the suburbs. Tents backed onto each other with only a few feet between them and paths ran past like streets. The only interruption to this system were the thick string lines that cut through the pattern of tent after tent, and all the Pete's made do.

Smokey stopped tailing Vaughn and instead watched as he wandered deeper and deeper into the tent city. As Smokey watched he snatched the collars of the next two Petes that passed him by; one in each hand. Smokey bent his long and angular torso so that the cloud that he puffed with such insistency made them cough.

"Don't let him leave." Smokey ordered to the Pete in his left hand.

Pete nodded and instantly eyed Vaughn and narrowed his gaze. Smokey let him go and with his now free hand found a cube in his pocket, twisted it and took the unsuspecting Pete in his right hand with him through a tangent.

Pete let out a quivering exhale, rubbing his neck where Smokey's cold fingers had touched. There was still a waft of Smokey in the air and that was enough to push Pete to work, following closely behind Vaughn.

Vaughn caught the first Pete he could, one carrying an armful of empty water bottles that all fell and bounced off each other.

"Hey buddy." Vaughn said, bending down with Pete to help him pick up the bottles. He spoke gently like he would to a stray dog he didn't want to scare away. "Let's ditch this place yeah? Get our pay, go on a

long trip? Remember we said we'd leave together, right? So, let's get going."

Pete piled all the bottles up neatly and rushed off from Vaughn, trying hard to keep his eyes on the ground.

There were some Petes that were strangely different than the others, the way you notice an old toy has been used much more than the same toy you just bought brand new. Vaughn even started to notice their fingers; some were missing the same index finger as his own Pete had, others were missing thumbs, pinkies or ring fingers. A few had stopped and slipped off their shoes and socks to nurse the wound of missing toe.

Some of them had bandages with dark black bloodstains. Others had such smooth skin on their nubs that would have taken years to heal.

Three Pete's had fully healed nubs where their fingers used to be, they were lugging stacks of paper, making notes on selected pages to perhaps later pin up along a string line.

These were also the Petes that spared the least amount of eyesight on him, daring Vaughn to talk to them.

"Pete!" Vaughn exclaimed to an uncaring clone. "You've got to explain this to me man, I'm lost."

"Vaughn, is it?" Pete spoke, looking to one of the others.

"From the Time Asylum." Answered RePete.

"Not supposed to be here." RePeter added.

Vaughn shook his head.

"Look, the soulless thing, you can knock it off."

"It's an interesting occurrence, yes." Said RePete.

"Can one of you just tell me what's going on? What happened to you?" Vaughn was worried. He felt the stiff wind of Smokey returning. But the triplets just looked at each other, confused.

"What are we going to do with him?"

"Right, ok. Got it. You're all late for your daily lobotomy." Vaughn hopped to his feet and took off for the opening of the arena and the horizon. He wove between tents, as not to be seen by Smokey when he returned. He worried that he might not be as composed as he was before he left.

Vaughn almost made it to the edge of the field where the stands had crumbled away, leaving an open gap for him to escape through. But suddenly there was a gust of wind and a thud a few yards in front of Vaughn that had him duck and dive behind a tent. He expected Smokey but instead two more Petes landed firmly on the ground, each grasping the arm of another figure just like them but with a bag over his head.

With a great deal of hostility, they dragged the quivering Pete between all the tents, lifting him up whenever his feet gave way.

Vaughn couldn't help but follow, wanting to both watch and rescue.

These Petes marched up to one of the larger tents, brushed past the tent flaps and Vaughn lost sight of them.

Should he go in? Even as one of the larger tents, it wasn't any bigger than his own bedroom.

Vaughn crept around the outside of the tent, finding that through the thin mesh he could make out most of what was happening.

Inside the tent was dark, especially to the hooded Pete. So when his hood was ripped off and a bright light was switched on and aimed in his eyes he found his was more blinded then before.

All Pete knew was that he was sitting in a cold steel chair at a cold steel table, his left hand still throbbing where a thumb should've been.

"I'm going to start while you still can't see, it'll be easier for you that way." A RePete began.

"Who...?" The trembling Pete whispered.

"Play it." RePete ordered. As RePeter took the cassette tape from his pocket and slipped it into a player. Vaughn had to now strain his ears harder to hear what was being said as unsettlingly smooth music started to play.

The music was loud. It left the tent and all the surrounding Pete's hesitated as they heard Nat King Cole's voice sing *Unforgettable.* Each note a sting in their minds and memories.

"No doubt you recognize my voice." RePete spoke loudly over the music. "I can't do anything about that, but I ask you not to be alarmed."

Pete's eyes were darting back and forth, trying not to hit the light and to see who was speaking to him. But the voice came from behind

the light. He knew that song, unlike all the others outside, the music filled him with some joy and happy memories. It was only when the song ended and the song played again did Pete find it unnerving.

"You remember this song, don't you? My mother used to play it for me when I was little, it was the first song I learnt to play. In fact, whenever I was angry or sad, she just played this song and made it all go away."

The voice moved, sitting down opposite him, still too hard to make out.

"When she died." RePete continued. "Someone else played it for me. A man who promised her they would take care of me when she was gone. Asim, he took care of me."

The song ticked over and the first few notes begun again as RePete leaned in, putting his face in front of the light, and Pete finally saw who he was speaking to.

"He took care of us." RePete growled. "And do you know what happened to him?"

If Pete wasn't so shocked he would have shaken his head.

"What's the last thing you remember?"

Pete let the music wash over him as he recalled anything before the moment the hood went over his head. As the height of Cole's voice rose and his vibrato tingled Pete's skin, he saw flashes in his mind. His own face staring back at him. A thousand times over. He thought the faces were just in his mind, but when he looked around the room, they hadn't gone away.

He felt his chest tighten, suddenly he couldn't breathe right. He reached for his throat and found only his own hands wrapped around it.

His mind had locked it away, but as Nat King Cole sang, he found the dark memories just as unforgettable.

"That... that was all real? Pete gasped. "It really happened?"

"Not only did it happen to you. It happened to everyone else. Only thing is, everyone else wasn't so lucky. Asim is gone, Pete. He's gone because of you. They all are."

Pete tried to shut it out, holding his hands over his ears and closing his eyes. RePeter stepped up behind him and held his hands down behind his back, gripping his freshly sliced nub and squeezing. RePete slammed Pete's face against the cold steel of the table.

"MILLIONS OF PEOPLE PETE!" RePete yelled. "NOT ONE OF THEM COULD BREATHE. NOT ONE OF THEM COULD MOVE! BABIES. WOMEN AND CHILDREN. ASIM. ALL YOUR FRIENDS. PEOPLE WHO DID NOTHING WRONG. BUT BECAUSE YOU WERE STUPID. SO DAMN STUPID. YOU WERE SELFISH. YOU ONLY THOUGHT OF YOURSELF AND LOOK WHAT YOU DID PETE! LOOK WHAT HAPPENS WHEN YOU THINK YOU KNOW BETTER. YOU THOUGHT YOU COULD CHEAT? YOU THOUGHT YOU COULD MAKE THINGS GO YOUR WAY? WELL CONGRATULATIONS PETER. YOU DID IT. NOW YOU'RE ALL THAT'S LEFT!"

The music rose to its crescendo of a climax, but they switched it off prematurely and the tent fell silent.

RePete stopped yelling and sat back down in his seat. RePeter let go of his hands and moved back to his station behind Pete.

Pete didn't lift his head. He kept it down and cried until his heart ran out of tears.

"Now, you're not as unlucky as everyone else. Someone out there looked at our situation and showed a little mercy, despite what we did. He freed the first of us. He is a blessing from the highest of places and he is the only reason we are here. If he was here what would you say?"

"Thank you." Pete whispered. "I would say thank you."

"But that's not enough, is it?"

Pete shook his head; of course, it wasn't.

"That's not enough at all. We can never repay our debt, not even for saving one of us. And our savior didn't just save one of us. He couldn't, he wouldn't stop there. No, he saved thousands of us. And do you know what he asks for in return?"

Pete shook his head.

"All he wants is for us to be like him and help him save everyone else."

Pete cried again, his bottom lip trembling as his brain struggled to comprehend such charity and goodness.

"Hey, Pete." RePete said, this time without authority but as one brother to another. "We're not trying to scare you here. I'm you, remember? We're just trying to make you understand it like we do, that's all. Because it's a big deal, isn't it?"

Pete nodded, wiping his eyes.

"Exactly. Here. I bet your hungry. Do you want some food?"

RePeter collected a plate and placed it softly in front of Pete, a fresh juicy burger surrounded by lots of chips. The food was fresh and hot as steam rose off of it and tantalized Pete's senses. Pete made for it but was stopped by RePete's voice. His own voice.

"Just before you take a bite of that tasty burger. I kind of need to know what you think. Just be honest and let us know where your head's at. Are you with us?"

To Pete, completely drained and exhausted, it wasn't even a question. "I'm with you."

"Good." RePete smiled. "That's great. That means we can be friends. Eat up and then we'll continue."

Vaughn slunk back against the edge of the tent. He held his head in his hands, wishing he could tear it off his shoulders and throw it just so he didn't have to deal with what was going on inside.

Vaughn hadn't noticed, but another Pete was sitting beside him. Passing by he had heard the music and had stopped to clamp his hands tight around his ears. He was doing such a good job he hadn't even heard the music stop.

Vaughn turned just as Pete did and they both yelped, not expecting to see one another.

Vaughn backed up, his face was everywhere he looked, he had to get away from them all. None of them was the Pete he knew, just shameful doubles.

Vaughn saw a trail that led out of the stadium and into remnants of the city that once was. The trail had just as many string lines and after

a while Vaughn didn't even try to move out of the other Pete's way, just knocking past them, unaware that he might be followed.

He came out to the huge stadium car park and saw a few Pete's walking across it and off into the mist of the haze. He followed them curiously as they were dragging someone between them. Perhaps it was someone new, someone with a different face for a change.

He followed them until they reached a big building with a wide mouth of an entrance and square cut steps leading up into it.

Vaughn saw them drag this person up the stairs. He was hooded and limp and they all disappeared into the building with Vaughn following.

As Vaughn walked the steps he had an inkling that he might've been forced up these stairs himself not so long ago. His inkling was proven right when he reached the top.

It was covered by a sheet now, standing there, as still as ever. Still humming. Still.

But it couldn't be.

Vaughn walked up to it, stepping into the jaws of the foyer and with an unsteady hand grabbing a ripple and pulling down the sheet. He found it staring him in the face.

The man was still vibrating. The two cubes in his hands grey and dusty but still touching at the corners. The man was dusty, his skin flaking but never peeling off. All the hairs on his head were standing up and his teeth were so close together that they jittered and chipped away at each other. He was shaking so slightly, so constantly, and so horrifically that his brain had boggled, and bits were sliding out of his nose at an incredibly slow rate.

And his eyes. His eyes had glossed over. So little light left but still light in there somewhere, somehow, and smoke had started to seep free from the darkened tear ducts.

He was staring straight ahead, and Vaughn was in the line of sight.

In shock he stumbled back, shivers and chills fighting for possession of his skin as he took step after step until…

His foot found nothing to step on.

Vaughn fell.

He toppled back. Almost flipping over and he slammed neck first in the jagged plastic pile.

The pile shifted like sand in an hourglass and Vaughn sifted between the gaps of the swamp of the colorful, square toys.

He squirmed and tossed, reaching up and trying to hoist himself out, but that only sunk Vaughn further. For a pool so solid he sure was drowning quick.

So, this is how I go? Vaughn thought as a rush of cubes washed over him filling his mouth and blocking his air. *This is how I die?* He thought of O'seus' last words, that he was meant to do something, and here he was. Drowning in a pit of cubes.

Pathetic.

He couldn't see the outside now, only square breaks between cubes of light from above as he sank deeper and deeper, his last arm still sticking out and feeling for anything, an edge, a ladder, a rope...

A hand.

He grasped it. His fingers digging into a wrist and Vaughn felt himself rising, cubes rolling off him as he rose further. There, hanging over the edge of the pit, was a familiar face and a familiar hand.

This Pete pulled him up just enough until Vaughn could reach the edge of the marble floor until he was able to do the one chin up his body was capable of. He heaved his chest over the edge and rolled himself out.

Pete fell back too and they both lay of the floor of the open foyer, deeply panting.

Vaughn realized he had fallen backwards into the open stairway and into to the bottom floor that had been filled with confiscated cubes all those centuries ago.

He guessed they never got the chance to pour in the concrete.

"Thanks." Vaughn managed to get out between breaths.

"No problem." Pete panted back.

"Why d'you help me?"

"Because you were in trouble." Pete said, all matter of fact. "I was following you and I saw you fall in."

"You were following me?"

"Yeah. You're the first person who… you know…"

"What?"

"That doesn't look like me." Pete admitted. "Besides *the savior*. But I can never make out what he looks like."

"Hold up, the savior?" Vaughn figured he couldn't possibly be talking about Smokey. "The lanky guy with all the smoke?"

Pete nodded.

Behind them they heard doors opening and closing. Vaughn peaked and saw Pete's assisting Pete's from room to room. Some Pete's looked quite dazed as they came out, a lot less frantic as when they went in.

The Pete that had saved Vaughn backed up, not liking this place at all, and he made for the way out. Vaughn hopped up and followed him down the steps where they stood outside.

"What goes on in there?" Vaughn asked.

Pete just shook his head.

"Not anything good I guess."

"I show me what I did." Pete added. "Then I am allowed to stay."

"Right."

"But I don't want to stay." Pete said, turning right to Vaughn and standing a little too close, Vaughn could see his own tired face in the reflection of Pete's puppy dog eyes. "I don't like it here."

"Dude, me neither." Vaughn shrugged. "That's why I'm getting the hell outta here as soon as I can."

"Are you going now?" Pete asked.

"Yeah."

"Can I come then, please?"

"Sure, but soon. This place is giving me the creeps."

Vaughn looked around, trying to get his bearings. He tried remembering which direction he had come from, which way the stadium was and which way anything worth going to would be.

"STOP THEM!"

Vaughn and his new Pete whipped their heads around to see who had yelled. All Vaughn saw was a crowd of Petes emerging from the haze. They came from every angle, their shiny eyes like big demon eyes in

the darkness. They came from out of the building behind them; they looked down out of buildings.

They were everywhere.

Any of them could have yelled it. To him, none seemed any different to the others.

But Pete knew. He spied the slightest twitch of anger in his own face. A RePete who was holding out his fully healed four-fingered hand, pointing at himself and Vaughn.

"HE. CAN'T. LEAVE!"

Vaughn took off, ready or not Pete quickly followed. Making for the widest gap in the inclosing circle of Pete's, they both ducked past unprepared doubles, knocking into one another. Vaughn and Pete made a lucky break for it.

The once expressionless and dull faces now turned hostile and Vaughn found it harder to push past any Pete, RePete or RePeter in his way. They tried to grab him, dive for him and when they failed, they chased after them.

They both skipped between the onslaught of Petes, jolting under string lines and busting down any string too slow to get out of their way. Vaughn felt like he was in a dream again, his legs at half power, struggling to push through the air the faster he wanted to go.

Ahead of them the herd compounded and stormed towards them, no room to avoid, so Vaughn and Pete slammed their feet, skidded and darted sideways to slip down a different street that headed to a wide birth of buildings heading out towards nothing.

"Why do you have to be so fast?" Vaughn shouted at Pete, who was so much faster, and he was not only running ahead of him but at every moment gaining on him.

They neared the end of the street, with an army of Pete doubles, triples and quadruples close behind. Soon they could see what lay beyond the city. A gap had opened and it looked like an earthquake had torn down the other half of the city. The ground slopped down steeply, almost immediately, into a deep valley where the haze of the Far coated all like an ocean, a thick mist of the unknown.

Pete had gotten nabbed by a vicious Pete and was frantically wriggling him loose, so Vaughn made it to the edge first and stopped once he saw the sudden drop. But when Pete caught up, he didn't hesitate - flying right past Vaughn. Pete took off from the slope with a giant leap, throwing himself down the sheer slope and sticking the landing, running even faster.

Vaughn didn't have time to be impressed, he could hear it; a thunderous rumbling of feet.

Behind him the stampede was gaining on him, herd storming down every path and converging on him at the edge of the city.

Vaughn's hands gave up waiting for him and did it themselves, whipping back and thrusting Vaughn off the edge. He tumbled and rolled, probably faster than he could have run, and somehow caught up with Pete.

Behind them the stampede slowed and came to a stop at the top of the slope. As soon as Vaughn and Pete slipped into the thick haze of the gorge, the herd thought them lost for good.

They kept running. Vaughn kept up with Pete, but preferred to keep his friend out in front so he could hide his exhausted face, puffed up red and panting. As long as he was close enough not to lose him in the haze. He was loving the feeling of shoes again.

They kept up their pace, with no way of knowing if they were still being followed. They ran until they could no longer see the buildings towering behind them. And then a little further.

Slowing to walk, things came into view. Some trees that stood like stone, sudden walls and the top halves of street signs poking out of the ground. As easily as each thing came into focus, it faded away as they passed it all by.

Fleetingly massive buildings stood tall and stretched up to meet with other skyscrapers. They lent on each other for support. There were no entry doors at the base of each building, as though they had all sunk into the ground. All the glass windows had long ago shattered, so the

wind blew through entire floors and sounded like a hollow bottle when blown across the top.

Pete wandered, filled with less wonder than Vaughn, as though he was looking for something. Whenever they came across a string line that ran through the ancient streets, he diverted and walked in opposition to it.

However, Vaughn couldn't help getting distracted and rushed to catch up with Pete before losing him in the haze.

Finally, Pete came to a stop on his own as he stared down to where the ground had also stopped.

"What is it?" Vaughn asked.

"Thirsty?" Pete asked back.

Vaughn was thirsty, and Pete nodded towards the ground in front of them. Vaughn bent into a crouch and reached out to what filled the void. It was icy cold and it stuck to his finger for a second before slipping back into the river.

The water rippled out, strange ripples, slower than they should be, as though the water was custard.

"Don't drink it." Pete warned.

Vaughn wiped his hand on his pants and stuck it under his armpit to defrost his fingers.

"All right what the hell is this place? Where are we? Is any of this even real?"

"I hope not." Pete replied.

The two of them continued, walking beside one another along the river's edge. They crossed under the jelly river through a tunnel, so dark that they accidentally and momentarily touched hands. Then on the other side they walked, following painted lines on the roads.

Vaughn couldn't help thinking he was still being fooled, this Pete was being so nice to him. Vaughn had to keep reminding himself he was just another double, that the real Pete's blood still stained his jumper.

"So are we going to talk about any of it?" Vaughn asked.

"Do we have to?"

"How are there so many of you? How did you get here? You said you landed here, who brought you here?"

"Well, the savior rescued me a couple of days ago, and…"

"Stop calling him that. What's Smokey's real name?"

"We just call him the savior."

"What did he save you from?"

"They call it…." Pete tried to say it but scrunched his mouth shut and shook his head.

Vaughn allowed his brain to catch up.

"Hang on. *The Incident*?"

Pete's eyes went wide and filled with tears.

"That thing everyone was talking about? That was you?" He didn't even let Pete answer, Pete wiped his eyes and kept walking. Having no real explanation for Vaughn, his guess was as good as any.

"But why didn't you tell me?"

"When? While we were running for our lives?"

"No, at the Asylum." Vaughn stepped up close, so Pete could see his face.

"I've never been to an Asylum."

"Not you, the other… ah forget it."

Pete's face was as apologetic as it was blank. His mind rolled back into his head and Vaughn could see he was living through it all again; everything that they did to him inside that tent.

They walked a bit longer and somehow Pete grew quieter and smaller. Vaughn knew what he was feeling, he had felt it himself. For so much of his life he had felt that way and for so much more he had wished he had told someone. Gotten it off his chest.

"When I was eight." Vaughn started, he spoke in a way that didn't need anyone else to be there, he could have told it to the void. "When I was eight, there was this spot. At the edge of a thin gorge atop a mountain. We used to go up there to jump across and anyone that didn't jump was called a wimp, you know. The older kids would jump first. Well, I thought they were much, much older. I think back and they were

giants. But they must've been only thirteen or something, hassling us younger kids to jump too.

I was fucking terrified, I hadn't jumped before, and it was actually a really long way down. We shouldn't have been allowed up there but still... there we were."

Vaughn stopped only to screw up his face and bite his lower lip.

"Brandon! That was his name! Brandon was in my year, but I barely knew the kid. Anyway, it was his turn to jump."

Vaughn stopped again, Pete lent forward as they walked to see Vaughn's face, as he went through it again in his mind. He was walking Pete through it as they walked endlessly onwards.

"So, it was Brandon's turn to jump." Vaughn said again. "He gets to the edge; he doesn't leave himself enough room for a run-up. The other kids are shouting *jump, jump, jump*. But he doesn't jump, he steps. He must've thought too much about it. His body kicked out a leg and went to place it where there was nothing but air.

So, Brandon starts to fall. And I'm just behind him. I'm within reach. But my hands stay at my sides."

Vaughn stopped, pulling the end of his sleeve to his eye to wipe a tear that doesn't come. He expected to cry, but anger shook in his hand and all Vaughn did was press his thumb so hard into the corner of his eye that things went fuzzy.

"For weeks the school and town and everyone was real shook up. Some kids said they were traumatized and got the attention they needed. The rest called me a wimp, a pussy, butter fingers. They said I panicked, and that it was my fault.

And then... then they started to say that I *let him fall*, that I didn't want to grab him. They called me *Limpfingers*. They called me that for years."

"Why are you telling me this?" Pete sniffed.

"I don't know, to make you feel better or something? To let you know that other people suck too, who knows? We're friends and I don't want you feeling guilty for stuff you couldn't control."

"We're friends?" Pete said weakly.

"Well, yeah. Course. You saved me and I saved you. That's friend shit. We're way beyond acquaintances."

Pete ducked his head down. He was trying to hide a grin.

"So, where are we going?"

"Well, I was thinking we'd see if there was anything left out there and if not…"

Vaughn pulled out of his pocket the old, worn cube stolen from Ida and the slightly blood-stained cube he had carried for far too long. "… we use these bad boys to find someplace else. I mean, if you don't wanna go anywhere specific or have some friends or family you wanna see or…"

"No." Pete blurted. "I wanna go with you. Where're you from?"

"Oh, well, we can do Fracture for a little while I guess. It's not that bad, really. But I'm putting my foot down, I don't wanna spend one more fucking second at that fucking Time Asylum."

"You're from the Time Asylum?"

"You know about it?"

"Who doesn't?"

"Huh." Vaughn was impressed. Even this far out in time and space, that bedlam of a party was still making waves. "Well, maybe."

"I mean, we don't need to worry about it now." Pete offered.

"Figure it out later?" Vaughn nodded.

"You bet." Pete nodded back.

The two friends walked in a comfortable silence. Walking like they were putting distance between themselves and their pasts more than their pursuers.

How far they would walk through these fading streets was unknown, perhaps they would walk and find nothing with no choice but to use the cubes they had and hope they could navigate time and space safety.

Neither of them said it, but they both were thinking the same thing. That they were doomed to leap on nothing but faith through time or walk until their feet were raw and their stomachs were empty.

They were doomed. Or at least they thought they were. They would have been correct too, if it were not for one of them innocently following the strange trail of yellow spray-paint on the ground.

"Hey what is that... oh fuck. No. NO!"

Vaughn caught sight of it too late and freaked out. Pete figured he had just stepped in something foul, but to Vaughn he had been leading them some place fouler.

Vaughn looked around for any sign of a quick exit in the haze and a familiar voice sounded from within it, coming from the orange glow that grew brighter and warmer as they grew closer. The fire crackled and smoked as the large man beside it hunched his shoulders back to crack his spine and stood to greet them.

"Hello again." O'seus said low and slow. "Do you see what I meant about your fated path?"

"Fuck you and fuck fate."

"Vaughn who is...?"

"Doesn't matter." Vaughn scowled at O'seus. "He's just a prick who messes with other people's lives like they're toys."

"Vaughn, I admit in my efforts to fix things I could have made a bad decision here or there. But everyone I brought and guided here to help me had only the purest of intentions."

"And what about Smokey?"

O'seus sighed deeply and looked off into the haze, towards the ruins of the stadium.

"Like I said, everyone I recruited had only the best of intentions and goodness of heart. But that man - Smokey, as you call him, I have absolutely no idea where he came from."

Vaughn suddenly felt the cold shrink around his jeans and cling to his legs.

"Vaughn, please. Let me explain." O'seus pressed.

"Explain what?" Vaughn spat.

"You are not supposed to be here. I want to help you get to where you're supposed to be."

"Wait." Vaughn stopped, letting his furrowed brow rest for a second. "Where is it you think I'm supposed to be?"

O'seus left his seat by the fire and approached the two boys.

"Fracture."

Vaughn felt a release run through him.

He could go home, home to a place he never thought he'd be aching to return to. He had doubted he would ever make it back there himself, even with a hundred cubes. With no clue how to use them he'd wind up in a volcano or the middle of the ocean before he saw Fracture again.

"Ok. I'll let you take me home."

"Good."

O'seus smiled and nodded, like he knew Vaughn would come around and was merely curious when. Vaughn wrapped an arm around Pete and stepped towards O'seus who was busy taking out a cube from his coat and doing a few calculations in his head.

But he stopped when he saw them together. He put his hand out and stopped them both.

"What? What is it?" Vaughn stammered.

"He's what." O'seus said solemnly, looking at Pete, still under Vaughn's arm.

"Nope. If you're taking me home, you're taking him too." Vaughn said firmly.

"I'm afraid not."

"Why not?" Vaughn and Pete said together.

"He has caused enough trouble for one timeline. I can't let him break another."

The words were painful because they were right. Vaughn looked at Pete, his friend, his one in a million. And that was exactly the problem.

"He'll behave himself." Vaughn persisted, not looking Pete in the eye. "He'll keep his head down. Just live a normal life, not bother anyone…"

"Vaughn." O'seus pleaded. At this point, it was obvious Vaughn was just trying to convince himself.

"Either he stays, or we all stay." O'seus said. "At this point you know you will leave with me. Why fight it?"

"I hate hearing that crap." Vaughn said through gritted teeth.

"He's too much of a risk."

"You're not even looking at him." Vaughn spat. "Why do you talk like he's not even here? He's right there and you're still saying this shit!"

"That's because the moment we leave, there's a possibility that things will begin to change. This place will fade, and he will with it." O'seus said coldly, now purposefully not letting an eye dart to Pete. Vaughn felt his hand dive back into his pocket, to the newspaper tear out. He wondered if he'd feel the ink change under his fingertips.

Pete was shaking. He looked at his hands as though they would turn transparent at any moment.

Vaughn felt his heart drop and his jaw shake, wanting to scrunch into a frown. He looked at Pete, looking back at Vaughn like a puppy he was ditching on the side of a highway. He didn't know what was happening or how to stop it. It was clear they were going nowhere if Pete came along.

"You agree with him, don't you?" Pete mumbled.

"Pete…"

"You think I'm too much trouble? You think I'm a risk."

"I don't know…" Vaughn said in a low tone, finally turning to Pete and taking his hand. Vaughn only just now noticed that this Pete was missing the same finger as a friend he had once known. Still gross.

Vaughn shot a look at O'seus. He was serious, they weren't going anywhere with Pete. He spent all this time looking for Pete but O'seus was his way home.

"But… I… I want to go with you, you said we would." Pete mumbled.

"I know buddy, I know."

"Please?"

"You can't." Vaughn balled up his face to keep it from busting. "You're a screw up. You're a walking catastrophe. If I let you leave this place… then, well… you'd just ruin everything, again."

Pete felt his cheeks well up and he blubbered. Vaughn caught him as he sobbed. He wrestled to get out of his arms, but Vaughn hugged him anyway.

Pete shoved him off, and Vaughn stumbled backward. Eyes down and apologetic.

He backed away to join O'seus. As he did Vaughn took the slip of mangled paper from his pocket. The invitation still read the wrong date, at least from his perspective.

He sighed and scrunched it into a small ball then flicked it into the fire but didn't bother to watch it burn. O'seus put out his hand and took the cube from Vaughn and begun to turn it.

Pete couldn't watch, he felt he only had seconds left to live and he didn't want to spend it watching them leave. He also couldn't stand to look at Vaughn. He couldn't believe just how wrong he was about him.

O'seus was halfway through turning the cube.

Pete felt the haze begin to swallow him up. He felt the dread of the cold, trying to live out here alone, hiding from everyone, hiding from Smokey, hiding from himself.

O'seus bit his tongue, as he was careful to count each twist and turn for what was going to be a massive jump.

This is it, the look on Pete's face said. All hope had escaped him. He was as good as dead and better off as nothing.

"Hey Pete."

Pete cocked his head up just as O'seus made the final rotation of the colored toy and it clicked into place. Vaughn was looking right at him with a sly grin.

"Catch!"

˙Go to Page 150

As a vortex swallowed up Vaughn and O'seus, a cube with the slightest bits of Pete's blood still on it, came flying out of the air and landed in Pete's hands. Then they were gone in a wink.*

Pete brushed back his tears and stared at the cube in his hands with a sudden strange wind cooling the tears on his face.

He started to laugh.

Vaughn had played him - he had played them both.

He knew how they worked but he hadn't ever held a working cube of his own before, and he wished he could follow. He wished he could have stayed with his friend, his only friend.

He knew Vaughn was a true friend; no one could have faked that.

He looked at the cube and thought of where he'd like to go.

He knew he was leaving this place, but he knew deep down that he had nowhere he felt he would be welcome. He had destroyed his present, his future. He only had the past, a past he didn't belong to anymore.

But there was a place he did belong to, a place he knew where everyone was welcome.

Not only was it the same place that would keep him safe from Smokey but was also the same place he knew the only person he truly wanted to see again would be.

He saw it by the fire. Vaughn had missed and the crumpled-up piece of newspaper was still intact. *November 15th, 1990* he read. Even if his estimates were off by a few months, Pete didn't care. He trusted so much that he would find Vaughn somehow. His friend, who had saved him.*

---

*Go to Page 179

$\diamondsuit$

Chapter Thirty-Eight:
Still Time

The coming winds were silenced by a lack of that to blow.
Hammond appeared some seven feet in the air and noticed how slowly he descended to the ground.

Vaughn appeared beside him, hand on his shoulder and his shadowed face staring a deep and endless void back at Hammond.

This place wasn't much of anything, and they had landed a thousand miles from what anyone would call *something*. A slight rise of an anthill would appear as a mountain here, but the ground was smooth and entirely reflective. In fact, it wasn't ground at all. The ocean had solidified, but it wasn't ice, instead it was just too slow to move at all or let them sink. All they could see was orange. Orange sky, orange water, orange air. And above, Vaughn recognized the streak of orange sunlight still painfully glowing above their heads.

Hammond still held his hat in his hands, crinkling the edges as he wondered where they were.

"Where are we?" Hammond asked, playing with his sunken cheeks in his reflection.

"Nowhere."

"I don't like jokes Pratt."

"Oh." Vaughn said as he reached up to the rim of his hat. "I'm not Pratt."

As slow as time allowed Vaughn lifted his hat, the shade following behind and Vaughn's face came back into the light, eyes on Hammond. Eyes Hammond surely wouldn't know.

"Ahhh thank fuck!" Vaughn moaned loudly.

Vaughn tossed the hat aside and ruffed up the thin, short hairs on his head. The hat drifted freely through the air as if strings held it up. It would take days for it to come down, days that weren't going to come.

"That feels GOOD! Can't tell you how hard it's been keeping up that act."

"What are you talking about?"

"I'm *not* Pratt." Vaughn snapped.

Hammond finally let go of his loose cheek and gave Vaughn a good hard look. Vaughn gulped hard, almost choking.

"No, you're Pratt." Hammond surmised after some time.

"I'm not!"

"You don't think you are, but you are him. Or someone that simply took his place."

"I'm not Pratt. I'm Vaughn."

"Who cares? A new face, a new name. It's just one more change."

"My name is Vaughn!"

Hammond went quiet, as he realized he was in an entirely different conversation than he first thought.

"Ok *Vaughn*, could you give me a cube so I can get us out of here?"

"No."

"No? Vaughn says no? Did Mr. Vaughn bring us nowhere on purpose? Where did Mr. Ashton take us?"

"Somewhere where you can't do shit to nobody no more."

Hammond sucked in air and felt it thicken in his throat and choked it down like swallowing a plastic bag. He could feel how stiff moving was, sensing a force he could not see. It was not something he understood.

Hammond screwed his nose up, it really screwed up. The cartilage had broken, and it sucked into his face like a frightened turtle. Vaughn winced as Hammond let it go and it popped back out again.

"Ok you little prick. The joke's over."

Hammond stomped over to Vaughn in a sudden burst that he wasn't ready for. But the air was like jelly. His foot caught mid-air and swung down so slowly he held his breath until it landed and almost passed out.

Vaughn took a simple, slow step back.

Hammond's ankle shattered as he thrust it to the hard surface of the sea. There he fell, nursing his ankle. He groaned and rubbed the bits of chalk-soft bone beneath his tissue thin skin.

"What in the world…?" Hammond growled at both Vaughn and the pain. "Where have you brought me?"

"I'm not sure yet, I'm figuring it out as I go."

"Don't waste my time mystery boy and give me that cube so I can do some good with it." Hammond said through gritted teeth. He let go of one hand from his ankle to hold up and point at Vaughn, still assuming he would give it up under orders.

"No. I've done enough enabling with you. Following you around, waiting for you to get where you're going. You see I had to wait. I knew I couldn't change what I had seen before. What I knew had to happen."

Hammond let go of his ankle entirely, letting it drop. He rolled over to his knees and looked down at the water, afraid he would sink and when he didn't, afraid that he wasn't.

Vaughn stepped back again, and Hammond snarled, shuffling on his knees towards Vaughn, occasionally dropping forward onto his hands for balance. His yellow stained eyes never leaving Vaughn.

But the faster he shuffled, the slower he became. Vaughn simply stepped backwards and out of his reach.

"And what are we waiting for now huh?" Hammond snarled. "Leave me if you're going to! Why test me? Don't toy with me!"

Vaughn stepped back once again as Hammond stalked him, laughing through the pain as he felt each bone break, just waiting in turn to shatter. He swiped at Vaughn, who scampered out of the way as slowly as he could, each time slower and slower - easier and easier.

Yet, with each vicious, bloodthirsty grab Vaughn grew more and more worried. As each attempt grew less of a threat, Hammond's persistence grew feverishly frantic. The only thing that wasn't slowing down.

"What can I say to get this out of your system?" Hammond pleaded. "What are you waiting for? You have all those fucking cubes, you could have gone by now, but you haven't. What do you want?"

"I don't want anything. I don't want one side to win, I don't want to kill anyone, and I don't want to let you go."

"You don't get it do you? Or you're too stupid to see. You've already picked a side, and its mine, isn't it?"

Vaughn said nothing, but his face said it all. No shade to hide it anymore.

"I get it. I see what this is about. You're worried you're turning into me. You want to know if you have a choice, if I had a choice. You know, sometimes I wonder if maybe they're right, that our fate is laid out for us and that maybe I am this monster they see me as.

Maybe they didn't turn me into this, maybe I was supposed to be this, maybe this is what I was all along. And if that's the truth, then I really had no real choice at all!"

Hammond made another grab for Vaughn, but his legs took a tumble, his fall almost broke through the slow water. Quickly he scrambled up to stand again like it didn't happen. Quickly taking so long that Hammond's veins rose, and his skin went purple. Quickly wasn't quick enough.

"If I'm wrong and they're right. If there is no free will, only destiny. That means you're judging me for something I cannot help. Cursing me for what I am cursed to be. In a world as cruel as this, won't you be the bigger man and just let me be!"

Hammond's rotting eyes had taken hold of Vaughn. He was drawn in and sweating ice. He couldn't dodge Hammond's next attempt without slowing his speed. He was getting frantic, and Vaughn was getting clumsy. He was slowing down by speeding up. Now just out of reach.

"Look. LOOK! Look at what all this has done to me. I'm withering away in front of you. Don't you have any heart. Don't you have any pity?"

Hammond lunged from too far away, and his second ankle snapped with it. Hammond barely noticed and kept at him, crawling towards Vaughn. As far as Vaughn could run, Hammond would never stop hunting him. He would tire before Hammond's mind would give. He knew he could out-slow him, but Hammond's chase was hungry; he was foaming at the mouth.

"Change? Ok, you want me to change? Is that it? Why? So, you can believe that there's hope for you? There's no hope for you *mystery boy.* You're like me. I know it, you know it. It grates on you, watching them jump, I see it in you, it hurts you every second you see them in the wrong place at the wrong time. But you want to be like them, you want to live a happy-go-lucky existence. Well, I'm sorry to be the one to tell you this but that's not in the cards for people like us. We, who know the truth. We who suffer the grim burden."

Hammond spat as he crawled, first spit, then bone from his jaw and chunks from his cheeks.

"You want me to change? I'll change! Oh, I'll change. I'll mutate, transform, metamorphosis and evolve because of them. No matter what, they won't stop they just HHHEHHHHAHEHE they just won't fucking stop. And it gets to the point you just want to just NAIL THEIR FEET TO THE GROUND IF IT WOULD MAKE THEM STAY IN ONE PLACE!"

Hammond, out of breath, but still crawling, launched himself up from his stomach to his knees. There he knelt, swaying with imbalance. The world had slowed around them now. Hammond was kept upright by slow motion more than balance. His words left him and floated slowly to Vaughn, hanging in the air for hours in between.

"You are like me. Admit it. You're just like me."

"I'm not!" Vaughn said. "Underneath all your anger, all your hatred, all your rage, there's just a scared old man worried he's losing something he doesn't even know he has."

"Damn right I'm scared! It's the scariest thing there is! I'm fucking frightened out of my wits! Everyday. Aren't you? I hate them and I know you hate them too."

"I don't. I don't hate them, and I'm not scared of them. I thought I was, once, but I'm not. You see, nobody knows how all this works, so there's no reason to act like it. So I figure I'll try living in the unknown instead of trying to define the unknowable."

Hammond tried to lick his lip as he felt it dry and harden, his tongue as heavy as a bag of concrete.

"Wherever they go, I'll find them. There's nowhere I can't be there's no time I won't go. I'll never stop hunting them."

"And that right there, that's the difference between you and me." Vaughn sighed. "Why I can change, and you can't."

"Why?"

"Because I'm not an asshole."

Vaughn's cube was already spun, but the effects took their time. Hours passed as the goo of the tangent leaked from the cube and slowly enveloped Vaughn. He suffered the pain, the folding, the collapsing, never taking his eyes off Hammond until he was nothing, Until he was matter. Until he was gone.*

Hammond's yellow tinged eyes fell to ocean below him, he saw them looking back. They said everything they needed to at that last moment.

He saw all his confusion, all his pain, all his anger, and all that hate. All of it.

All that was left was fear. In the end, he was just a scared old man, left to freeze in time.

All over the world, the wind felt softer. With every breeze the trees would react in delay, the ocean's ripples no longer extended to the coastlines of each country. Stillness sat in the air, whoever was left took longer to reach their destinations, they found the days were stretching and the nights seemed to never end.

The clocks had nothing to say and kept it all a secret, but you could feel it. The few that were left didn't dare speak of it, not wanting to be found strange or out of touch. A disillusionment of reality they would call it. But the silence built, the low resonating gossip found an echo at the bottom and sounded up on high. The world was in silent agreement; something was indeed a little off. And if you were quiet enough, you could hear it; the universe was coming.

But no one could answer why. They all felt dazed, suffered a disassociation with the rest of the world. As if they had all left a concert

---

*Go to Page 330

and had that resounding ringing sound of your eardrums screaming their last notes before dying. A general hum wafted over life all.

The sky was stained orange, and the oceans were a perfect mirror, reflecting the color back. This color pallet hung in the air, painted over their eyes, like the way you see the world tinted just before dusk sets in. The air tasted of dead fruit. The water no longer quenched any thirst, barely touching your tongue as you poured it into your mouth. Evaporating into thin air, not by the heat or the sun, but as though the molecules were collapsing on the way down.

The voyager landed and fell hard on his side and for a moment lay in the dirt, the curve of his helmet digging into the ground.

He laughed, ecstatic to be in one piece, barely noticing the impediment of time dragging each motion back with stronger and stronger force. The heat was unbearable, the earth was baking, and the sun cooked his uniform. A small pool of sweat collected in his helmet, and he watched the beads run down the plastic mold towards his face. He was too tired to move, but the growing pool of sweat rose to his eye and the salt stung.

He wore one of Steins prototypes, a Wyla patented mercury suit, and despite the heat he didn't dare take it off, for he figured it was all that was keeping him alive.

For what futuristic parasites or hazardous toxic air awaited him if he did?

He managed to get onto his feet and unclasped his helmet. He felt the heat of the place wash over him like a hot towel. He needed shade. He needed water.

There were dark shapes all around him, they had sunk into the red earth, but there were taller ones ahead on the early horizon. Perhaps tall enough to find shade.

As he got closer, he could spot the definitions, the cut of the blocks. There were buildings, huge skyscrapers with windows missing. From certain angles, you could see straight through the massive blocks where sunlight broke through to the shade and burnt the ground even redder.

The voyager struggled to walk normally. The suit was wide between his legs, and he had to hobble a little, less bending his knees and more bouncing from one foot to the next. He came to a wire fence with a wide-open gate and stumbled through it.

He tried to move faster, but the faster he hobbled the less distance he covered. He figured he had been walking for weeks from nowhere to nothing. But now beneath his feet he could feel a crunching. The ground was soft in parts and uneven.

The voyager looked down and saw he had been walking along a line of crops and sticking out of the ground were thousands and thousands of carrots. They had sprung up loose and were white, with fine hairs on their bald tops.

He kept on, further into the field and he could sense others around him. In the distance, many were on their hands and knees pulling up the carrots. They hurried to their feet and scattered.

He didn't see her coming - she was too slow. Not so suddenly, she knocked against his spherical helmet. The voyager was shaken, his feet stepped around each other, becoming their own obstacles and he tripped and fell.

In the reflection of his helmet the voyager could see the old woman approach and lord over him, leering at the mess he had made.

"Did you find what you were looking for?"

✦

Part Four:
ORANGE

"**A**H. FUCKING. DAMMIT!"

Vaughn felt his knees dig into crusty sand and dirt. Wherever he was it didn't matter, he was mad at it.

All he could see was bright orange anyway. It was dry, rough, and quiet. So quiet.

Vaughn wriggled with frustration and clenched his fists until it hurt his palms. He wanted to tear up the earth. He wanted to writhe endlessly until it just stopped happening.

"Can I just ONCE! STOP GETTING. PUSHED. AROUND!"

Those fists of Vaughn's, so tight, balling it all up - just as mad as he was - beat at the ground.

Sometime later they made contact.

"What the fuck...?" He breathed.

Raising his fists up to inspect them. They seemed normal. He closed and opened his fist slowly. Further out all he could see was orange. The orange dirt and the orange light, the orange clouds and orange sky.

The sun streaked across the sky like a splash of paint rather than keeping to a circle. It shone still, like normal, he supposed.

In the distance was a skyline of skyscrapers so dark they seemed like painted backdrops, but not all were still standing. Some buildings had toppled or fallen, and others had bent to lean on the buildings beside them for support.

Walking again through a time and place Vaughn knew nothing about, he found himself blocked by a wire fence and he ran his fingers along it as he followed it to the east.

All the while Vaughn was dropping in and out of thought. He went for ages not thinking anything at all and then snapped back and thought of nothing but the fleeting last moments he had spent at the Asylum.

Events seeming too much to deal with all at once. His brain fed it back to him in pieces. At that moment, he was stewing on the piece that remembered the face of the Historian. Every little detail slipped into his mind just as he found the opening in the fence.

He had come to a gate, ripped off its hinges, and swinging above it was a busted neon sign. It hung by its wiring, and he wondered how long it had been since it lit up. The sign was square with an orange triangle of neon glass in the middle.

Vaughn passed through the gate and now walked towards that city skyline.

As he did he felt a crunch beneath his feet, like satisfying dead leaves. Vaughn felt with each crunch a bit of satisfaction that calmed him; the little therapy that comes with a small taste of destruction.

He was careful though. Along the ground every seven or eight steps he spotted dead birds, already half covered in orange dirt. He didn't want to crush any of those between his toes.

Stark sun and cold shadow split this endless field of dirt in half. Vaughn walked on the edge of the sunlight keeping to the shade. The weird streak made an ever-weirder shadow that didn't match its source.

Overhead he saw a cluster of birds, white birds that flew in unison. They were circling overhead with nowhere better to go.

Getting closer, Vaughn made out a few buildings, made of stone and still standing. He saw people too, little grey figures in the distance, bending over every few steps. They moved in no rush or awareness of Vaughn.

He made for them, and even more figures came in focus.

Vaughn could see they were carrying baskets in their arms, and when they bent they were pulling things from the ground.

The ones in the shade pulled white and grey carrots, long and thin like weeds. The cnes in the sunlight pulled the tops, but the bottoms crumbled.

That's what Vaughn had been stepping on and crushing; carrot ash.

"Hello!" He called out. Those few that heard Vaughn pretended not to and just kept on pulling carrots.

Vaughn got clcser. Close enough to see their faces. At least they had faces, Vaughn thought.

"Hello?"

"Do not talk." One woman said, holding a full basket of carrot stubs. She was trying very hard not to look him in the eye.

"What?" Vaughn was taken aback. "Hey...hey! I'm talking to you! Yes you!"

But the woman turned and slowly headed away.

Vaughn ran. He had to find someone who would listen to him. Someone to answer his questions. He ran towards the next figure in the distance. He ran kicking back sand with his tired and swollen bare feet. He ran until his legs ached and he had a nagging stitch in his side. Vaughn ran and ran.

A peg-legged man came up beside him. He hobbled slowly, both his legs were cut short at the shin and his wooden stumps were uneven. This man walked up beside Vaughn as he ran with all his might. He stopped and watched, seeing Vaughn's legs tear themselves apart while the peg-legged man stood perfectly still, if not slightly leaning to one side.

Vaughn caught sight of the man watching him and toppled his footing, tripping up and falling forward. He took his time to do so, hitting his head over the course of an hour.

The peg-legged man waited.

"How did you... what was I... why wasn't I...?" Vaughn's head throbbed and he kept seeing double.

"Hi!"

"Hi." Vaughn said uneasily, trying to keep his eyes open. "Where am I?"

The peg-legged man shrugged.

"Who are you?"

The peg-legged man shrugged again.

"It's really orange here?" Vaughn said, starting to get delirious. He kept thinking he was talking to a man with no legs.

"Yes." The peg-legged man smiled, able to answer his question.

And with that, Vaughn fell unconscious.

He slept a week's worth of sleep. His mind processed and catalogued all he had seen, the Asylum, the cubes, the explosion, the court, the fights, the panic and then that peculiar White Cube.

And that Historian, his face stained his memory. He couldn't strip it from his mind. The sunken cheeks and those yellow eyes.

The haze around his face clouded Vaughn, as he was drawn closer to his reach. He batted away the arm, but Hammond had him by his shirt.

Vaughn fought it off, but he was weak. His arms flailed uselessly as Hammond pulled Vaughn into his breath. Relentlessly strong, Hammond had him at his neck - eyes staring into eyes. As he spoke soundless words, the skin on his cheeks flaked and blew into Vaughn's mouth. He choked on them.

He coughed.

He spluttered.

He woke.

Vaughn was still there, on the ground where he had fallen. The peg-legged man crouched awkwardly beside him.

"How long was I out?"

"A few seconds, maybe."

"You're kidding?"

Vaughn was still tired. He was that kind of tired that drained you so much that you just feel like ugly crying. He wanted to sob until someone put his head on a pillow or smothered him with one.

"Who are you?"

"Lewis."

"Lewis?" Vaughn confirmed.

"Larry."

“Larry?”

“Lorne.”

“Lorne?”

“Lincoln.”

“Stop it!”

“Sorry.”

“Don’t you know?”

“I have trouble.” The peg-legged man muttered. “Remembering things.”

“But you remember that.” Vaughn jeered. “I’m just gonna call you L.”

Vaughn got to his feet as L stood back up, swaying back and almost falling. Vaughn was dazed himself, nothing made sense here. Sense was something he had been lacking for a while now.

“You’re one of them, aren’t you.” L asked.

“One of what?” Vaughn pried.

“A time… um… mover.” L stammered. “You move from time… to time?”

Vaughn nodded, but only just. It was enough. L beamed, very proud of himself.

“Do you know any other time movers around here?” Vaughn asked.

Vaughn pulled the cube out of his apron to prompt L. The bloodstains were chipping off, dry like paint. It must’ve been empty now. He had never been so betrayed by a single thing so much in his life. First Pete, now this.

No. First Jake, then Pete, and now this cube.

“How about this? Have you seen any of these?”

“Not allowed.”

“Who says?”

L shrugged.

“I don’t think I like this place.” Vaughn sighed, looking around and seeing nothing but disappointment.

“Neither do I.”

“Then leave.”

"Not allowed."

"Of course. Why'd I even ask?" Vaughn squeezed his cube to take the pressure off his jaw that clenched every time he got mad. "I guess this is the last one."

Vaughn tossed L the cube. It hurtled through the air so slowly that Vaughn accused it of making fun.

Eventually the cube landed into L's hands, and he rolled it from palm to palm.

"You can have that one if you want." Vaughn offered lazily.

"No thank you." L said, rolling it from his left hand onto the floor and nudging it back to Vaughn. "There's lots of them in her room."

"Wait. What did you just say?"

Vaughn had L march him back into the city where the people still moved, following seeded lines of earth and twisting carrots from the ground.

The farmers walked without purpose, stopping only to recall the single-minded reason they had started long ago. They ripped the carrots from the ground, spending unspendable brain cells trying to decode the mystery of how it ended up in their hands.

The more astute and aware of the strange farmers became the least content. They were gracefully frantic, like anxious Tai Chi masters. They panicked in the streets, screaming without a sound at the sight of Vaughn or maybe just the recollection of their own memories.

And towering over them all was a great skyscraper. Its shadow split the farmlands just as it was split through the center. The pipes in the concrete walls had frozen and cracked, and now those cracks had run along the entire twenty-third floor and sent the top half of the building tumbling down in a free fall. Dust and chunks of rubble shot out at a tremendously slow speed, and within maybe a few months the building would crush them all.

They came to a stone building that had survived better than most.

This building was familiar, yet he couldn't recall. It was half buried in the ground and all the window glass had long since shattered and disintegrated. An enormous sheet, easily the size of a circus tent,

floated up to the sky like a sail caught in a slow wind. But it was not until Vaughn stood right beneath the building and looked up that he realized where he was.

Above the buried doorway, someone had carved five laws. But they were different, someone had altered them, scratching out words and leaving what was left as scripture.

Today is Today
The old are the law
You are not safe
Do not talk
Do not make yourself part of history

"What the hell is going on?" Vaughn whispered to himself. Not that L could or would answer with any authority.

"We shouldn't be here." L blurted, like he had just woken up and hadn't just led Vaughn all the way there. "We shouldn't... she'll come."

"Who's she?"

"The old are the law." L read from above.

"No no, don't lose focus. You said there were cubes in here, didn't you? Didn't you?"

"I don't know what I said. I get a little confused sometimes." L shied away from the windows. All were dark and whistling eerily in the wind, either beckoning them in or warning them of what was to come.

"You ok staying here then?" Vaughn backed away from L like he would a dog, as if L would try to follow or run away the moment he left. "I'm going in. If there's a cube I've gotta go in."

L stood solid, surprisingly rigid as Vaughn held on his sleeve to keep him from moving. His peg legs had found a firm footing. Vaughn sighed loudly and let go. He looked deep into the open window, recalling the tiled floor on the other side and trying to rack his brain around how long it had been since he was last here. Both in his sense of time and the world's.

"I'm going in. Ok? Stay here until I come back. I'm coming back, remember that. I'll be back before you know it."

"Got it." L said assuredly.

Vaughn couldn't be sure if he did, but there was no time to test his memory. Vaughn stepped through the open window and into the dark building.

L surrounded his eyebrows to his nose, concentrating on the spot where Vaughn had stood moments ago. A vein pulsed on his temple and ripped him a headache, but he only frowned tighter.

"What are you doing?" Someone said.

"Concentrating." L answered.

"Sounds like fun." It was a woman's voice. "What's your name?"

"L." He answered, smiling that he remembered something.

"Ok L, what are you concentrating on?" She said.

"I… I don't know."

"Sure you do. You just have to think about it." The woman stood beside him and looked where he was looking. "Why were you looking there?"

"Because something was there and now it's not."

"Was it really?" She said. "That's interesting. What could have been there?"

L looked to the ground, but she lifted his chin.

"How about, who could have been there?"

"Who? Who? There was a who!"

"There was?"

"There was! Yes. He said he'd be back."

"Did he say when?"

"Before I know it." L repeated softly, twisting a smile. He had remembered again, perhaps he would remember even more.

"Let's take care of that *know* part, shall we?"

Vaughn followed through into the tiled entry room. He remembered the icy touch of the tiles when he came here last to glimpse the court making up all their rules. Again, he got this sweet relief from the grit of dirt and sand. With the cleanly swept tiles cooling his feet, he felt like he was walking on ice.

He took a moment to look at himself. Under his apron his pajamas were beyond needing a wash. His white shirt was brown and yellow under his arms. It had been soggy since almost drowning in the quarry, through his constant sweating made a major contribution, to the sogginess. His boxer briefs had torn in between his crotch and his underwear had been riding up around his junk and chaffing like crazy.

Every time he wiped his brow his wrist or palm came back with a black smudge. He didn't know if he was wiping it on or off.

The big doors to the auditorium were open and Vaughn could see the tall podium stands had toppled like dominos all towards the center of the bowl like room. Some had crushed the judge's podium.

Above him the glass dome, minus the glass, let in the bright streak of sunlight. The light was broken in half by the massive sheet still attached at one corner. Vaughn was standing underneath it as it poked up in the sky like a tissue out of the box, a massive tissue, wafting slowly.

Ducking under toppled stands, and careful not to slip and slide to the center of the auditorium, Vaughn looked around. He did an entire lap but finding nothing. Every step he took he felt the tiles giving way, his footprints molding into marble as though it were clay.

I've just got to get one cube, if I can go back before it all, before the Asylum, before Atticus recruited me, before everything, Vaughn thought. *If I go back before it all, hide away for however long and let my past-self go to the Observatory and then I can just take my own place and go on like nothing ever happened.*

Vaughn was done with it all. Looking for Pete had caused more problems, trying to save him only made things worse. He still ached inside thinking about Pete and how he didn't have the same chance as Vaughn to go back to his normal life.

But what could he do? The Far was a seemingly unreachable place, and perhaps it was. Perhaps it was a myth, a legend told to tourists by tourists. If Smokey had taken Pete in search of it, maybe he got lost trying.

Vaughn even felt a little warmth at the idea of waking up in his own bed again. Going to work at a normal job where the guests weren't breaking his brain with their philosophies and debates. He wanted the simple back. Simple drinks, simple minds, and simple problems.

He had lapped it, the whole auditorium, and nothing. Well, something. One door on the far-left side was not like the others, but it made Vaughn uneasy.

It took away those warming feelings of getting his old life back, the one he hated so much. This door told him *no*.

As, sprayed on the door in dripping, yellow, spray paint, dripped fresh and the letter F reaching all the way to the floor, were those words again.

Limpfingers.

Don't go, follow me, it seemed to say. *You're so close.*

Vaughn sighed. It hadn't led him wrong yet, and maybe this would be the last one. He took the handle, feeling it crinkle under his strength. On the other side of the door was an office, simple, plain. Yet all the books on the shelves were scratched, erasing the titles. Vaughn went to take one out and it crumbled so easily in his hand, leaving dust behind.

He rested a hand on the back of the chair, and he felt the wood creak and wither quickly.

The floors were the same. His footsteps had imprinted behind him, making an easy trail. Everything was withering so easily, breaking down as though it was long overdue.

The only thing in the room not ready to crumble was the plain white dome, set on the middle of the desk. Silent, foreboding. Waiting. Vaughn recognized it, just like the ones that had chased him in the future, or the past. Spitting news footage in his face and scanning identities. He curled his lip at it.

Vaughn eyed it as he kept inspecting the room. There must be something in here worth looking for, otherwise what was the graffiti for?

Then he spied it, in the corner wall, beside the bookshelf, a crack in the plaster. Vaughn nudged aside the bookshelf. Easily it sanded itself into sawdust as he pushed.

Behind it someone had scratched at the ashy plaster and made a hole, and there in the wall were hundreds and hundreds of cubes.

Hundreds.

Vaughn smiled, reached in and took one that sat atop the pile; one more pronounced than the rest. The one he drew out first was oddly different to the others. It had faded in color somewhat more and there was an engraving on the side. He didn't care. It felt heavy. Heavy enough for one last trip and then he would chuck it.

He only needed one. But his hands figured he should take more, just in case.

"You shouldn't go around touching what isn't yours." A creaky voice said.

Vaughn cocked his head back and saw standing in the doorway, with L in her grip, was an old lady.

She was dressed in a starkly clean black coat, without a speck of dust or sand on it. But her collar was filthy with white crumbs.

She held a freshly picked carrot to her mouth with her free hand and gnawed at it hungrily.

"Hi!" L said cheerily to Vaughn, never minding her grip on his shirt. "I think… we know each other… right?"

'Who are you?" Vaughn asked. "You let him go."

"I think I'll hang on to him for a little longer." She croaked, taking another big chomp, the carrot mulch spilling from her loose and gummy grandma mouth. "My name is Ida. Who are you poking around in my things?"

"I just want one. You've got a lot. Please, all I wanna do is leave."

Ida raised a lip, her wrinkles folding over themselves like waves crashing over waves.

"Why would anyone want to leave?" She asked.

"Why wouldn't they? Where even are we? *When* are we? This place is all kinds of fucked up. Who are all those people out there? Why are they acting so strange?"

"They come here looking for the furthest point in time."

Vaughn gasped.

"You mean…this is… the Far?" He breathed, as though he would scare the idea off like a frightened bunny.

"No. Like I said, they come looking for it, but they'll never find it. I can't let them." Ida said and bit into another chunk of carrot. "I won't. My job is to keep the ones that come here safe."

She nodded to L, eyes wondering to the ceiling.

"What have you done to him?"

"It isn't all that effective, this one needs it done again and again to keep him safe." Ida slowly slapped the back of L's head and he whimpered, almost falling as he stumbled back and forth on his peg legs.

"I love carrots." She said. 'Don't you?"

But Vaughn was silent. Not that he had much opinion on carrots either way.

"My family figured it out, that carrots could grow almost anywhere. It's what kept us going. Carrot soup, carrot cake, carrot everything. They help you see better and they're a healthy snack. Without my farm, everybody out there would starve. I've given them a fighting chance."

"You have all those cubes, just let them leave. Let me leave, I won't come back I swear!"

"Leave!" Ida snapped. Carrot flew from her gums as she spouted rage over Vaughn. It now hung in the air, suspended. "Leave and do what? Destroy us all in the blink of an eye? This is all we have left, and you want it gone too, now how's that for hypocritical. They show up here whenever they come from, and I take care of them.

Me. I take care of everyone here. These visitors, they're messing with things that aren't supposed to be messed with. They will cause another extinction. It's safe, this is safe. The safe choice. Do nothing, be invisible. Eat carrots and do nothing. Affect nothing. We survive by adapting, and so I adapted.

That cube you're holding, by chance that is the very cube that destroyed them all. I found it, after the smoke and ash cleared, lying there, acting all innocent, buried in the dirt. It survived all that time, all that destruction. The only survivor. You think they are tools of

mankind, but they are weapons of the devil and he is determined. What you are holding is the cube that destroyed the world. Now give it here!"

Ida stomped into the room, still clutching L and blocking the only exit. Vaughn was scared at first, but then he sized her up.

She was an old woman, frail and brittle. If she fought back at all Vaughn was sure he could outmatch her. Vaughn shook his head and tucked the cube in his pocket.

She sighed, stepping up to the desk and nudging the white dome with her finger. It buzzed to life, making whirring noises as though it was warming up.

"In the old days, these Ogles had quite a few handy uses. Television, music, cleaning, that sort of thing."

So those are Ogles? Vaughn thought.

"I figured out one of its other special secret uses." Ida spoke in a clean and clear voice.

"Function: Perfect Citizen."

The Ogle came to life. It started spitting out images and noises as he had seen it do before, spinning with no sense of direction until Ida jerked L in front of it. It pulled focus on his eyes and locked him in a trance of rapid-fire projections. Ida even let go and L didn't budge.

"What are you doing to him?" Vaughn asked, knowing what it felt like to have those things project images in your eyes. Knowing it wasn't pleasant.

"We are forever victims to determinism. We think we have free will, but we do not. How could we? If everything that has ever happened to us will affect what we will do next. But, without a past and without our memories, we are free. We base our decisions on nothing but our will. I'm setting him free."

A tear fell from L's eye. He wished he knew why he was crying.

"But I can smell the naughty ones and believe me you smell worse than the others. I'm afraid you can't stay here." Ida cursed him. "No, you can't stay here at all."

Fuck this. Vaughn thought.

He charged at the old woman with all his strength, but he barely grazed her. Ida somehow moved out of his path and a soft hand touched his exposed neck and Vaughn slammed hard to the floor. Bits of floorboard flaked off like smoke.

He kept at her, rushing to his knees and swinging a punch at her stomach. But the punch merely geared up, while she had already calmly flicked him between the eyes and sent him out into the open auditorium. He smacked his back up against a toppled podium stand.

How? She was just an old woman.

"Ah, curious, aren't you?" Ida said, walking out into the auditorium and reveling in the acoustics. "Time slows down around these parts. I'm guessing you've noticed."

Vaughn scraped his molars together and rose to his feet. He was never a fighter, but he always figured he'd be able to hold his own against someone his size. But she was in a different class.

He kicked, and she caught it, pushing him back and he hopped backwards, his body light. He bounced like he was on a trampoline, the floor sinking under his bounce. Again, he slammed back into the stands.

There was no use, she had something on him. She was too much. Behind her in the office he could see L still entranced and out of it. What little he remembered was quickly fading. Even the first letter of his name.

"I'm sorry." Vaughn said to his strange friend. "I tried."

He turned and ran for it, dodging under toppled stands and podiums to get to the doors, to get away. Ida caught up to him easily. She spouted nonsense, more self-righteous thoughts and ideas. She had time and he knew there was no getting away from her. She was just too fast.

No. Vaughn thought. *She wasn't. She was too slow.*

Vaughn slowed his run to a jog and suddenly what was taking him minutes to duck under or jump over now he was dashing through in seconds.

It was hard though. As he felt himself moving faster, he naturally sped up and immediately slowed. Ida was noticing and slowly swung her carrot holding fist at him, clonking against his head as though it was a brick.

He kept on. He could see the outside light slipping through the open window. He had to get away.

Vaughn tried it again, this time slowing to a walk. Suddenly he was Superman. Gliding through the air as though he were running.

Easily he out-walked Ida. It hurt to concentrate on it. Keeping such a slow pace he shot out of the auditorium, shot out of the window and he was off. He dawdled at such a record pace he flew past the farmers, crushing carrots and kicking up dust.

Behind him Ida screamed and cried. But Vaughn was just too slow for her.

Vaughn had made it to the edges of the carrot fields. He stopped to catch his breath, finding it almost impossible to order his body to run faster to stop.

He had gone far enough, and he figured he could make time to leave now. But as he went to pull out his cube, that's when he felt it.

A siren screeched planet wide, and a rampant wind hurled the sands of the desert up in the air and out in every direction. A wind with no source. Something was beginning to end.

A bird crashed into the dirt right in front of him, and then another and another. The air was getting harder and harder for them to flap their wings, so they simply lost their height.

All the farmers dropped their carrots to shield themselves from so many falling birds. They came down hard and unpredictably, yet slowly.

Quickly the sand in the wind slowed, clustering so thick it became harder to see. The farmers left their baskets and wandered out in search of one another, not fearing the grazing of sand against their cheeks nor the danger of the laws they were forced to follow.

They instead stumbled through the world, joining the thousands fumbling in near blindness for someone to touch, a hand to hold as the world scared them one last time.

Vaughn felt the pressure of the atmosphere run through him like a terrible cold flush. The blood in his veins was slowing too.

He squinted to see. Stumbling through the sandstorm was a slow-paced figure. Vaughn tightened - worried Ida had caught up to him. But as the figure grew closer, he could see it was someone else.

A person dressed in a bulbous suit. Shiny, white and with a fishbowl like helmet. This out of place astronaut had a logo on the chest that read *Volta*.

Between them, three thousand two hundred and sixty-five grains of sand drifted in the air, for a long enough time to count. Vaughn thought of nothing to say or nothing to do. Even in the slow motion of time, his hands were still quicker than his mind. He waved to the spacesuit-man.

The out of place astronaut lifted his arm and with a strange enthusiasm he waved back.

Suddenly the grains were moving so slowly he could barely say they were moving at all. Then he noticed it happen. The astronaut had stopped moving all together, his arm frozen in its shape. It horrified Vaughn, feeling his own body clamp up, he could barely push a breath out of his mouth or pull one in. As slow as his body was, his mind was still sharp, and he watched it all crawl by in what felt like years. His hands were helpless, no longer able to dig the cube out of his pocket to get him out of there. They were useless and he was helpless.

All he could do was watch.

If he could have, he would have had a horrified expression on his face. But in the time it took for the horror to take hold and wring him senseless, the feeling passed over him like a cold, wet towel.

Surrounding Vaughn were the last moving pieces of sand as a slight wind seemed to have picked up in his vicinity.

He felt two arms wrap around his torso and he looked down to see one of those hands was holding a cube that was spinning and humming

a fraction at a time. The light, that would normally pulsate from it so rapidly to exhaust its power, now glazed over the cube like a thick jam.

A tangent seeped out of the cracks of the cube like water pouring out from a bottle. Vaughn felt his torso stretch towards the vacuum, dragging him and the owner of the arms around him along for the ride.

Vaughn passed through the time tangent so slowly that he could observe his body being folded into all kinds of uncanny shapes and positions, each time getting smaller and smaller until his body and his mind were molecules, atoms, quarks and matter.

Someone had pulled him out of there while there was still time.[*]

---

*Go to Page 582